The
Literary
Life
of Cairo

The Literary Life of Cairo

One Hundred Years in the Heart of the City

Edited and Introduced by
Samia Mehrez

The American University in Cairo Press
Cairo New York

First published in 2011 by
The American University in Cairo Press
113 Sharia Kasr el Aini, Cairo, Egypt
420 Fifth Avenue, New York, NY 10018
www.aucpress.com

Dar el Kutub No. 2266/10
ISBN 978 977 416 390 6

Dar el Kutub Cataloging-in-Publication Data

Mehrez, Samia
        The Literary Life of Cairo: One Hundred Years in the Heart of the City / by Samia
    Mehrez.—Cairo: The American University in Cairo Press, 2011
        p;   cm.
        ISBN 978 977 416 390 6
        1. Arabic Literature—History and Criticism. I. Title
        892.709

1 2 3 4 5 6   15 14 13 12 11

Designed by Fatiha Bouzidi
Printed in Egypt

For Cairo and her authors

Contents

Acknowledgments

When I first started the research on this project, I never imagined that I would find such a staggering amount of literary material on Cairo, whose sheer size and scope, even after considerable editing, still ultimately dictated the decision to publish two volumes instead of one: *The Literary Atlas of Cairo* and *The Literary Life of Cairo*. I am therefore first and foremost utterly grateful to Cairo's authors, who, in this context, are *the authors of Cairo*, the city that readers will encounter and experience through this collective atlas. Without these authors' inspiring works and their willingness to be part of this literary map, the literary atlas project, now in two volumes, would simply not have existed.

In order to complete this project within a year as I had envisioned, I requested and was granted leave without pay from the American University in Cairo (AUC). I have been supported throughout the year by several grants that allowed me to dedicate all my time to researching, compiling, translating, editing, and producing this work. I am indebted to the Ford Foundation Egypt and the Netherlands Cultural Fund in Egypt for their instant interest in and support of *The Literary Atlas of Cairo* proposal. I am equally grateful to the Arab Fund for Arts and Culture for their generous funding of this project. Mark Linz, director of the AUC Press and Ibrahim El Moallem, president of Dar El Shorouk, both made an immediate commitment to support and publish this work based on my initial proposal. I wish to thank them both for their insight and confidence and sincerely hope that the end product lives up to their expectations. Kamal Abou Deeb's and Barbara Harlow's enthusiastic letters of support for the atlas project are most certainly behind the generous support I have received. The introductory material to *The Literary Life of Cairo* was written at the Rockefeller Foundation's Villa Serbelloni in Bellagio, Italy, where I was a resident scholar in August 2010. I wish to thank Professor Pilar Palacia, director of the Rockefeller Bellagio Center, and the entire staff at the villa, for having made my stay so heavenly. Special thanks also to my resident colleagues and their spouses at the center who made my residency a most memorable and fun one, and whose interest in and comments on my presentation of the atlas project spurred me on to finish my task.

My concentrated and rather lonely year of work on this atlas could only have been sustained through endless conversations with friends and colleagues, who listened tirelessly over and over again to how the manuscript was coming along: its structure, its contents, its stories, and its problems. I want to thank Huda Lutfi, Joseph Massad, Nashwa Azhari, Mona Prince, Randa Shaath, Sherif Boraie, Iman Ghazallah, Ragui Assaad, Heba El-Kholy, Mona Abaza, Kamal Fahmy, and Neil Hewison for their kind willingness to read, comment on, and provide suggestions of new texts to be included in the *Atlas*. Their enthusiasm and encouragement have meant the world to me as I raced through to finish what an internal university grant committee had evaluated as an impossible task to complete within the proposed timeframe. I also wish to thank AUC students Andrew Heiss, Alex Ortiz, and Sarah Hawas, who enthusiastically agreed to translate some excerpts in the literary atlas project, two of which are included in this volume. I want to seize this opportunity to correct an oversight in *The Literary Atlas of Cairo*, the first volume in this project, where the translation of the excerpt from Mohamed Salah al-Azab's *Repeated Stops* should have been under the name of Alex Ortiz rather than my name.

Artist and photographer, Amr Khadr has been my main interlocutor with regard to the details of the atlas project. He is also my partner in the *Literary Cairo Installation*, a multi-media exhibition that will be based primarily on the literary material amassed in this *Atlas*. Amr's unique visual work on Cairo and his profound interest in literary representations of the city have allowed us to map out a new project that would integrate the literary and the visual in what we think may be an unprecedented endeavor. I am grateful to him for sharing his visual experiences of Cairo and for providing me with an extensive repertoire of images from which to select an appropriate cover for both volumes.

The challenge to finish this ever-expanding project could not have been possible without the enthusiasm, hard work, and motivating feedback throughout from my research assistant, Amira Abou-Taleb, who made sure at every juncture that I would be on schedule, working ahead of me, and spurring me on to produce more work for her to do on time. As always, her meticulousness, her intelligence, and her sharp, practical common sense were indispensable to producing this now two-volume work.

I also wish to thank AUC librarians Jayme Spencer and Ola Seif and members of their respective staff, who graciously allowed me to use the Main

Library and the Rare Books and Special Collections Library when the libraries were practically closed and the staff were preparing to move both libraries to the AUC New Cairo campus.

Mr. Samir Khalil was single-handedly responsible for typing both the English and Arabic manuscripts. I am thankful for his patience, thoroughness, and dedication even as the excerpts kept increasing in number beyond his initial expectations of the workload and the time frame required for producing it.

The AUC Press editorial staff has been tremendously supportive. I particularly wish to thank Nadia Naqib and Elizabeth Kelley, who have been most helpful at various stages of the production of the manuscript. I initially feared and had been warned that the process of seeking permissions from authors, translators, and publishers across the globe would be an absolute nightmare. Indeed, this proved to be the most time-consuming and mind-boggling aspect of the entire project. I am indebted to all the authors, publishers, and translators who granted me permission to reprint the material included in this volume. Without their cooperation, promptness, and enthusiasm, this work would have never seen the light.

Finally, I want to thank my son, Nadim, whose love for Cairo anchors us both in this, the mother of cities.

Introduction
Cairo, Mother of Cities,
Again and Again

The Literary Life of Cairo was not initially intended to be a separate volume. It was supposed to be part of *The Literary Atlas of Cairo*. But, once I had compiled the complete manuscript, even after I had already excluded a considerable amount of material I had selected for the project, it became clear that it would be impossible to publish in a single volume. The publishers immediately told me that I would either have to cut the material in half, or that we would have to publish it in two volumes. Although the two-volume solution didn't initially appeal to me, it still seemed better than cutting down on the material itself. At first, I was rather concerned about how and where I would divide the manuscript, since it was originally conceived of as a single volume. However, to my surprise, the ten sections of the manuscript very conveniently divided themselves into two fairly independent yet complementary literary maps of the city. The four longer sections included in *The Literary Atlas of Cairo* focus on literary representations of Cairo as a physical space and the transformations that its built environment has undergone during the twentieth century. In contrast, the seven shorter sections that make up *The Literary Life of Cairo* all represent Cairenes' lives and human relations across the city's literary topography. These two very general levels of mapping Cairo in modern Arab works of the twentieth century now each stand alone. However, they also dialogue with and inform each other in multiple ways that readers will no doubt discover if they read both volumes, which are collectively referred to as: the Literary Atlas project. Given this complementary relationship between the two volumes from the very start, it is important, and only fair to readers of

1

The Literary Life of Cairo for me to share with them, as I did with the readers of *The Literary Atlas of Cairo*, the elements that stood behind and propelled this project, to which I will refer hereafter as the literary atlas project.

Many reasons have come together to motivate this now two-volume work, some professional and others personal. Both, however, are thoroughly and intrinsically linked and interconnected since they were simultaneously shaped during a very particular moment in time. Perhaps the first professional moment in the development of this project was in May 2005 when I was invited by my colleagues Iman Hamdy and Martina Rieker to present a paper at the Cairo Papers Symposium at the American University in Cairo (AUC) titled "Transformations in Middle Eastern Landscapes: From Modernism to Neo-liberalism." I gladly accepted the invitation because, first, as a scholar of Arabic literature, a field routinely marginalized by the dominant social sciences, I was happy to see that the space for interdisciplinary conversation was both possible and welcome; and second, again as a scholar of Arabic literature, I was convinced that many of the issues raised in the social sciences and in urban studies are in fact represented in literary texts that have provided some of the most eloquent and perceptive readings of urban and social reality and its transformation in a form, language, metaphor, and idiom that are part and parcel of such transformations.

The paper I presented at the symposium was entitled "From the *Hara* to the *Imara*: Emerging Urban Metaphors in the Literary Production on Contemporary Cairo."[1] This paper eventually became the cornerstone for an entire seminar on "Cairo in the Modern Literary Imaginary" that I taught twice at AUC, once in Arabic in 2006 and then again in English in 2007. Both seminars provided magnificent testing grounds for the literary atlas of Cairo project and I remain indebted to the group of students who attended them, for their sharp discussions, valuable contributions, and excellent papers, one of which earned a distinguished university award.[2]

But, as I attempt to reconstruct the beginnings of this project through the new and inspiring professional directions it has brought me, I sense that it was equally motivated by a more deep-seated personal anxiety, for it coincided to a great extent with the ever-approaching date of the relocation of the American University in Cairo campus from Cairo's throbbing downtown Tahrir area to its present location in New Cairo. The old campus witnessed my student years at AUC as well as eighteen years of my professional life in the institution.[3] This imminent displacement from the city of my childhood, school years, social life, and professional growth—not to mention emotional attachments and a lifetime of memories—all brought forth a sudden desire to try to capture this ever expanding space all at once before I was uprooted from it, so to speak. My anxiety was driven home when, as I started working on the atlas project immediately after AUC had relocated to New Cairo, I received an e-mail from Faculty Services at the university announcing, for the first time ever, a walking tour of downtown Cairo for members of the AUC community. I must admit that I was horrified at the implications of the idea since it suddenly transformed bustling downtown Cairo into a museum, a thing of the past, which we could now watch as spectacle when, for most of the twentieth century, AUC had been part of the very making of its modern history.

This general nostalgia was further aggravated when I began to reflect on the new Open Museum project undertaken by the state in the heart of Islamic Cairo and its implications and consequences for life in the old city. After having been the microcosm of the entire Cairene society until the early decades of the twentieth century, the *hara,* or alley, of Islamic Cairo has become the margin to the center, a dwelling place for the predominantly poor and underprivileged. The historic heart of Cairo has visibly declined and its more affluent residents have moved elsewhere in search of more favorable conditions. The Open Museum project has effectively meant that Islamic Cairo has been emptied of its remaining social life and has been transformed into a playground for tourists where monuments and relics of the past are now the focus of the state's Islamic heritage industry and touristic modernization projects.

As these transformations begin to redefine the old city, similar projects of gentrification are in the making for the modern colonial center of the city, which has lost its earlier splendor and has become a *sha'bi* ('of the people' or 'lower class') area, and which now needs 'cleaning up.' In a paper entitled "Cairo's Downtown Imagined: Nostalgia and/or Dubaization," sociologist Mona Abaza maps out the mounting speculation concerning the future of the Khedival, Belle Epoque, downtown Cairo that is known in Arabic as Wist al-Balad, on the edge of which lay the AUC campus that moved to New Cairo in September 2008. Abaza traces the mega multinational projects to revamp Wist al-Balad—with Paris as an ideal to be emulated—that will involve moving the main landmarks of the downtown area: the Mugamma' (the main administrative bastion located in Tahrir Square), the Egyptian Museum, and the Stock Exchange headquarters. These lucrative beautification and gentrification plans, which are motivated by a nostalgia for Belle Epoque Cairo, lead Abaza to ask the critical question that has yet to be answered about the actual life and socioeconomic fabric of the downtown area: "How then will the investors deal with the uncontrollable public space occupied by the 'riff-raff,' beggars and ambulant sellers as understood amongst official circles?"[4] This question, along with my own personal anxieties and nostalgia about displacement from the heart of the city, seems to have prompted the need I felt for mapping Cairo from the sources I knew best and have come to lie at the very heart of both *The Literary Atlas of Cairo* and *The Literary Life of Cairo*.

I have been asked how long it has taken to research, identify, edit, and partially translate the selected excerpts that comprise this literary map of Cairo. There are two answers to this question. The immediate answer is one year: a very special year during which I was completely immersed in producing the map, in putting it together, so to speak. It was also during this year that I came to understand what exactly I was trying to map or, to put it differently, what the works themselves were telling me I should map. This one year was crucial for defining the very parameters of the atlas project as well as my own understanding of the different facets of urbanity and the levels of urban experience that I was trying to represent. But the real answer to the question is that it took more than three decades of reading, teaching, and writing about Arabic literature in order for me to feel familiar enough with Cairo's ever-changing literary topography to dare to map it.

Franco Moretti's *Atlas of the European Novel: 1800–1900* has been a great source of inspiration for my literary atlas of Cairo project as well as my teaching on Cairo in general, since it articulated in very concrete terms precisely what I wanted to do:

> Geography is not an inert container, is not a box where cultural history 'happens,' but an active force, that pervades the literary field and shapes its depth. Making the connection between geography and literature explicit, then— mapping it: because a map is precisely that, a connection made visible—will allow us to see some significant relationships that have so far escaped us.[5]

Despite the differences between Moretti's project and my own, it remains self-evident, to me at least, that we share the conviction that literary geography as he put it, can "change the way we read novels," and, I would add, can equally change the way we read the space in which these novels came into being. Even though Moretti's *Atlas* encompasses space in literature (Jane Austin's England, Balzac's Paris, Dickens's London, and so on) as well as literature in space (libraries, distribution of literature across space, among others) while the literary atlas project confines itself to space in literature only, my project, like his, understands literary geography as a means to pose new questions and look for new answers. Indeed, literary geography provides analytical tools that dissect the text in an unusual way and foregrounds, as Moretti put it, "the only real issue of literary history: society, rhetoric, and their interaction."[6]

The relationship between literature and geography, writers and the space that they and their narratives occupy, has been succinctly articulated by Gamal al-Ghitani, one of Egypt's major writers and literary architects of the city, in the following terms:

> Fundamentally, writing is linked to a specific place, the history and past
> of this place, and the spirit of this place. To be interested in time, and the
> passage of time, is to be interested in a specific place as well. For space and
> time are indissolubly tied. Place contains time. That is why remembering a
> certain event, at a certain date, cannot but evoke the place, the space in which
> we were at that given moment. . . .
>
> It is for this reason that the relationship between a writer and a place is very
> important, because place implies time, history, society and human relations.[7]

Even though representations of 'real' space in literature are fundamentally an imaginative construction, they will necessarily provide, through narrativity and temporality, a map of real material geopolitics and histories as well as a complex network of human relations across literary topography. In "Semiology and the Urban," Roland Barthes described the city as "a discourse and this discourse is truly a language: the city speaks to its inhabitants, we speak our city, the city where we are, simply by living in it, by wandering through it, by looking at it."[8] Not only is the city a "discourse" and a "language" but it also "speaks to its inhabitants"; not only is the city constituted of signs that need to be deciphered and read, but those very signs signify differently for the city dwellers who behold and decode them. Indeed, urban semioticians and planners have moved away from trying to identify universal features of the urban experience and have placed the emphasis on the readers of the city whose cultural and social positions will determine the very visibility and legibility of the cityscape.[9] The city is not simply a physical presence that writers reproduce; rather, the city is a construct that continues to be reinvented by its inhabitants—in this case, its writers—each according to his or her experiential eye and personal encounter with it. At this level, the city emerges as an actor with real agency that embodies and structures social power as well as political, economic, and symbolic processes. As the writers come to represent the city in literature, they, in turn, become architects of its history whose literary works reconstruct and re-map the city. Even as writers provide us with the familiar landmarks of the city, ultimately these same physical landmarks take on, or lose signification for each one of them depending on the time in which the place and space are written.

Given the dominance of the realist tradition in Arabic literature in general and Egyptian literature in particular, it is no surprise that Cairo, whether it is the historic city or the modern metropolis, should be the main 'real' and metaphoric space for much of the literary production during the twentieth century. Urban space, for the writers of the city, has been a major architect of its social, economic, and political fabric. In this literary production, Cairo becomes a protagonist whose existence is indispensable for the existence of the narratives themselves, not to speak of our own reading and decoding of these works. Hence, the city becomes a text that is constantly rewritten, a space that is continuously reconstructed/deconstructed through its ever-shifting, ever-changing signs.

During the twentieth century, specifically since the 1960s, Cairo has witnessed an accelerated pattern of physical expansion beyond its historic Islamic neighborhoods and its modern colonial ones. As the renowned historian of the city of Cairo, André Raymond has noted:

> Cairo's impetuous growth in the past half-century complicates any image
> one might try to form of it. The traditional city of the late Ottoman era
> and the two side-by-side cities of the colonial era have been absorbed into a
> whole so diverse as to prevent any simple conclusions. The faces of the city
> blur; its centers are many and mobile. But this 'fragmented' Cairo can still be
> reconstituted into more or less coherent wholes, each clearly revealing deep
> social differences.[10]

Many factors have converged to produce this image of 'fragmented' Cairo: the socialist, centrally planned, and public-sector dominated state economy of the Nasser regime of the 1960s was abandoned for an 'open door' one during the Sadat period (1971–81) that encouraged the private sector and Arab and international investment. This, together with rural–urban migration, led to the appearance of informal and illegal housing during the 1980s, as well as the 'ruralization of urban areas,' the deterioration in living conditions and infrastructure in the old city, and class inequalities and urban problems both social and economic.[11] The state's laissez-faire policies, not only within the economic field, but also in the field of urban planning, have resulted in the uncomfortable coexistence of skyscrapers and multi-million-dollar commercial centers side by side with shantytowns and informal settlements. The mega-city of Cairo has also experienced new patterns of geographic, economic, and social mobility: the influx of an immigrant rural population, the rise of professional and labor migration to the Gulf, new internal migration to the factories in satellite cities or coastal tourist developments, the emergence of new patterns of investment and consumption, the disintegration of the 'traditional' social fabric, and the emergence of new urban affiliations and solidarities.

Both *The Literary Atlas of Cairo* and *The Literary Life of Cairo* constitute an unprecedented literary intervention that tries to 're-construct' Cairo and Cairenes' lives from what André Raymond has called its fragments and its many mobile centers. Through a careful selection and juxtaposition of reconstructions and representations of the city of Cairo in Arab literary works throughout the twentieth century, this two-volume work provides a literary topography of the sociocultural, political, and urban history of the city by bringing together some one hundred works by Egyptian and Arab writers who represent several generations of men and women, Muslims, Copts, and Jews, citizens and lovers of the globalized metropolis, writing in Arabic, English, or French about the city of Cairo. Not travelers, but writers who are city dwellers and residents of Cairo whose reconstructions of its literary geography and experience with its urban topography can indeed render the cityscape legible, whether that representation is in Arabic, English, or French. As these writers undertake to represent the city in literature, their representations map out many of the changes in the 'fragmented' city's geopolitics and its urban fabric while tracing spatial and social forms of polarization as well as new patterns of inclusion and exclusion within the borderless boundaries of the expanding mega-city. As such, this two-volume work compliments and dialogues with many other existing publications about the city of Cairo, in both the humanities and social sciences, and specifically in the fields of history, sociology, anthropology, architecture, urban planning, migration studies, cultural studies, gender studies, and development studies, all of which have explored similar issues, problems, contradictions, and challenges in Cairenes' lives.

Through their thematic organization, the two volumes of the literary atlas project trace, with equal depth, both the developments that have taken place over an entire century in modes of literary production as well as the unique historical cross-section of the actors within the Cairene literary field. From the pre-modern prose style that imitates the classical form and structure of the *maqama*,[12] to the elevated neoclassical style of the *début du siècle*, to experimentations with a third language that combines the written and spoken Arabic at levels more attuned to the needs of modern narrative texts, all the way to creative uses of the vernacular and everyday street lingo—all these forms of fictional expression, as well as those developed by anglophone and francophone Arab writers, are an integral part of the city's literary geography. Likewise, throughout the *Atlas*, readers will experience the extent to which class, gender, race, and ethnic background condition and shape these literary reconstructions of the cityscape at both the diachronic and synchronic levels.

On another level, the sections that constitute *The Literary Life of Cairo* and *The Literary Atlas of Cairo* are meant to open up new lines of inquiry and new ways of reading Cairo, one of the globe's largest historic, multicultural urban centers through a century-long literary production by its writers. For example, as I was working on the atlas project, I was asked to participate on a panel during the inaugural festivities for the AUC campus in New Cairo. I volunteered to present a piece on the representation of AUC in Arab literary works through some of the selections I had collected for the manuscript.[13] It was a surprisingly interesting and rewarding experience, for by tracing AUC's appearance in narratives of the twentieth century, one discovers a fascinating development in the nature of the space accorded to this institution in the national imaginary: from being on the margin of Egyptian society to occupying its very center, from being 'other' to becoming an integral part of the writer's and the nation's very identity. Inversely, through these same representations we are able to read the transformations that have occurred in Egyptian society at large during the twentieth century. Indeed, the sheer physical presence of AUC in the heart of downtown Cairo as one of the main axes of the city's bustling Tahrir Square made it a landmark in narratives whose protagonists' stories, or parts of them, unfold in downtown Cairo. Works by Ihsan Abdel Quddus, Edward Said, Radwa Ashour, Ahdaf Soueif, Ahmed Alaidy, Mahmoud Al-Wardani, Yasser Abdel Latif, Mekkawi Said, May Khaled, Mourid Barghouti, among others, all map the downtown area with reference to AUC and the history it has participated in making.

And yet all these representations are reconstructions of 'real' space that do not always necessarily coincide with real geography. In trying to map out the coincidences between real and imagined space in Naguib Mahfouz's work, specifically in his *Trilogy*, which is set in Gamaliya, the writer's own neighborhood, Gamal al-Ghitani concludes:

> Mahfouz consciously mixes the real places with streets that exist solely in his imagination. The city then becomes a cobweb of the real and the imagined.

It is an imaginative landscape, constructed of elements so real that we occasionally confuse them with the city itself. Mahfouz gives himself the freedom to merge the real and the imagined, which converge in a city that comes eventually to serve as a representation of his characters' lives.[14]

A literary geography of Cairo then, but, which Cairo would this literary atlas represent? And how? These were the difficult choices that had to be made in order for this project to materialize. Given my own area of expertise—modern Arabic literature and more specifically narrative literature—it was obvious to me from the start that I would focus on the representation of Cairo in twentieth-century narrative works by Arab writers. But beyond my own field of study there were two crucial determining factors in the choice of material for the atlas project. First, as Benedict Anderson has argued in *Imagined Communities*, there is an intrinsic relationship between the birth of the imagined community of the modern nation and the new structures, forms, and languages that developed with the novel and the newspaper, for "these forms provided the technical means for 're-presenting' the *kind* of imagined community that is the nation."[15] It is through these new structures of representation that readers came to imagine themselves as a community even if they had never and would never see each other. This imagined community is cemented through a "presentation of simultaneity in 'homogenous, empty time,' or a complex gloss upon the word 'meanwhile.'"[16] The novel, then, imitates the nation to a great extent, not only through setting, temporality, character, and event, but also through language. For the purposes of compiling both *The Literary Atlas of Cairo* and *The Literary Life of Cairo*, it seemed appropriate to use narrative literature in constructing a literary geography of Cairo precisely because it allows, through its very form and structure, the representation not only of real material geopolitics and histories but a complex network of human relations across literary topography as well. One could imagine another atlas of Cairo that focuses solely on poetry for example, however, given the dense, elliptical nature of poetic language, the end product, no doubt very interesting, would have been substantially different.

The second issue that needed to be resolved was the time frame for the project. This was perhaps an easier decision to make given my choice of the novel as the dominant literary form in the atlas as a whole, for not only is the novel related to nationalism and the rise of modern national imaginings, but it is related equally to urbanity and the centrality of the urban experience both of which have become increasingly dominant in twentieth-century Arab narrative literature. Whether we choose to consider the canonical beginnings of the Arab novel during the first decade of the twentieth century or the more hybrid and cosmopolitan popular fiction from 'below,' there is no denying that the literary geography of the city gradually came to dominate the fictional space, so much so that it prompted Gaber Asfour, one of the Arab world's most prominent literary critics, to label the twentieth century "the time of the novel" *(zaman al-riwaya)*.[17] Naguib Mahfouz was among the first to lead the way during the first half of the twentieth century, with most of his novels set in Old Cairo. Gradually, however, as urban space expanded, and as Old Cairo lost much of its distinctive social and economic fabric through the exodus of its population to the modern metropolis, writers of the city, including Naguib Mahfouz himself, migrated or were displaced to other locations, mapping out many of Cairo's new boundaries and their accompanying social changes and economic developments.

The Literary Life of Cairo and *The Literary Atlas of Cairo* map out these migrations and displacements and attempt to reconstruct Cairo as it grows, changes, and expands through its representation in literary works over a century. In collecting, editing, organizing, and translating at least one third of the material that constitutes this project, I tried to let the city speak, to use Roland Barthes' formulation: I tried to let the city emerge from the literary works, in 'fragments,' in bits and pieces that, when juxtaposed against each other, would provide a map, would actually "speak to us" as Barthes said. Even though the texts themselves are excerpts from the authors' novels, their juxtaposition and arrangement in both volumes are my own. The act of selection and juxtaposition implicates me at a second degree in the reconstruction of Cairo's literary geography and suggests that the map that is about to unfold before the readers is but one of many possible maps that would ultimately depend on the perspective of the 'cartographer,' or the city dweller—myself— and how the city 'spoke' to me.

The Literary Life of Cairo: One Hundred Years in the Heart of the City is the second of the two-volume atlas project. Unlike the first volume *(The Literary Atlas of Cairo)*, which focuses on the literary geopolitics of the cityscape, this volume immerses the reader in the complex network of socioeconomic and cultural lives in the city across that literary geography. *The Literary Life of Cairo* comprises seven sections, all of which have emerged out of the preoccupations of the literary texts themselves. The first section, "Icons of the City," introduces readers to representations of some of Cairo's prominent profiles, both political and cultural, and their impact on the city's literary geography, from King Farouk to the popular, leftist, blind singer and composer of the second half of the twentieth century, Sheikh Imam Issa. Just as authors have represented public iconic figures through their literary works, they have also invented new ones, perhaps little known, and have bestowed upon them the status of city icons by writing them into their literary texts. The second section is entitled "Cairo Cosmopolitan," and includes a spectrum of literary reconstructions and readings of the city by its multiethnic, multinational, and multilingual writers across class, gender, and generation. The various excerpts in this section contest and unsettle the whole notion of cosmopolitanism by telling the complex story of how various ethno-religious communities from considerably different social and economic classes cohabited within the same urban space. Cairo's controversial cosmopolitan face is further revealed in the third section, "Going to School in Cairo" that includes daunting representations of colonial school experiences as well as startling contrasts of postcolonial educational realities. The representations of schools, learning, and education in general are of particular importance to the literary atlas project as a whole since they all provide us with fascinating insight into the very making of the intellectual and literary elite that is the producer and shaper of the two volumes themselves. The fourth section, "The Street is Ours?," maps out representations of Cairenes' numerous moments of political participation and oppression in such detail and quantity that these literary representations become the fictional alternative to constrained political activism on the real street. It is as if the constraints that stifle political culture in Egypt on the real street are undone within the imaginary text. The fictional narrative becomes the 'real' arena of contestation and resistance, one that cannot be silenced with batons and tear gas, physical torture and electric shock waves. The fifth section focuses on "Women in the City" and explores the space accorded them within the city's literary geography across history and class. Through the experiences of these different women, readers will encounter multiple faces of Cairo that have everything to do with these women's locations within the city. The sixth section delves into "Cairo's Underworld" to place the city's marginals on its literary map. Given the conscious and central role of creative writers as 'underground historians,' it is no surprise that their works painstakingly represent these silenced and unwritten faces of the city, which are so crucial to understanding Cairo's modern history.

Finally, the seventh section, "Cairo's Drug Culture" foregrounds the century-long representations of the very interesting and well-established relationship between writing and drugs, as well as the history of places, paraphernalia, and products in the drug world across class and time, from the salons of the divas of the early twentieth century to intellectual consumer dens, all the way to street kids and their drug culture. Mapping the culture of drugs in the city through literary representations across a century is of considerable importance and significance, since it traces the changes that have taken place in drug consumption, state politics, class attitudes, as well as local and global practices and networks. Like the first volume, each of the sections in *The Literary Life of Cairo* has an introductory section that leads the readers into the selections and establishes some of the important connecting points between them.

If readers of *The Literary Life of Cairo* find that the city as an urban space is missing from the general structure, they will want to read the first volume, which focuses primarily on this topic. *The Literary Atlas of Cairo: One Hundred Years on the Streets of the City* begins with a prelude that walks the readers into the city and defines the relationship between the city and the authors of its literary geography as articulated by them in their works. In the first section, "Mapping Cairo," readers will see the city expanding and changing, for the material presented here traces the city's accelerated physical growth from its once historic Islamic center at the beginning of the twentieth century to its haphazard, unplanned, informal settlements of the latter part of the same century. This is obviously not a 'real' map of Cairo but rather, the map that has emerged from the literature itself. As such, the map says as much about the writers of the city as it does about the city itself: who goes where in the city, whether the different 'fragments' of Cairo are connected, where the boundaries are, and who trespasses them. The second section is entitled "Public Spaces" and focuses on the representation of some of Cairo's landmarks, from the ancient pyramids to the postmodern malls, as they are reconstructed in the texts. These literary representations render the cityscape more legible, for suddenly such physical landmarks, which are part of the built environment, take on new and divergent levels of historic, cultural, and political signification as they are written by different authors. The third section, "Private Spaces," escorts the readers into the privacy of homes and intimate spaces in the city and provides an inventory of domestic rituals, hierarchies, and relationships. The juxtaposition of these private spaces against each other provides a unique glimpse into the contrasts and contradictions in Cairenes' domestic lives as we move from extended aristocratic abodes to displaced individuals' rundown rooms. "On the Move in Cairo"—the fourth section in *The Literary Atlas of Cairo*—attempts to map out how the lives of these radically different Cairenes intersect as they move about the city in both private and public transportation that provides the link between the public and the private, the outer and inner spaces of *al-Qahira*, the vanquishing city whose inhabitants constantly have to invent new ways to survive in it. Each of the sections in this volume is prefaced by a brief introduction that serves as a layout of the major axes, patterns, and issues that are raised by the selected literary excerpts.

Together, *The Literary Atlas of Cairo* and *The Literary Life of Cairo* produce a literary geography of Cairo that goes beyond the representation of space in literature to reconstruct the complex network of human relationships in that space. Unlike Moretti's actual physical maps of nineteenth-century novels, these two volumes provide mental, imagined maps that can then perhaps be traced physically by the readers themselves. As readers discover the major axes, patterns, and issues that are raised by the selected literary excerpts within each section, they will also begin to read across the sections and will trace new and interesting, as yet unwritten, relationships, thereby producing new maps of the cityscape and becoming themselves active authors of Cairo's literary geography. They are not just Baudelairian *flâneurs* who partake of and observe the city,[18] but motivated and implicated participants in reading and mapping the intricate literary geography, life, and lexicon of the city. Beyond this immediate level, it is important for readers to remember that the literary map of Cairo that unfolds in these two volumes is one that is constructed in translation. The representations of the city in Arabic, English, and French original texts for over one hundred years are here mediated through translation into another language. To be aware of this complex linguistic fact is to realize that embedded within both *The Literary Atlas of Cairo* and *The Literary Life of Cairo* is an equally valuable and unique atlas of literary translation that has yet to be written.

Just as the selections span the history of the relationship between literary producers and the city, as well as modes of representation of urban space, the English translations themselves provide an interesting glimpse into the transformations that have occurred in the field of Arabic literary translation and the roles and tasks of the translators of Cairo throughout the twentieth century: from the more literal and heavily annotated translations of the first half of the twentieth century to increasingly free-flowing renditions that oscillate between foreignizing and domesticating the original texts.

Almost twenty years ago, I had written an article entitled "Re-writing the City: The Case of *Khitat al-Ghitani*." It was a modest attempt at reading the changing faces of Cairo and the transformation of the city's signs through the works of Naguib Mahfouz and Gamal al-Ghitani. To put it very generally, *Khitat al-Ghitani* is a prophetic re-mapping of modern Cairo that lays out the oncoming defeat and downfall of the city victorious, *al-Qahira*. In this work, al-Ghitani parodies the great topographical texts of Islamic historiography known as the *Khitat* and produces his own 'fictional' history of the modern city.[19] As I started working on the atlas project, I was struck by how long the idea of mapping Cairo may have been brewing in my mind. Twenty years ago it was a mere chapter in a book, written by one person. Today it has become a collective work about 'The City Victorious' produced by almost one hundred writers over an entire century.

Notes

1. This paper eventually became chapter eight in my book *Egypt's Culture Wars: Politics and Practice* (London: Routledge, 2008; Cairo: American University in Cairo Press, 2010), 144–67; it has been republished *in Cairo Contested: Governance, Urban Space, and Global Modernity*, ed. Diane Singerman (Cairo: American University in Cairo Press, 2009), 145–73.

2. Amira Abou-Taleb, a graduate student in the department of Arab and Islamic Civilizations, won the Leila Fawwaz Award in Arabic Studies at AUC in Spring 2006 for her excellent paper, "Women in the City: Gender, Class, and Space."

3. New Cairo is a new city that was established by presidential decree in 2000 at the southeastern edge of Greater Cairo. It is part of the newly formed Helwan governorate and is home to several private schools and universities, including the American University in Cairo's New Campus, which was officially inaugurated in February 2009. New Cairo has been a place of escape for Egypt's upper-middle and upper classes from the noise and pollution of Cairo. Many of its residences are luxury villas and condominiums located in housing developments and gated communities.

4. Mona Abaza, "Cairo's Downtown Imagined: Nostalgia and/or Dubaization," unpublished paper presented at the Center for Middle East Studies, UC Berkeley, in December 2009.

5. Franco Moretti, *Atlas of the European Novel: 1800–1900* (London and New York: Verso, 1998), 3.

6. Moretti, *Atlas*, 5.

7. Luc Barbulesco and Philippe Cardinal, *L'Islam en questions* (Paris: Grasset, 1986), 143.

8. "Semiology and the Urban," in Neil Leach, ed., *Rethinking Architecture: A Reader in Cultural Theory* (London: Routledge, 1997), 168.

9. Hana Wirth-Nesher, *City Codes: Reading the Modern Urban Novel* (Cambridge: Cambridge University Press, 1996), 7.

10. André Raymond, *Cairo: City of History*, trans. Willard Wood (Cairo: American University in Cairo Press, 2001), 361.

11. Tarek Aboul Atta and Mahmoud Yousry, "The Challenge of Urban Growth in Cairo," in Carole Rakodi, ed., *The Urban Challenge in Africa: Growth and Management of its Large Cities* (New York: United Nations University Press, 1997), 111–49. See also Raymond, *Cairo: City of History*, 337–77 and Eric Denis, "Urban Planning and Growth in Cairo," in *Middle East Report*, no. 202 (Winter 1997), http://www.jstor.org/view/08992851/di011543/01p00442/0 (accessed 20 May 2006).

12. The *maqama* is an Arabic literary genre of rhymed prose with intervals of poetry and is characterized by rhetorical extravagance. It centers on a trickster figure or roguish character whose wanderings, experiences, and exploits are conveyed by a narrator.

13. For the full text of the presentation on "The Representation of AUC in the Arab Cultural Imaginary," see AUC Memories, http://www1.aucegypt.edu/ncd/onthemove/aucmemories/contributors.html (accessed 10 October 2009).

14. Gamal al-Ghitani, *The Cairo of Naguib Mahfouz* (Cairo: American University in Cairo Press, 1999), 14.

15. Benedict Anderson, *Imagined Communities: Reflections on the Origin and Spread of Nationalism* (London: Verso, 1983), 30.

16. Anderson, *Imagined Communities*, 30–31.

17. Gaber Asfour, *Zaman al-riwaya* (Cairo: GEBO, 1999).

18. The term flâneur basically means 'stroller,' 'lounger,' or 'loafer,' and has been used by the nineteenth-century poet Charles Baudelaire to describe a gentleman stroller of city streets who is at once part of and apart from the cityscape, someone with a key role in understanding and portraying the city. Since Baudelaire the idea of the *flâneur* has accumulated significant meaning as a referent for understanding urban phenomena and modernity.

19. The historiographical genre of *khitat* persisted well into the nineteenth century and was especially developed in Egypt. Perhaps two of the most prominent examples of this genre and among the most influential are *Khitat al-Maqrizi* (fifteenth century) and *al-Khitat al-tawfiqiya* by 'Ali Mubarak (nineteenth century). The word *khitat* is the plural form of the word *khitta*. Both derive from the Arabic verb *khatta/yakhuttu*, meaning to write, to plan, to lay out, to draw (as in a map). The plural form, *khitat*, came to designate an Islamic genre of historiography, distinguished by its spatial organization; a form of social history and topography of the provinces of the expanding Islamic empire that felt the urgency of keeping records of its newly established towns. In so doing, *Khitat al-Ghitani* undermines the authoritative voice of the historian and proposes to challenge it by imitating it. This symbolic gesture allows al-Ghitani to line up with some of the most noted historians thereby assuming, just like them, an equally authoritative role and voice in the city. More importantly however, *Khitat al-Ghitani* remains a fictional not a historical *khitat* and can therefore stand for an alternative historical record and an alternative cultural map.

Icons of the City

Every city has icons that constitute part of its memory and its history; they may be exceptional architectural or physical structures of the built environment or they may be people who are readily recognized as having some outstanding role or significance in the political or cultural life of the city. This section focuses on the latter kind of iconography by bringing together literary representations of some of Cairo's, if not the entire country's, most important national and cultural icons: individuals whose impact and imprint have clearly marked the collective literary imaginary during and beyond the twentieth century.

National figures have an important signification in literary texts, for the tones and modes of their representation betray the authors' own political and ideological leanings. Among the national figures who occupy a very special space in literary representations of the first half of the twentieth century is the figure of Saad Zaghloul, the icon of the 1919 revolution who headed the delegation, or wafd, that demanded Egypt's independence from the British high commissioner in November 1919. Rather than grant Saad Zaghloul his request, the British government deported him to Malta in March 1919 along with three other members of the delegation. Indeed, Saad, as he is intimately referred to by the Egyptian people, is *the* hero of national resistance and independence. Unsurprisingly, Saad Zaghloul is a familiar, and much celebrated, icon in the Mahfouzian oeuvre, since the author himself, who was then eight years old, is practically the son of the 1919 revolution. But, aside from Mahfouz's work, many references to Saad Zaghloul occur across this literary atlas, beyond Mahfouz's work and outside the bounds of this section. What remains quite striking in many of these representations of Saad is his physical absence from the text: he is talked about, hailed, admired but seldom seen or described as a physical presence. And yet despite his absence as a literary persona he remains omnipresent as a force, for he was able to mobilize the entire nation. As Robert Solé's narrator succinctly put it in *Birds of Passage* when Saad was deported, "The next day, Egypt rose in revolt." Nationwide demonstrations and strikes by students, civil servants, merchants, peasants, workers, and religious leaders both Muslim and Christian became a daily affair. Hundreds died for Saad and the national cause so that finally British fear of continued mass protest led to Saad's release two weeks after his arrest.

The other national figure who looms large in literary representations of the second half of the twentieth century is of course Gamal Abdel Nasser, the icon of the 1952 revolution. Unlike the symbolic literary representations of Saad Zaghloul—in which he is discussed, but never figures as a character— representations of Nasser are ambivalent and inspired by his sheer stunning physical demeanor, oscillating between love and fear, adoration and skepticism. Pitted against the image of this national godfather is the monarch that Nasser and the Free Officers ousted: King Farouk, represented in Ahmad Hasanein's excerpt from *And Cairo Burned* as isolated, unpopular, cowardly, corrupt, selfish, and nationally impotent.

In *Walking Through Fire*, Nawal El Saadawi describes her first face-to-face encounter with Nasser, 'the lion,' in the story of the 1952 revolution in almost mythical terms:

> When I looked into Gamal Abdel Nasser's face I found him more attractive than in his pictures. The cameras could not catch the strong glimmer in his big, black eyes. His skin was brown, the color of fresh silt brought down by the Nile. He was tall, very tall, with a slight stoop to his shoulders like my grandmother and my father, walked slightly bent, taking long strides. Was he carrying the same load they had carried throughout their lives?

Nasser was at once the son and the father, the determined leader of the future and the broken peasant of the past: "His voice was magnificent: strong, mature, sometimes thundering with anger like a wild Pharaoh; at other times soft like that of a peasant fed only on dry bread and cheese," says the narrator in Saadawi's text.

As the Free Officers' regime grew increasingly repressive toward its opposition, these radically opposed and contradictory descriptions of Nasser were to be further exploited in literary representations of him. The very same "strong glimmer in his big, black eyes" described by Saadawi becomes in later texts, not a source of determination and hope but one of threat and fear. In her epic novel *In the Eye of the Sun*, Ahdaf Soueif captures the intense intimidation Nasser's very presence would inspire at a concert by the diva Umm Kulthum singing the lyrics of "al-Atlal" (The Ruins) during the 1960s, prior to the 1967 Arab defeat in the war against Israel, where one of the lines of the song, "Give me my freedom, let loose my hands," is feared in case it is misinterpreted by Nasser as being a reference to his regime's increasingly repressive policies: "For a moment the audience is apprehensive. Would he perhaps think that this was a veiled reference to his Mukhabarat? How very audacious she is. Who else would have dared to sing this stanza—even though it is in a love song?"

And yet, Nasser's image as father of the nation continued to dominate literary representation even after it had been broken by defeat and his staged decision, very quickly withdrawn due to massive popular demand, to abdicate power: Soueif's young protagonist, Asya, watches Nasser's televised abdication speech and comments, helplessly distraught: "OK, maybe you are responsible. In fact, of course you are responsible. But how can we let you go? What shall we do without you?" The image of the Egyptian people as abandoned children in the aftermath of Nasser's attempt to step down is further accentuated by his sudden and untimely death in 1971, leaving the narrator of Latifa al-Zayyat's *The Search* caught between anger, disappointment, and grief: "Nobody, whoever they are, has the right to orphan a people."

Nasser's larger-than-life image in numerous literary texts contrasts quite dramatically with under-representations of both of his successors, Sadat and Mubarak. In Naguib Mahfouz's *The Day the Leader was Killed*, news of Sadat's assassination in 1981 only elicits further character assassinations on the streets of a city already boiling with rage against him: "The hell with him! Death saved him from madness. Anyhow, he had to go. This is what happens to those who imagine that the country is nothing but a dead corpse." Indeed, when Mahfouz first announced publicly, the title of his book *The Day the Leader was Killed,* it is known that he was called in by Mrs. Sadat, who feared that the text would be unsympathetic, perhaps even permanently damaging to President Sadat's image, especially if the criticism came from the writer who was reputed to be his 'staunch supporter.' She pleaded with him to postpone publication but he declined.

As for literary representations of Mubarak, they remain almost totally absent, certainly because of his continuing presence in power. However, there is one hilariously funny parody of the entire Mubarak era rendered in Ibrahim Issa's satiric and initially banned novel *The Assassination of the Big Man.* Issa's thriller represents the tragi-comic reality of the contemporary Egyptian field of power, both locally and globally. The novel opens with the discovery that the president of the republic has been stabbed to death in his own bed with a dagger that had been hanging on the wall in his bedroom. The president's private secretary summons key members of the cabinet for consultation. As they arrive at the presidential palace, their inner thoughts and consciousness are revealed to the reader in a series of flashbacks that expose the corruption, mediocrity, and ridicule of the political apparatus as well as the ministers' anxieties and fears for their fragile positions within the political field. One of these satiric episodes transforms the failed attempt on Mubarak's life in Ethiopia in 1996 into an attack on the President by the lions at the zoo, which pounce upon him and his guests:

"Get up and run, Mr. President."
When the President heard this, his youthfulness that had been lost during his eighty years of age shot forth. With the sole desire to save his skin, he quickly got up, held himself steady, looked at the lions and mumbled, stuttering and awestricken:
"Incredible! Incredible!"

The icons of the city are not limited to its political leaders. Indeed, the literature is full of representations of cultural figures that are endowed with national prominence and significance. Such is the case with Edward Said's *Homage to a Belly Dancer*, where he starts by tracing the beginnings of the careers of two such cultural icons: Umm Kulthum, *kawkab al-sharq* (The Star of the East) and Tahia Carioca, "the finest belly-dancer ever," both of whom performed at King Farouk's wedding in 1936. Even though Umm Kulthum is not one of Said's favorite singers, he still recognizes her, as do all Egyptians and Arabs, as "a national symbol, respected both during the monarchy and after the revolution led by Gamal Abdel Nasser." As for Carioca, the central icon of his homage, she is elevated, perhaps for the first time ever, to a stature identical to that of the exceptional Umm Kulthum: an equally "remarkable symbol of national culture."

Another prominent example of these urban cultural icons is Sheikh Imam Issa, the blind composer and singer who put to music the political protest poems by leading vernacular poet Ahmad Fuad Nigm, and who, as part of the frequently detained and imprisoned duo Imam–Nigm became *the* icon of political dissent during the 1970s. Not only memorialized in oral collective memory, in *Broken Spirit*, Mohamed Mansi Qandil inscribes this rogue-like, blind bard into the written literary text as the Sheikh makes his way to a student rally at Cairo University in1968. He is represented as "a fragile man who alighted from the train like a soft morning breeze. The prison mats had eaten at his body and the humidity of the old stone walls of his abode had affected his bones."

Just as authors have represented public iconic figures through their literary works, they have also invented new ones, perhaps little-known, and have bestowed upon them the status of city icons by writing them into their literary texts. One such example, which has preoccupied more than one author, specifically those of the 1960s and 1970s, is Shuhdi Atiya al-Shafie, a leading figure in the Egyptian communist movement during the 1940s and 1950s who died of torture in Abou Zaabal prison on June 15, 1960 at the hands of the Nasser regime, which he supported until the very last minute. Shuhdi's brutal murder became a moment that would be forever engraved in collective literary memory by more than one Egyptian writer. *In Heads Ripe for Plucking*, Mahmoud Al-Wardani reproduces Shuhdi's obituary, as it was published in *al-Ahram* newspaper on June 20, 1960, thereby immortalizing him and his atrocious death for future generations:

As for you, our dear departed, we eulogize you thus:

A youth who, stabbed with spear and sword, fell to a death
that bears the stamp of victory, though victory was not his.
Swathed he was in death's blood-red garments, but no sooner
had day dawned than they were the green silk of Paradise.
Easy it would have been to elude death, but it was
the bitter dues of dignity and valor that drove him to face death.
A soul that shuns shame as though it were
a sin worse than heresy on the Day of Judgment.

As Shuhdi is resurrected and engraved in literary texts of the city he becomes one icon in a lineage of unnamed and unwritten citizens. This is the case of Mansour, the self-appointed car attendant at the downtown campus of the American University in Cairo (AUC) during the 1970s and 1980s. AUC's physical presence as part of the vital downtown space embroiled it in one of the country's most dramatic historical moments: the assassination attempt on Egypt's former minister of interior Hasan al-Alfi in August 1993 by members of the Islamic Jihad. In that bloody incident AUC lost Mansour, its self-appointed car-park attendant, who used to park all AUCians' cars (including my own) on Sheikh Rihan Street and had all the keys in his pocket. The bomb that was meant for the minister killed

Mansour instead. This tragic and senseless moment is movingly captured in Ahdaf's Soueif highly acclaimed novel, *The Map of Love*, where she writes Mansour's unrecorded death into history as part of the collective memory of the university and that of the city at large. Mansour, the self-imposed car-attendant, known only to the elite students of the AUC, is transformed into a city icon, part of its very built environment, one that only the literary text can capture and eternalize.

Robert Solé

from *Birds of Passage*

SABRI AND HIS COMRADES saw the world in a different light from 23 November 1919 onward. That was the day on which a delegation or *wafd* led by Sa'ad Zaghloul Pasha had called on the British high commissioner and demanded independence. National independence! The workers saw this as the remedy for their misfortunes: the British had to be kicked out.

Being an ex-minister, Sa'ad Zaghloul did not put it to Sir Reginald Wingate as discourteously as that. He and his associates were not savages, after all. "Britain is the strongest of the great powers, and the most liberal," the Wafdists explained diplomatically. "In the name of the libertarian principles that guide her, we ask to be her friends." But everyone got the point.

His Majesty's Government responded in March of the following year: Sa'ad Zaghloul and three of his associates were deported to Malta. The next day, Egypt rose in revolt.

Sabri took to the streets in company with several thousand students who had come to demonstrate in his part of town—a surprising encounter between vociferous intellectuals and an illiterate peasant struck dumb with emotion. Five of the students were felled by a burst of machine-gun fire in Sayida Zeinab Square. Sabri bore one off in his arms, severely wounded in the stomach, and laid him down in the lee of a shop with a broken window. Before he died the young man took a handkerchief and moistened it in his blood.

"Here," he muttered, "take this to Sa'ad Zaghloul."

"Stiff with dried blood," recounts the author of *An Officer's Career*, "that handkerchief remained at the bottom of my father's pocket."

A week later Sabri went with several comrades to Opera Square, where they tried to persuade the cabbies to go on strike. They were out of luck. The cabbies, who had no wish to lose the custom they derived from the Sunday races at Gezira, responded with a volley of oaths. The two groups were on the point of coming to blows when an extraordinary procession of carriages and motor cars entered the square: some Egyptian women, the majority veiled and several of them pashas' wives, were parading through the streets in support of independence. The workers gave them an ovation.

But events in Cairo paled beside what happened in the provinces. At Beni Soueif a mob invaded the court and seized the British judge before proceeding to wreck the government offices. At Madinet al-Fayoum, Bedouin attacked the British garrison and inflicted many casualties—four hundred, according to some reports.

On 18 March, when the cabbies and carters of Cairo finally struck, Sabri went to Shubra with a sizable delegation to encourage other workers to follow their example. They went first to the Alma cigarette factory, then to the Sednaoui furniture factory, and finally to the Batrakanis tarboosh factory. At the last port of call, Sabri climbed on a chair and harangued the labor force with particular vehemence: "I know these Batrakanis. My brother Rashid had worked for them for years. Can't you see how they're exploiting you and sucking your blood?"

Batrakani tarbooshes had at last seen the light early in 1919. Initially hampered by the war, Édouard Dhellemmes and my grandfather had found their plans thwarted by the prohibitive rise in manufacturing costs at Lille. This compelled them to fall back on Cairo. Premises of adequate size were available on the outskirts of Shubra, but they had had to equip them, obtain the raw materials, and recruit men capable of adapting themselves to industrial production.

The manufacture of tarbooshes did not seem especially complicated. The woolen material was felted by being churned in a cauldron containing hot water and soap powder. It then went into a mold, had its nap raised with teasels, and was shaved. All that remained was to dye it and give it the requisite appearance. Preliminary experiments indicated, however, that it was difficult to achieve an even finish when shaving and dyeing the felt. As for the product's durability, that could only be ascertained by use.

"We're behind enough as it is," Georges told his French partner. "The Italians and Czechs are busy moving into the places left vacant by the Austro-Hungarians, and we must be wary of that little local factory at Kaha. It's improving its products and charging rock-bottom prices at the same time."

So Batrakani tarbooshes were launched on the market without more ado. My grandfather, who was more of a salesman than an industrialist felt confident that he could combine the advantages of his various competitors. He would produce a tarboosh that was cheap thanks to local labor costs, but lend it an exotic touch with the aid of an equivocal form of words: "*Fabrication à la française.*"

The *Versailles* sold for 400 piasters a dozen, with a discount of up to twenty percent, the *Marseille* cost 350 piasters, the *Clemenceau* 320.

The Shubra factory had only just gone into full production when the Cairo riots broke out and some ringleaders invaded the premises. Production ceased and the workers walked out, not to return that day. On the morrow they claimed to have been stopped en route to the factory. Georges was furious, and he wasn't the only one.

"I'll put this fire out with a blob of spittle!" declared a British official in Cairo.

But the fire continued to spread, and His Majesty's Government grew impatient. Finally, on 24 March 1919, the war hero General Allenby was appointed high commissioner for Egypt and the Sudan, with instructions to restore order. Two weeks later he announced the release of Sa'ad Zaghloul.

Sabri was apprised of the news by a great hubbub that shook the whole of Sayida Zeinab. He raced down the dilapidated stairs of his tenement building, four at a time, and ran out into the street, where he hugged passersby in a state of euphoria and high excitement. The fuul vendor was already capering around his little cart. Taxis sped past filled with uniformed Egyptian soldiers waving flags. Sa'ad Zaghloul's name was shouted, chanted, and sung ad infinitum.

The next day a vast procession left Bab al-Hadid headed by cadets from the military academy and the chief of police. All Egypt paraded past, from judges of the native courts to Muslim theologians, from Coptic priests to stage actors and employees of the street-watering company. The demonstrators cheered Sultan Fouad as they passed 'Abdin Palace, but did he really deserve their plaudits? That same morning he had swathed himself in the caftan of his ancestor Muhammad Ali—which was too big for him—and solemnly declared, "Whenever I feel the blood of that genius flowing in my veins, I feel myself burn with love for our beloved country." The inhabitants of his beloved country were promptly requested to "desist from demonstrations which have, in certain places, provoked regrettable consequences."

A huge crowd awaited Sa'ad Zaghloul's arrival at Bab al-Hadid station, singing, shouting, and fainting in a frenzy of anticipation. Sabri and his comrades waited for several hours. At last, after numerous false alarms, they had to face up to it: their hero would not be coming that night. Sorely disappointed, the demonstrators broke up into groups and dispersed into the neighboring streets.

Rashid's brother was not far from the Ezbekiyah Gardens when the people around him broke into a run. Instinctively, he followed suit, then heard two shots ring out.

Sprawling on the ground with his cheek against the warm asphalt, Sabri saw the pool of blood beside him steadily expand. He hadn't felt himself fall; now he was watching himself die. A spate of images traversed his mind's eye during the long minute that followed, and among them was that of his son Hassan, three months old, whose face he scarcely knew.

Translated from the French by John Brownjohn

Ahmad Hussein

from *And Cairo Burned*

FAROUK'S FACE TURNED YELLOW when he heard the gunshots: bam, bam, bam!

"What is that, Polly?"

"The army officers are firing gunshots. The guards have retaliated."

At that moment, King Farouk's wife and sisters appeared, in a state of fear and anguish. They started screaming, all at the same time,

"Farouk, Farouk, they're going to kill us. They have started firing."

Farouk yelled back, "Where is Ahmad Kamel? Where is the chief of guard? I do not want any resistance. Tell the guards not to retaliate. We will only lose our lives. Everyone has abandoned me: the English have not responded, the American ambassador only guaranteed my personal safety. What is happening? What is going on? I don't understand anymore. Where is the prime minister? He told me that he was on his way."

"The prime minister came this morning but the army forces did not allow him to come in."

"They barred the prime minister from entering? But what do they want? What do they mean? They must want to kill us. Have you seen the canons surrounding the palace on all sides, Polly?"

"And the tanks."

The king's sisters and daughters dashed around, screaming, "Father, father, save us. You must do something."

The palace protocol officer announced that the prime minister had arrived so the King dismissed his daughters and sisters and called in the prime minister. As soon as Farouk set eyes on him, he hurried toward him anxiously as if wanting to embrace him out of fear and horror.

"Do they want to kill me? Why are they shooting? Have I not done everything they asked for? What more do they want? I'm ready to grant them what they want, within reason. Why are you so late? I've been waiting for you since nine o'clock this morning."

"I did come but some of the officers did not have orders to allow me in. So they barred my entry."

"They barred you?! Why? What do they want? I don't understand."

"When I went back to my office, I found the president of the Revolutionary Council waiting for me. He handed me this ultimatum. Would you allow me to read it to you, your Majesty?"

"Go ahead . . . go ahead, Pasha. You know how much I trust you. I have always considered you like a father to me. You are my guardian and the guardian of my throne. You are the one who put me on this throne. Do you remember? But let's put that aside for now. Go ahead, read please. Let's hear their new demands."

"'Due to the complete chaos that the country has witnessed of late in all domains as a result of your incompetence and intervention with the constitution and your violation of the people's rights . . . .'"

"What is this, Pasha? How can you allow them to address me in this tone? I forbid you to address me in this way!"

"Forgive me, your Majesty, but I have been asked to deliver this ultimatum to you. Please understand the reality of the situation we are in. Please try to understand."

"Speak, go ahead."

"'. . . the people no longer feel that their lives, or property, or honor are safe. The reputation of Egypt has been smeared worldwide because of your persistent unbecoming behavior: the traitorous and the corrupt have found safety and refuge during your reign for their exorbitant wealth and their despicable excess at the people's expense. This has been amply demonstrated during the War of Palestine and its aftermath: the defective weapons and the ensuing trials in which you unashamedly intervened, thereby tarnishing the truth, unsettling people's faith in justice, and helping traitors to scheme further: allowing some to gather wealth and others to go beyond bounds. How can it be otherwise, when people but follow in their king's footsteps. For all these reasons, and on behalf of the army that represents the people, I ask your highness to step down and surrender the throne to the Prince Heir, Prince Ahmad Fuad, no later than twelve o'clock noon today, Saturday 26 July, 1952 (the fourth of Dhu-l-Qa'da 1371) and to depart from the country before six o'clock in the afternoon of the same day. The army holds your Highness responsible for the consequences should you choose not to comply with the people's wishes."

Farouk was so dumbfounded that he did not even realize that the prime minister had finished reading the ultimatum. He kept staring at the prime minister, who said, "I believe that you no longer have a choice. You have no way out but to abdicate if you want to remain alive and safeguard your throne for the prince heir."

Farouk exploded. "But is this what you promised me? When I charged you with forming a government did you not tell me that the leaders of the movement were a group of young officers and that you would be able to deal with them and put them in your back pocket? Did you not tell me that they had no demands beyond the purge of my entourage?"

"This is what I had imagined. I was surprised by the presence of the army in Alexandria and when I came to meet you, they did not allow me. Then the commander of the army asked to meet me and he handed me this ultimatum. Now you have to concede to the ultimatum and surrender the throne to your son. You have no choice. I have already warned you that your entourage will be a cause of trouble to you."

"You never warned or cautioned me. You are just like the rest. All you wanted was power. So long as I was in power, you supported me."

The prime minister interrupted, "I have not come here to argue with you. I care for your life and for the throne that your father entrusted me to protect for his descendants. The army commander is impatiently awaiting me. What shall I tell him?"

"Tell him that I accept and will abdicate. This has always been my wish. I have always hated power and its ways. I have gambled and lost. A gambler must assume the losses like a good sport. I was preparing to finish off these officers before they got me but they beat me to it. Let it be. I surrender. Congratulations to them. Tell them to prepare their documents and make sure that everything will proceed legally and that the rights of my son will be honored. I entrust this to you. I must have an honorable departure. I will leave on the *al-Mahrusa* yacht. The canons must be fired; the Revolutionary Council must be there to bid me farewell along with the American ambassador."

"But why the American ambassador?"

"He has promised to protect my life and safeguard my honorable departure. Can you protect me at that moment? Can you safeguard my life and my honorable departure? How do I know that they won't shoot at the *al-Mahrusa* after I am on board?"

"I can assure you that after your abdication they will be more anxious than you to ensure your safe departure from the country. The army commander assured me of this. They are committed to having everything proceed peacefully. The shooting of the guards happened by mistake."

"Anyway, these are my conditions. There is one more. Polly does not want to leave me and I cannot do without his services. They have to allow him to leave with me."

"I will transmit your wish to them, your Highness."

Translated by Samia Mehrez

Nawal El Saadawi

from *Walking through Fire*

FROM THE MEN'S WARDS arose a clamor of voices hailing the revolution. From the women's wards came the sharp shrilling of 'yooyoos' rising over the roar of male voices. Patients continued to stream out dressed in white cotton shirts, walking in their rubber slippers. The hospital nurses and cleaners were not long in joining the demonstrations of joy. They could be seen running amid the throngs in the corridors dressed in their white uniforms and caps, wearing white rubber shoes or sandals. After a moment's hesitation the doctors joined in. They did not run but walked to preserve their dignity, dressed in their short white coats with stethoscopes dangling down from their necks. The crowds flowed into the front courtyard of the hospital. After a short while the students arrived followed by the nurse trainees, the cooks, the workers in the laundry section, and the janitors from the dissecting hall.

My body propelled itself into the crowd, moved by a will of its own. I began to shout with them "Long live the revolution!" Batta waddled along in her high heels echoing "Long live the revolution?" (with a Parisian 'r'). A funeral coming out of the hospital came to a stop. The men carrying the coffin put it down on the pavement and mixed with the crowd shouting "Long live the revolution!" and the women who a moment ago had been mourning the defunct started to shrill out 'yooyoos' instead of shrieks.

. . .

On 26 July King Farouk boarded his royal yacht for the last time. He stood on deck dressed in his white naval uniform looking down at the sea of Alexandria, the sea in which I had swum when still a child. I could remember my father standing on the northern balcony and saying "Down with the King." Now the king had fallen from his throne. He had been replaced by his infant child Ahmed, with a Tripartite Trusteeship Council to manage court matters until he grew up.

I was five years old when King Fouad died in 1936, and the young boy Farouk came back from England to inherit the throne. The streets of Alexandria resounded to the shouts of "The King is dead, Long live the King!" The radio was singing King Farouk, king of the country, light of our eyes, flower of our nation. From the balcony the white round face of the child-king looked out over his people. He had become king overnight, knew nothing about the dark corridors of power and politics, was quickly surrounded by the three forces that wielded power: the court, the British, and al-Azhar, by the three men who embodied these forces: Ahmed Hassanein, Ali Maher, and Sheikh al-Maraghi.

How did the child Farouk develop into a king no different from his father, into a corrupt, licentious assassin? Now here he was standing on the deck of his yacht taking a last look at Egypt, a look full of sadness and regret. Maybe he would have been better off had he not been born the son of a king. People in my village used to say, "To be a sultan keep away from the sultan." Do sultans and kings suffer from a disease which is like cancer, where the sick cells devour the healthy ones, where greed and madness devour the self? King Farouk's greed and ambition knew no limits. He even tried to become the caliph of all Muslims and receive his crown from the hands of God.

After King Farouk was forced to leave Egypt, Muhammad Naguib became the first Egyptian to rule since King Mena in ancient Egypt. He had the features of a peasant, rough and simple with an open smile. His voice was gruff, which made him sound like a man of the people.

At the beginning of the revolution, an amnesty was decreed for all political prisoners and colleagues of ours who belonged to the Muslim Brothers, or the Wafdist Party, or to no party at all. They were all released from prisons and concentration camps, all except the Communists who were not included in the amnesty. Safeya's brother Asaad and Rifa'a, who was engaged to Samia, remained in prison. Zakariya Muhieddine, who was one of the Free Officers in the revolutionary movement that came to power, made a declaration in which he said that Communists were social criminals and not members of a political movement. Samia pouted in disgust and said, "You call this a revolution, Nawal? They're no more than a bunch of soldiers who carried out a putsch to replace British colonialism by American imperialism."

One of the first measures carried out by the new regime was the promulgation of an agrarian reform which fixed the ceiling for land ownership at two hundred feddans. In addition, each child was allowed to own fifty feddans.

In the month of July 1953, that is one year later, titles, political parties, and the monarchy were abolished and Egypt became a republic.

The atmosphere in the country changed. People used to walk along with grim, silent faces. No one said good morning or smiled at passersby. Now the streets had changed. People there behaved as though they were at home. They chatted, smiled, said good morning, shook hands with complete strangers, asked about one another's health, about recent events, congratulated one another for the change of regime, discussed, tried to foretell future events, kept expecting changes to happen every day.

In the morning on my way to the medical school my ears would pick up some of the comments people made: "At last God has set us free." "Could anyone have believed that the king's throne would collapse overnight." "Now, uncle, there is nothing called pasha or bey. Pasha is not an Arabic word, it is Turkish, we inherited it from the reign of the Osmanlis and the Mamelukes." "Do you mean to say that from now onward we'll really be free?" "Long live Muhammad Naguib!"

But as expected, the old forces and their political parties refused to surrender. The pashas and landlords were not prepared to give up the land they owned without a fight. They gathered around Muhammad Naguib. They formed a powerful front which claimed that its aim was to defend democracy, freedom, and the right to form political parties. This front grouped together the leadership from the Wafd, the Muslim Brothers, and the Communists despite the feuds that had always existed between them, for in the political game enemies often unite against a common enemy who has become a danger to them. The same thing happens in children's stories. The cat and the mouse join hands against the lion or the tiger.

But the lion in this story had not yet appeared openly on the scene. The revolution was announced on the radio by Anwar al-Sadat and at the same time many pictures of Muhammad Naguib were published in the newspapers. But my father spotted the lion standing in the photograph next to him. He pointed at him and said, "This man is the real leader of the revolution, Nawal."

At the beginning people used to hail Muhammad Naguib, proclaim his name. No one knew Gamal Abd al-Nasser. I asked my father, "How did you discover that?" He answered, "From his eyes." So I looked at his eyes in the photograph. Big, dark, wide open eyes looking straight out of the picture from under a broad obstinate forehead. His sharp nose stood out in his face, slightly hooked. His thin lips were pressed together with determination or in anger, an anger that had kept growing since he was a child. Muhammad Naguib's features next to him looked ordinary, childish, as though he had not seen very much in his life.

I met Gamal Abd Al-Nasser face-to-face for the first time in 1962 during the National Congress of Popular Forces. The revolution was moving forward, mobilizing to strike down the remaining bastions of feudalism and comprador capitalism and had announced what were called the Socialist Decrees. But my father did not witness these events. He had died three years before. When I looked into Gamal Abd al-Nasser's face I found him more attractive than in his pictures. The cameras could not catch the strong glimmer in his big, black eyes. His skin was brown, the color of fresh silt brought down by the Nile. He was tall, very tall, with a slight stoop to his shoulders like my grandmother and my father, walked slightly bent, taking long strides. Was he carrying the same load they had carried throughout their lives? They had never bowed under it. He too looked as though he could carry it with the same dignity with which my father had carried the load of feeding nine children, their mother, his mother, and a sister who was divorced and lived in the village with her.

Translated by Sharif Hatatah

Ahdaf Soueif
from *In the Eye of the Sun*

Scene 11

Friday, 9 June 1967: Evening

President Nasser addresses the nation. From somewhere private. No audience. No applause, There he is: the big square head, the magnetic eyes, the massive shoulders, the pause before he speaks. What have you done to us, chief? Oh, what have you done to us?

"I tell you truthfully and putting aside any factors on which I might have based my attitude during the crisis, that I am ready to bear the whole responsibility for what has happened. I have taken a decision in which I am asking you all to help me. I have decided to give up completely and finally every official post and every political role and to return to the ranks of the masses and do my duty with them like every other citizen.

"In accordance with Article 110 of the Provisional Constitution promulgated in March 1964 I have entrusted my colleague, friend and brother Zakariya Muhieddine with taking over the post of president and carrying out the constitutional provisions on this point. After this decision, I place everything I have at his disposal in dealing with the grave situation through which our people are passing."

They've got you now, they've got you. They've wanted to for fifteen years and now they have. A terrible sadness. A desolation. Asya sobs in front of the television. Kareem and Deena sit mutely miserable. Their father and mother go into their bedroom, saying nothing and closing the door. And is this a time to go away? OK, maybe you are responsible. In fact, of course you are responsible. But how can we let you go? What shall we do without you?

Last winter Asya had seen him; not just passing by in a motorcade as she—as everyone—had often seen him, but much closer, in a concert to celebrate the new session of the National Assembly.

It had been a top-notch affair. In the huge, domed Festival Hall of Cairo University, Ummu Kulthoum would sing for the president and his guests. The stalls, the boxes, the circle and the galleries were full to capacity when 'Abd el-Nasser had walked in at half past eight. In the whirlpool of bodyguards, photographers, and ushers surrounding him, he was the still center; he stood out. Taller than any man there—except possibly his friend Field Marshal 'Amer who kept abreast with him but was colorless and bland. The eye immediately went to the magnificent head and shoulders rising above the crowd. The heart leapt in his presence. His raised hand waved in greeting, the black eyebrows and the eyes crinkled up with a smile. The audience rose to its feet in an ecstasy of applause. ("But what about the purges? Here, in this very university?" whispered a quiet voice in her head. "What about the concentration camps? The torture of both the leftists and the Muslim Brotherhood?" I don't know. I don't know. Maybe he never knew of it. How can one man know everything? "What about Salah Nasr and the Mukhabarat, the huge intelligence organization that has been turned against the people?" What do I know of government? How do I know what he knows? He nationalized the canal, he got rid of the British Occupation, he gave us back our dignity— and at home, what about the clinics he's building everywhere? What about the High Dam? What about electricity for the peasants and land reform and education? He has to be a good man.) When he reached the middle of the front row he turned and faced the audience. His smile was wide and shining. He raised both arms above his head. 'Amer sat down abruptly. Nasser clasped both hands together and beamed around the auditorium. He gave one last wave, then turned and sat down next to the field marshal.

Ummu Kulthoum stands in a long gray gown of French dentelle, with the famous dark glasses on her thyroid-bulged eyes and the famous long silk handkerchief clasped in her right hand. The legendary voice soars and drops in the concert-hall. Up and down and around and up and down and around:

O my heart, do not ask where is love.
It was a fort of my imagination—and it fell.

Let's drink together over its ruins
Let's drink and let my tears slake my thirst—

A thirty-two-line lyric is made to last for two hours.

My yearning for you burns into my side
And the seconds are live coals in my blood.

Give me my freedom! Let loose my hands!
I have given you my all and held back nothing.
I ache with your bonds drawing blood from my wrists
Why do I hold on to them when they have availed me nothing?
Why do I hold on to vows you have broken
And this pain of imprisonment when the world is mine?

For a moment the audience is apprehensive. Would he perhaps think that this was a veiled reference to his Mukhabarat? How very audacious she is. Who else would have dared to sing this stanza—even though it is in a love-song? Then the chief is seen to laugh and clap his hands and the audience goes wild, "Tani," "Encore," "Bis," they cry. And it is only when she has repeated the stanza four times that they allow her to go on:

Where from my eye is a magical lover?
In him is dignity and majesty and bashfulness.
Confident of step he walks a monarch,
Unjustly beautiful, melodiously proud,
His enchantment is perfumed like the breath of gods,
His absent gaze is the dream of nightfall.

Don't go. Oh, please don't go. Stay and we'll all sort it out together. I can't bear how sad you look. I can't bear what they've done to you. It can't be that bad. Nothing can be that bad. We'll all sort it out—together.

11 p.m.

The people of Cairo are pouring into the streets. They are heading for 'Abd el-Nasser's house in Heliopolis. They are begging him to stay.

Saturday, 10 June 1967

'Abd el-Nasser announces his decision to submit to the will of the people. He will remain as president.

Field Marshal 'Abdul-Hakim 'Amer is given the choice of departing immediately for any country in the world. He refuses and barricades himself in his villa with his family, his bodyguards, and his close friends.

Mohamed Mansi Qandil

from *Broken Soul*

WE WERE LIVING IN a period when time stood still; it simply died. Hours disintegrated and minutes decomposed. Everything turned into gray dust that spread over the river like froth, strangling the fish and multiplying the weed of the Nile. My father told me that politics is a losing game. I don't know how he had found out that I had started playing the game.

On that autumn evening, everything was quiet, but the darkness was thick. Memories of many gloomy evenings cluttered and obstructed vision. Muted stars and a faint moon, aimless clouds. Everything always begins with this kind of murk. It was strange for Alaa al-Hamaqi and me to meet that evening and to walk the city streets; they seemed wider because of the dark and the houses looked less dismal. In the distance voices were heard trying to make sense of what had happened: murmurs of shock, fear, and apprehension. We didn't know what to do except continue walking aimlessly on the asphalt of the city streets in the midst of dust and dirt. Fatma had left and the city had become mine alone. There were no regrets. I suddenly said, "I am very scared. I feel I am walking naked, unable to protect my body."

Alaa said, "We are all scared, but is this normal?"

I was shuddering and not quite understanding his words, not quite grasping all that had happened. I said, "I wonder whether Abdel Nasser had done us wrong or whether it was we who wronged ourselves. Why did we believe in him so much? I wonder if he believed in us."

Old, bitter questions that could neither be answered nor avoided. Alaa spoke as if in a trance, as if his very words were the night that surrounded us and enveloped the city making everything fragile, unreal, and difficult to explain. Faint shadows and lights, tears, strange supplications, and an unsteady twilight, fragments of memories of fear.

"Do you know what Abdel Nasser wanted us to be? He wanted us to be like green grass that budded and grew but was grass nonetheless: identical stems resembling each other with no difference. He wanted us to all bend with the storm and accept trimming and weeding and absorb the fertilizer we received. He did not want us to be different, to bloom like wild flowers or thorny bushes. He made sure we got the right fertilizer but he also knew when we were ripe for pruning. Sometimes he seemed like an obsessive father who thought his children would never mature. That is why he worried about dry seasons, increasing prices, and radical ideas."

He fell silent. A group of people rushed forth from a side street screaming in agony: men, women, and children. They moved like a block in the dark adding a new shudder to our already weary bodies. We tried to look at each other but the darkness was thick. Were we weeping? We talked in quiet coldness and with tormenting reason. I felt the irony when I said, after they had all disappeared, "It was his right. Who wants to rule a dry arid land? The amazing thing is that he did not see us. Do you remember how he looked at us when he waved his hand to salute the crowds? How could he see us when there were millions in front of him? Once I stood with my friends to greet him when he visited town. When he drew near we started cheering and chanting his name. He turned and looked at us. But did he really see us? Did he come to us with the intention of seeing us?"

We were moving through the night amid the swarms of bodies. Sweaty, undistinguishable faces with the same voice that chanted his name. The same chanting, the same rhythm undifferentiated even at this very moment, at this degree of grief and loss. The voices were undistinguishable: not like the crackle of branches, the breaking of waves, or the rustle of palm leaves. Just grass, murmuring, bent over under the heavy storm.

Alaa al-Hamaqi said, "He was the only tree among us. He stood upright with his strong military body unaffected by any siege. He raised his hand high like the ancient Egyptian sacred trees that are painted on the murals of the temples. Then he would start talking. His voice was magnificent: strong, mature, sometimes thundering with anger like a wild Pharaoh; at other times soft like that of a peasant fed only on dry bread and cheese. He would make a sudden joke. And when the grass roared with laughter he would remember that he was the only tree and he would stand upright again."

Which of us had been speaking? And which one listening? And all those who dashed around us and then disappeared, were they in a state to hear any other voice? I spoke again, trying to be audible.

"He was a strange man! Even though he had imprisoned my father, I was incapable of hating him. Even my father loved him, for he was able to enroll me, thanks to him, in the faculty of medicine, like the children of the elite. He hit us hard so we would run to him for refuge from him, even inside prisons. Even when they were being tortured they chanted his name. They believed that what was happening to them was a kind of bitter misunderstanding."

Finally, it became impossible for us to walk alone. All the streets were filled with all kinds of people. Something had suddenly broken. All the ancient grief leaked through a hole in the soul. Qur'anic verses intermingled with chants from the Book of the Dead. He and I tried to escape to a side street but we collided with dark bodies. We passed by a coffee shop as it was dimming its lights and preparing to close. But before the lights were out, I looked at Alaa's face and found it faint and gleaming with the trace of tears. Before we were submerged in the dark, I asked myself: did he also see my faint and gleaming face?

We were walking toward the basement, the last refuge, the place to which I went for the first time with Alaa after the political meeting at the university. A student, two years our senior, lived there. We kept walking down, hoping that the steps that led us downward would separate us from all the voices. We were sure that the rest of the group was waiting for us and the remains of the colored pencils with which we wrote the slogans on the bulletin boards, the remains of cardboard and stencil pamphlets, and the sound of anger and protest. We will find everything scattered along with the skeletons and long bones painted in red and blue; books by Grey and Cunningham, Sufism, politics and economics. Everything will be ready as if we were about to meet for some debate. We would listen to the latest song by Sheikh Imam who, despite his blindness, saw everything; we would prepare for a conference or a meeting or a small rally that would begin inside the university before spilling out onto the streets of the city. I had followed Alaa al-Hamaqi since the very first day and felt that we were caught in a strange, thrilling, and fearful game. Since that day, together we studied and breathlessly pursued the flicker of a lost dream.

We knocked at the door as we usually did. The door was opened. They were all waiting for us. Their eyes were red and tired. Each wiped his face and put on a mask of strength in front of the others. We looked at each other as if suddenly realizing the truth. Alaa was the only one to speak.

He murmured, "Who would believe that he has died?"

Translated by Samia Mehrez

Mohamed Mansi Qandil   37

Edward Said

from *"Homage to a Belly Dancer,"* in *Reflections on Exile*

THE GREATEST AND MOST famous singer of the twentieth-century Arab world was Um Kalthoum, whose records and cassettes, fifteen years after her death, are available everywhere. A fair number of non-Arabs know about her too, partly because of the hypnotic and melancholic effect of her singing, partly because in the worldwide rediscovery of authentic people's art Um Kalthoum is a dominant figure. But she also played a significant role in the emerging Third World women's movement as a pious "Nightingale of the East" whose public exposure was as a model not of feminine consciousness but also of domestic propriety. During her lifetime there was talk about whether or not she was a lesbian, but the sheer force of her performances of elevated music set to classical verse overrode such rumors. In Egypt she was a national symbol, respected both during the monarchy and after the revolution led by Gamal Abdel Nasser.

Um Kalthoum's career was extraordinarily long, and to most Arabs it was the highly respectable while romantic tip of the eroticism typified by the belly-dancer. Like the great singer herself, the belly-dancers routinely performed in films, theaters, and cabarets, and on the ceremonial platforms of weddings and other private celebrations in Cairo and Alexandria. Whereas you couldn't really *enjoy* looking at the portly and severe Um Kalthoum, you couldn't do much more than enjoy looking at fine belly-dancers, whose first star was the Lebanese-born Badia Massabni, also an actress, cabaret-owner, and trainer of young talent. Badia's career as a dancer ended around World War Two, but her true heir and disciple was Tahia Carioca, who was, I think, the finest belly-dancer ever. Now seventy-five and living in Cairo, she is still active as an actress and political militant and, like Um Kalthoum, the remarkable symbol of national culture. Um Kalthoum performed at King Farouk's wedding in 1936, and the lavish party was also Tahia's debut. It gave her a prominence she never lost.

During her heyday as dancer *extraordinaire* Tahia Carioca embodied a very specific kind of sexiness, which she rendered as the most smooth and understated of dancers, and as a highly visible *femme fatale* in Egyptian films. When I looked up the actual number of films she made between the early forties and 1980 I was able to find 190 titles; when I asked her about them in Cairo during the spring of 1989, she couldn't remember the exact figure but opined that the sum was well over two hundred. Most of her early films included at least one dance number—every Egyptian film that did not pretend to be 'high drama' (only a handful did) had to include a song-and-dance routine. This was a formula rather like second-act ballets in nineteenth-century-Paris opera performances: ballets were put on whether or not they fitted the story. In Egyptian films an announcer would suddenly appear on screen and name a singer and dancer; the scene would reveal itself (often gratuitously) to be a nightclub or a large living-room; then an orchestra would strike up the music, and the performance began.

Tahia did such scenes. But they were no more than crude shorthand sketches for her full-scale cabaret performances, the only one of which I actually witnessed I shall forever remember with startling vividness. It took place in 1950. An enterprising schoolmate had discovered that she was dancing at Badia's open-air casino alongside the Nile in Giza (today the site of a high-rise Sheraton), tickets were obtained, and four awkward fourteen-year-olds arrived on the appointed evening at least two hours before she was to begin. The daytime heat of that June day had pretty much dissolved into a balmy, slightly windy evening. By the time the lights went out for the star turn, Badia's was full, all forty or so tables packed with an entirely Egyptian audience of middle-class aficionados. Tahia's partner for the evening was the singer Abdel Aziz Mahmoud, a stolid-looking, bald gentleman in a white dinner-jacket who walked out, planted himself on a wooden-and-wicker chair in the middle of the primitive stage, and began to sing to the accompaniment of a small takhta, or Arab orchestra, seated off to one side. The song was "Mandil el-Helou" ("A Pretty Handkerchief"), whose innumerable verses celebrated the woman who draped it, cried into it, decorated her hair with it, on and on for almost a full hour.

There were at least fifteen minutes of this before Tahia suddenly revealed herself a few feet behind the singer's chair. We were sitting about as far away from the stage as possible to sit, but the shimmering, glistening blue costume she wore simply dazzled the eye, so bright were the sequins and spangles, so controlled was her quite lengthy immobility as she stood there with an entirely composed look about her. As in bull-fighting, the essence of the classic Arab belly-dancer's art is not how much but how little the artist moves: only the novices, or the deplorable Greek and American imitators, go in the appalling wiggling and jumping around that passes for 'sexiness' and harem hootchy-kootch. The point is to make an effect mainly (but by no means exclusively) through suggestiveness, and—in the kind of full-scale composition Tahia offered that night—to do so over a series of episodes knitted together in alternating moods, recurring motifs. For "Mandil el-Helou" Tahia's central motif was her relationship to the largely oblivious Abdel Aziz Mahmoud. She would glide up behind him, as he droned on, appear as if to fall into his arms, mimic and mock him—all without ever touching him or eliciting any response.

Her diaphanous veils were laid over the modified bikini that was basic to the outfit without ever becoming its main attraction. The beauty of her dance was its connectedness: the feeling she communicated of a spectacularly lithe and well-shaped body undulating through a complex but decorative series of encumbrances made up of gauzes, veils, necklaces, strings of gold and silver chains, which her movements animated deliberately and at times almost theoretically. She would stand, for example, and slowly begin to move her right hip, which would in turn activate her silver leggings, and the beads draped over the right side of her waist. As she did all this, she would look down at the moving parts, so to speak, and fix our gaze on them too, as if we were all watching a separate little drama, rhythmically very controlled, reconfiguring her body so as to highlight her semi-detached right side. Tahia's dance was like an extended arabesque elaborated around her seated colleague. She never jumped, or bobbed her breasts, or went in for bumping and grinding. There was a majestic deliberateness to the whole thing that maintained itself right through even the quicker passages. Each of us knew that we were experiencing an immensely exciting—because endlessly deferred—erotic experience, the likes of which we could never hope to match in real life. And that was precisely the point: this was sexuality as a public event, brilliantly planned and executed, yet totally unconsummated and unrealizable.

Other dancers might go in for acrobatics, or slithering about on the floor, or modified strip-teasing, but not Tahia, whose grace and elegance suggested something altogether classical and even monumental. The paradox was that she was so immediately sensual and yet so remote, so unapproachable, unobtainable. In our severely repressed world these attributes enhanced the impression she made. I especially recall that once she started dancing, and continuing through the rest of her performance, she had what appeared to be a small self-absorbed smile, as if she was privately contemplating her body, enjoying its movements. Her smile muted whatever tawdry theatricality attached to the scene and to her dance, purifying them by virtue of the concentration bestowed on her innermost and most self-abstracted thoughts. And indeed, as I have watched her dancing through at least twenty-five or thirty of her films, I have always found that smile, lighting up the usually silly or affected setting—a still point of the turning world.

That smile has seemed to me symbolic of Tahia's distinction in a culture that featured dozens of dancers called Zouzou and Fifi, most of them treated as barely a notch above prostitutes. This was always evident during periods of Egyptian prosperity, the last days of Farouk, for instance, or when the oil boom brought wealthy Gulf Arabs to Egypt; it was also true when Lebanon was the Arab world's playground, with thousands of girls available for display or hire. Most belly-dancers would appear in such circumstances to go to the highest bidder, the night-club serving as a temporary shop-window. The pressures of a conservative Islamic culture were to blame for this, as were the distortions produced by uneven development. To be a respectably nubile woman was usually to be destined for marriage without much transition from adolescence; to be young and attractive has therefore not always been an advantage, since a conventional father might for that very reason arrange a wedding with a 'mature' and well-off man. If women didn't fall within those schemes, they risked all sorts of opprobrium.

Tahia belongs, not to the easily identifiable culture of B-girls and fallen women, but to the world of progressive women skirting or unblocking the social lanes. She remained organically liked, however, to her country's society; because she discovered another, far more interesting role for herself as dancer and entertainer. This was the all-but-forgotten role of almeh (literally, a learned woman), spoken of by nineteenth century European visitors to the Orient such as Edward Lane and Flaubert. The almeh was a courtesan of sorts, but a woman of significant accomplishments. Dancing was only one of her gifts: others were the ability to sing and recite classical poetry, to discourse wittily, to be sought after for her company by men of law, politics, and literature.

Tahia is referred to as almeh in her best film, one of her earliest, *Li'bet il Sit* ("The Lady's Ploy," 1946), which also stars the greatest of twentieth-century Arab actors and comedians, Naguib el-Rihani, a formidable combination of Chaplin and Molière. In the film, Tahia is a gifted young dancer and wit, used by her rascally parents to ensnare men of means. Rihani, who plays an unemployed teacher is fond of her and she loves him, but she is lured by her parents into a get-rich scheme involving a wealthy Lebanese. In the end, Tahia returns to Rihani—a rather sentimental conclusion of a kind that few of her other films permit themselves. She performs a short, but wonderfully provocative dance in the film, but that is meant to be an almost minor affair compared to the display of her wit, intelligence, and beauty.

Subsequently Tahia seems to have been fixed by film directors in a coarser version of this role, which she repeats in film after film. She is the other woman, a counter to the virtuous, domestically acceptable, and much less interesting female lead. Even within those limits, Tahia's talents shine through. You believe she would be more interesting as companion and as sexual partner than the woman who gets married to the leading man, and you begin to suspect that because she is so talented and so sexy, she has to be portrayed as a dangerous woman—the almeh who is too learned, too smart, too sexually advanced, for any man in contemporary Egypt. By the fifties Tahia had become the standard woman-as-devil figure in dozens of Egyptian films. In *Shabab Imra'a*, considered a later classic, she plays the role of a tough but sexually starved widow who rents a room to a handsome country bumpkin recently come to Cairo as an Azhar student; she seduces and marries him, but when he meets the angelic daughter of a family friend, he awakens from Tahia's Circe-like spell, denounces her, and leaves her for the safe, boring younger woman. In an otherwise undistinguished parable there is one great scene, in which Tahia pulls her young husband away from a street celebration that features a young belly-dancer who has captivated the inexperienced student. Tahia takes him into their house, sits him down, and tells him that she will now show him what real dancing is like. Whereupon she treats him to a private performance that positively smolders, proving that, middle-aged or not, she still is the finest dancer, the most formidable intellect, and the most desirable sexual object around.

Mahmoud Al-Wardani

from *Heads Ripe for Plucking*

AGAINST MY WILL, I am still stuck to the iron bridge. Yet in those first few minutes in which I open my eyes seeking out the dew of dawn just before the merciless sun rises, in these very minutes lies what rest is to be had from the whole day. There is no pain whatsoever then, rather a mellow drowsiness, a languor, the slow opening of the eyes before they make out the details of the scene that has long arisen before me: fields that stretch out until hemmed in by the mountain's looming shadows over there, and here are the hills that every morning support the sun on their tips, while I receive it submissively.

Shuhdi Attiya al-Shafie
Attiya al-Shafie and his family announce the passing of their dearly beloved, the pride of youth, Mr. Shuhdi Attiya, whom they have lain in his final resting

place. And to those who paid their condolences, they say: We shall not thank you, for to thank you would not do justice to your loyalty in this situation. It is to you that the memory of Shuhdi belongs, you are its guardians.

As for you, our dear departed, we eulogize you thus:

A youth who, stabbed with spear and sword, fell to a death
that bears the stamp of victory, though victory was not his.
Swathed he was in death's blood-red garments, but no sooner
had day dawned than they were the green silk of Paradise.
Easy it would have been to elude death, but it was
the bitter dues of dignity and valor that drove him to face death.
A soul that shuns shame as though it were
a sin worse than heresy on the Day of Judgment.
Al-Ahram, June 20, 1960

Abd al-Hamid Haridi

Today, for the first time in more days than I can remember, they did not take us to do hard labor on the mountain. They usually made us carry from the ward to the mountain even those of us who would drop because of the regular feasts of torture prescribed all morning. Then we would divide among us the allotment of stones our companions were supposed to hew, which we carried in the reed baskets, as well as bringing back our companions with us at the end of the day.

Today, though, they did not let us out.

This could only mean one thing: that there were new 'guests' assigned to arrive today or early tomorrow morning at the latest. We remained locked up in our cells until we overheard the voices of the jailers outside answering in indistinct words the commands of a row of officers who were themselves yelling. When, the following day, they had us vacate our cell and reallocated us to the rest of the cells, we ascertained that Cell Two had been set aside for the newcomers. We had discussed the situation the night before, and all the evidence indicated that these were the accused in the Shuhdi case in Alexandria.

We, the accused in the Fouad Mursi case, had already inaugurated the first 'reception banquet' at the Abu Zaabal Prison Annex on 17 November, 1959. Our first feast of torture took place during the two following days, when we arrived at Abu Zaabal Prison, presided over by Sergeant Hasan Mounir, the brutish chief warden who personally executed the whipping order on those thrown on the wooden 'maiden.' It was only two days later that the second reception banquet took place, when two hundred more prisoners from different organizations and cases arrived, which meant that the clampdown was expanding and hence that the torture would continue. It was the second reception banquet that witnessed the murder of Farid Haddad, the handsome doctor from Shubra, at the hands of the executioners who assaulted him while he was tied up with sticks and belts, until he breathed his last. He had not meant to provoke them, but then he was proud of his history as a Communist activist. As for Muhammad Mounir Mouwafi, the nationalist captain, they had a special reception for him after he was released from the Military Prison and beat him up when he was all alone at night so that he went a little crazy. Mouwafi had served as a liaison officer between the Free Officers' government and the battalions of Communist freedom fighters during the 1956 War in the Suez Canal zone. He was one of the most nationalist officers and the most loyal to Nasser.

So, it seemed this would be the fifth reception banquet, though the preparations for it were different and it looked like it would be a grand party—as befitted Shuhdi and his group.

Nur Sulayman
They'd packed the inmates of every three cells into a single van, and that was how I found myself in the same van as Shuhdi. When the convoy moved, we started chatting about this sudden transfer. Part of Shuhdi's speech for the defense in court, spoken on behalf of all the accused, argued that the government must take responsibility for our lives until the verdict was pronounced. This was because reports had reached us about the unrestrained brutality of the butchers who had surpassed their predecessors, the butchers of the monarchic period.

The first thing Shuhdi said in the van was that the fact that it was al-Halawani himself—the chief warden of Hadara Prison in Alexandria where we had spent the first months of our detention—who was handing us over to another prison was disquieting. We were therefore to expect a tough reception, whichever prison we were taken to. Despite the high esteem in which I held him, I couldn't help bursting out, "What I find hard to understand is how a nationalist government like President Nasser's would actually take it upon itself to sanction the torture, humiliation, wounding, and murder of Communist nationalists who stand by it. It was we in the Democratic Movement for National Liberation who printed their pamphlets back at the time when they were just a small organization. Then in the summer of 1952, which I will never forget, only two weeks after the Free Officers' coup, I myself took part in the efforts at conciliation during the strikes and sit-ins of the workers at Kafr al-Dawwar. Don't you remember, comrades? Do you, Shuhdi, remember when I asked to meet you urgently to point out that the Free Officers' having put to death the workers Mustafa Khamis and Muhammad al-Baqari had landed us in a quandary? Ignoring the issue in our propaganda was unacceptable, just as continuing to support the officers necessitated that they at least not kill the workers! That's if we wanted our propaganda to be consistent. You, Shuhdi, answered that we must not condemn Khamis and al-Baqari but rather defend them as wronged and condemn their execution. At the same time, we were to defend the nascent regime and also to go on showing up the conspiracy that targeted the Free Officers' movement in order to forge a rift between it and the workers. And we were also to persist in our call to shield the movement from its enemies who were primed to bring it down, more so after it got a grip on things and succeeded in expelling the king. You also said it was an exceedingly difficult task but that history would not forgive us the betrayal of the two innocent men whose blood had stained the hands of the movement. And here I say to you, Shuhdi, that the officers of this selfsame movement now torture and aim to liquidate us after the arrest campaign of the new year, which hardly spared any member of a Communist organization. This regardless of the differences between the organizations, some of which supported the Free Officers' movement that has now become a revolution—especially after the Bandung Declaration—as we in the Democratic Movement for National Liberation did, while others rejected it as a form of military Fascism, this being the position of the minority in the Communist movement."

"In any case," Shuhdi replied, addressing us all, "we should stand firm and face whatever lies ahead of us with utmost forbearance without succumbing to the provocations of the executioners." With a smile he gestured toward some of us who had caught the tail end of the monarchic period and the beginning of the Free Officers' era when prisoners were literally put in shackles. I knew that Shuhdi was among those who had undergone the shackling, but what exactly did he mean? Was he implying that our conditions now were better? I almost laughed outright. "History may lag until you get fed up," Shuhdi continued, "but in the end it progresses. It is no longer possible for any power to take history back to the pre-Bandung era. All over the world, a new movement has been born, the aims of which embrace dozens of anti-colonial and newly independent African and Asian peoples. Likewise, Nasser announced the nationalization of the Suez Canal and challenged the most arrogant and ruthless of imperial powers. We in turn stood by him, nor would it have been conceivable for us not to support him. None of the measures he took in the country could have been undertaken except by a nationalist government that we must back and support. The problem is that we need, simultaneously, to uphold our call for democracy, the annulment of martial law, and wresting our rights and the rights of all the political forces to independent organization."

I couldn't help losing my temper with Shuhdi as the van we were carted in rattled us while we sat spread out on its floor under patches of sunlight filtering through the narrow metal slits. "I'm a worker and not a theoretician like you," I said. "We've been supporting the regime for eight years, and the regime that we supported is now deliberately liquidating us. There can be no other meaning to what is happening. There are some who have in fact been killed: Dr. Farid Haddad, the medical doctor from Shubra and the finest of young men, is not the only one. Didn't the story reach us in Hadara Prison? He said to that dog, Younis Marei, 'I am an Egyptian Communist who believes in socialism.' Younis Marei answered, 'Oh, made in Russia, you son of a bitch?' And they dashed at him with the butts of their rifles. He screamed at Younis, 'You fascist dog!' And he spat at him before succumbing to a cudgel that fractured his skull so that he dropped dead. The prison doctor sullied his profession's oath when he wrote in his report that the death was of natural causes following heart failure. What can this mean? Is this not liquidation, murder?"

Appeasing my anger with his warm and charming smile, Shuhdi answered with his familiar gentleness, "What do you want then, Nur? Are we to denounce a nationalist government and call for its downfall? What would we say to people? True, we are against the government's militaristic inclination to arrogate exclusive power, and against the regime's executioners who incite it with all their might toward a rift with us."

There we were, rehearsing again the same talk we'd been going over ever since Shuhdi delivered his political plea at the Military Tribunal before the Lieutenant General Abdallah Hilal. He had, on the one hand, declared our support for the nationalist government and, on the other, held the court responsible for safeguarding our lives until sentencing. However, Lieutenant General Hilal did not take the trouble to respond and ignored the demand.

Where were we heading then? Where was the sluggish van headed in the midday inferno? As my companions fidgeted, the handcuffs clinked.

Translated by Hala Halim

Mohamed Mansi Qandil

from *Broken Soul*

THERE WERE A FEW remaining days in the academic year that promised to be out of the ordinary. The trip had only been a short time away from our feelings of anger. Once again all the promises of war fell through and the protests filled the university campus on a daily basis: bulletin boards, flyers, pamphlets, and demonstrations that erupted suddenly inside lecture halls. It became normal for us to meander our way to the university amid the throngs of bodies of national security forces with their shields, helmets, and heavy clubs. We used to meet in the basement every evening to write the slogans and the material for the bulletin boards, but also to study. Alaa al-Hamaqi said that the time had come for us to prepare for a political conference with the participation of all the faculties and to draft a statement to be signed by all, demanding a clear position on the war. Alaa then announced the surprise, "Sheikh Imam himself will sing . . . and this will spur everyone on."

We all cheered. But in the midst of the euphoria we heard one colleague exclaim, "But this is suicide!"

Hamaqi turned to him angrily and so did we. But he repeated insistently, "National security forces are outside and the Islamist groups inside. Where do we go from here?"

This time it was I who replied heatedly. "The authorities are supporting the Islamists but the masses are on our side. In a patriotic situation like this we cannot be divided."

Hamaqi looked toward me in admiration and the anger subsided. Our colleague fell silent in total intimidation.

We were up all night preparing slogans. In the morning we went to the train station to meet Sheikh Imam who, as we found out later, had started out at dawn. He had called for dawn prayer at Hosh Adam and then got on the train. He was a fragile man who alighted from the train like a soft morning breeze. The prison mats had eaten at his body and the humidity of the old stone walls of his abode had affected his bones. He walked along with us, almost stumbling because of our quick pace. He made sarcastic comments about his own real blindness and the blindness of the sighted. His skin was taut against his bone structure, as if his very cells were in constant motion. He was sad because his collaborator, the poet Ahmad Fuad Nigm, was not with him. They had arrested him only, leaving the blind Sheikh Imam free. This was very frustrating for him. He tried hard to make trouble but they ignored him and did not arrest him. This made him all the more angry. We walked attentively by his side. Many students from other departments came and the place overflowed with angry chanting. Lectures came to a halt and the senior professors left hurriedly while the more junior took refuge in their offices. This time no one could stop us from storming the main auditorium. We escorted Sheikh Imam to the podium immediately and he sang *Shatt al-qanal shatti wa-l-ard 'arabiya* (The Shore of the Canal is Mine and the Land is Arab). He fueled our feelings of anger against all. We applauded him wildly and we swayed, chanting the refrain along with him. We interrupted him with cheers so he smiled and stopped singing then picked up again. With his fragile body and his oud upon which he leaned he was able to capture everyone's attention. He took us away from ourselves and his voice mixed anger with love, the desire for revenge with the bitterness of separation. The tone of his voice overflowed with unique sadness: vast lands, deep fractures, stunted plants, endless dreams and short-lived romances, a thirst for justice and a thrill for the future. His Adam's apple protruded as if it were another nose on his face. He pursed his lips and dug his fingers into the chords and tapped the floor with his foot. The strangely moving rhythm filled the space. How did these images enter his dark world? How were they formed? How did they acquire color? How can he have mustered so much emotion? He stopped and we all fell silent. The final reverberations of his voice were still hovering in mid air. When he started to wipe his perspiration there was wild applause and requests for encores. He said laughingly that this is a political not artistic meeting, and we suddenly remembered that we had not yet begun.

Translated by Samia Mehrez

Naguib Mahfouz
from *The Day the Leader was Killed*

Elwan Fawwaz Muhtashimi
Let this be a festive occasion and let's forget our worries for an hour or so. But how when there are a hundred chinks in the door? What is the River Nile

trying to intimate? And the trees? Listen carefully. They're saying, Elwan, you poor fellow, trapped within four walls, Randa is coming back to you in the guise of friendship and small talk, in the guise of undeclared love resting on twin pillars of steel and despair, and shrouded in vague dreams. No persecution from family, no hope, and no despair! March at a brisk military pace, for today is soldiers' day. The café is packed with wordmongers. Here there's no satisfaction and no action. A transistor radio, brought along for the occasion, is placed on one of the tables between us. Just like on the day the late president broadcast his defeat in June 1967. The late President was greater in his defeat than this one in his glory was the first thing I heard. This reminds me of what my grandfather once said: We are a people more given to defeat than to victory. The strain that spells out despair has become deeply ingrained in us because of the countless defeats we have had to endure. We have thus learned to love sad songs, tragedies, and heroes who are martyrs. All our leaders have been martyrs: Mustafa Kamel, martyr to struggle and sickness; Muhammad Farid and Saad Zaghloul, both martyrs to exile; Mustafa al-Nahhas, martyr to persecution; Gamal Abd al-Nasser, martyr to June 5. As for this victorious, smug one, he has broken the rule: his victory constituted a challenge which gave rise to new feelings, emotions for which we were quite unprepared. He exacted a change of tune, one which had long been familiar to us. For this, we cursed him, our hearts full of rancor. And, ultimately, he was to keep for himself the fruits of victory, leaving us his *Infitah*, which only spelled out poverty and corruption. This is the crux of the matter.

We were caught up in the heat of arguments as the loudspeaker and transistor radio broadcast the details of Victory Day celebrations to whoever cared to listen. And, as usual, time got the better of us until, suddenly, strange voices could be heard.

"The traitors . . . the traitors," cried the broadcaster's voice.

Tongues grew paralyzed and eyes were averted as heads crowded around the transistor radio. The broadcasting of the celebrations came to a sudden halt, and then some songs started to be broadcast.

"What happened?"

"Something unusual."

"He said, 'The traitors, the traitors, the traitors!'"

"An invasion!"

"Of whom?"

"Honestly, what a stupid question!"

"The songs being broadcast indicate that . . ."

"Since when has logic meant anything?"

"A little patience!"

We had no desire to go back home. We all just huddled up in an urge to remain all together in the face of the unknown. We had a quick meal of macaroni for lunch and then sat there waiting. Following a brief but violent period of time, the broadcaster announced that there had been an abortive attempt on the president's life, that the president had left, and that the security forces were in full control of the situation. And, once again, there were songs on the radio.

"This, then, is the truth."

"The truth."

"Think a little."

"Certain facts cannot be concealed."

"But they can be delayed."

"Who are the assaulters?"

"Who but those involved in the religious movement?"

"But he was sitting in the very midst of soldiers and guards."

"Listen, they've started to broadcast national hymns."

Suddenly, there was a new broadcast announcing that the president had been slightly injured and that he was getting full medical attention at the hospital. Our hearts leaped up at the thought of increased chances of new possibilities. Time came to a halt, changed its tune, and emerged with a brand-new look on its face.

"The man has been injured. What then?"

"Get ready for prison."

"A definite return to terrorism."

"He'll survive and seek revenge."

"Will we be hearing the Qur'an after the hymns?"

We whiled away the time that was weighing heavily upon us. Jokes were cracked and then the recitation of the Qur'an began. At first, we turned pale. It's true then. Amazing! Actually true!? The man's finished? Who would've believed? Why do we sometimes get a feeling that the impossible is actually possible? Why do we imagine that there exists a reality other than death in this world? Death is the true dictator. The official announcement comes to us like a final statement. I wonder what people are saying? I'd like to hear what is being said around us in the café. I pricked up my ears. There is no power or might save in God. To him alone is permanence. The country is in obvious danger. He doesn't deserve this end, whatever his misdeeds. On his day of glory? A plot. Surely there's a conspiracy. No doubt. The hell with him! Death saved him from madness. Anyhow, he had to go. This is what happens to those who imagine that the country is nothing but a dead corpse. No, it's a foreign conspiracy. He doesn't deserve this end. It was the inevitable end. He was a curse on us. He who kills will ultimately be killed. In a split second, an empire has collapsed. The empire of robbers. What is the Mafia thinking about right now? I returned to my seat, torn by conflicting feelings of despair, fear, and joy. Vague hopes however overhead, hopes of unknown possibilities, hopes that the prevailing lethargy and routine would, at last, be shattered, and that one could start soaring toward limitless horizons. Tomorrow cannot be worse than today. Even chaos is better than despair, and battling with phantoms is better than fear.

This blow has rocked an empire and shaken fortresses.

By evening, I realized I had started dozing off. All this talk had exhausted me. I felt like taking a walk. There's a trace of death on every passerby. Suddenly, there I am in front of Gulstan's villa. Anwar Allam's car is parked there, awaiting its owner. Sexual desire of every sort takes possession of me and, with it, an irrepressible urge to kill.

Translated by Malak Hashem

Ahdaf Soueif
from *The Map of Love*

"'Am Abu El-Ma'ati." I say, "aside from the school, are there any problems in our village. About the land laws?"

"No, ya Sett Hanim. Everyone knows you are a gracious lady and you preserve the memory of your grandfathers. But it would be good if you came to us for a while."

"But what can I do about the school?"

"Come and see. Talk to people. Talk with the teachers and judge for yourself. And when you come back you can talk to the government."

"Me, ya 'Am Abu el-Ma'ati, I talk to the government?"

"And why not? Why shouldn't you talk to them? You're here in Cairo and the whole world knows who your father was—a thousand mercies and light upon him. Your father was a basha—even though they abolished titles, the whole world knows he was a basha and a man of understanding."

"Ya 'Am Abu el-Ma'ati, I don't know anyone in the government." I see myself going to look for 'the government.' I wouldn't know where to begin. There is a big ministry compound in Shari' el-Sheikh Rihan. I see myself going there and I am pulled up short by the memory of Mansur. Mansur was my friend and he was the car-park attendant at Shari' el-Sheikh Rihan between the American University and the ministries. For years I went to the American University to attend concerts, to see films, to use the library, to meet friends. As I crossed the intersection with Shari' el-Qasr el-'Ayni I'd be scanning the street ahead and he would emerge, short and stocky, stockier as the years went by. There he would be, his arm uplifted, his colored woven cap on his head. "Leave it just. Leave it," he would say. "Don't worry."

"How are you, ya Mansur?"

"How are you, ya Sett Hanim?" The keys would change hands. And later, when I came out there he would be again, with my keys and a few courtly words, pointing out where he had parked the car. Mansur was famous. He acquired two assistants; but he was always the one who had the keys. He was the one who was always there, until one day the bomb the Jama'at meant for el-Alfi, the Minister of the Interior they hated, had found Mansur instead. And now all that was left of him was a pale brown stain on the wall of the university. A stain that would not scrub off.

Ibrahim Issa
from *The Assassination of the Big Man*

IT WAS THE COMMEMORATION of two hundred years since the establishment of the National Zoo. The president wanted a breathtaking world-class celebration in an attempt to prove his commitment to nature and the environment. Since this had become a fashionable political concern of late, an international committee was formed to oversee the celebrations. Tens of millions of pounds were earmarked to import new and threatened animal species for the zoo, for the reconstruction and redesign of animal cages and shelters, the re-digging of artificial lakes, fresh supplies of water for the entire garden, new uniforms for the zoo workers and guards, and a special security company that would supervise the modifications and innovations with special attention to the monkey rockery and the importation of new African monkeys specifically for this occasion. One well-silenced incident marred these celebratory preparations, when the country sent a group of animal trainers to Germany to attend special courses in training lions and elephants. After they had completed their course work and were returning to the country two weeks before the inauguration, their airplane crashed and they all died. This necessitated the collaboration of trainers from the National Circus especially for the lion cages that had been custom-designed by an Italian master. The president invited many international figures renowned for their commitment to animal rights and decided to take all of his ministers to the inauguration to underline his and their good relations with animals.

A carnivalesque mood dominated the zoo: it was filled with flower arrangements, decorative paper hangings, and fluttering colored banners and ribbons. The orchestras played dance and ceremonial music through-out the gardens and three celebrities performed live with tens of students from the Institute of Ballet. They addressed special thanks and respect to the American movie star who had dedicated her life to saving animal furs and skins all over the world. The president was overjoyed at the sight of the lion cages, especially when he saw their imposing bodies, thick coats, strong fangs, sharp claws, legendary whiskers, and their body curves that looked like they had been chiseled by the hands of a sculptor. The ministers and guests were all taken by this awesome sight, particularly when the lions started roaring like kings who had ruled all the jungles of the world. The lion keepers were three young men in their late twenties. They were athletic, muscular, and well-dressed. They stood in front of the lions and circled around the spacious cage that had two (apparently) small doors with internal locks. The president, his guests, and the ministers stood together at the end of a narrow, meter-long stretch of lawn. The minister of agriculture was explaining something to the president and one of the guests was talking about the origin, genealogy, and natural habitat of these lions when suddenly everyone froze, at once breathless and speechless. The doors to the lion cage were unlocked, as if by remote control. Two lions jumped in complete and exact synchrony as if they had been rehearsing the moment for thousands of years. They jumped across the meter-long stretch of lawn that separated the president from the cage. One of the lions clawed the president's shoulder as he jumped, making him fall to the ground, just as a third lion leapt out of the cage. The ministers stumbled one after the other and were overwhelmed by the thundering chaos. Some fell on top of others, while some stampeded the bodies of those who had fallen. Blood started to spurt from the bodies of many international guests; the American movie star who had dedicated her life to animal rights was paralyzed by fear and passed out in the arms of a man who was standing by. They fell together, unnoticed by anyone, in the midst of hundreds of balloons that had surrounded the cage. One lion grabbed someone's neck then turned around and clawed another; another lion stood roaring on his two hind legs as people ran and swayed and fell and got up again and ran backward with their eyes fixed on him. Only one of the protocol officers remembered the president who lay on the ground in front of the lions. He ran toward him with his helmet and red baton until he got to him, breathless and staggering. Strangely he found the president fully conscious with a minor tear on his suit. The officer dragged the president for a couple of meters on the ground. The lions realized that the president had escaped so three of them focused their attention on the officer who was dragging the president on the ground in his torn suit in the midst of the sand, the grass, and the dust. The lions started moving toward them when the officer's arm grabbed the president's. He was astounded at the lions' attention and deliberate movement toward them as if they were aiming at him, confused and horror-stricken as he was. He turned to the president who was still on the ground and yelled,

"Get up and run, Mr. President!"

When the president heard this, his youthfulness that had been lost during his eighty years of age shot forth. With the sole desire to save his skin, he quickly got up, held himself steady, looked at the lions and mumbled, stuttering and awestricken.

"Incredible! Incredible!"

Then he started running as fast as he could, racing the winds of death and the claws of murder. The ministers saw the president running and suddenly the importance of running dawned upon them. Tens of them, in their formal suits, white shirts, shiny shoes, open heart surgeries, and seventy years of age, started running as fast as they could as the lions followed them with confidence.

When the president caught sight of the monkey rockery he felt that it was God's will to preserve his life for the sake of his people. So he jumped and was followed by his ministers, guests, reporters, and cameramen as if there were a master plan to counter the lions by using the monkeys.

Seven lions arrived at the fence of the rockery. They clawed their way to the top of the fence and started to walk along the wall, scrutinizing the crowded scene of the president and his entourage amid the rocks where one monkey fondled the president's head and another snatched at his vest while still a third sat on his lap, as he crouched peacefully among them shuddering and caressing their coats and backs. The lions could only see the redness of the monkeys' rear ends that hid the heads and bodies of the humans.

The lions stood on their hind legs, one after the other, taking turns in sustaining the loud, angry, thundering roar.

Translated by Samia Mehrez

Cairo Cosmopolitan

Cairo's cosmopolitan legacy has forever been overshadowed by Alexandria and its constructed, and of late contested, cosmopolitan history. However, the fact remains that Cairo, like Alexandria, has attracted multiple ethno-religious communities and can boast an exceptionally rich literary output in several languages by members of those communities who have historicized the tangled textures of multi-cultural lives and experiences in this city. Indeed, whether we choose to focus on the city's colonial past or its postcolonial present, Cairo, as the throbbing, ever-expanding mega city, has always been a magnet for communities from different ethnic and religious backgrounds, including Greeks, Italians, and Armenians among others, communities of Jewish and Christian origin, not to mention, of course, the city's main and growing Coptic minority, a population that is estimated at ten million of the country's eighty million inhabitants. As the national capital and the major political and economic urban space, Cairo also represented a beacon of opportunity for other Arab visitors, whether they were Syro-Lebanese immigrants (predominantly Christian) or young Arab students, who flocked to its religious and secular institutions of learning. At the same time, Cairo was, and continues to be, an alluring destination and perhaps a false refuge for local, individual, and communal migration as well as forced displacements. Like Alexandria, Cairo is marked by the diversity of languages that punctuated its literary output throughout the twentieth century, which together provide extraordinary insight into these communities' lives as they intersected with or diverged from each other.

The various excerpts in this section tell a complex story of how various ethno-religious communities from considerably different social and economic classes co-habited within the same urban space. The representations that are collected here unsettle the nostalgic and quite unreal image of the 'kosmopolite' or 'the citizen of the world' and reveal the inter-communal conflicts, problems, and differences that very often obstructed the much celebrated and idealized cosmopolitan experience. And yet, in the majority of these excerpts, we witness a considerable nostalgia for this eroded semblance of the cosmopolitan, examples of how individual members of different ethno-religious communities trespassed communal boundaries and defied community values. Ihsan Abdel Quddus's classic *I am Free*, written during the late 1950s, after the Egyptian Jewish community had dwindled in the wake of migration to the newly established Israeli state and the advent of the Free Officers' regime in Egypt in 1952, exemplifies such romanticized notions of living together. Despite initial violence between residents of the Jewish neighborhood of Dhaher and their Muslim neighbors in Husayniya, once the neighborhoods themselves begin to expand, and apartment buildings of Jews and Muslims begin to rise face-to-face and side-by-side, friendships started to develop between members of the two communities. Amina, the young, rebellious, middle-class Muslim girl, befriends her new Jewish neighbors, Fortuné and Elie, and skips school to be part of their liberal world, where she is given French lessons by Fortuné and dancing classes by Elie and, to dispel her shyness, is told that "upper-class Muslim women all danced and that magazines wrote about them and that a girl who didn't know how to dance in this day and age was not considered upper class."

Indeed, in more than one instance, Cairo's ethno-religious communities are portrayed as exemplifying far more liberal and at times utilitarian values, specifically where gender relations and women in particular are concerned. Through this kind of 'openness,' they are represented as capable of moving up the social and economic ladder much more easily when compared to their more conservative Muslim counterparts. In Fathy Ghanem's *A Girl from Shubra*, the Italian hairdresser, Emilio Sandro, living in the middle class, largely Christian neighborhood of Shubra, is torn between desire and trepidation as he envisions his daughter Maria at the heights of wealth and power thanks to her exquisite and seductive beauty: "Who knows, she may become Madame Pompadour of Egypt and, just like her, rule Egypt as Madame Pompadour ruled France during the time of King Louis XV." As for the upper echelons of Jewish and Christian society, we witness multiple forms of permissive social contexts that are practically alien to the majority of Egyptian or Cairene society. For example, Colette Rossant's Jewish narrator describes her grandmother's elaborately and painstakingly prepared "*jour de reçevoir*, her day to receive [women] guests in the afternoon for a game of poker or canasta," after which the women would be joined by the men for dinner and would later play "high stake games of poker until the wee hours of the morning."

Such intra-communal open, even libertine, mores are pitted against inter-communal conservative values and xenophobic forms of othering. In Bahaa Abdelmegid's *Saint Theresa*, khawaga Luca, the Jewish-Greek atelier owner loses Sabina, his Catholic-Italian girlfriend because of her father, "a conservative Catholic, [who] felt that it was impossible for a Christian to marry a Jew." In many other instances these elite islands of cosmopolitan social diversity and practice are represented as guilty of racism and condescension. This is amply demonstrated in Chafika Hamamsy's descriptions of the exclusively British Gezira Club during the 1940s and 1950s, where she provides a blatant example of British racism from Edward Said's autobiography *Out of Place*:

> Edward Said in his autobiography remembers with a certain measure of
> bitterness his early encounter with Captain Pilley [the Gezira Club British
> Administrator], who, having caught him in an out of bounds section of the
> club, told him with disdain, "Arabs aren't allowed here and you're an Arab."

The second half of the twentieth century witnessed the gradual disappearance of the large ethno-religious communities of Cairo. Only a handful remained. Those found themselves isolated, impoverished, and alienated from a new political and social reality in which they no longer had a space. Alaa Al Aswany's moving rendition of Madame Zitta Mendès, the dazzling Greek dancer who was the mistress of the narrator's father, is a case in point. The magical world that Madame Zitta had inhabited in the 1950s and had captivated the narrator as a child gradually collapses. Years later in 1996, the narrator stumbles over her and, initially, hardly recognizes her at Groppi's café, seated at the 'foreigners' table':

> The foreigners' table at Groppi's. All of them are old—Armenians and
> Greeks who have spent their lives in Egypt and kept going until they are
> completely alone. Their weekly date is at seven on Sunday mornings, and
> when they cross empty Talaat Harb Street, walking with slow, feeble steps,
> either propping one another up or supporting themselves on their walking
> sticks, they look as though they had just arisen from the dead, brushed off
> the grave dust, and come.

The image of cosmopolitan Cairo as a paradise lost for characters who seem like "they had just risen from the dead" contrasts quite sharply with representations of 'cosmopolitan' Cairo in thoroughly uplifting writings by Arab authors who came to the city as relatively privileged young students. In

Mohamed Berrada's *Like a Summer Never to Be Repeated* the young Moroccan narrator, Hammad, represents Cairo as a hegemonic regional presence that is nonetheless endearingly familiar, through its cultural and intellectual legacy:

> If he chose Cairo rather than Damascus, as others had, it was because of the many scenes his memory had accumulated from films like *Long Live Love*, *Forbidden Love*, and *Love and Revenge* and songs by Abd al-Wahhab, Farid al-Atrash, Asmahan, and Umm Kulthum. The names of certain writers—Taha Hussein, Tawfiq al-Hakim, al-Manfaluti, and Ahmad Lutfi al-Sayyid—had also snuck into his soul through the reading he undertook on his own in Bab Shala Library, close to Muhammad V School.

Similarly the young Bahraini student in Ghazi al-Qusaybi's *The Apartment of Freedom* dismisses the idea of being 'estranged' in Cairo:

> Cairo was the capital of all Arabs, the center of Islam, God's jewel on earth, the mother of the world, as Egyptians (who also called it Egypt!) referred to it; the Cairo of Gamal Abdel Nasser, and Voice of the Arabs, resistance against colonial powers; the Cairo of hope, the Cairo of the nationalization of the Suez Canal. . . .
>
> And the girls! The girls! Beautiful like movie stars; like Iman, his favorite actress; liberated like the girls in the films and Ihsan Abdel Quddus's novels.

However, the euphoria that surrounds Cairo as *the* cosmopolitan experience par excellence is unsettled by representations of cosmopolitan experiences that the city has failed and thwarted either because of political reasons or the failure of some of the characters to accept and assimilate into their new urban context. The tragic story of Roxanne, Shuhdi Atiya's widow, is movingly captured in Mahmoud Al-Wardani's *Heads Ripe for Plucking*. Roxanne was a Greek born in Egypt, who went against her parents' desire to see her married to a Greek and fell in love with Shudi Atiya al-Shafie, the well-known communist leader who was constantly in and out of prison until brutally tortured to death in detention in June 1960, leaving Roxanne wailing at the gate of Abu Zaabal Prison: "How could you have allowed them to kill you, Shuhdi? Why did you let them kill you, love? My God! They're a pack of dogs. Murderers, yes, murderers." Likewise, the downside of Cairo's 'cosmopolitanism' entraps Shaker, in Yasser Abdel Latif's *The Law of Inheritance*: Shaker came to Cairo in the nineteen thirties in the aftermath of the High Dam and the displacement of the people of Nubia to their new homes where he simply felt completely alienated. But in the end, he remained a misfit in Cairo and was eventually bundled up by members of the Cairo Nubian community and sent back to the village in the South.

And yet, by and large, all the excerpts in this section seem to reveal that the modern urban experience is one that unsettles and remaps boundaries between different ethno-religious communities by introducing new inter-communal affiliations and inter-class solidarities within the urban context. In Alaa Al Aswany's *Yacoubian Building* the two dubious Coptic brothers, Abaskharon and Malak, are thoroughly part of the rooftop underworld of the dilapidated luxury building. It is their class, not religious affiliation, that makes them part of that disadvantaged community. Similarly in Hamdi Abu Golayyel's *Thieves in Retirement*, Abou Gamal, who only rents out rooms in his house based on Upper Egyptian kinship, takes in Atef the Copt. Even though Atef is stigmatized and derogatorily nicknamed 'Koftis' for Copt, he becomes part of Abou Gamal's empire of the poor. Cairo thus imposes a new subaltern cosmopolitanism that in turn demands new forms and principles of living together, ones that various communities invented and re-invented throughout the twentieth century.

Ihsan Abdel Quddus

from *I am Free*

AL-DHAHER WAS THE Jewish neighborhood, with only a few scattered Muslim families. The futuwwas of Husseiniya used to raid al-Dhaher, which was bordered by a number of large barren areas and deserted streets. They used to hurl stones and rocks at its inhabitants until the police intervened. The Jews were always beaten during these raids that had no other purpose but religious fanaticism and the ultimate hatred of Jews, not to mention the fantastic stories that circulated about their habits, their daughters, and their sons. Likewise, when the Jews had an opportunity to lay their hands on a Muslim in their neighborhood, they would capture and torture him and then return him to his relatives almost naked.

This continued to happen, until a miracle occurred. The uninhabited areas that served as borders between Husseiniya and al-Dhaher were transformed into a modern street called Farouk Street where both neighborhoods met. Muslims and Jews became neighbors and their homes and apartment buildings rose face to face. Suddenly peace and friendship reigned: Muslims and Jews lived side by side. Urabi, the futuwwa of Husseiniya announced his repentance and opened a modern coffee shop at the end of Farouk Street where all of his clients were respectable effendis.

Despite this, however, the Abbasiya girls continued not to frequent al-Dhaher. Marie the dressmaker used to go to their homes to make their clothes for a daily fee. But Marie also bought property and expanded her business and no longer went round to the homes but received her clients in her own home.

Amina was not just a client of Marie's but a friend of her daughter, Fortuné, a girl of her age, tall, slim, and beautiful with seductive feminine eyes, a broad smile, and a brisk walk that rocked her entire body and shook her locks from right to left. She had no other sign of Jewishness except the delicate hook nose and two rather big ears.

Amina and Fortuné's friendship was circumscribed by the fact that the former felt more privileged: she was not a Jew with a dressmaker for a mother. But despite these differences, Amina loved Fortuné and her conversations that opened up new horizons were certainly more interesting than those that took place during other kinds of visits, or zar occasions, or the ladies' carriage in the *Khalig* metro. She used to talk to her about movies, about fashion, about Paris, about dancing, about what was published in foreign newspapers, and about men and women. Fortuné's conversations about men and women were always open and daring, causing Amina to blush in shyness.

Amina loved the life that Fortuné had. She was free to go out and come home whenever she wanted, to meet young men, to go wherever she wanted. Her mother, Marie, was a dressmaker and Fortuné was still a student, but she gave private lessons in French to some upper-class girls for a nominal fee. Her brother was employed in a bank but he also used one of the rooms in their apartment, which he equipped with a gramophone and music records, to give dance lessons to students from Fuad al-Awwal High School in exchange for twenty piasters for each dance. Amina used to wonder if she could ever be like them and make her own living.

Fortuné was surprised at Amina's visit in her school uniform and bag when the school day was not yet over. But she made no comment and welcomed her warmly. They sat and chatted side by side on the sofa. Then Amina asked her for a French lesson. Soon, Elie, Fortuné's brother arrived from the bank and joined them in conversation and updated them on the latest dance competitions in which he participated and the party that took place at San Stefano in Alexandria and the other one at Cabaret Kit Kat in Imbaba. He then offered to teach Amina how to dance.

Amina refused but Fortuné encouraged her and assured her that upper-class Muslim women all danced and that magazines wrote about them and that a girl who didn't know how to dance in this day and age was not considered upper class.

Finally Amina surrendered, laughing timidly. She felt nothing as the young Jewish man held her waist, placed his chest against hers or his legs between hers. She was completely focused on the dance steps that Elie was teaching her and was aided by her musical ear and agile body. In one hour Amina was dancing as if she had been born to dance the tango and the foxtrot.

Elie said to her, "Mademoiselle Amina, I want to congratulate you! If we were dance partners we would have outdone Fred Astaire and Ginger Rogers."

Amina laughed at the joke.

Translated by Samia Mehrez

Fathy Ghanem

from *A Girl from Shubra*

SEÑORA MATILDA WAS THE wife of the hairdresser, Emilio Sandro. She was not jealous or angry about the relationship between her husband and Princess 'H' or Madam 'M' even though she was a devout Catholic who went to Saint Theresa Church every morning with her daughter Maria and went to Father Lorenzo for confession every week.

The huge gap that separated the Sandro family in Shubra from the society of princesses and palaces stripped ethical values of their signification and meaning. No matter what, the servant remained a servant and the princess a princess. What Sandro engaged in was diffcrent in its meaning and importance from a relationship between equals: a prince and a princess or a servant and another. . . .

This did not mean that Señora Matilda felt that she belonged to the society of slaves for she was the wife of a respected man among friends, acquaintances, and neighbors in Shubra. Elsa, the wife of old Orlando, the head waiter at the Golden Scarab Club in the Pyramids area was her upstairs neighbor. He served the king himself when he came to the club. He had a weak heart and when he came home during the early hours of the morning he would climb up the stairs to the fourth floor. When he would reach the third floor where the Sandro family lived, he would collapse and his black suit would be drenched in sweat. His voice would cut through the silence of the night as he yelled, "Elsa, Elsa!" Elsa would come down to help him walk up the remaining steps. Sometimes, Maria would help him and would be shocked at his ailing body, so different from how it appeared in the afternoon when he went down smiling and dignified like a great military commander.

Orlando died early one morning and Señora Matilda looked at herself in the mirror and saw an old, flabby body. She said to herself that Elsa had become a widow and that she was a dangerous woman who would not shy away from doing wrong. She feared her and feared for Sandro.

Maria overheard her father yelling at her mother sarcastically, "I, Emilio Sandro, who has the most beautiful princesses and women in the country at my fingertips every day am interested in Elsa!"

Matilda yelled back, "Yes, danger can only come from the likes of her!"

Matilda defined the boundaries of the world through Shubra: Saint Theresa Church, the Italian Club with its spacious gardens, and the swings that Maria played on as Costa the Greek and his wife Nina—who lived across the street from Maria's room—chatted with Matilda and drank beer on Sunday while they waited for Emilio to come back from an appointment with one of the princesses who had summoned him suddenly. From time to time, Costa would push Maria on the swing and she would scream excitedly until her face flushed and would ask him to stop the swing but he would push her higher and higher still and she would fly in the air and the wind would push away her dress, uncovering her thighs and overtaking her with a sense of pleasure. Alfredo, the son of Marco the mechanic was, in Matilda's mind, the prime candidate to marry Maria. His father owned a workshop that brought in a fortune like gold, and a villa at the end of the street with a garden that housed marble statues. The boy would not go to Italy and would not be lost like Mario, Maria's brother, the victim of her husband's dreams of fame and glory—for Sandro believed that the Duce represented the highest hope for Rome and for his own personal glory. He was profoundly convinced that in the near future the Duce would enter Egypt as a conqueror on his white horse and would reign like Julius Caesar over Cleopatra. If today he was the hairdresser in the royal court, tomorrow he would become Mussolini, the great Duce's representative in a country where the princesses will become the slaves of the new Roman master. Today he is the servant but tomorrow he will become the master. He had paid heavily, and in advance, for the glory of Rome and the glory of the Duce, for he had sent his son Mario to Rome to join the Blackshirts, after which he went to Ethiopia as a soldier in the Duce's army. There, he died. This was the first crack in the edifice of glory and fame that Emilio had tried to sell to his wife Matilda. Now she wanted to escape these dreams of glory and contented herself with her kingdom in Shubra. The streets of Shubra had witnessed Mario in his black shirt on his motorbike as he zoomed through with energy and youth. As for the Duce's glory, it had transformed Mario into a legendary spirit that fluttered around Mussolini but it all brought unending grief that descended upon Matilda's head. She was angry that Sandro clung to shallow glory, that he was proud of Mario's heroism. She used to blame her husband and accuse him of having abandoned Mario, leaving him to die in faraway lands inhabited by savages who fought with swords and daggers. Only God knew what they had done to her son until he died; only God knew what they had done with his corpse that they could never retrieve.

But Sandro also grieved for the loss of his son even though he still believed in the road to glory. Boasting about his son actually alleviated some of his grief and helped him avoid his wife's blame for not having kept Mario in Egypt, when he could have easily obtained the Egyptian citizenship through the Palace and secured a decent life for their son.

Maria used to overhear her mother blaming her father and would be disturbed by what she heard. Sometimes she would join her mother in blaming her father and at others she would rebel against her words and tone. She made sure to confess to Father Lorenzo and ask him to pray for her forgiveness. She would always be anxious when her parents quarreled about her future, for she was a single child—now seventeen—whose femininity had come to maturation. Secretly she was also jealous of the attention her parents gave to Mario's memory, which seemed to surpass the attention they gave her. She used to try to dismiss this shameful jealousy by showing grief and by suddenly bursting into tears from time to time at home or upon seeing a scene of soldiers in a film she would be watching at the movie theater with Costa and Nina. But quickly she would forget everything, when Costa would whisper to his wife in Arabic because she didn't speak Greek and he didn't know any Italian and both, as her mother said, were stupid and would never learn the other's language. . . .

One day Sandro said to one of the princesses as he was styling her hair, "Your Highness, a girl called Rozina who is a neighbor of ours left for France and became a star in Paris. I cannot believe that she has become this successful when my daughter Maria is a thousand times more beautiful."

The princess replied sarcastically, "You have come to the wrong precinct for such matters. The King has a huge administration whose responsibility is the affairs of beautiful girls, whether singers or dancers or otherwise . . . ."

The words of the princess kept echoing in Sandro's mind. He would churn them and try to imagine what they meant, as he thought about the strategies used by members of his community to become closer to the king and his court. There was Petro, who had become an inseparable companion of the king in all his evening outings after he had been the driver of the royal sports car fleet that included Maserati, Ferrari, and Lamborghini. Señora Matilda remembered the days of her childhood in Azarita, Alexandria where she was born and where Petro and his sisters used to play with her on the rooftop. She said that Petro's sisters paved his way to the king until he became of great esteem and power among ministers and heads of Egyptian families, sought out by top administrators. Fortune smiled upon the beauties. The princess was right, for the king's men followed the news of beautiful girls. No sooner did a new young beautiful singer or dancer appear in one of the nightclubs than her photograph would be before the king. If he liked her, the girl would, for a long time, have a say in the royal court and would have accounts in the banks and would end up like Petro's sisters—marrying one of the wealthy Italian, Greek, or Jewish business men who wanted to cement their relationship with the court to protect their economic and industrial investments. Beautiful Maria deserved much more than that and will come to possess abundant wealth, complete protection and security for her future, and she will accede to the highest status in the country. Who knows, she may become Madame Pompadour of Egypt and, just like her, rule Egypt as Madame Pompadour ruled France during the time of King Louis XV. But those thoughts were like playing with fire and he could not gamble with his daughter and sacrifice her . . . .

Translated by Samia Mehrez

Midhat Gazalé
from *Pyramids Road*

Abraham lived in Egypt for a time; Joseph was Pharaoh's minister there; Moses "was trained in all the wisdom of the Egyptians" (Acts 7:22) . . . . Jesus found refuge on the banks of the Nile.
Christian Cannuyer

AT SCHOOL, MY BROTHER and I discovered strange new names that were foreign to our ears, such as Chalem, Levy, or Bensoussan. My father explained that these names belonged to the Jewish people, a community we had never before come across. They all spoke French, though Matzner and Falk spoke German when they played together. The mystery became thicker when Maurice Bensoussan asked me to his birthday party. His grandmother spoke Spanish and served little strange-tasting biscuits called *rosquettes*. My confusion reached its peak upon learning from Falk that his grandparents spoke something called Yiddish.

Most of my classmates went neither to church nor mosque, but to the synagogue, a word that sounded mysterious and somewhat foreboding. On Friday evening, I often bumped into them in the center of Cairo, where most of us lived. They were on their way to the synagogue with their parents and wore little caps on the back of their heads that were secured with little metallic pins. More than once, I had hoped that Bensoussan would ask me to accompany him, but he peremptorily replied that, not speaking Hebrew, I would not understand what was going on.

Upon learning that a rabbi gave him private Hebrew lessons, I became very frustrated at the thought that he was learning something that I was not. Having decided to emulate him, I asked my mother to arrange for the rabbi to come to our house and teach me Hebrew. Needless to say, I never learned Hebrew, and it was not until one of my close friends married several years later that finally discovered what the inside of a synagogue looked like.

Our next-door neighbors were Jewish, and their children also went to the Lycée. Both were particularly brilliant, and Molly, the younger of the two, always made it to the top of her class. No sooner had she finished her homework than she came knocking on our door, asking my mother if I had also finished mine and if she could come in and play. We spent hours in my room, busily playing at all sorts of games. I would show her my latest inventions and sometimes make them up as I spoke. She would show me her drawings and let me read her poems.

Their religious holidays were different from ours, though they sometimes coincided, Passover with Easter, and Hanukkah with Christmas. During Passover, they ate unleavened bread that looked slightly burnt and tasted vaguely like the eucharistic host. I remember my mother cautioning us never to get close to their apartment if we carried bread, for fear of infecting them with something called yeast. That word elicited in our minds the pungent smell of milk that had curdled in the heat of summer. For some reason, we were immune to that sort of predicament and the Jews were not. We therefore took great care not to contaminate them.

Molly had just learned the Seder, a kind of question and answer game they played during Passover, where the smallest child in the family asked his parents why the bread was baked without yeast, why food had to be soaked, why they had to drink lying down and eat bitter herbs. Molly resolved to teach me the game, and we took turns at questioning and answering each other.

The Seder stories had to do with the suffering their people had endured upon being forced by Pharaoh to leave Egypt. I could not quite fathom what terrible crime they had committed. Except for their strange habits and their lack of fluency in Arabic, they were very much like the rest of us. I was troubled, though, by her account of the plagues that befell my country in response to their prophet's imprecations. I had learned in catechism that God was love and forgiveness, and knew no vengeance.

Be that as it may, I was relieved at the thought that these events were a thing of the distant past, since Molly's people had safely returned to Egypt by now, and the little Jewish girl could freely play with her Egyptian neighbor.

During Hanukkah, the Jewish Festival of Lights, our neighbors lit one candle of a nine branch candelabra on the first day, two on the second day, and so on, during eight days in a row. The ninth candle served to light the other eight. Once, due to grave family circumstances in Alexandria—one of the grandmothers with dying—they had to leave unexpectedly. They were in the midst of Hanukkah, and had only lit four candles. As my mother offered her sympathy on our doorstep, Molly's mother asked her if she wouldn't mind lighting the remaining four candles as she handed her the silver candelabra. My mother of course accepted and promised to light the candles diligently. She was extremely superstitious though, and I have a sneaking suspicion that once entrusted with that mission, she feared some terrible misfortune would befall our family should she not fulfill her promise. She placed the candelabra atop a console in one of the rooms, remarking that it looked rather nice after all. The following day, as I walked into the room to bid my Mother good morning, I found her kneeling on a pillow in front of the candelabra. I did not interrupt her, for she was praying. She repeated that ritual every morning. No sooner had the eighth candle burned out than the doorbell rang. The neighbors were back, and the grandmother had miraculously recovered. "You are a saint, Madam Gazalé," exclaimed Molly's mother as she kissed mine.

Bensoussan invited me to his Bar Mitzvah, which he described as the equivalent of our First Communion. I was dismayed not to attend the ceremony at the synagogue, for I was only invited to the party that took place in his apartment. Bensoussan was very excited as he opened several envelopes that contained monetary gifts, and lined up an impressive collection of wallets and Parker fountain pens, as well as four or five wristwatches.

For my First Communion, I received mostly books, with the exception of a single fountain pen, a gift of my mother's closest friend Carolina, a Romanian Jew. My mother had told her that the First Communion was a kind of Bar Mitzvah. I used to call her Tante Nina, for we always called our parents' closest friends Uncle or Aunt. It was several years before I realized that Tante Isis, Tante Angèle, and Tante Emilie were my father's sisters in actuality, whereas Tante Nina, Tante Becky, Tante Waheeda, and Tante Rose were not related to our family. The thought that Tante Nina and Tante Becky were Jewish and Tante Waheeda Muslim never crossed my mind.

In the course of the coaching that we received before the big day, Father Augustin Buisson, a Canadian priest, told us the story of Napoleon who, upon being asked whether his coronation or the Austerlitz victory was the most beautiful day of his life, simply replied, "My First Communion." I therefore woke up that morning repeating to myself that I was about to experience the most beautiful day of my life. The Grand Mass at St Joseph's was awesome, and I shivered irrepressibly as the big bells rang. The girls sat on the left side of the aisle in their virginal wedding-like dresses and white gloves, with the mother of pearl rosaries wrapped around their missals. We sat on the opposite side, proudly sporting our white silk armbands wrapped around the left arm, on the heart's side.

It was a beautiful day indeed, for my grandfather, who seldom left the big house, attended the service and gave me ten gold pounds. A fortune! Also on that day, I met Yvette, a frail and sensitive young girl whose family had just moved into our building. She taught me the Lambeth Walk and I offered her a huge serving of chestnut filled *mont-blanc* that Molly's mother had baked for the occasion, and an equally large portion of cream-filled *kunafa* that my own mother had baked. I believe she kissed me on the cheek.

Chafika Hamamsy
from Zamalek

THE BRITISH, WHO AFTER the defeat of 'Urabi in 1882 became the 'protectors' of Egypt, very soon realized the beauty of the island and managed to obtain a piece of land there, where they created the Gezira Sporting Club. The site was presented by the Khedive Tewfik to the British High Command in the early 1880s, carved out of the Khedivial Botanical Gardens—hence the acacias and jacarandas that adorned it. In the 1940s the club boasted an eighteen-hole golf course—one of the best in the world—two swimming pools, several tennis courts, squash racquet courts, a club house, a pergola, which surrounded the pools usually referred to as 'the Lido,' and a dining room where typical British meals were served. Welsh rarebit, and steak and kidney pie were offered for lunch, hot scones and raisin cake for tea, and trifle for desert. Membership at the club was originally restricted to the British—in other words, the resident general (later to become ambassador), his staff, and British military personnel of officer rank only—as it was originally meant to serve the British Army of

Occupation. Gradually, however, Egyptian high officials were offered memberships, and these 'happy few' of the early 1920s could, if they chose to, have a taste of the English way of life.

'The club' or the 'Gezira,' as it was often called, was a little piece of Victorian England, where proper decorum *à l'anglaise*, discipline, and high standards of sportsmanship were preserved. In the late 1930s, a new club secretary, Captain Eric Charles Pilley, came on the scene. He was the last of a long line of eminent gentlemen entrusted with the formidable responsibility of protecting and preserving this British entity created in the heart of Cairo. He followed in the footsteps of Captain Humphreys of the mounted infantry and Haywood Walker Setton-Carr (1859–1938), who set the rules and made sure they were respected. Captain Pilley was the epitome of Britishness. Tall, gray-haired, with steel-blue eyes, which glared down at any unfortunate native gardener who encountered his displeasure, he toured the grounds all day long on his bicycle and maintained by his presence the exact orderliness of an already extremely orderly set-up. His aloofness was legendary, and his distrust of natives equally well known, and yet he was perceptive enough to know where to draw the line and whose toes not to tread upon.

Edward Said in his autobiography remembers with a certain measure of bitterness his early encounter with Captain Pilley who, having caught him in an out of bounds section of the club, told him with disdain, "Arabs aren't allowed here and you're an Arab." Such behavior can only be ascribed to Captain Pilley's innate British snobbery for, although he was well aware that Edward Said was a club member, he also knew that he was not a pasha's son but just an 'out of place' little boy. Offspring of Egyptian members were usually not antagonized by Captain Pilley as long as they behaved themselves and followed scrupulously all rules and regulations. For instance, children under the age of sixteen were never allowed into the big swimming pool or on the right hand side of the Lido, the side with awnings that were drawn everyday at noon and pulled back after sunset. Dogs were never allowed on the grounds but were kept in kennels provided for them, and under no circumstances were non-golfers to tread the greens. Children had to leave the club at sunset and were not to bring friends along who were non-members.

To survey his domain and keep the youngsters in check, Captain Pilley had a second in command, a Mr. Williams, otherwise known as 'the Control.' Mr. Williams was a short and stocky man whose diffident manner barely concealed a powerful determination to be obeyed. Under the pith helmet he wore all year round, he had a rubicund face but lips that seldom smiled. He patrolled all day from the playground, where nannies and young children were segregated, to the tennis courts, the swimming pools, and the dining room to ensure that Captain Pilley's instructions were followed to the letter. He knew each member and every member's offspring and was known to have, on occasion, politely requested a non-member who had 'trespassed' to "please leave quietly and make no fuss." Both he and Captain Pilley commanded the youngsters' respect and the club under their aegis was indeed a well-controlled place.

Captain Pilley lived on the grounds in a lovely British-style house, surrounded by perfect lawns with bougainvilleas of many colors creeping up the walls. In fact, the whole club was often perceived as his private garden with acacias, jacarandas, and poincianas planted at strategic points to ensure that pink, blue, and purple would contribute to the harmonious effect of perfect landscaping.

From the very early days of the club's existence, the major social events held there were races and polo matches. One of the first races took place in the mid-1880s. Jockeys were imported from England but in time Egyptian-trained riders joined in, and the heavy European horses were replaced by the swift and agile Arabian ponies.

Attendance at the races was always considerable and looked forward to by the British colony and Egyptians as well. As for the polo matches, ten or twelve were held every year, and as early as 1908 a 'challenge' cup was offered by Seif Allah Yusry Pasha, Princess Chivekiar's second husband.

In the early 1920s, very few Egyptians were club members. Those invited to join were usually men who had distinguished themselves in their chosen field of activity, but were not necessarily pro-British. Had that been required, few Egyptians would have wanted to join, as anti-British sentiment, though not always apparent, was very much part of the Egyptian consciousness. It stands to reason, however, that a very vocal anti-British official would not have been sought out as a desirable element in this exclusive—and one might add, elitist— group. On the whole, however, politics was not an issue which concerned Egyptians as much as social standing within the framework of society at the time. To become a club member was assuredly a status symbol perfectly acceptable to an Egyptian candidate as recognition of personal achievement. To be sure, not much use of the membership was made by these families in the early 1920s and 1930s, as most

Egyptian men, with notable exceptions such as Seif Allah Yusry Pasha, did not attach much importance to sportsmanship, while wives and children did not even consider it as a social option. Hoda Sha'rawi, the famous Egyptian feminist, founder in 1923 of the Egyptian Feminist Union, wrote in her memoirs that she never went to the Gezira Sporting Club; neither would she go to a restaurant for a meal or attend mixed parties. These were frivolous occupations that ran counter to the norms of the education she had received and the class to which she belonged. It was one thing to cast off the veil in a grand gesture which had tremendous sociopolitical implications, quite another to reject wholesale the traditions of her social milieu. This is all the more surprising because, according to the account she gives of her life, she was indeed far more emancipated than most ladies of her time and deeply involved in political pursuits. She was encouraged by her husband, 'Ali Sha'rawi Pasha, to become the first president of the Wafdist Women's Central Committee. For a lady who befriended Eugenie Lebrun, wife of writer, feminist, and politician Hussein Rushdi Pasha, and frequently attended her 'salon,' this reluctance to go the Gezira Sporting Club may have seemed anachronistic but only indicated that her adherence to tradition ran very deep. Therein lay her strength, for not all women of the next generation shared this clarity of vision and were able to navigate successfully the rough waters of modernism's tidal wave.

With the advent of World War II, the younger generation of the time, cooped up in Cairo for the summer since Alexandria and most coastal towns were considered dangerous, discovered under the watchful eyes of their governesses the joys of swimming in the pool or playing tennis. Virtually overnight, scones and jam, Welsh rarebit, and steak and kidney pie became household words. A brand new world opened up for these young Egyptians, a world of British discipline paired with a certain measure of emancipation, if not freedom. Soon enough, for these boys and girls aged ten to fifteen, the club became a focal point in their life. It is quite surprising that Egyptian families allowed their offspring so much freedom within the confines of the club, or allowed them to go there in the first place. It must have been a case of global emulation, a pattern followed by the Zamalekites, as well as others, with zest and alacrity. Another reason must have been that there was precious else they could do since the only other outlet for pent-up energies in the heat of the summer months would have been the Grotto Gardens, so named after the grotto that housed an aquarium, surrounded by patches of green lawns and well-traced alleys. There was nothing much one could do there except for an occasional game of hide-and-seek, during which the hiding always took place behind a lone tree with pursuit easily and successfully concluded! Despite its beauty, the garden had an oppressive atmosphere because of the eerie silence of its surroundings, or perhaps because of the gloomy aquarium from the ceiling of which bats hung, like so many stalactites, both ominous and repulsive.

Colette Rossant

from Apricots on the Nile

MY GRANDMOTHER HAD MANY friends and relatives. Among her friends and family members were eight women who had known each other since they were children. A few, like Tante Marie, were widows with children; others had husbands who worked for my grandfather or were old friends of his. The eight spent hours on the telephone every day, exchanging gossip, talking about their children, or complaining about their servants, cooks, or daughters- and sons-in-law. Each woman had *son jour de recevoir*, her day to receive guests in the afternoon for a game of poker or canasta. Later, in early evening, their husbands would join them for dinner; after dinner, the women and the men would play high-stake games of poker until the wee hours of the morning. Hundreds and sometimes thousands of Egyptian pounds would pass hands, all in good fun.

I hated these days, since my life would be turned upside down. Grandmaman's day was Saturday, every eight weeks. Preparations started the day before. Early in the morning, before the sun got too hot, the whole household would be put to work cleaning the house, washing the terrace, and cooking a feast.

First the windows of the living room were flung wide open. Then the oriental rugs were picked up and tossed over the veranda railing. Abdullah would whip the dust off the rug with great energy, using a reed beater shaped like a four-leaf clover at the end of a long stick. While he beat, he sang a song. I would hear him and immediately appear in my nightgown and beg Abdullah to let me try. Within five minutes I would be covered with dust from head to toe. Suddenly my grandmother would appear, screaming at Abdullah that he had absolutely no brains allowing me to do something so unladylike. She would grab me by the arm and banish me back to my rooms, ordering Aishe to give me a good scrubbing in the bathtub.

Afterward, the rugs would be put back in place, the furniture would be dusted, and four or five card tables would be set in the middle of the living room. Great quantities of flowers would arrive, and Lucie, who was considered the artist of the family, would arrange them around the room. No one was allowed in the salon for the next twenty-four hours.

For poker day, the 'good' silver, the most ornate and heavy cutlery, came out of the drawers, and the silver coffee service, which every Egyptian family seemed to have sitting on a silver tray on a sideboard, would be polished.

Aishe and the porter's wife would be given the task of polishing the silver. I would sit with them, listening to their gossip about the men servants of the adjoining houses. Between polishing and gossiping they would munch on dried melon seeds, placing them between their front teeth and cracking them open. I learned very quickly how to do it, a habit to which my grandmother strongly objected. When they were afraid to eat the seeds because she was too near, they chewed on *mastic*, a sort of resin, transparent and hard as a stone, which would, after heroic chewing, turn into a sticky white paste. When I was six, Aishe tried to teach me how to chew, but my baby teeth hurt so much that I quickly abandoned the idea, to the great relief of my grandmother, who loved to say about those who chewed, *"Ils ressemblent à des vaches espagnoles"* ("They look like Spanish cows"). I still don't chew gum and often try to stop my own grandchild Matthew from chewing bubble gum and blowing bubbles with it. Matthew thinks I am odd. "You're not an American, Grandmaman," he likes to say with a little smile as he tries to entice me to buy him some bubble gum.

On Fridays before poker days, Grandmaman and Ahmet would go together to the market, not in the open carriage, as when Grandmaman went to market with Abdullah, but in my grandfather's car. Ahmet sat next to the chauffeur, and I—when I was allowed to accompany them—would be in the backseat next to Grandmaman. On our return, my seat would be filled with packages, and I would be squeezed in front between the chauffeur and Ahmet.

The scene at the market was quite different when Ahmet was with us. My grandmother was more subdued and would stand quietly to the side while Ahmet argued with the vendors about prices and quality of the food. However, one day a shattering event occurred; it might easily have destroyed my grandmother's favorite pastime had not Ahmet saved the day. We were standing between the poultry vendor and the watermelon vendor when suddenly Ahmet started to scream at a young man next to us, accusing him of stealing his money. A fight ensued, and suddenly it grew ugly. The crowd that gathered seemed hostile, and the man turned his attention to my grandmother and began hurling insults at her. I will never forget the fear on Grandmaman's face. She took me in her arms, enveloping me as if to protect me, nearly choking me while Ahmet and the watermelon man tried to calm the young man and the crowd. The police arrived, searched the young man, found Ahmet's wallet on him, and arrested him. They then escorted us back to the car. This was the only time I was allowed to sit in the back. My grandmother held me tightly, and I could feel her body still trembling from the fear that that incident had provoked. That night my grandfather scolded my grandmother and Ahmet and forbade Grandmaman ever to go shopping at the market again. For the next two months Grandmaman sent Ahmet to shop alone, but she missed the adventure of going to the market and soon resumed her weekly trips. I, however, had to wait a full year before I was allowed to accompany her.

STUFFED VINE LEAVES

WASH A 450-G/1-LB JAR OF VINE LEAVES under cold running water to rinse off the brine. Place in a bowl, cover with boiling water, and let stand for 5 minutes. Drain and cool.

MIX 450 G/1 LB CHOPPED LAMB with 200 g/7 oz raw rice, 20 g/¾ oz chopped parsley, 65 ml/2½ fl oz olive oil, 50 ml/2 fl oz lemon juice, 1 tablespoon cumin, and salt and pepper to taste. Mix well. Spread out the leaves. In the center of a vine leaf place 1 tablespoon of the meat-rice stuffing. Fold the base of the leaf up and over the stuffing, fold in the sides, and roll the leaf tightly to make a cylinder about 6 cm/2½ in long and 1–2 cm/½ –¾ in thick. Continue until you have used all the stuffing.

COVER THE BOTTOM of a heavy saucepan with loose vine leaves. Place a layer of stuffed vine leaves, close together and seam side down, along the bottom. Arrange another tightly packed layer on top of that, continuing until all the stuffed leaves have been added. Cover with 3 or 4 loose vine leaves. Pour in 50 ml/2 fl oz olive oil and 450 ml/¾ pint chicken stock. Cover and bring to the boil. Lower the heat and simmer for 45 minutes. When cooked, arrange the stuffed leaves on a platter and pour 50 ml/2 fl oz lemon juice over them. Serve hot or cold with yogurt or tehina. This makes about 30 to 40 vine leaves.

With the poker-day cleaning and marketing done, the kitchen would be thrown into turmoil. Grandmaman herself would prepare her famous *sambusacks*, large aubergines would be charring on the primus, several legs of lamb would be marinating on the counter, and on a small table Aishe and the chauffeur would be stuffing grape leaves with a mixture of rice and chopped lamb. If I sat quietly near Aishe, I was allowed to stay in the kitchen and help roll the grape leaves. Meanwhile Ahmet would be preparing a ballottine of duck to be served sliced with a dark, smooth jelly. I loved to watch as Ahmet deftly cut the duck's back so it lay flat on the kitchen marble, then slowly and carefully deboned it. He would remove the duck meat, mince it with spices, and add pistachio nuts. The duck skin would then be rolled around the stuffing, and Ahmet with a needle and thread would sew it shut, making it look like a fat sausage. The scent of the roasting duck would permeate the house and make me very hungry. After a while, I would forget myself and begin chatting away, asking questions or begging a taste of something, often stealing some pistachios that Ahmet painstakingly had shelled that morning. Ahmet, in an unusual fit of exasperation, would then throw me out of the kitchen, and I would roam the house like a lost soul. I felt once more abandoned, for it seemed to me that I was nowhere welcomed.

APRICOT PUDDING

PLACE 225 G/8 OZ DRIED APRICOTS in a bowl. Cover with warm water and allow to soak overnight. Drain. Place the apricots, 4 large eggs, 50 ml/2 fl oz double cream, 1 tablespoon rum, and 100 g/4 oz sugar in a food processor. Process until the apricots are puréed. Butter a 1.2-liter/2-pint mold. Pour the apricot purée into the mold. Place the mold in a larger pan filled with hot water and bake in a preheated 180°C/350°F/gas mark 4 oven for 45 minutes, or until the point of a knife inserted in the middle comes out clean. Cool and unmold on a round platter. Garnish with mint leaves. This will serve 4.

My aunts prepared desserts. Tante Fortuné made her special dish of prunes stuffed with walnuts in a brandy syrup; Tante Lydia made a sort of multicolor tower of Jell-O that would invariably fall after the first person helped himself. It would look a mess, but Grandmaman never said anything because, as she explained to me one day, Lydia did not know how to cook. Tante Becca would bring a dish of her light, crisp, and golden *zalabya*, which I would gobble down if no one was looking.

Saturday morning, the remaining dishes were prepared. For the *mezze*, small pieces of lamb's liver were fried with onions and cumin; they would be sprinkled with lemon juice and minced parsley and served cold. *Hummus*, the traditional chickpea dish, was decorated with slivered almonds. There were also tiny artichoke hearts marinated in olive oil, fried ground chicken balls, and, in season, cold tender broad beans. Grandmaman's contribution to the *mezze* were "mimosa eggs," hard-boiled eggs stuffed with egg yolks mashed with mayonnaise and herbs, which I hated but which were very popular with the ladies. There were always thin slices of *batarekh*—salted dried roe of the gray mullet preserved in a sort of waxy skin—on thin toasts. Olives, black or green, would fill silver bowls, as would cucumber pickles. These dishes were served on the terrace while the table in the dining room was made ready for the dinner. Limoges dishes were brought out under the eyes of Grandmaman, who would repeat endlessly to everyone, "Be careful, be careful! These are my best dishes!"

On this day the jewels came out, heavy diamond-studded bracelets, arms full of gold bangles (by the age of ten, I had already ten of them), sparkling diamond rings. Grandmaman did not approve of diamonds and never wore hers. She would say of women covered in diamonds, "They look as if they are wearing a crystal chandelier!" I remember years later, when one of my uncles was trying to marry me off, he would always point out the quality of the pretenders by telling me how many karats my diamond would weigh.

My grandmother would tell me, just before the guests arrived, to go and get dressed, comb my hair, and, mainly, put some shoes on. Whenever I came back from school or was at home on weekends, I walked around the house barefoot or I wore *shib-shib*, the flat slippers that Aishe bought for me at the market. They made a flapping noise whenever I walked.

Sometimes a new person would be introduced to the group, and I would be proudly paraded in front of them. "My granddaughter," my grandmother would say to that day's new addition; "She is half French, you know," as if that qualification would add a new dimension to who I was. Then the whispers would start that always upset me, "She is an orphan, you know... Really? No, I did not know.... Well, not quite, her mother ... you know ... Alexandria ... Beirut ... left the child here with Marguerite. ...." And it would go on for several minutes. The women would look at me with pity, which I resented terribly, especially when my aunt Lydia would ask her younger daughter, Renée, who was just a year older than me, to come and say hello. Renée, tall, thin and blond, would gracefully make the rounds, and I would be forgotten as the women exclaimed in their chanting voices, *"Elle est adorable . . . comme elle est mignone!"* ("She is adorable`... how pretty she is!").

The food was served twice on that day. When the ladies arrived around four o'clock, they would be served tea with petits fours from Groppi's, the famous Swiss pastry store in Cairo. Then they would sit around the four tables and begin to play. At each table was a member of the family. Grandmaman was always in a black lace blouse, and her pearls looked regal. She had told me the story of that pearl necklace: that my grandfather had given her a strand of pearls for each of their nine children. It went several times around her neck, and while waiting her turn she would often play with the pearls as if making a signal to her canasta partner. "The pearls will be yours, Colette," she always said, "when you grow up and act like a real lady." Like Grandmaman, the others at the card table would also be all dressed up. Tante Fortuné was the one I admired the most. While everyone else was in black, her dresses would be of red silk covered with large blue roses, or of green velvet edged in gold. My grandmother was horrified. For her and her friends, once you got married you wore subdued colors, and by the time you were forty you wore black or gray. But Tante Fortuné would laugh and employ an argument that Grandmaman could never object to, "My husband loves it!" Years later at my own wedding, Tante Fortuné arrived in a black dress with an enormous red bow tied to her hips. The younger generation loved it, and she was the toast of the party.

While the women were playing, Renée and I were often asked to pass around little tea sandwiches, while Abdullah, dressed in his best gallabiya, would glide through the tables and ask which the women preferred, tea or coffee. The silver coffee set would be brought in, and European coffee, which was then very fashionable, would be served.

STUFFED COURGETTES AND RED PEPPERS

HALVE ABOUT 450 G/1 LB small courgettes and scoop out the centers. Cut the tops off 4 red sweet peppers and remove all the seeds.

MIX 450 G/1 LB CHOPPED BEEF with 450 g/1 lb chopped veal; add 3 tablespoons pine nuts, salt and pepper to taste, 2 minced garlic cloves, and 2 tablespoons olive oil. Fill the courgettes and the peppers with the meat. Place side by side in a pan. Drizzle with 2 tablespoons olive oil and add 450 ml/¾ pint chicken stock to the pan. Bake in a preheated 190°C/375°F/ gas mark 5 oven for 45 minutes. Serve hot or cold with yogurt. This is enough for 4.

Within half an hour, though, we were forgotten. Renée would go back to her floor, and I would roam around the house, trying to find someone to talk to. Aishe was always too busy helping Ahmet; Ahmet would not allow me in the kitchen, and if I returned to the living room, my grandmother would signal me to get out and usually would say, "You are distracting the players!" I would end up in my room, sulking until dinner was announced.

Robert Solé

from *Birds of Passage*

A FEW MINUTES' WALK from Shepheard's, Georges Batrakani's office was situated on the third floor of a handsome building overlooking Opera Square. Two clerks in shiny over-sleeves were lethargically at work beneath an enormous ceiling fan. My grandfather occupied an adjoining room redolent of cigar smoke and eau de Cologne.

He burst out laughing when the Frenchman wondered why so many European women should be sitting, apparently at a loose end, on the terrace at Shepheard's.

"Ah no, my dear sir, it isn't what you might think. Those ladies are British officers' wives. They were authorized to come to Egypt to spend a few days with their spouses, but many of the latter are detained in the Suez Canal or out in the Western Desert. So the ladies are enjoying a solitary, enforced holiday—the hotels are crammed with them. The British authorities have been obliged to prohibit any further landings of women not resident in Egypt. I note that *you* were granted an entry visa, incidentally."

"Yes," Édouard said with a smile, "thanks to a little wire-pulling."

The Dhellemmes cotton mill at Lille had been in a state of suspended animation since the outbreak of war. Édouard, who had inherited some shares from his father, occupied a marginal position in the firm. Called up in 1915, admitted to hospital with a bad bout of pneumonia after only a few weeks, and finally demobilized, he had traveled to Cairo to explore the Egyptian market on the advice, and with the assistance, of a cousin in the diplomatic corps.

"If I were you," Georges Batrakani said slowly, puffing at his cigar, "I'd take an interest in the tarboosh."

Édouard looked mystified.

"That's right, the tarboosh—the fez, if you prefer. Until war broke out that sector was dominated by some fifteen Austrian firms with an annual turnover of more than thirty thousand pounds. Not bad, eh? Well, the Austrians aren't entitled to sell anything here, not now, and the representative of their consortium, Brüder Stross, has just been asked to sell up. That leaves a gap to be filled—even outside Egypt, perhaps, because Morocco, Tunisia, and Tripolitania also import Turkish headgear, albeit of a different shape."

Georges asked the Frenchman to excuse him for a moment. Going next door, he opened a cupboard and took out four capacious cardboard boxes. One of the clerks jumped up and helped him to carry them in.

Georges opened one of the boxes and removed a big, cup-shaped cap of red felt with a black tassel hanging down the back. "This is the *Watani*, the standard product." he explained. "It's worth the equivalent of two francs twenty-five. Then there's the *'Abbasi* at three francs fifty. Next we have—note the difference!—the *Excelsior*, priced at five francs. But the king of Austrian tarbooshes and the most elegant, beyond a doubt, is the *Eagle* here. Feel the material, feel how soft and silky it is. You see? The *Eagle* is well worth its thirteen francs!"

For the next few minutes, Édouard Dhellemmes felt like the target of an experienced huckster. A salesman to the marrow, the Levantine seemed capable of selling anything, even other people's wares. His velvety voice might almost have persuaded one to devour those silky tarbooshes like so many luscious fruit.

"You see, Monsieur Dhellemmes, prices have soared since imports ceased. Today, tarbooshes cost two or three times as much as I indicated just now. The result is that certain Jews and Syrians in Cairo have given up wearing them. They've adopted Western headgear, which is considerably less expensive."

"So the tarboosh is threatened with extinction."

"You must be joking! The present situation is clearly temporary. The Egyptians have worn the tarboosh for more than a hundred years. They'll never be able to dispense with it. This form of headgear has become a national attribute."

Georges Batrakani reverted to the Austrians, whose business methods he had observed closely and with undisguised admiration.

"Commercial travelers used to come from Vienna every year. They came to see their customers and note their special requirements. They not only studied changing fashions; sometimes they actually initiated them. There are fashions in tarbooshes, you see, and different ways of wearing them."

My grandfather proceeded to launch into a brilliant account of the evolution of the tarboosh in Egypt. Returning to his cupboard, he removed a number of engravings and spread them out on his desk side by side.

"Here's Muhammad Ali, the founder of the reigning dynasty. Look at his strange headgear; you could scarcely call it a tarboosh. Under 'Abbas and Said—there they are—the fez began to acquire shape and height, but it still had no lining. Now look at Sultan Hussein, the present sovereign; it was the British who introduced the tall, rigid tarboosh lined with straw, which has the merit of retaining its shape. No need to press it every day like the old-fashioned tarboosh: once a week is enough."

"So tarbooshes need pressing?"

"Of course. There are tarbouchiers all over town who will brush and press them for you."

More and more interested, Édouard Dhellemmes plied my grandfather with questions. "But you know the Egyptian market so well, Monsieur Batrakani." he said at length. "What's to prevent you from manufacturing tarbooshes yourself?"

Georges stared at him in amazement.

"Manufacture tarbooshes of this quality here? Out of the question! One needs excellent cloth, one needs machinery and qualified personnel. Above all, one needs method and organization. Where would you find all those things in Cairo? Ask anyone: Egypt has neither the resources nor the vocation to be an industrialized country. You manufacture the tarbooshes in France, and I'll sell them for you here."

After talking for another good hour, they arranged to meet a little while later at the entrance to the American Cosmograph, where Yolande and Maggi would join them.

Opera Square had been sluiced with bucketfuls of cooling water, and a gentle breeze was dispersing the last of the noontide heat. In a thoroughly exuberant mood, Édouard went off to buy some Turkish cigarettes on the other side of the square. He was feeling more and more at home in this charming, teeming city. At the risk of poisoning himself, he proffered a coin to an itinerant vendor who, with a big glass pitcher propped on his hip, sang the praises of his carob- and tamarind-flavored drinks while clicking some little copper cups between his fingers.

Having drained his cup at a gulp, Edouard made his way down a neighboring side street. The tarbouchier's establishment Georges had mentioned was a diminutive shop whose counter was arrayed with copper molds of various sizes. Customers entered, removed their tarbooshes, and handed them over without a word. The shopkeeper picked up one of the molds, sandwiched the headgear between the two halves, and turned a handle. A cloud of steam went up. A few minutes later the tarboosh was removed, stiff as a board and still steaming.

Delightedly, Édouard headed for the Ezbekiyah Gardens, of whose giant banana trees he had heard great things. A strange sight awaited him outside the entrance. The balconies of several nearby houses were occupied by half-naked women calling, singing and making obscene gestures manifestly designed to entice foreign soldiers.

Édoward walked on. For want of anything better, he would have preferred the forlorn Englishwomen on the terrace at Shepheard's. His spirits rose still higher at the thought of his imminent reunion with lovely Maggi of the slim brown hands.

Translated from the French by John Brownjohn

Alaa Al Aswany
from "Mme Zitta Mendès, A Last Image,"
in *Friendly Fire*

1961

On Sundays my father would take me with him to her house. The building, which was immensely tall, was situated halfway down Adly Street. The moment we went through the main door a waft of cool air would meet us. The lobby was of marble and spacious, the columns huge and round, and the giant Nubian doorkeeper would hurry ahead of us to call the elevator, retiring, after my father had pressed a banknote into his hand, with fervent thanks. From that point on, my father would wear a different face from the one I knew at home. At Tante Zitta's house, my father became gentle, courteous, playful, soft-spoken, tender, afire with emotion.

Written in French on the small brass plaque at the door of the apartment were the words "Mme Zitta Mendès," and she would open the door to us herself, looking radiant with her limpid, fresh, white face, her petite nose, her full lips made up with crimson lipstick, her blue, wide, and seemingly astonished eyes with their long, curling lashes, her smooth black hair that flowed over her shoulders, and the décolleté dress that revealed her ample chest and plump, creamy arms. Even her finger and toe nails were clean, elegant, carefully outlined, and painted in shiny red.

I shall long retain in my memory the image of Zitta as she opened the door—the image of the 'other woman' enhanced by the aroma of sin, the svelte mistress who draws you into her secret, velvety world tinged with pleasure and temptation. Tante Zitta would receive me with warm kisses and hugs, saying over and over again in French, "Welcome, young man!" while behind her would appear Antoine, her son, who was two years older than I—a slim, tall youth whose black hair covered the upper part of his brow and the freckles on whose face made him look like the boy in the French reading book we used at school.

Antoine rarely spoke or smiled. He would observe us— me and my father—with an anxious look and purse his lips, then make a sudden move, standing or going to his room. He always seemed to have something important on his mind that he was on the verge of declaring but which he'd shy away from at the last minute. Even when I was playing with him in his room, he would apply himself to the game in silence, as though performing a duty. (Just once, he stopped in the middle of the game and asked me all of a sudden, "What does your father do?" I said, "He's a lawyer" and he responded quickly, "My father's a big doctor in America and when I'm older I'm going to go there." When I asked him disbelievingly, "And leave your mom?" he gave me an odd look and said nothing.) Antoine's disconcerting, difficult nature made my father and me treat him with caution.

So there we would sit, all together in the parlor. My father and Tante Zitta would be trying to hold an intense conversation and Antoine would be his usual aloof self, but I'd be giving it all I had: I'd flirt with Tante Zitta and surrender to her kisses, her strong, titillating perfume, and the feel of her warm, smooth skin. I'd tell her about my school and make up fabulous heroic deeds that I'd performed with my fellow students and she'd pretend that she believed me and make a show of astonishment and fear that I might get hurt in the course of one of these amazing 'feats.'

I was very fond of Tante Zitta and colluded totally with my father when each time on the way back he'd impress on me that I shouldn't tell my mother. I'd nod my head like a real man who could be relied on and when my mother, with her apprehensive, reluctant, alarming eyes, would ask me, I'd say, "Father and I went to the cinema," lying without either fear or the slightest sense of guilt or betrayal.

Zitta's magic world captivated me. I keep it in my heart. Even her apartment I can summon up in detail now as a model of ancient European elegance—the large mirror in the entrance and the curly wooden stand on which we would hang our coats, the round polished brass pots decorated with a lion's head on either side for the plants, the heavy, drawn drapes through which the subdued daylight filtered, the light-colored patterned wallpaper and set of dark brown armchairs with olive-green slip covers, and, in the corner, the large black piano (Zitta worked as a dancer at a nightclub on Elfi Street, which is where, I suppose, my father must have met her.)

Tante Zitta would go into the kitchen to get the food ready and my father would draw Antoine and me close and put his hands on us and talk to us like an affectionate father chatting with his sons during a moment of rest. From time to time he would shout out in mock complaint about how long the food was taking and Zitta would answer laughingly from the kitchen. (I now take these touches of domesticity as evidence that my father was thinking of marrying her.)

The luncheon table was a work of art—the shining white table cloth, the napkins ironed and folded with offhand elegance, the polished white plates with the knives, forks, and spoons laid round them in the same order. There would be a vase of roses, a jug of water, sparking glasses, and a tall bottle lying on its side in a metal vessel filled with ice cubes. Tante Zitta's food was delicious and resembled that at the luxurious restaurants to which my father would occasionally take my mother and me. I would eat carefully and pretend to be full quickly, the way they'd taught me at home, so that no one might criticize me, but my father and Tante Zitta would be oblivious to everything, sitting next to one another, eating, drinking, whispering, and constantly laughing. Then my father would urge her to sing. At first she would refuse. Then she'd give in and sit down at the piano. Gradually the smile would disappear and her face would take on a serious expression as she ran her fingers over the keys and scattered, halting tunes rose from the keyboard. At a certain point, Zitta would bow her head and close her eyes as though trying to capture a particular idea. Then she would start to play. She would sing the songs of Edith Piaf—*Non, je ne regrette rien* and *La vie en rose*.

She had a melodious voice with a melancholy huskiness to it and when she got to the end she would remain for a few moments with her head bowed and her eyes closed, pressing on the keys with her fingers. I would clap enthusiastically and Antoine would remain silent, but my father's excitement would know no bounds. By this time he would have taken off his jacket and loosened his tie, and he would clap and shout, "Bravo!", hurrying to her side and planting a kiss on her forehead, or taking her hands in his and kissing them. Experience had taught us that this was a signal for me and Antoine to leave. Antoine would get up first, saying as he moved toward the door of the apartment, "Mama, we'll go outside and play." I can see now—with understanding and a smile—the face of my father, flushed with drink, alight with desire, as he searched impatiently through his pockets, then presented me and Antoine with two whole pounds, saying, as he waved us toward the door, "Tell you what. How about some ice-cream at New Kursaal after you've finished playing?"

1996
The foreigners' table at Groppi's. All of them are old—Armenians and Greeks who have spent their lives in Egypt and kept going until they are completely alone. Their weekly date is at seven on Sunday mornings, and when they cross empty Talaat Harb Street, walking with slow, feeble steps, either propping one another up or supporting themselves on their walking sticks, they look as though they had just arisen from the dead, brushed off the grave dust, and come.

In Groppi's they sit at one table, which never changes, next to the window. There they eat breakfast, converse, and read the French newspapers until the time comes for Sunday Mass, when they set off together for church.

That morning they were all in their best get-up. The old men had shaved carefully, polished their two-tone English shoes, and put on their three-piece suits and old ties, though the latter were crumpled and crooked. They were wrapped in ancient, heavy overcoats whose colors had faded and which they removed the moment they entered the restaurant, as convention required.

The old women, those once skittish charmers, were wearing clothes that had been in fashion thirty years ago and had powdered their wrinkled faces, but the old men without exception were careful to observe the rules of etiquette, standing back to allow them to go first, helping them to remove their coats and to fold them neatly and carefully, and pulling out chairs so that they could sit down, after which they would compete at telling them curious and amusing anecdotes. Nor had the women forgotten how to let out *oohs* and *aahs* of astonishment and gentle, delicate laughs.

For these old people, the Sunday table is a moment of happiness, after which they surrender once more to their total and terrifying solitude. All they have left is likely to be a large apartment in the middle of the city, coveted by the landlord and the neighbors. The rooms are spacious, the ceilings high and the furniture ancient and neglected, with worn upholstery; the paint on the walls is peeling and the bathroom, of old-fashioned design, is in need of renovations the budget for which remains forever out of reach; and memories—and only memories— inhabit every corner, in the form of beloved black and white photographs of children (Jack, Elena) laughing charmingly, children who are now old men and mature women who have immigrated to America, speak on the telephone at Christmas, and send tasteful colored postcards, as well as monthly money orders, which the old people spend a whole day standing in long, slow lines to collect, counting the banknotes twice just to be sure once they have finally cashed them, and folding them and shoving them well down into their inside pockets.

Despite their age, their minds retain an amazing capacity to recall the past with total clarity, while inside themselves they harbor the certainty of an impending end, always accompanied by the questions, When? and How? They hope that the journey will end calmly and respectably but terrifying apprehensions of being murdered during a robbery, of a long, painful illness, or of a sudden death on the street or in a café haunt them.

That particular morning, I noticed something familiar about the face of one of the old ladies. She was sitting among the old people, her face embellished with a heavy coating of powder and on her head was a green felt hat decorated with a rose made of red cloth. I went on watching her and when I heard her voice I was sure. It must have looked strange—a staid man in his forties, rushing forward and bending over her table. I addressed her impatiently, "Tante Zitta?"

Slowly she raised her head toward me. Her eyes were old now and clouded with cataracts and the cheap glasses she wore were slightly askew, giving the impression that she was looking at something behind me. I reminded her who I was, spoke to her warmly of the old days, and asked after Antoine. She listened to me in silence with a slight, neutral smile on her old face and for so long that I thought I might have made a mistake, or that she had completely lost her wits. A moment passed and then I found her pushing herself up with her hands on the table, rising slowly until she was upright, and stretching out her arms, from which the sleeves of her dress fell back to reveal their extreme emaciation. Then Tante Zitta drew my head toward her and reached up to plant on it a kiss.

Translated by Humphrey Davies

Samia Serageldin
from *The Cairo House*

"Gigi, I'm worried about Madame Hélène, It's been months since we've heard from her. Not since Papa's fortieth."

Ever since Gigi had left for England, Madame Hélène often went to stay in her apartment downtown, for weeks, even months, at a time. She didn't have a telephone in the apartment, so she couldn't be reached, but she would call from time to time. It was unusual for her not to get in touch for so long. Gigi realized that she had been so unsettled by turmoil in her own life that she had not kept track of the time that had elapsed since Madame Hélène last called.

"I sent Ibrahim the doorkeeper over this morning with a message," Mama continued. "Just to make sure that she wasn't ill or in need of something. He came back a while ago. He said he tried ringing the doorbell for a long time, but no one answered. What's really worrying me is that he said the apartment door was sealed with wax. He tried to get some information from the doorkeeper but it was a new man who didn't seem to know who she was. All he knew was that when he was hired the apartment was empty and had been sealed by the superintendent of the building."

"I don't understand it," Gigi shook her head, "She would never leave just like that without letting us know. And where would she go? She always used to say that if she were seriously ill or dying, she would go to the Italian Hospital in Abassia." Madame Hélène had often mentioned that they would take care of her there because her husband's family had been major benefactors of the hospital for generations. She had said to ask under her married name, Fernandini. "I'll go over there right now." Gigi picked up her car keys.

Guilt is a strange thing. All the while she was driving to the hospital Gigi kept remembering the exquisite lace collar Madame Hélène had made by hand for her thirteenth birthday, a lace collar the governess must have pored over for hours with her weak, boiled-egg eyes. It had been all she had to offer, a labor of love. She expected Gigi to wear the lace collar over a velvet dress, the way she had in years past. But Gigi was thirteen, and in the past year the last vestige of the little girl had given way to the self-conscious teenager. For her birthday she wanted to dress like other girls her age, in a bright sweater and matching, short skirt that had been Gina's present from a trip to Europe. Guilt is a subjective thing. For some of us it is not breaking great commandments but small acts of thoughtlessness that continue to haunt us.

For some reason an image came to her mind, an image of Madame Hélène watching a soccer match on television with Papa. Madame Hélène was nearsighted to the point of near-blindness and had not the first idea of how the game was played, but she had heard that the goalkeeper for the red-shirted Ahli team, Aldo, was Italian, like her dear departed husband. From that day forward she sat through every match in which Aldo played. Papa would be hunched forward in concentration, clutching his pipe till his knuckles turned white, and every time there was a burst of excitement from the commentator Madame Hélène would pester him with: "C'est Aldo, Monsieur Shamel?" He would answer patiently that it wasn't Aldo, Aldo was the goalie.

Gigi had only a vague idea where the Italian Hospital was, and got quite lost trying to find it. By the time she managed to get there it was past nine o'clock at night. The hospital was a large, turn-of-the-century building surrounded by a pleasant garden of overgrown magnolias. It took Gigi a while to rouse the night guardian, then to be taken to the head nurse.

"Was she a relative of yours?" The Italian nurse in her crisp white cap asked as she ran her finger down the list of names.

"No, my governess. But she raised me, she was family."

"Fernandini, Fernandini. No, There's no one here by that name."

"Please check under her maiden name then. Dumellier. Hélène Dumellier. Although I'm sure she would have used her married name."

"No Dumellier either."

"She has to be here. I mean, she has nowhere else to go."

"Wouldn't she have called you?"

"Of course. Unless she were too sick, or confused."

"We certainly have plenty of senile old women here. Some of them may not know their own names, but there's no one here who's not accounted for in the records."

"Are any of them French? I don't know how old she is exactly but she must be over eighty. She has bulging blue eyes and long silver hair that she wears in a bun rolled in the back. She has a bit of a humped back and she smoked quite a lot, so her teeth are very stained, but she still has most of them."

The nurse shrugged. "Old ladies all look alike."

"Can I look in the ward?"

"Our patients have gone to bed for the night."

"Please. We're very worried about her."

"Go ahead and look around then," the nurse conceded grudgingly. "The women's geriatric wing is through that archway to the left. There's a night light in every room, and most of the bedside lamps stay on all night, so you'll be able to see. Not that you'll find her."

Gigi walked along the corridors, peering into room after room after room. The smell of disinfectant and old age was inescapable. The two or three occupants in each room all looked alike, especially those who were asleep. At the door of each room Gigi called softly: "Madame Hélène? Madame Hélène? C'est moi." One or two answered in French, but that meant nothing, the Italian community in Egypt spoke French routinely.

In one of the last rooms on the corridor a sleeping woman in a pink, knitted bed jacket bore a resemblance to Madame Hélène. Gigi's heart skipped a beat. "Madame Hélène?" she called quite loudly, to wake her. "C'est moi."

The woman snorted in her sleep and raised her head. "Viens, ma petite," she beckoned.

Gigi hurried to the side of the bed and leaned over her.

"Viens, ma petite, que bellina," the woman mumbled, reaching out to pat Gigi's cheek. But even as she sat on the edge of the bed to let her face be stroked, Gigi knew it was not Madame Hélène. This woman had sweet brown eyes and no teeth. In a minute her hand dropped to her side and her head feel back on her pillow and she started snoring peacefully again. Gigi wondered who she had been dreaming of, a child or grandchild.

Gigi went back to the head nurse's office so drained that the woman took pity on her. "Look, you said she was very old. Have you considered that in all probability she's resting in peace?"

Gigi slumped down in the chair. "Yes. But she always said that if anything happened to her she would be brought here for the final rites, then taken to the Italian Cemetery to be buried."

"She was Catholic?"

"Of course."

"It would have been recently?"

"A month—two months at the most."

"I can check the records at the Italian Cemetery in the morning. Leave me a telephone number and I'll let you know if I find out anything."

"Would you? At least if I knew that she's buried properly—it sounds awful, but it's better than not knowing what happened to her, wondering if she's alone and suffering somewhere."

"Of course, I understand. I promise I'll let you know if I find any trace of her. Now you'd better go home, it's very late."

Over the next few months Gigi called the Italian Hospital several times. It was always very difficult to get through to the head nurse, and when she did she was always told that there was no news. When she did hear of Madame Hélène again it was in the last place, and from the last person, she would have expected.

Mohamed Berrada

from *Like a Summer Never to Be Repeated*

The Threshold of Bab al-Hadid Station

Hammad read what he had written on a white sheet of paper ten years earlier:

> Bab al-Hadid Square. August. The midday sun blazed as he stepped out of the train station in Cairo, his suitcase in one hand and a cardboard box containing a dark blue suit he bought the night he left Paris for Rome in the other. He wasn't yet seventeen. . . .

He paused for a moment and let his thoughts wander: Why begin with Bab al-Hadid Square? Wouldn't it have been better to begin with his family's farewell in Rabat or with boarding the boat in Casablanca on 13 July 1955 heading for Marseille, or at dawn in the train station in Paris on his way to Rome?

There were many possible beginnings. Hammad supposed that the clamoring image of Bab al-Hadid Square, swelling with activity, cars, the yellow tram, and people, had lodged itself in his mind, especially after he had arrived there several times and seen it in the film *Bab al-Hadid* depicted from a perspective that blended reality with the dreams and illusions of the sensual actress Hind Rostom, with her relaxed, light-footed gait. Besides, there was no absolute beginning, he said to himself. What he was going to write was clothed with imagination, interjected in time and space, and constructed from words. And it would soon be razed by other memories as they burst out suddenly from some corner of his unconscious. He thought a little and added: I'll write what I remember then edit it and embellish it creatively until I have an ample account, into which I'll have woven all that insists on inhabiting the page lest it fade in my memory.

Hammad was almost seventeen when he decided to travel to Cairo to finish school, as Arabic education in the private schools set up by the Nationalist Movement did not include the baccalaureate and tightened French authority meant it was limited.

If he chose Cairo rather than Damascus, as others had, it was because of the many scenes his memory had accumulated from films like *Long Live Love*, *Forbidden Love*, and *Love and Revenge* and songs by Abd al-Wahhab, Farid al-Atrash, Asmahan, and Umm Kulthum. The names of certain writers—Taha

Hussein, Tawfiq al-Hakim, al-Manfaluti, and Ahmad Lutfi al-Sayyid—had also snuck into his soul through the reading he undertook on his own in Bab Shala Library, close to Muhammad V School. Only now, as he walked out into Bab al-Hadid Square carrying his suitcase and suit in the scorching August sun and clamor of the street, the like of which he had never experienced in quiet Rabat, did he understand that he was entering an unknown world which bore no relation to the city he saw in those chic, romantic films. He looked right and left and turned around, following the brown figures in gallabiyas of all colors with cotton skullcaps on their heads despite the heat, the women, who were mostly wearing black milayas, and a few men in European-style suits and red tarbooshes. It was a very different mix to the one he had left behind in his own country. There was also the yellow tram that cut through the middle of the square, and the pushcarts and bicycles that never seemed to stop. He tried to ask for the address of the North African Lodge where a friend who had arrived a year earlier was staying. He used what classical Arabic he knew to ask a man in a striped gallabiya with a white turban on his head, "How do I get to the North African Lodge in Agouza, please?" He spoke quickly and falteringly and the man had to ask him to clarify what he was saying a number of times. The exchange failed so he tried again with other people. Passersby gathered round to get a good look at this guy who appeared to be an Arab but couldn't speak Arabic. When Hammad recalled that awful episode, he couldn't remember exactly how he finally got to the North African Lodge in Agouza or how he handled being lost before finding his friend Nabih, who embraced him warmly and cried, "Cairo celebrates. Welcome. Praise God you're well." The words coming out of Nabih's mouth had the same accent as the people Hammad had spoken to in Bab al-Hadid Square and heard in films. So his friend, who was laughing loudly and slapping his back exuberantly, had mastered the Egyptian dialect. Nabih laughed a lot as he listened to Hammad's account of Bab al-Hadid Square and his problems communicating. "Don't worry," he said, "We'll teach you Egyptian in a week. You'll be a nightingale. No offense but, as they say in Morocco, you're like an Arab in a strange land!" Some students began to emerge from their rooms to say hello and ask about affairs in Morocco and news of the struggle. One of them was Abd al-Qadir. He was tall, slim, and good-looking with smooth brown skin. Hammad quickly recognized him, for he had been the hero of a romance at the Muhammad V School before traveling to Egypt. He had acquired a reputation after writing a letter to a pupil he liked, which began, "Love dropped from the sky. You must acknowledge it." The pupils passed the letter around secretly and watched the two of them walking among the other girls and boys in the fifth form. There would be further romances for Abd al-Qadir in Cairo, for he seemed made to dress elegantly, flirt with girls, and stay up late as was the custom in Cairo.

When Hammad asked his friend Nabih about a student called Barhum, whether he had arrived yet from Morocco, Nabih said he had turned up a month ago with his friend Alaa. Their risky attempt to escape on foot to "North Morocco" had been a success. Hammad was delighted. He had made friends with Barhum through an exchange of letters after reading a prose poem of his in a Moroccan magazine and finding it echoed some of his personal feelings. They met up in Rabat and formed a strong friendship through mutual literary interests and the prospect of escaping to Egypt: Hammad via a trip to France organized by the Department for Youth and Sport, which was under French supervision, and his friend across the borders between the two Moroccos of the time: Spain and France.

In the evening, Barhum returned from the cinema to a surprise, and years full of talk and banter began. When he introduced him to his friend Alaa, the trio that would live and do everything together for the next five years—and survive beyond through friendship and shared memories—was complete.

Translated by Christina Phillips

Ghazi Abdel Rahman al-Qusaybi
from *The Apartment of Freedom*

THE QUESTIONS THAT WERE on his mind were never ending and without any answers that he knew of. Now the pilot occupied his thoughts with a new question. Perhaps this was the point of the contest: to try and brush away from the passengers' minds many other disconcerting issues so that they may concentrate on one single non-disturbing question, even if it seemed a bit strange, "How much fuel is this airplane carrying?" This was the question asked of the passengers. They were told that the passenger who got the right number or the closest to it would get a prize. The flight attendant went round distributing the questionnaires. Each passenger took one and became absorbed in thought.

Likewise, Fuad became absorbed in thought. How many gallons is this airplane carrying? A question he had never thought about before. Can one compare it with a car? He knew that a car could easily use up twenty gallons but the airplane was much, much bigger than a car. It carried more than one hundred passengers with heavy luggage just like his. He smiled broadly to himself as he thought about his luggage: four heavyweight suitcases besides his overstuffed carry-on. He remembered his brother Khalil's comment, "What is this? Is he going to the moon? Or the North Pole? Why all this luggage?"

But his mother had insisted that he take with him everything he might need in "strange lands." Among the needs were many strange items: bath towels, tea bags, scented soap bars, chocolate bars and cookies, a transistor radio. He smiled as he imagined all these things sitting in his suitcases. But the smile eventually disappeared when he imagined himself standing in front of the customs officer in Cairo Airport.

He had heard a lot about customs officers and how they searched bags and fiddled with everything and how they would only allow you to enter if you paid up. Paying up was a perplexing issue. His brother Nasser had said to him, laughing, "Just imagine: you are going to Cairo to study law and you will begin your life there with a bribe that the law punishes. Imagine yourself a prisoner at the police station. Do you know the sentence for bribery? At least a year! Ha, ha, ha."

Ha, ha, ha. This was not funny at all! It was a real problem. His experienced friends who had come through Cairo Airport had confirmed that one left only when one paid and paying meant bribery and bribery was a crime. True, he had never heard that someone had been arrested at Cairo Airport because of bribery, but who knows?

He remembered Nasser giggling, "I don't know how you will manage in Cairo when you can drown in a puddle! God help you! I wish I were there to watch: immigration, customs. You'll be in a real fix! Ha, ha, ha."

Ha, ha, ha. It all seemed like a joke to his two brothers but he couldn't see what was funny. He was still sixteen, twenty years younger than Nasser and ten years younger than Khalil. They were used to traveling. But for him, this was the first time on his own. On all previous trips there was always someone older to look after his travel arrangements, to deal with the endless complicated bureaucracy, and to arrange for everything until he departed from Bahrain Airport. Nasser had accompanied him to the airplane but now he was alone, with no one to look after him. He had to rely on himself. He had to remember that he was beginning a new stage in his life. He had become a man and he had to deal with the problems of displacement and estrangement like a man.

Displacement? Estrangement? But he didn't feel he was about to be estranged. He was going to Cairo. How can Cairo be displacement? Cairo was the capital of all Arabs, the center of Islam, God's jewel on earth, the "mother of the world" as Egyptians (who also called it Egypt!) referred to it; the Cairo of Gamal Abdel Nasser, and Voice of the Arabs, resistance against colonial powers; the Cairo of hope, the Cairo of the nationalization of the Suez Canal. With the thought of nationalization everything receded: questions disappeared, anxieties evaporated, and fears were overcome. The memory of the historic speech was still engraved in his soul. The strong, overpowering tone still rang in his ear, "A decree from the President of the Republic to nationalize the International Suez Canal Company and render it a national Egyptian company."

The Suez Canal? No, the canal of decolonization, the canal that brought forth a bright tomorrow which the Egyptian revolution was making for all Arabs.

He was now on his way to Cairo of the revolution, Cairo of Gamal Abdel Nasser. He was deeply moved as he imagined himself in the same city as Gamal Abdel Nasser. Who knows? Maybe one day they will be brought together on the same street. He may see him with his own eyes. He may shake his hand and talk to him. Why not? Did Gamal Abdel Nasser not reply to all the letters sent to him by the high school students in Bahrain? Had he not autographed his photos as they requested? True, the signature was just a stamp but it was Gamal Abdel Nasser's signature. He must have signed the original himself.

His smile broadened when he remembered Mr. Headley, the English language teacher. He got upset every time Gamal Abdel Nasser was mentioned. The students were keen on upsetting him by bringing Gamal Abdel Nasser into all discussions. Mr. Headley would come into class to find, written on the board in English, "Long Live Gamal Abdel Nasser." He would look at the board and then turn to the class.

"I know it is useless to ask who has done this. The handwriting is appalling and 'live' is not spelled like this, and 'Abdel Nasser' should be spelled differently."

He would sigh and wipe the board clean. On another day he would find Gamal Abdel Nasser's photo on the wall. With the well-known British reserve, he would stroll calmly and remove it from the wall and put it in front of him on the table.

"The owner of this thing may have it back after I leave."

At that very moment, one of the classmates would suddenly raise his hand.

"Mr. Headley, did you listen to Gamal Abdel Nasser last night? He spoke for more than three hours."

"Poor listeners!"

Another classmate would say, "Look, Mr. Headley, a signed photograph of Gamal Abdel Nasser that I just received today. Would you like to see it?"

"No, no! I know what he looks like. I thought that only movie stars sent autographed photographs of themselves."

The class hour would pass in arguments about Gamal Abdel Nasser. The students would score three points at the same time: they would defend Arab nationalism, they would upset the colonial teacher, and the hour would pass with no work done.

But these amusing memories could not make him forget practical matters: will someone meet him at the airport? Where will he live? And how will he meet up with his friends who had arrived in Cairo before him when he didn't know their address? He tried to answer these questions calmly, one after the other. His father had sent a telegram to Ustadh Sherif who was supposed to look after him in Cairo and he will certainly send someone to the airport if he did not come himself. In the worst case scenario, he did have Ustadh Sherif's address in Dokki and he could always go directly to him. As for his accommodation, certainly Ustadh Sherif will have arranged for that before his arrival. As for his friends, they will be staying in the Islamic Conference Residence and there was no doubt that he could get the exact address from Ustadh Sherif or from the residence itself. It was quite simple.

But deep inside him, he knew that it was not simple. He imagined himself alone in Cairo with its three million inhabitants. How many people did he know there? Ten, at the most; a drop in the ocean. He imagined himself lost in the midst of the crowds, lost in neighborhoods with strange names: Agouza. What a funny name. Where did it come from? Had an old woman ('agouza') lived there? Is it the oldest neighborhood in Cairo? And what was the story behind Nawal Street where Ustadh Sherif lived? Was there a woman whose name was Nawal who still lived on that street? And what about Garden City? How could Gamal Abdel Nasser overlook this British name after the end of the colonial period?

He knew so much about Cairo before even seeing it. He saw it in the movies and in the newspapers and other visitors had talked to him about it. His Egyptian elementary and high school teachers never wearied of talking about Cairo. The information kept accumulating: the Andalus Garden was the most beautiful in the Middle East, the zoo was the second best worldwide after the London Zoo, there was a huge flower clock in Cairo, a talking clock, and in Helwan there was the Japanese Garden, the likes of which didn't exist in Japan itself. Manama? You can put it all on one street in Sayyida Zeinab. Bahrain? You could hide it all in Shubra and never find it again.

And the girls! The girls! Beautiful like movie stars; like Iman, his favorite actress; liberated like the girls in the films and Ihsan Abdel Quddus's novels. A few years ago, a girl from a well-known family in Bahrain had refused to wear the face veil and caused a huge uproar. How many unveiled women were there in Bahrain? Not more than twenty. Most of them were Christian and Jewish Iraqis. But in Cairo, all the girls were not veiled except for the peasant women and the elderly. And who would be interested in them anyway. Girls! He let his imagination run wild. Will he have a girlfriend? Will they go to Cinema Metro (the best movie theater in the world)? To Andalus Garden? To the zoo? How will he meet his girlfriend? At the university there was a lot of mixing so, as they told him, it should be simple. But he still had a whole year in high school, a year with no mingling. But there was no reason to give up hope. He might get to know a girl in the building where he will live or in the one across the street. He heard from his colleagues that friendships often began with a fleeting smile that, like a butterfly, fluttered across the street from one balcony to the other.

But there was one thing he knew he would never do and that was deal-ing with professionals, despite the appetizing descriptions, despite the many accounts that he had heard. Some were young, and so kind and well-behaved that you couldn't tell them apart from regular girls. But he knew that he couldn't fall in love with a body that was sold for money. With a handful of dirhams both the buyer and the seller can be dishonored. He remembered Jarandul, the night district in Bahrain, a hateful gift from the colonizers. He remembered the fright that came over him when one of his friends had suggested that they visit one of the brothels in that district. He will have a girlfriend in Cairo. He will never, never, never have a relationship with a professional.

Once again he came back to reality. The problem of the visa took over his thoughts. He didn't have a visa in his passport but he will be given a tempo-rary visa at the airport after which he will get residence as the experts had told them. Why worry? Ustadh Sherif will arrange for everything, as he had assured his father more than once. He had come to know Ustadh Sherif three years ago when he was the high school principal (and the president of the edu-cational delegation in Bahrain). There was general consensus that he was the most active school principal the institution had known in its entire history. During his stay in Bahrain, he was able to consolidate relationships with many people even though he was only there for two years. He got to know his father and they became friends. He convinced his father to send him to Cairo to study. Ustadh Sherif's problem was that he was very strict. Will he enjoy his stay in Cairo when he had such a guardian?

The flight attendant interrupted his thoughts when he asked him if he had filled out the questionnaire. He answered in the affirmative as he quickly jotted down: ten thousand gallons. Will he win? And what might the prize be? He decided he would make of this competition the omen for the trip: if he won, or scored close to the winner, it would be a good omen. But if he did not win, then lo for the visa problems, the customs, and the accommodation!

Translated by Samia Mehrez

Mahmoud Al-Wardani
from *Heads Ripe for Plucking*

Roxanne

She had no option but to leave her daughter Hanan with her mother in Alexandria and follow from a distance in the trail of the fourth and last van after the convoy had set out shortly before dawn. Fatigue and driving at night had rattled her body, which felt as if it was coming apart. She would have dozed off had it not been for the striking desolation of the desert in the early morning hours at the beginning of the road to Abu Zaabal Prison with which she was familiar from Shuhdi's successive imprisonments. She felt like lighting a cigarette but resisted the temptation as one of the soldiers might catch sight of her and harass her.

Ever since Shuhdi was arrested and transferred to Hadara Prison she had moved from Cairo to Alexandria where she was staying with her father and mother. She devoted all her time to him, following up with the lawyers and braving no end of trouble going back and forth between the prosecutor and State Security to get a permit to visit him, each foisting the responsibility for issuing the permit on the other. She did not see Shuhdi all through the trial except once in the courtroom as he was standing among his companions in the dock. His eyes were shining, she thought, as he sent her kisses in the air. They managed, though, to steal a few minutes in which their hands touched across the iron dock like two teenagers.

Roxanne, a Greek born in Egypt, went against the grain of the upbringing her parents were keen to give her among her peers in the Greek community when she fell in love with the senior inspector of English language in secondary schools who was constantly in and out of prison. From the minute she met him at one of the seminars at the House of Scientific Research, something about his broad shoulders and towering height made her fall head over heels for him. Shuhdi overwhelmed her with his tenderness, enveloping her completely. The daughter they had after two years of marriage was the spitting image of her father, so much so that all Roxanne needed to do to have dreams of Shuhdi was to look at her face before going to bed.

The five years she had so far spent with him were fraught, but he always made it up to her during the spells when he was out of prison. He would make sure they often dined out alone together which, as he knew, made her very happy. His rare gentleness so bound her to him that she craved his approval. It was he who chose to name their daughter Hanan, meaning tenderness. Roxanne and Hanan: he drew them closer into his captivity, folding them both under his wings.

She became adept at organizing protest campaigns and contacting lawyers and the press, her English and French, as well as her Greek of course, being an asset in this respect. But Shuhdi's imprisonment this time was different from any other before. She had taken on the task of going every week to report on the latest to the families, lawyers, and those of his comrades in the movement who were still free, and staying in contact. But this transfer was much more worrying: the circumstances made her expect treachery. Setting out before dawn, she drove after them, keeping at a reasonable distance so as not to lose sight of the last van. She could not bring herself not to go: I'll just find out which prison they're taking him to, and there's no difference really between Abu Zaabal Prison and any other jail, she reasoned.

The sun had now risen and, feeling the sting of thirst, Roxanne stretched. It was another hot day and the humidity made it all the more sweaty and tedious. She felt sticky and wished she could have a warm bath and go to bed after making sure her husband was safe. She stretched again and lowered the window on her side.

The silence of the soldiers guarding the entrance to Abu Zaabal zone, the point beyond which she could not go further, caught her attention. Shortly afterward a motorcade of jeeps overtook her. Then the sound of the bugle echoed from afar and her heart sank at the surprise. Something must be up this sticky, damp morning. She lowered the car window on her side halfway and looked right and left.

The sun was everywhere and the daily noise of cars had started. Seeing that the whole world was up and about gave her courage to light a cigarette.

She sat smoking furtively and felt the heavy numbness of the first cigarette. She said to herself she wouldn't leave before finding out what was behind the motorcade of jeeps that had driven past a little while ago. It might be a routine inspection by the Prison Authority; then again it might have been deemed necessary that its officials should be there to deliver this particular group of prisoners. Time went by sluggishly, and feeling weary, she lowered the window halfway again. As long as Hanan was with her grandmother, she had nothing to worry about. The important thing now was to set her mind at ease about Shuhdi then she would go to the lawyers so that everyone would know that the whole case had now been transferred to Abu Zaabal.

It seemed to her she had dozed off for a few minutes. She saw him— Shuhdi. He had misplaced his eyeglasses and stood blinking with his hands outstretched. Still he was laughing as he said,

"Hand me my glasses."

This was his habit whenever he woke up. The eyeglasses were right in front of him on the dining room table. She kept trying to raise her voice to caution him that he was about to bump into the table. Someone was shackling her and pressing down on her mouth. She suppressed her gasp when he actually bumped into the table and started to fall slowly to the floor. She finally summoned the strength to get rid of whoever was shackling her and took Shuhdi's head in her arms. Shuhdi was silent but she felt his warm, sticky blood.

She opened her eyes. The hand with which she had held his head to her was still warm; she raised it and gazed at it. Her palm was white and her fingers were slender as always, yet she still felt the stickiness of warm, wet blood almost preventing her from moving her fingers freely. She lit another cigarette with the same furtiveness, then had to move it to the other hand which had not touched Shuhdi's head in her fleeting dream and was less sticky.

She saw them in the distance coming out of the prison gate. They were a number of guards on their way home, it seemed, after their shift was over. She stubbed out the cigarette and hurried out of the car. She was not sure how to act as she went toward them. But then she caught sight of one of them, who seemed so young he looked like a boy. She went up to him, driven by an irresistible force, until she had almost bumped into him. She tried to raise her voice, "What happened? Tell me what happened."

She couldn't tell whether the sight of her scared the boy or whether he was so startled to see her in front of him that he couldn't help blurting out what had terrified him only a moment ago. His shift had ended midday, and he was standing above the quarry with his machine gun pointed at the prisoners ever since they went down. He saw the high officials and the very tall man they'd taken aside and beaten violently until he'd fallen to the ground then was dragged around. Next he saw them hurrying to leave the place in their cars without the bugle marking their departure. He found out later that one of the prisoners called Shuhdi had been beaten to death. To Roxanne, who had picked him out of all the soldiers and jailers, he answered, "Seems a guy called Shuhdi died. Heard them say one of the prisoners called Shuhdi died."

Fortunately for her, the car was nearby. She headed for it before she could drop to the ground. She held up until they had left. Then she burst into a long fit of weeping without the slightest sound escaping her. "I knew it in my heart," she mumbled as her tears fell profusely. She felt her heart shudder as though it was as heavy as a stone. "How could you have allowed them to kill you, Shuhdi? Why did you let them kill you, love? My God! They're a pack of dogs. Murderers, yes, murderers."

Translated by Hala Halim

Bahaa Abdelmegid

from *Saint Theresa*

THE KHAWAGA LUKA, the owner of the tailor shop, was of Jewish origin. He had come to Cairo from Greece a long time ago but didn't emigrate with those who went to Israel after the founding of that nation. He did not have an advanced education, but he spoke Arabic and English fluently. He wasn't an ordinary-looking man: he was handsome and the sun gave him a beautiful bronze color. He smiled a lot, and his fine black hair fell in long locks over his forehead. He was on the tall side, and had a physique that suggested regular exercise. He wasn't married and he was scrupulous about praying at the synagogue on Adli Street. Saturday was his private day when he retreated from daily life for the Sabbath and Girgis would come to him to prepare his food and then leave.

He was twelve when he arrived in Alexandria with his mother Sasha, after his father, who had been living there on his own, died. His mother had come to claim what remained of his father's business, but she only found debts. She traveled to Cairo and tried her luck at dancing and acting, but never fulfilled her dream of success, having instead fallen in love with a failed director. She soon realized that he wanted her for his own gratification—and for that of others. She was an alcoholic and suffered for years before regaining her self-confidence. She had brief flings with men who passed through her life, until she finally settled down with a taxi driver who loved her very much. He insisted that she leave the burlesque houses behind, and he supported her and her son. She hated for Luka to see her with a man other than his father, although the child had accepted the new situation without raising a fuss. But when he realized that the driver wanted to marry his mother, he heatedly objected and left the house. She ended the relationship in disgrace after the driver's wife came and accused her of being a home wrecker, declaring that Western women cause nothing but trouble and their bodies are like public property. Some of Luka's mother's friends offered to loan her some money, so she rented a studio to cut clothes, which she had some experience in. With time she mastered the trade of tailoring and became well known in upper-class Egyptian circles. Her son was able to retain the shop's good reputation after his mother's death.

Luka usually went to Alexandria every Sunday morning and came back on the last train. At one of the birthday parties he was invited to there, he met an Italian woman named Sabina. They danced all night and he told her about his longing for a kindred soul who would understand him and could share his life in Cairo. They parted and agreed to meet again.

The relationship between them grew stronger. Each took an interest in the other's life. They would go to the beach, where she surrendered to his flirtations and kisses. He told her, "You have become an important part of my life," and asked her to marry him. Sabina was delighted by his embrace of her at that moment but she was caught off guard since she did not want to get married now and wasn't certain about her feelings toward him. Marriage was an eternal bond that only God could break. So she put off giving him an answer, thanks to the fact that the decision wasn't hers alone to make: there was her father whom she had to consult. "I'd like to get out of the water," she said. "I want to go; I've stayed too long."

"But you didn't tell me what you think! I want to hear your answer now."

"Not now. Let's not talk about it. I don't have an answer ready. I'll give you one soon."

Sabina's father gave his daughter the freedom to act as she wished in the affairs of her life. At first he did not forbid her from becoming friends with Luka, but because he was a devout Catholic, he felt that a Christian woman marrying a Jew was an impossibility. One Sunday evening while they were listening to the radio and sipping tea she asked him, "Do you want some dessert?"

"Thank you, no dessert. I'm trying to cut back on sugar, as you know."

"I know, I was just testing your willpower."

"You know well the extent of my willpower."

"And are you aiming that willpower of yours in my direction?"

"Not exactly, but I do want to see an end to that relationship."

"The end, as Luka proposed, is marriage."

"And what do you think about it?"

"Would that change your position?"

"Well, you know I am opposed to it."

"That's what I always expected."

"Have you been straightforward with him about it?"

"I didn't have a chance to explain: he was happy and optimistic. I didn't want to hurt his pride at the same moment he was asking me to share my life with him. I couldn't do something that I wouldn't want done to me."

Sabina's father was ready with his response, which he made as if he were making an important statement: "The Jews have no future! Their lives are constantly threatened, ever since Hitler declared war on them, when they were like mice hiding in ditches and underground. Of course Luka is a fine young man, but I don't want you and your children to end up in the gas chambers!"

"You are talking about a history that ended fifteen years ago; this is 1958! Luka doesn't want to go to Israel or anywhere else. He's become an Egyptian. Regardless of what you believe about his religion, I will try—maybe I'll even succeed—in making him Catholic."

"Sabina! My final word is that I do not consent! Luka is threatened by death at any time. Abd al-Nasser won't leave any Jew in Egypt, since he's at war now with the great powers. Didn't England steal the Palestinians' land and give it to the Jews? Didn't Israel preside over attacks on Egypt in the War of '56? Didn't—"

"Father, can we drop the subject?" responded Sabina in agitation.

Each one looked at the other. Then a deadly silence came between them.

. . .

Luka's circumstances changed after the October War. He hadn't sided with Israel against Egypt, but he felt something break apart inside him, and he couldn't understand what it meant. The days of the 1967 War hadn't gone too badly for him, in spite of his feelings of loneliness and fear. One night, as he was returning from work, he imagined that someone was following him. The air was cold and most of the shops had closed up early. He quickened his pace, looking for a way to escape. He entered the Estoril restaurant and left by the back door that opened onto the Qasr al-Nil passageway. He found himself on Talaat Harb Street, and continued in the direction of Talaat Harb Square.

Now he was certain he wasn't imagining it, and that the man was trailing him like his shadow. He lit a cigarette; the smoke trailed upward and hung motionless in space. He felt his heart pounding faster. He wanted to disappear from sight, to hide somewhere—even in a garbage bin—but failed to find a place. Then suddenly he remembered Emmanuelle, a Greek friend of his mother who lived on Talaat Harb Square in the Groppi Building. He headed in that direction and finally reached the building; he climbed the stairs without looking behind him and knocked on the door. After a few moments that felt like an eternity, a gray-haired old woman opened the door. Traces of past beauty remained on her face, despite her filled-out features. Without hesitation, he slipped through the crack in the door, sweat pouring off him and fear coursing through his limbs.

"Luka, how nice to see you . . . . What's wrong? Is someone after you? What's happened?"

"No—nothing."

"Relax, I'll get you a glass of water."

"No, no, I don't want any water. Just look out the window for me, but don't let anyone see you. Take a look: is there a tall man wearing a black jacket standing in the square or on the street below?"

With slow, heavy steps, she walked to the window and cautiously pulled back the edge of the curtain; then she came back, wearing the same worried expression. Although she had seen someone standing in the square, she pretended she hadn't, so as not to tax Luka's nerves any more than they already were.

"There's no one there," she said calmly. "Don't worry about it: maybe it was a pickpocket, or an admirer following you."

"No, it's not a pickpocket. I know I'm being watched—but *you* know I have no contact with Israel nowadays. They tried to recruit me, but I refused. Maybe at first I felt some sympathy for Israel, and I had some delusions about the idea of establishing a state for Jews, but now I mind my own business. I have nothing to do with anything. I want to stay in Egypt, I don't want to travel to Israel, and I don't want to be a spy."

"The Egyptian secret police aren't stupid, Luka, so be careful."

Emmanuelle was also Jewish, and while she was still alive, his mother had frequently asked her to take care of him. She would ask about him and knew all about what he was doing, but as she grew on in years and Luka's visits to her became less frequent, she began to forget about him. Although her sons had immigrated to Israel, she preferred to remain in Egypt; she knew the country well, and had spent the most beautiful years of her life there. Now she lived a quiet life in downtown Cairo. What would she find in Israel? The life she had left in her wouldn't allow her to start over again. She led a settled life in Egypt: she woke up in the morning, went out to the street, bought the papers and some magazines, drank her morning coffee at Groppi's or at the Continental in Opera Square; she met some of her friends, and then went back home at lunchtime. Before the 1967 War, when the Mossad had tried to recruit Luka, he went to her, trembling in fear, to ask her for advice. They spoke a lot about the nation, about Egypt, Greece, and Israel, about their shared sorrows and divided sympathies. About how they had suffered because the government was afraid of them, and because it treated them as a source of anxiety, even though their nationalist sympathies had been shaken in the face of the dream of Greater Zionism. They came to the conclusion that night that they had no nation other than Egypt: they loved its Nile, they felt affection for its people, and they spoke its language. As for Israel, let it be what it is. Emmanuelle had saved him that night, and on other nights when panic seized him. With him, she lived through his aborted love story, and her being there was one reason why he didn't go to pieces after Sabina's escape to Italy.

After he had calmed down a little, he asked her, "Do you think the Egyptian secret police know about the Mossad's attempt to recruit me?"

"I don't think so; the government's been preoccupied with the corruption that led to the defeat. Forget the whole thing for now. I'll make some dinner for you and then you can go to sleep. You shouldn't go back out on the street at such a late hour." Then she gave him a small prayerbook with pages from the Old Testament and told him, "Read these words before you sleep, and you'll fall asleep restfully and quietly. It will put your fears to rest."

Luka lay down and read, "The Lord is my rock, my fortress, and my salvation. . . . In Him I find my refuge, my rescue, and my deliverance from evil. . . . For waves of death have surrounded me . . . floods of perdition have frightened me, the heights of the chasm encompassed me. . . . In my anguish I have called out to the Lord, and cried out to my God, and from His temple, he has heard my voice. . . . The earth trembled and shook because of his wrath."

Luka didn't sleep that night, and the jinn danced on the edge of the blanket while in his head he imagined them hanging from the window curtains. Memories leaped into his imagination like a movie reel projected onto the ceiling of the white room: Sabina, who had left forever, without giving him the opportunity even to say goodbye. He had only seen her from afar walking up the ship's gangplank: she was wearing a diaphanous blue dress with a white hat. Sabina seemed fragile and defeated. Despite the harbor crowds, he was able to get close to the ship just at the moment it pulled away from Alexandria, the moment the past separated from the present, the moment history ended.

Alexandria, which she was passionate about, and which she loved to draw in her nature sketches. He remembered how she used to take him with her on trips to the ruins on the city's outskirts, how she used to dream of rebuilding the Library of Alexandria and its lighthouse. She would laugh, saying, "I want to immortalize Alexandria in my paintings—and you can immortalize me with your love." Oh, Sabina! Why did you leave?

Her father had told him, "If you marry her, you will marry her as a Christian; I don't want to marry off my daughter to a Christ-killer." "But I didn't kill Christ—I never laid eyes on him," Luka thought. "I'm not the traitor Judas. Why am I burdened with the guilt of my ancestors? I wasn't there when they condemned Christ. I didn't see them when they raised him on the cross, leaving him to hang there between heaven and earth."

Luka put his face between his hands, then floated in the extreme darkness as he imagined that the words of Sabina's father were true, and that they were dragging him to the gas chamber, and that he was choking to death. Then, as they burned Sabina and her children before his eyes, the stench of burnt flesh filled his nostrils, and terrible visions followed one after another until he fell asleep.

Translated by Chip Rossetti

Yasser Abdel Latif
from *The Law of Inheritance*

SHAKER WAS A FOURTH or fifth degree relative to my grandfather, but, in the remote villages of the south, such a distance in the degree of family relations is eradicated through the more important tribal kinship and blood ties.

He had a pitch-black complexion, unlike the people of Nubia whose skin color was lighter. In the 1930s, after forced migration and the displacement of the people of Nubia, he could not find a place for himself. So he came to Cairo, where my grandfather and his nephew Fathi had settled for about twenty years and where they now had homes and jobs.

Shaker had not had any education except in the Qura'nic school of the kuttab that was called khalawat in Nubia. The sheikhs, like their students, had a Nubian accent when they spoke Arabic, whereby the guttural letter 'ha' was pronounced as a regular 'h' and the 'ayn' was transformed into a 'hamza,' while the masculine gender became feminine and vice versa. Despite this, Shaker spoke proper Arabic and he quickly mastered the Cairene dialect, where my grandfather, with the help of some acquaintances, found him a modest job as a custodian in a small bank that was owned by local foreigners.

Shaker rented a small room in Bulaq Abul 'Ila and brought his wife Sultana from the village to share his life and the little he had. It was a quiet life. Seven years later, during which Shaker had grown old and thin while Sultana remained fresh and young, they had their only son, Ahmad. Under her thin, dry skin Sultana hid a strong and sturdy body that could withstand time, which led her Cairene neighbors to describe her as the eater of her husband's meals.

Shaker would often meet up with my grandfather. They would sit on the pavement of Wadi al-Mulk coffee shop on Abdin Square. My grandfather would be in his stylish gray suit and Shaker in his simple gallabiya, which exposed his thin, bony body. They would sit from mid-afternoon till the calm of the night in that quiet spot in Cairo during the thirties. They would chat for hours, moving between Arabic and Nubian with great ease and depending on the level of secrecy dictated by the subject of conversation or the level of abstraction. Given their intimate relationship with the language, Nubian was for everyday matters and family affairs, which allowed for secrecy among strangers, while Arabic was for more public matters of an abstract nature since Nubian, in its simplicity, hardly possessed an abstract lexicon. Most of the conversation would be about religion, in which they were both very interested, each in his own way. Even though he was a practicing Muslim, Shaker never set foot in a mosque and never performed group prayer—believing that, at the end, we will be resurrected as individuals.

When our female relatives, who had moved to Cairo, visited my grandmother they would criticize my grandfather, the educated Effendi and civil servant, for his relationship with that vagabond Shaker who was known for his eccentricities since the days of the old country (that's what it came to be called). The difference between the two men had become clear and disquieting, even for the culture of the Nubian ghetto that was normally tolerant of passing friendships across class and levels of education for the sake of race and tribalism. My grandmother used to mumble in Nubian in defense of her husband, basically arguing that blood could not turn into water, recalling the prophet's teachings about blood relatives. The older and wiser women told the story of an accident that took place in the old days when the men raced each other across the Nile waters in the old country. My grandfather was going to drown and die and it was Shaker who had saved him from certain death. My grandfather defended his friendship with Shaker by saying that he was a man of culture, that he read and owned books despite his poverty and limited education. He also stressed Shaker's knowledge of their tribe's genealogy with its births and deaths which encompassed every individual in the family tree, those who remained in the old country and those who migrated south to the Sudan or north to Cairo and Alexandria after the Aswan barrage had been made higher.

But with time, my grandfather became quickly disappointed in his friend: Shaker's general condition deteriorated in a way that confirmed people's suspicions. Shaker had joined a Sufi order that he claimed fought against black magic. It was most probably an underground group like many others that operated in various pockets in Cairo during the interwar period and conducted its activities under the guise of a Sufi order. Out of curiosity, Fathi, my grandfather's nephew once went with Shaker to a hadra, one of their religious festivities. When he returned, he said that the hadra was not like any other he had known in the south or in the north for those attending were not seated on the ground like brothers of an order but were respectable gentlemen seated at a round table with someone as modest as Shaker, and led by an awe-inspiring sheikh. As soon as he saw Fathi he ordered him to leave the hadra for they did not allow consumers of alcohol in their midst. Fathi swore that he had not touched any alcohol—by pure coincidence—for three nights. He could not understand what drove the angry sheikh to expose such a personal secret. Beyond Fathi's brief encounter with Shaker's relationship to this Sufi order, the latter's world remained closed with its secrets to the closest of people to him, including my grandfather who frequently tried to find out what exactly he was doing. Shaker's repeated answer was that he, in particular, should stay away from this world.

Shaker dedicated his entire being to the activities of this group. He gradually began to neglect his family duties and was frequently absent from work. He grew thinner and his complexion grew darker. He would wander about the street like a fleeting ghost among the imposing downtown buildings or in the darkness of the alleyways in humid Bulaq. He was fired from his job because of his continued absence so the crisis spilled over to his basic household needs. It became clear that Shaker was no longer fit for a regular job, for his spiritual obligations took over his entire being and left him completely estranged from earthly matters. Sultana sought the help and support of relatives. Here, my grandfather intervened for the last time in Shaker's life: he forced him to leave Cairo and to return to the south, having bundled up his tatters along with Sultana and little Ahmad and a small metal trunk full of old books.

Translated by Samia Mehrez

Alaa Al Aswany
from *The Yacoubian Building*

LIKE A VICTORIOUS WARTIME general who enters in triumph a city he has conquered after bitter fighting, Malak Khilla appeared on the roof of the building to take possession of his new room in a happy and vain-glorious mood. He was wearing his blue people's suit that he kept for special occasions and had hung around his neck a long tape measure that was for him—like an officer's pips or a doctor's stethoscope— the distinguishing mark of his professional status as a master shirt-maker. That morning he brought with him a number of workmen to get the room ready—a smith, an electrician, a plumber, and some young male assistants to help them.

Master craftsman Malak muttered a prayer of thanks to the Virgin and Christ the Savior, then stretched out his hand to open the door to the room for the first time. The air inside was musty because it had been closed for a whole year following the death of Atiya the newspaper seller (some of whose effects Malak found and had one of the boys collect in a large cardboard box).

Now Malak stands in the middle of the room after opening the window and letting sunlight flood the place and issues detailed instructions to the workmen as to what they have to do. From time to time, one of the residents of the roof stops and watches what's going on out of curiosity. Some watch for a short while, then move on. Others offer Malak their congratulations on taking possession of the new room and shake his hand, wishing him well in his enterprise.

Not all the residents of the roof, however, are so well mannered. After less than half an hour, word has spread on the roof and soon two individuals appear who do not seem to be the least bit eager to welcome the new arrival—Mr. Hamid Hawwas and Ali the Driver.

The first is a civil servant in the National Sanitation Authority whose boss got angry with him and transferred him from his home town of El Mansoura to Cairo, so he rented a room on the roof where he lives alone, expending all his energy for more than a year now to get his arbitrary transfer cancelled and return home. Mr. Hamid Hawwas is a major writer of official complaints, and finds a genuine and all-encompassing pleasure in selecting the subject of the complaint and formulating it eloquently, then writing it out in a neat, easy-to-read hand and subsequently following it through to the end at whatever cost this may impose upon him, for he considers himself to be responsible to some degree for the proper performance of all public utilities in any area in which he may be residing, or even passing through. He always finds the time to make a daily round of the District Administration, the Governorate, and the Utilities Police, during which he pertinaciously and single-mindedly follows up on the complaints he has made against street vendors who may stand in locations far distant from his place of residence but whom, as violators of the law, he nevertheless believes it to be his duty to pursue with one complaint after another, never tiring and never despairing, until the Utilities Police finally move and arrest them and confiscate their goods—at which point Mr. Hamid watches from a distance, feeling the ease of conscience of one who has gone that extra mile to do his duty in full.

As for Ali the Driver, he's an alcoholic, over fifty, never married, who works as a driver at the Holding Company for Pharmaceuticals, going straight from work every day to the Orabi Bar in El Tawfikiya, where he eats and sits sipping a drink until midnight. Loneliness and the cheap alcohol to which he is addicted have had their effect on him, making him gross, violent, and ever in search of a quarrel on which to expend his aggression.

Mr. Hamid Hawwas approached Malak and greeted him, then opened the conversation in an extremely refined way by saying, "About this room, my friend. Do you have a contract from the owner of the building giving you the right to use it as a commercial establishment?"

"Of course I have a contract," answered Malak excitedly, and he pulled out of his small leather purse a copy of the contract that he had signed with Fikri Abd el Shaheed. Hamid took the piece of paper, put on his glasses, and examined it carefully. Then he handed it back to Malak, saying quietly, "The contract is invalid in this form."

"Invalid?" repeated Malak, apprehensively.

"Of course invalid. According to the law the roof is a common resource for the residents and a common resource may not be rented out for commercial purposes."

Malak didn't understand and stared angrily at Mr. Hamid, who went on to say, "The Court of Cassation has issued more than one ruling on the issue and the matter is closed. The contract is invalid and you have no right to the use of the room."

"Yes, but all of you are living on the roof, so why not me?"

"We are employing our rooms for residential purposes, and that is legal. You, however, are exploiting your room for commercial ends, and that is illegal and we cannot allow it."

"Okay. Go complain to the owner of the place since he's the one who gave me the contract."

"Certainly not. The law itself forbids you to make use of the room, and we, as injured residents, are obliged to prevent you."

"What does that mean?"

"*It means you'd better get a move on and scram or else!*"

These last words were spoken by Ali the Driver in his husky voice as he looked challengingly at Malak. Laying his hand on Malak's shoulder in a clearly threatening way, he went on, "Listen, sonny boy. This roof is for respectable folk. You can't just turn up here in your own sweet time and open a shop, with workers and customers looking at the ladies going in and out. Got it?"

Malak, who now felt the danger of the situation, responded quickly, "My dear sir, all my workers are educated people, praise God! They're the most polite and discreet people in the world. And the people living on the roof and their ladies have my utmost respect."

"Listen. Forget the chit-chat. Pick up your stuff and get going!"

"Dear me! What's going on? Are you going to behave like ruffians or what?"

"That's it, momma's boy, we're going to behave like ruffians."

As Ali the Driver said this, he pulled Malak toward him by his collar and gave him a slap to announce that battle was about to commence. He conducted his quarrels with ease and proficiency as though he were carrying out simple, routine procedures or practicing a sport of which he was fond. He started with a well-placed head butt at Malak followed by two punches to the stomach and a third, powerful and audible, that struck his nose. A thread of blood flowed down Malak's face and he tried to resist by aiming a useless, symbolic punch at his opponent but it missed. Then as violent blows fell on him, he started screaming in protest and chaos reigned, while the workmen, not wanting problems, quietly fled and people gathered from every direction to watch. Abaskharon appeared suddenly on the roof and started screaming and wailing for help and the fight continued until Ali the Driver succeeded in expelling Malak from the room.

Mr. Hamid Hawwas had slipped away at the beginning and called the Emergency Response Police from the telephone in the cigarette stand on the opposite side of the street from the building and it wasn't long before a young police officer and a number of policemen and goons took everyone involved into custody—Malak, his assistants, Abaskharon, and Ali the Driver.

Translated by Humphrey Davies

Hamdi Abu Golayyel
from *Thieves in Retirement*

"So, YOU'RE LIVING NEXT to Koftes, aren't you?"

Taking me unawares with this bit of information, Abu Gamal chose a tone of voice appropriate to someone who has rendered an honorable service. Although I did my best to appear annoyed and upset, in fact I all but gave him a kiss. For having Koftes as a neighbor in this house specifically as good as guaranteed some degree of security and a natural, normal life inside your apartment. You could talk to yourself and laugh without any embarrassment, you could turn up the volume on the radio louder than necessary and dance if you felt like it, and have your friends over just to exchange the latest shades of gossip and all of you could hoot as noisily as you wanted while you consumed forbidden substances. More important than any of this, having Koftes there meant I could finally enjoy the sensation of pitying someone else.

Pity. The resort of the slothful. Pity allows you to come to terms with the disasters in your own life by dwelling on the catastrophes of others. Pity cons you into believing that you are a truly generous person. That you are noble and courageous, with nothing to lose but a sympathetic gaze that you part with easily and deliver sincerely. Pity is the sign of power. The sign of that generous impulse to give unto others that left me when I left the Bedouin, for everyone else was always stronger and I was always the one cut out for shows of grief and likely even some tears.

According to the dictionary, the word *koftes* approximates the English 'Copt' or 'Copts' or the French 'Coopti,' and they all mean what we call in Arabic qibti in everyday speech *ibti* or in other words someone of the Coptic religion or a person from ancient Egypt. When applied to Adil, however, it meant something else, something beyond an insult. Hearing it, he would erupt as if he had just gotten an invisible bite from a snake. And because our ears are highly trained at picking up whatever wounds us, he was erupting constantly.

. . .

Adil is a clever guy, blessed with the caution of a person faced with having to eliminate potential hazards all too often. Simply on the basis of his experience and expertise in this area he could have gotten on just fine, keeping to himself and keeping from mixing with the inhabitants at No. 36. But because he was so uncertain of being worthy of their confidence, together with his inflated respect for the worth of confidence itself, living quietly among us was out of the question. *The more convinced we are of the difficulty of obtaining some thing, the greater grows its worth in our eyes.* Here was a thought that Gamal wrote down, once.

Adil exists in a state of permanent fear. It may well be that those who live in fear cannot be free, or perhaps they're never able to take firm decisions and act. But there's no denying that these folks are the ablest of anyone at discovering what their own strong points are in the eyes of those around them. Adil's neighbors truly feared his presence—you know how you act when you don't know someone, how you take care to conceal details of what you do every day? You don't necessarily suspect that person of deliberately concealing some hidden power. But there's an anxiety that gnaws at you when you feel you have to be on guard against someone you know is weak but you can't be sure what naughtiness he might be capable of. Adil fought back against this fear by constantly going too far out of his way, sacrificing his comfort for the sake of making his neighbors comfortable. Not simply to gain their confidence but also to prove to himself that he was not that alien person who merits suspicion, who gives you the creeps and makes you constitutionally cautious.

He followed Abu Gamal closely. Stuck with him like his shadow. This wasn't a question of simple parasitism; after all, it was a fruitful attachment. Abu Gamal always had something nearby that he wanted repaired: the door to the chicken coop, the spigot in the stairwell, the ceiling fan or the drain. Not only was Adil at his beck and call. Adil, in fact, was skilled in a number of technical fields: carpentry, painting and decorating, plumbing, electricity. He fixed everything with great dedication and nobility. At first, Abu Gamal's reaction was to take it all as a down payment on a friendship that was only to be expected from this new resident. As the days went on, though, the older man began to look upon Adil's constant self-renunciation as no more and no less than father-right—that right he'd been deprived of when he was afflicted with disobedient offspring, a right due him as a man of a certain age who coveted the respectful gaze of others.

Adil didn't work. Or, let's just say that he didn't last where work was concerned. And so, at 8 a.m., Abu Gamal would wake him up, and after they partook communally of Um Gamal's breakfast, the daily round of work commenced. They'd look into the state of the hut that housed the chickens, continue with a quick tour around the building's utilities, and round out the day by cleaning and sprinkling the strategic stretch in front of the house. Then Abu Gamal would settle himself into his chair and begin telling his life story to Adil, who sat at his feet. This wasn't the life story that everyone in the vicinity already knew, but rather a tale of escapades that Abu Gamal was hoping everyone would hear.

Translated by Marilyn Booth

Going to School in Cairo

THE REPRESENTATIONS OF SCHOOLS, learning, and education in general are of particular importance to both *The Literary Atlas of Cairo* and *The Literary Life of Cairo* as a whole, since they all provide us with fascinating insight into the very making of the intellectual and literary elite that is the producer and shaper of the two volumes themselves. The educational system we encounter in these excerpts is the natural product and outcome of at least one hundred years of Egyptian modern history that are themselves shaped by Egypt's colonial history and the impact of cultural imperialism on the Egyptian and Arab elite in particular. The contradictions and colliding school values, pedagogies, and visions that emerge on the educational map of Cairo throughout the twentieth century and beyond trace the tribulations involved in the making of a literary elite as well as account for their effect on that same elite's subsequent intellectual locations and literary positionalities in both the *Literary Atlas* and *Literary Life of Cairo*. "Going to School in Cairo" deliberately confronts pre-revolutionary Egyptian traditional religious and secular schools with their contemporaneous missionary and colonial British and French private ones; two parallel systems of education that continue to co-habit even after the 1952 revolution with the colonial turned entrepreneurial, globalized, private education steadily gaining more and more ground and sway at the turn of the twenty-first century to the detriment of an increasingly nonviable national educational system that can no longer serve millions of underprivileged Egyptian youth.

The excerpts in this section clearly show how schooling in the city has always been, by and large, class-based, with the lower and middle class students predominantly attending modern state-run or traditional religious schools while the upper class students and those from the aristocracy are predominantly formed within missionary/colonial systems of education. These mostly autobiographical or pseudo-autobiographical texts are intriguing because they offer detailed reconstructions of school curricula, languages, classmates, teachers, songs, and last but not at all least the relationship of these schools to the streets and life of the city. Indeed, there is a world of difference between the schooling of Naguib Mahfouz's protagonist Kamal Abdel Gawwad and his experience of the city in *Palace Walk* and that of Prince Hassan Hassan. Whereas little Kamal attended the Khalil Agha neighborhood school in bustling Gamaliya in old Cairo, Hasan, who lived with his great aunt in her palace, was sent to the English School in the desert on the outskirts of Heliopolis. Kamal walked to school and meandered and daydreamed his way to and fro, witnessing street fights between school gangs, street vendors, and billboards while hopping on and off streetcars and tramways. In stark contrast, Hasan is sent to school by car and only experiences the metro for the first time in his life the day he rebels against being a boarder at the English School. Whereas Kamal studied in Arabic, learned the Qur'an from the Sheikh at school, and was taught to revere Islam and its icons, students who went to the colonial schools only studied in English and French, reading British and French history and curricula. Such was the case for Edward Said, who attended a private British colonial school in the posh neighborhood of Zamalek and was convinced as a child that "schoolteachers were supposed to be English" and was taught to sing hymns like "All Things Bright and Beautiful" and "From Greenland's Icy Mountains" every morning. Likewise, Midhat Gazalé who attended the French Lycée and studied from a French history book intended for France's Third Republic schools was taught that: "Our ancestors, the Gauls, were intelligent and brave." While Kamal's imagination was formed through his middle-class surroundings and environment, students in colonial and missionary schools were part of a "melting pot where dozens of different nationalities rubbed shoulders, whether they were pupils or teachers, amidst a rambling community of refugees from all over Europe." Kamal is immersed in Egypt's national liberation struggle while Leila Ahmed was taught to sing the British national anthem that included the words "God save our gracious king" and was brought up oblivious to "the issue of Palestine and Israel" for "it was something happening elsewhere, somewhere 'out there.' and it had no bearing at all, at least insofar as [she] was aware, on relations among Jews and Muslims and Christians where [she] lived."

Despite its massive alienating effects colonial-type secular education does become an aspiration for the literary elite, especially as more traditional pedagogies of learning are portrayed as sinking further and further into their own traditionalism. Taha Hussein, the Dean of Arabic Letters, describes his experience at al-Azhar in the following dismal terms:

The four years I had spent at the Azhar seemed to me like forty, so utterly drawn out they were. They wore me down. It was like being in a pitch black night when heavy piling clouds admit no gleam of light.

It is precisely at this juncture that Hussein makes a radical change in his education dropping out of the religious institution of al-Azhar for he discovers "the name of the 'university'" which he had not heard before. He asks himself: "What might the university be?" Hussein of course eventually teaches at Fouad al-Awwal University (renamed Cairo University after the 1952 revolution), later becoming *the* minister of higher education who introduced free education for all.

During its heyday, Cairo University was *the* national and regional magnet that attracted students, both male and female, from all over the Arab world. It was the locus for major avant-garde, progressive intellectual and political movements. Moroccan literary critic and author Mohamed Berrada offers a succinct representation of the symbolic status that Cairo University commanded for several generations of Egyptians and Arabs during the first half of the twentieth century:

Hammad got to know the gate of Cairo University, its tall dome, and the chimes of its famous clock on his way to the zoological gardens. He waited longingly for the end of the summer so that he could enter the complex, which symbolized a dream he had entertained since he was a schoolboy in Rabat.

But this towering institution of learning gradually loses its glamour in the post-1952 years, suffering its first blow with the 1954 university purge, when all professors reputed to be, or suspected of being against the Free Officers' regime were dismissed and replaced by newly appointed stock that would toe the line. Increasingly, this free and secular university became subject to state and security intervention and surveillance and was reduced to a huge factory for rote learning and policing that was at the receiving end of an already crumbling, obsolete school system. The prominent cultural critic, Ihab Hassan, who ended up leaving Egypt altogether, describes his national baccalaureate examination thus:

The baccalaureate examinations resulted annually in a national trauma. Harsh, exigent, and inflexible, more French than English in their centralized character, these exams, lasting two weeks, remain the most strenuous I have ever endured. Administered across the nation in vast, silent tents, with endless rows of numbered desks and sawdust on the ground, the ordeal—indeed its very place—exuded dread. Watchful monitors prowled the aisles of that city of the living dead, construing any communication, any whisper, as an attempt to cheat.

This deadly, constraining atmosphere spills into the national university system itself, ultimately killing the very spirit of the 'university' to which the generations of Taha Hussein and Mohamed Berrada had aspired. Since national education took a plunge during the second half of the twentieth century, we have witnessed the rise and proliferation of private, international, globalized schools and universities that are today entrusted with shaping the Egyptian elite and socializing it, in ways frightfully similar to the colonial school legacy. The earliest model of these universities is of course the American University in Cairo (AUC), which opened its gates in 1919, initially as a Protestant missionary school, only eleven years after the establishment of Fouad al-Awwal University in 1908. In *I am Free*, Ihasan Abdel Quddus describes how alien and estranging the liberal atmosphere on the campus of AUC initially seemed to his middle-class heroine Amina and how "young women mixed with the young men, how they sat in little groups to chat (always in English), how they would lounge on the lawn next to the young men leafing through a book or telling stories with signs of general happiness at the beginning of the academic year." But Amina finally integrates and adopts the liberal, modern model of the 1950s.

However, this modern model of the 1950s will be overthrown in the 1970s and 1980s with the Islamization of Egyptian society that will cut across social and economic classes. Indeed, Miral al-Tahawy's main character in *Blue Aubergine* at the end of the twentieth century offers a radical inversion of the liberal model of Amina provided by Abdel Quddus: at the university, all that al-Tahawy's protagonist sees when in the lecture hall is "the arrow pointing to the mosque." Rather than the university providing a space for her self-discovery and growth, "She weeps and ties back her hair. She lengthens her head covering every day so that no details are revealed. When the din of the lectures subsides, alone she follows the arrow and sits against the wall."

As more and more elite students seek to partake of the privileges of private education, disadvantaged students have to contend with the rapidly deteriorating conditions of university life, including national university student residences. When the women students in the dorm complain to the supervisor about a dead rat that was served in their collective supper pot, she responds: "Praise your Lord that the food is free of charge. People don't have a drop of oil in their homes, or a lump of sugar or even a piece of bread, and you're refusing to eat good food." No wonder then that the cab driver in Khaled Al Khamissi's *Taxi* skeptically concludes: "Me personally, I say to everyone around me, don't send your kids to school, don't send your kids to school, like it was my only mission in life."

Naguib Mahfouz

from *Palace Walk*

KAMAL LEFT THE KHALIL AGHA SCHOOL in the afternoon, bobbing along in the swelling current of pupils who blocked off the road with their flow. They began to scatter, some along al-Darrasa, some on New Street, others on al-Husayn. Meanwhile bands of them encircled the roving vendors stationed to catch them at the ends of the streets that branched out from the school. Their baskets contained melon seeds, peanuts, doum palm fruit, and sweets. At this hour, the street also witnessed fights, which broke out here and there between pupils forced to keep their disagreements quiet during the day to avoid school punishment.

Kamal had only rarely been embroiled in a fight, perhaps not more than twice during the two years he had been at the school. He had avoided fights, not from a lack of disputes, which actually were plentiful, nor because he disliked fighting. Being forced to renounce fighting caused him profound regret, but the overwhelming majority of the other pupils were much older, making him and a few of his companions aliens in the school. They stumbled along in their short pants surrounded by pupils over fifteen, many close to twenty. They plowed through the younger boys pompously and haughtily, sporting their mustaches. One of them would stop him in the school courtyard for no reason and snatch the book from his hand to toss far away like a ball. Another would take a piece of candy from him and pop it in his own mouth, without so much as asking, while carrying on a conversation with someone else.

Kamal's desire to fight did not desert him, but he suppressed it out of fear of the consequences. He responded only when one of his young companions provoked him. He found that attacking them vented his stifled rebellious feelings. It was a way to regain confidence in himself and his strength. Neither fighting nor being forced to refrain was the worst insult the aggressors could inflict. There were the curses and bad language that reached his ears, whether or not intended for him. He understood the meaning of some of the expressions and was cautious with them. Others he did not know and repeated innocently at home, thus stirring up a storm of outrage and indignation. This led to a complaint to the school disciplinarian, who was a friend of his father's.

It was nothing but bad luck which decreed that his adversary in one of his two fights was from a family of known toughs living in al-Darrasa. On the afternoon following the battle, Kamal found waiting for him at the door of the school a gang of youths armed with sticks, forming a ring of terrifying evil. When his adversary gestured to point him out, Kamal grasped the danger lying in wait for him. He fled back to the school and appealed to the disciplinary officer for help. The man tried in vain to dissuade the gang from its objective. They spoke so rudely to him that he was forced to summon a policeman to escort the boy home. The disciplinarian paid a call on Kamal's father at his shop and told him of the danger menacing his son. He advised him to attempt to resolve the matter prudently and diplomatically. The father had recourse to some merchants he knew in al-Darrasa. They went to the home of the toughs to intercede for him. Thus the father made use of his well-known forbearance and sensitivity to soothe their tempers. They not only forgave the boy but swore to protect him like one of their sons. The day was not over before al-Sayyid Ahmad sent someone to them with several presents. Kamal escaped from the sticks of the toughs, but it was like jumping out of the pan into the fire. His father's stick did more to his feet than tens of others would have.

Kamal started home from school. Although the sound of the bell signaling the end of the school day brought a joy to his soul unmatched by any other in those days, still the breeze of freedom he inhaled lightheartedly outside the school gates did not obliterate from his mind the echoes of the last class, which was also his favorite: religion. That day the shaykh had recited to them the Qur'an sura containing, *Say it is revealed unto me that a group of the jinn listened* (72:1). He had explained the passage to them. Kamal had concentrated his attention on it and raised his hand more than once to ask about points he did not understand. Since the teacher was favorably disposed toward him on account of the extraordinary interest he displayed in the lesson as well as his excellent memorization of Qur'an suras, he was much more open to the boy's questions than he usually was with his pupils. The shaykh had undertaken to tell him about the jinn and their different groups, including the Muslim jinn, and in particular the jinn who will gain entry to paradise in the end as an example for their brothers, the human beings. The boy learned by heart every word he said. He kept on turning the lesson around in his mind until he crossed the street to get to the pastry shop.

In addition to his enthusiasm for religious studies, he knew he was not just learning it for himself alone. He would have to repeat what he had grasped to his mother at home, as he had been doing since he was in Qur'anic kindergarten. He would tell her about the lesson and she would review, in the light of this new information, what she had previously learned from her father, a religious scholar trained at al-Azhar mosque university. They would discuss what they knew for a long time. Then he would teach her the new Qur'an suras she had not previously memorized.

He reached the pastry shop and stretched out his hand with the small change he had hung on to since morning. He took a piece of pastry with the total delight he experienced only on such a sweet occasion. It made him frequently dream of owning a candy store one day, not to sell the candy but to eat it. He continued on his way down al-Husayn Street, munching on the pastry with pleasure. He hummed and forgot he had been a prisoner all day long, not allowed to move, not to mention play or have fun. He was a sitting duck to be struck at any moment by the teacher's stick raised threateningly over the pupils' heads. In spite of all this, he did not hate school totally, since his accomplishments within its walls brought him praise and encouragement. His brother Fahmy was impressed because he did so well, but Kamal did not even receive one percent of his brother's appreciation from his father.

On his way, he passed by the tobacco store of Matoussian. He stopped under its sign, as he did every day at this hour, and raised his small eyes to the colored poster of a woman reclining on a divan with a cigarette between her crimson lips, from which rose a curling plume of smoke. She was leaning her arm on the windowsill. The curtain was drawn back to reveal a scene combining a grove of date palms and a branch of the Nile. He privately called the woman Aisha after his sister, since they both had golden hair and blue eyes. Although he was just going on ten, his admiration for the mistress of the poster was limitless. How often he thought of her enjoying life in its most splendid manifestations. How often he imagined himself sharing her carefree days in that luxurious room with its pristine view that offered her, in fact both of them, its earth, palms, water, and sky. He would swim in the green river valley or cross the water in the skiff that appeared ghostlike far off in the picture. He would shake the palm trees till the dates fell around him or sit near the beautiful woman with his eyes gazing at her dreamy ones.

He was not good-looking like his brothers. He was perhaps the one in the family who most resembled his sister Khadija. Like hers, his face combined his mother's small eyes and his father's huge nose, but without the refinements of Khadija's. He had a large head with a forehead that protruded noticeably, making his eyes seem even more sunken than they actually were. Unfortunately, he had first realized how strange he looked when a schoolmate teased him and called him a two-headed boy. Kamal had been enraged, and his anger had gotten him into one of his two fights. Even after he taught the boy a lesson, he was still upset and complained of his unhappiness to his mother. She was upset because he was. She tried to console him, telling him that people with large heads had large brains and that the Prophet (peace upon him) had a large head. To resemble the Prophet was the ultimate that anyone could aspire to.

He tore himself away from the picture of the smoking lady, and gazed this time at the mosque of al-Husayn. He had been taught to revere al-Husayn, and not surprisingly the holy martyr's shrine provided his imagination with countless sensations. Although his high regard for al-Husayn—matching the high status his mother in particular and the family in general accorded him— derived from al-Husayn's relationship to his grandfather, the Prophet, Kamal's knowledge of the Prophet had not provided him with what he knew about al-Husayn and the events of his life, nor did it explain the way his soul always hungered to have the saga of al-Husayn repeated, so he could draw from it the finest stories and the deepest faith. This centuries-old saga had found in Kamal an attentive, passionate, loving, believing, grieving, weeping listener. His suffering response was eased only by the fact that the martyr's head, after being severed from his immaculate body, chose Egypt from all the world for its resting place. Immaculate, it came to Cairo, glorifying God, and settled to the ground where al-Husayn's shrine now stands.

Kamal frequently stood in front of the shrine, dreaming and thinking. He wished his vision could penetrate it, to see the beautiful face. His mother assured him it had withstood the vicissitudes of time, because of its divine secret being. It had preserved its bloom and beauty, so that it lit up the darkness of its abode. Although unable to fulfill his wish, he stood there for long periods, communing with himself. He expressed his love and told his problems to the Prophet's grandson. These arose from his vivid daydreams about the jinn and his father's threats. He would implore al-Husayn's assistance for his exams, which he had to take every three months. He would usually conclude his private audience with a plea for a visit in his dreams. His custom of passing by the mosque both morning and evening had somewhat lessened its impact on him, but the moment his eyes fell on the shrine he would repeat the opening prayer of the Qur'an, even if he passed by repeatedly in a single day. Indeed, the shrine's familiarity could not rob his breast of his splendid dreams. The sight of the towering walls still evoked a response from his heart and the lofty minaret still called out to his soul, which quickly answered.

Reciting the Qur'anic prayer, he cut across al-Husayn Street and then turned into Khan Ja'far. From there he headed for Bayt al-Qadi Square. Instead of going home by way of al-Nahhasin, he crossed the square to Qirmiz Alley, despite its desolation and the fears it aroused in him, in order to avoid passing by his father's store. His father made him tremble with terror. He could not imagine that a jinni popping out at him would frighten him any more than his father screaming at him in anger. His distress was doubled, because he was never convinced of the appropriateness of the stern commands with which his father pursued him in his attempt to keep the boy from the fun and games he craved. Even if he had seriously wished to yield to his father's wishes and had tried to spend all his free time sitting quietly with his hands folded together, he would not have been able to obey that haughty, tyrannical will. He furtively took his fun behind his father's back whenever he felt like it, at home or in the street. His father knew nothing of this, unless a member of the household, exasperated when Kamal got out of hand and carried things too far, informed on him.

Kamal had gotten a ladder one day and climbed onto the arbor of hyacinth beans and jasmine, high above the roofs. His mother, seeing him there poised between earth and sky, had shrieked in terror until she had forced him to come down. Her concern over the consequences of such dangerous sport had won out over her fear of exposing him to his father's severity. She had told her husband what Kamal had been up to. He had immediately summoned him and ordered him to stretch out his feet. He had beaten them with his stick, paying no attention to Kamal's screams, which filled the house. Then the boy had limped out of the room to join his brothers and sisters in the sitting room. They had been trying not to laugh, except for Khadija. She had taken him in her arms and whispered to him, "You deserved it. . . . What were you doing, climbing the hyacinth beans and bumping your head against the sky? Did you think you were a zeppelin?" Except for such dangerous games, his mother shielded him and allowed him as much innocent play as he wanted.

He was often amazed to remember that this same father had been sweet and kind to him not so long ago, when he was a small child. Al-Sayyid Ahmad had enjoyed playing with him and from time to time had treated him to various kinds of sweets. He had done his best to lighten Kamal's circumcision day, hideous though it was, by filling his lap with chocolates and candy and smothering him with care and affection. Then how quickly everything had changed. Affection had turned to severity, tender conversation to shouts, and fondling to blows. He had even made circumcision itself a means for terrifying the boy. For a long time Kamal had been confused and had thought it possible they might inflict the same fate on what he had left.

It was not just fear which he felt toward his father. His respect for him was as great as his fear. He admired his strong, imposing appearance, his dignity that swept everyone along with it, the elegance of his clothing, and the ability he believed him to have to do anything. Perhaps it was the way his mother spoke about her husband that put him in such awe of him. He could not imagine that any other man in the world could equal al-Sayyid Ahmad's power, dignity, or wealth. As for love, everyone in the household loved the man to the point of worship. Kamal's small heart absorbed its love for him from this environment, but that love remained a hidden jewel, locked up inside him by fear and terror.

He approached Qirmiz Alley with its vaulted roof, which the jinn used as a theater for their nightly games. Although it frightened him, he preferred going that way to passing by his father's store. When he entered the cave-like space he started reciting, *Say He is the one God* (Qur'an 112:1), in a loud voice that resounded in the gloom beneath the curves of the roof. His eyes looked eagerly ahead at the distant mouth of the tunnel where light shone from the street. He quickened his steps, still repeating the Qur'an sura to keep from thinking about the jinn, for jinn have no power over anyone who arms himself with God's verses. His father's anger, once it flared up, could not be averted, even if he recited all of God's Book. He left the vaulted section of the alley for the other half. At the end he could see Palace Walk and the entrance of Hammam al-Sultan. Then his eyes fell on his home's dark green wooden grilles and the large door with its bronze knocker. His mouth opened in a happy smile at the side variety of amusements this place harbored for him. Soon the boys from all the neighboring houses would run to join him in his wide courtyard, with its several chambers, surrounding the oven room. There would be fun and games and sweet potatoes.

At that moment he saw the Suarès omnibus slowly crossing the street heading for Palace Walk. His heart leapt. Pleasure at his own cleverness filled him. At once he tucked his book bag under his left arm and raced to catch it. He jumped on the back steps, but the conductor did not let him enjoy his pleasure for very long. He came and asked the boy for his fare, giving him a suspicious, challenging look. Kamal told him ingratiatingly that he would get off as soon as it stopped but could not while it was moving. The conductor turned from him and yelled to the driver to stop the vehicle. He was angrily scolding Kamal, but when he looked away the boy seized the opportunity to tread on the instep of his foot, take a swing at him, and hop to the ground. He shot off in flight. The conductor's curses that followed him were filthier than balls of mud with stones inside. It had not been a deliberate plan or an original one. He had simply been delighted to see a boy do it that morning. When he got the chance to try it himself, he did.

Translated by William M. Hutchins and Olive E. Kenny

Hassan Hassan

from In the House of Muhammad Ali

MY STUDIES WERE TO be resumed at the English School in Heliopolis, ten minutes away from Marg by car. The school had none of the charms of Leighton Park. Set in an unpicturesque desert on the outskirts of Heliopolis, it seemed to be all brick, stone, and hardened sand. However, the atmosphere was not unpleasant. I settled down to work with my usual extra math lessons and tried to make the best of it all. After two terms of satisfactory if not brilliant reports—"Doing his best," "Trying hard," "A certain amount of progress"—Miss Machray asked me if I would like to become a boarder at school. I was horrified at the thought, not that the school was so bad, but I loved living at Marg after all these years of moving around. We did not talk about it again and I took it for granted that the subject had been shelved. But at the end of the Easter holidays Aicha mentioned casually at supper that I was going back to school on Saturday. I explained that only boarders were going back on Saturday, and that I, as a day-boy, would be going back on Monday.

Then Miss Machray very calmly said, "But you are a boarder now and therefore going back on Saturday."

I was amazed and asked why this should be, since I had so clearly expressed my desire to stay at home. No explanation was forthcoming and I was told that the decision had been taken "all for my own good." Nothing I could say could draw out a better reason or change the matter.

So on Saturday I went to school as a boarder, but I was resentful: here was my reward for doing my best; very well, henceforth I would work badly and perhaps this would convince 'them' that I had better results when I was living at home. But now it was no longer going to be a matter of studies, but a question of discipline. How did I dare discuss my great-aunt's decisions? I protested my respect and affection for her (which were perfectly sincere) and said that all I wanted was to be under her roof, but my stubbornness was considered an intolerable act of insubordination.

The struggle waged on, the school authorities were consulted, end-of-term reports were bad. I was in disgrace. I had heated arguments with Miss Machary, who I think may have been more understanding than her loyalty to Great-Aunt Nimet allowed her to show. One day I was sent to call on Aunt

Behidje (Princess Omar Toussoun) and what I thought was to be an ordinary visit turned out to be one long, public dressing-down, with a sermon on the evils of pride. It started with, "Il paraît que tu es orgueilleux," and it went on and on. I was completely taken back, as I had never been taxed with this supplementary sin, and I listened in humble and astonished silence while the storm raged on. And of course there was no question of allowing me a word in self-defense; one listened to one's elders but did not converse with them unless invited to. Rhetorical questions, of which there were plenty, were not to be taken advantage of.

A few days later I was back at school, but with unprecedented boldness I telephoned Marg and asked for a car to fetch me as I wanted to speak to my great-aunt. During the drive back my courage ebbed and my usual shyness got the better of me. After an hour's waiting in an anteroom I was reduced to a nervous state. When finally admitted to my great-aunt's presence, I stood mute while her wrath in no uncertain manner was unleashed upon me. Fortunately, it was mainly in Turkish, which I did not understand too well, but the tone was eloquent.

Chastised and vanquished, but unrepentant, I was driven back to school. There I decided on a plan of action. But for this I had to bide my time until I was eighteen, when, according to the law, I had the right to dispose of my person but not my inheritance. When the moment arrived, I had a final interview with one of the professors in charge of me and, seeing that nothing could be done (he sniggered, "What can you do? A palace revolution?"), I bade goodbye to my two best friends, Brian S. D. and Nevil F., and walked out defiantly by the front entrance of the school. This was against regulations—only parents and teachers were allowed that way. I took the Metro for the first time in my life and arrived in town. From there I set off on foot for Bab al-Luq Station to board a train to Ma'adi, a residential district south of Cairo, where my sister Hadidja was living.

I took her completely by surprise, still in her green satin bed, her maids drawing curtains, bringing breakfast on a tray, and without more ado I told her I had come to stay. She immediately telephoned Marg to inform them of my presence in Ma'adi. The news was very coolly received. She was told that my personal belongings would be sent over immediately, and that she herself was in disgrace, as it was obvious that she must have instigated the whole affair, since I was too much of a simpleton to take such a step by myself.

Like all family decisions of the period, these were final, dramatic, and irrevocable. Without much thought to consequences, and with all the usual ingratitude of youth to previous generations, I had crossed the Rubicon into adult life, where I was to find myself more than a little lost and bewildered. The whole world was open to me and, without knowing it, I was shedding the protection I had enjoyed since childhood. My new-found freedom was to provide me with only superficial joys and eventually to lead me into chaos.

Taha Hussein
from *The Days*

THE FOUR YEARS I had spent at the Azhar seemed to me like forty, so utterly drawn out they were. They wore me down. It was like being in a pitch black night when heavy piling clouds admit no gleam of light. It was not the poverty that oppressed me, nor my inability to do as I pleased. Those were familiar enough in the lot of students seeking knowledge in the noble Azhar.

Rather, it was seeing around me tens and hundreds suffering what I suffered, enduring what I endured, with even their most modest desires beyond their attaining. They had come to accept it quiescently, accustoming themselves to it, in the firm conviction that wealth and comfort and ample living were not part of the student's fate, and that poverty was, in fact, the proper condition of earnest effort and diligent achievement. To be rich in heart and spirit, rich in knowledge, was better and more useful than to have hands and pockets filled with material means.

The dismay that filled me gave me the sharpest distress. It enveloped my whole existence and dogged me in every part of my being.

It was a life of unrelieved repetition, with never a new thing, from the time the study year began until it was over. After the dawn prayer came the study of Tauhid, the doctrine of the divine unity; then fiqh, or jurisprudence, after sunrise; then the study of Arabic grammar during the forenoon, following a dull meal; then more grammar in the wake of the noon prayer. After this came a grudging bit of leisure and then, again, another snatch of wearisome food until, the evening prayer performed, I proceeded to the logic class which some sheikh or other would conduct. Throughout these studies it was all merely a case of hearing reiterated words and traditional talk which aroused no chord in my heart, nor taste in my appetite. There was no food for one's intelligence, no new knowledge adding to one's store. The Azhar upbringing had nurtured me in the sort of talent it required: I had become competent to understand what the sheikhs repeated. But all to no point.

I bethought myself that there were four more years of this ahead. With the four that had preceded them they would count like eighty. I pondered the fact that I would have to go on with these studies in the same old way, going through the ins and outs of all this Kalam, this discursive 'theology' which I could not stomach, so unavailing did I find it.

It was in the midst of all this that the name of the 'university' was first mentioned. I had not heard this word before and, initially, a peculiar sense of strangeness possessed me. All I knew was the mosque in which I was spending all my daylight hours and half the night besides. What might the university be? How might it be different from this mosque of mine, or from those many mosques which I frequented with their sheikhs? I had found some relaxation, in fact, in going to and fro among the mosques within that quarter of the city. For many of the sheikhs took their studies and their students off to them, in preference to the Azhar, from time to time.

It was not long before I had some inkling of what this word 'university' signified, enough at least to know that it was not a school like other schools. The feature I found most significant was that the lessons to be had there did not at all resemble Azhar studies—not remotely so. It was not to be only a place for the turbaned style of students: there would be those who sported the tarboosh, perhaps in greater force than the turban wearers. For the latter, thanks to their Azhar skills, could never match up to other knowledge or busy themselves with the trivialities in which 'the sons of the schools'—as they used to call them in those days—wasted their time.

These tidings about the 'university' put me into a state of apprehension. Perhaps my anxiety would give me away and my ardor might quickly be dispelled. Destiny might have for me something to hear other than those familiar, endless, wearisome sequences of Azhar lore. Yet I was possessed the while with gnawing doubts which sorely tormented me and which I could in no way explain to my friends and intimates.

Would this university accept me among its students once it was established? Or would it send me back disconsolate to the Azhar because I was blind and, for blind folks, the Azhar was the only path to learning? Such painful doubts made my nights sleepless, my couch restless. I could only take counsel with myself, for I was too shy to talk about my plight with anyone. It gave me great distress to have people talk about it to me, as oftentimes they did.

So I lived betwixt and between insistent fears and dim hopes in intermittent alternation. I let myself lie low awhile to get some respite. At length, when the university was established and I became a pupil there, my fears abated and a glad anticipation filled me with happy satisfaction. When that day I went to my Azhar classes, I had no ear for anything the sheikhs were saying. I did not understand a word, preoccupied as I was with what was in store in the evening. My mind had no register either for them or for their studies. I was present, as it were, in *absentia*, during the forenoon's lesson in language. It was the first time I had been so sleepily alert. I did not wait for the afternoon prayer but went off to the university with my two companions, when the rhetoric class ended. Each of us had ready the guinea we had perforce to pay for permission to attend the classes. It was an odd thing, in our eyes that we had to buy learning with money, small though the sum might be. It was unfamiliar and uncongenial, too. We were used to the Azhar practice of having provender of daily loaves for our pursuit of learning, solving in part our subsistence problems. Paying that guinea was a hard business, but the hardship of doing so was simply a measure of how much we were in love with what it purchased.

The theme of the first university studies I ever heard was Islamic civilization. My first impression was the utter contrast with everything in the Azhar and impressive it was! The professor, Ahmad Zaki, began the class with words the like of which I had never heard in the Azhar. "Gentlemen! I greet you in the fellowship of Islam, and I say, 'Peace be upon you and God's mercy.'"

In the Azhar I had been used to a different from of words from the sheikhs. They were not directed to the students but addressed to God ("His be the might and the majesty") in praise and adoration. The sheikhs did not greet the students, they "called down blessing on the Prophet, his family and companions every one"!

It impressed the newcomer, too, that the professor did not say when the study began, "The author—God have mercy on him—said . . . ." He broached the subject by speaking for himself, not reading from a book. What he said was clear and needed no explanation, being straightforward and lucid, and free of qanqalah, or citation and counter-citation, obviating mere contention. How altogether strange and new it all was, exciting my mind and revolutionizing my whole way of thinking. With my two companions and, indeed, all the students around—and how many there were—I was gripped with fascination. When the session was almost over, the professor announced that he would repeat the lesson again, after some minutes, to allow the many students to hear it who had not been able to get into the room. When the first relay of students made their exit, I had no mind to do so and stayed in my place to hear the study a second time.

That night I did not sleep. I heard the muezzin call the dawn prayer but did not rise from my bed. The Azhar lay like a load on my mind and I stayed in my room till high forenoon. Had it not been for the class in literature in the 'Abbasid riwaq, I would have remained there till evening.

I attended the literature class but from the start had no relish for it. I stammered when the sheikh questioned me on a point. Whereupon, he turned angry and asked me what I was doing with the two picking baskets in my head—my two ears that is. That brought me round to my wonted concentration and for the rest of the lesson I got everything he said. In the grammar class that followed I gave the professor just one of my baskets, or perhaps only part of one. For I was living only for the evening hour, savoring the lesson I would then be having from Ahmad Zaki Bey, on the subject of ancient Egyptian civilization. I heard what was being said, but took nothing in. My mind was impervious and I could not imagine how it was possible for people to busy themselves with such topics.

When the third day's lesson came, my ardor was keener and sharper than ever. It was to be by an Italian professor, and in Arabic—an Italian talking to Egyptians in their own language, learnedly, about a theme of which I and my Azharite contemporaries had never even heard till that very day. And when we did—my friends and I—we failed to take it in. "The Literature of Geography and History" it ran. But what were our ears, and our inward comprehension, to make of its strange sounding?

What was this word 'literature,' 'belles lettres'? and what had it to do with geography and history? We were present at the session but comprehended precisely nothing. Indeed, we actually heard nothing.

Professor A. Tuwaidi, a great scholar, was a slim man with a very feeble voice. The students nearest to him failed to get what he was saying and there were very many present. The low voice, too, gave rise to some commotion. So the first lecture went for nothing. While the professor toiled in its delivery the students strained in the effort to hear. The University was obliged to choose the student with the strongest voice and the best delivery to pick up what the professor said and relay it, just as somebody does in the mosque prayer following the imam.

But before that third day passed after the opening of the University I had experienced a sudden and total change in my life.

Translated by E.H. Paxton

Ihab Hassan

from *Out of Egypt*

AT THE GRILLED, lead-hued gate of the school, which shut at five minutes past eight with frightening finality and opened mercifully again at five minutes to four, the parental Rolls or Daimler might wait for the most privileged pupils. But once inside, these abandoned all hope. Jostling with the rest, they relied on their wits, fists, and unbreakable skulls—a quick, sharp blow with the head to the enemy's nose bridge—to absolve themselves daily of cowardice, effeminacy, or simply good breeding. In the brief recreation periods, the younger boys played el-beel (marbles), viciously throwing their nickle leaders at a triangle full of bright, multicolored spheres. Older boys played fudbal (soccer) with a makeshift lump of old socks, delighting to kick each other in the shins. Lunch was a predatory affair, wolves and hyenas, the stronger or hungrier fighting for inedible gobs of glutinous matter while el-alpha (the monitor), disdained by all, tried to establish some order of precedence around the table. (For many, poorer pupils, this was their only meal for the day.) Extracurricular activities? Suspect. Character development? Absurd. The fit survived, and everyone studied grimly or else fell by the way.

Not quite ten, I entered the lowest grade of Saidiah. The youngest boy in class, I wore short pants; a new, red tarboosh (fez) barely concealed hair parted on one side. I sat at a rickety, sepia-colored, wooden desk, ink-splotched and carved-up by the canifs (pen knives) of all my predecessors. When the teacher stepped briskly into class, we all clattered to our feet and saluted, hands to fezzes, standing till he ordered us seated. The lesson began, and as in schoolrooms around the world, excitement and misery mingled in the period, which sped or dragged till a hand-rung bell struck the hour.

Directly behind me sat Tawfik, the class bully. He was fair, almost creamy of complexion, not particularly muscular. But he could glare ferociously or snarl, displaying a snaggle tooth, and he fought with reckless glee. At once, he began to smile at me, making a slow, pumping motion with his hand, his thumb and index forming a circle. I smiled affably back. Afterward, I discovered the meaning of his lewd, homosexual gesture. We fought, of course, and I lost—gashed lip, blood filling my mouth, ribs aching for a week— though not so badly as to brand myself a pansy nor so well as to discourage future strife.

That first year in school became my initiation to social reality. It certainly wrenched, remade, my character. I woke every morning with fear in my guts, in my feet; I ended each day with an infinitesimally stronger sense of my endurance. I could not share my pain with my parents; I could not stay away from school. The year passed, the next came, the misery remained. Then one day I made a stunning discovery: I had lost my fear. I discovered also that by striking out first I could win most fights. Sensing, really believing, that I had nothing to lose, I found that I had accidentally won everything, almost everything. Suddenly, I began to excel in my school work, standing near the top of my class. Suddenly, too, I became popular: boys asked me to join their secret bands and warring gangs, practicing roughhouse pranks. I declined, my old bitterness stronger than their new-fangled flattery.

Tawfik and all those boys who had bullied me for an eternity began to fade from my awareness. They also faded into a lower 'form.' (At Saidiah, the higher achievers were segregated into the same classroom or form within each grade. Thus pupils bound for the university moved from first form, first grade, to first form, second grade, until their last year in secondary school, first form, fifth grade.) But a few others—Talat, Ibrahim, Roshdy—remained within the tight, invincible circle of friendship through my school and university years, until exile, marriage, age dispersed our ways.

Though I belonged to no racial or religious minority in Egypt, I was tormented more than if I had been a freak. What have the tormentors of my boyhood become? No doubt, some have grown into upstanding men, model fathers to their sons. Were they to recall the pain they once inflicted on a boy, they might now wince and squirm. Or was that pain but some exchange for a lack they themselves as boys endured? Lack or warp, something there tempts us to indulge a nameless evil; we torture purely, like art, for its own mysterious sake.

. . .

Increasingly, I discovered in Saidiah an outlet for my energies. I endured its dreary, disinfected classrooms and execrable lunches because the world opened itself to me again as it had on those long, silent afternoons when I read at al-'izba. At Saidiah, though, the autodidact in me encountered odd and exacting masters.

Most pupils perceived only the ludicrous quirks of their teachers. One, dubbed "The Klaxon," kept tapping his hip pocket during class to check on his wallet; another, called "The Clutch," reached for his crotch and glared to stress a point in the lesson; a third, nicknamed "The Bullet," fired chalk pieces with the accuracy of a high-powered rifle at nodding or chattering boys. Other teachers, however, evoke images of richer hue.

I recall Mr. Miller who taught us the King's English, and conveyed a certain hurt radiance even to the rowdiest spirit. His pale, pinched face and distant sunken eyes rendered all the horrors of W. W. Jacobs' "The Monkey's Paw," and his flashes of mock braggadocio infused in *King Solomon's Mines*, *The White Company*, *Montezuma's Daughter*, *The Coral Island*, *Kidnapped*, and *The Prisoner of Zenda* a delightful irony without impairing their romance. He had a taste for things Gothic, a gentle way of shaming obscenity into silence. He may have also inspired me to the first prize I ever won at school: a handsome combination desk calendar and writing pad, inscribed, "For Excellence in English."

I did well in all subjects—except Arabic. Once, my total points in the marking period earned me second place even though I had failed Arabic. The headmaster came as usual to congratulate the three top pupils in class. He called on the first, and walked up to his desk to shake his hand; he called on the third, and did the same. Then he called on me. Pausing as if in great perplexity, he lowered his brown, watery eyes and softly asked: "Why, my son? Are you rumi (Greek or Roman, any foreigner really)?" I did not fail Arabic again, though I never did more than pass it; and when I missed Highest Honors on graduation from secondary school, I blamed it bitterly on my battered native tongue.

Highest Honors were attained by placing among the top ten students in Egypt in the nation-wide baccalaureate examinations. The 'top ten' were separated from one another by a few points, sometimes only by half a point; and often, when two or three pupils tied for the same place, the ranking would skip, say, from first to fourth, keeping 'the ten' only ten. I placed thirteenth, which guaranteed me entrance to any university, but not the inscription of my name in golden letters on a plaque, hanging in the main hall of the Saidiah Secondary School. (To this day, I regret the omission with a small, occasional twinge that takes my self-irony by surprise.)

The baccalaureate examinations resulted annually in a national trauma. Harsh, exigent, and inflexible, more French than English in their centralized character, these exams, lasting two weeks, remain the most strenuous I have ever endured. Administered across the nation in vast, silent tents, with endless rows of numbered desks and sawdust on the ground, the ordeal—indeed its very place—exuded dread. Watchful monitors prowled the aisles of that city of the living dead, construing any communication, any whisper, as an attempt to cheat. This brought instant retribution: a red mark in the corner of the examination book, assuring failure. Punctually at the end of each exam, the head monitor screamed maniacally his command: "Pens at rest! Pens at rest!" Any delay in obeying this doomsday cry brought again the red stigma of failure. Thus we raced against time as well as each other, raced ultimately against our own selves.

Failure meant a year lost and, far worse, shame. Students who failed sometimes committed suicide; others, in fearful anticipation of the event, would flee their homes, or simply collapse. Thus the great battles of Egypt were fought not on the playing fields of its public schools but under its examination tents. Were these battles really won? I have known piercing intellects among my classmates who have either emigrated or remained to find their minds brutalized by bureaucracy. I have known others who lost hope and quietly lapsed into cynicism, sloth, sensualism. Is the school itself to blame for this? Is Egyptian society? In some rude, outlying districts of Upper Egypt, an intelligent school child may aspire to a world centuries, literally centuries, ahead of the world its family inhabits.

Leila Ahmed

from *A Border Passage*

IN SENIOR SCHOOL the day started with our standing outside the hall in rows according to our houses; the teachers stood on a raised, covered arcade facing us. The youngest children would be in front, and house prefects would walk up and down the lines checking that we were quiet and properly dressed, our ties and socks straight. Once all the teachers were there, there would be a pause, and then a hush would fall over everyone and the headmaster would sweep out of the school building and onto the arcade, his academic robes flowing behind him. Mr. Brent Price. A new headmaster appointed by the powers in London, he had replaced Mr. Whiting, who had been there many years, much loved by students and parents alike.

On Mondays we would troop up the stairs and into the hall for assembly. The headmaster would make various announcements and generally give a short speech. We would then sing hymns; my favorite was "Teach Me, my God and King." I loved in particular the first stanza and two others:

Teach me, my God and King,
In all things thee to see
And what I do in any thing
To do it as for thee.

A man that looks on glass
On it may stay his eye;
Or if he pleaseth through it pass
And then the heav'n espy.

A servant with this clause
Makes drudgery divine:
Who sweeps a room, as for thy laws,
Makes that and th'action fine.

I wonder now why this last stanza was as arresting to me as it was; I had never myself had to sweep the floor. Perhaps it helped make sense of what I know I sometimes vaguely puzzled over, why it was that some people were servants and how it was that apparently they were not unhappy about it.

We would conclude with the Lord's Prayer. The hymns, referring only to God and specifically chosen from among those that made no reference to Jesus, were, like the Lord's Prayer, considered by the school to be interdenominationally monotheistic and thus as acceptable for Muslim and Jewish children as for Christians. On special occasions we also sang the national anthem—the British one, of course. It included the words "God save our gracious king," and "Send him victorious, happy and glorious, long to reign over us." So far as I recall, we sang them entirely unselfconsciously. We must have stopped singing it after the Egyptian Revolution, 26 July 1952, but I seem to remember that we sang "God Save the Queen" for a time, too; Elizabeth ascended the throne a few months before the revolution.

. . .

On weekdays other than Mondays we would not go into the hall for assembly. After we had lined up outside and after the headmaster had made his usual entrance, he would make a few brief announcements and then declare, "Jews and Muslims fall out!" At this point, Christian students would troop into the hall to pray and sing Christian hymns, while we Muslims and Jews had the time to ourselves, usually about twenty-five or thirty minutes during which we would walk about with our friends on the school grounds or out onto the playing fields as far as the fir and oleander copse.

This became the time that Joyce and I would spend together. Joyce, who had straight black hair and bright, mischievous brown eyes, had been my best friend from the time I first came to the English School at the age of six, when she also was six. I remember our friendship not, as with Gina, for the games we played but for the way things were between us, the way we would know, for instance, just exchanging glances, what the other thought. And the way we saw things the same, as if we stood together on the edge of things, outside the ordinary stream of life, observing from a space of our own, seeing below the threshold of words that the rules by which adults lived and with which they tried to contain what we thought were not grand and infallible, as the adults would have us believe they were. Joyce was Jewish, and I know that we discussed to our satisfaction what it meant that people were of different religions, and that we watched quizzically (I remember exactly Joyce's expression) the antics of adults, and that we observed, exchanging glances, the convolutions into which they sometimes got on the subject of different religions. At home I was told about Jews what I was told about Christians, that we all believed in the same God but had different religions because people had to be the religions into which they were born. I expect that Joyce was told something similar, probably with the same additional explanations that I got in response to further persistent questioning. It would go something like this: "Are all three religions exactly the same?" "No, not exactly. There are differences, but they are in essence the same." "But are they all exactly equal?" "Well, no, ours is best." "Well then, why doesn't everybody else convert?" "They can't do that. People have to belong to the religion into which they're born." "But if ours is best?" "Well, it's best for Muslims, dear. Why don't you run off and play now?"

The issue of Palestine and Israel was something happening elsewhere, somewhere "out there," and it had no bearing at all, at least insofar as I was aware, on relations among Jews and Muslims and Christians where we lived. In my own perception it would be only after Suez that these would change. But my own perceptions were those of a preteenager and obviously reflected attitudes in my own home and community, and not necessarily those of the country at large. Elsewhere in the country and in Cairo, as I know now (not from memory but from history books), other currents and feelings were afoot, and already for several years before the revolution there had been hostilities and incidents against Jews.

I recall a few details of the kind of play Joyce and I engaged in, for instance, the secret society we formed consisting of just the two of us and modeled, I expect, on the secret societies in Enid Blyton's books. We had a secret symbol, the letter K (because it came between her first initial and mine), which we wore on buttons we made for ourselves by writing the letter on a piece of material and wrapping it around a button and tying it there, attaching it to our clothes with a safety pin; we explained its meaning to no one. We also had secret signs and a secret written language, but it was such a labor composing and deciphering notes in this language we did not resort to it often. I remember, too, that we roller-skated together, and that Joyce broke a front tooth one day when we were skating in the school rink, and that she got up and did not cry, in spite of all the blood—she had also cut her lip—and that we were scared as we ran to the school matron. And I remember her new tooth, whiter than the others, and how she worried that people would know she had a false tooth.

My skipping a grade separated us to some extent, but it did not end our friendship. We kept up our habit of spending that first half hour of the school day together, walking in the school grounds and talking. And we continued seeing each other outside school, Joyce sometimes coming to Ain Shams and I sometimes going to her home, though more rarely, because it was an apartment and we were more confined there. They lived on the main boulevard in Heliopolis, opposite Cinema Roxy, an open-air movie theater to which we would go together. During the intermission we would buy Coca-Colas and the delicious fresh round sesame bread (called semeet) sold there with slices of Greek cheese in wax paper, enjoying as well as the film we had come to see, the always pleasant evenings of Egypt in the seasons in which open-air cinemas were open. Invariably, though, Nanny came with us, as I was not allowed to go anywhere without her, even to the rare parties (usually birthday parties). Later, this would cause me enormous embarrassment since no one else went places with their nannies. Some girls at our school had even stricter families, though, and they were simply not allowed to visit anyone who was not family.

The films we saw were almost always American, and when they were not American they were British: *On Moonlight Bay*, *Fantasia*, *The Secret Life of Walter Mitty*, *Hans Christian Andersen*, *Annie Get your Gun*, *Seven Brides for Seven Brothers*, *The Greatest Show on Earth*, *Lassie*, *The Man with the Golden Arm*. We rarely went to Arabic films, which we did not like, except for those of the famous comedian Naguib el-Rehani, which we loved. Arabic movies, like Arabic music, were looked down on in our circle, although when I say this, I don't know who exactly I mean: my parents rarely went to movies, Arabic or Western. (Now I love old Egyptian movies. Egypt was the Hollywood of the Middle East, and in the thirties and forties, anyway, produced some wonderful films.)

Besides the movies we also went to the Heliopolis Sporting Club, where we swam and sat on the Lido and drank Cokes. Sometimes we took walks in Heliopolis, from Joyce's house to the Baron Empain castle, right next to my aunt Aisha's house, and sometimes I took walks in that area with my aunt Aisha, too, with her great, big, handsome gray dog, Wolf. The baron, a Belgian, was the man who had thought up Heliopolis, buying desert land and designing its layout and persuading the government to build wide European-like boulevards with palms and varieties of trees and grass down the middle, and selling plots of villas. The result was an attractive European-style suburb, called in Arabic Masr el-Gedida, New Cairo. Empain amassed a vast fortune and built himself an extraordinary castle that, in all the years that I knew it, was totally deserted. A peculiar, haunting landmark, its grounds were dominated by flights of steps on which stood stone vases and sculptures, and there was little green except for some ornamental palms. Rising above them, the rose-colored castle with its complicated turrets looked exactly like the castles of dribbled sand on the beach.

Midhat Gazalé

from *Pyramids Road*

THE LYCÉE FRANÇAIS WAS a melting pot where dozens of different nationalities rubbed shoulders, whether they were pupils or teachers, amid a rambling community of refugees from all over Europe—Jews, antifascists, White Russians, etc. The Lycée nonetheless abided by the demanding curricula of the French Ministry of Education, requiring my little Egyptian schoolmates to recite parrot-fashion the famous opening paragragh of Emest Lavisse's classic French history book intended for France's Third Republic schools:

> Our ancestors, the Gauls, were intelligent and brave. They were not able to defend themselves against the Romans. Gaul was conquered by the Romans fifty years before Jesus Christ despite the beautiful defense put up by Vercingetorix. Gaul remained under Roman rule for more than four hundred years. It became educated and rich. It became Christian.

Our Lycée, in a building designed by the French architect Victor Erlanger, was located in a section of town called Bab el Luq, nicknamed "Babel look" for it housed an unusually large number of private schools of different nationalities. The American University in Cairo, known as the AUC, was immediately adjacent to the Lycée Français, within a stone's throw of the Collège des Frères, the Italian and German schools, and others.

Strangely, we never mingled much with our AUC neighbors. Our basketball teams had been rivals since time immemorial, taking turns at winning the annual college championship. The Lycée students were outwardly discreet, with the girls wearing natural-colored cotton uniforms that barely revealed the hem of their skirts. The kids next door wore extravagant colors, taking for role models American movie stars of the day. The boys were Mickey Rooneys, and the girls Judy Garlands. They involved themselves in numerous extra-curricular activities, a luxury we could not afford, given the amount of reading that was required of us daily.

The large majority of students came from well to do 'European' families who lived in the center of town or its immediate vicinity, within walking distance of one another and of their respective schools.

My closest friend Robert Farhi and I were barely eleven when we discovered that we were both in love with Madame Moulin, our history teacher. Her Christian name was Germaine, a slightly old-fashioned choice by today's standards. When I told that story to the beautiful and talented French actress Fanny Ardant, she confessed, amid one of her legendary laughs, that Germaine Moulin sounded like a name out of the French Resistance. Not so much because it reminded her of the mythical and heroic Jean Moulin, but because Germaine called to mind an adolescent messenger wearing a long ample skirt and rolled down socks, riding a rusty bicycle on a rural pathway with the Germans lurking behind the bushes in their drab green uniforms.

Considering that we were 'inseparable,' Robert and I decided to share Madame Moulin. The secret name of our brotherhood would be GRV, our initials joined to hers (throughout my Lycée years, my first name was Victor). We carved the secret logo on our school benches and on the bark of trees, we drew it in the courtyard sand and on our copybooks, and we sealed our conspiracy by uttering the magical word every time we shook hands, in the manner of knights out of our fair teacher's history book mixing their blood.

It was Madame Moulin who taught us the first rudiments of ancient Egyptian history, the object of her passion and soon of ours. La Phalène bookstore carried a seemingly endless collection of pharaonic postcards, and I never failed, upon receiving my pocket money, to buy one or two, and neatly paste them down in chronological order in a little copybook: the Old Empire with the Pyramids of Giza, the Middle Empire with Sesostris (one of my grand uncles was named Sesostris), and above all, the New Empire with the emblematic figures of Thutmose, Hatshepsut, Akhenaton—said to be the precursor of monotheism—his beautiful wife Nefertiti, the mythical Tutankhamen and the greatest of all, Ramesses II. Having reached Cleopatra, my copybook ran out of gages, but the history of ancient Egypt had come to an end anyway.

Thereupon, I mustered all my courage and decided to show my album to Madame Moulin. She tucked it under her arm, and invited me for tea at five o'clock at her apartment, promising to diligently examine my magnum opus and return it to me that afternoon.

. . .

Her apartment, which was heavy with the fragrance of bitter-almond floor wax, was very different from ours. Whereas my parents insisted on having nothing but French-looking furniture, hers was furnished with oriental antiques, probably gleaned from the Khan el Khalili souk. I had visions of Sheherazade emerging from behind an arabesque screen when Madame Moulin appeared, wearing a straight gray skirt and a white cotton blouse with a tiny silk scarf tightly wrapped around her neck. She sat next to me on a soft Turkish diwan and slowly flipped the pages of my copybook, sometimes pausing to offer this or that comment. But I only remember the way she puckered her lips every time she uttered the word 'pschent,' her light perfume, the warmth radiating from her body close by, and the thin blue vein that ran under the translucent skin of her cheek. When the time came to take leave, I shyly asked her if she would care to keep the copybook. She gave me a soft kiss on the cheek, promising always to cherish that memento of her dearest-ever Egyptian pupil.

Monsieur Marie, our math teacher, was redoubtable. His oral interrogations invariably began by chalking up a problem on the blackboard then proceeding with the roll call in alphabetical order. Upon being called, we sheepishly went to the blackboard and embarked upon our own flight of fancy, praying that it would contain enough substance to escape the ultimate sanction, the zero mark. Such a performance entailed a two-hour consigne (detention) in the permanence, a sinister classroom where the habitual inmates went straight to their perennial seats, and the zero achievers sat in silence under the watchful eye of Monsieur David or Monsieur Neemetallah, a true sadist. Another sadist was Monsieur Bradke, a supervisor of nondescript origin whose specialty was tugging ears or pulling the short hairs of the temples while vigorously shaking his hand to exacerbate the pain.

. . .

Hundreds of White Russian immigrants, many of whom belonged to the defunct aristocracy, had found refuge in Egypt when the revolution broke out in their country thirty years earlier. Princess Wolkonski, our English teacher, belonged to the Czar's family. She looked fearful with her flame-red wig tightly tucked under the black turban she never parted with. The word was unkindly passed down from generation to generation that the poor woman had lost her hair overnight when the revolutionaries massacred her family. She was one of a handful of survivors, a very young one at the time. I was one of her favorite pupils whereas my unruly brother was her bête noire, whom she regularly expelled from the classroom with the unvarying "Oy oy oy, quelle horreur de garçon!" Otherwise, she inflicted upon him le piquet, forcing him to stand at attention facing one of the corners of the classroom, head bowed and hands joined behind his back. The punishment usually lasted until the recess, unless she took pity on him and authorized him to return to his bench if he showed, or usually feigned, signs of fatigue. The princess taught me my first words of English, and patiently helped me shed my Egyptian accent, at least partly, for I believe I have kept indelible Russian traces to this day.

Counts Preobrajenski and Andreevski, both of whom once belonged to the Imperial guard, were employed as supervisors. They treated us with the brutality of Cossack officers, but we never dared complain to our parents. When their paths crossed Madame Wolkonski's, they bowed very low, clicked their heels, and kissed the tip of her haughtily outstretched hand.

Another Russian immigrant was our art teacher, Professeur Stoloff, who insisted on being addressed as 'Maître.' He was short and heavy, wore his long hair artistically unsubmissive, and never parted with his floppy black bow tie. Despite his frightening facial expressions and thundering voice, we never really feared him, and his art class was deliciously chaotic. Our undisputed mischief leader Chalem never ran out of imagination when it came to putting the plaster models to unorthodox use, such as having Apollo's statue mount that of Venus. Art grades did not weigh heavily in the overall annual score, which caused his class to be consistently half-deserted without the master noticing, or perhaps even caring. I was fairly good at drawing and enjoyed his comments on my work, which were always enlightening though never charitable. He would rub his chin and declare loudly enough for the entire class to hear, "Le dessin s'adresse à l'intelligence," ('Drawing rests on intelligence'), adding that given that premise, not one of us would ever make the grade.

The White Russian community organized weekly musical evenings, usually in Andreewski's apartment, whose walls were covered with sabers, medals, brightly adorned tunics, fur hats, capes, etc. The apartment was crumbling under an odd assortment of gilded icons, orthodox crosses, and other Russian memorabilia. They drank vodka, played the balalaika, and sang nostalgic songs in chorus. They also cried à lot. I remember Suzette—I believe her mother was Russian—once telling me that they had a lot to cry about, but that in general Russians loved to cry.

Laila Osayran

from *Colored Ribbons from My Life*

The Color Brown

I was so scared, I could not cry!

I woke up and pulled away the mosquito net. I washed and put on my uniform: a brown skirt and a beige blouse with a brown vest embroidered with the American College for Girls badge. My braids were badly done and without colored ribbons.

The color brown started to overtake my life after the festival of colored ribbons.

I am on the threshold of my tenth year. I am in Cairo in a spot that lay exactly in the middle on Queen Nazli (King Farouk's mother) Street. Within the confines of the boarding school, I wore these clothes for six whole years. Like me, all the other girls wore the color brown. We walked, moved, came and went all over school covered in this dark, ominous color. How brown became hateful! The fabric would change during the summer but the color remained the same.

Today, I hate the colors brown and beige. They never came near my body again.

The clean shoes were brown with no heels; the nails were cut and clean as well. The closet was tidy: all my clothes were numbered. The bed was made. The teacher-inspector went round the girls' rooms. The room had twelve beds for the youngest girls in the boarding school. They didn't know each other yet. All are Egyptian. I am the only one from Lebanon. I speak a different dialect. I am with them, without my mother's warmth.

The first day at boarding school with a Lebanese accent was difficult. And that family to which I was related was far away, an unstable entity. My main concern was my father. Had you been alive, father, would my life have witnessed this change? Would I now be deprived of you and of my mother?

The situation is frightening!

We line up. We go down to the dining hall. One hundred students. A teacher sits at the head of each table. The headmistress and the other teachers sit at a table apart. They have a different breakfast from ours.

We are second-class people. The younger ones among us are third-class.

We are all seated without a word. The situation is frightening! We stand up to leave. We go upstairs like sheep to the dormitory again where we wash our hands and mouths. The school day begins from a long dark corridor that leads to the school playground.

The girls in other classes meet up with their friends who attend day school. I stand alone. My schoolbag is new. I realize how unlike the old students I am. I see Mona's blue eyes and the cruelty of the other children who stigmatized me as an orphan.

I stand watching. I don't know anyone with whom to talk. None of them tried to welcome me. A frightening bell rang. Several lines were formed. We say good morning to the headmistress in English. She scolds us even before we have committed an offence. The situation is frightening! The whole school is frightening! The first lesson, the second, and the third. Break. I watch, alone. The old students huddle together. Girls, girls, girls, all wearing the same color, the same cut, almost the same shoes. The girls run off to buy chocolate. I don't buy any. I like chocolate but I don't buy any. I have no money. My mother forgot about break hour and the money. The day is spent in fear. I suffocate. We finish lining up. We eat lunch. We go back to our lessons. At four o'clock we gather around a big cupboard with small lockers in which each student places her afternoon snack.

All except me. My mother's aunt, who agreed to be my guardian during boarding school vacations, did not give me anything. I look confused and then I withdraw in shame.

The situation is frightening. We go to the classrooms and sit at tables large enough for six students. We work until seven. At eight we have dinner. By ten, each student is in her bed, lying still, under the mosquito net. The lights are turned off. Talking is forbidden. Moving is forbidden. We fear going to the bathroom. We say good night to the teacher in English. Day over.

Fearful silence. Cold. Tombs erected underneath the white mosquito nets. The teacher does several rounds in our dorm, hoping to catch a voice among us.

Mornings are frightening. Afternoons are frightening and evenings are frightening and sleep is frightening. How can anyone fall asleep? I could not cry from fear. I felt that heaven itself had fallen on top of my chest and that the walls had closed in on my body, pressing harder and harder. I confronted the first 'impossible' in my life. My father's death had represented the impossible without me quite understanding the meaning of impossible. Now my outspokenness was silenced because of this huge pressure, this new fear that descended upon me. I never understood why my mother wanted to construct this deadening loneliness around me. I am behind invisible bars. I am squashed under a low-lying ceiling. This truth stood before me in defiance.

After a week of this routine, I started to cry! My tears cut through my mornings in endless pain. I cried for three continuous days. My nose swelled. Miss Badr called me in to ask what was wrong. I told her that I wanted my mother. I became feverish. The school doctor came to see me. He did not say that I was 'spoiled' as one of the teachers did. Miss Badr warned me that she would tell my mother that my behavior was unsatisfactory. How will my mother know the truth? Maybe her aunt will save me. But she is also frightening like the school. She forbids me to tell my mother about a deep unease that I fail to describe in a letter. At school I cannot complain about my situation to my mother. All the letters that are written on Friday evening in the study room are read by the teachers afterward.

I found myself in an imaginary prison. I wept. I don't know how they allowed me to spend the weekend with my mother's aunt, who scolded me. I felt besieged. I had no one to turn to.

Translated by Samia Mehrez

Edward Said
from *Out of Place*

SCHOOLTEACHERS WERE SUPPOSED TO be English, I thought. Students, if they were fortunate, might also be English or, as in my case, if they were not, not. I attended the Gezira Preparatory School (GPS) from the autumn of 1941 till we left Cairo in May 1942, then again from early 1943 till 1946, with one or two longer Palestinian interruptions in between. During that period I had no Egyptian teachers at all, nor was I conscious of any Arab Muslim presence in the school: the students were Armenians, Greeks, Egyptian Jews, and Copts, as well as a substantial number of English children, including many of the staff's offspring. Our teachers were, to mention the two most prominent, Mrs. Bullen, headmistress, and Mrs. Wilson, the ubiquitous all-purpose general head teacher. The school itself was located in a large Zamalek villa, once intended for living on a grand scale, its main floor now converted into several classrooms, all of which were entered from an enormous central hall with a platform at one end and an imposing entrance portal at the other. The hall was two floors high with a glass ceiling; a balustrade surrounded another set of rooms located directly above our classrooms. I only ventured there once, and not very happily at that. These struck me as secret places where mysterious English meetings took place and where the redoubtable Mr. Bullen, a large red-faced man only rarely glimpsed on the lower floor, might be found.

I had no way of knowing then that Mrs. Bullen, the headmistress, whose daughter Anne was in the class immediately senior to mine, was in Egypt as a school concessionaire who held a franchise to run for the GPS British Council, not as an educator. After the 1952 Free Officers' Revolution the school slowly lost its European cachet and by the 1956 Suez crisis had become something else altogether. Today it is a career language training school for young adults, without a trace of its English past. Mrs. Bullen and her daughter later appeared in Beirut as principals of another English-type school, but they seem to have been even less successful than they were in Cairo, where they were dismissed for inefficiency and Mr. Bullen's drinking habits.

GPS conveniently sat at the end of Sharia Aziz Osman, our relatively short Zamalek street, a walk of exactly three blocks. The time I took to get there or to come home was always an issue with my teachers and parents, associated forever in my mind with two words, 'loitering' and 'fibbing,' whose meaning I learned in connection with my meandering, fantasy-filled traversal of that short distance. Part of the delay was to put off my arrival at either end. The other part was sheer fascination with the people I might encounter, or with glimpses of life revealed as a door opened here, a car went by there, or a scene was played out briefly on a balcony. As my day began at seven-thirty, what I witnessed was invariably stamped with night's end and day's beginning—the black-suited ghaffeers, or evening watchmen, slowly divesting themselves of blankets and heavy coats, sleepy-eyed suffragis shuffling off to market for bread and milk, drivers getting the family car ready. There were rarely any other grown-ups about at that hour, although once in a while I'd see a parent marching along with a GPS child, dressed in our uniform of cap, trousers, and blazer, all in gray with light-blue piping. What I cherished in those dawdling walks was the opportunity to elaborate on the scanty material offered me. A redheaded woman I saw one afternoon seemed—just by walking by—to have persuaded me that she was a poisoner and (I had without specific comprehension heard the word recently) a divorcee. A pair of men sauntering about one morning were detectives. I imagined that a couple standing on a balcony overhead spoke French and had just had a leisurely breakfast with champagne.

. . .

School always began in the big hall with the singing of hymns—"All Things Bright and Beautiful" and "From Greenland's Icy Mountains" were the two that recurred most frequently—accompanied at the piano by omnicompetent Mrs. Wilson and directed by Mrs. Bullen, whose daily homilies were simultaneously condescending and cloying, her bad British teeth and ungenerous lips shaping the words with unmistakable distaste for the mongrel-like collection of children who stood before her. Then we filed into our classes for a long morning's lessons. My first teacher at GPS was Mrs. Whitfield, whom I suspected of being not really English, though she mimicked the part. Besides, I envied her name. Her son, Ronnie (Mrs. Wilson had a son, Dickie, and a daughter, Elizabeth; Mrs. Bullen had Anne, of course), like the Wilson children, was enrolled at GPS; all of them were older than I, and this added to their privileged remoteness and hauteur. Our lessons and books were mystifyingly English: we read about meadows, castles, and Kings John, Alfred, and Canute with the reverence that our teachers kept reminding us they deserved. Their world made little sense to me, except that I admired their creation of the language they used, which I, a little Arab boy, was learning something about. A disproportionate amount of attention was lavished on the Battle of Hastings along with lengthy explanations of Angles, Saxons, and Normans. Edward the Confessor has ever since remained in my mind as an elderly bearded gentleman in a white gown lying flat on his back, perhaps as a consequence of having confessed to something he shouldn't have done. There was never to be any perceived connection between him and me, despite our identical first name.

These lessons in English glory were interspersed with repetitive exercises in writing, arithmetic, and recitation. My fingers were always dirty; then, as now, I was fatally attracted to writing with an ink pen that produced an ugly scrawl, plus numerous smudges and blots. I was made acutely conscious of my endless infractions by Mrs. Whitfield in particular. "Sit up straight and do your work properly"—"Don't fidget," she then added almost immediately. "Get on with your work." "Don't be lazy" was the habitual clincher. To my left Arlette was a model student; to my right it was the ever-obliging and successful Naki Rigopoulos. All around me were Greenvilles, and Coopers, and Pilleys: starchy little English boys and girls with enviably authentic names, blue eyes, and bright, definitive accents. I have no distinct recollection of how I sounded in those days, but I know that it was not English. The odd thing though was that we were all treated as if we should (or really wanted to) be English, an unexceptionable program for Dick, Ralph, and Derek, less so for locals like Micheline Lindell, David Ades, Nadia Gindy, and myself.

All our time outside class was spent in a little enclosed yard completely shut off from Fuad al-Awwal, the bustling main street into which Aziz Osman—our house sat at the bottom left-hand side—ran. Fuad al-Awwal was lined with shops and vegetable stands; it carried a healthy flow of traffic as well as an extremely noisy tram line and occasional public buses. Not only was it distinctly urban and busy, but it welled up from the older parts of Cairo, crossed into Zamalek from Bulaq, traversed the quietly wealthy and smug Gezira island, where we lived, and then disappeared across the Nile into Imbaba, another teeming antithesis to Zamalek, with its quiet tree-lined streets, its foreigners, and its carefully plotted, shopless streets like Sharia Aziz Osman. The GPS's 'playground,' as it was called, constituted a frontier between the native urban world and the constructed colonial suburb we lived, studied, and played in. Before school began we would line up by class in the yard, and then again during recess, lunch, and dismissal. It is a sign of how last-ing was the impression on me made by those exercises that I still remember *left* as the side nearest the school building, *right* as the Fuad al-Awwal side.

We stood there supposedly to be counted and greeted or dismissed: "Good morning, children" or "Good-bye, children." This seemed a polite ritual camouflaging the travails of being in line, where all sorts of unpleasant things took place. Forbidden to utter a word in class except in answer to the teacher's questions, the line was simultaneously a bazaar, auction house, and court, where the most extravagant of offers and promises were exchanged, and where the younger children were verbally bullied by older boys who threat-ened the direst punishment. My particular bane was David Ades, a boy two or three years older than me. Dark and muscular, he was ruthlessly focused on my pens, my pencil box, my sandwiches and sweets, which he wanted for himself, and was fearsomely challenging to everything I was or did. He didn't like my sweaters; he thought my socks were too short; he hated the look on my face; he disapproved of my way of talking. Coming to or leaving the school represented a daily challenge to me, of how to avoid getting caught or way-laid by David Ades, and for the years I was at GPS I was quite successful. But I could never escape him in the class lines, when despite the supervising teacher's presence, pushy, ruffianlike behavior was tolerated and Ades would whisper and mutter his threats and general disapprobation across the row of fidgeting children that kept us mercifully apart.

I have retained two phrases from Ades in my memory. One I parroted for years thereafter, "I promise you"; the other I haven't forgotten, because it frightened me so much when he uttered it: "I'll bash your face after school." Sometimes separately, often together, both were pronounced with fervent, not to say menacing, earnestness, even though it must have been at most a month after he first hurled them at me that I noticed how empty and unfulfilled they both were. Despite its soporific and sometimes repressive class atmosphere, the 'school' that Ades promised to bash my face 'after' protected me from him. His older brother Victor was a famous swimmer and diver who attended English Mission College (EMC) in Heliopolis; I admired his performances at meets around Cairo to which GPS took us, but I never liked the look of him any more than I ever warmed up to David, who would occasionally ask me to play a game of marbles with him.

I tried out both phrases at home—"I promise you" on my sisters, "I'll bash your face after school" in front of a mirror. (I was too timid to use it on a real person.) In the bickering squabbles I had with the two oldest of my younger sisters, "promising" meant trying to get something on loan ("I promise you I'll give it back") or working hard to convince them of some preposterous "fib" I was telling ("I promise you I saw the crazy poisoner with red hair today!") But I was prevented from pronouncing it as much as I wanted by Auntie Melia, who said I should vary its idiotic insincerity and monotony by saying "I assure you" instead.

For some infraction in class when I was eight I was sent out of the room by one of the women teachers (there weren't any males) who never used physical punishment except for a few polite taps of a ruler on our knuckles. The teacher left me outside the door, then summoned Mrs. Bullen, who with a dour expression on her face jostled me along to a staircase leading up from the main hall. "Come along now, Edward. You've got to see Mr. Bullen upstairs!" She went up ahead of me. At the top of the stairs she stopped, placed her hand on my left shoulder, and steered me toward a closed door. "Wait here," she said, and then entered. A moment later she was back, signaling for me to go in; she then closed the door behind me, and I was, for the first and last time in my life, in the presence of Mr. Bullen.

I was instantly frightened of this large, red-faced, sandy-haired and silent Englishman who beckoned me toward him. Not a word passed between us as I approached him slowly where he stood near the window. I remember a blue vest and a white shirt, suede shoes, and a long flexible bamboo stick, something between a riding crop and a cane. I was apprehensive, but I was also aware that having reached this nadir of awfulness I must not break down or cry. He pulled me forward by the back of my neck, which he then forced down away from him so that I was half bent over. With his other hand he raised the stick and whacked me three times on the behind; there was a whistle as the stick cut the air, followed by a muffled pop as it hit me. The pain I felt was less than the anger that flushed through me with every one of Bullen's silently administered strokes. Who was this ugly brute to beat me so humiliatingly? And why did I allow myself to be so powerless, so 'weak'—the word was beginning to acquire considerable resonance in my life—as to let him assault me with such impunity?

That five-minute experience was my sole encounter with Bullen; I knew neither his first name nor anything else about him except that he embodied my first public experience of an impersonal 'discipline.' When the incident was brought to my parents' notice by one of the teachers, my father said to me, "You see, you see how naughty you're becoming. When will you learn?" and there was not in their tone the slightest objection to the indecency of the punishment. Father: "We pay a lot of money for you to go to the finest schools; why do you waste the opportunity so?" as if overlooking how he had in fact paid the Bullens to treat me in this way. Mother: "Edward, why do you always get yourself into trouble like that?"

So I became delinquent, the 'Edward' of punishable offenses, laziness, loitering, who was regularly expected to be caught in some specific unlicensed act and punished by being given detentions or, as I grow older, a violent slap by a teacher. GPS gave me my first experience of an organized system set up as a colonial business by the British. The atmosphere was one of unquestioning assent framed with hateful servility by teachers and students alike. The school was not interesting as a place of learning but it gave me my first extended contact with colonial authority in the sheer Englishness of its teachers and many of its students. I had no sustained contact with the English children outside the school; an invisible cordon kept them hidden in another world that was closed to me. I was perfectly aware of how their names were just *right*, and their clothes and accents and associations were totally different from my own. I cannot recall ever hearing any of them refer to 'home,' but I associated the idea of it with them, and in the deepest sense 'home' was something I was excluded from. Although I didn't like the English as teachers or moral examples, their presence at the end of the street where I lived was neither unusual nor unsettling. It was simply an unremarkable feature of Cairo, a city I always liked yet in which I never felt I belonged.

Ihsan Abdel Quddus

from *I am Free*

AMINA ENROLLED AT THE American University.

She did not know why she chose this particular university. Perhaps because she hated the prospect of being with the Abbasiya youth in the same university and they had all enrolled at Cairo University. Perhaps also because she had no ambition to become a civil servant and was not interested in preparing herself for a particular profession like a lawyer, or a doctor, or a teacher, for she wanted knowledge that would prepare her for life itself. Perhaps she wanted more freedom and she had heard from her friends in al-Dhaher that the American University protects personal freedom from antiquated eastern traditions and from religious discrimination and people's gossip and rumors that surrounded all her actions and perturbed her life.

Her father was not against her enrollment at the American University and he did not bother to find out about the differences between it and the national university. Had he known that the Egyptian state did not recognize the degrees awarded by the American University he may have tried to dissuade her, for he could not imagine that his daughter would attend university for a reason other than becoming a civil servant. But he did not know. The only thing that had occurred to him was that Amina had chosen this university because it was closer to home, so that she could walk back and forth to campus.

Amina took her first steps into the university. She was uncertain, as if she were learning how to swim for the first time. She was afraid of drowning even though she was sure she wouldn't, for the water was shallow and she stood on firm ground.

She tried to act natural as if she were not afraid of drowning, as if she had been liberated of traditional ways that continued to impose a veil of chastity on her face every time she found herself besieged by the gaze of male students she did not know. She would imagine that they were gazing at her lips so her mouth would tremble, or that they were gazing at her cheeks so she would blush, or that they were gazing at her body so she would falter and stumble as if burdened by the weight of their gaze.

She tried to act natural and to look at her male classmates straight in the eye but she couldn't, and so she would peek at them from the corner of her eye when they were unaware of her gaze. She also tried to act natural when she found herself sitting beside a young man in class, almost rubbing shoulders; his leg, if he shifted just a bit, would touch hers. But again she couldn't and she answered his greeting with a whisper, like a slave from the harem greeting the sultan. She didn't look at him again nor did she allow for any further conversation.

On that first day at the university she was something other than herself and what everyone knew about her. She was neither daring nor forward nor stubborn. She felt like a spirit from the ancient east among this foreign milieu into which she had hurled herself, as if she were touring the city of New York: dumbfounded, scared, and hesitant. After a few hours she felt she was suffocating. She was suffocating because of the dress she had spent days preparing for this occasion; she was suffocating because she had tied her hair into a bun since five o'clock in the morning, having filled it with hairpins and small barrettes that weighed her head down so that she had a headache; she was suffocating because of all the decorum she imposed on her every move so that she looked like a puppet. She wanted to be rid of all this and be able to look natural like she was during her al-Saniya schooldays: to be able to speak, laugh, and eat sandwiches.

She saw how the young women mixed with the young men, how they sat in little groups to chat (always in English), how they would lounge on the lawn next to the young men leafing through a book or telling stories with signs of general happiness at the beginning of the academic year. She tried to partake of their happiness but she lacked the courage and tried to conceal her cowardice with a degree of haughtiness and feigned conceit.

No one helped her overcome the alienation that was strangling her, for the young women students were all graduates of the American College for girls and she was the only one from al-Saniya, a national public school for girls. They considered her somewhat strange and perhaps they deliberately ignored her because of her beauty and the kind of threat that represented for them. The new male students, on the other hand, were alienated and intimidated like her and hesitated for long before daring, with God's help, to approach any of the women.

She was brought out of this distress by a voice that called out to her in English from behind as she was strolling on campus:

"Hey you . . . wait!"

Translated by Samia Mehrez

Mohamed Berrada

from *Like a Summer Never to Be Repeated*

HAMMAD GOT TO KNOW the gate of Cairo University, its tall dome, and the chimes of its famous clock on his way to the zoological gardens. He waited longingly for the end of the summer so that he could enter the complex, which symbolized a dream he had entertained since he was a schoolboy in Rabat. He and Barhum had inquired about the names of the teachers, first-year curriculum, and teaching methods, and began preparing for this next difficult stage after they passed the tawjihiya.

The first few weeks were characterized by excitement and eagerness to attend every lecture and visit the library regularly to read reference books. The process of getting to know other students was slow as there was no occasion designed to facilitate it. Hammad and Barhum noticed that the level of beauty among the female students was below average, or approached it with difficulty. There were students from Egypt, Saudi, Jordan, Syria, and Malaysia but communication was almost nonexistent. Each person was like an island. The teaching method of most teachers did not permit students to participate in the discussion or present their thoughts. Hammad remembered how Dr. Shawqi Daif would spend the whole period dictating his lectures on the history of literature, so in the winter term Barhum stopped attending this elementary class and asked Hammad to take notes for him.

Later on, in the third year, the students agreed to ask Dr. Shawqi to set time aside for questions and discussion. He listened to their request, took off his spectacles, was silent for a while, then said that his dictation was the essential foundation and it was up to them to go to the sources and references if they wanted more. As for discussion, it was pointless at this level. He replaced his spectacles and continued dictating. Nevertheless, most students approved of dictation and relied on rote learning to guarantee success. This was the principle followed by the majority of teachers, with the exception of Suhayr al-Qalamawi, Abd al-Hamid Yunus, Shukri Ayyad, and Dr. Ibrahim Hammouda, who taught Qur'an rhetoric and informed the students that he would alternate between dictation and explanation and that they must distinguish between the two processes through the change in his voice. Sometimes he would notice students continuing to write when he was explaining. "Are you writing?" he would shout. "Didn't you notice the change in my tone of voice? Are you an idiot?"

The syllabi were long and their contents did not cover the relationship between literature and life that Hammad and Barhum, who were endeavoring to write short stories and poetry, had hoped to explore. They realized that what concerned them and what they were striving for lay outside the Arabic Language and Literature Department. It was a realm that could be entered via the cafeteria of the College of Arts, where a group of journalists, young writers, and, in particular, beautiful female students from the Sociology or French Literature Departments, would meet. Here leaders from all over the Arab world would come alive and debate, and occasionally literary and art get-togethers were organized to which rising names of the day were invited. Hammad remembered listening to Salah Abd al-Sabbour reciting his poem "I Shall Kill You," which was inspired by the Tripartite Aggression. Here too the talents of the singer Safinaz Kazem, who would perform songs by Fayrouz, were unveiled. Just as the Arabic Language Department was surrounded by an aura of gravity and high 'academic' standards, so the cafeteria of the College of Arts teemed with rebellious voices, questioning and plunging headlong into politics and writing projects. The North African Students' Club was another window onto the literary and intellectual scene in Cairo. Its organizing committee invited Ahmad Abd al-Muti Hijazi to recite poems from *City without a Heart* and the young critic Ragaa al-Naqqash to deliver a lecture on new criticism. The apartment opposite the North African Students' Club was the site of the Modern Egyptian Writers Association, whose president was the late Mustafa al-Sihrati. There Hammad met Naguib Surour, who had returned from the Soviet Union, and invited him to play a game of table tennis.

. . .

Hammad visited Cairo University again in December of 1971. He was living in Paris, preparing his thesis on the critical works of Muhammad Mandour, and needed some sources and to speak to Mandour's wife, the poet Malak Abd al-Aziz. When he entered the university library, he noticed signs of decay and neglect as he examined clippings and moved about the hoards of books and magazines. He visited the Arabic Language Department and inquired about his teachers, and paid his respects to those who were still there. The corridors and classrooms were bustling as usual with all kinds of people. He tried to visualize himself in this space that had so enchanted him as a student. Maybe something had changed deep inside him. Perhaps his experience at the Sorbonne had dampened his passion. Nevertheless, he thought that Cairo University deserved more attention in order to maintain its place in a fast-changing world. He felt a melancholy take hold of him during that visit. Nasser was dead and the Sadat era had begun dubiously, full of speeches and

canny public statements. The anxiety was clear in his friends, who anticipated bad things and predicted that some of the positive accomplishments
of Nasser would be dissolved. They would relate a joke that epitomized the
mindset of 'the leader of believers.' The joke was that at the crossroads the
driver would ask Sadat whether to go left or right. Sadat would ask the driver
which way Nasser had gone. He would reply that he had turned left, so Sadat
would tell him to signal left but turn right.

Miral al-Tahawy
from *The Blue Aubergine*

Two Girls in Block Four at the Women's Hall of Residence

The high building did not inspire either of them to throw themselves off it.
They wanted to but they didn't. The first was unable to because they had only
taught her to look at the world from swings going up and down, and not to fly
or fall. Her name, as you know, was Aubergine, which she had recently short-
ened to the letter *nuun*. The second was putting off suicide for the time being
too, so that she could plait her frizzy hair into rows of little braids and sing
to her lover: "Our souls have been lovers since before the world began." Her
name began with the letter *saad*.

There were other girls in the building, rushing between narrow rooms
with pale yellow walls and bunk beds just wide enough for their dreams.

They can laugh, or cry, or count the number of insects cooked in the
meals, and protect themselves against vomiting with glasses of tea and dry
bread. They can hear the corpulent cleaning ladies arguing and swearing in
the corridors every morning as water smelling of disinfectant swirls in under
the door, and the smoke from burning rubbish outside creeps through cracks
in the windows. The bell for the morning meal rings, and the supervisors
inspect the cleanliness of the bathrooms in a cacophony of stern voices. In
room number 81, block four, of the women's halls of residence, four girls
will share glasses of tea and smile for four long years to come. When they go
out they pass the storerooms, the cafeteria, the telephone booth, the visiting room, and the administration and security offices. Then they encounter
three main doors, which everyone must go through. Once outside, the Nile

is not far away, and the university even nearer, and on the pavement, where other young women are walking, there is enough space for the newcomers to walk alongside.

"N" did not know, as she sat at her papers with a pen in her hand, that when she placed its nib at the start of the road, it would soon get lost in a maze it will take a hundred years to find a way out of. The young man's name was Ziyad. The girl had no name but she could have been called *nuun*, a convex semicircle, like a bowl with a drop falling into it. The first man in her life, panting down the corridor changing the posters on the walls, tapping a rhythm on the bench with other students as he sings bits of songs that are not easy to memorize and that invariably tell of prisons and bathrooms and fresh breezes and glad tidings and the wretched toiling masses. She tries every day to overcome her nervousness. She will open her eyes confidently, she will stretch out her hand to hold his and she will not be afraid. She will lift up her face so he can see how beautiful she is and without shyness or embarrassment she will talk to him about her father, "He was a political activist and spoke like you do about corruption and disappointment." She will tell him that he died, of a hemorrhage, and maybe elicit a pat on the shoulder. She will tell him about the scars on her face, knowing quite well that her eyes are brimming up with the sadness of all her defeats, and hopefully he will hold her face in his hands and say to her as they run along the pavement, "I love you."

But he is always moving quickly, coming and going, and he never gives her the opportunity to say something. He only remembers, after four long years, that she was always there. "You are very pure," he tells her, "which is something generally quite rare, a respectable girl." For four years no one feels she's really there. She digs deep into her innermost self, and is "polite and refined." She regularly practices how to suppress her dreams, and she accustoms her eyes to making those submissive bows and curtsies with which she lives her life, humbly, as they had always wished her to be. She regularly talks to herself about her mistakes and she forgets how speech can sound, because she has been silent for so long. All she sees in the lecture hall is the arrow pointing to the mosque. She weeps and ties back her hair. She lengthens her head covering every day so that no details are revealed. When the din of the lectures subsides, alone she follows the arrow and sits against the wall. The mosque consists of a corner between two walls. To the right is a cafeteria and the smell of coffee drifts over; to the left a narrow passage leads to the women's toilets. A wooden board makes a third corner, and a curtain covers the entrance. There is no one here except herself and another student in a black niqab whom she always notices praying the late morning prayer. After a number of other non-obligatory performances, she sits to read the Qur'an in a low voice. She might speak to her, after finishing her prayers, about the torment of the grave, or the portents of the Day of Resurrection, or give her a book about the evils of women displaying their bodies, or selected passages for morning and evening contemplation. She lengthens her dress, and starts to wear gloves, and becomes too chaste to shake hands or even speak.

. . .

In the lecture room the girl who lives above my bed was ignoring me with a vengeance. This time I sit next to her. I nibble my fingers and tell her how boring it is waiting for the lecturer to arrive. She does not comment. I continue, "The syllabus doesn't really need anyone to explain it." She does not reply. Me again, "Have you summarized any of it?"

She looks at me coldly. Does she know I love him like she does? Does she resent my very existence? I leave her when the boys gather around her and hand out cigarettes, and slap one another's hands at the wisecracks, and drum on the benches and sing songs I don't know the words to. They talk about the revolution and the workers in Kafr al-Dawwar and the Uprising of the Starving, and they swap the latest jokes about caviar and coop chicken.

I say some morning prayers with Maha until the lecturer walks in wearing his smart jacket and brightly colored tie. He takes off his glasses and smiles, "Good morning." He spouts forth on the segregation of roles in society, and digresses into gender differentiation, moves on to class differences, and defines the meaning of justice. She applauds vigorously, then follows him to his office, and everybody sees her sitting opposite him as she takes a cigarette and he lights it. She smiles mysteriously as the smoke twists into the air.

Alia puts the rug down between the two bunks as she leans against the bed and confronts Safaa. I am standing in the middle of the room.

"He's a charlatan," says Alia. "He doesn't know the meaning of anything he says." She objects fiercely, "Ignorance and backwardness are the only things that stop people thinking because then they refuse to accept other ways of looking at the world."

"On what basis do you think he's progressive, Safaa? Because of the cigarette he lit for you?"

"Is the smoking all that bothered you? Even you, Alia, are so narrow-minded?"

"All charlatans talk about justice and freedom and then use it as an excuse for rejecting values."

"Backwardness, backwardness, just a pretense. The true values we need are justice and freedom, not backward ancestral rituals."

"She doesn't think about him and he loves her," I said to Alia. "She's too busy with her progressive professor. She doesn't deserve his toenail." I said it with sorrow and some scorn seeped into the compassion in her eyes. Maha's voice drifted down from the top bunk, humming a sad song.

The girl who shares my bunk plaits her hair like a villager stepping out of a tin bath, and wears clothes from the nineteenth century. They probably belong to her mother who she's always writing letters to. Her headscarf gets longer every day and she opens her mouth with the sanctimonious pomposity of an Azharite in a fez. She sounds like my father when he used to talk about grace, which the Lord protects from fading, slapping my face so hard to teach me good manners and modesty that his handprint glowed red on my cheek. He did not want me getting any ideas into my head about wearing that dress and teasing the neighbor who used to whistle at me in his spare time and blow me kisses.

Our neighbor was the first man to talk to me about Marx and the rotten bourgeoisie and the patriarchal system and sexual freedom. He offered to give me lessons in philosophy and psychology one school year, and then he stuck his hand under the table and Satan took hold of my body. In those days I still feared the Lord who can see us, but I did not believe that patience is the key to the door of Paradise, or that the most beloved of His servants are the poor, or that he who is content in this world shall dwell contented in the hereafter, but he who scorns shall be scorned. The girl who lies on the bed below me is trying to add new chapters to my father's knowledge, "Say, if the people of the villages believe and are pious We shall pour upon them blessings from the heavens." She hung the verse on the door of the room. And she stuffs her talk with the story of Switzerland as a prosperous society where there is a lot of suicide, and the diseases and plagues that afflict rich countries. And she wearies me with her pious mumblings every evening to soothe her pain and apprehension. That's why she was the first one I served the musaqqaʻa. I could see it clearly. I held it up in front of her eyes, a little rat, fried and spiced along with the slices of aubergine in the huge pot they used to feed the thousand mouths in our concentration camp.

"Eat it," I said. "Rats aren't unclean. It's more halal than that force-fed American chicken they don't even pray over when they slaughter it. Go on, eat it."

She held her breath and put her hand over her mouth. I knew she was going to vomit.

Alia took charge of the situation and sent a petition with dozens of signatures. The manager spat into her handkerchief when she saw it, then she swallowed and said, "Praise your Lord that the food is free of charge. People don't have a drop of oil in their homes, or a lump of sugar or even a piece of bread, and you're refusing to eat good food."

We dip bread into dark tea and keep our hunger at bay until we forget. I read some long articles on justice and the revolution, and the distribution of wealth and Marx and Ali Ibn Abi Talib, and I wrote down all the slogans we needed for a great wall poster. Then I slept, with a clear conscience.

Her voice echoes down the corridor:

"I will not allow you to make such vile accusations."

"May I know where you spent the night?"

"With relatives, friends. It's none of your business."

"Yes it is. It's my job. And you don't have any relatives."

"Your job is to make sure I respect other people's rights, not to meddle in my private life."

"You should behave yourself, young woman."

"My behavior is beyond any suspicion, and even if it weren't, it's none of your business. I have a conscience and a mind."

"We don't need any of your wicked behavior here."

The two voices grew louder and I ran out of the room into the corridor, "Forget it, miss." The girl with the braided hair grabs my hand and removes it abruptly from her shoulder. She yells at me, "I haven't done anything wrong for you to have to apologize on my behalf." Alia says exactly what I said to the supervisor and leads Safaa into our room instead of me.

She was not crying. "That supervisor's a bitch pretending to be virtuous," she said. "She picks on whoever she wants." She smoked a lot and threw the stubs next to the bed. Then she took off her clothes without telling us to close our eyes, and wove little plaits in her wet hair. She flicked another stub onto the floor and went out. "Was she with him?" I asked Alia. She did not answer. Maha was saying, "Khalid came round last night. He said he would speak to my mother. I asked him not to. I'd be no good as a wife to anyone."

We could sense tears in her voice, and the echo of her words remained as Alia talked about the kind of love that doesn't exist anymore, and her health and jasmine and death. Then we were all silent for a long time.

Translated by Tony Calderbank

Miral al-Tahawy 159

Khaled Al Khamissi

from *Taxi*

I WAS IN UNIVERSITY Lecturers' City in Saft el-Laban, right behind Cairo University, beyond the railway tracks. The place is a perfect example of Egypt's urban planning, for Saft el-Laban is a village which borders on farmland and, because of the brutal expansion of Cairo, high-rise buildings made of breeze block have parachuted in on the unfortunate village, imports from the cities and the embodiment of disgusting architecture. People from outside have descended on the village and the university lecturers' compound had also landed there from Venus, surrounded by a large wall to prevent the earthlings from entering.

While I was leaving this 'city' (and of course 'city' here means no more than a collection of a few apartment blocks inhabited by people from Venus) towards Saft el-Laban, and after carefully examining the architecture and the inhabitants I realized the extent of the disaster. The place was a real monstrosity of an indeterminate nature. A beautiful woman walked past me wearing a long rustic dress and earrings hanging from her ears. She was headed away from the city, her feet leading her toward a market place that was the dirtiest I have ever seen in my life.

From behind the market there began to appear legions of children coming out of school, a first wave of primary-school girls, all in Islamic headscarves, then a wave of boys all wearing uniforms of faded brown. They passed around me on every side as though I were a disembodied errant spirit, and I felt some tension, although usually the sight of children fills me with delight.

I caught sight of a taxi from the city and I ran toward it to escape, after besmirching my face in this salad bowl of humanity.

"Where would you like to go?" asked the driver.

"Anywhere. Just get me out of here!" I said.

"I'm going in the direction of the university."

"Then go," I said.

The driver did not set off as I had hoped, for the road was packed with dozens of minibuses without number plates, driven by devils of the tarmac. On my right I saw a boy about four years old come up to a slightly older girl and take her hand for her to help him cross the crowded street. He seemed frightened and a part of his uniform was torn. She seemed confident that she could find a way safely through the vehicles with this boy.

I too felt safe and my tension at the chaos subsided.

"See how sweet the kids are?" I said.

"They sure are sweet, but their parents are mad," he said.

"What do you mean?"

"They're mad sending their children to school."

"What do you expect them to do with them?" I said.

"The kids go to school and don't learn a thing. The parents keep on coughing up for private lessons from the age of ten upward. In the end the parents are penniless and the kids don't find jobs. I mean, it's sheer stupidity.

"Then you find those kids filling the streets all day long as you can see, kids going to school, kids coming back from school, petrol and pollution, dirt and noise, for nothing.

"Me personally, and a few of my friends with me, we pulled our kids out of education after primary school, and we save their private lessons money for them. When the boy or the girl reaches 21, we'll give them all the money we would have given to the private tutors. I swear it's better for the kid to start his life with a little money in hand, rather than with some meaningless education, education that didn't teach them anything in the first place.

"Me personally, I say to everyone around me, don't send your kids to school, don't send your kids to school, like it was my only mission in life."

"But my parents," I said, "they spent everything they had on my education and they didn't leave me any money, and through my education I've been able to work and live."

"That was in the old days," said the driver. "That was in the sixties. Today the only motto is 'Get smart, make money,' and for your information 90 percent of people live off business, not from anything else.

"We'll leave our kids some money to open a small shop or a kiosk or as an advance payment on a taxi.

"Today there's no industrial training that's any use or any agricultural training that's any use or any business training. And don't forget that kids, poor things, expect the best and think that they are well and truly educated, when they don't even know how to read. The only thing they learn in school is the national anthem and what good does that do them?"

Translated by Jonathan Wright

The Street Is Ours?

This section brings together a rich selection of representations of Cairenes' moments of uprising, demonstrations, resistance, and protest on the streets of the city. These are juxtaposed against equally detailed representations of consecutive regimes' repression of and violence against Cairenes' lives and freedoms for over more than a century. The tension between public protest and state brutality throughout the twentieth century and beyond is perhaps the explanation for the rhetorical question that makes up the title of this section.

The material in this section posed one of the greatest challenges in the *Literary Life* because of the staggering overabundance of literary representations of public protest, as well as the detailed descriptions of individual and collective experiences of detention, imprisonment, and torture. Indeed, anyone familiar with the general quiet and calm that seemed to dominate Cairo streets during some of the most critical moments in recent Arab history will be struck by the over-representation of iconic scenes of public protest in literary texts of the period. It is as if the constraints that stifle political culture in Egypt on the real street are undone within the imaginary text. The fictional narrative becomes the 'real' arena of contestation and resistance, one that cannot be silenced with batons and tear gas, physical torture and electric shock waves. Given the surplus of representation and remembrance of such moments of protest, one is inclined to say that the near absence of political activism on the street is displaced onto the endless possibilities of the literary world. Hence, we discover multiple representations of the same moment of protest, written over and over again by several writers from very different generations, positions, and backgrounds, who are themselves participants, eyewitnesses, and chroniclers of these moments.

Among such striking examples during the second half of the twentieth century are the Bread Riots of 1977, when Cairenes took to the streets to demonstrate against price hikes, and the demonstrations against the American-led Gulf War in 1991, both captured in many texts from considerably different perspectives. The variety of representations of these moments alone could have made up this entire section and would have provided a fascinating spectrum of histories. However, for the sake of an overall picture of the entire century, many of these excerpts have not been included. What I have tried to preserve, despite the editing, is the highly revealing contrasts that so many of these representations offer. For example, the 1919 revolution and massive demonstrations on the streets of the city are rendered very differently in Naguib Mahfouz's *Palace Walk* and Huda Shaarawi's *Harem Years*. In Mahfouz's text, readers will see only male members of the Abdel Gawwad family involved in the national uprising against the British colonialists while the female characters, Amina, the mother, among them, are given an apathetic, conservative, and politically naive role that is epitomized in Amina's protest against her son Fahmy's hatred of the British occupiers: "Why do you despise them, son? . . . Aren't they people like us with sons and mothers?" Amina's apolitical innocence stands in stark contrast to the militant voice of Huda Shaarawi writing about exactly the same moment of protest: "We women held our first demonstration on 16 March [1919] to protest the repressive acts and intimidation practiced by the British authority." True, Amina is imagined by Mahfouz as a middle-class sequestered housewife, while Huda Shaarawi belonged to cosmopolitan, liberal aristocracy but it is important to register the different chronicles and imaginings of participation in the 1919 revolution. This is but one example of many other sharp contrasts that readers will discover throughout the following excerpts.

One of the most ambiguous moments in these literary representations is the 1952 revolution that brought the Free Officers to power. This is a moment that oscillates between deep suspicion and exaggerated elation depending on the position of the authors and the milieu that they are representing. In Robert Sole's *Birds of Passage*, the Syro-Christian, privileged minority characters, see the Free Officers as "communists—communist and uneducated oafs. They'll send this country to the dogs." But in Idris Ali's *Poor*, the underprivileged, working-class characters hail them as "revolutionaries—and much better than the king and his retinue!"

Just as the excerpts in this section give voice to these multiple positions, they also trace, with equal candor, the shifts that have taken place during the twentieth century and beyond in the very raison d'être of uprising. Whereas texts of the first half of the century provide an archive of slogans against the British colonial powers, texts of the second half of the same century become a record of slogans against consecutive national regimes from those of Nasser to Mubarak, whose decreasing credibility and increasing ruthlessness are viewed as identical to, if not worse than those of the former British occupiers. In Hala El Badry's *A Certain Woman* the main character, trapped in a student demonstration in 1990s against the Mubarak regime, envisions a replay of British brutality against Egyptian demonstrators in 1946, "Would they dare to shoot us, as it happened at Abbas Bridge?" Similarly, the Islamist students of Cairo University demonstrating against the American-led 1991 Gulf War chant:

Rulers, traitors, men of straw!
How much did you sell the Muslims' blood for?

Worse still, in Mona Prince's *Three Suitcases for Departure*, student demonstrators against the Gulf War at Ain Shams University are suspended and accused of "high treason" and are told by the president of the university, "You deserve death, not suspension."

While the motives of protest in the first half of the century were primarily nationalist and political in nature, demonstrations during the second half of the century predominantly trumpet economic frustrations and discontent even when motivated initially by political circumstances, both local and regional. In Mahmoud Al-Wardani's *Heads Ripe for Plucking*, demonstrators during the 1977 Bread Riots denounce President Sadat's outrageous, extravagant lifestyle, given the increasing impoverishment of the people and the sudden hike in prices:

He dresses like a bridegroom
While we sleep ten to a room.

However, the turn of the twenty-first century has witnessed accelerated movements of protest against the regime's internal and external policies, especially in the wake of the American Invasion of Iraq, as well as the Israeli occupation of Palestinian cities of the West Bank and Gaza that were marked by renewed massive protests by the Egyptian youth from across the ideological and socioeconomic divide. One very striking aspect of this renewed youth involvement is captured in Palestinian poet, Mourid Barghouti's autobiographical text, *Checkpoints*, where privileged American University (AUC) students, led by Barghouti's own son, Tamim, break all the stereotypes that had for long framed them as indifferent, spoilt, affluent, and alienated youth and spearhead Cairo's largest demonstration against the American invasion of Iraq, successfully seizing Tahrir Square, the state's most well-guarded bastion in the heart of downtown Cairo.

The hot summer of 2005 marked a historic mobilization of civil society organizations and groups from across the political and civic spectrum under the general umbrella of the "Egyptian Movement for Change," all primarily demanding the end of Mubarak's rule and opposing the possible succession of his son, Gamal. These protest movements have been followed in recent years by regular and sustained sit-ins in front of Parliament by various sectors of disgruntled, impoverished, and severely underpaid civil servants whose long overdue and legitimate demands have largely been ignored when not simply silenced by the ever-ready brute force of national security. These successive sit-ins have been marked by new creative forms of public protest that have captured nationwide, if not worldwide, attention, announcing a real shift in the practice of political culture on the streets of the city. They remain too raw, however, to have surfaced in the literary texts but it will certainly not be long before they are represented.

Just as the forms of political protest have changed over the century, so, too, have the state's diabolical methods of repression and torture. The magnitude of human rights violations is carefully and movingly recorded in many of the excerpts in this section, where the writers, themselves victims of these violations in many instances, expose the lawlessness of the state's detention practices through the experiences of their respective narrators. Latifa al-Zayyat, Nawal El Saadawi, Sonallah Ibrahim, and Sharif Hatatah are but a handful of Egyptian writers whose prison narratives have engraved these silenced horrors onto a collective memory. In particular, Sonallah Ibrahim's *The Smell of It*, considered *the* cult text of the 1960s, aired the "smell" of political repression in a new literary language characterized by a bareness that violated the complacent and complicit literary standards of the time. Despite the fact that the text was immediately banned, it continued to be published outside Egypt and was circulated throughout the Arab world and beyond, confirming the author's own statement, in a belated introduction to the complete Moroccan edition of 1986, in which he considered the text's survival despite its banning "a lesson to be heeded by the state apparatus in the Arab world" and a challenge to the "familiar scissors which cut all that might trouble the sensitive feelings of the readers."

The details of detention, humiliation and torture that may have shocked the readers of the sixties become even more nightmarish when graphically and bluntly represented in Hamdy el-Gazzar's turn of the twenty-first-century text *Secret Pleasures*. Here readers witness the Internet torture scene of a young woman at the hands of a mercilessly sadistic police officer who derives sexual pleasure from her increasing physical pain and humiliation. All these accounts of violence and repression take place within closed spaces, behind closed doors, in police stations and detention sites, all hidden from public view and only recently documented thanks to mobile phone cameras. What is horrifyingly new in the state's human rights violations is that they are now committed in public, shamelessly, deliberately, for everyone to witness, and be warned. The most shocking instance of such public state brutality was the beating to death of twenty-eight-year-old Khaled Said at the hands of two undercover policemen in Alexandria on June 11, 2010. Khaled's completely disfigured face and his final plea to the ruthless murderers "Please leave me, I'm going to die!" mobilized thousands of Egyptians all over the country, who took to the streets to denounce state violence and declare him the first martyr of the renewed Emergency Law. The campaign in solidarity with Khaled Said's family and against state violation of human rights and freedoms culminated, after a whole century of state torture and oppression, in the most depressingly eloquent slogan that flew over the Internet and was enacted by thousands of young Egyptians, including the residents of Cairo:

Iddi dahrak li-l-shariʿ (Give your back to the street)

Naguib Mahfouz

from *Palace Walk*

"ENGLAND PROCLAIMED THE PROTECTORATE of its own accord without asking or receiving permission from the Egyptian nation. It is an invalid protectorate with no legal standing. In fact, it was one of those things necessitated by the war and should end now that the war has ended."

Fahmy dictated these words, one at a time, deliberately and in a clear voice, while his mother, Yasin, and Zaynab followed this new dictation exercise Kamal was tackling. He concentrated his attention on the words without understanding anything he wrote down, whether he got it right or not. It was not unusual for Fahmy to give his younger brother a lesson in dictation or some other subject during the coffee hour, but the topic seemed different, even to the mother and Zaynab.

Yasin looked at his brother with a smile and remarked, "I see these ideas have gained control of you. Has God not inspired you with any dictation for this poor boy except this nationalist address that could get a person thrown into prison?"

Fahmy quickly corrected his brother, "It's an address Sa'd gave in front of the occupation forces in the Legislative and Economic Assembly."

Yasin asked with interest and astonishment, "How did they reply?"

Fahmy said passionately, "Their answer hasn't come yet. Everyone's anxiously and apprehensively wondering what it will be. The speech was an outburst of anger in the face of a lion not known for restraint or justice." He sighed with bitter exasperation and continued, "This angry outburst was inevitable after the Wafd Delegation was prevented from making their journey and Rushdi resigned as Prime Minister. Sultan Ahmad Fuad disappointed our hopes when he accepted the Prime Minister's resignation."

Fahmy hurried to his room, returning with a piece of paper, which he unfolded. He presented it to his brother and said, "The speech isn't all I've got. Read this handbill, which has been distributed secretly. It contains the letter from the Wafd Delegation to the Sultan."

Yasin took the handbill and began to read:

"Your Majesty,

"The undersigned, members of the Egyptian Wafd Delegation, are honored to represent the Nation by presenting these concerns to Your Majesty:

"Since the belligerents agreed to make the principles of freedom and justice the basis for the peace treaties and announced that peoples whose status had been altered by the war would be consulted about self-government, we have taken upon ourselves an effort to liberate our country and to defend its case at the Peace Conference. Since the traditionally dominant power has disappeared from the arena and since our country, with the dissolution of Turkish sovereignty over it, has become free of every claim against it, and since the Protectorate, which the English proclaimed unilaterally without any agreement from the Egyptian nation, is invalid and merely one of the necessities of war, which ends with the end of the war, based on these circumstances and the fact that Egypt has suffered as much as could be expected of her while serving in the ranks of those claiming to protect the freedom of small nations, there is nothing to prevent the Peace Conference from acknowledging our political freedom pursuant to the principles it has adopted as its foundation.

"We submitted our request to travel to your Prime Minister, His Excellency Husayn Rushdi Pasha. He promised to assist us, confident that we expressed the views of the Nation as a whole. When we were not permitted to travel and were confined within the borders of our country by a tyrannical force with no legal authority, we were prevented from defending the cause of this distressed nation. When His Excellency the Prime Minister was unable to bear the responsibility for retaining his post while the will of the people was obstructed, he resigned along with his colleague His Excellency Adli Yeken Pasha. Their resignations were welcomed by the people, who honored these men and acknowledged the sincerity of their nationalism.

"People believed that these two men in their noble stand in defense of liberty had a powerful ally in Your Majesty. Therefore no one in Egypt expected that the final solution to the question of the journey of the Wafd Delegation would have been acceptance of the resignation of the two ministers, which will further the purposes of those desiring to humiliate us and strengthen the obstacle placed in the path of the delivery of the Nation's plea at the Conference. It also makes it appear that we consent to the perpetuation of foreign rule over us.

"We know that Your Majesty may have been forced for dynastic consideration to accept the throne of your illustrious father when it became vacant on the death of your late brother Sultan Hasan, but the Nation, for its part, believed that when you accepted this throne during a temporary, invalid protectorate for those dynastic considerations, you would not be deterred from working for the independence of your country. Resolution of the problem by accepting the resignation of the two ministers who demonstrated their respect for the will of the Nation is impossible to reconcile with the love for the good of your country to which you are naturally disposed or with your respect for the wishes of your subjects. Therefore, people have been amazed that your advisers have not sided with the Nation at this critical time. That is what is requested of you, O wisest of the descendants of our great liberator Muhammad Ali, so that you will be the mainstay in the achievement of the Nation's independence, no matter what the cost to you. Your zeal is too lofty to be limited by the circumstances. How did it escape the attention of your advisers that Rushdi Pasha's resignation guarantees that no patriotic Egyptian will agree to replace him? How did it escape them that a cabinet dedicated to programs contrary to the wishes of the people is destined to fail?

"Pardon, Your Majesty, if our intervention in this affair seems inappropriate. In other circumstances perhaps it would be, but the matter has now gone beyond consideration of any concern other than the good of the Nation, of which you are the faithful servant. Our Sovereign holds the highest position in the country and therefore holds the greatest responsibility for it. The greatest hopes are placed in him. We will not be misrepresenting our advice to him if we implore him to take into account the views of his Nation before reaching a final decision regarding the current crisis. We affirm to His Majesty that there is no one among his subjects, from one end of the country to the other, who does not seek independence. Obstruction of the Nation's request is a weighty responsibility which Your Majesty's advisers did not consider with the necessary care. Therefore, our duty to serve our country and our loyalty to Our Sovereign have compelled us to bring to the attention of His Majesty the feelings of his Nation, which hopes fervently for independence now and greatly fears what the agents of the colonial party may do to it. The Nation has a right, which it seeks to exercise, for its sovereign to be angry when it is angry and for him to side with it. This is the goal the Nation has chosen. . . . And God is capable of granting that. . . ."

Yasin raised his head from the handbill. There was an astonished look in his eyes and his heart pounded with a new excitement. He shook his head and exclaimed, "What a letter! . . . I doubt I would be able to send anything like that to the headmaster of my school without being severely punished."

Fahmy shrugged his shoulders disdainfully and said, "The matter has now gone beyond consideration of any concern other than the good of the Nation." He repeated the words from memory, just as they appeared in the handbill.

Yasin could not keep himself from laughing. He observed, "You've memorized the handbill. . . . but that doesn't surprise me. You seem to have been waiting all your life for a movement like this in order to throw your whole heart into it. Although I may share your feelings and hopes, I'm not happy about your holding on to this handbill, especially after the cabinet has resigned and martial law has been proclaimed."

Fahmy said proudly, "I'm not just keeping it. I'm distributing it as much as I can."

Yasin's eyes widened in astonishment. He started to speak, but the mother spoke first. She said with alarm, "I can scarcely believe my ears. How can you expose yourself to danger when you're such an intelligent person?"

Fahmy did not know how to answer her. He felt the awkwardness of the situation his recklessness had created. Nothing could be more difficult for him than discussing this matter with her. He was closer to the heavens than he was to convincing her that he had a duty to expose himself to danger for the sake of the nation. In her eyes, the nation was not worth the clipping from his fingernail. The expulsion of the English from Egypt seemed easier to him than persuading her of the necessity of expelling them or inducing her to hate them. Whenever the subject came up in a conversation she would remark quite simply, "Why do you despise them, son? . . . Aren't they people like us with sons and mothers?"

Fahmy would reply sharply, "But they're occupying our country."

She would sense the bitter anger in his voice and fall silent. There would be a veiled look of concern in her eyes that would have said if it could have spoken, "Don't be like that."

Once when he was exasperated by her reasoning, he had told her, "A people ruled by foreigners has no life."

She had replied in astonishment, "But we're still alive, even though they've been ruling us for a long time. I bore all of you under their rule. Son, they don't kill us and they don't interfere with the mosques. The community of Muhammad is still thriving."

The young man had said in despair, "If our master, Muhammad, were alive, he would not consent to being ruled by the English."

She had responded sagaciously, "That's true, but what are we compared to the Prophet, peace and blessings on him? . . . God sent His angels to assist him."

He had cried out furiously, "Sa'd Zaghlul will do what the angels used to."

She had raised her arms as though trying to fend off an irresistible calamity and shouted, "Ask your Lord's forgiveness. O God, Your mercy and forgiveness!"

That was what she was like. How could he answer her now that she had realized the danger threatening him because he was distributing the handbill?

All he could do was resort to lying. Pretending to dismiss the matter lightly, he said, "I was just joking. There's nothing for you to be alarmed about."

The woman spoke again entreatingly, "This is what I believe, son. How I would hate for my hopes in the person with the best sense of all to be disappointed. . . . And what business of ours are these affairs? If the pashas think the English should be expelled from Egypt, let them expel the English themselves."

Throughout the conversation, Kamal had been trying to remember something important. When the conversation reached this point, he shouted, "Our Arabic language teacher told us yesterday that nations gain their independence through the decisive actions of their sons."

The mother cried out in annoyance, "Perhaps he meant big pupils. Didn't you tell me once that some of the other pupils already have mustaches?"

Kamal asked innocently, "Isn't my brother Fahmy a big pupil?"

His mother replied with unaccustomed sharpness, "Certainly not! Your brother's not an adult. I'm amazed at that teacher. How could he have succumbed to the temptation of discussing something with you that wasn't part of the lesson? If he really wants to be a nationalist, he should address such talk to his sons at home, not to other people's children."

This conversation would have grown progressively more heated had not a chance remark intervened to change its direction. Zaynab wanted to gain her mother-in-law's approval by supporting her. She attacked the teacher and called him "a despicable mosque student to whom the government gave a responsible position despite the changing times."

The moment the mother heard this insult aimed at students in Islamic universities like al-Azhar, she was distracted from her former concerns. She refused to let the remark slip by unchallenged, even though it had been said to support her. She turned to Zaynab and said calmly, "Daughter, you are disparaging the best thing about him. The religious shaykhs carry on the work of God's messengers. The man is to be blamed for exceeding the boundaries of his noble calling. He should have contented himself with being a student at a mosque and a religious scholar."

Yasin was not blind to the secret behind his stepmother's change of direction. He quickly intervened to erase the bad impression left by his wife's innocent remark.

Translated by William M. Hutchins and Olive E. Kenny

Huda Shaarawi

from Harem Years

WE WOMEN HELD OUR first demonstration on 16 March [1919] to protest the repressive acts and intimidation practiced by the British authority. In compliance with the orders of the authority we announced our plans to demonstrate in advance but were refused permission. We began to telephone this news to each other, only to read in *al-Muqattam* that the demonstration had received official sanction. We got on the telephone again, telling as many women as possible that we would proceed according to schedule the following morning. Had we been able to contact more than a limited number of women, virtually all the women of Cairo would have taken part in the demonstration.

On the morning of 16 March, I sent placards to the house of the wife of Ahmad Bey Abu Usbaa, bearing slogans in Arabic and French painted in white on a background of black—the color of morning. Some of the slogans read, "Long Live the Supporters of Justice and Freedom," others said "Down with Oppressors and Tyrants," and "Down with Occupation."

We assembled according to plan at the Garden City Park, where we left our carriages. Having agreed upon our route and carefully instructed the young women assigned to carry the flags and placards in front, we set out in columns toward the legation of the United States and intended to proceed from there to the legations of Italy and France. However, when we reached Qasr al-Aini Street, I observed that the young women in front were deviating from the original plan and had begun to head in the direction of *Bait al-Umma* (The House of the Nation), as Saad Zaghlul's house was called. I asked my friend Wagida Khulusi to find out why we were going toward Saad Pasha's house and she returned saying that the women had decided it was a better route. According to our first plan we were to have ended our demonstration there. Reluctantly I went along with this change. No sooner were we approaching Zaghlul's house than British troops surrounded us. They blocked the streets with machine guns, forcing us to stop along with the students who had formed columns on both sides of us.

I was determined the demonstration should resume. When I advanced, a British soldier stepped toward me pointing his gun, but I made my way past him. As one of the women tried to pull me back, I shouted in a loud voice, "Let me die so Egypt shall have an Edith Cavell" (an English nurse shot and killed by the Germans during the First World War, who became an instant martyr). Continuing in the direction of the soldiers, I called upon the women to follow. A pair of arms grabbed me and the voice of Regina Khayyat rang in my ears. "This is madness. Do you want to risk the lives of the students? It will happen if the British raise a hand against you." At the thought of our unarmed sons doing battle against the weaponry of British troops, and of the Egyptian losses sure to occur, I came to my senses and stopped still. We stood still for three hours while the sun blazed down on us. The students meanwhile continued to encourage us, saying that the heat of the day would soon abate. Some of the students departed for the legations of the United States, France, and Italy, announcing that the British had surrounded the women in front of Saad Pasha's house. I did not care if I suffered sunstroke—the blame would fall upon the tyrannical British authority—but we stood up to the heat and suffered no harm. The British also brought out Egyptian soldiers with sticks.

. . .

The women rebuked the soldiers. Some were moved to the point of tears. Eventually Russell Pasha arrived. "You have conducted your demonstration in defiance of orders. Now that you have done what you set out to do you are requested to return home." I answered, "We read in *al-Muqattam* yesterday that the authorities had granted permission for the demonstration. Why do you now stand in our way?" He replied that permission had not been granted and the news was false. Yielding in the face of force, we made our way to our carriages. After departing from the scene we called on some of the foreign legations to inform them of events and to register protest against the Protectorate (imposed by the British in 1914) and martial law. We received courtesy but nothing more. Before returning home we promised to hold another demonstration.

Translated by Margot Badran

Latifa al-Zayyat
from *The Open Door*

LAYLA'S DOOR FLEW OPEN and in rushed Mahmud, still in his outdoor clothes. "You're just sitting here, when the whole city's boiling over?!" Layla, well aware of her brother's tendency to exaggerate, just smiled and gave her legs a little shake. "Boiling over with what?"

"The government's gone and cancelled the treaty, the '36 Treaty."

As she jumped to her feet she could feel the blood rushing hotly into her face. "You're joking!"

"Turn on the radio and you'll hear it for yourself!"

She shot into the front room, intent on switching on the radio, but as she passed her brother she stopped with a sudden impulse to fling her arms around him and give him a kiss. But she turned aside as an abrupt shyness came over her, and merely gave him an embarrassed smile.

She could not get to sleep that night. Her whole body pulsed with excitement as she lay on her back, wide awake, as if awaiting something that she was sure would happen.

The next morning Layla was late getting to school. The bell was already ringing as she arrived. Passing through the main entrance, her demeanor stiffened, as if she were in wary anticipation of some particular event. As she glanced round, though, her features relaxed and she took off at a run. The bell was still ringing, but the pupils had not yet formed themselves into the usual line. Girls were scattered in small knots across the courtyard, and she began to flit from one group to another in some confusion, without knowing why she did so. The words that flew into her ears tumbled directly into her heart; a shiver that began in her feet ran all the way up her body, until it came to concentrate in her head, leaving a prickly feeling down to the ends of her hair.

"Bring down the girls who've gone up to the classrooms! No, no work today, none of the girls will work." "Aliya, go see about the first-year girls, reassure them if they're scared." "Scared? They're all fired up!" "Yes, they're even bolder and braver than the older girls." "We're every bit as ready as the boys are." "Girls, girls—girls have just as many feelings about it all!" "We have to show what we feel!"

The bell rang and rang, supervisors and teachers clapped their hands, but the girls remained scattered in their little groups. Layla found her own friends.

"Come on over here, Sitt Layla!" called out Adila. "Come see your cousin, she doesn't want to go!"

Layla looked astonished. "Go? Go where?"

"The demonstration, of course."

"You're all going out there, to join a demonstration?"

"Of course we're going. The whole city's jumping with excitement, all the schools will join in, why shouldn't we show how we feel, too?"

Discussion stopped suddenly as the headmistress appeared in the courtyard, but the bell went on ringing, its shrill urgency outdoing all. The small groups fell together into a single, huge, human mass, each knot of girls bolstering the next, and the shouting rose.

"Down with imperialism! We want weapons—weapons!"

The headmistress approached the microphone. Woman's job was motherhood, she said. Woman's place was in the home, she said. Weapons and fighting were for men.

A stifling silence fell heavily over them, but just for a moment. A dark figure, her short curls bouncing, her shoulders wide and firm, broke the ranks. Her black eyes shone as she crossed the yard and mounted the four steps that divided the students from the headmistress. She stood in front of the woman. Her voice shook as it came through the microphone.

"Our esteemed headmistress says that woman belongs in the home and man belongs in the struggle. I want to say that when the English were killing Egyptians in 1919 they didn't distinguish between women and men. And when the English stole the Egyptians' freedom they didn't distinguish between men and women. And when they plundered the livelihood of so many Egyptians, they didn't stop to think whether *that* belonged to men or to women."

Yells went up from the crowd, and students skittered about, hugging each other. As the voices rose they became one, "Down with the English! Weapons, weapons—we want weapons!"

The headmistress stepped back.

"She's great!" Layla said to her friend Sanaa.

"Yeah, that's true toughness. Could you do something like that?"

Layla laughed as she closed her eyes and tried to imagine herself in such a situation. "I wish." Then, a moment later, "What's her name?"

"Samia Zaki. She's in her prep year, science division."

By unspoken agreement Samia was now the leader, and the pupils followed her to the school's main gate. Samia pounded on it and the girls followed her example, but it remained tightly shut. The rhythmic slogans stopped as the would-be demonstrators broke up into groups, gesturing, shouting to each other. But all grew quiet as they heard a muffled commotion in the distance. They listened as it rose gradually into a deafening shout. One girl took the steps at a run.

"It's the boys—the students from Khedive Ismail School."

The girls gathered again into one mass and the shouts rose again in unison, slogans batted back and forth from the boys outside to the girls inside and back again. "No more imperialism!" "Down with the agents of imperialism!" "Weapons, weapons—we want weapons!" "We'll die so Egypt lives forever!" The girls hammered harder and harder on the gate and one of the boys climbed up the school wall. "Get away from the gate," he called. The girls drew back and the gate began to give way under a succession of blows from outside.

. . .

The boys stepped back to clear a space for the girls, who pushed forward to take the lead in the procession. The boys fell in behind them. On either side of Khayrat Street passersby stopped and gathered, the owners of the little shops along the street emerged to watch, and so did the children who peopled the side streets. Faces filled the windows above the street, and balconies were crammed with watching figures. Layla walked on, staring round, fear vying with embarrassment to assail her. She was afraid someone she knew would catch sight of her; she felt an embarrassed shyness about her full body and was sure that every pair of eyes on the street was focusing on her. The rhythmic yells surged like waves and abated, the first wave chased by a second, the pair coming together into one swell. Applause, the watching women's trilling zagharid, all of those hands waving, hundreds of eyes sparkling, bodies everywhere, rising and falling in mad leaps. Mouths open wide to shout, drops of sweat glinting on a broad forehead, feet pounding, flags and banners fluttering, tears streaming down, and always the pushing, the pushing, on and on.

Blood pulsed into Layla's head and she felt a surge of energy. She felt alive, at once strong and weightless, as if she were one of those birds circling above. She pushed through the lines and found herself scrambling onto classmates' shoulders, heard herself calling out with a voice that was not her own. It seemed a voice that summoned her whole being, that united the old Layla with her future self and with the collective being of these thousands of people—faces, faces as far as she could see. Then that new voice was lost, caught up in thousands of others, and she slipped down from her perch.

A pair of eyes was drawing her, staring in mute insistence, in an unyielding appeal that enveloped her, to stifle the wells of strength in her body and spirit. She kept moving forward but she felt the eyes follow her with unabated pressure, as if they were aimed at the back of her neck. Layla saw herself at home, at the dinner table, her father's face darker than usual, twisted in anger, his hand out threateningly, her mother's paled lips. A fierce shudder ran through her body and at once her legs felt as though they would collapse. She whipped around. She saw her father. Yes, he was standing there, in that spot where she thought she had seen him, on the pavement at Lazoghli Square, next to the café. Even from here she could see his teeth as he chewed furiously on his lower lip.

Behind her the crowd pushed forward without mercy, pushing her further from her father, his face very dark indeed, and away from the image of her mother, her lips even paler now. Her father vanished from sight and she saw only the crowd of thousands, and herself melting into the whole. Everything around her was propelling her forward, everything, everyone, surrounding her, embracing her, protecting her. She began all of a sudden to shout again, in that voice that belonged to someone else, a voice that joined her whole self to them all.

Layla's father was still chewing on his lip as he opened the door. He opened it silently, impassively. He was equally cool as he closed it. Only then did he bring out the slipper concealed behind his back. He tried to throw her to the floor but her mother slipped between them. He pushed his wife away and she stood motionless to one side, her lips quivering. He yanked off Layla's shoes and against her feet sounded the slap of the hard slipper. As it hit against her legs and then her back, Layla could hear that slap mingling with the sound of a woman's laugh on the stairs outside, the screaming of a newborn, and her mother's choked sobbing. She heard her father's voice, shouting at her mother—"shut up!"—and again, the crack of the slippers, one blow after another, a momentary silence between each, a pause, suppressed breathing, then the slap ringing out again. Then there was the rustle of her book bag as she dragged it across the tiles, the squeak of teeth on leather as she clenched the bag in her mouth, her father's steps receding, the sharp sound of his door slamming, her mother's steps coming near, the sensation of her hands punctured by the iciness of the floor tiles as she crawled on hands and feet to her room.

Inside, she braced herself and got to her feet in time to close the door in her mother's face. She turned the key in the lock. She dragged her feet across to the chair that faced the bed and collapsed onto it. She seemed unable to breathe; she put her hand to her neck. She stood up slowly and practically ran across the room, whispering, "Where can I go? I can't possibly stay here." As if blinded, she knocked into her bed, the wardrobe, the chair. Her mother was knocking on the door, tapping, tapping, lightly.

Translated by Marilyn Booth

Ahmad Hussein

from And Cairo Burned

THE ANGER OF THE crowds in Abdin Square rose to a boiling point in response to the scope of the celebrations and the number of orchestras that were playing in the square and inside the palace.

The army trucks, big and small, filled with officers, could be seen as they started to assemble in the square. The excitement of the crowds increased. The sight of the impressive army officers in their uniforms was like a matador's red cloth that fuelled the raging bull whenever its excitement subsided.

People started booing every army truck that arrived. The booing turned to slander.

"Long live the martyrs of the police force!"

"Aren't you ashamed of yourselves?"

"Is this the only thing you're good at?"

The people chanted the well-known and cherished slogans:

"Death to the traitors! Death to the British!"

"We want weapons . . . we want weapons!"

"To the Canal . . . to the Canal!"

By the afternoon, the huge square was packed and there was no more space for more people. Like a lake whose waves have risen and overflowed on its sides creating running streams, so the dense crowds poured from the square into downtown Cairo, chanting loudly in front of the foreigners, the news agencies, and the foreign consulates. Soon, the heart of Cairo was transformed into a human block: students, workers, police officers, and Free Officers.

The ground began to shake under their feet and the weather itself seemed to change from the impact of the heated breath of hundreds of thousands of angry citizens. One gaze from among the thousands fell upon a distasteful scene: a senior army officer in uniform publicly drinking alcohol on the terrace of Casino Opera. The voice of the beholder addressed the senior officer, saying, "Not only are you cowardly and incapable of resistance, but worse you sit and get drunk as you watch the bodies of the martyrs!"

The senior officer replied in anger, "Shut up, you ill-mannered scoundrel! I am free to do whatever I want."

The 'ill-mannered scoundrel' rushed toward the officer, whose chest and shoulders were decked with military medals. The crowds did not have time to realize what had happened until the tables of Casino Opera started flying about and breaking in mid air. Moments later flames of fire began to eat at the Casino's wooden walls and its glass façade, fuelled by the bottles of alcohol and the wall paper, the wooden decor and the stage curtain.

The crowds went wild with joy as the flames rose in the air, devouring everything in their path, while the black smoke collected in the sky above the square. The fire was coming out of their very chests, burning everything that had troubled them throughout the past weeks since the resistance battle that had started at the Suez Canal where martyrs had fallen in Ismailiya, Suez, Port Said, and al-Tall al-Kabir while these nightclubs were packed with their good-for-nothing clientele.

The neighboring shop-owners dashed off to the main fire station that was only some meters away from the Casino for help. The firemen and the soldiers dragged their feet and started whispering among themselves. Were they not part of the police force that had been attacked a day ago? Were they not part of the wounded people, were they not human beings of flesh and blood, with emotions and feelings? Today was a day of anger and the expression of that anger. Why were they not showing anger, dragging their feet like that when danger was but footsteps away and Casino Opera itself was in flames?

Finally the firemen arrived and unhurriedly started setting up their hoses. The water gushed forth forcefully, battling the flames.

Someone yelled, "Cut the hoses . . . cut the hoses!"

The crowds rushed to cut the hoses.

The policemen stood by and watched what was happening without lifting a finger, and the firemen were not upset that their hoses had been ripped apart. The pressure of the water fizzled and made puddles of water on the ground. The crowds were elated, with a sense of pride and victory.

"Death to the traitors!"

"Long live the people with the police force!"

"Long live the people with the fire brigade!"

"To Cinema Rivoli, to the English House!"

It seemed like the crowds had been transformed into an automated machine: anyone could press a button and make it work.

Minutes later, Cinema Rivoli was in ruins and the head of the secret police, General Ibrahim Allam, stood watching the scene without lifting a finger to protect or save the movie theater.

The flames spread to Suleiman Pasha Street: the À l'Américaine, Cinema Metro, Cinema Miami.

The owners of the movie theaters and the neighboring shops screamed, "Where is the police force? Where is the government?"

They ran away to save their skin in fear of the wild, angry people. . . .

Shukri was horrified at what he saw as he approached the edge of the city and stopped his car. Impossible to believe! It must be a nightmare and not reality. He was seeing something more like what he saw in the movies that represented the burning of Rome, London, or San Francisco.

Would this be the fate of Cairo?

They had always dreamed of a popular uprising, of a people's protest, but they had never imagined that this would be translated into the seizure and burning of the people's institutions and the country's capital. . . .

The thick smoke started blocking his nostrils, and heaviness filled his chest; the signs of horror increased as he approached the heart of Cairo: a lot of hustle and bustle, groups and scattered people running without control, cars, cattle and individuals carrying goods and furniture, a mix of necessities and needs.

Shukri sought an explanation: is it collective migration or are these stolen goods and merchandise? Shukri became depressed. These must be stolen goods without a doubt.

The number of cars loaded with such goods increased. But another kind of cars started to clog the street on their way out of Cairo. They were foreigners, pashas, notables, all trying to save their skin.

"No, this is not the Cairo I left last night. This is not at all the beautiful, dazzling bride. This is not even angry, restless Cairo. This is a wild Cairo that has lost its mind and is trying to kill itself."

When he was finally at the edge of Cairo in Mahatta Square the tragedy became clearer before his eyes: scattered flames lit the sky and danced on the horizon. As for the square itself and Ibrahim Street that had been dark and deserted, they were both clogged with suffocating smoke that became more eerie as ghost-like figures started to emerge, here and there, repeating as they ran:

"The army is on the streets . . . the army is on the streets!"

Translated by Samia Mehrez

Idris Ali

from *Poor*

July
1952
The Tanks

THE SAME TANKS THAT filled the streets during the January fires amass again to occupy strategic sites, including the royal palace in Abdin Square where you used to play, back when the crown prince Ahmad Fouad was born. Like the fires, another puzzle. They call them the 'Free Officers.' The 'Blessed Revolution.' You've been curious ever since the bookseller told you about the Russian Revolution and how it came about and who led it. Here, the revolution springs up while everyone is fast asleep. Like all children, you cheer on Muhammad Naguib and you play with paper, folding it to make the king's face look squashed, then unfolding it so it looks like four pigs. Still, you're confused by what is happening. You go to the book-seller who greets you cheerfully, "It's happened, boy!"

"Is this the revolution?"

"They beat us to it, but we share the same interests and there are comrades among their ranks."

He tells you their names and begins to explain to you the steps that this promising future will take. The shantytown of Turguman will turn into rows of clean homes. There will be food in every mouth, a job for every citizen. Mosques and churches will be converted into schools and hospitals. Eventually, Egypt will become heaven.

The company employees feel the same joy, and so does your father. But the foreman is distressed by the depression that has come over the pasha. One of the junior employees leads a campaign to support the revolution and, in contrast to the others who express their satisfaction in low whispers, he begins to raise his voice. Fouad al-Shami informs the pasha about what the employee was doing and the man is fired. Other employees intercede on his behalf, because he was poor and supported his father. The bodyguard tells them angrily, "We come here to work. To be productive. We're not here to shout slogans. I won't allow anyone to waste work time with idle talk."

Talk about the revolution may have died down at the company out of fear of Fouad al-Shami and the pasha, but the patrons at the café across the way never stop their loud discussions. Supporters versus opponents. And all the while the radio blasts uninterrupted reports. One person they called a Wafdist leads the opposition, "Listen people: these guys are soldiers, they know nothing about politics or how it's done on the inside."

"But they are Egyptians."

"So? Were Mustafa al-Nahhas and Fouad Serag Eddin Turks then?"

"Brother, the king robbed this country blind!"

"By the way, the Free Officers are no saints themselves. . . ."

"Who said they were? But they are revolutionaries—and much better than the king and his retinue!"

"The king can go to hell! But these guys need to withdraw their tanks and go back to their barracks, and leave the country to those who know how to run it!"

Abduh the hashash jumps into the fray as only stoners can, bellowing, "Shut up and listen!"

They grow quiet, expecting as always with him to hear the latest joke he'd heard or made up. Laughing, he says, "Did you hear the one about the imam of Sultan Hassan mosque?"

"What did he do?"

"He walks out of the mosque and runs into a tank. He blocks the way and asks the driver, 'Who do you think you are?' The officer points at the tank. So he asks him again, 'So what exactly are you going to do for us?' The officer raises his middle finger in the old man's face and says, 'This!'"

The café rolls with laughter and sarcastic comments. "That's what they've always given us!"

"At least we're used to taking it by now!"

"That's why us civilians are always walking down the street rubbing our asses."

"That's why they used to execute people by impaling them."

"They couldn't complain—they'd die comfortably being so used to it."

The stoner adds, "You know what that smart-ass old man told the officer?"

"What?"

"'Stick it up your mother's ass, you son of a whore!' Then the officer flattened him with the tank."

One of the customers asks in disbelief, "Are you still high from yesterday?"

"Not on your life. Go to where it happened and see for yourself. All the sheikhs of the neighborhood are building a tomb for the imam who was murdered."

When Abduh the hashash and the Wafdist disappear, the café patrons fall silent. Their disappearance is suspicious. Whoever ridiculed, or whoever criticized, disappeared. And whoever showed their support was fired.

Confused, you ask your friend about what is really going on. You ask when you will receive a better place to live. He tells you confidently while handing you a book, "It's just a matter of time, that's all."

Yet time goes by and nothing changes. You remain as you are, eating nothing but fava beans day and night, living in the same shitty room with its disgusting bathroom. Sharbat still suffers from life's adversities. What is new is that the revolution has stirred up clashes.

One day you find yourself riding on a horse cart, circling the streets and shouting, "O Naguib, you tricky, tricky man! O Naguib, you double-talking man!" There's tumult in the streets as the radio announces that Naguib has resigned. You go to the bookseller seeking to be illuminated, but his stall is closed. You go back the next day, thinking he might have been sick, but the stall is now gone. When you ask the adjacent vendor about what happened, he asks suspiciously, "How do you know him?"

"He's my friend."

"Get out of here, boy, before they take you away like they took him."

Translated by Elliott Colla

Robert Solé
from *Birds of Passage*

MY GRANDFATHER REFUSED TO be pacified.

"They're communists—communist and uneducated oafs. They'll send this country to the dogs."

The officers who overthrew Farouq on 23 July 1952 had been quick to abolish all local titles: Egypt had no more beys or pashas. That was a crime for which Georges Bey would never forgive them.

"And to think my idiot of a brother-in-law is still a count! Count my backside!"

Three months later the uneducated oafs added insult to injury by promulgating a new agrarian law. From now on, no one could own more than two hundred feddans of cultivated land.

"If that isn't communism, what is?" protested Georges Batrakani, who owned nearly four hundred.

"In communist countries assets are requisitioned without compensation," Makram retorted coolly. "You'll be indemnified."

"Come off it! Their indemnities are paid in treasury bonds redeemable in thirty years. I'll never see the color of their money."

"You'll be indemnified, I tell you. In any case, before the requisition order comes into force you're entitled by law to sell a hundred feddans to your children and the balance to small farmers."

"Don't play the innocent! The fellahin don't have the wherewithal, you know that perfectly well. They'd sooner sit back and wait for the state to present them with what it has stolen from us. As my brother Ferdinand used to say . . ."

Makram, whose sight was deteriorating, couldn't roll himself a cigarette in the gloom. He went over to the window to take advantage of the flashing Coca-Cola sign.

"And you know perfectly well, Georges, that the ownership of land in this country is outrageously inequitable. Sixty-odd landowners own one-twentieth of all the cultivated land."

"I'm not one of the sixty."

"But you're one of the five hundred who own more than one-tenth of the land, and there are two million seven hundred landowners in all."

"So what? Are you a communist too?"

The man in black preferred to remain silent when their arguments took such a turn. He recalled the conversation they'd had in this very same office soon after 25 July.

"A fundamental change has set in, have you noticed?" Georges had asked.

"Of course, and I welcome it. For the first time in centuries, Egypt is being governed by Egyptians."

"Yes, yes, but I'm talking about something more profound, more serious. Haven't you seen Naguib's head?"

"What's the matter with his head?"

"He doesn't wear a tarboosh! No Egyptian head of government has ever appeared in public without a tarboosh."

"Naguib's a general. He wears a peaked cap, it's only natural."

"No, you don't understand. He doesn't have the head for a tarboosh, nor do the officers in his entourage. That's serious, Makram, very serious. You never know where you are with such people."

"We know where we've been, anyway, and that's reason enough to forge ahead," the Copt replied with a smile. "The main change I've noticed is that these bikbashes are slim and athletic. The reign of the obese is over."

"Never fear, they'll put on weight in just the same way as your beloved Wafd grew fat on power. The officers are calling for the party to be purged."

Dismissed from office after the burning of Cairo, Nahas Pasha had gone off to recuperate at Vichy with his wife the celebrated Zouzou who was suspected of selling favors and manipulating cotton prices. The military putsch had caught them in mid cure. Nahas boarded the first available plane to Cairo. Arriving there at one a.m., he knocked on General Naguib's door in the middle of the night, convinced that he and his officers were waiting to entrust him with power. Their only response was to invite the Wafd to purge itself thoroughly, like the other parties, and Nahas himself to abstain from all political activity in the future.

"You didn't take my worries about the tarboosh seriously," said Georges. "Those communists want to deprive the nation of its headgear, that's obvious."

People were, in fact, beginning to debate the merits of the tarboosh. "It's a relic of the past," declared certain members of the new regime. To ingratiate themselves, some Muslim scholars had unearthed ancient fatwas that permitted the faithful to wear hats or caps as long as they weren't designed to cast scorn on religion or patriotism.

"What cheek!" was my grandfather's comment. "When I think that the tarboosh used to be regarded as a symbol of nationalism and Islam! I used to be criticized for manufacturing them on the grounds that I was a khawaga; now we're told that the Arab used to wear hats with brims in times gone by, and that the tarboosh originated in the West—that it's the ancestor of the Phrygian bonnet!"

To open his newspaper, with its bold red headlines, was a proceeding that made Georges quail every morning. One never knew what those trails of blood portended. One day it would be a fifteen per cent cut in rents; the next the abolition of the notorious waqfs, or inalienable private assets; the day after that a wave of arrests. The hangman of Alexandria, a patriotic soul, had telegraphed the new rulers as follows: "Am prepared to hang traitors free of charge."

My grandfather cursed himself for having publicly congratulated the king on his birthday the previous 11 February. Together with some thirty other companies (Gattegno, Air Mist, Hannaux, Savonneries Kahla, etc.), the firm of Batrakani & Sons had inserted a full-page advertisement in the *Progrès égyptien*. It conveyed a desire "to place at the foot of the throne the expression of their most respectful good wishes and their infinite gratitude."

"Gratitude for what?" Makram said sarcastically. "For having allowed four hundred businesses in Cairo to be burnt or looted on Black Saturday?"

The Coca-Cola sign was flooding the office with red-and-white light.

"It's a civilized revolution, you can't deny," the Copt went on. "Not a drop of blood has been spilt. They've allowed Farouq to sail for Capri in his yacht, complete with his family and his private fortune."

"Much good that does me! Farouq was a fool. He had all the makings of a big success. People admired and flattered him when he arrived here in thirty-six. They applauded him even during the war, in spite of his escapades, but he was a sick man. A glandular problem . . ."

"He was spoilt by his entourage."

"Not only by his entourage, Makram Effendi! I shall never forget that Nahas of yours, kowtowing to him as boy of seventeen. 'Your Majesty, I have a privilege to request of you; May I kiss your hand?' A fine crew, your Wafdists!"

"A new era has begun, Georges."

"Yes, no more Wafdists, just uneducated oafs in uniform munching fuul sandwiches in the palaces where they've installed themselves. They're going to send us all to the dogs. To the dogs, d'you hear?"

Translated from the French by John Brownjohn

Ghaleb Halasa
from *The Novelists*

THE RADIO WAS BROADCASTING the "Rabbat al-Buyut" (Homemakers) program and Samia Fahmi was explaining a recipe for an okra dish. The broadcasting was suddenly interrupted and military march music started. Ihab saw Helmut and Qasim standing at their respective office doors. Helmut said, "What happened?"

Ihab replied nervously, "It's war!"

At that very moment the voice of the radio broadcaster announced that large numbers of Israeli airplanes had attacked military posts inside Egypt and that forty planes had been shot down. Helmut came out of his office, asking, "What happened?"

Ihab told him what he had heard, so he said, "Leave the newspapers and let's listen to the radio broadcasting."

The radio broadcaster stopped and Samia Fahmi came on once again with the recipe for the okra dish. It was very complicated. Helmut asked, "What is she saying?"

Ihab replied, "She's explaining a recipe. I think they need some time before they can change the programming."

Abbas arrived at that moment, carrying breakfast, and said, "What's the story? Did something happen?"

Ihab said, "We're at war."

"Are we in Tel Aviv yet?"

"In six hours."

At that moment the sirens went off. The broadcasting was interrupted and military march music started. Abbas said enthusiastically, "It's serious. We're going to get rid of Israel!"

Qasim embraced Abbas. "Brother, our people are unwavering!"

The phone rang and Helmut told Ihab that it was for him. Ihab heard Zeinab's voice. She was excited. She said that the Egyptian Army had entered Israel and that it was advancing in the Kontilla region and that we had shot down forty air planes. She added, "We're the ones who started the war. Dayan said so and the whole army has marched into the Sinai."

"Fantastic!"

"The Syrian and Jordanian armies have also joined the war. I have to go. I'll call again in a little while."

As he put down the receiver, Ihab remembered Ismail: What will his reaction be to this amazing situation? He told Helmut and Qasim what Zeinab had reported. Helmut said, "It seems that the situation is dangerous."

Qasim said to Ihab, "Will America stand by and watch Israel come to an end?"

Ihab replied, "What can it do? It has global interests."

Abbas placed the food on a low table in front of the radio set. There was cheddar cheese and red Italian onions and olives and bread. Ihab could see Helmut typing his daily report at the typewriter. He called him. "Please join us for breakfast, Mr. Helmut."

He replied, "Thank you. Please report every news item to me."

Qasim said to Abbas, "Come and have breakfast with us."

"Thank you, I've already eaten."

Qasim said to Ihab, "You used to criticize us because we bet on Abdel Nasser."

Ihab said, "Reality itself dictates who we should bet on."

"And what has reality dictated?"

"What has it dictated?"

"It dictated the termination of Israel."

Ihab replied, knowing full well that he had a lame argument, "This is only the beginning."

Qasim was a member of the Democratic National Liberation Movement known as HADITU (in abbreviated form) that was the first to demand disbanding the communist movement. Most communist movements broke off with HADITU for they were close to the Free Officer's before the July coup. It was said that the Free Officers printed their flyers in HADITU's secret print shop and that some of the movement's members had joined the Free Officers. After the July coup, they acted as if they were part of the Free Officers' movement. Even though Abdel Nasser had detained them in 1959 they still remained loyal to him and campaigned to dissolve the communist parties because Abdel Nasser would implement democracy. They prided themselves in their unfounded statements that the Soviet theory about the transformation of capitalism into socialism was in fact theirs and that the Soviets had taken it from them.

Qasim was one of those who had been detained in 1959 and released in 1964 on the occasion of Khrushchev's visit to Egypt. Now he demanded of Ihab a clear confession that HADITU was always right but Ihab was not ready to make such a confession.

The patriotic tone that gushed forth from the radio interrupted their conversation. They were re-broadcasting the 1956 war songs: "*Wallah zaman ya silahi*" (It's been a long time, my weapon), "*Hanharib*" (We will fight), "*Da' qanali*" (Leave my Canal), and "*Allahu akbar fawqa qayd al-mu'tadi*" (God is greater than the attacker's might). The military march music continued, followed by Ahmad Said's raucous voice, "Advance, brother, on Tel Aviv. Destroy the cowardly enemy . . . " not to mention the slogans delivered by enthusiastic broadcasters and hysterical female announcers, and military statements that said nothing in particular but seemed to imply the most amazing military feats.

Another phone call from Zeinab: She said that the Egyptian army had advanced inside Israel and that the Syrian army had arrived at Lake Hawleh. She said she would wait for him at home at two o'clock. He told Qasim what Zeinab had reported. Abbas, who had been listening, jumped up cheering, "Allahu Akbar! God is great!"

Helmut came out of his room and asked, "What happened?"

Ihab repeated what Zeinab had said. Helmut listened with a frown on his face and then said, "I hope it's true."

Qasim replied, "It is certain."

At that very moment one of the drivers walked in and said to Helmut, "Mr. Helmut, no more Jews. Jews kaput."

Helmut smiled and walked back into his room.

"Israel is finished, guys."

Abbas said, "Good riddance!"

Until two o'clock in the afternoon, nothing was really clear. Ihab left the news agency and walked along Brazil Street. The siren went off announcing an air raid; the cars came to a halt as they waited for the all-clear. At the corner off the main street there was a small, popular coffee shop where the doormen and servants in the neighborhood hung out. An old Nubian man in a white gallabiya and head turban stood in front of it. He looked at the sky, shading his eyes with his hands and said, "The boys didn't get to Tel Aviv it seems."

Ihab said to himself: this is typically what doormen do when they watch a football match. A young man whose gallabiya's slit neckline revealed his thick chest hair said, "How did you know that they didn't get there?"

The old man replied, "The radio didn't say."

The young man said, "It's top secret information."

Zeinab had gotten home before him. Lunch was ready on a table in the living room along with a bottle of rosé wine. She got up and hugged him when he came in, sighing: "Ihab!"

He sighed back, imitating her, "Zeinab!"

"Ihab!"

He replied, imitating Abdel Wahab in the famous *Qays wa Layla* Operetta, "Zaynaaab."

Zeinab laughed and poured herself a glass of wine and gulped it down straight up. Her face gradually turned dark red. She poured another glass. Ihab said to her, "Easy sweetheart. You're wild enough as it is."

She replied energetically, "I'll show you how wild 'wild' can be."

She took a sip of wine and said, "Give me a kiss, you charming guy."

He said, "No, honey. I'm too shy!"

She answered, "You, shy? Come on, give me a kiss."

He held her close and they embraced for a long time. Suddenly he said to her, "By the way, what's the news?"

She replied as she indulged herself in the food, "We won!"

"What does that mean?"

She looked at him and said: "I don't know. There are conflicting reports and announcements."

"What are they reporting?"

"Our Air Force has been bombed."

"Who bombed it?"

"Who do you think?"

Then she added: "Major General Amer was flying so they couldn't bomb the Israeli planes."

"What about the forty planes we shot down?"

She whispered, "We didn't shoot down anything."

Ihab's lips were moving soundlessly. She said, "But our forces are advancing inside Israel."

"Advancing? What are you talking about?"

She said, "This afternoon I'll go back to the news agency to find out what's happening."

They resumed eating in silence, then they lay side by side on the bed without touching. They both felt that they were hiding a shameful lie. During this loaded silence, Zeinab started to weep. Ihab watched her without saying a word. He then pulled her toward him. She buried her head in his chest and her entire body shook as she continued to weep.

Translated by Samia Mehrez

Latifa al-Zayyat

from *The Search: Personal Papers*

I WENT TO GREAT lengths consciously to pluck out the remnants of my husband from my being, assessing the experience of my marriage objectively, making the connection between the general and the particular. I split the woman I am into two parts, one that is dying and one that flees in distress, as in 1966, the year after my divorce, I wrote a play entitled *Buying and Selling* that was never published.

Suddenly, my husband fell from my emotions as if he had never existed and, with him, the play I wrote that had seemed to me, in the shadow of the way events developed, pure heresy as the 1967 defeat knocked me down and marked the dividing point between two phases, two lives. Words became emptied of their meanings, all words, and wrapped in the cloak of history and economics I seek in facts shelter from words, all words, head bowed and eyes cast down for fear of meeting other people's eyes. I am the soldier, martyred, not knowing from where the betrayal came; I am the soldier coming back naked in the fevered heat of the sun across the Sinai desert; I am the one who arouses sorrow; I am the object of ridicule and every joke that people tell hurts like an arrow in my heart. O my God, how many arrows you have showered upon me as I dragged on in my failure, my rancor and my desire for revenge as words lost their meanings, all words. What I have suffered as an individual dwindles away to nothing compared to what people as a whole have suffered. I do not exempt myself from responsibility: How did I not say 'no' more often than I did? How could I have been so ineffectual? A few days after the defeat, the Fiction Committee at the High Council for Culture held its meeting, which was attended, quite unusually, by about fifty eminent writers. I said, "Every one of us is responsible for this defeat. If we said no to wrong whenever it was done, we would not be faced with defeat now."

The hall tensed as I spoke, some accepting what I said and some rejecting it. Dr. Hussein Fawzi protested that nobody was able to say no, and anyone who did would find themselves in prison. Insisting that we take responsibility for the defeat, I replied, "If all the intellectuals said no, they wouldn't be able to put us all in prison."

There was a crucial moment of silence and someone asked: What happens next? Still caught up in their dreams, the leftists—including myself—were expecting another Vietnam. Tawfiq El-Hakim said that Abdel Nasser was not better than the Prophet, prayers and peace be upon him, and suggested that there might be a peace treaty like the one Mohamed made at Hudaybiyya. He told his version of the story, right up to the moment when the treaty was to be signed. Mohamed paused as he went to sign and instead of signing himself Mohamed the Prophet of Allah, as he usually did, he just signed his name: Mohamed ben Abdel Muttaleb. El-Hakim captivated us with his story, telling it as only he can, and I realized that the story was a fake only as I stood in front of the iron gate at the High Council for Culture. The truth slapped me in the face: The most miraculous thing about the Prophet was that he was illiterate. He never signed his name. I felt the weight of the betrayal when the Secretary of the Socialist Union said, in a meeting she held in the University College for Women, that the Israelis had come into Sinai like rats into a trap and were fated to die there. My heart sank. I felt choked and unable to breathe. My brother Mohamed, who had come back from abroad on 6 June 1967, dragged me out of the ground-floor flat where we were taking shelter and, in the dark, whispered in my ear. I did not know why he was whispering when nobody else could hear, until I realized that what he was saying could be said only in a whisper: "The Egyptian army has pulled back to the Suez Canal."

Refusing to believe that everything was over so quickly I said, in a tremulous voice: "Perhaps it's a plan to draw the enemy in."

My brother Mohamed shook his head. The pounding of his heart rose to my ears and I could not bear the droning sound of his words. At that point, words lost their meaning. Like a wounded animal in search of shelter I went up the dark stairwell to my room, where I shrouded myself in a blanket on the bed. Like salt the unbroken stream of tears hurt my eyes. Weaving flimsy threads, I pushed the knowledge away from me and hung it from them so it did not touch me, fled from the burden of a truth heavier than I could bear . . . When I heard the voice of El-Quwani asking, in the name of Egypt, his voice choked with tears, for a ceasefire in the United Nations Security Council, I realized there was nowhere left to run to and I burst into tears, wailing hysterically. My brothers, Abdel Fattah and Mohamed, as torn apart as I was, tried to calm me down. My sister's husband, Mohamed El-Khafif, said, "She's right."

He would have liked to be able to burst out crying as I did. He wept without tears and I threw the cigarette lighter at the television screen, as Abdel Nasser backed down in his speech to Zakariya Muhieddine. Lowis Awad said to me, "What legal right does he have to do that?" The legality of Nasser's assigning power to a successor preoccupied him as he strolled around his room at the offices of *Al-Ahram*. It seemed to me that his preoccupation with this legal point, when the boat was sinking, was not relevant in the least and appeared to be a way of skirting the main issue. I did not realize until later on that Lowis Awad had grasped the kernel of the whole problem: by what legal right was all this going on? Mohamed El-Khafif asked what the television set had done wrong when the lighter whistled past it, then he and I set off, without saying a word, and picked our way down to the side street in the dark.

In our quiet side street, we found other people feeling their way like us in the dark, some still in the clothes they wore around the house. When we reached the main street, a bus pulled up next to us. The driver had decided to go to Manshiyet El-Bakri, where Abdel Nasser lived, so we took the bus to Qasr El-Aini, near the People's Assembly, where thousands of people were gathering.

I found myself in the street again, among people, after having been away from them for a long time. The street was not the street I had known in the days of the revolution, and the people were not the same. This time I found myself in the dark, wounded like the others, weighed down like them by doubt, not knowing where we were going, our future enveloped in a thick, unwelcome darkness.

With the greatest difficulty, we found our way to the People's Assembly by the back door. I found my brother Mohamed Abdel Salam El-Zawat, who was the General Secretary of the People's Assembly at the time, drafting the resolution that the Assembly had published at dawn that night, entitled "We Say No to Gamal Abdel Nasser." Mohamed El-Khafif and I helped El-Zayyat draft the resolution, which took some time. We left, past four in the morning, after he had read it out by candlelight in the main hall and the Assembly had passed it.

No sooner had I thrown myself upon my bed, torn apart, exhausted, than I found myself sitting up suddenly, a question eating at me: Was what we did right? I threw myself back on my bed again. What other choice did we have, now that the time of questions without answers had begun?

I did not cry the night Gamal Abdel Nasser died. My mother set a pile of handkerchiefs in front of her as she watched the television and everyone cried, but the defeat of 1967 was with me, and the Black September massacre of the Palestinians. I was gripped by bouts of sharp, conflicting feelings. A mixture of sorrow and anger made the tears freeze in my eyes, and a blend of regret for today and fear for tomorrow kept me until morning, waiting for what I feared, although I did not know precisely what the true nature of this was.

I did not hear about Abdel Nasser's death until the news was broadcast. Abdel Nasser was laid out on his bed, dead, as the eye doctor darkened the room and shone the light in my eyes. O my God, how long has the light been piercing my eyes? The doctor shone the light in my eyes and began to talk about the financial problems he had with his wife to a mutual friend, turning to my eyes from time to time, then plunging in to enumerate all the clothes and pairs of shoes he had bought for his wife as the light shone in my eyes. In a nightmarish trance, I fancied that the world had stopped and that I would die in this chair, with the light shining in my eyes. Abdel Nasser is in his shroud on his bed, dead, and the light is trained on my eyes. What is harsher than light in the eyes? When I came home and my mother told me the news, the pile of white handkerchiefs stacked up in front of her, I did not cry. I cried days later.

I stood on the balcony of our house, looking out at a gathering of wailing women dressed in black, confused men, children howling out the death of Abdel Nasser as they beat their breasts. Tears sprang to my eyes as I said in an audible voice, "Nobody, whoever they are, has the right to orphan a people."

Translated by Sophie Bennett

Hala El Badry
from *A Certain Woman*

MANY A TIME HAVE I swallowed bitter tears of pain and choked on them without making a sound. It was as if a knife were stabbing me in the back despite the comfortable cotton kilim covering the car seat. It was the lifelong fingerprint left by the demonstrations of 1973. The superficial pain was gone, but inside there was a wound that I felt as if it were lashing the skin with an electric current every time I felt anger. I adjust the way I sit, knowing that there's no use doing anything about it.

"Watch out, Nahid. Come here."

I leaned my whole body against him as he pulled me to the entrance of an apartment building,

"Thanks. The belting I got almost stripped the skin off my back. That soldier was rushing after me like a blind bull."

"Are you injured?"

"No, it's just a little pain that'll go away soon."

"This apartment building is a godsend. We'll rest for a few minutes then catch up with everybody in Tahrir Square."

"I know the streets of Doqqi very well. But what are we going to do about the bridges? We'll be caught at University Bridge and even if we crossed Gezira at Galaa Bridge, we'll still have Qasr Al-Nil Bridge."

"Let's get out of here first. It's a good plan. We've managed to provoke them and our message has reached the people."

"Would they dare to shoot us, as it happened at Abbas Bridge?"

"No, Egypt was occupied at the time."

"What's the difference? At least then they were fighting an enemy they knew. Now who are we fighting?"

"The goal is clear. First, a war in which we liberate Sinai, then we'll settle accounts."

"There are so many things that I didn't understand but it seems the tear gas and the belts in the hands of Central Security soldiers have explained some of them to me."

"What happened to you? You used to be so apolitical."

"It seems that each of us needs to take a clear stand so we wont be invisible to the regime which thinks of us as no more than scarecrows at best. Let's get out of here."

"Don't be in such a hurry. We've still got time and we'll all meet up, God willing."

"I don't hear anything going on outside."

"Wait. Stay here. I'll see what's happening outside and come back."

Just crossing a threshold cut me off two worlds: the stage and the auditorium. He crossed it and I stood in the dark, waiting. Now I know that I have stood at thresholds, never having the ability to cross. Where did that seed that lived inside me all my life come from? When was it created? Was it born at that moment or has it been slowly pushing its way inside for years? Did change play a role in this? Or did fate leave the decision up to me and I couldn't make it?

Yasir went to the melée outside. He was gone for a long time. I got tired of standing so I sat on the staircase, enveloped by a cold loneliness which I tried to dispel by hugging my knapsack. Fears assailed me with questions which I started to answer in defense of myself and the demonstrations: all we are asking for is our right to kick the enemy out. Why are they surprised by our demands? They sent Alexandria University Engineering students to the front and that was the last we heard of them. In a dramatic tone, as if we were a bunch of reckless kids, they said, "You want war? Quit school and join the army."

The young men couldn't back out. There was an uneven confrontation and then a deathly silence, as if we were the enemy. They planted their spies everywhere around us. We no longer knew with whom we were speaking or eating or attending lectures or singing at picnics. When we have some peace of mind and forget about them and tend to our lives' immediate concerns, looking forward to moments of truth or communication, one of them volunteers, "Nahid, why are you talking to him? Don't you know he's an informer?" Every day one group produces incrimination evidence against another. What's happening today is proof of their failure to divide us, to sow hatred and suspicion among us so we'd reap nothing, so our voices would get lost. Yasir's been gone a long time. Where did he go? Was he hit by the soldier's stones or their clubs? Did he clash with them and get arrested?

Days later I found out that a police car had picked him up as soon as he crossed the threshold. They took him to the jail in Muhammad Ali's Citadel that still reeked of the massacre of the Mamluks, to add his name to the names of prisoners and revolutionaries inscribed on its walls throughout its history. He had wanted to stay a little longer, to make sure it was safe. Did I, in my impatience, push him to go out? It was a question that gave me many a sleepless night for years afterward, even though there was no trace of it on his face when we met later on.

A spark of defiance grow inside me as I waited, until I found myself possessed of such an immense energy that I dashed out onto the sunshine without casting a last glance at the lobby where I hid. I didn't know what it looked like and I never found that building afterward. I didn't find Yasir in the street, but I found a crowd of students thundering angrily, "War, nothing but war." I also saw white smoke rising in circles in the street, which reminded me of childhood stories of Ummina al-Ghula and her constantly bubbling cauldron in which wayward children were cooked.

I soon found myself in the midst of a wave of marching students swelling flood-like, my fingers clasping with the fingers of a young man I didn't know. When our eyes met I understood. I turned to the person holding my other hand. It was another young man I didn't know. Unconsciously the waves had become one solid block. The soldiers tried everything to break it up, to no avail. In the midst of that block I forgot who I was and learned what it meant to be a mere atom in a large entity. It was a feeling I had looked for all my life but it had been like a mirage, flirting with me from a distance, rising the closer I got to the earth's surface, riding a warm mist and appearing real to me, but when I ran toward it, it disappeared into nothingness. But now the block was rolling forward, our feet beating the ground wildly and rhythmically as if to unseen African drums. Our heads were raised like sunflowers toward the source of strength. It was as if Ra, the god of the sun, was once again sitting on his throne and we marched toward him, anxious not to lose sight of him.

Translated by Farouk Abdel Wahab

Mahmoud Al-Wardani

from *Heads Ripe for Plucking*

I was slain too when I was a boy . . .

By 10 A.M. THE BUS taking us on the trip hadn't moved. The chaperones were sitting up in front after they'd checked on us one by one, again and again, then had us get off the bus to do a headcount all over again. We were all first-year pupils, but from different classes. I'd turned fifteen that day, 18 January 1977, and was planning to celebrate my birthday with my classmates as soon as we reached Port Said. Once we got there, the chaperones would let us loose on the town until the evening, as they always did on trips, and go off on their own, after arranging with us to meet at the bus at the end of the day.

The headmaster arrived finally and when we heard the engine start we went wild. When we'd reached Manial Street, we started cheering the driver on:

"Clever driver:

Take us to Qanater!"

Nagi, whom we all knew because he'd had to repeat the grade since he was often absent and played hooky, cheered, "Long live Mr. Azmi! Long live Mr. Rakha! Long live Mr. Abd al-Wahid!"

He didn't cheer for the fourth chaperone, Tawfiq Aydarus, whom we all hated and even wished to see dead because of his cane—he used it to give a beating to anyone who crossed his path during break time.

We finally reached the end of Manial Street, and when the bus swung in the direction of the Muhammad Ali Palace, it suddenly ground to a halt. But we just went on singing at the top of our voices. I was happy I had thirteen pounds that my mother had somehow managed to cobble together for me. Until last night, my dad was dead set against giving me more than the five pounds he'd decided on. My mom, though, slipped me an extra eight pounds, saying that I should buy whatever I needed, and not to worry about bringing any money back with me. Still, if I could buy two kilos of American apples and a tube of Signal II toothpaste, she'd be pleased, but if I couldn't that was fine too—the important thing was that I should take care of myself. I made my calculations carefully: a checkered BVD shirt, a pair of jeans (Lee, Wrangler, or FUS), and a pack of Marlboros that I'd smoke there to celebrate my birthday. But I had to keep enough on me to buy mints or chewing gum before I went home because my mom couldn't help crying when she smelled cigarettes on me, but she never told my father who though nothing of beating me even though I was a grownup now.

The bus was parked a long time. I craned to see past the classmate sitting beside me and found the street teeming with angry-looking people. They were pouring in from the side streets, gathering and crossing the Nile shouting. When the bus started up amid the loud honking of cars, one of the chaperones barked instructions that we all stay put in our seats. The crowds outside were thickening and though I couldn't catch what people were chanting it was clear they wanted to band together. They were the ages of my father, uncles, and cousins. The bus swerved and I recognized al-Sadd Street in Sayyida Zaynab district. I saw women in gallabiyas and black wraparounds, some barefoot with children clutching at their hems, rushing out of the intersecting alleyways ahead of us. Then the bus came to a standstill and the bald driver turned to us and slapped his palms together.

A long time passed. Some of the pupils were smoking in the back of the bus, having taken their cue from the chaperones. In fact, three of the chaperones had slipped out, one after the other, leaving only one teacher on board. After a while, we shoved that chaperone out as well and one of us forced the door open and we all followed him out shouting. We melted into the huge crowd around us. All I had with me was my bag, which was empty except for the sandwiches my mother had given me. Nagi and Umar, the only two pupils from my class on the trip, joined me as I cut through the crowd. Everyone around us was shouting agitatedly and I couldn't figure out what it was all about. When we'd made it to the top of Port Said Street we found pupils from the Khedival Secondary School, Sabil Umm Abbas School, and the Hilmiya Commerce School gathered. They were chanting after someone:

"Gihan, is it true
that Ford fucked you?"

I found it really funny and was chuckling as I watched them, but they looked pretty serious. The world seemed vast just then and the three of us felt we could do just as we pleased. We looked at each other and burst out laughing and clapping. Then we cheered along with the others:

"Gihan, is it true
that Ford fucked you?"

The crowd was growing by the minute and the public buses and trams had stopped. "Looks like we won't be going on that trip," Umar said, leaning over and raising his voice above the din. Nagi and I answered in unison, "We're on the trip!"

We laughed again and, still close together, surged forward with everyone around us toward the square. There we found people holding up a boy wearing eyeglasses who was chanting:

"He dresses like a bridegroom
while we sleep ten to a room."

I was sure the boy meant Anwar Sadat: he was the best-dressed man I'd ever seen, and slim and always happy, his ready smile showing off his white teeth. The people knew just who was meant but they weren't afraid of Sadat; if anything, it just made them chant louder. The crowds were lining up in front of the Sayyida Zaynab Police Station, their cheering growing frenzied as they repeated after another man they held up who was waving his fists:

"They had us down to tattered clothes
and now they take our bread loaves."

What they were saying hit the mark and they were not afraid of anyone, not even of Sadat or State Security, so I chanted along. As for the Sayyida Zaynab Police Station, its notoriety had reached us all the way in Manial. Woe be to anyone who even came near it! Our classmates had told us stories about people they knew who'd been whipped and beaten, sometimes even killed, in that place. I tried to get a glimpse of its façade and made out some people carrying huge pipes or maybe logs of wood and shoving them forcefully against the outer gate of the police station. The chanting grew louder as everyone egged them on to break the gate:

"Give us democracy,
Our life's a misery."

Suddenly, bullets flew from somewhere, hitting in the first round the ones who were trying to break down the gate. I caught sight of their silhouettes dropping at a distance while others turned round to flee. A stampede in the opposite direction had begun. It was essential that Nagi, Umar, and I stick together, what with the pressure on all sides and the risk of tripping and falling to the ground any minute. Nagi shouted in his croaky voice, "Hold on to each other! Careful now."

I was scared and felt hungry when another round of shooting started. I knew the relatives of two people who'd died in custody in the Sayyida Zaynab Police Station. The superintendent of that police station would park a van with its back to the Sharq Cinema in Sayyida Zaynab Square during the matinée. Then he'd pack the van with pupils playing hooky and keep them in custody for two or three days. I let myself be carried along with the rushing crowd, while making sure I kept my grip on Umar's hand. But my eyes watered as the pungent smell intensified and rose in my throat. I tried to run and pulled Umar to get away from it. It was clear, in any case, that I had to forget about the trip. Right beside me I saw a man running and holding up his arm splattered with blood, which made me grip Umar harder and practically drag him along. The chanting had died down, giving way to screams and curses on the government and the president. When my feet stumbled on the tram rails I realized we'd managed to get away from the battlefield and the gunshots, the reports of which still echoed.

Translated by Hala Halim

Radwa Ashour
from *Warm Rock*

WHO'S POUNDING AT THE door like this? Shams left the dishes she was washing covered in soap, rinsed her hands, and hurried to open the door as she dried them. Munira's face looked disconcerted.

"What's wrong?"

"Sayyid just came back from the university and he said that the security forces have encircled the campus and were not allowing anyone in. He heard that the students who were inside have been arrested."

"What a disaster! And where's Sayyid?"

Shams asked the question but she was really thinking about Ali.

"He's gone to alert his friends and I have forbidden him to come near the university so that he doesn't get caught."

Shams got her stockings and her shoes and started putting them on.

Munira asked her, "What are you going to do?"

"At least I can try and find out what happened and ask about the children's whereabouts."

"Shall I come with you?"

"It's not necessary," Shams replied, as she dashed out on the street thinking that Ali always got himself into trouble. True, he was kindhearted, but he was also rash and hot-tempered. Why were they arresting them? God protect us! She was drenched in sweat despite the nippy January wind. She wiped her face with her handkerchief as she kept an eye on the road through the bus window so as not to miss the university stop.

The bus crossed over al-Gami'a Bridge but did not continue on its usual route. It turned to the right and the driver said that the street was blocked. He stopped, so she got off. She walked toward the statue of Nahdat Misr and walked past it quickly toward the university at the end of the street that was practically deserted. From a distance she could discern the dome and the clock tower; she also began to see crowds in front of the university walls. She hurried along with the sole thought of getting there. They were not students but soldiers, a wall of soldiers: hundreds of tightly packed gray helmets, hundreds of heavy black shoes, the khaki uniforms and the shields and clubs. Shams continued moving toward them. Her heart beat; she heard it and continued. What have they done to the children? She moved forward.

"Do not come any closer, lady!"

"My son is in the university."

"The university is closed."

"But my son is inside."

A black shoe moved a step forward and a threatening hand with a club was raised.

"Cut it out and get going, lady!"

She turned around silently and walked back toward the statue. Her throat was dry and so was her worried heart. They were standing like a wall so what could she do? She was afraid, not of them but for the children. When she got to the statue, she turned left and walked alongside a flower nursery at the edge of Urman Gardens. "I will get to the university from the other side," she said. "But what if they stop me?" She sighed and walked on. In the narrow side street she saw the parked military trucks with the soldiers inside. She started counting the trucks. "Is this a war?" she asked herself disapprovingly as she wiped the sweat from her face and neck. "What if they stop me? I will say that I work in the administration," she thought. "What if they ask me?" She slowed down as she tried to find an answer.

At the crossroads she was confronted with the same wall of helmets, shields, and heavy shoes.

"Do not come any closer, lady!"

"But I work in the university. I am a nurse in the day clinic."

"There is no work now at the university. The university is closed."

"I'm going to cash my salary. The feast, as you know, is only two days away. We're getting early pay this month."

"Ok, wait here."

The soldier left his post to verify the information. How did she get this idea?! How did she lie with so much confidence? She sighed and thought, "God is generous!" The soldier came back and the human block in front of her gave way a little to let her pass through, as if it were a narrow door that opened in an armored wall. She went through and the block returned to place. Shams walked on until she found herself alone inside the area encircled by the soldiers.

She went into campus through a small gate right next to the big metal gate that was closed. She had never entered the campus before but she used to see it when she went past it on the bus, flooded with sunlight and the bustle of the students inside and outside the walls. Young men and women wearing all kinds of clothes and colors, walking back and forth or talking to each other or laughing against the backdrop of the old two-storey buildings and the domed auditorium and the clock tower. When she used to see them like this she would think of the university as a big garden where boys and girls had a good time. It was difficult for her to imagine them in classrooms, for she had only seen that once, in a film. The hero and heroine were both students. They sat side by side in the lecture hall and whispered to each other. Others laughed quietly so that the instructor who was busy lecturing would not hear them.

She looked around her and could hardly recognize the place. There was no sunshine and no human beings: it was as if, standing alone under this cloudy sky, she was in a graveyard in their village at dusk. What to do? She spotted a slim young man emerging from one of the buildings on his way down the couple of steps that lay between the door and the ground. She ran toward him and met him halfway. She asked him, out of breath, "Are you a student here?"

He answered, with reserve, "I work in the administration. The university is closed."

If she doesn't ask him, she may not find anyone else to ask.

"My son was in the sit-in and I don't know what happened."

He did not answer her and looked as if he were going to walk away. What if he left now? Her eyes were focused on his face.

"The security forces stormed the campus at dawn and arrested all the boys and girls who were here."

"Where did they take them?"

"I don't know."

He left her and walked away. Shams felt her legs give way, for she had only half-believed the news when she first heard it. She was hoping that the children were being punished inside the university. What to do now? She stood still in her place hoping to find another person she could ask. The clock struck once and then a second time and on the third strike she started to walk slowly toward the gate.

It wasn't a wall but a circle. As she watched the huge number of security forces that were spread out beyond the university and its buildings to her right and to her left, Shams thought to herself that never in her life had she seen so many soldiers. It was as if it were wartime! She continued walking until she got to them. They made way for her to pass and she noticed as she walked by—now that she was outside the boundaries of the circle—how young the soldiers were. Their faces were burned by the sun, their khaki uniforms were faded, and their bodies that, from a distance, seemed upright and straight were slack with fatigue. What do they have against the children? She almost asked them but she didn't and went on walking. She will walk home. What to do? If the children's father were alive he would have explained things to her and would have helped her out. If Bushra were in Cairo . . . should she send her a telegram to ask her to come? She would worry her unnecessarily and Ali might get home before she arrived. She didn't know what the matter was with this girl; she grew thinner by the day as if she were brooding over some burden. After a couple of days she will come home to spend the feast with them. Ali will have returned before then. Insha'allah he will have returned before then. When she got to the end of the bridge in Manial the voice of the muezzin resounded in the place through the loud speaker at the nearby mosque. She felt this was a good omen. "It's the call for noon prayer," she thought to herself as she slowed down her pace and mumbled "*Aziz Allah a'dham wa-l-'izzatu li-Llah.*"

Shams repeated the same sentence as she stood on the balcony when she heard the afternoon prayer. She was waiting for Ali to return or even Sayyid who might have news. Since she got home she had been reproaching herself for not persisting in asking that young man about the children's whereabouts. She should have also asked the soldiers; one of them may have told her something. Had they taken them to prison? Which prison? She spotted Sayyid as he appeared on the street. She opened the door and stood waiting on the stairway. She grew impatient and hurried to meet him at the gate. He walked up with her and almost collapsed on the first chair in view but she told him that it would be better for them to stand on the balcony until they see Ali, for he may return any minute now.

In a low voice that sounded as if he were confessing to a crime Sayyid said, "Auntie, my sister Amina was also at the sit-in but she told my mother that she was staying with a friend for a few days to study."

"Amina too?!" Shams asked him earnestly hoping that he might reconsider what he had just announced. But when he confirmed the news she exploded at him in anger, "You are older and you are her brother. You should have advised her instead of covering up for her. You hurl yourselves into problems and you never think of us. Your father will give us hell!"

But she still went down with him to help him break the news to his mother and father. She left the apartment door ajar "so that Ali will know that I'm home if he comes back."

As she had expected, Abdel Tawwab was furious and bewailed that he has lived to see the time when young girls are imprisoned with prostitutes. He said, "Who knows . . . they might become prostitutes at the end. Didn't they lie to their parents and spend the night in the same auditorium with young men at the university!" His face was red as he slapped one hand into the other. Munira cried silently as if she were responsible.

Shams intervened. "Remember God, Abdel Tawwab. Amina is mature and the best of young women. True, she was wrong to have lied to you but she didn't go to a brothel. She was at the university demonstrating against the government. Who knows, maybe she was just watching and they took her along with the others."

But Abdel Tawwab was not listening. He kept repeating that he has lived to see the day when young girls have become loose women and that Munira had failed in bringing up her daughters. Then he turned to Sayyid as if he had suddenly remembered that he was there and slapped him on the face, screaming, "You son of a bitch! You are responsible! How dare you let your sister sleep at the university with men? And I had been thinking that you have become a man. Damn this rotten offspring."

He spat on the floor. Like Abdel Tawwab, Munira and Sayyid, Shams was taken aback when Madiha, who was still in high school, said to her father, "You are wrong, father. There is no reason for this scene. My sister, Amina, was not in some cheap nightclub. She was at the university fighting for the future of the country."

Her words fell like fire on the barrel of gunpowder that was Abdel Tawwab. He went wild and threw himself upon her trying to hit her as he growled incomprehensible words. Shams tried to stand between them but he pushed her out of his way. His yelling merged with Madiha and Munira's weeping. Shams and Sayyid's words were lost in between. Then everyone calmed down and silence prevailed.

Translated by Samia Mehrez

Ibrahim Aslan
from *The Heron*

Yusif al-Naggar began to feel the effect of the small bottle of rum and asked the bartender to bring him another. He'd completely forgotten about Fatma until he searched in his pockets for a box of matches. His fingers stumbled upon the key to the flat. He thought of her, but the echoes of the chanting demonstrators rang in his mind, softly, ceaselessly. He didn't know what had come over him exactly, or what had made him come to the bar to drink alone. He thought of the young, dark woman he had seen being carried on the crowd's shoulders, her hair wrapped in a scarf, and he was fascinated by her bravery—a bravery he didn't possess—and by the visible anger that had transformed her features. That child-like woman.

. . .

Emerging from the bar onto Alfi Street, Yusif couldn't see a thing, because the lights of the cabaret marquees had been extinguished. On the way to Orabi Square, he didn't notice anyone save for the old parking attendant on the other side of the square. He headed along the sidewalk until the corner with the government bookstore and saw the storefront smashed in and the books scattered everywhere. From the tall steel birdcage, he could see the street littered with broken glass and fragments of rock. There wasn't a single storefront, window, door, or billboard that hadn't been demolished. Twenty-sixth of July Street seemed completely deserted. He could hear nothing but the occasional sound of cars speeding by, fleeing. He crossed the street and found himself in front of the public bathrooms near the Supreme Court. He hurried down the stairs and urinated. Then he headed to Ramsis Street and turned left between the Music Institute and the Telephone Building.

At al-Galaa Street, he ran into a mass of people. The façade of the *al-Ahram* newspaper building had been destroyed, and he heard people saying that the paper storehouses of *al-Akhbar* had been torched as well. Yusif walked along the darkened street behind al-Galaa Maternity Hospital and returned to 26th of July from the direction of Bulaq. In front of the Ali Baba Cinema, he saw the soaked, burnt shell of a bus that had been pulled into a small side street. Small children were climbing on top of it, crawling through its windows and pounding on it with rocks and iron bars. They were ripping out bolts and pieces of metal and throwing them into the road. They were ripping out the seats and throwing them through the doors. Yusif al-Naggar shuddered.

From where he was standing, he could see white and brown clouds of smoke swirling around red columns of fire in front of Abu'l-Ela Bridge. He followed the long alley behind al-Sultan Mosque and came out at the Television Building along Maspero Street. The wooden billboards had been burnt, some were still hanging by their metal clamps, and some had been thrown down into the street. The flames had jumped onto the scrap wood barriers next to the new Sixth of October Bridge. Piles of tar and gravel were also on fire, sending scraps popping, exploding against fences, the edge of the sidewalk, into speeding cars. Groups of people were hurrying around warning others about the danger. He returned to the foot of the bridge and saw that the flames were leaping into the thick, green clumps of weeds growing next to the water. Heading toward Omar al-Khayyam, he glanced at the furious whirlpools of the river through the openings between the bridge's sections. Continuing on his way toward Imbaba, he realized that he hadn't seen a single soldier or bus since he'd left the Regal Bar. The glass storefronts and neon signs in Zamalek were smashed as well. The signs dangled one after another in front of the doorways, between the tree trunks and streetlight poles, and on the stones of the wide sidewalk. He passed the Officers' Club, came to the Zamalek Bridge, crossed it, and turned right along the river's edge on his way back to Kit Kat.

When he got there, he found everything just as he'd left it: the doorways lit, the fruit carts, the liver and parts carts, the coffee mill, Sadiq and his brood of children gathered around the television, the fuul restaurant, Usta Badawi the barber, the department store, Khawaga's kiosk, the bookstore, Sgt. Abd al-Hamid, and the crowded doorway at the café. He walked to Hommous's to refill his butane lighter, then went to the grocery and bought another bottle of rum, putting it, wrapped in paper, in the outer pocket of his jacket. His buzz had worn off and he wanted to get drunk again. He knew he wouldn't run into anybody if he took a circuitous enough route. He crossed the street while looking at the vegetable and fruit sellers, who, sitting cross-legged with

their heads wrapped in scarves, were burning a pile of shredded palm-leaf baskets. They were making tea and trying to warm themselves. And there were
some people at the bus stop. Yusif al-Naggar stood directly in front of the
house facing Hawa Alley, then took two steps down the stone stairs. Stepping
to the right, he sat down under the squat stone wall.

He hid himself under the moist, drooping castor trees with their heavy,
dark leaves and started to drink the deep red rum.

A stench was rising in the air. The breeze carried it from beyond the river,
through the tall trees and over the distant houses still wet with rain.

Translated by Elliott Colla

Salwa Bakr

from *"Zeenat Marches in the President's Funeral,"*
in *My Grandmother's Cactus*

. . . HE WROTE DOWN EVERYTHING that Zeenat had to say to the President: she
told her whole story, from how d'you do to farewell, from the very moment
of her father's death when she was little until after she was widowed, while
still a maiden not yet taken by her groom, who had died in a fire along with
the owner of the shop in which he worked. She also told him how she had
got on after that, staying with her only brother. But after he had married and
been tied down at the neck by a heap of children, she left him, and left behind
the quarrels, every day and the next, with the children's mother, and went to
live on her own in the shack. And she told him, too, that she had tried to get
work more than once, to no avail. Her latest attempt—applying for work as a
cleaning woman in the school near her home—had ended in rejection because
she didn't know how to read or write. Then, after she had thanked him for
the three pounds in many and moving words, and similarly for the eighteen
pounds, and after she had implored God's protection for him—from her heart,
in appropriate fashion—she said to him, "Begging pardon, and it's not that I
set no store by them, but the three pounds aren't enough to cover anything,
because a kilo of meat costs nearly a pound now, and a kilo of lupines has gone
up to fifty piasters." Over and above that, there was the medicine she bought,

which the doctor had advised her to keep taking, and it cost a mint. She told him also that she was on her own and was embarrassed to ask help from any creature on earth, whatever the circumstances. Thus she was requesting of him precisely what a sister would ask of her brother, a child of her father, and "the one in need from the one who is able": to raise her pension just a little, so it would cover the demands of the world.

Then she asked Abduh the barber to tell the President, in full detail, her story of what had happened on the day of the procession following the Friday prayer service, about the behavior of the soldiers, who as far as she was concerned were devoid of good upbringing and honor; but Abduh the Barber refused. He refused unequivocally, on this point specifically, because it might result in the letter not reaching the President of the Republic if someone other than he were to open and read it. Abduh proposed adding at the end a few lines of poetry that he still remembered from his primary school days, but Zeenat rejected this, stating that the President would understand the words as they stood, and there was no need to bring the poet into it. So Abduh made do with a prose finale in which he emphasized that the people, all of them, were behind the Hero-Leader in the firm stand he was taking against imperialism and reactionary elements.

Zeenat was very pleased with the letter. She was confident that the President would, without a doubt, respond to her and take the necessary steps concerning her request, for this was a letter to end all letters, and she dreamt that the pension would be raised to five pounds. Indeed, and in light of this possibility, she had drummed up in her mind's eye the bare bones of a new plan for her life. Moreover, a somewhat unsettling thought kept tugging at her. The five pounds, if they really were to materialize in her hand at the start of each month, were bound to cause a major shift, a real change in her life. Perhaps they would even help to make her perennial dream come true: that dream which never left her, of marriage and becoming a mother. True, in terms of realities, there was a lot standing in the way of that dream, for time was rushing by and she wasn't getting any younger, and she had passed the age of demand, and because even when she had been at the age of demand, after the death of her bridegroom, no sort of creature had given her a look because she had (more's the pity!) "no lolly, no looks and nothing at all." Maybe, though, the five pounds would stimulate someone to consider her. If the truth be known, Zeenat's eye was on an elderly street sweeper whom she saw from time to time sweeping the main street by which she sat to sell her wares. From him she had learnt that many years ago he had cleared out, leaving his wife and children behind, and come to Cairo; to this very day they had no idea of his whereabouts. A few expert glances were enough to tell her that there was a good chance of extracting a child from his loins. She thought the five pounds might tempt him where nature, which had formed the features of her face and body, had failed.

But as the proverb says, "The world is deceptive and illusory, and it never lasts for a soul." Thus has Zeenat remarked, over and over, ever since that ill-fated day in which Abduh the barber brought her the momentous news, several days after sending the letter on which they had collaborated to the President. She had gone to see him in the shop to ask whether an answer had come from the president of the Republic, for she was using Abduh's shop as her address since it was clear and well-known and the postman couldn't possibly miss it. Presently, the barber—for whom Zeenat had waited by the shop—came into sight at the end of the lane, his face pallid, as yellow as turmeric, slapping himself on the cheeks just like a woman would do. At the time Zeenat's reaction was that he must have wet himself, especially when she saw him lunging for the radio like a madman, turning the dial as he screamed, "The man has died, the President had died, folks! The President has passed away, people!"

At that moment Zeenat was aware only of her hand grasping Abduh's collar and a strange anger erupting from inside her, an overwhelming anger that made her swear at him, and say to him, "Shut up! Damn it, Abduh, shut up! Take those horrid words out of your mouth . . . ."

But the folk of the street, all of them, had gathered around her, their glances telling the bitter truth which Zeenat refused to believe: and the tears said the same—those tears streaming down every face as if someone had pushed a button to start them flowing. It was enough for Zeenat to see the disheveled hair from which the women's head coverings had fallen, and the men's hands, slapping together in grief, to be convinced that this was no dream. There seemed to be nothing to do but scream; so she screamed at the top of her voice, and let out an impressive cry, and then collapsed in a faint.

Zeenat, at the hour of the funeral, did many things. At the start, she went round the various alleys gathering the women, to slap their faces in grief and wail. She walked in their midst until they reached the wide main street, the route of the funeral procession. There Zeenat saw many folk and, since with the crowds it looked like the Day of Judgment, she murmured the appropriate thing, the "To God alone is all might and strength." She came to realize that the President had been dearly beloved by many—children, women, young fellows—and she began to feel even sorrier. She would start sobbing and whimpering like the children, then switch back to the wailing and mourning of the women. "What a loss, your youth, my beloved. . . . Snatched away before your time, O prince!" "A thousand mercies be upon you, beloved of us all, beloved of the whole world.'

Then suddenly she remembered the letter and the pension. She tried to imagine what would happen to them now. Tired out by the fast pace of her thinking and unable to arrive at a reasonable mental picture of it all, she rushed forward recklessly, leaving the women behind, and began running in the direction of the bier, shoved and knocked all the while by shoulders and hands and heads. She had decided to get a close look at him, to touch him with her very own hand. The bier got larger in her eyes, larger and larger, and his features grew distinct, and she realized that she had got very close indeed. She flung herself forward amid the crowds with great force, pushing this one and that, giving not a single thought to what might happen to her. When she got within two steps or less of the bier, hands began to reach out toward her, slapping her to prevent her from moving any further. But she surged forward again and again while they restrained her, holding her back over and over. Suddenly she felt the salty taste of blood on her lips and felt as if she had lost her nose completely.

Some say that the madness which possessed Zeenat at that moment was real. But she herself says, whenever she reviews those moments and her eyes take on a calm, sad look, that at the time she was remembering how long she had waited on the day of his procession, after the Friday prayers, and what had happened to her that day. Thus, and with no consciousness of what she was doing, she began to return the kicks and slaps directed her way with stronger blows, and whenever possible she sank her teeth into anyone who struck her.

As for the contents of the police report which they wrote out for her, she said that she had bitten the fat man—the one in the white silk shirt—in the hand because she had had an inkling that he was smiling during the funeral procession. She had looked him full in the face when his walking stick tapped the portrait of the President she was carrying, and she saw him smile as he looked in her direction.

It is said that years after this report had been drawn up at the police station, Zeenat (who had not stopped repeating to herself the phrase 'illusory and deceiving world') was detained for several days in another police station because of her participation in the turmoil which broke out when the government raised the price of bread; and that at the time she had said, over and over, "A thousand mercies be upon you, beloved of all the folk," in addition to many things that need not be mentioned here.

Translated by Marilyn Booth

Mona Prince

from Three Suitcases for Departure

WE HAD TO DO SOMETHING. My friends and I had started to get involved in political matters, and we agreed to stage a march at the university after the semester break, which had already been extended for a month as a precaution against any student protests. For security reasons, several well-known student activists had been arrested, as well as many whom the university suspected could be potential protesters.

It was the first Monday after the break. My friends and I left the faculty of literature and met up with another group of students on our way to the department of law. We formed lines and held up banners with our slogans:

No to the invasion of Kuwait!
No to American interference in the Arab World!
Down with Zionism!
Jerusalem for the Arabs!

Samira, Soha, Safa and I were in the front. Yusuf, Ali, and Osama were next to us. Hussein, who cared so deeply for his country at the time, led the march.

The university closed its gates, just like it usually did on these occasions that "threatened the safety of the university and of Egypt," as the security officers were fond of saying. The university guards stood ready with their walkie talkies, watching the situation develop—only seconds away from calling up, God forbid, the Central Security Forces, who would respond to the criminal transgression of the students' protest.

I was surprised then—although I no longer am now—that the majority of the students didn't care about what was happening to themselves or to their country. They masked their eyes and busied themselves with vacations and parties. I cursed them then—now I only pity them. I turned away and joined in the chanting and singing. *Biladi, biladi, laki hubbi wa fu'adi*: My country, my country, you have my love and my heart.

That was the first time I had participated in student demonstrations with my friends. My relationship with Abd al-Rahman and with Sanjay before him had distracted me from anything. Perhaps I was just like those students I had cursed. Because it was my first protest I didn't realize what the consequences would be.

The march ended and we returned to our classes. I was shocked when they suspended Samira, Hussein, and me. Suspension wasn't something new for Hussein—he had been suspended and arrested before—but this had never happened before to Samira and me. We went together to the university administrator to ask about the reason for the suspension.

"I suspended you because you interrupted classes and destroyed the grass that we just paid 500 pounds to plant," he told us.

"We didn't walk on the grass, and we definitely didn't stop any classes. All the students are getting ready for their parties and vacations anyway!"

"What you did is considered high treason. You deserve death, not suspension."

The intensity of my anger almost pushed me to laughter, but Samira glared over at me. The administrator turned to her and said, "You're even wearing red. That means you're a communist."

Samira asked him what 'communist' meant, and I was floored by her naive response, which quickly ended the discussion.

We were suspended for a month. I didn't tell my family right away. My father was in Cairo and I didn't want to worry him. I knew that he would never approve of what I had done. He was a firm believer in minding your own business—as if my business had no connection to the real world and its problems.

I went back home that day and didn't talk to anyone. I went to my room and barricaded myself there, pacing back and forth until dinner, when I finally came out to tell what had happened. *You have no right to get involved in these things, my girl. Mind your own business! There's no reason for people to do this. Even if someone took part in a demonstration fifty years ago, today they can re-arrest him whenever anything pops up. Why are you causing all these problems for yourself and our family? You're going to ruin your future. There's no point in throwing it all away! You aren't going to change anything—you're going to wear yourselves out for no reason.*

I ran back to my room to take refuge within its deaf walls. I called up Abd al-Rahman to tell him what had happened.

"They're right. Listen to them."

His answer shocked me. How could he say something like that?! I ended the conversation and slammed the handset down. *They're right. Listen to them . . . .*

We didn't accomplish anything. We had actually strayed down dark and forbidden paths. Were they right? Had we really made a mistake?

Questions . . . questions . . . questions . . . .

Translated by Andrew Heiss

Alaa Al Aswany
The Yacoubian Building

THE STUDENT PROTESTS HAD been going on in most faculties since early morning. They interrupted studies, closed the lecture halls, and then started moving around in large numbers shouting and carrying banners condemning the war in the Gulf. When the call to the noon prayer sounded, about five thousand male and female students lined up to perform the prayer in the forecourt in front of the auditorium (boys in front, girls behind), led by Brother Tahir, Emir of the Gamaa Islamiya. Then the congregation said the prayer for the dead for the souls of the Muslim martyrs in Iraq. Shortly afterward Tahir climbed to the top of the stairs facing the auditorium and stood there in his white gallabiya and impressive black beard, his voice emerging loud from the PA system.

"Brothers and sisters, we have come today to stop the killing of Muslims in our sister country Iraq. Our Islamic nation is not yet dead, as its enemies would wish. The Messenger of God—God bless him and give him peace—has said in a sound hadith, 'Good fortune will remain with my nation till the Day of Resurrection.' So, brothers and sisters, let us say our word, loud and clear, so that those who have placed their hands in the filthy hands of our enemies, polluted with the blood of Muslims, may hear. Youth of Islam, as we speak the rockets of the unbelievers are pounding our sister Iraq. They pride themselves that they have devastated Baghdad and turned it into ruins, saying that they have sent Baghdad back to the Stone Age by destroying the generating stations and water plants. Now, brothers and sisters, at this very moment, Iraqi Muslims are being martyred, their skins shredded by American bombs. The tragedy was made complete when our rulers submitted to the orders of America and Israel and instead of the armies of the Muslims turning their weapons on the Zionists who have usurped Palestine and befouled the el Aqsa Mosque, our rulers have issued orders to Egyptian troops to kill their Muslim brothers and sisters in Iraq. My brothers and sisters in Islam, raise high your voices with the word of Truth. Speak it loud and clear, so that those who have sold the blood of the Muslims and piled up their looted wealth in the banks of Switzerland may hear it."

The slogans rang out from all sides, chanted by students carried on others' shoulders and taken up with huge enthusiasm by thousands of throats:

"Islamic, Islamic! Not socialist and not democratic!"
"Khaybar, Khaybar, all you Jews! Muhammad's army will return!"
"Rulers, traitors, men of straw! How much did you sell the Muslims' blood for?"

Tahir made a sign and they fell silent, his voice rising, thundering with anger, "Yesterday television screens around the world showed an American soldier as he was preparing to fire a rocket to kill our people in Iraq. Do you know what the American pig wrote on the rocket before he fired it? He wrote 'Greetings to Allah'! Muslims, they mock your God. What then will you do? They murder you and violate your women. They ridicule your Lord, Almighty and Glorious. Do your self-respect and your manhood count for so little with you? Gihad! Gihad! Gihad! Let everyone hear what we say! No to this dirty war! No to the killing of Muslims by Muslims! By God, we shall die before we let the nation of Islam become a tasty morsel in the mouths of its enemies! We will not be shoes that the Americans can put on and off as they please!"

Then in a voice choking with emotion Tahir chanted, "God is Most Great! God is Most Great! Down with Zionism! Death to America! Down with the traitors! Islamic, Islamic. . . ."

The students raised Tahir onto their shoulders and the huge throng turned toward the main gate of the university. It was the demonstrators' goal to get out onto the street so that other people could join the demonstration but the Central Security forces were waiting for them in front of the university and the moment the students went out into the square, the soldiers, armed with huge sticks, helmets, and metal shields, attacked them and started beating them savagely. The screams of the female students rose and many students fell and were beaten, their blood flowing over the asphalt, but the masses of students kept pouring in huge numbers through the gate and many got away, bursting out and running far from the soldiers, who chased after them. These students managed to get past the square in front of the university and re-formed at the bridge. Additional platoons of Central Security soldiers fell on them but they charged in their hundreds toward the Israeli embassy and there large numbers of Special Forces troops started firing tear gas grenades at the students, the pall of gas rising till it covered the whole scene. Then the sound of heavy gunfire rang out.

Taha el Shazli took part in the demonstrations throughout the day and at the last minute was able to escape as the security forces at the Israeli embassy started seizing students. Following the plan Taha went to the Auberge Café in Sayeda Zeinab Square where he met up with some of the brothers, among them Emir Tahir, who presented a review and evaluation of the day's events. Then he said in a sad voice, "The criminals used tear gas grenades as camouflage and then fired live ammunition at the students. Your brother Khalid Harbi from the Law Faculty achieved martyrdom. We resign ourselves to God's will for him and ask Him to forgive him all his sins, enfold him in His mercy, and reward him generously in Paradise, God willing."

Those present recited the Fatiha for the martyr's soul, all feeling fearful and oppressed. Brother Tahir then explained the tasks required of them for the following day—contacting the foreign news agencies to confirm the martyrdom of Khalid Harbi, tracking down the families of the detainees, and organizing new demonstrations, to start from a place the security forces did not expect. Taha was charged with the task of writing wall posters and putting them up early in the morning on the walls of the faculty. He had bought for this purpose a number of colored pens and sheets of sturdy paper and he shut himself into his room on the roof and devoted himself to his work, not coming down to the prayer area to pray the sunset or evening prayers, which he performed on his own. He designed ten posters, wrote them out, and did the drawings for them, finishing after midnight, at which point he felt extremely tired. He told himself that he had a few hours ahead of him in which to sleep, since he was supposed to go to the faculty before seven in the morning. He prayed the two supererogatory prostrations then turned off the light, lay down on his right side, and recited his customary prayer before sleeping: "O God, I have raised my face to You, placed my back under Your protection, and entrusted my affairs to You, in desire for You and in awe of You. There is no refuge from You or escape from You but through submission to You. O God, I believe in Your Book that You sent down and in Your Prophet that You sent." Then he fell into a deep sleep.

After a little, thinking he was dreaming, he awoke to confused noises, and, opening his eyes, could distinguish shapes moving in the darkness of the room. Suddenly the light was turned on and he saw three huge men standing by the bed. One of them approached and hit him hard across the face. Then the man seized his head and turned it violently to the right and Taha saw for the first time a young officer, who asked him jeeringly, "Are you Taha el Shazli?"

He didn't respond, so the goon struck him hard on his head and face. The officer repeated his question and Taha said to him in a low voice, "Yes."

The officer smiled challengingly and said, "Playing at being the big leader are you, you son of a bitch?"

This was a signal and the blows rained down on Taha. The strange thing was that he didn't protest or scream or even protect his face with his hands.

His face remained expressionless under the impact of all these surprises and he submitted totally to the blows of the goons, who took a firm grip on him and pulled him out of the room.

Translated by Humphrey Davies

Alaa Al Aswany
from *The Yacoubian Building*

TWO HOURS LATER A small truck loaded to the brim with cylinders of cooking gas was making its way toward the Feisal area in the Pyramids district. In the driver's seat was Dr. Mahgoub and next to him Taha el Shazli. Brother Abd el Shafi had taken up position among the cylinders piled in the back of the truck. They had shaved off their beards and dressed themselves as workers distributing gas, the plan being for them to carry out a visual inspection of the site at least one hour before the operation, then stay in the street in a perfectly normal way until the National Security officer left his house. In the time between his exiting the door of the apartment block and his getting into his car, they were supposed to delay him by any means available to them, then open fire with the three automatic rifles hidden under the driver's seat. They were also provided with stern additional instructions. If the officer was able to get into his car before the plan had been implemented, they were to cut him off with their truck, then throw their whole supply of hand grenades at him at once, abandon the truck, and each run in a different direction firing into the air so that no one would pursue them. If they suspected that they were being observed, Dr. Mahgoub (as the emir of the group) had the right to call off the operation immediately, in which case they were to leave the truck in any side street and return to the camp separately using public transport.

As soon as the truck entered the Feisal area, it reduced speed and Brother Abd el Shafi started banging with his wrench on the gas cylinders to announce their arrival to the residents. A few women came to their balconies and windows and called out to the truck, which stopped more than once, Abd el Shafi carrying the cylinders to the residents, taking the money, and returning to the truck with the empties; these were the instructions of Sheikh Bilal, who was concerned that they have good cover. The truck arrived at Akif Street where the officer lived and a woman asked for a cylinder from her balcony, so Abd el Shafi took it to her. This provided an opportunity for Mahgoub and Taha to inspect the place at their leisure. The officer's car—a blue, late-seventies Mercedes—was waiting in front of the entrance to the building. Mahgoub carefully studied the distances, the neighboring shops, and the exits and entrances. When Abd el Shafi returned, the truck sped off to a point away from the site, where Dr. Mahgoub looked at his watch and said, "We have a whole hour. What do you say to a glass of tea?"

He spoke in a cheerful voice as though to instill confidence into them. The truck stopped in front of a small café in a neighboring street, where the three sat and drank mint tea. Their appearance was completely ordinary and incapable of provoking any suspicion. Mahgoub noisily sucked tea from his glass and said, "Praise God, everything's okay."

Taha and Abd el Shafi responded in a low voice, "Praise God."

"Did you know that the brothers in the Gamaa Council have been watching the target for a whole year?"

"A whole year?" asked Taha.

"I swear, an entire year. Investigations are difficult because the high-ranking officers in National Security go to enormous lengths to conceal themselves. They use more than one name, have more than one residence, and sometimes they move with their families from one furnished apartment to another, all of which makes it almost impossible to get to them."

"What's the officer's name, Brother Mahgoub?"

"You're not supposed to know."

"I understand that it's forbidden but I'd like to know."

"What difference would his name make to you?"

Taha fell silent, then looked at Mahgoub for a moment and said irritably, "Brother Mahgoub, we've started the gihad for real and maybe God will honor us with martyrdom and our souls will rise together to their maker. So can't you trust me a little, as we stand at death's door?"

Taha's words had an impact on Mahgoub, who was very fond of him, so he said in a low voice, "Salih Rashwan."

"Colonel Salih Rashwan?"

"A criminal, an unbeliever, and a butcher. He used to take pleasure in supervising the torture of Islamists and he's the one directly responsible for the killing of many brothers in detention. In fact he killed with his own revolver two of the best of the youth of Islam, Brother Hassan el Shubrasi, the Emir of Fayoum, and Dr. Muhammad Rafi', the Gamaa's spokesman. He boasted of killing them in front of the brothers in detention at the El 'Aqrab prison—may God have mercy on our innocent martyrs, bring them to dwell in the mansions of His paradise, and unite us with them without mishap, if God wills!"

At five minutes to one the gas truck pulled up on the other side of the street from the entrance to the apartment building. Abd el Shafi got down, went up to the driver's cabin, took a small notebook out of his pocket, and pretended to go over the accounts with Mahgoub the driver. The two of them busied themselves with an audible discussion of the number of cylinders sold, appearing entirely natural, while Taha grasped the door handle in readiness. The entrance to the building was in clear view in front of him and he felt as though his heart was almost bursting it was beating so hard. He tried hard to focus his mind on a single point but a roaring waterfall of images swept through his mind's eye and a minute passed in which he saw his whole life scene by scene—his room on the roof of the Yacoubian Building, his memories of his childhood and his good-hearted mother and father, his old sweetheart Busayna el Sayed, his wife Radwa, the general in charge of the Police Academy condemning him for his father's profession, and the soldiers in the detention center beating him and violating his body. He burned with longing to know whether this was the officer who had supervised his torture in detention but he had not been frank with Mahgoub about this desire in case the latter should feel uneasy about him and exclude him from the operation. Taha kept staring at the building entrance, the memories rushing past in front of him, and then the officer appeared. He looked the way they had described him—portly, with a pale complexion, the traces of sleep and his hot bath still on his face, walking calmly and confidently, a cigarette dangling from the corner of his mouth.

Taha quickly opened the door, got out onto the street, and headed toward him. It was his job to detain him however he could till the others could fire at him. Then Taha would run and jump into the truck and throw a hand grenade to cover their flight. Taha approached the officer and asked him in a voice that he strove to make seem ordinary, "Please, sir, which way is No. 10, Akif Street?"

The officer didn't stop but pointed haughtily and muttered, "Over there," as he continued toward his car.

It was he. He was the one who had supervised his torture, who had so often ordered the soldiers to beat him and shred his skin with their whips and force the stick into his body. It was he without the slightest doubt—the same husky voice, the same dispassionate intonation, and the familiar slight rasp due to his smoking. Taha lost all awareness of what he was doing and leapt toward him, letting out an inarticulate, high-pitched cry like an angry roar. The officer turned toward him with frightened eyes, his face pinched in terror as though he realized what was happening, and he opened his mouth to say something but couldn't because successive bursts of fire suddenly erupted from the automatic rifles, all of them striking the officer's body, and causing him to fall to the ground, the blood gushing out of him. Taha disobeyed the plan and remained where he was so that he could watch the officer as he died; then he shouted, "God is great! God is great!" and leapt to return to the truck. Something unexpected occurred, however. Sounds of glass being violently broken were heard on the first floor and two men appeared who started shooting in the direction of the truck.

Taha realized what was happening and tried to get his head down and run in a zigzag course as they had taught him during training so as to get out of the line of fire. He was getting close to the truck, the bullets flying around him like rain, but when he got to within two meters he felt a coldness in his shoulder and chest, a coldness that burned like ice and took him by surprise. He looked at his body and saw the blood covering it and spurting and the coldness was transformed into a sharp pain that seized him in its teeth. He fell to the ground next to the rear wheel of the truck and screamed in pain. Then it seemed to him as though the terrible pain was vanishing little by little and he felt a strange restfulness engulfing him and taking him up into itself. A babble of distant sounds came to his ears—bells and sounds of recitation and melodious murmurs—repeating themselves and drawing close to him, as though welcoming him into a new world.

Translated by Humphrey Davies

Mourid Barghouti
From *Checkpoints*

TAMIM LEFT CAIRO FOR Boston on 20 August 2001. Just twenty-one days later, on 11 September 2001, the Twin Towers were blown up. He was obliged to live in an atmosphere of persecution directed against Arabs and Muslims in the United States instead of experiencing its social, scientific, cultural, and literary environment. What helped him to do so was the political openness of Boston and of New England in general. It is a fact that must be acknowledged that he was not subjected to harassment during the entire period of his residence there and that it was, for him, a normal period, with a certain measure of tension that should not be exaggerated, during which he was able to pursue his studies, teach his students, and read for the comprehensive exam that would precede the research and writing phases of his dissertation.

He took the comprehensive exam, passed, and returned to Cairo to do his research. He would take his laptop in the mornings and go to the library of the American University in Cairo, located a few steps from our house in Shari' al-Falaki, and there he would spend most of his time, racing to obtain the greatest academic benefit in the shortest possible time.

This was early in 2003 and America's around-the-clock preparations for the invasion of Iraq were speeding up.

It seemed certain that Bush would launch his attack on Iraq within two or three days.

Egyptian opposition activists had agreed via the Internet and cell phones to go to Tahrir Square in the heart of the capital at noon on whatever day the offensive started in order to demonstrate against the war.

The U.S. and British embassies are located not far from Tahrir Square, as is the American University.

At the American University, on the morning of Thursday, 20 March, a small number of students were trying to come up with a way to let the others know that the shelling of Baghdad had in fact begun during the early hours of the morning, so as to get them out to demonstrate without waiting for the agreed upon time.

They decided to set off the fire alarm.

Students and teachers rushed out of their classrooms to see what was going on. News of the war spread. They set off spontaneously for Tahrir Square and occupied it before the government could put its fortifications in place. A little later, the Cairo University students and waves of local citizens poured in. The government had lost control of the situation.

The Egyptian government spends millions of pounds to protect this particular square and only very rarely in recent history have the students of Cairo University been able to get to it, because the security forces close the university's gates on demonstrators and imprison them inside the campus, making it impossible for them to get out.

The government found that the square had fallen early, and to a threat from an unexpected direction. The students of the American University are mostly children of the ruling class or of the social elite that has the means to pay its fees, and in the estimation of the security apparatus nothing is to be feared from such people. The state went crazy.

Tamim returned from the demonstrations at night and said he expected to be arrested. He spent the night at another house and nothing untoward happened.

He returned the following day.

We became less cautious and he slept at home.

At dawn, five Egyptian security officials forced their way into our house.

Through the partly opened door, the figure of a man in civilian clothes could be seen.

"We want Tamim al-Barghouti and we want to search the house."

"Who are you?"

"State Security."

"Where's your permit?"

"Open the door immediately."

"I want to see the written permit. This is kidnapping."

When the first man heard us insist on seeing the permit, he took a step to the right, bringing into our field of vision the man standing directly behind him—a soldier wearing gleaming black body armor that gave him the appearance of a two-meter-tall metal bar and who looked as though he were about to set off for the battle front. His index finger was on the trigger of his weapon. He said nothing. He jerked his body one step to the left and another of his colleagues appeared behind him—a huge leaden twin, who didn't speak either and whose hand, like his companion's, was ready for anything.

"There's no reason to be alarmed. Just a couple of questions. We'll bring him back to you in an hour or so."

They're inviting him for 'a cup of coffee,' I told myself.

No matter the differences in terms and methods from one Arab country to another, such people are always gracious when inviting their prey to be their guests and they will always be bringing them back in an hour or so at the most. Men and women have spent decades in the cells of the Arab regimes without ever finishing that damned cup of coffee.

We got the message.

The message of fear or, rather, of intimidation.

In dictatorships, local industry's finest product—the best made, most hard-wearing, best packaged, and most quickly delivered to the home—is fear.

Impotent, Radwa and I would watch them as they took Tamim down the building staircase, their guns pointed at his back.

Thuggish authority is the same, whether Arab or Israeli. Cruelty is cruelty and abuse abuse, whoever the perpetrator.

What hurts most is the lack of a clear legal mechanism for what follows the arrest.

They don't tell you where they've taken him. His place of detention remains unknown to you—such places are many and they are scattered throughout Cairo. All you can do is look through your telephone list for the name of someone influential who may be able to direct you.

As to what happens to him there, it's no different from what any foreign occupation would do to a citizen who had the miserable luck to fall into the hands of its security forces. Humiliation, slapping, torture with hot and cold water, being hung from the ceiling with your arms behind your head, electric shocks, and sleep deprivation. None of those things may actually be done to him, but fear that they will is used deliberately to bring about the desired effect.

The night before his arrest, we were with Edward Said and his wife Mariam at the house of our friend Huda Guindi in Zamalek. Edward was talking to Tamim about his dissertation, asking him about his professors at Boston University, and telling him what he knew about them.

The following morning, Edward and Mariam were on their way to a resort on the Red Sea coast for a holiday when Edward found out via a phone call from a friend what had happened. He phoned me in the utmost fury.

"What can I do? Tell me how I can help."

"No one can do anything, Edward. Things will take their course."

Tamim, who had been given his rights in Palestine, a country he didn't know, would lose them in Egypt, the only country he knew.

He was born in Cairo to an Egyptian mother and educated at Egyptian schools, from the Happy Home kindergarten to al-Hurriya School, to Cairo University, to the American University in Cairo, where he obtained his master's degree. On arresting him along with hundreds of other students, the Egyptian security authorities would treat him as a foreigner and 'advise' him to leave the country, unlike the Egyptian students, who typically would spend a few weeks or months in the detention centers, after which they would be released. If a male Egyptian marries a woman from the furthest reaches of Eskimo Land, Egyptian law automatically grants her and her children Egyptian nationality. At the time, this same right was not granted to a female Egyptian who marries a non-Egyptian.

Tamim was forced to leave Egypt.

Translated by Humphrey Davies

Khaled Al Khamissi

from *Taxi*

ONE OF THE DIRECT social effects of the Kefaya opposition movement on the streets of Cairo is that it pushed up the taxi meters on demonstration days. Of course by meters I mean the taxi fares because the meter is there just as an ornament to embellish the car and to tear the trousers of customers who sit next to the driver.

On that particular day I was on Shooting Club Street in Dokki and heading downtown, standing looking for a taxi. Whenever I waved to one and shouted out, "Downtown," the driver would brush me off and keep on driving. That was strange. It took me back to the days of the 1980s when finding Ali Baba's treasure was easier than finding an empty taxi. You only have to look back at the cartoons of that period to see how taxi customers like me suffered from the 'yellow towel' folded over the meter. Please God don't bring such days back! Now you stand out for less than a minute to ride a beautiful taxi and you can choose from among dozens of vehicles, except that day, until one driver obliged, stopped and asked seven pounds for the trip. "Why?" I shouted.

"There are demonstrations and the world's turned upside down and it'll take me an hour to get you there," he answered. "I tell you, seven pounds won't be enough. I'll do it for ten pounds." To cut a long story short, I agreed to pay ten pounds for the trip, for which I usually pay three pounds.

It was indeed impossible to move. The cars were bumper to bumper and on top of each other on the street, moving not an inch, as though we were imprisoned in a giant garage.

"What's up?" I asked.

"Demonstration." said the driver. "Dunno why. There are about two hundred people holding banners and around them about two thousand riot police and two hundred officers, and riot police trucks blocking everything."

"All this crowd for two hundred people?" I said.

"The crowd's not from the demonstration, and it's not much of a demonstration in the first place. In the old days we used to go out on the streets with fifty thousand people, with one hundred thousand. But now there's nothing that matters. How many people are going to step out of their front door for something no one understands? And the government's terrified, its knees are shaking. I mean, one puff and the government will fall, a government without knees." He laughed out loud.

"You think the government needs legs?" I said.

"Nothing doing with the government, puffed up with false pride. But the problem's with us," said the driver.

"How so?" I said.

"You know what was the beginning of the end?"

"What?"

"The 18th and 19th of January," he said.

I was stunned by this answer, which I was hearing for the first time. I had expected many conventional responses, but the 18th and 19th of January! This was new, and I wondered whether the driver knew that the demonstrations on those days, which President Sadat called 'The Uprising of the Thieves,' took place in 1977. I don't know for certain why this stupid question came to my mind but I put it to him anyway. "What year was that?" I said.

"In the 70s, I mean about 1979," he said.

"And why was that the beginning of the end?"

"Those were the last serious demonstrations on the streets. In the 1960s we did many protests and in the 1970s before the 1973 war they were very frequent. After that Sadat, God curse him wherever he goes, issued decrees that put up the price of everything. The world turned upside down. People understood politics and they went out on the streets and made Sadat go back on his word. At the time we heard he'd taken fright and fled to Aswan and was saying that if he was overthrown properly, he'd flee to Sudan, the coward. My God, anyone could have seized power that day, but there wasn't anyone, just a bunch of wretches wanting prices to come down.

"In Abdel Nasser's time we went on demonstrations that made a real impact and suddenly we would find him there among us in Tahrir Square. He hadn't gone off to Aswan or even gone home. That's what happened after the Defeat, can't remember exactly when."

"I still haven't understood why the 18th and 19th of January were the beginning of the end." I interjected.

"After that the government realized that it had to get its act together, and that these demonstrations had become a serious danger to them. The 18th and 19th of January were not just anything, that was the start of a revolution, but you know what, it wasn't completed. And since then the government has planted in us a fear of hunger. It's made every woman hold her husband by the arm and say to him, 'Mind you don't go out. The kids will die.' They planted hunger in the belly of every Egyptian, a terror that made everyone look out for himself or say 'Why should I make it my problem?', so that's why the 18th and 19th of January were the beginning of the end."

Were the 18th and 19th of January really the beginning of the end? And what is this end that the driver was talking about with such simplicity and such certainty?

Translated by Jonathan Wright

Sharif Hatatah

from *The Eye with an Iron Lid*

THE HOARSE VOICE AMPUTATED his moment of joy.

"Put your clothes on."

He dressed quickly, in a white shirt and gray trousers, still swaying slightly. Then he slipped on a new pair of socks and the open black shoes. He fingered the coarse growth of beard on his face mechanically and then stood up.

"I'm ready."

The small group crossed over the spaces of rough sand, between the walls and low flat buildings. Everything looked half-asleep, relaxing in the warm sun. A few men in blue tunics sprayed water from their buckets on the ground with slow, indifferent, desultory movements, as though they belonged to another world. He felt Eweiss's fingers grow tight on his arm as they seemed to approach their objective. The instinctive movement of the jailer as he feels himself in the vicinity of his superiors. They suddenly emerged in front of a low building with windows and doors covered in a fine wire mesh. Then they continued along a narrow path bordered on both sides by potted cactus plants, some long and pointed, others short and swollen like blow-up water-skins. They passed through the main entrance in the middle of the building, their footsteps sounding on the polished wood floor, then turned left and came to a halt in front of a dark-green baize door with a round brass knob.

Eweiss knocked lightly on the door twice, as though his very life depended on not disturbing whoever was inside, and stood motionless, holding his breath, as though awaiting a great event. Aziz heard an indistinct voice say,

"Come in." Eweiss swung the door wide open and took two steps inside. He lifted his right arm in a salute, his rigid hand moving up and down in small, tense vibrations which refused to subside, said something in a low voice, and beckoned him to enter. Aziz stepped forward, followed by Mohammed.

The room contained a small group of people who were talking and smoking. Behind the desk sat a tall man wearing spectacles with very thick lenses which concealed his eyes, so that nothing appeared expect two indistinct dark circles. His face was white-skinned, more circular than oval, and pitted with small holes like the legacy of some pimply adolescent stage. They were thinly scattered all over, but denser on the nose and cheeks, and interspersed with tiny blackheads about the size of a pin. The mouth was coarse and thick-lipped, and seemed hardly to open even when he spoke. An expressionless face on which it was difficult to detect what might indicate anger, or content, cruelty or kindness. A meaningless face, rigid as a tool, like the head of a hammer, that can be held back in mercy or left to fall on its victim by the will of others.

On his left side, almost at his elbow, sat a gray-haired man, with small eyes that moved rapidly in all directions, a sharp nose, and two huge flop-ears that kept up a continuous slight tremble like instruments made for listening. The face of a rat on a human body so shrunken that it seemed to disappear inside the clothes. The neck, thin and wooden-like, was kept motionless, as though the continuous movement of the eyes and ears were enough for him to register all that was happening without a need to turn his head in one direction or the other. He sat bolt upright on the left side of the desk in a position that indicated his profound respect and even awe for the other people in the room. In front of him were a swollen file, a ream of white paper, and pens of different sizes and colors.

In one of the corners of the room, near a window overlooking the small garden, another man stood smoking silently. He was leaning with his elbow on a high oval pedestal raised on fine elongated legs. On the pedestal was placed a bust of Orabi, with his coarse peasant features, his bushy whiskers, and the squat Turkish fez covering his head. The man and the statute seemed to share a common disinterest in what was going on in the room, both gazing at some distant horizon, registering the conversation as it went round without the slightest hint of any reaction.

On a sofa covered with dark-red velvet sat Hegazi, with his cold blue eyes and blonde mustaches, his chin resting on a large hand. By his side was the bald-headed commandant, his gold-rimmed spectacles glinting slightly, and his wide, thin-lipped mouth tightly compressed like a slit.

When Aziz entered there was a short silence. He could feel all eyes in the room examining him with hidden care, like being weighed on a delicate scale. Only the man leaning on the pedestal continued to gaze at something in the distance that only he could see, as though he had not noticed the arrival of a newcomer in the room. The man behind the desk pointed to a large, comfortable looking armchair. Aziz lowered himself slowly into the dark-red depths, feeling his muscles relax to the soft, warm touch of the velvet. He stretched his legs under the desk, like a traveler resting after a long journey. The man nodded his head imperceptibly, upon which Eweiss withdrew through the door, followed by Mohammed. There was a moment of silence before the man asked in a clear voice, "Dr. Aziz, I believe?"

"Yes."

He paused for a moment, and stretched out his hand with a slim silver cigarette-case which opened suddenly under the pressure of his fat thumb. "Tic," the metallic click resounded like a sharp warning.

"Cigarette?"

"Thank you. I do not smoke."

"Coffee?"

"Yes, with pleasure."

He pressed on a bell-button beside him. A dark man in a blue tunic sidled through the door.

"Medium sugar?"

'No, just a smell.'

The prisoner in the blue tunic withdrew noiselessly on his bare feet. The man placed his swollen, thick hands flat on the desk and leaned forward. The small, gray-haired clerk by his side picked up one of his pens, removed the metal cap, opened his file, and waited.

"I wish to ask you a few questions."

"Please go ahead."

"Your name?"

"Aziz."

"Your full name?"

"Aziz Omran."

"Married?"

"Yes."

"What is your wife's name?"

"I no longer remember it."

"How can that be?"

"I have not seen her for years."

"How can you forget your wife's name?"

"Sometimes I forget her, and at other times I can almost touch her with my fingers."

His tone rose slightly.

"Do not try to mislead us. That will not be in your interest. Answer my questions directly. I want to know the truth."

"The truth. Since when this search for the truth? I am telling the truth, but maybe it is not the truth that you want."

"Do not try to maneuver. You will not be able to hide anything."

"I have nothing to hide. Everything must be said."

"We are in agreement, then. Now tell me the name of your wife, and her address."

"I told you, I do not remember."

"I cannot believe you. You are lying." The voice showed a trace of irritation.

"I am not lying. A man can forget what he does not wish to remember."

"Have you got children?"

"Yes, one child."

"Where is he?"

"Forgotten with his mother."

"You mean to say you have forgotten your child also?"

"He is like all children, and yet different. I remember his large black eyes, thoughtful with a flame that never dies down."

The man in the blue tunic came in through the door and placed a cup of coffee on the desk. Aziz held it for a moment in his hand, feeling the warmth under his fingers, and the exhilarating smell of coffee and cardamom creeping up his nostrils. He took two sips. His head made one delicious, stimulating turn, and then settled down again. For the first time, the eyes of the man near the pedestal shifted their look to Aziz's face. Their eyes met in a quick glance, and then broke away, like swords touching in the first moments of a duel, each opponent feeling out the other. Hegazi crossed his legs, and stared at the man in the corner as though waiting for some signal. The prosecutor busied himself lighting a cigarette from his small lacquer and gold lighter. There was a sound of tapping fingers from somewhere near the bust of Orabi, followed by a silence only broken by the slight scratch of the pen on paper.

"We want to reach a better understanding than this. Why are you so intent on being obstinate? Do you not want to finish with the situation in which you now find yourself? We want to ensure that justice is done, and you must help us."

"Whose justice?"

"The justice of law."

"Which law? The law used by those who have everything against those who have nothing?"

"You are therefore against the law?"

"No, not all laws. I am against the law of jungle."

"Do not change the subject. I am questioning you, and it is you who are supposed to answer."

"As you wish."

"You say your name is Aziz. Yet here I have documents which show that your name is not Aziz."

"Documents? I know nothing about your documents."

"We took them from your house."

"I have no house."

"We brought you from your house in Ein-Shams."

"Maybe it was someone else. I was walking in the road. Your men surrounded me and brought me here."

His fist landed on the desk suddenly and his voice rose in anger.

"You are lying again. You were in the house."

"I told you I am not lying. I have no home. My home has been destroyed, and I move around in the streets and lanes of the city."

"Our investigations have proved that you are a medical doctor. Yet what you say means that you a vagabond. Explain the contradiction. Are you a medical doctor or not?"

"Yes, I am."

"And where do you work?"

"Everywhere. I treat sick people."

"An ambulatory doctor! Don't you have fixed premises?"

"I have no fixed premises."

"You are being evasive, and this will not help you in any way."

"You are questioning me and I am answering."

The man looked at the papers in front of him.

"Our investigations also show that you had other activities."

"I work to feed myself. Sometimes I dig in the fields, or tan leather, or weave silk."

"But there papers show that you keep changing your name. Sometimes you are called Aziz, at others Hassan, or Magid. Why is that so?"

"I know nothing about the papers you mention. But it's true that I change my name."

"Why?"

"Because I am a hunted man."

"And why are you hunted?"

"I do not know why. I move from prison to prison and from one cell to another. And when I am finally released eyes follow me everywhere, and your men hunt me down without respite."

"You know the reason, but you are pretending."

"I do not know the reason."

"The papers in front of me prove the opposite of what you say. This document, for example." He held out one of the papers across the desk. "Is it not in your handwriting?"

Aziz examined the lines written neatly one below the other in a broad, square hand. He felt the faces move nearer, close in on him, waiting for the quarry to fall. He pushed the paper aside.

"I have never seen it before."

He could hear their breathing now like the panting of an animal lying in its lair.

"And these papers typed on stencil?"

"I have not seen them before."

"This notebook. Is it not yours?" He took hold of a little green notebook, flipping slowly through its pages, and read aloud in a regular, almost monotonous tone, that neither rose nor fell,

"'Mostapha.' 'Andolouse.' Who is Mostapha?"

"I do not know."

"Have you got an appointment with him on 6 April at five p.m.?"

"I said I do not know him."

"We will find out about that very soon." He flipped over another page with his fat thumb.

"'Hussein.' 'El Limoun.' 'End of the table.' What do you mean by that?"

"That notebook is not mine."

He tapped rapidly on the desk with nervous fingers. The man in the corner, who was now almost crouching, drew nearer.

"On the page dated 8 April you have noted down, 'committee. The sea as usual.' Why did you write this?"

"I do not understand anything of what you are saying."

"Dr. Aziz, how long are you going to insist on your denials? Do you not think that you are making your position more and more difficult? Turn around and look behind you."

Aziz turned his head. Next to the wall at the end of the room were two large, open trunks crammed with documents. Next to the trunks were piles of book and a typewriter.

"We found all this in your house."

"I have already said that I do not understand what you are talking about."

"What about the books? Are they not yours?"

"No."

The dark-skinned man, who was now standing about two steps away from where Aziz was sitting, moved toward the pile of books. He bent down, picked up a small lot tied with string, and carried it to the desk. Now the questions came quickly, like the lashes of a whip.

"These books. It looks as though you have read them carefully." He stopped at one of the pages of the book in front of him. "The same handwriting as the notebook and some of the documents. 'Liberty is never a gift. It is never attained except through struggle.' What do you mean?"

"Those are not my words."

"Even if they are not your words. What do you think of them?"

"I agree."

"And do you agree to everything that is written in these books and documents?"

"I would have to read through them first in order to answer your question."

"You say this book is not yours. And yet in it there is a handwritten dedication to you." He opened the cover page and pushed it towards Aziz.

"Read."

"To my friend Aziz. In memory of our first encounter. Hussein."

"Who is this Hussein?"

"I do not know him."

"But he wrote this dedication."

"I have no friend called Hussein, and this book is not mine."

"But our information tells us you do."

"What proof have you?"

The breathing in the room suddenly stopped. Like a drop of water changed into ice in mid-air, Aziz felt his heart drop into an empty space. Everything seemed to become lost, to disappear, to cease its existence, as he heard the words. Everything except the twitch of muscle in his neck like a slaughtered bird.

"Hussein told us that he dedicated the book to you."

The cell surrounded him with complete darkness. From time to time he could hear the sound of footsteps outside, and muffled voices approach then move away, or the cough of sentinel trying to chase the sleep away from his eyes. The khamaseen winds blew with an almost uninterrupted whistle, cut through at infrequent intervals by silence. Sometimes the whistle would grow into a howl like that of some animal lost in the desert sands. The fine particles of sand crept under the lower edge of the door, filling his nose and mouth with the taste and smell of grit, and smothering his respiration.

Sleep had deserted him completely, and the days passed like one wave after another breaking on an unknown shore in a monotonous, slow, unchanging movement, with no difference between them. Today was like yesterday, and tomorrow would be like today. Everything in the room remained immobile, the same. He needed four steps to traverse the length of his cell, and only two and a half for the width, counted by the clink of his chins. The floor sloped slightly toward the door, and the door was dark green, with a small, round, iron-rimmed opening two-thirds of the way up. The opening was closed by a metal lid that dropped down, like an eye which sometimes opened to watch, its iron lid lifting silently so that it could observe and register. A cold eye that waited patiently. The ceiling was low, and seemed to drop lower, gradually pressing on his body with a growing weight, and the walls were a dirty white, almost yellow, traversed by fine rivulets of humidity, and stained all over their surface by spots of blood, or coffee-brown-colored fingerprints. Each time he noticed some minute detail that looked new, he would contemplate it, study it carefully for hours, his interest quickened by the feeling of something discovered in the putrefied, perpetually stagnant water of his existence. The taste of salt on the tip on his tongue when he licked the whitewash on the wall, a procession of small ants following their devious path from the corner of the window down the wall, then across the black tarmac floor round the legs of the square table, and finally up one of the legs to its top in search of the crumbs of bread, anything seemed sufficient to arouse his interest in the all-enveloping monotony of the narrow cell.

He was now used to the smell of urine and rot that rose in sudden waves from the rubber bucket squatting in a corner of the room, waves that had no particular frequency, but could pour out at any moment, in the middle of the night, when the wind blew cold and strong around the walls, or at midday in the suffocating heat when he stood over it, his legs apart, emptying the hot yellow urine accumulated in his bladder, then they would come strong and overpowering with slow putrefaction of years. He became used to the nause-ating odor that crept down to his guts from under his nose and mouth, where his head lay on the pillow, each time the dark-brown bugs were crushed under him as they crawled in heavy slowness, leaving a stain of red hemorrhage. He became used to the smell of stale, sour sweat in his clothes, and the animal

odor of a creature imprisoned in a cage excreting the wastes of its body day
after day in the place where it lived.

He became used to all these smells. Sometimes he revolted against them
from the very depths of his being, and at others he felt a feeling of pleasure,
almost of ecstasy when they crept through the air. For they were the odors of
his own existence, the odors that meant he was alive.

Translated by Sharif Hatatah

Raouf Musad

from *The Ostrich Egg*

Cairo, June 1983

THIS IS MY SECOND SUMMER in Cairo—and in Egypt—in thirteen years, since I
left for Poland in 1970. The temperature is high but it remains bearable if compared to Baghdad's scorching heat or Beirut's heavy humid summers. . . .

Cairo, Mid-June 1983

The commemoration of the 1967 defeat. We had been released from the prisons and detention camps in April 1964. We were looking forward to working
with the regime (this was the agreement when we dissolved the party). We
had done so while in prison but in politics, like in life itself, there are interests
and favoritism. The poorer members of the party found themselves on the
street, jobless, or in menial positions while the more affluent members were
posted in important positions. To be fair, some of the poorer members foisted
their way into some jobs because they had been leaders within the party. The
rest fell under the horses' hooves.

Today, I met Nasr by pure coincidence. He was originally a simple
mechanic with limited cultural background. I got to know him during my
time in the Oasis detention camp. He was about my age (in his mid-twenties).
He was not with me in the same cell but we were in the same ward (ward number one). We became inseparable friends. We smoked our cigarettes together
from the same wooden filter that he made with his clever hands; he helped
me with the gardening in the nursery, which was new to me. I used to tell him

about the books I had read and the films I had seen. He had a beautiful soft voice and a naturally timid demeanor. He had arrived at the Oasis detention camp before me and knew it inside out with its written and secret laws and the complex relationships between the detainees. He also knew how to make cigarettes when they could not be had, and he managed to get his hands on tea and sugar and all the other good things that make up the daily dreams of the detainees. From him I came to know about love stories and desire in the camp . . . how people reacted when a hidden relationship was discovered, the limits of what was acceptable and what was forbidden. There was the young handsome university student who was 'loved' by two inmates. There was the young man with the serious face and a feminine body. He was the most desired but was betrothed to someone else. Most of the relationships were platonic in nature since there was no privacy and it was almost impossible for two men to be alone together. The cells in the Oasis detention camp were big and crowded. Sometimes twelve detainees lay on mats side by side so that each could hear the others' every movement in the cell whether he wanted to or not. But the long duration of the detention created a kind of tolerance and acceptance. It was a normal thing for two detainees to seek to be alone in the nursery (only a stone's throw away from the gaze of the others) or at the far end of the yard where they would smoke and chat for a long time. No one would intrude on them or interrupt their privacy. Nasr had told me that he had been "in love" with someone who had been transferred to Fayoum detention camp. He spoke about his love for that person quite naturally. There was no sense of disgrace or loss of 'masculinity.' He said that it was the first time in his life that he had felt this way. He did not speak about details but I was able to read between the lines. There was no active and passive partner but rather a mutual desire to communicate with each other and to set free the fantasies of the already imprisoned body in tattered rotten prison clothes, fed on disgusting food, surrounded by barbed wire and the loss of hope in ever leaving and seeing the streets once more. A special relationship grew between us. We looked after each other, exchanged simple things that we owned and agreed on times and places to meet. Here I am, meeting him by coincidence after many years. No, actually, I had met him before, immediately after we were released. He had given me directions to his workplace (the family workshop). I had gone to see him there. He had not changed much. I felt he wanted to avoid me. Perhaps he was ashamed of his clothes or his simple, dilapidated work place. We decided to meet in a coffee shop he chose in his working class neighborhood in the evening. We had tea and talked about life after prison: the difficulty, the projects, who we had met among our detention comrades. I did not recognize in him the Nasr I had known. He was closed and troubled. We parted with the noncommittal invitation, "Do come by again." But I never did. I regretted having contacted him to begin with. And here I was meeting him again by coincidence after all these years. We found refuge from the bustle of the street and the crowds at a small coffee shop. I was preparing to leave on a trip to Sudan (the first one since we had left in the 1950s, fifteen years ago in a tormenting attempt to recapture the past). He listened to me attentively. He did not say much about himself. We discovered that we both had not married yet and laughed at the similarity. We did not speak about prison, or about the past. We were in the midst of the ugly present. When we separated we did not agree on another appointment. He did not ask for my address or my phone number and did not volunteer anything to gratify my curiosity. He did not even know that I had written a book about the High Dam. Perhaps he was ashamed of himself for I had made some of my dreams come true: I wrote and I traveled. But he had remained in his workshop. I watched him disappear in the Cairo crowds. It was his same old gait.

Translated by Samia Mehrez

Sonallah Ibrahim
from *The Smell of It*

"What's your address?" said the officer.

"I haven't got one," I said.

"Where, then, are you off to? Where are you going to stay?" He looked at me in amazement.

"I don't know." I said. "I have no one."

"I can't let you go off just like that," said the officer.

"I used to live on my own." I said.

"We have to know your whereabouts," he said, "so we can come and see you each evening. A policeman will be going with you."

And so we went out, the policeman and I, into the street. I glanced round curiously. This was the moment I had continually dreamed of throughout those past years. I searched within myself for some unusual sensation, of pleasure or joy or excitement, but found none. People were walking and talking and moving quite naturally, as though I had always been with them and nothing had happened.

"Let's take a taxi," said the policeman.

I told myself that he wanted to have an outing at my expense. We went to my brother's place. On the stairs we met my brother, who told me he was just going away, and that he had to lock up the flat. We walked down and went off to a friend's.

"My sister's staying here," said my friend, "and I can't take you in."

We went back into the street. The policeman began to grumble; a savage look came into his eyes. I thought to myself that he wanted ten piasters.

"We can't go on like this," he said. "Let's get along back to the station."

At the station there was another policeman. He said, "You're a real problem and we can't just let you be."

I sat down in front of him, putting my suitcase on the floor, and lit a cigarette. Night came and he said he was unable to do anything. He called over a third policeman and said to him, "Lock him up," and they led me off to a locked room with a fourth policeman standing at the door. He searched me and took my money and pocketed it. They then put me into a large room which had a wooden bench raised slightly above the floor along the walls. I seated myself on the bench. There were many men there and all the time the door was being opened to let in yet more. I felt a pricking on my neck. I put my hand up to my neck and felt a wetness. I looked at my hand and found there was a large blob of blood on my finger. The next moment I saw dozens of bugs on my clothes. I stood up. For the first time I noticed the large splodges of blood that stained the whole of the walls.

One of the people there laughed and said to me: "Come here."

Some of the people were sitting down on the floor. One of them had spread out a torn blanket on the floor. I found myself a small corner on the very edge where I sat down, resting my chin on my knees.

"Why don't you go to sleep?" the owner of the blanket said to me, but there wasn't room for my whole body to lie down on it.

"I prefer to sit like this," I said.

Someone else asked me, "Drugs?"

"No," I said.

"Larceny?" he said.

"No," I said.

"Murder?"

"No."

"Bribery?"

"No."

"Forgery?"

"No."

At a loss, the man lapsed into silence and proceeded to give me odd looks. I began shivering with the cold, then I stood up and walked about a little. I sat down again. Tired from the way I had been sitting, I shifted my position. One of the men produced a blanket which he had kept folded up under him and began preparing for sleep. I began amusing myself by hunting for the bugs that were running along the floor and killing them. Suddenly I lowered my head over my chest. I didn't want them to see my face. They had begun to give themselves up to sleep. In front of me an old man had stretched out to sleep on the bench. The policeman opened the door and called out to him, "There's someone asking for you."

The old man came back carrying a blanket and a pillow and stretched himself out on the bench, covering himself up with the blanket and leaning his head against the pillow; soon he was asleep, breathing loudly and paying no attention to the bugs.

Alongside him there sat a man who was staring into my face, his hands plunged into the pockets of his overcoat, which was undone, his chest naked, for he was wearing nothing under the coat. Suddenly this man let out a strange frightening howling sound; he got up and approached me swaying; he laughed into my face, then sat down alongside me, staring in front of him distractedly; then he gave another howl, and a young, heavily built man got up and struck him in the face.

"Don't hit me," said the madman, lifting his arm to protect his face. Blows from the young man rained down on him. I heard his bones crack. He fell down where he was, breathing heavily. The others laughed.

The owner of the blanket pulled it over himself and spread it out with his hand over a plump young boy who was sleeping beside him. I saw the boy's face before it was covered over by the blanket. He had a bronze complexion and full lips. He was immersed in sleep, his knees flexed. The man encircled him with his arm under the blanket. He began moving until he was right up against him. I watched his arm under the blanket as it moved over the boy's body, stripping him of his trousers. The man's thighs pressed against the boy's back. Alongside the boy sat the heavily built young man who had struck the madman. He was following what was taking place underneath the blanket, raising his eyes continually to meet mine. After a while the movement under the blanket quietened down. The cover shook and the boy sat up, wiping his eyes as he roused himself from sleep. He began looking down between his thighs. I dozed off as I sat there, then came to again. I didn't see the heavily built young man, then I caught sight of his thighs from under the blanket. He was asleep, hugging the boy to him. I got up and walked about, and the blanket shook. The young man dragged it from off the boy and wrapped it all round himself. The boy slept on, his thighs naked.

The darkness began to lighten. I watched the light of dawn spread. At last they opened up so we could wash. They took the boy away to make him clean out the courtyard. The rest brought out food and breakfast.

The boy appeared at the door and asked, "Haven't you left me anything?"

"No," said the heavily built young man.

The policeman began calling out names. I heard my name, I took up my suitcase and went out. I found my sister waiting with the policeman of yesterday. He handed me a small book bearing my name and a photo of myself. We went out, my sister and I, to the street.

"Do you want anything to drink?" said my sister.

"I want to walk," I said.

Translated by Denys Johnson-Davies

Nawal El Saadawi
from *Memoirs from the Women's Prison*

I HEARD THE SOUND—like an explosion—of the door breaking. Their metallic boots pounded the floor in quick rhythm like army troops bursting forth in the direction of battle. They attacked the flat like savage locusts, their open mouths panting and their rifles pointed.

I could not see myself, but it seems that my appearance had changed, and so had my face and eyes. A devil must have been taking over my body. . . for I was no longer afraid. In the small sitting room, I stood before them, head held high, prepared to face them to death.

For a moment, they stood fixed, as if pinned to the ground before me. I must have appeared frightening to them, and I spoke in a voice which was also terrifying. "You broke down the door. This is a crime."

I don't know what happened then; perhaps my voice confirmed to them that I was a woman and not a devil. Maybe they were surprised that I was still in the flat and had not escaped.

They surrounded me, their breathing still heavy. Long, haggard faces damp with sweat. Open mouths panting. Noses curved like the beaks of predatory birds.

One band of them closed in, enveloping me like an iron chain, while another spread out in the three rooms. They searched through my drawers, and I saw one of them picking up the novel from my desk. I shouted furiously, "That's a novel! Leave it alone, don't touch it!"

But the man crammed it into a bag he was carrying. "This is another crime!" I yelled in rage. "How dare you snatch my novel from me? You have no business with it."

Another man began leafing through the private diary lying on my desk, reading bits from it, his hands toying with the small clock which I keep there.

I heard their chief saying, "Take her to the car, and we will catch up with you after we've finished searching the flat."

"Search the flat in my absence?" I asked him. "This is a third crime! If anything is lost, you are responsible."

We descended the five floors. All the doors to the flats were shut tight. Bewildered eyes peered from behind the small apertures. We stood waiting on the ground floor. The rest of the men and their chief—the officer—were still inside my flat, scattering and going through my papers and private belongings. Anger was collecting in my throat like a lump. One of my neighbors came near, and they pushed him away quickly with their rifles.

The officer appeared, surrounded by his men, still panting and carrying my papers. The armed procession left the building. At a distance, people were stopping in the street, gazing at the awesome parade, their eyes full of fear. A woman carrying a child cried out angrily, "Shame on you! Poking rifles in the face of a woman. Go fight Israel instead!" From a distance, a young girl waved to me, and I waved back.

In a flurry, the officer ordered the armed men to get into the vans. They clambered in, rifles on their shoulders. The officer led me to one of the vehicles and requested that I climb in to sit between him and the driver. I refused, saying "I'll sit by the window."

The officer looked at me in astonishment. For the first time. I took in his face: curly black hair, black eyes, a thick black mustache. Full lips parted to reveal very white teeth as he said, "That's not permitted. It's against instructions." His voice was harsh, but beneath the roughness I could detect a tone of weakness, and his eyes, despite their impenetrable gleaming blackness, held a note of passivity, a sort of submission to orders, or resignation to fate.

He tried to persuade me to sit between him and the driver, but I refused to sit between two men in this heavy heat. Two strange bodies oozing the sweat of hatred. It was absolutely necessary to impose my will from the start. I didn't know where they were taking me: to prison, or to my death? Nothing concerned me any longer except the issue of sitting where I wanted. Then let whatever would happen go ahead and happen.

The officer looked at me in the eye, and I fixed my gaze on his. I didn't blink, but he did, and looked at the ground. Perhaps he was thinking, and telling himself: even if my orders lack intelligence, I don't. There is no reason to stir up people in the street. Then, she's a woman and won't jump out of the door while the van is moving.

A look of despair came over his face. He got in ahead of me and seated himself next to the driver. I stepped up after him and sat next to the door.

The air moved as soon as the van was in motion. I took a deep breath. My will had won out. A simple matter, but as the first victory it was important.

People were still standing along the street. Some of the young men raised their hands and waved to me; I waved back. The officer jumped up in agitation on his seat, "Please don't speak to anyone."

"I'm not, I'm waving to them."

The van sped off. My throat is parched, my heart is still throbbing, although heavily. My limbs feel cold, although my fingers still work normally. The leather handbag is still on my shoulder, and the shoes still on my feet. From the car window, an invigorating breeze reaches my face, and before my eyes are Giza Street and the zoo, University Street and the cars, people on the street, everything around me as it was before any of this happened.

But I am no longer the same. Something momentous has happened, and in the wink of an eye I no longer belong to the world outside the van, nor to those people walking in the street, nor to the ones in their cars going home.

Returning home seemed like an impossible feat, or like being transported from one world to another. I opened my eyes, closed them, and imagined that I would reopen them and find myself in my home, the nightmare over.

I opened my eyes and found myself sitting in a van, beside a police officer. Behind me, I could catch a glimpse of the tips of rifles jutting out from the roof of the van. I was still unable to believe this scene. The officer removed his hat and placed it on his knees, wiped the sweat from his face and head with a large white handkerchief. "You really tired us out, doctor."

My eyes widened. Was he addressing me? Was I still this 'doctor'? My memory began to return . . . . I'd been sitting at my desk, writing the novel, and I heard the knock on the door, followed by more knocks before the door was smashed open with the noise of an explosion.

"Who tired out whom?" I asked in amazement. "You broke down the door. That's a crime punishable by law."

He smiled sarcastically. "What law? Didn't you hear yesterday's speech?"

"What speech?"

"The speech given by the President of the Republic . . . Sadat."

"I don't listen to speeches."

"If you'd heard it, you'd know everything."

"I'd know what?"

"You'd know why we came to you and where we are taking you."

"Where are you taking me?"

"Nothing at all! Just a question or two, and you'll return to your home."

"Interrogation!"

"No, no, simpler than that. Just a couple of questions, then you'll be home."

If that officer had told me that he was taking me to jail, perhaps the situation would have been bearable, or at least not quite so awful. At least I would have known where I was going. Knowledge, no matter what it reveals, is less painful than ignorance.

Ignorance is like death, or rather it really is death. If we were familiar with death then there would be neither death nor the fear of it.

Ignorance is fear. Nothing terrifies a person except ignorance. The amazing journey from the door of my home to the prison took several hours, during which I experienced the strangest ignorance in my life. It was exactly like being blind; it was as if they had bound a thick black covering around my eyes to shut out the light and the road so that I would not know where I was going. Each time I asked the officer where we were headed he replied with "Never mind, its nothing at all. Just an hour and you'll go home."

. . .

The van straightened out on the road, the sound of the motor monotonously regular and the officer's snoring audible over it. His lips hung loosely—thick lips, the lower one drooping over a full, square beard. His tunic, open at the neck, revealed a thick, pale neck, as his head bobbed and then fell on to a burly chest. Fine threads of white saliva ran down his lips, falling on to a bit of gold glinting on his chest.

I raised my head, looking toward the road. The lights of the barrages were reflected on the surface of the Nile, but they were still distant as the car turned off on to a road so dark and narrow that it looked like a subterranean passage. We turned off on to another road, still darker and narrower. The smell of the crops and the Nile disappeared. The odor of dirt filled my nose.

At the end of the gloomy vault I saw a long horizontal pole blocking the road. The car stopped before it. The officer opened his eyes suddenly in alarm and wiped his mouth off on his palm. From the roadside, a thin man appeared, his eyes gleaming and darting about like those of a highwayman. He scrutinized the officer and vehicle for a moment, then his hunched figure hurried over and pulled the pole with a rope, or perhaps it was a chain, so that it swung high enough into the air to let the van pass. It fell into place once again, and the road was blocked behind us.

The van moves at a crawl through a long dark passageway. The air is sluggish, and the darkness is getting heavier; it's as silent as a grave in this place. The walls are as high as the Cairo Citadel. The sky and the stars have vanished. The van came to a complete stop.

My eyes collided with a huge black door like the doors of forts and castles from the Mamluk era. Several armed men approached us, images of the angels who toss dead souls into hell straight from the Courts of Inquisition. Their long and sharply pointed rifles and bayonets reminded me of the needles which used to be plunged into the bodies of witches in search of the mark of the devil. Their eyes were like bits of glass, and I was surrounded by eyes gazing at me, front and back, head to foot.

One of them tapped at the huge door with his rifle butt. A bald head and two shifting, glassy eyes peered from the narrow aperture in the door. He raised his hand in greeting when he noticed the officer and bowed.

The gap in the door was the size of a dwarf, and the threshold was high. I raised my foot to step up. I am tall, and I couldn't enter without bending. I doubled over: a body entering the mouth of a grave, my white dress the color of the shroud. The officer's hands helped me to enter like the undertaker's hands would. It was as if I had seen this scene before, but when? Thick darkness, the odor of dust and rot.

I exerted pressure on my eyelids to open them, but they were already open. I saw a dark passage ending in a black shape, head wrapped in a white kerchief. Above the head was an electric light, like a single, open, red eye. The shape raised its hand in greeting. Its rifle butt hit the cement floor, and one metallic heel struck against the other.

A hole opened in the wall; the earth swallowed me.

Translated by Marilyn Booth

Hamdi el-Gazzar

from *Secret Pleasures*

Anwar Gabr

I picture being face to face with Anwar Gabr.

I collect my strength and willpower and I conjure him up to know him, to observe him, and to denude him of his official uniform. I make him walk like us: an insignificant person on the street, just like everyone else. . . .

I want him to come to me face to face.

Come, man.

He comes confidently and conceitedly, smiling with the arrogance of a terrifying military man. I see his face clouded and blurred, bolted, ready for hysterical laughter. I see him as he appeared before me on the internet.

For more than twenty hours I had been pursuing him, following the well-known search engines: Yahoo, MSN, Alta Vista, Maktoub, al-Mohit, Masrawi, al-Arabiya, al-Zaman, and so on.

I smoke like a madman, I eat at the cigarettes; I smoke and I sweat in the cold of my room. The nipping cold dawn wind enters through my window, which opens onto the street. If I shut it I will suffocate from the smoke of my constantly lit cigarettes. As I surf the internet to the north and to the south, to the east and to the west—if this world has any sense of direction or longitudes and latitudes—having lost all sense of my surroundings, I search with my hands and eyes, with all my senses and my brain, with nothing in my mind but the letters that constitute his name. Like a madman I search for his name in Arabic and Latin letters, in the open, denuding, and transparent virtual space. I search for him, for anything that has to do with him.

I am overtaken by bitter despair from the thousands of results that I find. The hormone levels in my blood rise to combat the danger. I defeat my despair and continue searching wildly as if I were going to eat the computer and gulp it up.

After fifteen hours of continuous, exhausting search, I found that small corner in the infinite world of images, sound, videos, and words. I must have tracked at least fifteen people who had the same name and more or less the same profession. Perhaps this is my final destination. With uncertainty, with doubt, and with suspicion I read the letters of his name and I look at his fuzzy face that has been filmed with a poor cellphone camera. Only the left side of his face is visible: a blurred profile.

Is this the person I want, the person I am looking for?

Maybe. I don't know.

What I see now is the face that stood in Shawqi's room, the same face that appeared in the video that is posted on one of the blogs.

The blog is small, with limited capacity and is free on Yahoo GeoCities. The colors are bright on the homepage, shining on braided ropes that appear along the length and breadth of the page as if they were decorating the façade of a house or shop or a new laundry joint. . . .

After a quick reading of the jokes on the blog, I found him. I found Anwar Gabr.

In the video that was of mediocre acoustic and visual quality he was a young man of about thirty in an ordinary shirt and trousers. He had a long black whip in his hand with which he was whipping a beautiful girl of about twenty.

He orders her, with repeated gestures of his right hand, to take off her blouse. The young man's face is bolted shut. The girl cries and shakes her neck left and right in refusal. The whip slashes against her chest lightly. The young man orders her again with a sign of his hand. The girl beseeches him with tears in her eyes and a soft wailing voice, her hands against her chest to cover it. The sound of the whip is louder this time as it falls on the girl's stomach and waist. The girl unbuttons her blouse with a submissive cloudy face. The young man smiles uncouthly as he eyes what protrudes from her bra: two full breasts with a deep exciting bronze cleavage between them. The young man gulps while the girl looks very ashamed and tries to hide her nakedness with her hands. She places both hands on her breasts. The young man hits her. The tip of the whip falls on her white bra. The girl howls and slaps her cheeks violently. The whip rises in the air and falls on her knees, then on her thighs in her baggy, white slacks. She screams. The young man holds the tip of the whip with his free hand. He threatens her with a sign of his right index finger. The look in his eyes is frightening. He is silent and looks at her angrily. The girl's eyes are filled with absolute horror. Slowly, the girl reaches around for her bra with trembling hands. She tries to take it off from the front but she fails. She looks at the young man, completely crushed. The young man's lips utter some inaudible insults. Slowly, hesitantly the girl reaches out to her back and undoes her bra with her tears streaming down her face as she gazes at the ground. The young man's mouth is open. He licks his tongue with pleasure. She has full breasts and two small nipples. Her chest shines and her eyes are completely hard, flooded with tears. The young man looks like he is nearing a climax. Suddenly he laughs and lashes the whip on the tile and then points it at her breast and nipples. The girl screams in pain and horror. The young man's body twists and turns as he moans as if ejaculating. His arm is stretched out completely as he lashes the whip and hits the naked breasts. It slashes her skin as she screams. The young man is drunk on the girl's horrified screaming. His body sways. He is drunk on the madness of pleasure. He screams and the lashes from the whip accelerate frantically. He moans and hits as hard as he can. The girl has rolled her body into a ball: her hands are over her head, her dark skin is marked with the lashes of the whip, the whip leaves lasting lines and circles and long dark red blotches. Her weeping will rip her apart. The lashes of the whip become more violent, they follow quickly and brutally one after the other on her body. Her entire small body has become a bulk of bleeding red from which sounds of supplication like those from the torture in hell are heard. The girl screams and screams from fear and unbearable pain.

Suddenly, the image stops.

Almost sixty seconds in the sadistic jungle of hell, enough to wrench one's heart and gray one's hair.

I got up from my seat terrified, placing my hand on my mouth. I ran to the bathroom and emptied my guts as my entire body shook with every convulsion of my stomach and gaping mouth and the food and drink that poured out of my entrails. I shuddered and almost knocked my head against the sink, practically pissing in my pants.

After I completely emptied my stomach, I took off all my clothes and stood under the shower, letting the water run on my body for more than an hour. I stood naked, trembling. I mumbled like someone hallucinating with fever. I hallucinated for a long time and then I collapsed. No one heard me: not my mother, not my wife.

I am not at all sure that the young man is Anwar Gabr. And I cannot fathom watching that horror once again.

I have not seen Anwar Gabr for the past fifteen years. Is it possible that if we subtract fifteen years from the face I saw on the damned video that it would be the same handsome, innocent face of the student at Abul Hol School?

I don't know. And it seems I never will.

Translated by Samia Mehrez

Women in the City

This section brings together literary representations of women in the city from different class and social backgrounds whose multiple roles are defined and shaped by the space they occupy or strive to inhabit in the city. The numerous roles that women play, as mothers, lovers, artists, house cleaners, prostitutes, students, and professionals are not uniform or identical in their constraints or limitations but rather, are conditioned to a great extent by the social space and context, that is, class affiliation, family background, and urban experience in general, of the women themselves. As one reads these representations, one cannot help but see the extent to which they unsettle preconceived ideas and stereotypes that have come to be attached to women specifically from Arab countries. Given that the representations of women in the city also span more than one hundred years, we are able to trace changes in the space accorded to women across the social spectrum. Similarly, at a synchronic level, we can discern the wide range of positions and possibilities that are available to women in the city at one and the same time. Through the experiences of these different women, readers will encounter different faces of Cairo that have everything to do with these women's locations within the city.

One of the fascinating and quite exceptional representations of a practically extinct role that was played by women for centuries is to be found in Tawfiq al-Hakim's 1933 *The Return of the Spirit*. The story of the cultivated singer, Maestra Labiba Shakhla, an almeh, who frequented the narrator's family, is reconstructed from the memory of a six-year-old child, Mohsin, who represents, to a great extent, the author himself as a child. Little Mohsin's mother had seen Maestra Labiba Shakhla at the wedding reception of one of her relatives and was "immediately taken by that famous artiste's manners and decorum, modesty and taste." Even though Labiba's fame name, 'Shakhla,' evokes playfulness and erotica, the Maestra is invited to the family home and becomes a regular member of the household entertainment and animated evenings of music, song, storytelling, and cuisine. Maestra Labiba's story is of great significance for several reasons. First, the very fact that she is a family guest represents an important statement about the status of such cultivated women artistes, not to mention the status of art in general, so much so that six-year-old Mohsin is allowed to partake of the Maestra's presence and her accomplishment and is influenced by her talent and humor in storytelling. Indeed, it is common knowledge that Tawfiq al-Hakim's distinguished career as a man of letters was inspired by encounters with artistes like Labiba Shakhla who shaped his imagination as they did little Mohsin's in *The Return of the Spirit*, leaving a definitive imprint on both the character in the novel and the author himself, whose career veered from that of a public prosecutor to that of a brilliant playwright, novelist, essayist, and leading public intellectual figure.

The freedom and respect that Maestra Labiba Shakhla possessed and the creative powers that she wielded stand in sharp contrast to Naguib Mahfouz's almost contemporaneous character Amina, the middle class, traditional, cloistered wife who inhabits the same city but has never set foot outside the bounds of her own house. Amina's ultimate dream was to pay a visit to the shrine of al-Hussein, which, with the help of her children, and behind the patriarch's back and in his absence, she does realize but not without paying a terrible price: she is banished by her husband from her home and sent back to her family as punishment for daring to violate his orders.

Unlike the obedient and dominated Amina in *Palace Walk*, Hamida the central character in Mahfouz's *Midaq Alley* is a young rebellious, headstrong, lower-class woman. Ironically, Hamida's underprivileged situation and disadvantaged social circumstances actually provide her with the prospects of much more mobility in the city. As a young, poor, and orphaned girl she is not bound by the same middle- and upper-class values of respectability for women and therefore enjoys far more space in the city, indeed, within and beyond the very same neighborhood that Amina of *Palace Walk* inhabits. Hamida ventures out of the alley and dreams of becoming like the well-dressed and prosperous factory girls and the more liberated Jewish girls, who had taken advantage of wartime Egypt and found new employment opportunities, thus acceding to more freedom and space in the city. But, Hamida's ambitious dream turns to disaster and the glitter of the city and its seduction ultimately lead to her death.

Likewise, Fathiya, the pretty and timid peasant girl in Yusuf Idris's *The Siren*, who marries Hamid the bawwab because she wants to come to Cairo, is doomed and transformed by the opportunities with which the city of her dreams tempts her. Her initial, daring bet, "Just you wait and I'll get even with

you, Cairo," is won at the end but not without taxing her original rural innocence. Even the middle-class literate women find the city's prospects hard to
resist. In Mohamed Salah al-Azab's much more recent *Frequent Stops*, Randa
finds herself succumbing to prostitution and uses her "ordinary appearance
and the ringed notebook that she presses to her chest" as a ploy against
"the Vice Squad officers who heavily patrol [the] area." For all these characters—Amina, Hamida, Fathiya, Randa—and despite their radically different
positions in the city, Cairo is 'the siren,' the alluring, seductive caller that
threatens and unsettles traditional mores and values, both urban and rural,
creating new creatures more fit than misfit for its challenges.

This is the case for many of the women we encounter in these literary representations. For example, we meet Umm Fathiya the Nubian "black bride
adorned with pearl necklaces," the motherly house cleaner for the three young
Moroccan students in Mohamed Berrada's *Like a Summer Never to Be Repeated*,
who drinks and smokes with "her Moroccan boys" but also scolds them for not
keeping in touch after they leave Cairo: "Is this acceptable, Hammad? Only
one letter in all these years. . . . Didn't we know each other well? Living together
is not taken lightly except by the illegitimate." In Sonallah Ibrahim's satiric
novel *Zaat*, we meet Umm Atef the Coptic housemaid, who is begrudgingly
employed by an increasingly Islamized Zaat, out of a sense of obligation to the
cause of national unity. Umm Atef is "short, skinny and covered in dust, her
clothes were dirty and infested with fleas and the soles of her feet were full of
cracks and ridges," but she is also thrifty and practical in her own way, devising
ingenious yet, from Zaat's perspective, disastrous methods of grouping, into
one bottle, different medical pills scattered among various half-full containers!

As these poorer women, single heads of impoverished households, accede
to freer circulation in the urban space, moving between their own modest
abodes and those of their bourgeois employers, they begin to refashion their
ways of dealing with the city to accommodate their employers' demanding
tastes and their own new and sometimes perplexing contexts. But, despite
their relentless efforts to re-tailor their own understanding of the city, Cairo,
the vanquisher, continues to crush them along with more privileged women
under relentless pressures: economic, social, professional, and religious. In
Khaled Al Khamissi's *Taxi* we witness the drastic transformation of a young,
initially veiled woman inside the cab as she undresses to fit the colliding and
challenging urban contexts that she must inhabit. As she takes off her veil in
the cab and reveals the hidden hair curlers beneath it, she explains to the dumbfounded cab driver that she tells her parents that she is employed in a hospital
when in reality she waitresses at an uptown bar. She concludes: "Frankly, I earn

a thousand times as much working [at the bar]. In a single day I can get in tips what I would earn in one month's salary in the moldy old hospital."

But women's mobility in the city is not without its risks and high cost. Whether we choose to look at the lower- or upper-class women, the city can have a crushing effect on these women's very being. No wonder then that there is a shared vision of the city from characters as radically different as Mahrousa the prison warden in Salwa Bakr's *The Golden Chariot* and Amira Abou-Taleb's slick, high-tech, professional narrator in *Barbed Silk*. In Bakr's text, Mahrousa becomes a warden in the women's prison after being abused, robbed, and finally abandoned by her husband and is ultimately reduced to begging on the streets of the city to feed her six children. Even though Abou-Taleb's narrator is accomplished and fulfilled on many levels: social, economic, and professional, she still senses "the weight of a heavy rock settle deep inside her gut . . . . The soul is dead. All that is left is a corpse that knows how to drive and has memorized the way to work." The very title of Abou-Taleb's text, *Barbed Silk*, is telling of the similarities between the text's 'successful' upper-class narrator's sense of the pressures of the city and Mahrousa's own experience in it as an underdog.

One fascinating aspect that cuts through all these representations of women in the city is the extent to which women occupy a special location in the languages(s) of the city. Throughout these excerpts we encounter a female language that reveals itself through the very consciousness of the characters: their dreams, their disillusionments, their expectations, their fears, and their disappointments. This century-long dynamic, ever-changing, and living female language is articulated through special idiomatic expressions, metaphors, images, slang, and streetwise lingo that are all specifically those of women in the city. Perhaps the most fascinating example in this regard is Ghada Abdel Al's best-selling blog-turned-book, made into a highly successful Ramadan TV series in 2010, *I Want to Get Married*, which is completely written in colloquial Egyptian Arabic and is littered with young, hip, women's slang.

It is important to note, however, that most of the literary representations in this section are ones produced by male writers about women in the city. With the exception of Ahdaf Soueif, Salwa Bakr, Amira Abou-Taleb, and Ghada Abdel Al, all other excerpts are by male authors. This means that most of the women represented here are doubly imagined; their world and language(s) doubly constructed from the perspective of the male authors. It should be an excellent exercise for readers to compare excerpts by male authors to those by female authors to determine for themselves points of conversion and diversion between the various representations of women's spaces, locations, and languages in the city.

Tawfiq al-Hakim

from The Return of the Spirit

MUHSIN WAS SIX YEARS old when Maestra Labiba Shakhla frequented his family's home. There was more than mere coincidence to the story of that artist and her close contact with the family. Muhsin's grandmother at that time was suffering from a nervous complaint for which no medicine or cure could be found. Many doctors had treated her without achieving any results. At last one of them, after trying everything, said, "The best thing for a state like hers is peace of mind, freedom from worries, and a cheerful outlook. Entertain her as much as possible. Pleasure and joy may improve her condition . . . "

"Entertain and delight her how, Doctor?"

"In other words, sing to her. Help her relax. Song and music are the best remedy for her."

The coincidence came after that. Muhsin's mother saw Maestra Labiba Shakhla at the wedding reception of one of her relatives. She was immediately taken by that famous artist's manners and decorum, modesty and taste. She found her exquisite. Shakhla likewise picked out Muhsin's mother in the crowd of ladies. A certain aloofness in her personality caught her eye. So they made each other's acquaintance. On that occasion Muhsin's mother mentioned the sick lady whose cure was music. She seized the opportunity and invited Shakhla to visit.

From that time on the Maestra Labiba Shakhla visited Muhsin's family every summer in Damanhur, accompanied by her troupe and their instruments. She would stay all summer with them, or part of it, as their honored guest. She revived her soul with the sights and air of the countryside while entertaining the ailing old lady and filling the house with joy and pleasure.

Those days that Shakhla and her troupe spent in the house of Hamid Bey al-Atifi were to be counted her best, as she said. Nothing disturbed them except al-Hajj Ahmad al-Mutayyib who sought her and the troupe from time to time for an urgent performance or a good contract.

For little Muhsin, especially, those days had been the happiest of his life without question. He waited for them all year long, counting the months on his fingers in anticipation of them. It was a matter of great joy to him whenever a month passed.

What sweet and innocent dreams they were! How agreeable the magnificent childhood mirage was that passed before the amorphous soul of this young fellow at that age. . . .

What pleased and flattered Muhsin most was to be considered a member of the performing company. Nothing would do except to sing, eat, sit, and squeeze in among the artists. Woe to anyone who did not specify he was a member of the troupe. Many a time he wept and raged because someone forgot to consider him a member of the chorus like Hafiza, Najiya, and blind Salm. . . . Time and again he had raged and stormed so they would teach him the argot used by them, the fellowship of artists. . . .

His incorporation into the troupe and his imitation of its members were such that he became known for his sincere respect for the leader, Maestra Labiba Shakhla.

Yes, he would not forget his happiness when he sat on the floor with the troupe around the maestra who was elevated on a large chair in the center, holding the lute in her arms. He would raise his eyes and gaze at her as though observing a goddess on a marble pedestal. Then he would turn his small head right and left to his colleagues in the chorus with an inner relief which could not be described or characterized.

At times he felt a strange sensation looking at that charming woman of about thirty, particularly at evening receptions or whenever she appeared decked out in glittering jewelry before invited guests and visitors who came especially to hear her at Muhsin's home.

He sensed at times that he understood vaguely Shakhla's charm. In reality, Labiba, in addition to her magical singing, had a merry nature and a light and graceful spirit. She provided her listener bliss and delight.

How much Muhsin loved to sit with her, flattering and praising her after he had spent the morning plucking and gathering bishop's weed which she would boil and drink to clear her throat. He would beg her, in return for that, to tell him some of her anecdotes which she would recount at length to him and the rest, without repetition detracting in any way from their charm.

"Tell me the cooking story," little Muhsin said to her in a pleading voice. She laughed and then pretended to frown, saying to him and those around her, "Cooking . . . What a scandal, Kids! . . . So whatever I forget, you remind me?"

The basis of the story was that the real cook got sick one day, and so Maestra Labiba suggested seriously and earnestly that she should take her place. She affirmed that no one had ever tasted anything more delicious than the food her hands would produce. She advised everyone to take care not to eat their fingers, since it would be so tasty. She asserted that she was a first-class cook. A person eating her Alexandria-style fish might well say that he had never eaten fish before in his life.

She stipulated that she be left alone to work. They led her to the kitchen and got her the vegetables, fish, and other necessary items. She began to work . . . but what work!

She had not spent five minutes in the kitchen until it started to look like the leftovers at the market in the afternoon. She got down all the copper vessels, trays, bowls, and containers which she put on the floor and scattered from side to side. There was no corner or spot without a tray, dish, or pot. Why all of this?

Perhaps she did not ask herself this question. No one dared approach the kitchen, because she had categorically refused assistance from every quarter, so that she might have all the credit for herself.

She left some empty cooking pots on the hot stove for a time, while she began to run here and there in the kitchen with a fish in her hand. She was crooning, "O Reviver, O you with the almonds. . ." while her feet stumbled over the trays and containers strewn in disarray over the floor.

Fish was also scattered throughout the place. No one can imagine how that happened with such speed . . . . There was fish on the floor, on the shelf in the bowls and in the basin under the spigot—as though the kitchen had turned into a fish market.

But Maestra Labiba Shakhla presumably paid no attention to the condition of the kitchen, for she was truly caught up in her work. Enthusiasm for it had grasped hold of her. She called out from time to time, with a laugh, "God, God, Darlings! Where's the audience now to watch Maestra Shakhla at the height of her power?"

At last she threw together a number of dishes. She came out of the kitchen with sweat dripping from her and food falling off her white apron. In the parlor she shouted, "All finished, Darlings! . . . I've stewed the eggplant . . . I've trimmed the ends of the okra . . . And the fish . . . O my spirit! I've fried it in a way to bewitch and enchant the mind."

She suddenly fell silent and her face went pale, because just then Dr. Farid appeared in front of her at the parlor door. He had been summoned to examine the sick cook. This Dr. Farid was one of Maestra Shakhla's most enthusiastic patrons and most avid listeners. He saw her frequently and heard her at wedding parties and soirées. No sooner had he seen her there in a kitchen apron with scraps dribbling off it than he shouted in astonishment, "God! . . . are you working as a cook here or what?"

But Shakhla, the moment she recovered from her surprise, turned tail and fled. She was covering her face with her hand one moment and slapping her side curls, the next. In a weak, choking voice she said, "Hide me! . . . Hide me. . . ."

This was not all that her volunteering to cook brought down upon her that day nor all that the Alexandria-style fish cost her. . . .

Another crisis threatened to prove more serious. Unknown to her, the fish was spoiled. She ate a lot of it as did all the members of the company because she had fixed it.

Unfortunately she and the troupe were booked that very evening to perform at a soirée in the home of one of the local notables.

She went and sang till the festivities were at a climax of commotion and joy. The guests were assembled and the excitement and agitation were intense. It was then that Maestra Labiba suddenly felt acute pains throughout her digestive system. At first she tried to conceal that for fear of a scandal, but she had hardly staggered to her feet when she saw that the whole company were all suffering from that indigestion. Each member of the chorus was leaning on another, writhing, her hand on her belly. She grasped the truth of the situation. It was a sight, as recounted afterward by Shakhla with her lightness of spirit, weeping and laughing at the same time. Immediately thereafter the guests witnessed all the members of the troupe, reeling and heaving. They rose quickly at the same moment, each with a hand on the belly. All the artists rushed off, clearing a way for themselves through the crowd, in search of a bathroom or rest room.

But the most pitiful sight of all in truth was that of Salm, the blind woman. Her colleagues abandoned her in that predicament. She stood in the center of the room pawing anxiously, one hand on her stomach and the other beating the air as she sought her way. She was calling out, "O what a disaster. Bring me a basin or a chamber pot. Those who love the Prophet, may God protect you one day." At first the invited ladies laughed at her, but then they came to her assistance.

The young Muhsin was not with the troupe that evening. Despite his tears and pleas his mother had not permitted him to accompany the artists. He had therefore to satisfy himself by hearing the story like the others from the mouth of Maestra Shakhla. She narrated and recounted it frequently in a diverting way. Muhsin would laugh at it with childish good humor and would be consoled by hearing that account. He would forget his wish to accompany them. Shakhla would scarcely finish her story before Muhsin quickly begged, without allowing her time for a cigarette, "Tell me the story of the Jewish wedding."

Maestra Labiba and her troupe had been invited to perform at a wedding party at the home of a well-to-do Jewish family. That was in the Coptic month of Tuba (approximately January) when winter is at its coldest. The Maestra sat in the center of her troupe awaiting the coming of the bride from her bath and toilette. Shakhla explained that one of the Jewish marriage customs was for the bride to bathe in cold water mixed with holy water sprinkled by the rabbi. After this bath, the bride is dressed and adorned. Then, it is forbidden for anyone who is not Jewish, whether Muslim or Christian, to touch her. If that occurs, it is necessary for her to bathe again in cold water.

Labiba Shakhla waited until the bride appeared. She strutted forward in her finery and jewels. She sat down in the place prepared. The festivities commenced and heated up. Then the climax approached. The wind was storming and rain came down cold and icy that night in a way without precedent in the city of Cairo. Labiba rose without thinking about it and went up close to the bride to admire her magnificent clothing. She wanted to scrutinize and check the fabric in the bride's gown. So she stretched out her hand and touched the bride. No sooner had she done that than an appalling cry rang out in the room, stunning her. Voices were raised in anger from every direction. Caught by surprise, she clutched her hand and stood frozen where she was. When she looked up she saw everyone—the bride, her family, and her attendants—had gone off, frothing and foaming, in spite of the roar of thunder outside. They were leading the bride to the bath a second time, the bitter cold notwithstanding.

The poor bride returned from the cold bath after a while. She was moaning and her teeth were chattering. Her male relations heard the commotion and came up to see what it was about. The women from the bride's family and the women guests hurried to them, yelling, "May Labiba be cut down! Labiba be burned! . . . Labiba touched her!"

Labiba heard that. She was cowering among the members of her troupe. Her body, was trembling in fright and terror. She had begun to recite to herself the Throne Verse from the Qur'an (2:255, al-Baqara). From time to time she peeked out to see whether the family's fury had abated. Then she would cling to those near her from the troupe and whisper, "Come a little closer, Najiya! . . . Hide me. Do me a favor. . . . Hold me, Salm. Have mercy on me. . . . Ransom me, Children! O Master Abu as-Su'ud, by your miracles . . . half a dozen candles . . . just let us get out of here unharmed."

Despite her own great fears, Salm tried to calm her. She whispered to her leader in a scolding voice, "Enough! What can they do to us?"

Najiya answered her in a whisper, "The least they can do is plunge us in that soot bath too."

Salm's teeth chattered and she said, "Shield us, lord . . . . What responsibility do we have for all this. . . ."

At this point the shouting had calmed down. It seemed the hosts of the wedding thought the stream should now return to its banks so the evening would not come to a bad end. They became quiet and signaled to Maestra Labiba to resume the singing and music. Shakhla decided to obey the order immediately to avoid causing some new problem and to distract them from what she had done. She straightened herself in her seat and commanded the troupe to take their instruments. She said to Najiya quickly, "Tune the lute for Hijaz-kar."

Then she raised her voice and sang, "The Critic's Ruse."

She had barely finished the opening when she heard whispering and commotion among the members of the troupe. She noticed Salm's voice calling out and drowning hers, "God! God! . . . Maestra Shakhla, you Egyptian . . . Pride of the kings!" Salm then bent over her and whispered, "God! . . . God! That's Discord-kar!"

Shakhla turned on her sharply, "What's come over you, girl?"

But Shakhla immediately realized she was singing off-key because of her fear and terror. She composed herself and smiled. "What shall I do for them? They brought this calamity on me. Sing, children; sing no matter how. Just let's get through this evening with our skins. . . . They can do what they please with 'The Critic's Ruse' when we're on the way home."

Translated by William M. Hutchins

Naguib Mahfouz
from *Midaq Alley*

LATE AFTERNOON . . . The alley returned once more to that hour of murky shadows. Hamida set out, wrapping her cloak around her and listening to the clack of her shoes on the stairs as she made her way to the street. She walked slowly, conscious of both her gait and her appearance, for she was aware that four eyes were examining her closely. The eyes belonged to Salim Alwan, the company owner, and to Abbas, the barber. She was well aware of her attire; a faded cotton dress, an old cloak and shoes with timeworn soles. Nevertheless, she draped her cloak in such a way that it emphasized her ample hips and her full and rounded breasts. The cloak revealed her trim ankles, on which she wore a bangle; it also exposed her black hair and attractive bronze face.

She was determined to take no notice of anything, simply to make her way from Sanadiqiya to Mousky Street. As soon as she was beyond the range of the penetrating eyes, her lips parted in a smile, her beautiful eyes quickly surveyed the activity in the bustling street. For a girl of uncertain origins she never lost her spirit of self-confidence. Perhaps her beauty contributed to her self-assurance, but this was not the only factor.

She was by nature strong, and this strength had never once deserted her. Sometimes her eyes revealed this inner strength; some thought it detracted from her beauty, others that it enhanced it. She was constantly beset by a desire to fight and conquer. This she showed in her pleasure in attracting men and also in her efforts to dominate her mother.

It also revealed itself in quarrels which were always flaring up between her and other women of the alley. As a consequence, they all hated her and said nothing but unkind things about her. Perhaps the most commonly said thing about her was that she hated children and that this unnatural trait made her wild and totally lacking in the virtues of femininity. It was this that made Mrs. Kirsha, the café owner's wife, who had nursed her, hope to God to see her a mother too, suckling children under the care of a tyrannical husband who beat her unmercifully!

Hamida continued on her way, enjoying her daily promenade and looking in the shop windows, one after the other. The luxurious clothes stirred in her greedy and ambitious mind bewitching dreams of power and influence. Anyone could have told her that her yearning for power centered on her love for money. She was convinced that it was the magic key to the entire world. All she knew about herself was that she dreamed constantly of wealth, of riches which would bring her every luxury her heart had ever desired.

In spite of her fantasies of wealth, she was not unaware of her situation. Indeed, she remembered a girl in Sanadiqiya Street who was even poorer than she. Then fortune sent a rich contractor who transported her from her miserable hovel to a fairy-tale life. What was to prevent good fortune from smiling twice in their quarter? This ambition of hers, however, was limited to her familiar world, which ended at Queen Farida Square. She knew nothing of life beyond it.

In the distance, she saw some of the factory girls approaching her. She hurried toward them; her unpleasant thoughts were now replaced by a smile on her face. In the midst of their greetings and chattering, Hamida gazed searchingly at their faces and clothes, envying them their freedom and obvious prosperity. They were girls from the Darasa district, who, taking advantage of wartime employment opportunities, ignored custom and tradition and now worked in public places just like the Jewish women. They had gone into factory work exhausted, emaciated, and destitute. Soon remarkable changes were noticeable: their once undernourished bodies filled out and seemed to radiate a healthy pride and vitality. They imitated the Jewish girls by paying attention to their appearance and in keeping slim. Some even used unaccustomed language and did not hesitate to walk arm in arm and stroll about the streets of illicit love. They exuded an air of boldness and secret knowledge.

As for Hamida, her age and ignorance had deprived her of their opportunities. She joined their laughter with a false sincerity, all the while envy nibbling at her. She did not hesitate to criticize them, even though in fun. This girl's frock, for instance, was too short and immodest, while that one's was simply in bad taste. A third girl was too obvious, the way she stared at men, while she remembered the fourth one from the days when lice crawled about her neck like ants. No doubt these encounters were one of the roots of her constant rebelliousness, but they were also her main source of diversion in the long days filled with boredom and quarrels. So it was that one day she had said to her mother, "The Jewish girls have the only real life here."

"You must have been conceived by devils!" her mother shouted. "None of my blood is in you."

"Maybe I'm a pasha's daughter, even if illegitimately."

The woman shook her head and moaned, "May God have mercy on your father, a poor vegetable seller in Margush!"

She walked along with her companions, proud in the knowledge of her beauty, impregnable in the armor of her sharp tongue, and pleased that the eyes of passersby settled on her more than on the others.

When they reached the middle of Mousky, she saw Abbas lagging behind them a little, gazing at her with his customary expression. She wondered why he had left his shop at this time of day. Was he following her on purpose? Couldn't he read the message in her eyes? She had to admit that despite his poverty he was presentable-looking, as were all those in his trade. Yes, his appearance pleased her. She told herself that none of her friends could hope to marry anyone better than Abbas.

Her feelings toward him were strange and complicated. On the one hand, he was the only young man in the alley who would make a suitable husband for her, while she, on the other hand, dreamed of a husband like the rich contractor her neighbor had married. The truth was she neither loved nor wanted him; at the same time she could not dismiss him. Perhaps his passionate glances pleased her.

It was her custom to walk with the girls as far as the end of Darasa and then return alone to the alley. She continued with them, stealing an occasional glance at Abbas. She no longer doubted he was following her intentionally and that he wanted to break his long silence. She was not mistaken. She had scarcely said goodbye to the girls and turned around when he made his way toward her. In a few quick steps he was at her side.

"Good evening, Hamida . . ." he said awkwardly.

She turned suddenly and pretended to be surprised by his appearance. Then she scowled and lengthened her stride without saying a word. His face reddened, but he caught her up and said in a hurt voice, "Good evening, Hamida . . ."

She was afraid that if she kept silent and continued to hurry they would reach the square before he could say what he wanted. She drew to a sudden halt and spoke indignantly. "What nerve! One of our neighbors, acting like a fresh stranger!"

"Yes, you're right, I am a neighbor but I'm not behaving like a stranger. Can't neighbors talk to one another?"

Hamida frowned and said, "No. A neighbor should protect a neighbor, not insult them."

"I never thought for one moment of insulting you, God forbid. I only want to talk with you. Is there any harm in that . . . ?"

"How can you say that? It's wrong for you to stop me in the street and expose me to a scandal."

Her words horrified him and he seemed stunned. "Scandal? God forbid, Hamida. I have only the most honorable intentions toward you. I swear by the life of Hussain. You'll soon learn that if you only give me a chance. Listen to me. I want to talk to you about something important. Turn off toward Azhar Street so we can be away from prying eyes."

Hamida exclaimed in feigned horror, "Be away from people? What a thing to suggest! You're right, you are a good neighbor!"

Abbas had now become a little braver as a result of her arguing with him and he demanded indignantly, "What's a neighbor's crime anyway? Has he got to die without saying what he feels?"

"How pure your words are . . ."

He sighed peevishly, showing his regret that they were approaching the busy square. "My intentions are completely pure. Don't rush off, Hamida, let's turn into Azhar Street. I have something important to tell you. You must listen. I'm sure you know what I want to say. Don't you feel anything? One's emotions are the best guide."

"You've gone far enough . . . No . . . No . . . Leave me alone."

"Hamida . . . I want to . . . I want you . . ."

"So you want to disgrace me before everyone?"

They had now reached Hussain Square and she crossed over to the opposite pavement and hurried off. She then turned down toward Ghouriya, smiling self-consciously. Hamida now knew what he wanted. It was just as he had said. She saw the spark of love in his eyes just as she had suspected it was there when he stared at her window. She knew his financial state was not impressive, but his personality was submissive and humble. This should have pleased her dominating nature; instead she felt no interest. This puzzled her.

What, then, did she want? And who would satisfy her if this kind young man did not? She knew no answer to this, and she attributed her indifference to his poverty. It was a fact that her love to dominate was a result of her love to quarrel, not the reverse. She had always resisted peace and quiet and found no joy in easy victory. Thus her confused feelings filled her with perplexity and distress.

Abbas refrained from following her, fearing that he might be seen. He started back home, his heart overflowing with disappointment, but not despair.

He told himself as he made his way slowly, oblivious to all about him, that she had at least spoken to him, and at some length too. If she had wanted to stop him, she could easily have done so.

It was obvious she did not dislike him and perhaps she was acting like any girl would. It could have been modesty that made her hesitate to make friends with him. He felt drunk with joy from some magic potion he had never before tasted. Abbas was truly in love and he felt certain his love for her would last a thousand years.

Consequently he felt no sense of failure from today's encounter. When he turned into Sanadiqiya, he saw Sheikh Darwish coming from the mosque of Hussian. They met at the end of the alley and Abbas moved to greet him. The old man, however, pointed his forefinger at him warningly and, gazing from behind his gold-rimmed spectacles, he said, "Never go out without a hat! I warn you against going bareheaded in weather like this, in a world like this.

Young men's brains are liable to dissolve into steam and fly off. This situation is well known in *alma'sah* and the meaning of this in English is tragedy and it is spelled t-r-a-g-e-d-y . . ."

Translated by Trevor Le Gassick

Naguib Mahfouz
from *Palace Walk*

A FEELING SPREAD THROUGH the household that they would have a day's reprieve from their oppressively prim life. Safe from their guardian's eye, they would be able, if they so desired, to get an innocent breath of fresh air. Kamal was of the opinion that he could do as he wished and spend the whole day playing, inside the house and out. Khadija and Aisha wondered if they might slip over to Maryam's house in the evening to spend an hour there having fun and amusing themselves.

This break did not come as a result of the passing of the gloomy winter months and the arrival of the first signs of spring with intimations of warmth and good cheer. It was not occasioned by spring granting this family liberty they had been deprived of by winter. This respite came as a natural consequence of a business trip, lasting a day or more, that al-Sayyid Ahmad made to Port Said every few years. It so happened that he set out one a Friday morning when the weekly holiday brought the family together. They all responded eagerly to the freedom and the peaceful, relaxed atmosphere the father's departure from Cairo had unexpectedly created.

The mother hesitantly dashed the girls' hopes and the young boy's high spirits. She wanted to make sure the family persisted with its customary schedule and adhered, even when the father was absent, to the same rules it observed when he was present. She was more concerned to keep from vexing him than she was convinced that he was right to be so severe and stern.

Before she knew what was happening, though, here was Yasin saying, "Don't oppose God's plan . . . . Nobody else lives like us. In fact, I want to say something novel. . . . Why don't you have some fun too? What do you all think about this suggestion?"

Their eyes looked at him in astonishment, but no one said a word. Perhaps, like their mother, who gave him a critical look, they did not take what he was saying seriously. All the same, he continued, "Why are you looking at me like this? I haven't contravened any of the directives of the Prophet recorded in the revered collection of al-Bukhari. Praise God, no crime has been committed. All it would amount to is a brief excursion to have a look at a little of the district you've lived in for forty years but never seen."

The woman sighed and murmured, "May God be merciful to you."

The young man laughed out loud. He said, "Why should you ask God to be merciful to me? Have I committed some unforgivable sin? By God, if I were you, I'd go as far as the mosque of our master al-Husayn. . . . Our master al-Husayn, don't you hear? . . . Your beloved saint whom you adore from afar when he's so near. Go to him. He's calling you."

Her heart pounded and the effect could be seen in her blush. She lowered her head to hide how deeply she was affected. Her heart responded to the call with a force that exploded suddenly in her soul. She was taken by surprise. No one around her could have anticipated this, not even Yasin himself. It was as though an earthquake had shaken a land that had never experienced one before. She did not understand how her heart could answer this appeal, how her eyes could look beyond the limits of what was allowed, or how she could consider the adventure possible and even tempting, no—irresistible. Of course, since it was such a sacred pilgrimage, a visit to the shrine of al-Husayn appeared a powerful excuse for the radical leap her will was making, but that was not the only factor influencing her soul. Deep inside her, imprisoned currents yearning for release responded to this call in the same way that eager, aggressive instincts answer the call for a war proclaimed to be in defense of freedom and peace.

She did not know how to announce her fateful surrender. She looked at Yasin and said in a trembling voice, "A visit to the shrine of al-Husayn is something my heart has wished for all my life . . . but . . . your father?"

Yasin laughed and answered, "My father's on his way to Port Said. He won't be back until tomorrow morning. As an extra precaution you can borrow Umm Hanafi's wrap, so anyone who sees you leaving the house or returning will think you're a visitor."

She looked back and forth between her children with embarrassment and dread, as though seeking more encouragement. Khadija and Aisha were enthusiastic about the suggestion. In their enthusiasm they seemed to be expressing both their own imprisoned desire to break free and their joy at the visit to Maryam, which had become, after this revolution, a certainty.

Expressing his heartfelt approval, Kamal shouted, "I'll go with you, Mother, and show you the way."

Fahmy gazed at her affectionately when he saw the expression of anxious pleasure on her face, like that of a child hoping to get a new toy. To encourage her and play down the importance of the adventure, he said, "Have a look at the world. There's nothing wrong with that. I'm afraid you'll forget how to walk after staying home so much."

In an outburst of enthusiasm Khadija ran to Umm Hanafi to get the black cloth she wrapped around herself when she went out. Everyone was laughing and offering their comments. The day turned into a more joyous festival than any they had experienced. They all participated, unwittingly, in the revolution against their absent father's will. Mrs. Amina wrapped the cloth around her and pulled the black veil down over her face. She looked in the mirror and laughed until her torso shook. Kamal put on his suit and fez and got to the courtyard before her, but she did not follow him. She was afflicted by the kind of fear people feel at crucial turning points. She raised her eyes to Fahmy and asked, "What do you think? Should I really go?"

Yasin yelled at her, "Trust God."

Khadija went up to her. Placing her hands on her shoulders, she gave her a gentle push, saying, "Reciting the opening prayer of the Qur'an will protect you." Khadija propelled her all the way to the stairs. Then she withdrew her hands. The woman descended, with everyone following her. She found Umm Hanafi waiting for her. The servant cast a searching look at her mistress, or rather at the cloth encompassing her. She shook her head disapprovingly, went to her, and wrapped the cloth around her again. She taught her how to hold the edge in the right place. Her mistress, who was wearing this wrap for the first time, followed the servant's directions. Then the angles and curves of her figure, ordinarily concealed by her flowing housedresses, were visible in all their details. Smiling, Khadija gave her an admiring look and winked at Aisha. They burst into laughter.

As they crossed the threshold of the outer door and entered the street, she experienced a moment of panic. Her mouth felt dry and her pleasure was dispelled by a fit of anxiety. She had an oppressive feeling of doing something wrong. She moved slowly and grasped Kamal's hand nervously. Her gait seemed disturbed and unsteady, as though she had not mastered the first principles of walking. She was gripped by intense embarrassment as she showed herself to the eyes of people she had known for ages but only through the peephole of the enclosed balcony. Uncle Hasanayn, the barber, Darwish, who sold beans, al-Fuli, the milkman, Bayumi, the drinks vendor, and Abu Sari', who sold snacks—she imagined that they all recognized her just as she did them. She had difficulty convincing herself of the obvious fact that none of them had ever seen her before in their lives.

They crossed the street to Qirmiz Alley. It was not the shortest route to the mosque of al-Husayn, but unlike al-Nahhasin Street, it did not pass by al-Sayyid Ahmad's store or any other shops and was little frequented. She stopped for a moment before plunging into the alley. She turned to look at her latticed balcony. She could make out the shadows of her two daughters behind one panel. Another panel was raised to reveal the smiling faces of Fahmy and Yasin. The sight of them gave her some courage for her project.

Then she hurried along with her son down the desolate alley, feeling almost calm. Her anxiety and sense of doing something wrong did not leave her, but they retreated to the edges of her conscious emotions. Center stage was occupied by an eager interest in exploring the world as it revealed one of its alleys, a square, novel buildings, and lots of people. She found an innocent pleasure in sharing the motion and freedom of other living creatures. It was the pleasure of someone who had spent a quarter of a century imprisoned by the walls of her home, except for a limited number of visits to her mother in al-Khurunfush, where she would go a few times a year but in a carriage and chaperoned by her husband. Then she would not even have the courage to steal a look at the street.

She began to ask Kamal about the sights, buildings, and places they encountered on their way. The boy was proud to serve as her guide and volunteered lengthy explanations. Here was the famous vaulted ceiling of Qirmiz Alley. Before walking beneath it one needed to recite the opening prayer of the Qur'an as a defense against the jinn living there. This was Bayt al-Qadi Square with its tall trees. She might have heard him refer to the square as Pasha's Beard Square, from the popular name for its flowering lebbek trees, or at times also as Shangarly Square, giving it the name of the Turkish owner of a chocolate shop. This large building was the Gamaliya police station. Although the boy found little there to merit his attention, except the sword dangling from the sentry's waist, the mother looked at it with curiosity, since it was the place of employment of a man who had sought Aisha's hand. They went on until they reached Khan Ja'far Primary School, where Kamal had spent a year before enrolling at Khalil Agha Elementary School. He pointed to its historic balcony and remarked, "On this balcony Shaykh Mahdi made us put our faces to the wall for the least offense. Then he would kick us five, six, or ten times. Whatever he felt like."

Gesturing toward a store situated directly under the balcony, he stopped walking and said in a tone she could not mistake, "This is Uncle Sadiq, who sells sweets." He refused to budge until he had extracted a coin from her and bought himself a gummy red candy.

After that they turned into Khan Ja'far Alley. Then in the distance they could see part of the exterior of the mosque of al-Husayn. In the center was an expansive window decorated with arabesques. The façade was topped by a parapet with merlons like spear points bunched tightly together.

With joy singing in her breast, she asked, "Our master al-Husayn?" He confirmed her guess. Her pace quickened for the first time since she left the house. She began to compare what she saw with the picture created by her imagination and based on what she had seen from her home of mosques like Qala'un and Barquq. She found the reality to be less grand then she had imagined. In her imagination she had made its size correspond to the veneration in which she held its holy occupant. This difference between imagination and reality, however, in no way affected the pervasive intoxication of her joy at being there.

They walked around the outside of the mosque until they reached the green door. They entered, surrounded by a crowd of women visitors. When the woman's feet touched the floor of the shrine, she felt that her body was dissolving into tenderness, affection, and love and that she was being transformed into a spirit fluttering in the sky, radiant with the glow of prophetic inspiration. Her eyes swam with tears that helped relieve the agitation of her breast, the warmth of her love and belief, and the flood of her benevolent joy. She proceeded to devour the place with greedy, curious eyes: the walls, ceiling, pillars, carpets, chandeliers, pulpit, and the mihrab niches indicating the direction of Mecca.

Kamal, by her side, looked at these things from his own special point of view, assuming that the mosque served as a shrine for people during the day and the early evening but afterward was the home for his martyred master al-Husayn. The Prophet's grandson would come and go there, making use of the furnishing in much the same way any owner uses his possessions. Al-Husayn would walk around inside and pray facing a prayer niche. He would climb into the pulpit and ascend to the windows to look out at his district surrounding the mosque. How dearly Kamal wished, in a dreamy kind of way, that they would forget him in the mosque when they locked the doors so he would be able to meet al-Husayn face to face and pass a whole night in his presence until morning. He imagined the manifestations of love and submission appropriate for him to present to al-Husayn when they met and the hopes and requests suitable for him to lay at his feet. In addition to all that, he looked forward to the affection and blessing he would find with al-Husayn. He pictured himself with his head bowed, approaching the martyr, who would ask him gently "Who are you?"

He would answer, before kissing his hand, "Kamal Ahmad Abd al-Jawad." Al-Husayn would ask what his profession was. He would reply, "A pupil in Khalil Agha School," and not forget to hint that he was doing well. Al-Husayn would ask what brought him at that hour of the night. Kamal would reply that it was love for all the Prophet's family and especially for him.

Al-Husayn would smile affectionately and invite him to accompany him on his nightly rounds. At that, Kamal would reveal all his requests at once, "Please grant me these things. I want to play as much as I like, inside the house and out. I want Aisha and Khadija to stay in our house always. Please change my father's temper and prolong my mother's life forever. I would like to have as much spending money as I can use and for us all to enter paradise without having to be judged."

The slowly moving flow of women carried them along until they found themselves near the tomb itself. How often she had longed to visit this site, as though yearning for a dream that could never be achieved on this earth. Here she was standing within the shrine. Indeed, here she was touching the walls of the tomb itself, looking at it through her tears. She wished she could linger to savor this taste of happiness, but the pressure of the crowd was too great. She stretched out her hands to the wooden walls and Kamal imitated her. Then they recited the opening prayer of the Qur'an. She stroked the walls and kissed them, never tiring of her prayers and entreaties. She would have liked to stand there a long time or sit in a corner to gaze at it and then circle around again, but the mosque attendant was watching everyone closely. He would not allow any of the women to tarry. He urged on women who slowed down and waved his long stick at them threateningly. He entreated them all to finish their visit before the Friday prayer service.

She had sipped from the sweet spiritual waters of the shrine but had not drunk her fill. There was no way to quench her thirst. Visiting the shrine had so stirred up her yearnings that they gushed forth from their springs, flowed out, and burst over their banks. She would never stop wanting more of this intimacy and delight. When she found herself obliged to leave the mosque, she had to tear herself away, her heart bidding it farewell. She left very regretfully, tormented by the feeling that she was saying farewell to it forever, but her characteristic temperance and resignation intervened to chide her for giving in to her sorrow. Thus she was able to enjoy the happiness she had gained and used it to banish the anxieties aroused by leaving the shrine.

Kamal invited her to look at his school and they went to see it at the end of al-Husayn Street. They paused there for a long time. When she wanted to return the way they had come, the mention of returning signaled the conclusion of this happy excursion with his mother, which he had never before dreamed would be possible. He refused to abandon it so quickly and fought desperately to prolong it. He proposed a walk along New Street to al-Ghuriya. In order to put an end to the opposition suggested by the smiling frown visible through her veil, he made her swear by al-Husayn. She sighed and surrendered herself to his young hand.

They made their way through the thick crowd and in and out of the clashing currents of pedestrians flowing in every direction. She would not have encountered even a hundredth of this traffic on the quiet route by which she had come. She began to be uneasy and almost beside herself with anxiety. She soon complained of discomfort and fatigue, but his desperation to complete this happy excursion made him turn a deaf ear to her complaints. He encouraged her to continue the journey. He tried to distract her by directing her attention to the shops, vehicles, and passersby. They were very slowly approaching the corner of al-Ghuriya. When they reached it, his eyes fell on a pastry shop, and his mouth watered. His eyes were fixed intently on the shop. He began to think of a way to persuade his mother to enter the store and purchase a pastry. He was still thinking about it when they reached the shop, but before he knew what was happening his mother had slipped from his hand. He turned toward her questioningly and saw her fall flat on her face, after a deep moan escaped her.

His eyes grew wide with astonishment and terror. He was unable to move. At approximately the same time, despite his dismay and alarm, he saw an automobile out of the corner of his eye. The driver was applying the brakes with a screeching sound, while the vehicle spewed a trail of dust and smoke. It came within a few inches of running over the prostrate woman, swerving just in time.

Everyone started shouting and a great clamor arose. People dashed to the spot from every direction like children following a magician's whistle. They formed a deep ring around her that seemed to consist of eyes peering, heads craning, and mouths shouting words, as questions got mixed up with answers.

Kamal recovered a little from the shock. He looked back and forth from his prostrate mother at his feet to the people around them, expressing his fear and need for help. Then he threw himself down on his knees beside her. He put his hand on her shoulder and called to her in a voice that was heartrending, but she did not respond. He raised his head and stared at the surrounding faces. The he screamed out a fervent, sobbing lament that rose above the din around him and almost silenced it. Some people volunteered meaningless words of consolation. Others bent over his mother, examining her curiously, moved by two contrary impulses. Although they hoped the victim was all right, they were grateful to see that death, that final conclusion which can only be delayed, had knocked on someone else's door and spirited away someone else's soul. They seemed to want a rehearsal free of any risks of that most perilous role each of them was destined to end his life playing.

One of them shouted, "The left door of the vehicle hit her in the back."

The driver had gotten out of the car and stood there half blinded by the glare of the accusations leveled at him. He protested, "She suddenly swerved off the sidewalk. I couldn't keep from hitting her. I quickly put on my brakes, so I just grazed her. But for the grace of God I would have run her down."

One of the men staring at her said, "She's still breathing . . . . She's just unconscious."

Seeing a policeman approaching, with the sword he carried on his left side swinging back and forth, the driver began speaking again, "It was only a little bump. . . . It couldn't have done anything to her. . . . She's fine . . . fine, everybody, by God."

The first man to examine her stood up straight and as though delivering a sermon said, "Get back. Let her have air. . . . She's opened her eyes. She's all right . . . fine, praise God." He spoke with a joy not devoid of pride, as though he was the one who had brought her back to life. Then he turned to Kamal, who was weeping so hysterically that the consolation of the bystanders had been without effect. He patted Kamal on the cheek sympathetically and told him, "That's enough, son. . . . Your mother's fine. . . . Look. . . . Come help me get her to her feet."

Even so, Kamal did not stop crying until he saw his mother move. He bent toward her and put her left hand on his shoulder. He helped the man lift her up. With great difficulty she was able to stand between them, exhausted and faint. Her wrap had fallen off her and some people helped put it back in place as best they could, wrapping it around her shoulders. Then the pastry merchant, in front of whose store the accident had taken place, brought her a chair. They helped her sit down, and he brought a glass of water. She swallowed some, but half of it spilled down her neck and chest. She wiped off her chest with a reflex motion and groaned. She was breathing with difficulty and looked in bewilderment at the faces staring at her. She asked, "What happened? . . . What happened? . . . Oh Lord, why are you crying, Kamal?"

At that point the policeman came forward. He asked her, "Are you injured, lady? Can you walk to the police station?"

The words "police station" came as a blow to her and shook her to the core. She shouted in alarm, "Why should I go to the police station? I'll never go there."

The policeman replied, "The car hit you and knocked you down. If you're injured, you and the driver must go to the police station to fill out a report."

Gasping for breath, she protested, "No . . . certainly not. I won't go. . . . I'm fine."

The policeman told her, "Prove it to me. Get up and walk so we can see if you're injured."

Driven by the alarm that the mention of the police station aroused in her, she got up at once. Surrounded by inquisitive eyes, she adjusted her wrap and began to walk. Kamal was by her side, brushing away the dust that clung to her. Hoping this painful situation would come to an end, no matter what it cost her, she told the policeman, "I'm fine." Then she gestured toward the driver and continued, "Let him go. . . . There's nothing the matter with me." She was so afraid that she no longer felt faint. The sight of the men staring at her horrified her, especially the policeman, who was in front of the others. She trembled from the impact of these looks directed at her from everywhere. They were a clear challenge and affront to a long life spent in seclusion and concealment from strangers. She imagined she saw the image of al-Sayyid Ahmad raising above all the other men. He seemed to be studying her face with cold, stony eyes, threatening her with more evil than she could bear to imagine.

She lost no time in grabbing the boy's hand and heading off with him toward the Goldsmiths Bazaar. No one tried to stop her. No sooner had they turned the corner and escaped from sight than she moaned. Speaking to Kamal as though addressing herself, she said, "My Lord, how did this happen? What have I seen, Kamal? It was like a terrifying dream. I imagined I was falling into a dark pit from high up. The earth was revolving under my feet. Then I didn't know anything at all until I opened my eyes on that frightening scene. My Lord . . . did he really want to take me to the police station? O Gracious One, O Lord . . . my Savior, my Lord. How soon will we reach home? You cried a lot, Kamal. May you never lose your eyes. Dry your eyes with this handkerchief. You can wash your face at home. . . . Oh."

She stopped when they were almost at the end of the Goldsmiths Bazaar. She rested her hand on the boy's shoulder. Her face was contorted.

Kamal looked up with alarm and asked her, "What's the matter?"

She closed her eyes and said in a weak voice, "I'm tired, very tired. My feet can barely support me. Get the first vehicle you can find, Kamal."

Kamal looked around. All he could see was a donkey cart standing by the doorway of the ancient hospital of Qala'un. He summoned the driver, who quickly brought the cart to them. Leaning on Kamal's shoulder, the mother made her way to it. She clambered on board with his help, supporting herself on the driver's shoulder. He held steady until she was seated cross-legged in the cart. She sighed from her extreme exhaustion and Kamal sat down beside her. Then the driver leaped onto the front of the cart and prodded the donkey with the handle of his whip. The donkey walked off slowly, with the cart swaying and clattering behind him.

The woman moaned. She complained, "My pain's severe. The bones of my shoulder must be smashed." Meanwhile Kamal watched her with alarm and anxiety.

The vehicle passed by al-Sayyid Ahmad's store without either of them paying any attention. Kamal watched the road ahead until he saw the latticed balconies of their house. All he could remember of the happy expedition was its miserable conclusion.

Translated by William M. Hutchins and Olive E. Kenny

Fathy Ghanem
from *The Man Who Lost His Shadow*

MY NAME IS MABRUKA ABDUL TAWAB. My late husband, Abdul Hamid Effendi, was a primary school teacher. I am still young and pretty. My figure is graceful: my hips are on the plump side, which pleases me, but my breasts, being small, annoy me. Men still stare at me and I like this. I'm vital, restless. I can't sit still even when I'm at home. I must cook, wash or sweep. In the evenings I go out to look for my son, Ibrahim, If I find him playing football, I drag him home by his gallabiya, to see that he does his homework. After that I bath, and comb out my hair. And then come the long hours in which I lose myself in the hatred devouring my heart.

My only emotion now is hatred—hatred for one man whose death I dream of—a slow lingering death with plenty of pain. I would like to knife open his belly, pull out his liver and grind it with my teeth. I would gouge out his eyes, or drink his blood.

The man is Yusif Abdul Hamid, my husband's son by his first wife.

Sometimes I wonder why I have come to hate him so much, and what will be the end of it. He obsesses me day and night. Sometimes when I look at

Ibrahim, his face blurs and becomes Yusif's. I feel an urge to smash his ribs, but then a faint voice whispers: Control!

It is a long time since I first saw Yusif. I was a little child. I knew nothing of the world. I was hardly ten and worked as a servant in a big house in Giza. I didn't know what being a servant meant. All I knew was that one day my mother had taken me from the village by train, with Sheikh Dessouki who chattered with her all the way. I paid no attention because of the strange things happening. This was my first train; the world which ran to meet the train was vast; at stations where we stopped people climbed up while others clambered down. And a rough man in blue serge approached us; my mother pulled me close to her. The man examined me with cruel eyes which made me frightened. He asked Sheikh Dessouki how old I was and examined our tickets. Then he went away, still staring at me for no reason I understood.

I stayed frightened as I climbed down from the train into the big city. The wide road with the speeding cars frightened me—they looked like the dwellings of ogres. And the people frightened me. They reminded me of the man on the train. Any moment they might seize me and ask my age—for no reason I could understand.

We boarded a train. I thought it was another train. My eyes could not focus on what was happening near me. I squatted on the floor near my mother's feet, holding the skirt of her dress. I would not lift my head whatever happened. I even stopped myself from crying. I was afraid that if I cried people would notice me.

We left the train and walked down a wide road lined on both sides by houses and gardens. The sight of greenery once more helped to calm me. Mother said not a word to me but went on talking to Sheikh Dessouki. They walked fast while I ran behind, clinging to my mother's dress, frightened she might forget me, and I'd be lost.

We reached a house with a garden. A black man in a big turban sat at the gate and Sheikh Dessouki asked him:

"Is Rateb Bey at home, Uncle Osman?"

The man's eyes moved between me and my mother:

"The Bey's gone out and not come back."

"And the old lady?"

"At home."

"I'll call on her, then."

Sheikh Dessouki left us to enter the garden. But he did not use the white staircase I had expected. Instead he disappeared round the back of the house while my mother and I sat down near the man called Uncle Osman.

He stared at us a moment, then said:

"Don't sit in front of the gate. Go and sit inside."

"Inside where?"

He pointed to where Sheikh Dessouki had vanished.

Mother seemed at a loss, so the man got up slowly.

"Follow me."

Half-way up the garden he pointed to a passage along one side of the house. He told us to go and sit at the end of it. We did as we were told, sitting down near a chicken-coop. A man in a white cap came out of a narrow door and stood in front of a pot cooking on the fire. From the pot came the smell of food and my mouth watered and my stomach rumbled.

Time passed while I looked at the chickens and smelt the food and stared at the man's strange cap. Every now and then he looked in our direction but said nothing. Then Sheikh Dessouki came out of the little door, beaming.

"The old lady agrees, Layla. If she proves good, she'll get sixteen shillings."

The sum astonished me. Sixteen shillings—a fortune! But who would the old lady be giving it to?

Mother got up and took my hand. We followed Sheikh Dessouki indoors and my fear came back. I didn't take in what I saw; it was like entering a magic world. We climbed up a long staircase till we reached an open door. Sheikh Dessouki coughed, knocked and told us to go in.

I saw an old lady whose face was as shining as the full moon, wrapped round as it was with a white shawl. My mother covered her hand with her black head-cover, before stooping to kiss the lady's hand, praying God to grant her long years and lasting bounty. Turning, she prodded my shoulder:

"Kiss your mistress's hand, child."

The old lady withdrew her hand before my lips touched it.

"What's your name, girl?" Her voice was feeble.

My mother quickly nudged me:

"Tell the lady your name."

I lowered my head.

"My name's Mabruka."

Mother, nudging me once more as if I had done something really bad, corrected me.

"Your *servant* Mabruka. We are all your servants, Madame. We live thanks to your breath and the breath of the great Bey."

Mother then began praying for the old lady, who said to Sheikh Dessouki in her faint voice:

"Enough—we have agreed."

The lady put her hand to something by her side, I did not know what. She looked at it, then said:

"It is not yet noon."

We then went down the stairs again and sat by the chicken-coop. Sheikh Dessouki left us to sit with Uncle Osman, waiting for Rateb Bey.

Sheikh Dessouki was gone a long time and the smell of food came to my nostrils. I was hungry but dared not ask my mother when we should eat. If I asked her, she'd be bound to slap me. That was her way with me and my brothers and sisters. So we never asked when we should eat or complained if we were hungry. We would wait till she brought us food. If she didn't bring it, we went to bed hungry and practiced patience.

A second man joined the man with the cap and both got busy. The new man put a red sash round his waist and began carrying out plates piled high with food, meat, watermelons and rice.

I watched him, astonished. My eyes were glued to him till he vanished behind the door. Hunger gripped me so that I almost munched a handful of mud.

But my pains did not last long. The man came out again, carrying a tray loaded with plates and loaves of bread. He put the tray before us and left, saying nothing.

The sight of so much food—lumps of meat, rice and mulukhiya—dazzled me. My mother seized a loaf and bit into it hungrily, then told me:

"Eat, child."

I ate and ate till my plate was empty and my stomach ached; but I was happy. When would I taste such food again?

"Mabruka," my mother said suddenly, "you're going to stay here."

I didn't understand what she meant and so kept silent as she continued:

"You'll stay with the old lady and serve her, you understand."

I said in terror:

"But mother, you'll stay with me?"

"Stay with you?" she snapped back. "What for? I go home to your brothers."

I was on the edge of tears. She looked at me harshly:

"You'll eat meat every day and wear clean clothes."

I knew she would hit me if I went on talking. I was afraid of her, but even more afraid of this large house. My pleasure in the food had vanished. It could not replace my mother or my brothers or my village and it could not remove my fear.

I said trembling:

"Mother, I'm scared."

She cursed me, saying how I was to be envied. If it had not been for my brothers and sisters she would herself have left the poverty and hunger of our village for this house of plenty.

Sheikh Dessouki came back smiling: it was time for him and my mother to leave. Tears came to my eyes and I clung to her, circling her tightly with my arms. She pushed me away and slapped me; then pounced to hug and kiss me. She was as upset as I was. She called to the man who had brought us the food (he was watching us from the window) and implored him to take care of me, making him swear to this in the name of God and the Prophet.

The man led me inside the house. At the same time my mother walked away with Sheikh Dessouki, muttering prayers on my behalf.

Translated by Desmond Stewart

Yusuf Idris

from *"The Siren," in Rings of Burnished Brass*

SHE CROUCHED WITHDRAWN, still knowing only what she had seen between the railway station and the block of flats, contemplating the dream become reality. Cairo, Cairo, much more magnificent than she had imagined or than her cousin had been able to describe, a thousand times grander and more wonderful. Could such crowds of people, such broad streets, such wide squares, really exist? Were people able to live in the midst of that dreadful crush of cars, that went so fast that they'd swallow you up if you were off your guard for a moment. The shops and the hoardings and the lights, all colors of the rainbow, flashing on and off, pulsating like single drumbeats through lines of music, the tumult, the uproar, the constant festivities. For it had seemed to her, when, after something of a struggle, Hamid had managed to drag her terrified, bewildered, half-mad, into the middle of the square before the railway station, that it must be some feast or saint's day or another celebration that she didn't know about, to make the people congregate in such vast numbers and make a noise that set her ears jangling. But Hamid had told her, laughing in a knowing way, "It's like that every day."

What a city, where people lived every day as if it were a saint's day or a feast.

Yet as she shrank behind the half-open door of the room, seeing from a distance now, and pondering, she began to notice in Cairo, condensed for her in the section of the street facing her, things that she would never for a moment have expected to find in the dream city. Poor people, properly poor, and hungry, and beggars; even in their village itself poverty did not exist in such extremes of ugliness. People lied and swore and were rude to each other, and there were thieves and pickpockets; theft made the existence of her husband and others like him necessary, and provided him with stories of incidents both in the neighborhood and far away, that he would relate to her.

The Cairo ladies, whom she had imagined at first to be without exception women of taste, reaching European standards of fashion and beauty, she now realized numbered many ugly ones among them. The majority would have been ugly, had it not been for the red and white paint that they daubed on their faces, and this made them take on color and shine like newly polished shoes and, she concluded eventually, left their owners even more ugly than they would have been without it. The abundance of these ugly women was such that she began to feel a sort of satisfaction with herself. In the beginning she had put her market value no higher than that of a maid to the least of them, but her self-esteem had risen to the point where she reckoned that if she had been dressed like them she would have become the center of attention, and been considered a real beauty as she had been in the village.

Hamid himself seemed to have some sense of his own importance and pride in his job, although she quite failed to understand the nature of his work when they told her about it. She supposed that he had something of the status of official night-watchman in the village who carried a gun and commanded respect and fear, but from what she saw of him at work, he looked more like a servant: inclining his head to her, rushing to carry out the orders of Mrs. So-and-So, being bellowed at and scolded by the owner of the building in unfamiliar phrases with words like 'dunce' and 'hypocrite', quite meaningless to Fathiyya, although she presumed that they were perhaps swear-words in Cairo.

Even so, she didn't like the attitude of lofty disdain which he adopted toward the owner of the building the day he tried to insist that Hamid let her work for them: Hamid refused outright, vowing that he himself would stop working for them if they tried to force her. It was a point of view that she couldn't accept when she thought of the pitiful way they lived, and their position in the scale of things, so low that it didn't allow them even the equanimity of spirit that comes from having five pounds to your name. This was an opportunity to have enough to live on and to buy a warm dress for winter, and it was more than likely that they would have been given a good meal from time to time. But Hamid refused, rash and capricious, and when she opened her mouth to argue with him he shouted at her, as if he owned the building and she was a tenant on the eighth floor.

The truth of the matter was that the economic justification for her desire to work was no more than a pretext, and what she really wanted was to get to know the people of Cairo better, to go into their homes and talk to them. Shut up in the room as she was, her shy introverted nature didn't allow her to do any such thing. Faced with the curious stares of the tenants who stormed the threshold, boring into her for a few moments as they scrutinized her appearance, the way she sat, her clothes, and then smiled or muttered vaguely or merely mocked, she became more closed in on herself and the chains tightened around her. They were chains of her own making; like the tenants of the building, the city around her was always on the move, surging forth, teeming with life, everything in it flowing along and coming together. But she to a certain extent, and her husband Hamid, were not only unable to abandon themselves to the city and its movement, to let it do with them what it did with the others, but were terrified and appalled by it, and recoiled more tightly in upon themselves.

She did, at least, but Hamid—and this dated exactly from the time he had married her and she had come to Cairo—had been able to free himself somewhat, moved about more easily, went to Sayyida Zaynab, to the suburbs, knew where you should change going to al-Husayn. It was not just where he went either, but his attitude of savoir-faire, his air of understanding what went on. He seemed to Fathiyya a different person from the dark silent shy youth from their village, who would turn his face away if he encountered a procession of women and girls carrying water jars early in the morning. Now he laughed and joked with the men at the garage, collected the rents and reckoned up the money to the last half penny, and even had friends who were natives of the city, not his relations or men from the same part of the country as him.

It was she alone who remained a prisoner in the room, bound by the narrow crack through which she saw he world of Cairo; and she sensed that the city was not a world, but a sea, shoreless and unfathomable. She was going along the brink, but if she once forgot and let her feet carry her on, that would be the end of her. What was frightening was that the sea was not tranquil and still, and did not adopt the same stance in relation to her as she to it; it was oppressive, a heavy sea, and thousands of hands stretched out from it, thousands of smiles beckoned from it, treacherous sirens calling to her, smoothing the way for her to plunge in.

Even the eager call of one of the tenants, with the money in his hands and the greengrocer's nearby, was a hand reaching out from the sea, paralyzing her with the terror of it and making her freeze where she stood. She withdrew further into herself until it was as if she had seen and heard nothing. She turned away covering her head, in flight, praying for a miracle to deliver her from the situation. Meanwhile the tenant, giving up, shot her a glance which she did not see, but she felt it, like a bullet in her head, and her ears picked up his muttered comments correctly interpreting the obscenities contained there.

She was shy, introverted, withdrawn: so be it, but life has its incontrovertible rules from which there is no escaping. With her first pregnancy Fathiyya had emerged from the room so that her world extended to include the entrance, and with her second child, which followed the first in a matter of months, it took in the pavement adjoining the building and the one opposite, then the street in both directions up to the square which opened out of it.

And now Fathiyya began to answer back, and even to initiate conversation. She ran errands and learnt to distinguish between the car bringing the doctor's son home from school and the one carrying the son of the man who worked for the radio. She knew all the gossip about the tenants from Hamid, and from others, and eventually it reached the point where she became Hamid's source of information about them and their affairs. The story of the midnight visitor who knocked at the flat of the airline employee, especially when he was on night duty at the airport, was only an intimation of what she came to know about the seamy side of life in Cairo, the scandals and intrigues that took place constantly beneath the respectable affluent surface. This is the exclusive province of the concierge, and still more of his wife, with her greater persistence and wiliness in these matters. Despite her narrowness of vision, she sees a lot especially in the night, and although her mind is small she can tell the difference between the sister of the man whose wife and children are spending the summer holidays in Alexandria, while he's up to his ears in work darling and simply can't get away, and his real sisters who visit the family throughout the year.

Oddly enough, none of this spoilt the dream in Fathiyya's head completely: she modified it, but she never lost sight of it. The great city remained great in her eyes, although she could see the bad things everywhere, and this was always her reply to Hamid when every now and then he came back cursing Cairo and everyone in it, having suffered this or that at the hands of one of its inhabitants.

If the ugly slime of evil lay at the bottom then salvation must lie in learning how to float. In this way Fathiyya learnt to do what the other thousands and millions of people crowded into Cairo did, floating as they floated in the great terrible surges of movement that rolled through the city.

The only things that ruffled the calm surface of her life sometimes were the tremors set up by the sudden emerging of the apparition which lay in wait for her and ambushed her in the thick of her many duties: the Man, naked, like a dreadful hand stretching out and threatening to pull her down into the mud and filth; and that voice assuring her that the end result of her being in Cairo would be to make her see that she was going to descend to forbidden territory with the Man and there was nothing she could do about it. These occasions left Fathiyya exploding with annoyance and irritation and disgust, and determined too that it should never happen, even if she paid with her life. Just you wait and I'll get even with you, Cairo.

Translated by Catherine Cobham

Mohamed Berrada
from *Like a Summer Never to Be Repeated*

Umm Fathiya
Like what else?

Like Umm Fathiya: "A black bride adorned with pearl necklaces."

No one could remember how they first got to know her or agreed with her that she would take care of the housekeeping at the flat they rented in 1957 in Zamalek. The flat was between the building's entrance and the basement; but then Zamalek was all alleys. With the regular arrival of the grant, it was inevitable that the three of them—Barhum, Alaa, and Hammad—would be left to themselves to face the phase of university and the trappings of bachelorhood, and to discover some of life's pleasures after a year of primitive living and poverty at the North African Lodge.

Umm Fathiya was in her forties. Her black skin was smooth and her long face was distinguished by small eyes whose pupils rarely stayed still and a smile that seemed to issue straight from her eyes. Her manner was natural and she spoke sweetly with the slight stutter that was common in Egyptianized Nubians. When she talked about her origins she wasn't clear about where she came from—Sudan or Nubia. She always wore a black gallabiya and a veil of the same color; bright colors were only seen when she took it off. She was quite small but her dynamism meant she filled the room.

Hammad was responsible for the food budget, therefore his relationship with Umm Fathiya was not free from wrangling, especially in times of difficulty, when money was scarce and the arrival of the grant was delayed. Each morning negotiations got going to reach an agreement over the contents of lunch and what would be left over for supper. On days of poverty they usually resorted to white beans and rice, which was dirt cheap, and tomato salad. Whenever Hammad gave Umm Fathiya ten piasters she would respond with the same phrase, which became proverbial, "Today I'm going to make something just right for you," and it was tacitly understood that the food that day would consist of a solid meal of rice and beans or potatoes or lentils. On days of relative abundance Umm Fathiya was versatile and conjured up what she had learned and perfected while working for Italian, French, and German employers: baked macaroni, potato gratin, purée, beefsteak with creamed mushrooms. . . . She was at her happiest and would scrounge a cigarette from Alaa Bey and enjoy herself as she laid the table and talked about the banquets and feasts she prepared single-handedly once upon a time. The three knights would sometimes get her to confess how she would drink beer and wine when her foreign employers persuaded her to. They would set aside a place for her to sit so that they could enjoy her stories while she sipped glasses of cold Stella. She would sit cross-legged on the floor and ask for a cigarette then grab the glass and raise it to the health of her Moroccan boys, "You're wonderful. God is great. I'm happy with you. You study hard and like having fun. Though sometimes you have too much. I see the signs when I come in the morning. Right Ustaz Barhum?" (Laughter.)

By the third glass, Umm Fathiya's expression would be merry and symptoms of light intoxication would show in her smile. She would speak more freely, especially when they asked her views on politics and Nasser, "What do you say, boys? You can laugh but I tell you, perhaps we'll get communism. Isn't communism the system that allows us to eat, have a house, and be treated in hospital for free? It's better than what we've got. We work so much but don't live well. So many people live wretchedly, poor them."

Laughter and enthusiastic remarks, "Bravo Umm Fathiya! You're a great political thinker. Where did you get this talk from?"

Umm Fathiya would giggle and lean on her right hand to hoist herself up.

"You're having a good time. You want to get me drunk. It's seven o'clock. Umm Hamdi will have sent her son to wait for me at the bus stop," she would say.

Thus Umm Fathiya's treasures were unveiled through her strong yet compliant personality and through her attitudes and experiences. Barhum, Alaa, and Hammad circulated some of her ideas and eccentricities among friends and she gained a reputation among the Moroccan students, especially those who visited the flat to meet her and enjoy her cooking. One day a group of friends were round and Umm Fathiya was in her element telling stories and answering questions. Perhaps the melody of Stella flowing in her veins let her drift off into make-believe and encouraged her to embellish her tales. One of them said to her, "Umm Fathiya, you're in your element, almost completely drunk. You should be in a film. We need to find her a director to appreciate her talents, right guys?"

"He said the movies . . . . All I know is that when I was only fifteen I acted in a film with Umm Kulthum, the film where she sings 'Lovers, They Ask Me,' you know?"

Laughter and disbelief. Umm Fathiya added, "By Hamdi's life, it's true. Go and ask Umm Kulthum. She'll tell you!"

When Hammad asked her about her roots, whether she was from Sudan or Nubia, and how she came to settle in Cairo, she would reply vaguely that she migrated with her father from Wadi Halfa when she was small. ("Have you heard of it? It's near Abu Simbel.") Her father was looking for work and his relatives in Cairo helped him out. He worked as a doorman until he died. She went to school for a short while then began working in houses, helping her mother: "Life depends on luck and on what kind of luck you have. After that my mother married me to an officer who was a horseman in the cavalry. He gave me my daughter Fathiya but died five years later. I brought Fathiya up and taught her, then she married a koshari-seller from Sayyida Zaynab. . . . That's the story. We're alive, thank God. We have enough."

In 1959, in their third year at university, they moved to a flat in Doqqi not far from the university. They lived in a two-story building, renting the first floor from Sitt Zaynat, who lived with her son and two daughters, also on the first floor. Sitt Zaynat was a thick-set woman who had a strong personality and was a good storyteller. Umm Fathiya was impressed by the flat and preferred it to the basement in Zamalek. When Eid al-Adha drew near, the three knights, together with two of their friends, decided to buy a ram to slaughter so that they could enjoy its tender meat and celebrate Eid in the Moroccan manner. Umm Fathiya's eyes widened and she smiled in wonder at the happy news. She quickly informed them that she and her half-brother, Radwan, would take responsibility for buying the ram at a price that would please them. Hammad suggested that he accompany her to the souk but she answered decisively,

"Don't trouble yourself. My brother Radwan is a butcher. It's his job. Just tell me if you want it slaughtered or if you'd like to slaughter it here?"

"Of course we want to slaughter it here, Umm Fathiya, so the neighbors know that we're making an Eid sacrifice. . . . See?"

It was a memorable day. Lots of noise and excitement. Master Radwan in his vest, peasant trousers, and cotton skullcap, with his knives and deep bronchial expressions, and the Moroccan students in shorts, fetching buckets of water and helping turn the ram to face the direction of Mecca. It was hung and skinned and the liver and fat were prepared so they could be rolled for the traditional breakfast on the morning of Eid in Morocco. Tapes of Andalusian music played and cups of mint tea were passed round. Umm Fathiya was as happy as could be and looked proud in front of her half-brother, Master Radwan. They decided to finish the ram that day. They cooked lunch then dinner and what remained was distributed between Umm Fathiya and Master Radwan, with a taste for Sitt Zaynat and her family. The next day Hammad informed Umm Fathiya that they were entering a week of asceticism during which they would remember white beans, rice, potatoes, and lentils!

In June 1960, the results of the College of Arts were announced. The three friends had passed and preparations to return to Morocco began. They sensed the emptiness and longing that leaving Umm Fathiya would leave in their hearts: her colluding smile, conversation, comments, little skirmishes, and the friendship that words could not describe. They could not leave without visiting her at her home behind Abdin Square, where she lived with her married daughter in a two-room basement. They found her presiding over a small room, surrounded by her female neighbors from the basement, her daughter Fathiya and her husband, and their son Hamdi, who was nine and seemed shy despite the signs of mischief in his intelligent eyes. "Welcome, please come in. The quarter celebrates. These are my boys but alas they're going home and leaving me." "You should go with them," said a neighbor. "That's what we said but she doesn't want to. She says she needs to raise Hamdi," said Hammad. She laughed. "No, I told them I would go on the condition that they live together in Morocco too, even when they get married. Then I'll live with them forever."

Umm Fathiya was proud of the visit and of her boys, who had obtained their degrees and would return to their country to take up important posts. She tirelessly related memories of the happy days that she had spent with them over three years: "Good kids, really. They get on like brothers and their house is always full of friends, boys and girls, right Ustaz Hammad? They're also moody. And the Egyptian girls, so sweet! But we only have one life, and is anybody taking anything from it anyway?" She turned to Hamdi. "Listen Hamdi. You must study hard like them so you can go to university and graduate and we'll be proud of you. Right? Please advise him. He just plays with a ball all day. . . ."

The visit drew on and they wanted to say goodbye but Umm Fathiya entreated them to stay for a meal of koshari, specially prepared by her daughter's husband. "You'll eat your fingers afterward," she said. They formed a circle around the low round table and the talk and laughter was nonstop. Hammad leaned over to Umm Fathiya and whispered, "Shall we go and get you a bottle of Stella?" She hushed him, laughing, and whispered, "No, dear! Do you want to expose me in front of the neighbors? Leave it until tomorrow when I come and see you off."

When Hammad returned to Cairo in 1964 for a few weeks he was eager to visit Umm Fathiya. She could hardly believe it and began scolding him, "Is this acceptable, Hammad? Only one letter in all these years. . . . Didn't we know each other well? Living together is not taken lightly except by the illegitimate." Hammad kissed her forehead and made excuses about work and looking for somewhere to settle and assured her that she was always in his mind and heart. He gave her a Moroccan kaftan of brocade and lace and urged her to put it on. Then he put a yellow belt made from Sicilian thread around her waist, so that she looked "beautiful and radiant like a bourgeois Moroccan woman." He laughed and said to her, "Don't worry. We'll take a photo and look for a groom for you!"

Like a snake, days curl up and wrap people in their vortex leaving nothing behind except new memories. Thoughts like these seduced Hammad in 1972 when he visited Cairo after years filled with work, travel, and adventures. He was coming from Paris, where he was living and preparing his doctoral thesis. As he looked down at the houses and buildings by the Cairo train station, the image of Umm Fathiya popped into his head. Goodness! He hadn't seen her for eight years. He would visit her first thing tomorrow he thought, hoping that she was still alive.

He was shocked to find that the basement she lived in had disappeared and a tall building had been erected in its place. He circled the quarter a few times and asked after Umm Fathiya and her family. With difficulty he located the doorman of the building next door, who told him that they had left three years ago. He had heard them talking about Afrah al-Angal Alley, behind Muhammad Ali Street, where they had found a room on a roof. Hammad was determined to find Umm Fathiya so he asked the way to the alley and began questioning residents house by house, offering descriptions, but no one knew

Umm Fathiya and the inhabitants of Afrah al-Angal had not grown in ten years! "Really?" "Yes. It's true," said a cobbler crouching in a small shop at one end of the alley. "I know everyone here without exception. It's my job. Some people have died but no one new has come, no."

Hammad spent three days searching for Umm Fathiya in the popular quarters without finding any trace of her. He was sure that what he was doing was completely useless in the vast and crowded city of Cairo without anything to go on. But he couldn't accept that Umm Fathiya was lost to him, for he was used to the idea that she would be around forever, that he could meet her whenever he visited or whenever he felt a yearning for her. In the last few years he had read about Nubia, visited exhibitions of Nubian statues and inscriptions, and watched documentaries about the area full of antiquities and Nile rapids. He pictured Umm Fathiya and surrendered to his imagination, pretending that she had not left all that beauty to live in a poor city quarter, neglected and separated from her birthplace. He was determined that this time he would talk to her about Ramesses II, who built underground temples and decorated tombs and caverns with inscriptions etched into the rocks. He intended to ask her to return to Nubia, or rather he wanted to suggest that he go with her to reclaim her roots, breathe the pure air of the oases and bathe in the clear waters of the Nile. Here no one knew her, and her family lived in wretchedness and poverty, while there her pores would open to the breezes, sun's rays, and songs. Across the plains of Wadi al-Subu, Wadi Halfa, and Abu Simbel, she could walk proudly with her suntanned skin and small body, which traced back to the descendents of Mandulis, the ancient god of Nubia. There she could wander about the thickets, the caves of Philae, and the sacred island of Isis, and realize her dream of a happy life that would compensate her hard work and didn't enslave the weak. Umm Fathiya, in his opinion, with her acumen, goodness, and love of life, deserved to be a princess in the pagan kingdom of Nubia, which upheld the freedom of living beings. Plants, trees, animals, people, and gods filled this space that was deeply rooted in ancient times and watched over the fate of God's creatures. Hammad remembered the caption beneath an ancient painting depicting the upper half of a legendary princess with a long neck, open mouth, and head raised to the sky: "The cry that this creature wants to hear, in vain, is a reverberating Hallelujah lost amid the everlasting silence."

At the end of that visit to Cairo, Hammad felt that he had lost something valuable: something that was a part of his accumulated self, in which he would seek refuge to combat triviality, turbidity, and feelings of extinction. In times that followed he tried again to look for Umm Fathiya but without success. Then he became fond of this unexpected ending. Perhaps it was better, he said to himself. Umm Fathiya was preserved in his memory bursting with vitality and splendor. Her words dwelled inside me and she was herself— the woman from an ancient soil and from the lowlands of Cairo, surrounded by a halo of talk, smiles, and laughter, thus simultaneously immersed in and separated from her surroundings. The fact that she worked for them was not all that brought him and his friends together with Umm Fathiya. What did you call the kind of relationship that mutated into magnetic moments, which barely twinkled in your memory before you became speechless with joy and happiness and something words could not describe? A relationship that had a date and time but soon transcended them and became an essential part of one's deepest self. Hammad accepted this ending because it meant that Umm Fathiya stayed in his memory, safe from old age and released from death. He could not imagine her as an old lady or lying in the hollow of a grave. She would always be as he knew her: sprightly, smiling, quick-witted, living in the heart of Cairo or slipping off to Wadi al-Subu to bathe in the sacred waters of the Nile and be enriched by the splendor of Isis.

Translated by Christina Phillips

Sonallah Ibrahim
from Zaat

. . . UMM ATEF. SHORT, skinny and covered in dust, her clothes were dirty and infested with fleas and the soles of her feet were full of cracks and ridges. She wore odd flip-flops because they had been begged from different places, and her eyes were always half-closed, which she claimed allowed her to see better. Her skin was a withered yellowish-brown color, full of wrinkles, and her age somewhere between forty and seventy. She walked quickly and inclined—in her politics as well as in her gait—to the right. A green cross was tattooed on the inside of her wrist and her bag of medicine, which contained Entocide for dysentery, Flagel for stomach bacteria and the urinary tract (certainly not the reproductive one), Andromide for her blood pressure, and asprin for headaches and any other ailments, never left her side.

After she had been cleaned up, by enabling her to take a full bath, forcing her to scrape her feet, and allowing her clothes a long soak, her finer qualities were revealed: scrupulously honest, a finely tuned sense of social awareness regarding her natural place sitting on the tiles, and a generous and indulgent spirit, for she never turned her nose up at a few scraps of bread with yesterday's leftovers or some potatoes and an orange, or anything she could take home to Atef, the light of her life, who suffered from epilepsy.

The two other lights in her life were the house she was building brick by brick in her village in Mallawi, for which she was collecting furnishings and utensils from the residences she frequented in Cairo, and her mother. It was on account of these two that she spent a week out of every month in the village. Zaat found this arrangement most convenient because it allowed her to seek Umm Atef's assistance twice a month instead of four times, thus permitting her to set aside some funds for projects of demolition and construction, and to pay Hagg Qurashy, first twelve pounds, then sixteen, then twenty, according to the continued increase in the rates the Umms charged. Unfortunately the arrangement did not last long, for it floundered on two rocks: the medicine and the cassette tape.

The most important piece of furniture in the living room, apart from the dining table, was the sideboard, which had been assigned a role not unlike that of a display cabinet in a boutique. Behind its glass doors was the silverware, later joined by the Pyrex set. On the thick sheet of glass that covered the top of the sideboard stood an expensive porcelain vase in which two plastic roses had settled. While some of these arrangements dated back to before the night of tears, the events and upheavals that followed and which faded the color of the roses and dirtied their leaves had imposed other more practical uses on the sideboard top. Tactical medicines (related to specific periods of treatment) had infiltrated the area, quickly followed by strategic medicines: for coughs and headaches, catarrh and flu, diarrhea and constipation, vomiting, bleeding, dizziness, indigestion, stomach cramps, high blood pressure, low blood pressure, skin inflammations, broken bones, cuts and burns, as well as painkillers, tranquilizers, sleeping pills, vitamin supplements, and antiseptics. It was not long either before the vase was sheltering, in the shade of the roses craning over its neck, other essential household supplies: a bottle of cologne, hair pins, Doaa's necklaces, a bottle of foreign perfume, a Japanese alarm clock, a clothes brush, two hair brushes, an old pair of tights, part of a tattered snakeskin belt, a comb, a hair slide, a sea shell, one of the smart leather-bound diaries the bank distributed for publicity, sticking plasters, a wooden key ring, a metal key ring, a metal water filter for the tap which had not been fitted yet, hair rollers, a plastic syringe, a small wooden statue of a tiger, a painted wooden spoon, a thermometer, half a plastic ruler, half an old strip of contraceptive pills, a bobbin of cotton, a set of needles of different sizes, a tape measure, a cigarette holder (all that remained of Abdel Maguid's attempt to give up smoking), an ashtray, a pencil, a small padlock, a jar of Vaseline, a pair of scissors, a bottle of shampoo, a piece of a broken plaster of Paris statue of the god of poetry Apollo, a small wooden dish containing a razor blade, a metal chain, a set of keys, a can of fly and mosquito spray and another for cockroaches, a battery, a sock, a few cassettes, the opening verses of the Holy Book engraved on a brass plaque, a flashlight with no batteries, and one or two other things as well.

It was only natural, then, that dusting the contents of the sideboard top, and putting everything back in its place according to some kind of system, was one of the main tasks of Zaat's domestic help. Unfortunately, however, this requirement did not take into account Umm Atef's high blood pressure, and the irritability, impatience, and ridiculous behavior that accompanies such a condition.

What happened, briefly, was this. One day Umm Atef noticed how few tablets many of the used bottles and vials of medicine contained and she resolved to make the dusting and replacing of them easier by an ingenious collection process based on a scientific classification according to the nature of the substance: she emptied the vitamins, painkillers, sleeping tablets, laxatives, and all the other kinds of tablets and capsules into two jars. She was also lucky enough to find a bottle large enough to accommodate the cough medicine, appetizers, antiseptics, and other liquids. In front of the tubes of ointment and creams, however, she stood incapable, and before she could reach a solution, Zaat discovered what had happened.

Zaat made a huge effort to control her temper in order not to lose Umm Atef. Nevertheless her reaction was enough to provoke the anger of the faithful Umm, who, while grudgingly accepting Zaat's point of view about the mixing of the liquids, was unable to understand it as far as the tablets were concerned, for it was still possible, in her opinion, to differentiate between them due to their colors and sizes. Umm Atef was plagued with doubt and began to suspect that there was more to Zaat's response than met the eye. Subsequent events would soon confirm her suspicions.

Not long afterward Umm Atef brought with her a tape of Coptic hymns which she asked if she could play on Doaa's cassette recorder. Zaat saw nothing harmful in the idea, for although she had put on the higab, she was not one of those fundamentalists who refused to have anything to do with the historic enemy. She also needed to keep in the good books of the pious Umm, for the local Umm market was experiencing a slump as a result of the flourishing Umm trade in the Gulf. Unfortunately, Umm Atef, like the majority of Egyptians, was hard of hearing, so she turned the tape up. Then she turned it up even more when she moved onto the balcony. At this point a clash seemed unavoidable.

Zaat could not bear loud noises (either because they reminded her of the humming hoard of machines at the Archives, or of Abdel Maguid, whose hearing had grown worse in recent years and who insisted on turning up the central transmission set which would make her, who had for so long struggled to obtain the set and add to its number of inches, undertake complex maneuvers to turn it down or off). She therefore asked Umm Atef to turn down the tape. When the Umm pretended that she had not heard, she turned it down herself. Umm Atef turned it back up secretly, louder than it had been before, and Zaat was obliged to express her request once again, first in words then in deed. At this point Umm Atef began to doubt that the matter had anything to do with hearing, but rather was about strife, sectarian, of course.

Was Zaat totally innocent? Who knows. We must not forget, though, that despite her tendency to mean well and her contempt for the trivialities of fundamentalism, she had previously offered a Christian sacrifice at the altar of the machines. And though it may be that she later discovered her transgression was linked to far more complex issues such as the world being divided into two camps, society into classes, tendencies into right wing and left wing, and Islam into Sunna and Shia, still we should not rule out that she might have been afraid lest the sound of the church hymns reached the neighbors, or at least that she had misgivings about the goals and motives of Umm Atef: was she attempting to win credit for her pious deeds at Zaat's expense or was she hoping to guide her Muslim mistress to the (true) faith. In any case the situation was liable to flare up at any moment. All it needed was a spark. It was not long before Sheikh Kishk's sermon provided it.

Umm Atef had decided to come to Zaat on Sundays instead of Fridays after passing by the church early in the morning to clean it and to take her share from the collection box. Zaat welcomed the change because it would allow her more time to keep out of the way of the machines (by apologizing for not going in on one of the days, and leaving work early on the other). When the first Sunday came around Umm Atef appeared with a new tape and looked for the cassette recorder, but Zaat had hidden it away on purpose. The woman had to bring up the subject directly: "By the Almighty, ya Sitti, I bought this tape with my own money. I paid the priest three pounds for it."

Zaat felt sorry for the Umm, who had sacrificed a third of her daily wage on spiritual nourishment, and she brought out the recorder. Umm Atef sat down on the floor beside it listening with interest to the solemn voice delivering the sermon. She did not listen for long, however, for the three-pound sermon only took up the first half of side one. The other half, and side two, were completely devoid of any sound whatsoever.

Despite her obvious misgivings, Umm Atef presumed that the sermon, of which in reality she had not understood a single word, had some particular importance that justified its length and price. Unfortunately Zaat did not allow the incident to pass without comment, for she saw an opportunity to revel in Umm Atef's misery: "The priest ripped you off. Either that or you've gone mad. Who in their right mind would pay three pounds for Sheikh Kishk?" Because she did not know the name of the reverend father (Umm Atef did not know it either) she had uttered the name of the Islamic preacher whose voice was, at that very moment, blaring out of the microphone above Doctor Fathy's emporium.

Umm Atef did not rise to the provocation but continued to work away silently while she weighed the matter over in her mind. It was not long before the thought occurred to her that she was the victim of some kind of trick. And because her faith was rock solid and events could not shake it, she directed her anger, as is usual in such cases, towards Zaat, considering what had happened as part of that eternal war that raged between the children of the two religions.

The two women therefore made ready for the inevitable finale which came on the same day. Instead of finishing off with the bathroom as she normally did, Umm Atef wanted to leave the kitchen till last. When Zaat objected, she could take it no longer. She picked up her bag of tools and left the flat without a word. She was never seen again. The stage was now clear for the entrance of Umm Waheed and her films.

Translated by Tony Calderbank

Mohamed Salah al-Azab
from *Frequent Stops*

THE FIRST MEETING WITH Randa and Yasmin was like this.

Yasmin stood down from the sidewalk in front of the Koshari Sheikh al-Balad restaurant on Abbas al-Aqqad Street and on the curb three cars away from her stood Randa.

Randa relied more on the customer's discernment and experience. She did not seem exceptional at all, what with her general, ordinary appearance and the ringed notebook that she pressed to her chest, which made many regular guys not take notice of her. This guaranteed her a kind of security from the Vice Squad officers who heavily patrolled this area in plainclothes, which granted her the opportunity to formally choose the acceptable guy so as not to relive the disgust she had felt during her first encounter with the 50-year-old butcher in his aged Lada. She had gotten into the car with him after he persisted in following her and saying, "Come sit with me for half an hour and take whatever you want!" He was very flaccid, and confessed to her that he had dyed his pubic hair.

As for Yasmin, she relied on the style of a 70s prostitute, with a few small modifications to keep up with the times: the exaggerated make-up, the chewing gum, the swaying posture, the constant peering around, the tight, revealing clothes, and the large handbag that, because of the general appearance, gave away what it contained.

Yasmin didn't worry much about the issue of the Vice Squad. She knew most of the officers, sergeants, and soldiers of the first and second police branches in Madinat Nasr, Heliopolis, and al-Nuzha by virtue of her professional domain, and she continuously presented them with sexual or monetary bribes, or played the intermediary between the officers and some of her important clients.

The two of you were on the prowl. When you noticed Yasmin and her distinct appearance, you said to Men'im:

"Very good . . . stop."

You motioned to her with your hand and she saw you. She pretended that she hadn't noticed a thing. After about two minutes she looked at her watch, huffed as if she had seen someone who was late to meet her, and then calmly began to move toward the two of you.

You came to a stop directly facing Randa. She thought that you two had stopped for her sake, and at the same moment that Randa opened the door on the right, Yasmin came from the outside, as a kind of camouflage, and opened the left door. Yasmin quickly came in and closed her door, saying, "Step on it."

Yasmin and you got out at the end of Abbas al-Aqqad by Inby oil company. After switching places so that she sat in the front seat next to Men'im and you rode in the back next to Randa, Men'im started the car. He said to Yasmin, who seemed more experienced, "How much do you two take?"

She looked condescendingly toward Randa and said, "What's this 'two of you'? Who's this? I don't know her!"

You traded looks with Men'im and the two of you laughed. He said, "When it rains it pours . . . "

Calmly, Randa said, "I want thirty pounds."

It seemed a simple and modest enough request, so you nodded your head at her, and asked, "What's your name?"

"Randa."

You noticed the small green crucifix tattooed on the wrist of her right hand, but pretended that you did not see it so as not to spoil the night.

Men'im said to Yasmin, "And you want the same."

She snorted as she pulled an LM cigarette out from Men'im's pack, "What, like this child? I'm not a virgin."

You tried to place your hand on Randa, so Yasmin twisted around and said to her, "Take his hands off of you, you silly girl . . . the money first."

Randa said, "I know that!"

You felt that she was naive, and that she had come here by mistake.

You gave her the 30 pounds, and Yasmin continued to snort and swear at the car jobs "that aren't worth it anymore" until Men'im gave her 50 pounds.

Men'im asked her name, so she said, "Yasmin."

And Randa asked you, "Do you have a kleenex?"

You took out a packet of Mini Flora brand tissues for her. She shook her head in refusal and raised herself a little off of the seat, then took out a packet of Fine tissues from the back pocket of her pants. She said, "I don't like Flora because they crumble."

Men'im had arrived at the 10th Zone, the area at the end of Madinat Nasr, and exited on the way to the Ahly football club. He parked on a dark side street. He turned off the car's headlights but left the engine running in preparation for any surprise, and each one of you closed the glass windows and locked the side doors.

You were all occupied when a cell phone suddenly rang to the polyphonic tune of "Don't go far, my darling." Yasmin took out the phone from her pocket, and said with interest, "How are you, my dear . . . No, I can't."

Men'im tried to talk, so she forcefully put her hand over his mouth and didn't take it away. She went on, "Half an hour and then come get me from in front of Sindbad amusement park . . . and there's a possibility I'll bring something sweet for you all."

She was silently listening and did not lift her hand from over Men'im's mouth. You felt it to be an insulting gesture—and from someone such as this!—and you said to yourself that if you were in his place you would slap her across the face. She said, "Ok beautiful . . . ok . . . bye!"

And she hung up.

Men'im tried to kiss her but she pushed him away violently.

"I don't like kissing."

So you said to Randa, "Why don't you talk to your friend; she's going to spoil the night for us."

Yasmin said as she turned her head and fixed her eyes on your unfastened pants, "It smells really awful. It's like the smell of socks."

So Men'im abandoned the issue of kissing her and you returned Randa's head to down below another time.

Suddenly Yasmin laughed, a loud and impudent laugh, and tugged at Randa's hair, "Just look at this! It's thin and white . . . it looks like a cigarette."

Randa pushed her head between the two front seats to look, half-laughed, and nodded her head to Yasmin.

Each of them went back to her partner. The sound of the evening call for prayer rose from the noisy loudspeaker of a nearby mosque, so Yasmin raised her head quickly and covered herself. Men'im said, "What?"

She said, "Wait 'til it finishes."

Shortly after she continued she laughed her impudent laugh another time, and said: "Did you see how quickly he came?!"

Men'im, aghast, said in his defense, "I came because I wanted to."

So she laughed and said, "They all say that."

Randa bent down once again over your open pants. A long time passed. From time to time she said to you, "Are you close?"

So you answered her, "Not yet."

Yasmin left Men'im completely, twisted her body to follow your situation, and presented professional advice to Randa, who had gotten bored. She said to Yasmin, "I'm tired . . . I've spent an hour going up and down and it's no use."

Yasmin pulled Randa's head over and whispered in her ear. Randa gestured to her in recognition, and after a little while you noticed that Randa had brought the tissue close to her mouth. While moving up and down she wetted it with her saliva, then rose suddenly and said, "Finally . . . it's over."

And you understood what Yasmin had whispered to her. You said, "What's over?!"

So she raises the tissue wet with her spit in front of your face, "Here you are. What's this, then?"

You didn't care much because you knew that you had taken your time and that the girl had gotten tired of you. You fastened your pants and tried to kiss her on the cheek, but she refused and said, "That's enough."

She straightened her clothes and took out a small mirror and a tube of lipstick. She applied it lightly, fixed her hair with her hand, and slouched in the seat, placing her right hand upon the left window.

Yasmin said to Men'im, who had begun to move the car, "Take us to Sindbad." And then she said to Randa, "Why don't you come with me on this job . . . it'll take exactly an hour and I'll give you 50 pounds."

Randa didn't accept or refuse. You noticed that she was indecisive and scared.

You tried to talk with her. She became shy, demurring, as if the two of you had met for the first time on Qasr al-Nil Bridge.

She said that she was studying at Helwan University without specifying which college. She said that her father works as a lawyer and that he wanted to force her to enter the Faculty of Law but she refused. She said that she practiced this as a hobby, "You know, I buy clothes and make up and pay the phone bill . . . and also sometimes I don't take money."

Men'im entered the gas station. She slumped down into the seat so as to hide her face.

You reached out your hand and opened the cover of the notebook that she had placed between you two as some imaginary barrier so that you wouldn't come closer to her. You find written within:

Mariana Aziz Kamel

The Third Year

Faculty of Law

Ain Shams University

The two of them got out at the Sindbad, and Yasmin grabbed Randa's hand while they crossed the highway. You got out to climb in the front seat next to Men'im.

After that you will see Randa and Yasmin together more than once in Abbas al-Aqqad and Makram Ebeid without either of them seeing you. You will see that Randa has shed her simple appearance and started to resemble Yasmin in her style of clothing and make-up. One time while you are with Hind in the Ramses Hilton Mall you will be going up the escalator with Hind in front of you and see facing you the two of them going down with three young Gulf Arabs. Randa will see you and act as if she doesn't know you.

Neither of you spoke a word during the long return trip along the airport fence. The sound of the car was loud and high-pitched. At the ramp to the Hykestep Bridge the car sank down into a pothole and shook violently. Men'im said, "I swear to God I came because I wanted to!"

You nodded your head to him in agreement and he sped up the car so that the two of you could go your separate ways as quickly as possible.

Translated by Alexander Ortiz

Ahdaf Soueif
from *In the Eye of the Sun*

We have not sent against his people after him a host from the sky and We shall not send. It is but one cry and they are extinguished. Woe to My people, no prophet is sent to them but they mock him. Do they not see how many We have destroyed before them over the centuries and they shall not return?

—AND THEY SHALL NOT RETURN. In a way they are right: the girls who wear those horrible long pastel-colored gowns, the gloves, and the angled veil; they've screened themselves off entirely, held on to their privacy. They're preferable anyway to the halfway ones, the ones who wear the long gown but leave their made-up faces bare and deck out their tarhas with bits of ribbon and colored braids—and yet how dismal it would be to think that it is for them and only for them that there will be forgiveness and great rewards. But that is what they think. They are certain of it. And there are so many of them in the university now. Of them and of the young bearded men in short white thobs. And on the other hand there are girls in short skirts and tight trousers and amounts of make-up that no one would have dreamed of wearing ten years ago when Asya was a student. She has three of the veiled girls in her classes—and they always sit in the front row. The first time she'd gone into her Seventeenth Century Poetry class she'd asked the sixty-three students to write a paragraph explaining why they had chosen to enter the Department of English. "And, ladies and gentlemen. I would be gratetul if you could give me an honest answer. Please do not write 'because I love Wordsworth'—particularly if you have never read him. I don't mind whether you like literature of not. I just want to adjust my teaching as much as possible to your needs—so it would help us all if you could give me a true, and brief, answer." And the answers came back, depressingly predictable—every single one of them to do with learning English in order to get a job in a bank or one of the new agencies or import companies—every single one jaggedly constructed or scarcely legible or managing to cram four grammatical errors into one sentence—and one had stood out by its simplicity. "I want to learn the language of my enemy." Asya had read the student's name out, and sure enough the girl who sat shrouded in the front row, dead center, had put up a gloved hand.

"This is yours?" Asya had held up the paper.

The hooded figure nodded. It was spooky talking to one of them directly— seeing nothing except the movement of a pair of eyes through the narrow slit of a white tarha.

"Why is English the language of your enemy?" Asya had asked. She knew the answer, but she wanted to hear her speak, to engage her in dialogue, to ask whether she did not think there was a commonality of human experience beyond politics, beyond forms.

The veiled head shook once silently and was still.

"I'm sorry?" said Asya, and nothing happened.

"Are you all right?" she had asked, and another—an unveiled—girl had spoken up.

"She cannot speak," she had said, "because the voice of a woman is a 'awra."

"How is she going to participate in seminars then?" Asya had asked. The class was silent. "Why did she not go to al-Azhar? Or the Girls' College? Then at least she would have been able to answer her teachers." Still silence. And the eyes watch her from the slits in the veil. "Very well, then." Asya had turned away. "We might as well begin. I think, rather than start with a long introduction about the age, we'll start with the poetry itself. Then, later, we'll try to find out *from* the poems about the age. Would you open your books, please, at page sixty-nine: 'When I consider how my light is spent—'"

That should be safe enough to start with, she had thought. The voice of woman is a 'awra. Of course, she'd always known that theoretically, but she'd never come across anyone for whom it was a living truth before. So as far as this girl—and the others who thought like her—were concerned she was doing a sort of porno-spread up here on the podium for the world to see. So now it was not only a class that wasn't bothered about literature, that didn't know English, that didn't know about sentences, that was too numerous to be taught properly anyway, but also a class holding people who were sitting and scrutinizing her and thinking she was doing something shameful by merely being there—something worse than shameful; something for which the fires of hell were being stoked in readiness. What if they knew—what if they had looked through the window of the cottage and seen a blond, blue-eyed man kneeling, his head between her thighs—

"They sent me a little delegation." she'd told Deena. "A delegation to say they could see I was a good sort really only it was a shame I was destined for hell."

"That's all right." Deena had said comfortably. "They do that with the ones they like. They did it with me."

"What did you say?"

"I said maybe God would show me the true path in His own good time. What did *you* say?"

"I said that I believe each one of us has to find his own way to Paradise. The thing is, they spook me, and I know if ever they had their way we'd all be finished—at least, I would—but I do have a kind of sneaking admiration for them. I mean, they've sorted out some kind of answer to what's happening all around us—all the manifestations of the West that they see here are no good for them, for the way of life they want to hold on to, the values they feel comfortable with, even to their standard of living. And their answer is genuine, it's not imported of borrowed from anywhere—"

"How genuine is it, though?" Deena had asked. "I mean, it's essentially an urban phenomenon—"

"But don't most of the young men come from the countryside"

"Yes, but they only get like this when they move to the cities—no, I don't see it catching on here like in Iran."

"Because we're not a warrior people like the Persians? We're essentially a submissive peasant race?"

"Well," Deena had smiled. "That's been true so far."

Salwa Bakr

from *The Golden Chariot*

As Mahrousa, the prison warder, lifted her head from a plate of honey, Safiyya the heroin addict began to massage the warder's face to stop the honey from dripping. After removing the hair and fine down growing round the chin, cheeks, and bridge of her nose with some plaited thread, she washed it in water without soap. Having removed these blemishes she was well pleased with the softness and glow on Mahrousa's face.

Mahrousa smiled at the thought of her face after this treatment and, in a hoarse voice, she began to sing a joyous wedding song remembered from the days of her youth some thirty years ago. Then she said, sighing sadly, "You know my dear Safiyya, when I was in the full flush of my youth my skin was so beautiful and smooth that a love bird could have picked up a crumb from it!"

"Amazing!" replied Safiyya, adding, "Worry and sadness is enough to wreck anyone in this life—even someone as beautiful as Badr al-Budur—and you have certainly had your fair share of ups and downs, may God help you."

Mahrousa pursed her lips and her face looked even more swollen than usual after the plucking. She sighed deeply and began a well-known mournful song, "The book of my life, my love . . . la, la la."

Then she stopped singing and began to speak,

"You know, if anyone else had gone through what I have and experienced life in the way I have, they would probably have committed suicide and died an unbeliever. By God, such is their right but, thank God, my heart is as pure as the white scarf wrapped around your head, Safiyya, and I have sought nothing but good for people. God rewards everyone according to his merits."

Safiyya agreed, saying, "You are right . . . God awards you your just deserts." Safiyya reminded her of the incident involving the murderess, Samiha who stole a bit of a broken fenugreek bottle from the prison hospital and hid it among her things. She intended to use it as a weapon during the endless battles with the other prisoners and was caught out by Mahrousa quite by chance. Safiyya praised her good heart because if any other prison warder had discovered such an offence the prisoner would have been in deep trouble with the prison authorities who would have imposed a heavy punishment. What's more, if Samiha had used this dangerous weapon, the authorities could have had a tragedy on their hands. Mahrousa was satisfied that slapping her across her ugly face was enough to put the fear of God into anyone, and sufficient to make Samiha mend her evil ways. Mahrousa swore by her mother in heaven that if Samiha engaged in any further activities which went against the prison rules there would be no alternative but to bind her hands and feet and pinch her with two dry date pits on the tender area of her thighs. This treatment, which was immensely painful and left the soft areas of skin severely bruised, was the very same deterrent that Mahrousa had often employed against her daughters if they did something serious which deserved a harsher punishment than the more usual slap.

Mahrousa's heart wasn't white like the prison scarf Safiyya was wearing, it was black like a cold wintry night overcast with clouds without a single shining star to lighten the gloom. The sun never rose in Mahrousa's heart to erase the black hatred which had settled there over time. This hatred was directed against people, life, time and, above all else, her husband, because he as good as killed her when she was in her prime and left her to shoulder all the responsibilities after stealing everything she owned. This included the gold she received when she married and the only piece of jewelry she possessed, an eighteen carat gold ring with a small carnelian red stone. He also stole her household effects which she had collected bit by bit, sweating blood as a housemaid from sunrise until well beyond sunset to make a living for him and their children and for which she received nothing in return but a broken heart. This husband had not an ounce of mercy and even told her once that he hated her because she was ugly and misshapen—or rather she was the ugliest woman ever created on the face of this earth. . . .

After suffering many years of torment with her sick husband, the gambler and sadist, he deserted her and completely disappeared, but not before robbing her of her only piece of jewelry which, as far as she was concerned, was as valuable as King Solomon's treasure and her only security against hard times. He stole the ring from her finger in the dead of night when she was stretched out like a corpse, fast asleep before the dawn of another exhausting day. She had come across the ring, which had a fake carnelian stone, quite by chance in the inside pocket of an old coat belonging to a Greek lady she worked for. She had been presented with the coat when the lady was forced to leave quickly when in 1956 foreigners were expelled from the country.

After he deserted her Mahrousa abandoned all hope of her errant husband ever returning. She was forced to move around from job to job because domestic work was no longer easy to find. The spread of electrical appliances and the tendency to choose practical furnishings enabled people to manage the daily chores on their own and dispense with servants.

At first Mahrousa took up cooking kushari made from rice, noodles, lentils, fried onions and spicy sauce which she sold on the pavement. But as soon as she managed to get back on her feet and save a little money she was pursued by municipal officials, demanding protection money and fees which she was forced to pay in order to get the necessary license to ply her trade in peace. The pavements were the property of the Government who doled out licenses to traders on a purely arbitrary basis. Mahrousa decided she had had enough of selling kushari after she discovered that the financial return was negligible; the taxes and bribes she was forced to pay exceeded her earnings and after she had paid off the wholesaler for the noodles, lentils and rice, which she bought on credit, at the end of the day she made no profit at all.

After that she went into 'manufacturing,' perhaps spurred on by the general trend of the 'open-door' economic policy which was meant to promote manufacturing but failed to build the factories to make the goods. The scale of Mahrousa's industrial plans differed considerably. She started picking up any discarded paper she could find on the street, thrown out by import-export dealers, and used them to make clowns' hats and paper fans. She fixed these onto sticks made from stripped palm branches, used to make cages, which had ended up on the rubbish dump in the market. She stuck the hats and fans onto the sticks with starch made from cooked rice then, in order to paint them, she boiled up left-over vegetables and scraps to make dyes which were brightly colored to attract children. Then, in this attempt to stave off destitution, she roamed the markets and saints' day festivals, selling her wares for a few pennies.

During this critical period of her life, a neighbor enticed her to work with him in a Punch and Judy show. Her husky voice was projected from behind the curtain and she played the part of the mother-in-law who is always stirring up trouble and dissension between her daughter and hen-pecked husband. Apart from her main role she also sang some ditties which brought laughter and mockery from the audience. Mahrousa found this work easy and was happy because it did not sap her strength or undermine her health, which had recently deteriorated. Chronic rheumatism had spread to her joints despite the fact that her work-load, apart from the show, was light and only involved cooking and occasional washing for her employer.

She was ecstatic about her new role in the Punch and Judy show because it made her feel loved by people, especially children, who laughed uproariously and screamed when it was her turn to sing. At last she was accepted after feeling alienated for so long, and earning a wage was an additional bonus. Her work was eventful to say the least: one day the owner of a large café surprised her by inviting them to give a show for a circumcision party. This was to be on behalf of a prosperous man whose son had been born after seven daughters, produced by three different wives; only the last wife had enabled him to fulfill his dream of producing the son from his loins who would succeed him and preserve his name for posterity.

Mahrousa made her mark in her new role and even contributed new ideas of her own; to the delight of her audience she told riddles, usually during the intervals. By extending the performance she was also able to attract bigger crowds and thus earn more money. A typical riddle she asked them might be, "What crosses the sea without drowning?"—and by the sea she knew the people understood she was referring to the River Nile. It was common to use this terminology and indicated the reverence and affection felt for this great river. One of the more witty members of the audience might then give the answer, "A buffalo calf in its mother's stomach because a buffalo can easily float in the Nile, even when pregnant," at which point Mahrousa would ask the audience to applaud this intelligent response while Punch played one of Hasab Allah's famous melodies by way of congratulation. Mahrousa would go on to deliver the second of four riddles which were the only ones she knew, asking her audience, "What hovers over a glass plate?" Then she got to the third riddle, which she considered the most difficult of all, which went like this, "A container within another container immersed in water; inside it are pearls and its outside is copper colored. What is it?" At this stage the audience would inevitably give the wrong answer but Mahrousa gave them more time to think during which she would circulate, collecting money. Only when she returned to Punch would she tell them the answer which was, "A pomegranate." Then she would throw out the last one which was, "Something which shines and glistens and hides between leaves." Then she would join with Punch in the second part of the show which followed this interval.

However, not long after, Mahrousa had to leave the work that she loved so much. She was astounded when the very man who played Punch, made it clear that he not only wanted to have sex with her but also wanted her to do it with other men. He was most insistent that she agree to both demands, planning to share with her the income she earned from prostitution in return for his protection and procurement of men for her.

After she left the Punch and Judy group Mahrousa and her children went through dark times. She was forced to beg in the streets to stave off the hunger of six little mouths which were constantly open, demanding food. She found work with removal men and her hopes were raised only to be dashed when she injured the vertebrae in her lower back. As if this wasn't enough, one night she was returning from her work in an apartment far out in one of the new suburbs of Masr Jadida, when she was raped by three soldiers, the same age as her eldest daughter. After gagging her and binding her with their army belts the gang raped her, leaving her in such a state that she would never know how she managed to get home. In the days that followed, Mahrousa rummaged around in dustbins for anything fit to eat. She got hold of some offal and discarded remains from a man who slaughtered and sold chickens which she stewed and gave to her children with bread. But God was to intervene and show mercy to this wretched woman. One happy day one of her husband's relatives, who was working as a staff sergeant in the prisons, was unexpectedly transferred to the women's prison. Having just heard that she had been abandoned by his relation and witnessed the misery and deprivation that she and her children had suffered, he went out and bought a tin of halawa made from the best ground sesame seed and syrup, some flat loaves of white bread, and a packet of tea which he sat and shared with them. Then after slipping three pounds into Mahrousa's hand, which were the only notes he had left in his pocket, he promised to try and find her a job which would give her a regular income and save her from begging on the streets. Hardly a month went by before Mahrousa was wearing the warder's uniform, a blue-grey overall; she was appointed because the authorities were impressed by her hefty size and the forbidding look in her eye that gave her a stern appearance, both of which, in their view, qualified her for the new post.

Despite the extraordinary experiences and suffering Mahrousa had already encountered in her life, her job opened her eyes to a world of human relationships wholly outside her previous experience; with the turnover of prisoners she was constantly exposed to new stories of tragedy. She became aware of the comforting truth that she wasn't the only oppressed woman in the world as she had thought, nor was she alone in suffering from misfortune; there were many other women to whom fate had dealt a terrible blow and had robbed of happiness and mercy. In her new profession she was required to be firm, strict, and authoritative which gradually gave her self-confidence and strength but this neither eliminated the blackness in her heart nor banished the bitterness from her soul. The lasting feeling of failure and the sense of an absence of justice in life which she harbored made her compassionate in her dealings with the prisoners. She was sympathetic to their plight, and had reached the conclusion that mercy should always come before justice; there was no hope for the human race without mercy, which, if allowed to surface in human relations, would go some way toward eradicating misery in life. For this reason she was honest with the prisoners and didn't oppress or exploit them. She didn't impose fines on them like some of the other warders nor did she expect them to render services for her without anything in return; even when Safiyya, the heroin addict, made her a crochet shawl she reciprocated by giving her a whole chicken which she had boiled herself at home and brought to the prison. She was also quite happy to accept presents from the prisoners on condition that they offer them freely and without expecting any special favor in return. On this basis she accepted the honey in which her face had been immersed a short time ago from a prisoner whose family owned a large number of hives in their village. Generally she would only stretch out her hand to accept something from the prisoners after satisfying herself that, weighed on the scales of justice, the gift had come through the door of love, mercy, and compassion, all qualities necessary to survive the terrible life in prison.

Translated by Dinah Manisty

Khaled Al Khamissi
from Taxi

"IF I TOLD YOU what happened now you wouldn't believe me," said the driver. "I've been driving a cab for twenty years but what happened now was one of the funniest things that ever happened to me."

"Go on then, tell me," I prompted.

"A woman in a face veil stopped me in Shubra and asked me to drive her to Mohandiseen. She got in the back seat and she had a bag with her. As soon as we were out on the Sixth of October Bridge, I saw her looking right and left, and then she went and took the veil off her face. I was watching in the mirror, because, look, I have a small mirror under the big mirror so that I can see what's happening in the back. You have to be on your guard. As the saying goes, better safe than sorry. Anyway, then I found her wearing a headscarf instead. I was surprised but I didn't say anything. A little later she took off her headscarf and she had done her hair in curlers. Then she started undoing the curlers and putting them in her bag. Then she took out a round brush and started combing her hair.

"I looked in the mirror in front of me, and she yelled at me, 'Look in front of you.' she said. 'What are you doing?' I asked her. 'None of your business. You drive and keep your mouth shut,' she shouted back at me.

"Between you and me, I thought of stopping the car and making her get out, but then I thought, "What's it to me?" So I held out to see what else she would take off. Next thing, I found her taking off her skirt. Nice, I said, we'll have a free view. I looked again and found her putting on a short skirt and thick black tights which didn't show anything. She folded up the long skirt and put it in the bag. Then she started taking off her blouse. My eyes were transfixed on the mirror and when the car in front of me suddenly braked I almost ran into it. She shouted at me like a mad woman, 'Hey, old man, shame on you, keep your eyes on the road.'

"I saw she was putting on a tight blouse and pretty too. Honestly, I didn't answer her. She put the other blouse in the bag and went and started getting out some make-up stuff and started putting on lipstick and rouge on her cheeks. Then she took out an eyebrow brush and started working on her eyebrows. In short, by the time I was coming off the bridge into Dokki she was a completely different woman. Another human being, I tell you, you couldn't say that this was the woman in the veil who stopped me in Shubra.

"She finished off by taking off the slippers she was wearing, taking out a pair of high-heel shoes and putting them on. I told her, 'Look, miss, every one of us has his peculiarities but for God's sake tell me, what's your story?'

"'I'm getting out at Mohieddin Aboul Ezz,' she said. I kept my silence and didn't repeat the question.

"After a while she started telling me her story, 'I work as a waitress in a restaurant there, respectable work. I'm a respectable woman and I do honest work. In this work I have to look good.'

"'At home and in the whole quarter I can't come or go without wearing that veil. One of my friends got me a fake contract to work in a hospital in Ataba and my family thinks I work there. Frankly, I earn a thousand times as much working here. In a single day I can get in tips what I would earn in one month's salary in the moldy old hospital.'

"'My friend at the hospital gets 100 pounds a month from me to cover up. She's a girl who looks out for herself. Every day I drop in at her place and get changed. But today it wouldn't have worked to go to her place so I had to take a taxi to change in. Any other questions, Mr. Prosecutor?'

"'Lady, I'm no prosecutor, and if I saw one, I'd fall flat on my face. But they say that he who cooks up poison tastes it. You changed in my taxi and I wanted to know why. Once one knows the reason, the wonder ceases,' I said, and thanked her for telling me the story. Now honestly, isn't that a strange story, sir?"

Translated by Jonathan Wright

Amira Abou-Taleb

from *Barbed Silk*

STARTING HER DAY IN reverse, she works her way back from the important business dinner she has to attend at 8:30 p.m. That means that the kids must be asleep by 8:00 p.m. so she can have ten minutes to get ready and the remaining twenty minutes to get to the dinner.

She won't have the usual time after they sleep to prepare for tomorrow's chores of shopping, preparing little Hind's outfit for the nursery's costume party, or baking the cookies she's supposed to take to the party. She must do all that before she leaves for work today. To go do the necessary shopping, she would have to leave the house as soon as the bus picks the kids up at 7:05 a.m. which is normally the time she uses to prepare herself for work. That means that she'll need to get ready and dressed for work before waking up the girls. She checks the time: 5:15 a.m. This gives her 45 minutes before their 6 a.m. wake-up time.

Standing under the hot shower, she stops thinking and watches the translucent steam twirl up mysteriously. Deep inside she pleads for time to stop, even if just for a few moments. She catches sight of the hands on the clock; they seem to mockingly speed up. The measly second hand runs even faster, in what seems to be direct defiance. In a hurry she concludes the morning prayer while her mind runs over shopping lists and possible outfits for the day.

The six o'clock hour is rapidly lost between breakfast preparations, hair brushing, repeated attempts at waking up the sluggish teenage daughter, an incessant search for the homework folder which—according to eyewitness reports—has miraculously hidden itself, clarifying the theory of why ballet shoes are not appropriate for school, and straining efforts to elucidate the concept of time and explain how a ninety-minute animated feature film cannot possibly be viewed in the remaining twelve minutes left before the bus. Between this and that, and so much more, the hour disappears. The clock strikes 7:00 a.m. announcing the onset of 'panic time,' where the voice gets louder and the smile scurries off to a faraway place where it can find shelter and respect. For five minutes the place turns into an utter madhouse, a jumble of running and yelling and cynical hands racing across the clock. The bus honk announces the culmination of the battle. A loud slamming of the door, preceded by a little shove. Exhale . . . .

Ten minutes of clean-up time to erase the signs of war. She takes a long, slow, deep breath and makes yet another plea for time to stop, but, being true to its usual self, it doesn't. As she goes off to do the day's grocery shopping, she thinks about what to make for dinner, and, more importantly, who will make the dinner. She wonders if dinner can acquire some self-independence tips from the homework folder. Oh well, she'll have to deal with that later.

The journey to work begins. She plans to use the forty-five minute commute from Maadi to Mohandiseen to relax. She looks forward to feasting her eyes upon scenes of the ever so graciously flowing waters of the majestic Nile and its historic Corniche. With a bit of soft music to relax—and to offset the blowing noise of synthetic air from the AC—all remnants of the earlier combat will soon be gone.

Amid her private world of little pleasures, a huge public transportation bus intercepts her line of sight. The bus is tilted, leaning uncomfortably toward the car, giving her the impression that the hoards of people stuck inside, with their bodies half-dangling, may soon start plummeting down upon her. Gloomy faces fill up the seats, the walkways, and any other vacuum the bus might have once possessed. Some faces stare straight at her, making her feel uncomfortable, like an alien from another planet. Others are too preoccupied with their own strife to even notice her. She senses the weight of a heavy rock settle deep inside her gut. She tries to swallow, but nothing can digest stone. The need for music is no longer there. The soul is dead. All that is left is a corpse that knows how to drive and has memorized the way to work.

Finally, at around 8:45 a.m., she arrives at the office. She embarks on the morning routine of individually greeting her male and female colleagues and kissing everyone, all of whom are of course graduates of foreign schools. It was a routine she never quite understood the point of. Maybe it's their way of boasting their Western liberal inclinations while maintaining affinity with Eastern traditions of warmth. Reaching her own office, she finally shuts the door, automatically reaches for the power button on the computer, and takes a sip of the hot Nescafé with its erupting bubbles of foam.

Task list: First, read e-mails. She finds an urgent request from the London office asking for the cost of a comprehensive advertising campaign for a client that needs the information the same day. As usual, they apologize for the short notice as the matter is out of their control. In her reply, she states that work will start on that project the next day as today's agenda has been pre-planned and the hours slotted are already barely enough. She apologizes for giving priority to her pre-set agenda and states that her avid commitment to meeting her deadlines is, unfortunately, out of her control. Internally, she asks one of the employees to start work immediately on the London project so that he can share with her the results before the day is done. That way she will ensure having the time needed to send him back to fix the methodological mistakes and errors of common logic that will inevitably be present.

Going back to the task list she realizes that the office meeting planned between the management team and the client has been moved to the client's office instead. She fumes in despair at such careless regard for other people's time but opts not to stir trouble as the client is as yet unaware of her plans to shatter his current advertising strategy which doesn't even match his marketing objectives to begin with. This idiotic change of venue will now cost her an extra hour of time as it takes thirty minutes just to get there. She goes on through her day reviewing and analyzing the field research results and getting into disputes with the television censorship officials over the new detergent ad showing the fallaha hand-washing the clothes in a tisht (plastic basin). The officials claim that the portrayal of the tisht in the ad demeans the nation's civilized image. She, in turn, attempts to question the censorship officials about their logic in allowing intellectually shameful TV serials to air daily at primetime; their approval of the use of profane and vulgar language in televised plays; their acceptance of the degrading portrayal of women as sex symbols in video clips; and their filling up of useful airtime with religious Q&A programs and fatwas that compete in their level of substance with the shallowness of fawazeer Ramadan. The agency's radio and TV liaison begs her not to ask those questions and promises to take care of the tisht issue in his own way, for he knows how to handle those officials and knows what it takes to make things right.

The rest of the day is spent putting out little fires here and there and placing the final touches on the new business pitch presentation to one of the country's largest mobile phone operators set for the following day. Seemingly failed attempts at explaining the basics of logic and professionalism are constant drags throughout the entire work day. Constantly failing and constantly hoping. She soon realizes the impossibility of making it home in time for the kids return from school and sends out an SOS text message to a friend. She looks out the window and finds the Nile still flowing graciously in its uninterrupted course, unfazed by time or the hands on the clock.

A five-minute break—a pause to ponder if you wish. She asks the office boy for a clear glass kubbaya for her tea. She prepares the tea, conjuring up a lesson in tea-making learned long ago; a lesson she had received once upon a day when time stopped . . . . Hot, boiling water in a clear plain glass; heat, haze, turbulence. A cold dry teabag; the cheap local kind. Elegantly and cautiously, she lowers the teabag and watches it plunge straight to the bottom. A few moments of serenity. Slowly and softly, thin sheets of red haze graciously seep out of the teabag and discreetly settle down, subtly forming a dark scarlet-red layer below the clear undisturbed top. She abruptly pulls the string and moves the teabag to watch the saga unfold. A volcano of curling red flames erupts in a frenzy, twirling and spreading its inferno in every direction, reflecting nature's innate tendency for insanity . . . . Another dream, another prayer.

She falls back into reality and leaves the office anticipating an exciting meeting with the client.

In a plush conference room on the thirty-ninth floor, thirteen gurus of the local and international marketing and advertising industry gather in a summit meeting, each boasting a victorious career history, preceded by a top-notch university degree, as a banner directing the rest to the soundness of his opinion. At the far corner of the room stands a silent window overlooking a Nile that carries on its deliberate and natural course. A Nile undeterred by heated arguments inside the room nor by the high salaries they represent. Nothing they can ever say could stop such eternal flow. Soft, sparkling golden waves impregnated by the rays of the sun bear in every turn the profound certainty of faith.

She takes her position at the head of the table and begins bewildering them with her innovative marketing theories. Concepts that were shattering barriers and clearing paths for innovative ideas that would multiply sales in ways they never thought possible. She challenges their minds, exhausts their wits, and secures a consensus among an assembly that rarely conforms.

In the halo of applause she is overcome by a profound sense of meaninglessness.

At the end of the final round everyone gathers for Nescafé and pastries. Peering out the window, she could hear distant whispers. She listens carefully trying to understand the meanings, struggling to decipher their mysteries, but alas, this type of expensive glass is absolutely air-tight, no gaps. She feels the iciness of the walls and the bite of the chilled artificial air pouring down the silent vents of a highly proficient air-conditioning unit. Amid a sip of coffee and another glimpse, she is lost.

The warm sun rays seep into her soul as she sits there by the riverbank, playfully kicking her feet in the water. A calm warmth gradually penetrates the folds of her turbulent being, filling up the void deep inside with that same serene certainty of faith.

By the riverbank she reflects upon that normal day that had passed a few days ago, bearing along with it the first glimpses of her forties.

She wonders if there was a way to go back to that sad day and locate it on the old-fashioned calendar—that thin, square sheet of calendar paper holding within it the tiresome memories of that day. How she wished for that thin sheet of paper announcing 18 January 2007 to find its place back onto the calendar, giving her a fresh new chance at reliving that same day—differently this time.

Another dream, another prayer . . . .

A light breeze tickles her face as she wakes up in her soft bed. The air carries the scent of white lilies which have bloomed overnight while she was deep within her purple dreams. The corners of the curtain dance to the lily-filled air in a gracious orchestration. She is dumbfounded by the amount of sensuality that can be experienced in such few seconds with eyes still half-exposed to the light of a glorious sunny morning. An unconscious smile settles on her face as she feels the warmth of the soft cotton bed linen engulfing her, and she sinks deep into the sheets like a child enjoying the soft spring sun. She settles her hand under the pillow as if it were a cornerstone holding her whole being in place. A blissful calm overcomes her.

A bold ray of sunshine invades her privacy in search of deliverance; it settles at the end of the room on the painting portraying the silhouette of a belly dancer and brings to life the sensual moves of her curling dress. The dancer's waist remains in the shadow, yearning for its turn under the lights. All those emotions overwhelm her and deplete her resistance; she subtly falls back into slumber, longing to awaken only to repeat the same experience again.

She dreams of his fingers sifting through her soft black hair, gathering the wild strands in a gentle crescent motion and reeling them safely home. He deliberately caresses her every inch in an agonizing confirmation of vulnerability and surrender. Warmth flows through her. She conjures up the scent of piping hot, fresh bread rolls, the kind served in posh hotels with the soft butter florets. As she opens up the hot roll the heat swirls rise up into the air and tantalize her with the homey smell of sour dough; she watches the butter subtly melt. He holds her kindly, he holds her strong, leaving her drowsy and sleepy once more.

Three beautiful daughters stumble into the room, one after the other, filling it with sincere bliss. She is overcome by a profound sense of humbleness as she experiences God's ultimate compassion and struggles to hold the tears back. Tears are like safety valves which overflow to release extreme force and restore internal balance. The little one holds up a drawing of a giraffe cut into shape by those cute tiny fingers that have fondly added the word 'mommy' in print, boasting their owners' latest acquired skill, reading and writing. The middle daughter performs a song that she has composed herself, and appears in her fragile, slender form like a delicate, scrumptious wafer. As for the eldest one, it is enough to see that killer smile of hers, a smile that fills the room with the spirit of pure goodness and joy . . . all three fly to the kitchen to prepare a special breakfast-in-bed in celebration of her special day while he goes out to buy fresh hot loaves of fino bread.

She reaches for the nightstand and grabs that stubborn book that refuses to end. As she reads it she is lost within the dunes of the Western Desert and lies amid the bareness and glory of the Siwa temples. She reads and dreams, and dreams and reads, finally giving way to the heaviness of her eyelids as she pulls up the fluffy goose-down duvet and surrenders herself to purple dreams . . . continuing her dream, she imagines him bringing to her bedside a glass kubbaya of tea, the smoky swirls rising up and tickling her nose, filling her with warmth. He asks her, "What do you feel like doing for your birthday?" She thinks; maybe she'd like to visit a museum or an art exhibit, maybe this could be her chance to purchase a painting or a piece of art . . . . No, no, maybe they'll go to the little bookstore café where they can cozily sip their mochaccinos and then wander around looking at the magnificent coffee-table books she never buys for herself . . . . Better yet, how about a trip to the desert where they can stay up till the break of dawn gazing at the desert stars and listening to the sweet sounds of oud strings . . . . Still, why can't her gift be a visit to the local orphanage where she would go, packed with little gifts, to see the smiles light up the beautiful tiny faces that so long for connection. Wait, what about a trip to Alexandria during a rough winter storm, they can walk along the corniche with the waves blasting against the rocks compelling her to seek refuge inside his woolen coat until they reach the room and light up a fire. She basks in her confusion and asks him to grant her time to think of what she'd really like to do for her fortieth birthday.

Awakened by the in-room breakfast commotion, she sits up in bed with her heart and arms opened wide, ready to greet a generous day.

As the day progresses, she is overcome by the brutal reality, a reality that tears the delicate purple-woven dream fabric to shreds. There, she sits in the middle of the loud group of friends he has invited over for a surprise birthday party. She wears a fake smile and hates herself, for she was never a fake. He presents her with an expensive brand name gift; the perfect aid for the busy modern woman: a sophisticated, sleek hi-tech deep-freezer. A gadget, she is positive, that would impress any of the women present. Feeling suddenly nauseous, she runs inside as the tears begin to fall.

She pleads to God to not have him follow her. How would she even begin to explain what she feels, what would she ever say. There it stands in front of her; the day she has long awaited has merely come and gone. The day signaling her entry into her fifth decade of life; a new beginning, one in which she, exclusively, can play the starring role. After forty years of perfecting supporting roles: from the well-behaved child to the hard-working student, the lovely sweetheart then the cordial wife, the high-flyer business woman all the way to the inspirational mom. For so many years she has patiently played her roles, one after the other, longing for the day she reaches forty, the peak of femininity, where she can finally indulge in the bliss of self-actualization. Oh my, how that beautiful woman inside her has longed for the day where she can simply and boldly step out into the light in pure abstract form, free of all roles.

Adjusting her posture with her feet still dangling in flowing Nile waters, she turns to look at the skyscraper behind her. The golden waves reflect sunshine onto that sealed window up on the thirty-ninth floor, sending rays that carry whispers of absolute esoteric faith; alas, the whispers cannot penetrate the clear, cold glass. Once again she finds herself inside the busy conference room staring out the plain glass.

The present jumps back at her with all its awful might. The cold air blowing down the expensive air conditioning ducts sends a chill down her back and her mind conjures up the sight of the ominous hi-tech deep-freezer. The lights inside her go out, she is left in deep morbid darkness with graveyard-like stillness that absorbs every sound. One last time she looks up at the sealed glass facing her; she can see the reflection of smoke from the hot tea as it playfully twirls up and slowly fades, giving way to the incessant, loudening noise of the hands on the clock.

Translated by Amira Abou-Taleb

Ghada Abdel Al
from *I Want to Get Married*

10–15 Reasons Why I Wanna Get Married (Don't Count Them!)
Sometimes I think to myself: why on earth do I wanna get married? I'm just fine the way I am: a respected medical doctor, I make . . . (uhh . . . forget it . . . you're gonna make fun of me). I'm basically OK: I eat, drink, sleep, go

out, go to the movies, I watch Rotana TV and I can't look away. So what's my problem?!

But then there are moments when I feel like I wanna get married—for many reasons. I'm sure that all girls, regardless of their class and cultural background, must feel the same way.

One of them might say: I wanna get married cause I wanna have kids.

A second one will say: I wanna get married so that no one will dare call me an old maid.

And a third one will say: I wanna get married to live it up and be free (stupid, but it's not me talking!)

A fourth one might say: I wanna get married to give birth to another heroic Saladin to revive the Arab nation! (Wow—why not?)

As for me, I have very different reasons. Not the grand, meaningful reasons (like "it's my right to want to get married because it's normal"). For me, it's small things that matter because they give taste to life, just like Mervat Amin said in that movie: *wa mada qitar al-'umr ya waladi khud illi ba'du bita' arba'a illa rub'* (Life's train has departed, my son—catch the next one at a quarter to four). It was a very deep movie.

Anyway, here are ten to fifteen moments when I really feel that I need a husband:

1. When the gas cylinder is empty and needs to be changed. That, of course, is one of the main household duties for a husband.

2. When I see a cockroach in the house and am totally freaked out and too scared to kill it. But it would really suck if he's also scared of roaches.

3. At lunch when my parents eat the two chicken thighs and leave the chicken breast for me. Even if he doesn't like chicken breasts, a chicken with two thighs will feed two people.

4. When I need to haul the mattresses up to the roof to air them. (I'll pretend that I just need him to help me out, then make him carry them all.)

5. At the movie theater when they separate singles from families. Get this: they get married and *still* go to the movies! It's not fair!

6. When I have to get on a minibus, he'll definitely protect me from harassment. That is, if he's not too busy harassing the girl sitting next to him.

7. When I come home after a fight with my supervisor and I need to take it out on someone. If I pick on my parents that would be haram and I'd be punished in hell—but not if I take it out on him.

8. When one of my girlfriends gets a call from her husband to tell her that she'd forgotten the food on the stove and the apartment caught fire. Why can't I have an apartment that catches fire too?

9. When I'm alone in bed at night (hey, no dirty thoughts!). At least he'll do something instead of me falling off the bed every night.

10. When my mom cooks something I don't like. When will I have control over the food and cook what I want? And if he doesn't like it, he can go eat at his mom's!

11. When mom stops me from putting my old stuff out on the balcony. When will I have my own balcony so I can fill it with old stuff and when will I have my own kitchen where I can save as many empty jam jars as I want?

12. When I crave prunes and no one wants to buy me any. Then I'll threaten him that I might be craving them because I'm pregnant and the kid might end up with a prune-shaped birth mark on the back of his neck if he doesn't get me prunes.

13. When I watch a Haifa Wehbe or Nancy Ajram music video and wish to God that someone was sitting next to me so I could tease him.

14. When I write something like this and don't have anyone to point out that I've written fourteen reasons but forgot to write number six.
(Ha—gotcha!)

15. Why don't *you* come up with number fifteen cause all this stuff got me thinking and now I'm a mess.

Anyway, so there you go, 10–15 moments when I feel I wanna get married. But there are also 100 other moments when I feel I don't want to—moments when I feel that I want to stay single.

Translated by Samia Mehrez

Cairo's Underworld

The rapid and haphazard growth of the city of Cairo has resulted in new patterns of geographic, economic, and social mobility. During the second half of the twentieth century, Greater Cairo was the site of successive waves of rural migration due to the centralization of institutions and employment opportunities in the capital. Uprooted and disadvantaged, these rural immigrants began to form new communities in a number of informal settlements on the margins of Cairo that have slowly transformed the face of the city altogether. The fragmentation of familiar spaces and the encroachment of unfamiliar ones led to new urban affiliations and communal solidarities. At the same time, life in the new urban context provided a heightened sense of mobility and anonymity, as well as an imminent sense of alienation and isolation. Furthermore, specifically since the 1980s, the state's neoliberal market policies, the privatization of the public sector, as well as of state assets and services, all led to rising levels of unemployment, especially among the youth, thus creating new forms and structures of urban poverty and misery.

Many writers, specifically since Naguib Mahfouz, the author of the city par excellence, have emerged either from Cairo's middle and lower middle classes or from its recent rural immigrant communities. In fact, since the mid-twentieth century, more and more writers from the city's low-income neighborhoods and *'ashwa'iyat* (informal housing settlements) have made these 'marginal' informal settlements the very center of their literary representations: Imbaba, Bulaq, Manshiyat Nasir, Dar al-Salam, and so on. Given the conscious and central role of these writers as 'underground historians," it is no surprise that their works painstakingly represent these silenced and unwritten faces of the city that are so crucial to understanding Cairo's modern history.

This section brings together a spectrum of literary texts about Cairo's underworld(s) whose juxtaposition across time reveals the transformations of both structures and representations of urban life from below as well as the transformations of the writers' own attitudes toward the city's underworlds. As Greater Cairo expands, so the lives and profiles of the truly disadvantaged multiply and diverge. In Mahfouz's *Midaq Alley*, urban poverty is represented as part of a rigorous hierarchical social order. Mahfouz's *hara*, or alley, is a microcosm of Egyptian society and contains within its walls and boundaries a representative spectrum of society at large who all cohabit the same space: from the affluent merchant to the professional beggar at the very bottom of this social ladder. Mahfouz's description of Zita the professional beggar is particularly interesting because it includes him in rather than excludes him from the structure of life in the hara. Even though he visits no one, and no one visits him, he does rent out a 'hole' from the bakeress Husniya, with whom he has sex, and he conducts his business—that of mutilating the miserable poor and creating cripples who are fit to join the profession of begging—in collaboration with the hara's 'doctor,' Booshy. As part of a rigorous social order, Zita is born a beggar, inheriting his profession from his parents, who were both also beggars. He reigns supreme over an underworld empire of cripples "who acknowledged his absolute sovereignty." As king of the underworld he walks the city alleys to "collect his dues" from the beggars whose artificial cripples he created and to update himself on their crippled state: "How is your blindness, So-and-so?" or "How is your lameness?" he asks. Not only is Zita doomed to be a beggar from birth but Mahfouz's representation of him is thoroughly negative throughout. At no point do we sense any empathy toward this underworld creature; in fact, he is described as evil and portrayed in terms that are completely sub-human:

> On the ground, almost directly beneath the little window, something is piled, no different from the floor of the room in color, filthiness, or smell, but possessed of limbs, flesh, and blood, and which therefore, despite everything, deserves to be called a human being.

Mahfouz's fatalistic and perhaps even judgmental rendition of urban poverty within the traditional structure of the hara is challenged through many other class-conscious readings of urban reality, which document new forms of urban misery. Rather than demonize the 'delinquent' urban poor, many later texts seek to expose the material conditions that stand behind such urban 'delinquency'; no longer represented as the scum at the bottom of a social order, these 'delinquents' are understood and written as human beings whose crushing urban existence has formed their singular and individuated underworld experiences in the city. For example, Mekkawi Said's *Cairo Swan Song* tries to understand the reasons behind the growing phenomenon of street children in the city by reading into the unbearable social and economic lives they lead. Hence, not only do we encounter Karim the runaway child who "learned how to get high off glue and rose through the ranks of a big gang of kids who hung out downtown begging and selling tissues," but we also understand the conditions of deprivation and abuse to which he was subjected that ultimately lead him to choose to live on the street. Similarly, Mohamed al-Fakharani exposes the horrific living conditions of the urban poor that make the street a safer place than 'home': "You will not go back to the shack now . . . your mother is probably in bed twisting her body of cruel hunger and her rotting liver as your father sits in the corner eating kabab and cussing at her. . . . He will not give her or you anything."

Likewise, in *Zeenat Marches in the President's Funeral*, Salwa Bakr invests her poor and completely marginal woman protagonist Zeenat with a personal drama, a personal dream, and a personal politics, all represented through the consciousness, idiom, and language of illiterate Zeenat, who quietly seized a tiny piece of government land to build a small shack with her own bare hands. In Yahya Taher Abdullah's folk-like tale, "The Story of the Upper Egyptian," the underworld of immigrant Upper Egyptians (vendors of vegetables, doormen, construction workers, hawkers) is endowed with communal solidarity and organization not to mention a nascent urban class-consciousness. As members of the community celebrate the circumcision of one of their young male kin with other urban craftsmen and artisans, one of the guests makes an ironic toast to the rich of the city, whose lives are constructed by the bare hands of this unrepresented community: "We and the Upper Egyptians put up the buildings and construct the Mother of Cities, but we don't live in the buildings, so greetings to those who live in the buildings."

The hope that Cairo will improve the fortunes of the dispossessed is shattered in all of these texts; the fantasy is transformed into nightmare as these new urban settlers discover the impossibility of realizing their dream. In Hamdi Abu Golayyel's *A Dog with No Tail*, the construction worker whose point of view shapes the narrative tells us that so many successive waves of young men from his village have come to Shubra neighborhood in Cairo to work in construction that it has become a tradition and right of passage after which they are expected to return to the village with a "few hard earned pennies." How these 'pennies' were earned may remain part of their own burdensome, undisclosed urban experience, which is masked, like the case of the narrator, in unrealized, phantasmagoric success stories in the city: "I myself would put in two or three weeks' hard graft in Shubra and on my return to the village tried my hardest to convince people that I was, in fact, a pilot in Cairo." The crushing force of the city is succinctly captured in Maguid Tobia's symbolic story "Five Unread Papers," where the entire urban experience is reconstructed through the voice of a dead narrator whose metaphoric "death" in the indifferent city is discovered only because of his "rotting smell" and five unread newspapers that lay at the door of his flat. Finally, when Cairo turns her back so ruthlessly on so many dreams of mobility, integration, and livelihood, her young are forced to seek salvation elsewhere. Hamid Abdel Samad's dramatic depiction of Egyptian young men waiting for days at the gates of the German Embassy to try to get a visa captures their tragic sense of abandonment in the Mother of Cities and their search for a new and perhaps even more hazardous dream of survival.

What remains unique, however, despite the harshness of all these underworld experiences, is the fact that literary texts are able to capture, beyond what the social sciences have to offer, the human face and depth of these urban miseries. The poor and the disadvantaged have faces, names, and individual stories to be told and represented. They are not simply countless, faceless victims, but people who have feelings, emotions, humor, and, most important of all, the creative energy to place the city's underworld squarely on its cultural map.

Naguib Mahfouz

from *Midaq Alley*

THE BAKERY IS NEXT to Kirsha's café, near Mrs. Saniya Afify's house. It is an almost square building, its sides built unevenly. An oven occupies the left side and the wall is lined with shelves. Between the oven and the entrance is a bench on which the owners of the bakery, Husniya and her husband, Jaada, sleep. Darkness would envelop the spot day and night were it not for the light issuing from the door of the oven.

In the wall facing the entrance, there is a small, wooden door which opens onto a grimy little outbuilding smelling of dirt and filth, for it has only one tiny window in the opposite wall overlooking the courtyard of an old house. About an arm's length from the window there is a lighted lamp, placed on a shelf, throwing a dim light on the place, with its dirt floor covered with various and indeterminate rubbish; the room looks like a garbage heap. The shelf supporting the lamp is long and stretches the entire wall; on it are bottles, both large and small, various instruments, and a great number of bandages, making it look just like a pharmacist's shelf, were it not so extraordinarily dirty.

On the ground, almost directly beneath the little window, something is piled, no different from the floor of the room in color, filthiness, or smell, but possessed of limbs, flesh, and blood, and which therefore, despite everything, deserves to be called a human being. It was Zaita, the man who rented this hole from the bakeress Husniya.

If you once saw Zaita you would never again forget him, so starkly simple is his appearance. He consists of a thin, black body and a black gown. Black upon black, were it not for the slits shining with a terrifying whiteness which are his eyes. Zaita is not a Negro; he is an Egyptian, brown-skinned in color. Dirt mixed with the sweat of a lifetime has caked a thick layer of black over his body and over his gown, which also was not originally black. Black was the fate of everything within this hole.

He had scarcely anything to do with the alley in which he dwelt. Zaita visited none of its people, nor did they visit him. He had no need for anyone, nor anyone for him. Except, that is, for Dr. Booshy and the fathers who resorted to scaring their children with his image. His trade was known to all, a trade which gave him the right to the title of 'Doctor,' although he did not use it out of respect for Booshy. It was his profession to create cripples, not the usual, natural cripples, but artificial cripples of a new type.

People came to him who wanted to become beggars and, with his extraordinary craft, the tools of which were piled on the shelf, he would cripple each customer in a manner appropriate to his body. They came to him whole and left blind, rickety, hunchbacked, pigeon-breasted, or with arms or legs cut off short. He gained his skill by working for a long time with a traveling circus. Zaita had, moreover, been connected with beggar circles since his boyhood, when he lived with his parents, who were beggars. He began by learning "makeup," an art taught in the circus, first as a pastime, then as a profession when his personal situation became worse.

One disadvantage of his work was that it began at night, or at midnight, to be exact. It was, however, a trivial disadvantage to which he had become completely accustomed. During the day, he scarcely left his den and would sit cross-legged, eating or smoking or amusing himself by spying on the baker and his wife. He delighted in listening to their talk, or peeping through a hole in the door and watching the woman beating her husband, morning and night. When night fell he saw them overcome with friendliness toward each other and he would see the bakeress approach her apelike husband and tease him and talk to him coyly. Zaita detested Jaada, despised him and considered him ugly. Apart from this, he envied him for the full-bodied woman God had given him as a wife, a really bovine woman, as he said. He often said of her that she was among women what Uncle Kamil was among men.

One reason why the people in the alley avoided him was his offensive odor, for water never found its way to either his face of his body. He happily reciprocated the dislike people showed for him, and he jumped with joy when he heard that someone had died. He would say, as though speaking to the dead person, "Now your time has come to taste the dirt, whose color and smell so much offend you on my body." No doubt he spent much time imagining tortures he could inflict on people and found a most satisfying pleasure in doing just this. He would imagine Jaada, the baker, as a target for dozens of hatchets striking at him and leaving him a smashed heap. Or he would imagine Salim Alwan stretched on the ground while a steamroller ran over him again and again, his blood running down toward Sanadiqiya. He would also imagine Radwan Hussainy being pulled along by his reddish beard toward the flaming oven and being eventually pulled out as a bag of ashes. Or he might see Kirsha stretched beneath the wheels of a train, his limbs crushed, later to be stuffed into a dirty basket and sold to dog owners for food! There were similar punishments that he considered the very least people deserved.

When he set about his work of making cripples at their request, he was as cruel and deliberately vicious as he could be, cunningly employing all the secrets of his trade. When his victims cried out at his torture, his terrifying eyes gleamed with an insane light. Despite all this, beggars were the people dearest to him, and he often wished that beggars formed the majority of mankind.

Zaita sat thus engrossed in the wanderings of his imagination, waiting for the time for work to arrive. About midnight he got up and blew out the lamp; a deep darkness took over. He then felt his way to the door and, opening it quietly, he made his way through the bakery into the alley. One his way he met Sheikh Darwish leaving the café. They often met in the middle of the night without exchanging a single word. For this reason, Sheikh Darwish had a particularly rich reward awaiting him in the Court of Investigation to try mankind which Zaita had set up in his imagination!

The cripple-maker crossed over to the mosque of Hussain, walking with short, deliberate steps.

As he walked, Zaita kept close to the walls of the houses. In spite of the blackness of the shadows, some lights still gleamed; thus someone approaching would almost collide with him before seeing his flashing eyes glinting in the dark like the metal clasp of a policeman's belt.

Walking in the street, he felt revived, lively, and happy. He only ever walked out here when no one but the beggars, who acknowledged his absolute sovereignty, were about. He crossed to Hussain Square, turned toward the Green Gate, and reached the ancient arch. As he swept his eyes over the heaps of beggars on both sides of him he was filled with delight. His joy was that of a powerful lord mixed with the delight of a merchant who sees profitable merchandise.

He approached the beggar nearest him, who sat cross-legged, his head bent on his shoulders and snoring loudly. He stood for a moment before him, gazing intently as though to probe his sleep and determine whether it was genuine or feigned. Then be kicked the disheveled head and the man stirred, but not in a startled manner, merely as though gentle ants had wakened him. He raised his head slowly, scratching his sides, back, and head. His gaze fell on the figure looking down on him; he stared up for a moment and, despite his blindness, recognized him at once. The beggar sighed and a noise like a groan rose from his depths. He thrust his hand into his breast pocket and withdrew a small coin and placed it in Zaita's palm.

Zaita now turned to the next beggar, then the next, and so on until he had completely encircled one wing of the arch. Then he turned to the other wing and, when he finished there, he went around the niches and alleys surrounding the mosque, so that not a single beggar escaped him. His enthusiasm at receiving his dues did not make him forget his duty to care for the cripples he created and he frequently asked this or that beggar, "How is your blindness, So-and-so?" Or perhaps "How is your lameness?" They would answer him, "Praise be to God . . . praise be to God!"

Zaita now went around the mosque from the other direction and on his way bought a loaf of bread, some sweets, and tobacco and returned to Midaq Alley. The silence was complete, only broken from time to time by a laugh or cough from the roof of Radwan Hussainy's house, where one of Kirsha's hashish parties was in progress. Zaita made his way past the threshold of the bakery as quietly as he could, taking care not to waken the sleeping couple. He carefully pushed open his wooden door and closed it quietly behind him. The den was neither dark nor empty, as he had left it; the lamp burned and on the ground beneath it sat three men.

Zaita made his way unconcernedly toward them; their presence neither surprised nor troubled him. He stared at them with piercing eyes and recognized Dr. Booshy. They all stood, and Dr. Booshy, after a polite greeting, said, "These are two poor men who asked me to seek your help for them."

Zaita, feigning boredom and complete disinterest, replied, "At a time like this, Doctor?"

The 'doctor' placed his hand on Zaita's shoulder and said, "The night is a veil, and our Lord ordained the veil!"

Zaita protested, belching out air, "But I am tired now!"

Dr. Booshy replied hopefully, "You have never let me down."

The two men begged and pleaded. Zaita yielded, as if unwillingly, and placed his food and tobacco on the shelf. He stood facing them, staring hard and long in silence. Then he fixed his eyes on the taller of the two. He was a giant of a man, and Zaita, amazed to see him there, asked, "You are an ox of a man! Why do you want to become a beggar?"

The man answered falteringly, "I am never successful at a job. I have tried all kinds of work, even being a beggar. My luck is bad and my mind is worse. I can never understand or remember anything."

Zaita commented spitefully, "Then you should have been born rich!"

The man did not understand what he meant and attempted to win Zaita's pity by pretending to weep, saying spiritlessly, "I have failed in everything. I even had no luck as a beggar. Everyone said I was strong and should work—that is, when they didn't curse or shout at me. I don't know why."

Zaita nodded. "Even that you can't grasp!"

"May God inspire you with some way to help me," the big man pleaded.

Zaita continued to examine him thoughtfully and, feeling his limbs, said decisively, "You are really strong. Your limbs are all health. What do you eat?"

"Bread if I can get it, otherwise nothing."

"Yours is really a giant's body, there's no doubt about it. Do you realize what you would be like if you ate as God's animals eat, on whom He lavishes good things?"

The man replied simply, "I don't know."

"Of course, of course. You don't know anything, we understand that. If you had had any sense you would be one of us. Listen, you oaf, there's nothing to be gained by my trying to twist your limbs."

A look of great melancholy came into the man's bullish face, and he would have burst out weeping again if Zaita had not spoken. "It would be very difficult for me to break an arm or a leg for you, no matter how hard I tried. Even then, you wouldn't gain anyone's sympathy. Mules like you only arouse indignation. But don't despair," (Dr. Booshy had been patiently waiting for this expression). "There are other ways. I'll teach you the art of imbecility, for example. You don't seem to lack any talent for that, so idiocy it will be. I'll teach you some ballads in praise of the Prophet."

The huge man's face beamed with delight and he thanked Zaita profusely.

Zaita interrupted him, "Why didn't you work as a highwayman?"

He replied indignantly, "I am a poor fellow, but I am good and I don't want to harm anyone. I like everyone."

Zaita commented contemptuously, "Do you wish to convert me to that philosophy?"

He turned to the other man, who was short and frail, and said delightedly, "Good material, anyway."

The man smiled and said, "Much praise to God."

"You were created to be a blind, squatting beggar."

The man seemed pleased. "That is because of the bounty of our Lord."

Zaita shook his head and replied slowly, "The operation is difficult and dangerous. Let me ask what you would do if the worst happened. Suppose you were really to lose your sight because of an accident or carelessness?"

The man hesitated, then replied unconcernedly, "It would be a blessing from God! Have I ever gained anything by my sight that I should be sorry to lose it?"

Zaita was pleased and commented, "With a heart like yours you can really face up to the world."

"With God's permission, sir. I will be eternally grateful to you. I will give you half what the good people give me."

Zaita shot a penetrating look at him and then said harshly, "I am not interested in talk like that. I want only two milliemes a day besides the fee for the
operation. I know, by the way, how to get my rights if you are thinking of getting away without paying."

At this point Dr. Booshy reminded him, "You didn't remember your share
of the bread."

Zaita went on talking: "Of course . . . of course. Now, let's get down to
planning the work. The operation will be difficult and will test your powers of
endurance. Hide the pain as best you can . . ."

Can you imagine what this thin and meager body would suffer under the
pounding of Zaita's hands?

A satanic smile played about Zaita's faded lips . . .

Translated by Trevor Le Gassick

Maguid Tobia

from *"Five Unread Papers,"*
in *Flights of Fantasy*

AT LAST I HEARD the occupant of flat seven telling the hall porter that there
was an awful smell coming from my flat. The porter said he too had smelt it,
and wondered what was its cause:

"Maybe there's a dead cat inside."

But he recalled that I don't keep cats in my flat; and that he hadn't heard
the sound of cats. (He felt that this was puzzling, and was puzzled.)

The man from flat seven thought the smell was awful, and told the porter
to ask the police to open the flat.

The police broke down the door with a clatter, so that the glass shook and
the echo of it reverberated around the sparsely furnished flat.

*The day I took the flat over I had liked the area's total peace and the gardens
around each building. I had wanted to live in al-Sayyida with the people of my village, but there wasn't a place there for me. When I inquired about a hotel in a quiet
street the prices had been more than I could afford. I continued to search but without
any luck. (This was exhausting and I grew exhausted.)*

Although the street is paved and always clean, nobody moves in it except street traders, porters, and beautiful cars. No children play in it. (I was aware that this was amazing, and was amazed.)

I got off the Sayyida train. There were lots of children playing in the street. I asked them the whereabouts of the flat of Mahmud—who is from my village—but they knew nothing. One of them, however, asked me:

"You mean Mahmud from Upper Egypt"

"Yes."

Instantly, they knew him, and a group of them guided me to his flat. I used to fold the quilt and spread it out over the straw mat and sleep in the sitting room. Sleeping there was comfortable, except for the heat and his fat wife who started to get annoyed by my presence. She would go to the bathroom deliberately several times each night, making a loud slapping sound with her slippers. Sometimes she would step on my fingertips on purpose so that I took to sleeping with my hands clasped on my chest. I heard her telling her husband that I slept like the dead, but he didn't reply. Once she kicked me in the head with her foot, which hurt, and I smelt the odor of her body as her nightgown touched my head. (I didn't like her smell, and was disgusted.)

They put the door they had knocked down to one side and started carefully toward my bedroom. They froze in their tracks . . . nauseated by the smell. They retreated in confusion. All of them, except the hall porter, who stood speechless where he was for several moments. He has only one eye: he looked at me with his good eye, and a single tear glistened on his brown cheek.

His good eye had stared at me in puzzlement as he said to me:

"All the people in this building keep little black statues of naked negroes, and dogs lying down with collars round their necks, and peasants playing the flute!"

One evening, his eye shining with astonishment, he whispered to me:

"They're all mad about these idols! The pearls in the negroes' noses are real . . . the collar around each dog's neck is stainless steel . . . the flute in the peasant's mouth is genuine bamboo!"

(He was truly astonished because he felt that this was truly astonishing.)

When he came into my flat he looked in every corner, then he smiled and said:

"You don't behave like them."

And a single tear glistened on his brown cheek.

I went up to the top of the Cairo tower. Long hours I stood there, comparing my size to that of the city. I gazed at the high buildings and watched the people scurrying to and fro and eating standing up. When the fat woman said to her husband that I slept like the dead, I moved to a hotel in Clot Bey street. I chose it because it was cheap. From the very first moment there, something strange happened: my ear grew and grew and workers came and extended the tramlines into it, so that the tramcars drove into it with their bells, the screeching of their wheels, their drivers swearing at the donkey-cart men, and their conductors rowing with the passengers. Fleets of these trams went into my head, never to return. (I hung a sign outside my ear saying "No Entry," but it didn't help.) Frequently, the electric cables would touch, and spark and crackle in my head! So I changed the position of the bed and slept with my right ear to the street (because it's hard of hearing).

After expending a lot of effort in the search, I discovered that an acquaintance of my father was building a house in the suburb of Heliopolis. I went to him and he promised me a flat with one bedroom and a sitting room. He took no key money and no advance of rent. He said he was doing it for my father's sake. (I thought this was surprising, and was surprised.)

The hall porter wiped away the tear which was glistening on his brown cheek—*the fat woman told her husband "your friend sleeps like the dead"*—the porter was confused by what he saw and said:

"The day he came here he seemed to be in good health."

At that time I was mad about women. And the men I knew from the village said: "The city woman is easy to get. Men like us from Upper Egypt are overpoweringly attractive to her. Our attractiveness to Cairo women is like that of the Egyptian man to European women." Immediately I began to look everywhere, up at every balcony and into every villa. I recalled my friend, Hashim. He had kept on borrowing money from everyone he knew until he was able to buy a small car; with the car he managed to marry a beautiful girl. Then he wanted to sell the car to pay off his debts. The girl's parents had to pay the debts themselves to put a stop to the scandal. They began to help him financially each month. One day, he told me that he accepted their money and rejected their contempt. (I felt that this was funny, and laughed.)

They started searching in the drawer of my desk and among my papers. I don't care. I've no secrets or love letters for me to fear the scandal of exposure. There are letters from the village full of talk about cotton and wheat and barley, and innumerable greetings from relatives and village folk. Everyone of them sends me a thousand, thousand greetings, "This letter to be delivered by hand to our beloved son."

I saw the top of a palm branch jogging along and ran to my mother. She was standing in front of the oven baking. I shouted that I had seen the palm; and she gave me two milliemes. Holding them, I ran to old Husayn on his donkey with the palm branch fixed high above the saddlebar. He doesn't cry his wares. He sells his dates in bunches of four.

When he came to the fourth letter, the police officer wanted to laugh (but didn't). My father was telling me the news of the village: after the usual thousand, thousand greetings from every relative and friend, he wrote that the mango tree which he had planted in front of our house had withered and died.

The officer put the letter down. He was disgusted by the smell. He looked at the faded wooden bed.

I was thinking: if this woman came to my wooden bed, it would be really good. She looked dazzling when she appeared on her balcony, and seemed even more attractive getting into the car, showing as she did so the better part of her pink, soft thighs. One night there was a power cut, and she came to my flat. I liked the smell of perfume about her. When the lights came on again, I liked the elegance of her dress. But her breasts sagged and her bottom and the flesh beneath her rubber corset were peculiarly fat. I noticed that she had a faint mustache beneath the powder under her nose. (This was repulsive, and I was repulsed.) She leant over to kiss me, but I was sad about the mango tree which had withered and died. I saw her face plastered with bronze powder, running after me at great speed while I ran away from it terribly slowly. I wanted to scream, but it stretched out its hand and ripped out my vocal chords and tore them to pieces and pulled me toward itself and tried to kiss me.

My grandmother scolded me. She told me that there was an evil spirit with a hideously mangled foot in the darkness of the larder—a spirit which breathed fire from its mouth into the faces of small children. She was afraid we would go in there and steal buns. And my mother was baking and I asked her for two millemes. And I felt that this was funny, so I laughed. And the porter thought it truly astonishing, and was truly astonished.

I wished I had gone back to the sitting room of Mahmud from my village. I complained to him about my new home. He was silent, and then said that it was better than the hotel. (His words were unambiguous, and I understood.)

At the fourth letter the officer had wanted to laugh but didn't. At the fifth, he began to raise his eyebrows: *My father was still going on about his sadness at the death of the mango tree. He wrote that its roots hadn't taken to the soil, and that the family and friends asked for nothing more than to see me in the best of health. He ended with a thousand, thousand greetings, and "The postage stamps were affixed in my presence and the envelope contains no money orders."*

The doctor came—*the fat woman said he slept like the dead*—and asked the hall porter to bring a bottle of eau de cologne from the neighbors. Then, taking out his handkerchief, he soaked it in the eau do cologne, and clapped it on his face, covering his nose. He approached the bed and started to play with my clothes, then with my chest and stomach. He pulled my eyelids and looked into my eyes for a long time. (But my eyes did not look at him.) He left the room and washed his hands thoroughly. Then he looked at the officer and said:

"The case has been dead for four to six days."

When they broke down the door they found five newspapers for five consecutive days, untouched on the floor. With his policeman's instinct, the officer thought and said:

"Then the flat has been empty for five days!"

And one of the neighbors said:

"Five papers he didn't read. He must be happy!"

They laughed, but they were overcome with nausea from the smell.

The doctor went on, speaking to the officer:

"Most probably he died from natural causes, but I have to take a sample from his intestines to be sure."

In distress, the hall porter cried:

"It's always the good ones who go!"

The officer assured the doctor that this precaution was natural.

In distress, the porter repeated:

"It's the good ones who go!"

My father answered tenderly:

"He who is good and does good deeds goes to heaven where there are rivers of honey. But he who is bad and does bad deeds, goes to hell, the most miserable of fates."

This puzzled me enormously. I didn't want a miserable fate, nor did I want to go to hell, because I would hate to burn forever. But, at the same time, I wasn't enthusiastic about heaven because I don't like honey.

(Now I know full well where I am. And I have a strong inclination to tell what I know . . . . Except that I am afraid of the consequences . . . . For, here too . . . .)

Translated by Nadia Gohar

Yahya Taher Abdullah

from *"The Story of the Upper Egyptian,"*
in *A Mountain of Green Tea*

The Story of the Upper Egyptian Who, Overcome by Fatigue, Went to Sleep under the Wall of the Old Mosque

He woke to a scream and found her by his head; she was weeping, wearing black, and carrying a dead child in her hands.

She said, "O So-and-so son of So-and-so, has the wide world become so restricted for you that you can find no place other than this in which to crowd out me and my children? You have killed my son, you who can't see where you're going. In order that my sorrow for my son may be lessened you must quit these houses before daybreak."

The Upper Egyptian went on rambling away, saying, "I came to the place and there was nobody there but me."

She shouted at him, "Were I not a believing genie, the daughter of a believing mother genie and of a believing father genie, I'd have ridden upon your shoulders for two lunar years as animals are ridden, you animal."

The Upper Egyptian let off a couple of farts and, collecting up the tail of his gallabiya and closing his teeth over it, he set off with the speed of wind, scarce believing that he had made good his escape from the female genie who dwells hidden away and whom no son of Adam sees except when she wants him to. After a time, believing he had escaped, he came to a stop and asked himself, 'How is it that I am leaving the mother of villages that holds within itself the bones of my ancestors? I shall go to him who has studied as well as al-Bukhari, to him who knows the Book of Allah by heart and who is held in awe by the jinn, and I shall complain of the female genie."

He said, "I found him sitting under the vine with the firewood ablaze in front of him. I made the distance between him and me a kassaba and a half, and I said, 'Peace be upon you.' When I didn't hear a reply from him I made the distance between him and me one kassaba and said, 'Peace be upon you.' And when I did not hear him reply, I went forward and made the distance between him and me half a kassaba, and I gave greetings but he replied not. Meanwhile the fire he had lit was still blazing. Having understood, I said, 'Then everything has ended. The Reaper has come before me and the matter is over and done with.' I scooped up some earth in the palms of both hands and scattered it over the fire and it died out. Then I sat down and wept."

The Great Hand, O my Emir, had marked out for him the way: two iron lines over which trains ran, with their wooden poles along which were stretched telegraph wires. When the Upper Egyptian found the way marked out in front of him, he walked along it. He continued to walk, with Allah's lands passing by, until he reached the Mother of Cities (Cairo), which he entered on the fifth day of Dhu 'l-Hijja, and the year was that of the wolf and the bears. In a sea of iron and fire he saw human beings hopping about and asking for alms, saw them on bicycles, saw them going on all fours, saw them in buses, in trams, in trolley-buses, saw them flying, saw them driving cars.

He stood and watched and marveled and forgot in what time he was until the man came and asked him about his identity. He said, "So-and-so the son of So-and-so."

Said the man, "I'm asking you about your identity card."

He said, "I've got an identity card."

Said the man, "Give it here."

The man took the card and said, "You're the person pictured in front of me; there remain the words that are written and this is a problem because I do not know how to read."

Said the Upper Egyptian to himself, "Seeing that he can't read and seeing that the words written are all about me and that it was I who said these words to the clerk writing out the identity cards and it was the clerk who wrote out my card, this then is my chance to show off." He said to the man, "I can read," and he proceeded to gaze at the card and to recollect all he had said to the clerk and to say it to the man, and it came as a surprise to him to find the man striking him on the mouth to make him shut up, so he shut up. The man, though, went on hitting him on the back of the neck while he was silent, and the man didn't stop hitting him until the Upper Egyptian, on his first day in the Mother of Cities, fell to the ground unconscious.

When he came to, he found around him some people whom he did not know and whose measure of evil and measure of good he did not know (evil is concealed and good is concealed within every soul and no one knows the hidden parts of souls, O my Emir, except Allah). He had to speak with them to find out their intentions, so he spoke, and they had to reply to his words and they did so. The Upper Egyptian understood that the people around him were onlookers, sympathetic, wanting to put things right, wanting to give advice. They said, "Forget it, the man's a policeman." They said, "You're here and not over there," and they advised him to change where he was living, and they said, "It's nothing, he's opened up your left eyebrow." Then they said, "As you're from Upper Egypt, tell us to which group of Upper Egyptians you'd like to go." They enumerated to him what his fellow countrymen did: they were vendors of vegetables, doormen, workers on building sites, hawkers. He said to them, "I've got no money for buying anything to sell." He said, "I own nothing but my body." They said, "Then go to the building workers," and they described to him how to get to them.

He went to the building workers. The day had ended and he found them seated around a fire they had lit. He gave them greeting and said, "I am So-and-so the son of So-and-so." They said, "Welcome, you're one of us." He told his story and they said to him, "What happened to you happened to Mr. Abdul Haleem." He ran his hand over his wound and groaned and said, "Would that my mother hadn't married my father." Having been seated, he lay down. They sat him up straight and made him drink some hot lentil soup and they rubbed his feet with warm water and salt and blamed him for coming on his own. They said to him, "The earth is all marked out, O So-and-so, and we do not walk here singly, and when we walk we are a people who know where the boundary is and we do not overstep boundaries." They excused themselves for their state of poverty and said, "Today is one day before the end of the week and so we do not possess the money with which to buy ground coffee to put on your wound." One of them got up and placed some ashes on the wound and they promised him to buy some coffee when they were paid their week's wages, saying that when tomorrow came to an end the week would have ended.

When the week ended, the Upper Egyptians bought coffee and packed it over the Upper Egyptian's wound and they bought a Mahallawi handkerchief and bound it round the wound. The weeks went by and a month passed, and the Upper Egyptian was cured of his wound and of his swollen feet, and life became good for him with his fellow Upper Egyptians, although he would, on moonlit nights, avoid them, going off to sleep early before the moon came out. He continued to move about with them from place to place, constructing with them buildings of bricks and steel and sand and cement, singing the red erotic mawwals, the blue mournful quatrains, and the nostalgic green laubali, when he would hear the sound of the waterwheels of the mother of villages. From among those who shared his perilous work he chose acquaintances of townsfolk who were artisans and lived in alleyways: blacksmiths and carpenters, men who laid paving stones, house painters. He would visit them in their homes and drink tea with them and their wives and eat sweet potatoes with their children.

Once they invited him to a circumcision party at which a singer performed to an arghoul, also a fair-skinned dancer who played the castanets so that people got into a great state of excitement. He was in as great a state of excitement as the others and had smoked hashish with the others who had also smoked hashish, and he remembered the distant mother of villages. Asking for Allah's mercy upon the souls of his forefathers, he went up to the microphone and took out a shilling note and ordered the singer to sing a song for the mother of villages and for the sons of the mother of villages, and he talked into the microphone and his voice boomed out, "Greetings to the Upper Egyptians, the men who put up buildings and construct the Mother of Cities," One of the artisans who was of the quarter got up and paid the singer and the dancer a quarter of a pound and spoke into the microphone and said, "O masters of crafts, it is the men from the Mother of Cities who construct the Mother of Cities." The craftsman's words grew louder and the dancer seated herself, kneading her white flesh, and the singer sang his song. A squabble almost broke out between the craftsman and the Upper Egyptian had it not been for a sensible Upper Egyptian who got up and paid the dancer and the singer half a pound and said into the microphone, "Greetings to everyone, greetings to all those Upper Egyptians and craftsmen who are present, greetings to the men who put up buildings and construct the Mother of Cities." A witty craftsman got up and hailed the Upper Egyptian and paid half a pound to the dancer and the singer and said into the microphone, "We and the Upper Egyptians put up the buildings and construct the Mother of Cities, but we don't live in the buildings, so greetings to those who live in the buildings.'

Thus the night ended well. From that night on, our friend the Upper Egyptian would tell himself, "It's true that we the Upper Egyptians put up the buildings, and also the craftsmen with us put up the buildings, and it's true too that I and the craftsmen don't live in the buildings, but we Upper Egyptians leave one of us at the door of every building we put up," and he asked himself, "When will my turn come to rest and sit on a wooden bench in front of the door of a building?"

Our friend went on living in the future after having discarded the past and forgotten the present. He made his calculations that Tayeb Mohammed had fallen down from on high and broken his neck and had lost his turn and that Mahmoud Saket had lost his turn when the Angel of Death had seized his soul as he slept; likewise Abdul Bari who, poor fellow, wanting to clear his throat, had coughed up his soul. "My turn will come to be a doorman before Abdul Haris and Abdul Malik and after Hajjaj, Mahmoud Zanni and Abdul Hakim."

On a sunny day, going up the wooden scaffolding that was tied together with ropes, on his shoulders a load of sand and cement, our friend, having discarded the past, forgotten the present and living in the future, said to himself, "When we finish putting up this building, Abdul Hakim will sit at its door and we shall proceed to put up the building at whose door I shall sit on a wooden bench."

On that day, O my Emir, the foolish Upper Egyptian lost his life, just as the foolish woman, the seller of milk, lost the milk.

Translated by Denys Johnson-Davies

Hamdi Abu Golayyel
from *A Dog with No Tail*

Dreams

The Doctor dreams methodically; every so often he is visited by a new dream. All his dreams come true. What are all the jobs he's done but dreams come true? He doesn't overreach himself, though. He has no desire to turn his life upside down; he merely seeks to improve his circumstances. Rolling in the dust of the building trade he dreamed of guarding trucks. Rather than spend sleepless nights guarding trucks he dreamed of traveling the country as a driver's mate. Instead of dozing before a garage of heavy-goods trucks he dreamt of his backside on the comfy bench outside the actress' building. And this was his greatest dream of all.

His name was Shinhabi, but he always felt the need to explain that "it's Sinhabi on my ID card." The medical moniker dated from his days in the pharmacy. He'd always had that strong body, the pale skin, and the green eyes, and when he took the time and cleaned himself up, you'd think him quite the gentleman. People who met him for the first time would be completely taken in. They wouldn't bat an eye to hear him called "Doctor." A perfectly shrewd friend of mine saw him in our village clad in a white gallabiya and suede jacket and thought he was a government vet.

The Doctor went to Cairo young. His father died and he didn't continue his education. He dropped out in his second year of high school, but he would have left even if his father had lived. His father had tuberculosis and not much else, aside from a mat to sleep on, a blanket, and two rooms with reeds for a roof. I knew him toward the end of his life: a thin robe wrapped around a hunched skeleton. I would see him every day, rolling out a cigarette as he perched on the mound in the middle of our village. It was said that the cigarettes loosened him up and I got the habit from him. To this day I won't enter the bathroom without my cigarette.

The Doctor was quick to get his affairs in order. He went off to work with his Nubian cousins on the work gangs all over Cairo and stayed at his aunt's buildings in al-Waili. Together with her Upper Egyptian husband she had been looking after a villa for an ancient Englishman, and when he died it went to her. She joined forces with her sisters' children, who lived back in the village, and in place of the old villa erected a tall, gaudily painted building. But the

Doctor had no time for the way his cousins made their living. It didn't sit right with him, so he went off to earn his living at the daily laborers' markets on the public squares and bridges: the first person from our village to discover Shubra and Mi'allim Matar's crew. His unshakably rude health qualified him to carry sand, gravel, cement, and tiles. He could lift two meters of red bricks and carry them to the top of the highest building in Egypt. Working alongside him in Bousta almost killed me. He was also the first person from our village to work as a loader for goods trucks, as a driver's mate, wiping down cars, hawking videotapes, and as a doorman.

Over the course of successive generations, the young men of our village have, without exception, made their way to Shubra. More than mere job hunting, it's something like a local tradition, a first step that every man must take at the start of his life: independence, self-reliance, and returning to the village with a few hard-earned pennies. Once a man has developed the beginnings of a mustache and a sense of self-worth, he travels to Shubra. For my generation the trip was an adventure for the brave and the bold. To miss out was to court disparagement of your intelligence and open-mindedness; your ability to pass beyond the limits of your world.

And every one of them, educated and unlettered alike, worked as manual laborers (the most contemptible and, by a considerable margin, the toughest of the professions) yet they were ashamed to work as doormen, loaders, and driver's mates, or even as craftsmen in the construction gangs. He'd carry dirt but he wouldn't work, that was the boast. However, when circumstances forced one of us into this life of labor, he'd do his best to conceal it from his very closest relatives. I myself would put in two or three weeks' hard graft in Shubra, and on my return to the village tried my best to convince people that I was, in fact, a pilot in Cairo. For the entire holiday I would assume the mantle of village intellectual. Rising late, towel slung over my shoulder, I would make my way down to the canal bank, with my toothbrush and toothpaste—the proofs of cultivation, culture, and an upward social trajectory—borne aloft.

The Doctor wasn't ashamed. He worked lots of different jobs. He cleaned cars, distributed videotapes, and traveled the length and breadth of the country as a truck driver's mate. Yet he never stayed in one occupation for long. He'd dream of a job for months, years even, familiarize himself with its smallest details, and finally decide that it was there, and there alone, that his future lay; a final solution to the grubbing around and ignominy he suffered in the building trade. He'd move mountains to get the work, but after a while, when he'd gotten so good at it you'd think he'd been born to it, boredom set in and he would turn his mind to another dream.

When he got hold of the night guard job we had just started working in Shubra. We were commuting workers, a little more respectable than usual, traveling up to Cairo, staying a while, then returning to the village. We knew nothing of Cairo beyond Ahmed Helmi Square, Salim's cafe, and the buildings where Mi'allim Matar's crew worked. We would sleep in the buildings or, when the mi'allim owed us wages, in his red Mazda pickup licensed for transporting workers. Usually there were no more than five or six of us, mostly from the village of Daniel in the Itsa Fayoum municipality. The Doctor, by virtue of age and experience, was our leader. We were all studying; he was the only one with time on his hands. He would sleep in the buildings, sit with us at the cafe, and trail after Matar. But he also turned his attention to the shops and stores, the homes and streets, hunting down the daily wage and the daily grind, working one day and sleeping ten. One morning, standing on the corner of Muniyat al-Seirig Street, he found the solution. An agency for heavy-goods vehicles was looking for a night guard. We used to walk the entire length of Muniyat al-Seirig to reach Salim's cafe before the crew bosses left. The agency specialized in cement trucks. Its vehicles went everywhere from Alexandria to Aswan. It was a modest little place and spattered with motor oil. At first glance you would think it was a workshop, but in his dreams the Doctor saw it as a means to escape the misery of day labor. Whenever we passed by he'd stop us in the middle of the street and then it would be, "If only everybody could get work like this. I swear to God it's the real deal. A fixed salary at the start of every month and on top of that, you're only working at night. The day is yours: sleep, work, run around the streets, it's up to you . . . ."

One fine day, I, the Doctor, and two guys from back home read a notice pasted on the metal door: WANTED: NIGHT GUARD FOR GOODS VEHICLES.

The agency's office wasn't open and no guard was in evidence so we waited and eventually someone appeared. The Doctor stepped forward, kissed his cheeks, and greeted him.

The garage owned about five large cabs and their trailers. Some went out transporting their loads around the country and the others stayed parked out front. The Doctor's task was to guard the parked trucks at night and his place of work was located beneath one of them. Every day, running up to the cafe to catch the bosses before they left, we would come across him yawning and stretching as he emerged from under a truck. As soon as he had started, the Doctor devised a plan to improve his lot. Instead of staying awake all night guarding the trucks, he found a way to sleep.

Muniyat al-Seirig Street, especially in the direction of Dawaran Shubra, was home to wild dogs that passed their daylight hours sunk in a deep sleep with forepaws outstretched. The Doctor put them to use. Each night he would beg a bunch of chicken legs from the poultry vendor on the corner. He'd tie them to a plastic bag, or a sheet of cardboard, or any old piece of paper so long as it was rough, then he'd place them beside his head and lie down. The moment he sensed movement in the street, he would stretch out his hand, half-asleep, and shake the legs. He'd ring them like a bell. Every dog in the street would set off toward him, barking their heads off, and swarm around the truck where he slept, a cacophonous canine riot terrifying to passing citizens. The passersby would take to their heels before they were devoured, the Doctor would replace the chicken legs, and the dogs would trot away.

And so it would go until morning. It only took a few days for the dogs to adjust and develop a firm bond with the Doctor. They knew exactly what was expected of them. The instant they sniffed out a passing shadow their voices would rise heavenward and they would descend upon him, at which point the Doctor would come to the rescue. Truth be told, he exploited this state of affairs in the worst possible way. He purposefully delayed his interventions, thus ensuring the passersby were frightened out of their wits. Just picture yourself for a moment, walking alone at the dead of night, suddenly confronted with an army of dogs attacking you from every side. The neighborhood was shaken to the core. Its residents were of one mind when it came to the danger of walking in the street after ten at night. And the Doctor slept. He slept and snored, making up for all those lost days and months. Those places where once he couldn't find a place to take a shit, much less lay his head, were now his and his alone. He could sleep anywhere and it was his right.

And when he'd glutted himself on sleep he began to cast his eye over the street. He noticed that across from his spot by the trucks, and stretching the length of the street, was a long line of cars. Asking no one's advice, and forgoing idle hours at Salim's cafe, he took up his rag and, recklessly putting his faith in the maxim that "no man can ignore you if you've cleaned his car for a month," he set to. By the time the sun had risen he'd polished off every car in the street. He cleaned up; he flourished; he grew fat. His reputation spread through the street and the neighborhood. Even his nights changed. Instead of sleeping courtesy of street dogs he began to spend happy hours prying into the lives of his neighbors, and in doing so he revived an old tradition. Back in the village we used to take great pleasure spying on newlyweds (Bedouin or peasant, it didn't matter) on their wedding night. We would creep up to their windows and watch everything, spending countless delightful evenings at the invitation of the Doctor. Directly opposite the office lay the apartment of a peculiar married couple. By day he was a respectable man of influence and she a lady of good repute, but by night? A complete farce. They had sex—extremely violent sex—every single day. I watched them once (well, several times), and was utterly unable to hold myself together, going to pieces as he, haughty and pompous, pressed on.

For some months the Doctor divided his life between guarding trucks and wiping cars, but the owner of the agency started to cramp his style. He confronted him about the car cleaning and warned him several times against taking liberties. Better he look to his job lest he send him back to the building trade. Then he gave him another responsibility: guard the trucks by night and wash them during the day. One morning, just as the Doctor was packing away his bedding from under a parked truck, an articulated truck from Suez pulled in and the driver's mate got down. He was swaying where he stood; off his face and a beer bottle in his hand. The Doctor quickly weighed his options: the owner couldn't stand him, and anyone who could drink to the point of inebriation was certainly earning more than a car guard who scarcely had enough to eat. Wasting no time he brought it up with the owner.

"I want to work in a cab."

"What, a driver's mate? "

"Yes. "

"Right, and you know all about that, do you? You've done it before? "

"If you want to learn, you'll learn . . . . "

"I'm finding it hard to employ you as a guard. I tell myself you're having it tough and you need the work. But because of that silver tongue of yours I'll take you on as a driver's mate. If you can do it, you can do it. If you're no good, show me your back and I don't want to see you around here again."

The Doctor vanished from the street. He left without telling a soul. The head of the agency informed me with relish, "He took off on a cement truck heading to Aswan. "

Translated by Robin Moger

Salwa Bakr

"Zeenat Marches in the President's Funeral,"
in My Grandmother's Cactus

HER NAME WAS SUPPOSED to be Zeenat, but everyone called her "Z'nat." Even Abduh the Barber, as he finished writing out a letter on her behalf to the President of the Republic—with whom she had persistently and tirelessly corresponded—would wind up what he was writing with the name "Z'nat Muhammad Ali," after fixing the pen firmly between her fingers, closing his hand over hers and moving both together so that the signature would truly be in her own hand. To make doubly sure, he would moisten the indelible copy pen with his saliva and color her thumb with it until a dense purple splotch had formed, enough to imprint a clearly distinguishable thumbprint over the letters of her name which they had written together.

One could certainly say that during the final years of the President's life a very special relationship had grown up between him and Zeenat, Yet, although the two of them had never come face to face during that period—and despite everything—it would be difficult to maintain that this was a one-sided relationship. True, they had not met, nor had it ever been feasible for Zeenat to converse with him, to tell him herself, in her own words, all that she wanted to say. Yet the ongoing relationship between them got to the point where she put together a plan: she thought it a detailed one, and absolutely watertight. But the passing of the days, and the hour of implementation, proved its failure—an outcome that had never entered her mind.

Moreover Abduh the Barber rebuked her in no uncertain terms and cautioned her against ever repeating that crazy deed of hers. This time God had shielded her, but it certainly would have been possible for them to have taken her away—to have taken Zeenat, herself—and hidden her beyond the sun, and even the blue djinnis would have been ignorant of where she dwelt. Abduh went so far as to call her stupid for having imagined that they would allow her even to get near, that near, to the President of the Republic, let alone to attempt to shake his hand—her hand in his—and give him the petition. Furthermore, had she forgotten the soldiers and plainclothesmen and guards, who would be surrounding him on all sides wherever he might go?

If the truth be known, Abduh's advice to Zeenat did no more than belabor the obvious; for Zeenat had experienced at first hand every word he said.

Despite the fact that she had concealed herself from the very crack of dawn on the corner of a certain street that she knew the President came along, every Friday after the prayer service . . . despite the fact that she had been able, as a result, to obtain a position at the very front of the crowd that flocked there to greet the President . . . (and this was, by the way, after one of the pupils from the school had written a brief letter which Zeenat intended to submit to the President, just a few quick, short words with no extras. Literally, the text read, "Z'nat says hallo, and asks what you've done about you-know-what?").

Despite all that, at the moment when she thought the president's car had drawn close enough to allow her to step out across from it, quickly, and rush forward to shake his hand and give him the piece of paper, she was startled to find dozens of rough hands, those of soldiers and other men, shooting out suddenly as if they had dropped from the heavens to fall precisely on her. The hands began pushing her away from the car and the procession so that she fell among feet, many of which (Zeenat noticed at the time) were encased in high leather boots. Against some were fixed pistols enough to butcher an entire town.

But this regrettable incident, and the hideous pains from which Zeenat suffered afterward, did not prevent her relationship with the President from continuing. Nor did it change her feelings about him one bit. The portraits of him remained exactly where they had always hung in her shack. Those pictures were the sole elements of decor in the hut, which Zeenat had constructed, entirely on her own, out of rocks, mud brick and tin sheeting, after she had succeeded in taking possession of a few meters of government land bordering the main road. She would sit before it in shifts from early morning until nearly sunset, waiting for the elementary school pupils to come in and out of the school building. It was actually three schools in one, since both girls and boys would go inside, one batch at a time, to have their lessons. Zeenat sold them molasses sticks, popcorn, lupine beans and small plastic toys which then became the happy lot of those who triumphed in games of chance, which they also bought from her.

As for sending the letters to the President, Zeenat did not waver one bit— proof once again that the relationship between her and the President had not been disturbed, and that indeed it remained serene as a summer day. As Zeenat saw it, the incident had taken place behind the President's back; had he been aware that the bastards, those very ones, had prevented her from giving him her salutations, and the piece of paper, then undoubtedly he would have sent them home, somewhere beyond the sun. For he'd understand, and know Zeenat's good intentions; he'd know that she couldn't possibly mean any harm to him. Otherwise he would not have answered her letters, as he did more than once, nor would her case have undergone consideration by the government, nor would he have sent the woman, an employee of the State, personally to inspect the shack and observe Zeenat's situation and ask her question after question about her state of affairs and how the world was treating her. That official had assured her, indeed, that her case would be dealt with over the next few months.

And the few months immediately following this visit gave Zeenat no reason to feel disappointed in the President. On the contrary, one could safely say that the plan she had sketched out (in the light of clarifications made by the woman from the government) had succeeded this time. Actually, it was a Development Strategy in miniature which Zeenat drew up for herself, its broad outlines encapsulated in the principle that—now and then—she would treat herself to a luxuriously large food intake. In order to activate the project, she would buy a small primus stove and an aluminum pot in which she could cook whenever her insides hankered after meat. She would also undertake to buy a fine corduroy gallabiya and beaded headband to replace the tattered gallabiya that she always wore. And before all else (and by the leave of the One and Only) she would pay back her foreseeable debts, which could be summed up in the two pounds she owed to Abduh the Barber (the final outstanding installment of an old debt, money she had borrowed from him to buy new goods to trade in). She would also take care of those debts she had not anticipated, consisting of a number of invitations from her brother, the children's father, to eat meat, and several fifty-piaster notes which he had passed on to her at the beginning of each month. Zeenat was determined to visit her brother with two kilos of meat in hand, once she had the money in her grasp. And before all else, a pair of top-notch chickens and a bottle of rosewater-flavored sherbet, as a sincerely meant gift to Abduh the Barber which would gladden her own heart, in recognition of the kindliness he had shown her and the service he had performed for her in writing the letters to the President of the Republic. For these were services that finally had been crowned with success, in that it had been stipulated that she would receive an exceptional pension, to the value of three pounds, fully and entirely. Because of those three pounds she had begun to go in person, and in all pride and confidence and esteem for herself and the President of the Republic, to the government cashier's office at the onset of every month, to take receipt of those three pounds after showing the necessary document of exchange, in addition to her identity card. Zeenat was very careful with this card: after it was issued to her, she had preserved it as if it were her own eyes, her most precious possession. There could be no greater proof of this than the fact that she kept the ID in a plastic cover which she had purchased for an entire shillin—a whole five-piaster piece. Moreover, she always stuffed the ID away under her mattress for safekeeping, and made sure, every so often, that it was still there. This was not only because of the pension. Once she had been able to stick it full in the eye of a municipality policeman. She had really given it to him, with all self-confidence, when he had tried to pick a quarrel and then fleece her while she was seeing to her own business. He began threatening to drag her to the police station because she had no identity card. Let down, he recoiled—the nape of his neck burning like a hot bread-round—after she had ridiculed and scolded him in strong language.

But the three pounds were not the grand finale of Zeenat's relationship with the President of the Republic. For despite the fact that Zeenat had received a sum of money of which she had never in her whole life dreamt—to the amount of eighteen pounds, since the executive order stipulating her acquisition of the pension had been issued with retroactive force, giving her the right accordingly to claim for the period of six months—and notwithstanding the indisputable fact that she had done wonders with this money—for she had bought some brand-new red bricks with which she finished the walls of the shack, after removing the rocks and tin sheeting, and she had knocked through a window so the breeze and sunlight could enter at their leisure—and had allowed herself a more prosperous lifestyle, so much so that she bought a whole chicken which was an utter delight to eat all by herself, not sharing it with any creature of God's earth . . . an unforgettable delight: that moment when she was steering the boiled flesh, mixed with cooked rice and moistened with its own hot broth, into her mouth . . . despite all of that, and in spite of the fundamental changes which had come into Zeenat's life (among them the increases she managed in the stock of goods in which she dealt, adding new categories, like pencils and erasers) . . . despite all of that, Abduh the Barber—"May his hands be graced, and may God protect the light of his eyes," as Zeenat, loyal and sincere friend that she was, always said—was constantly advising her to pick up the relationship where it had left off, and to persevere in sending her letters to the President. But, he said, the tone of grievance should be heightened even further and, she should make a specific complaint, asking for an increase in the pension on the basis that she was a helpless woman on her own with no one in the whole wide world to take responsibility for her, and no one to hear and honor her grievances except God and the President of the Republic.

And frankly, Abduh the Barber outdid himself in composing the new missives, surpassing even the strenuous efforts he had made in writing the letters of the first stage. Zeenat's receipt of the pension had been the crowning achievement of that phase, and it had happened because the pertinent law was clear and unequivocal on the question of Zeenat's right to the pension. And, from another perspective, the first letters had been justified because Zeenat had not yet received the pension. But now, compliance with a further request would be in the manner of an exception, and would have to be based on personal directives from the President of the Republic, who would be able to issue such an order once he sensed (by means of the words written to him) the reality of Zeenat's situation and her difficult circumstances—for these would melt even a heart of stone.

Thus, Abduh the Barber massaged his natural talents vigorously, working to extract the juices of his rhetorical faculties, trying to have such an effect on the president that he would issue the decree necessary to raise the pension. Apparently, though, the standard of what Abduh wrote was not up to par in one way or another, for not a single reply arrived from the Presidency pertaining to the outcome of fully nine letters which Abduh had written in the presence of Zeenat herself, and at her direction, on this matter.

Therefore, and just a few days before Zeenat heard the momentous news, Abduh the Barber had scaled the heights, reaching his rhetorical summit in the tenth letter to the president. It cannot be denied that Zeenat herself had a hand in writing the essential text of this letter, making exertions that are not open to doubt, after conferring with Abduh in his little shop for about three hours, to ensure that the discourse would emerge in the best possible shape and form. Abduh was obliged to write it all down several times, after Zeenat had gone on revising and redrafting the wording, furnishing Abduh with some new and impressively moving thoughts. The truth is that Abduh, though indeed a good-natured chap, could not have borne it so patiently all this time if it hadn't been the end of the month, when customers were wanting (for hardly any were putting their feet inside the door). But Abduh, too, was enjoying himself, for through writing Zeenat's letters he had discovered that he could utter passages that had a certain beauty, ones that were really extremely pleasing and which he himself found most moving—just as the results of his first pieces of writing had really strengthened his confidence in himself and in his great abilities in this sphere. Moreover, he had not forgotten Zeenat's gift to him, which provided a certain encouragement and which was, on the plane of mundane reality, a large male duck which Zeenat had fed (bit by bit, for the space of a week before presenting it to Abduh) dried beans, every evening at suppertime, until it got quite heavy and grew to nearly the size of a pelican. And along with it she had brought two bottles of sherbet, one rosewater and the other apricot. In any case, the gift—in its totality—came as a genuine surprise to Abduh, who had not anticipated that it would be quite this grand and expensive.

For the latest letter, Abduh had tried in the beginning to inject the traditional preamble—which he had written each time, constructing it around expressions of gratitude and praise, and phrases extolling the President of the Republic—with some of his political views concerning the current state of affairs, his opinion of the Americans and the British, the role of feudalism in alliance with colonialist imperialism, and other issues arising from the kind of talk of which Abduh was very fond. He tried to write this preamble in a way that would show the extent of his perusal of the newspapers, and the magazines too. From this beginning, he meant to move on to the subject of Z'nat and her request, ending with her hopes that the President's life be long and that he be graced with blessings, he and his children, as well as with an invoking of God to spare him the evil of his enemies and all their zealous proponents.

But Zeenat, 'She of the Plans,' was carrying around in her head a new concept of how they might frame the discourse, an idea that took shape through her daily sessions before the portraits of the President, as she sat conversing with them. For after his reply to her and after the episode of the three pounds, Zeenat had come to feel a very warm affection for the President of the Republic. She felt that he was her true support in the world, and deep down she sensed that his pictures kept her company, cheering her up in her solitude and removing the dreariness from her soul whenever she was alone in the shack. Thus she decided to talk to him frankly and to tell him all the things she had to say that were locked up in her soul. This is what she said to Abduh the Barber, who rejected the idea at first (as he considered this an interference in what was, after all, his area of expertise). But she begged him, and asked him to please do what would make her feel most comfortable. "Maybe the Lord would see fit to bring a spot of good luck to the very one who'd never had it." By that she meant the letter. Abduh, in the end, left her to say what she wished. He was afraid to do otherwise lest these particular words indeed be the salutary ones which would bring her benefit; and if he insisted on having his way, he might deprive her of it. After all, it was Zeenat who was the woman—the poor, helpless thing.

Translated by Marilyn Booth.

Mekkawi Said

from *Cairo Swan Song*

IT WAS A BOISTEROUS PARTY like all the rest. The foreign band was playing like a bunch of madmen and the noise from the speakers was shaking the chairs and the floor. I went out to the balcony and leaned against the wooden door. I stood there smoking, looking out over the beautiful Cairo night. The balcony stretched the length of the two rooms that the partygoers were congregated in and each opened out onto it. I wasn't the only one out on the balcony; other guests were hanging out in corners smoking pot or hash, and couples stood in the dark, one hand on their drinks, the other on each other's bodies. The clamor reverberated through the otherwise serene and lovely neighborhood, even though we were up on the fourteenth floor. The building's tenants were mostly students at the international private universities in the city—most of the foreign students were studying at the American University in Cairo—or else they were consultants or employees of the multinational firms operating in Egypt. The building was extremely well guarded, almost as if it were being kept a secret. Watch out if you've had a plate implanted for a broken bone, or if you've got a silver tooth, or if you're a woman, if you're using an IUD for birth control because the metal detector that's like a second narrower entrance to the building is certain to erupt in an excruciating whistle. You might not even get through without a certificate of quarantine from NAMRU.

I was leaning against the door of the balcony unable to look at the ground below. When I turned my head, I could see Marcia writhing, dancing, absorbed in the music. I could tell she was drunk. She was staring at me with an empty look, warning me against sneaking out unannounced. I wouldn't have been able to dance with her if she'd asked. I was sick with boredom so I tried to keep entertained by checking out the faces of the people there: half of them I'd never seen before, but the other half I knew. Some were students of mine, or I'd met them through Marcia, and there were some Egyptians and foreigners whom I'd met at cultural events. None of my close friends had come. Bloody Essam talked me into coming here and then didn't show up himself. I hadn't seen my German friend, Awad, either. I saw Diana and Evelyn, but I pretended not to, and went to say hello to some losers and exchange idiotic conversation with an idiot. I was drinking steadily and steadily receiving stolen kiss after stolen kiss from the foreign girls I tutored. I was totally out of it by then.

Exhaustion drove me to the study where I found Julia the maid. Clearly drunk at this point, I kicked her out like a tyrant. My mind was wrestling with gelatinous visions, my intestines were near bursting, and I had an awful headache. When I woke up in the morning, I was in Marcia's room and my elbows and feet were painfully sore. Marcia was sleeping at my feet, her legs spread, and her hair looking like tufts of felt. I slowly moved my feet from above her and kissed the part of her hair; my lips felt wet. A plan was just now beginning to crystallize in my mind. I was going to get in the shower and get out of there as soon as possible; no Nescafé, no coffee, no chitchat with Marcia. But as soon as I'd finished my shower and went back into the room to grab my keys from the bedside table, I saw a note written in English under my keys: It said something to the effect of "Wait for me. Don't leave before I wake up. Marcia." Those few lines made me scramble to get dressed so that I could get out of there immediately, hopefully before the maid woke up. I tripped over empty plastic bottles and beer cans causing a racket I couldn't muffle, but, fortunately, no one woke up.

Essam wasn't at home when I went to his apartment-cum-studio. I thought about going home, but it felt unwelcoming so I didn't. I sat in a cafe nearby and when I thought about Marcia, I got scared. I'd started this cat-and-mouse game with her a little while ago. I was part of her life, but it wasn't like I was her shadow. I came and went as I pleased, but she was a foreigner and our genetic make-ups were totally different. She might've got fed up with the game and grown used to me not being there. Someone else would just fill my place, and I'd met plenty who would've been happy to do so. I decided that I'd take my search for Karim seriously and make some time for the project even if it meant taking a break from teaching or not accepting any new students. If I couldn't find Karim, no matter what the reason, Marcia would probably take that to mean that I'd been stringing her along, especially since it wouldn't be the first time I'd let her down. And if—God forbid—Marcia and I did have a falling out, well then that would've made it impossible for me to maintain those beneficial relationships with foreigners who want to learn Arabic or even with the Arabs who want to live like foreigners.

I went back downtown and hung out in coffeehouses and on the street. I started with the spots I knew Karim frequented. I saw a bunch of kids just like him and I went up to them, and gave them money, and some of them told me that Karim had been carted off to the reformatory. I relaxed a little now that I had some solid information and I was sure he'd be back before long. Karim wouldn't be able to handle it and the teachers and administrators wouldn't be able to tolerate his mischief. My guess was that it would all be over in a few weeks at most; I could convince Marcia to wait patiently until he got out. Even though I'd met a lot of Karim's pals—older ones, younger ones, and ones his age—none of them seemed as reliable as he did. They were all—without exception—blind to any consequences. Karim was unique because he came from a solid background: a working class family. His father was a butcher in the Ezbet al-Nakhl neighborhood. He'd married several times and had a reputation as a bit of a stud. Every one of his wives, the ones he was still married to and the ones he'd divorced, bore him children; Karim was one of sixteen. Like most of his brothers and sisters, he'd never gone to school, but unlike them he hadn't learned a trade either. He'd been mistreated and abused, physically and sexually, from a young age, so he decided—as he told me many times—simply to let the wind blow him away. By that he meant that he'd be under nobody's control, not other people, or the government, or his family. He formed a gang of young kids in his neighborhood and they stole, kidnapped, and vandalized their way through Ezbet al-Nakhl. His father and brothers had beaten him till he'd had enough, so he ran away to downtown where he learned how to get high off glue and rose through the ranks of a big gang of kids who hung out around there, begging and selling tissues.

He'd been arrested more than once and dragged back home where they tried to discipline him with beatings and by burning him on the chest and back with a hot iron, but huffing had made his head more stubborn than rock. It was his intelligence that made it possible for him to lead kids older, bigger, and stronger than he was. He would stagger them out among the alleys and streets after the dawn prayer and then divide up the earnings with them after sunset as they lay down to sleep behind the unending rows of parked cars.

I met him at the Zahrat al-Bustan coffeehouse a year ago or more. He came up to me, covering his torso, with his right hand outstretched, and asked for half a pound so he could buy some food. I looked at him and I could see he was holding something I couldn't make out in his other hand under his tattered jacket. As I was reaching for my wallet, his hand moved a little, revealing the bottle of glue in the palm of his hidden hand. I pointed to it and put my wallet away, telling him I wouldn't give him any money. In fact, I scolded him for huffing and warned him about the danger of it. He smiled innocently, showing his yellowed, decaying teeth and listened closely to everything I said. Then he swore to me that he hadn't eaten a thing all day and I could sense he was telling the truth, so I caved and gave him what he'd asked for. He started avoiding our familiar faces after that even though we were regulars at that coffeehouse. One time, when I offered to buy him a strawberry juice, he just looked at me incredulously, and when he eventually did sit down, smiling, I tried to peek up the sleeve of his jacket. He noticed what I was doing so he brought out the bottle of glue, which had a little palm twig resting inside, and showed it off to us. I asked him what the stick was for, so he stirred the glue up and explained. We became friendly acquaintances after that.

Originally, I was interested in them as a recent phenomenon spreading through downtown Cairo. There was a striking number of these glue huffers, or 'street kids' as intellectuals and TV presenters liked to call them, but what really stoked my interest were two events that I saw with my own eyes, and though they were fleeting, they were unforgettable.

The first incident happened around noon on some holiday, those days when downtown Cairo is once again like the downtown of the 1930s that we read about. Everyone had gone to the parks, or the movies, or were sprawled in front of the TV. Downtown was abandoned to calm and silence. I was just one of a handful walking down its streets that day, a hash cigarette in my hand, smoking it with relish, enjoying the quiet and the cracking echoes of children's distant fireworks. I ignored the cops who greet you with a "Good health in the New Year!" hoping for some holiday charity. There were no other pedestrians out to notice the smell of my hash, no shop owners to give me dirty looks.

When I saw a body lying in a heap against the curb up ahead, I stopped in my tracks and peered at it: a boy of about seventeen, dressed in rags. The mud and dirt had done such a number on him that he looked like a miner or someone who made a living carting both coal and garbage. He was alive, lying there smoking the butt of a cigarette. A couple coming from the opposite direction were about the same distance away from the boy as I was. A pretty, giddy girl in a short skirt and a tight blouse, which crept up revealing her abdomen, was walking arm in arm with her boyfriend on a path that would lead them past the body on the ground. They got to it before I did, but they didn't take any notice of it. I didn't know what made the boyfriend look down at the ground as they passed the boy, nor did I know why he immediately turned back and started kicking him all over his body: in the stomach, the face, the arms, the legs, and all the while the boy didn't even defend himself. Nor did I know why the girl joined in, screeching at first, then kicking along with her boyfriend, and then trying, unsuccessfully, to drag him away. I ran over quickly and grabbed the boyfriend from behind to stop him from hitting the tattered pile that was bleeding on the pavement. He struggled against me and slipped out of my grasp. He stared at me in rage as he pointed to the boy, "Do you see what he's doing?"

At that point, I looked down at the rag splayed on the ground. I almost couldn't make him out against the background of the cement sidewalk. He was leaning forward like a puffed-up rooster getting ready to fight, but in the face of the boyfriend's wild-eyed insistence, I pulled the boy upright; he was masturbating, apparently indifferent to his bleeding wounds. He wasn't worried about us or what we might do to him, his red eyes wide open. And as we dragged him along the ground like a dead dog, he didn't struggle or resist. He seemed to enjoy us moving him. The girl was beside us crying and covering her face with her hands so she wouldn't have to watch. There was a coarse rope tied around the boy's wrist and I pointed it out to the boyfriend. I lifted the rope and saw that the boy's wrist was bleeding. It was only about twenty centimeters long; he'd probably cut it and run away from the detective who'd been marching him back to the police station. I told the boyfriend why the boy's wrist was tied. I'd seen it a lot: a group of three or four boys bound like this together, being led like sheep to the police station by a cocky detective. The boyfriend realized there was no point in taking the kid to the closest police station, or the juvenile hall, or even the gallows. So we let go of him and he fell over onto the ground. The weeping girl pressed her head against her boyfriend's shoulder and they walked along slowly, in the opposite direction as I did.

Marcia had listened in complete silence and chain-smoked two cigarettes as I told her what I'd seen. My story made her laugh joyous laughter, but she never explained to me what it was she found so funny.

The second incident happened in Tahrir Square, the biggest and most famous of all the squares in Cairo. It was a cold winter night so I lengthened my stride in hopes of getting home quickly. There was no chance of rescue by cab because the way home was against traffic on a one-way street. It was then that I noticed them from afar, shoving one another. There were three boys chasing another boy their age, pushing him to the ground. They were around ten years old. They started hitting the boy and ended up piling on top of him as he screamed loudly. I thought they were trying to rape him and I was shocked by their audacity. I ran over to them. There was no one out on that cold night, not even any policemen. The boy was still shouting as one of his assailants sat on his lower half and restrained his legs while another, seated on his upper half, held down his chest and one arm. The boy was flailing his free arm up and down until the third boy grabbed it. The third boy held a wet cotton rag in his hand and a bottle lay beside them. At first glance, it occurred to me that they were trying to force him to huff. It was when I'd finally reached them that I was surprised to find the third attacker frantically trying to wipe a tattoo off the forearm of the boy who was lying on the ground, crying out in pain. I started kicking them and pulling them off of him. The boy's arm was bleeding so I tried to cover his wound, while the other boys stood around me, staring in anger. I roared at them, "What the hell are you doing?"

The tallest one replied as he backed away, "We're wiping the cross off his hand 'cause he's a Christian."

I asked them if they were Muslims. When they nodded, I let go of the boy's arm and ran after them. I wasn't able to catch them before they got to the other side of the square. They were too far away. They started hurling rocks, which they got from God knows where, and though I had no problem dodging the rocks, I couldn't stop their taunts: "Dirty Christian!"

What was weird, and surprising, was that I never told Marcia that story, despite the fact that we'd been together a long time, and I usually just told stories to tell stories. I'd told stories that were more pointless. Yet, despite my love for her and our strong connection, or whatever other term described our relationship, I'd never told her; even after we'd begun working together on a project about these kids, I hadn't even used that as a pretext to tell her.

Translated by Adam Talib

Hamid Abdel Samad
from *Farewell, Heaven*

BEFORE I WENT TO the country, 'Germany' conjured up contradictory names and events: the Germany of Goethe and Rilke and the Germany of Hitler and Goering; ravished post-war Germany and the Germany of the economic miracle and reconstruction; Germany divided between East and West and its reunification without a single drop of blood. The Germany of work, order, and the signature phrase "Made in Germany"; not to mention the German soccer team that wins every game regardless of whether or not the team plays well. Germany, the land of Martin Luther and the land of freedom and unbridled desire; Germany, the land of the Franks—my relatives. Germany, the land of poets, philosophers, and heroes—a country that is no longer allowed to have heroes.

The only images of Germany I had seen on television were those of neo-Nazi protests in the streets and of the arson of refugee homes—and those of the collapse of the Berlin Wall in total peace. I had other impressions of

Germany from the film *al-Nimr al-aswad,* which showed us that any ignorant Egyptian could travel to Germany, become a millionaire, and marry the most beautiful women in the course of a few short years.

I read a lot of German literature, but I didn't know a thing about the current political and social conditions there. My general idea of Germany was positive, especially since they have no history of colonialism in our region. Even the Holocaust, the darkest moment of their history, is seen by us as a boon rather than a scandal, since the enemy of my enemy is my friend.

My first direct contact with Germany was full of bitterness and disgrace. I went to the German embassy in Zamalek to submit a request for a visa when hordes of young men gathered unexpectedly in front of the embassy gates and waited there as if they were circumambulating the Kaaba. Out of the thousands waiting outside, the embassy was only allowing fifty applicants to enter, and only a few of those would actually get a visa to enter the 'promised land'—those fifty had camped out in front of the embassy during the previous night, before the arrival of the flocks of pilgrims. The embassy security staff tried to drive the mobs away but they were unsuccessful since the men waiting in front of the embassy had nowhere else to go—it was easier for them to pursue a soothing mirage than to face their own painful reality.

I returned to the embassy after nine o'clock that night and found that there were twenty people already in line—I was number twenty-one. One of them wanted to visit his sister in Berlin and then 'disappear' there. Two of them, like me, wanted to study. Another wanted to marry an old German tourist he met at the hotel where he worked as a waiter. As for the others, they had no idea what they wanted to do in Germany or even why Germany in particular. Most of them were waiting in front of the German embassy for one reason alone—the line at the German embassy was far shorter than the lines at the American, French, or English embassies.

We were all promising young men whom Egypt could have needed, but instead our country had ignored us: our education was handed out to us like candy and we had received our diplomas in a staged spectacle. However, there was also an older man in his seventies among this group of young men. I wondered what this old man wanted in Germany. He wore a simple gallabiya and couldn't have been a businessman or someone who wanted medical tourism. "Maybe he needs to check up on one of his sons there," I thought to myself.

The young men began to chat and joke around to kill time, while the old man leaned against the wall of the embassy without saying a word. Most of the young men were ready for a long night and had brought blankets and pillows with them. They offered a pillow and blanket to the old man, but he refused angrily. I noticed that he didn't have a folder for submitting embassy requests and I wanted to tell him, but I feared the same violent response. Suddenly a man in his forties—I think his name was Khamis—appeared out of nowhere and in a matter of minutes erected a small kiosk in front of the embassy and began to sell tea and sandwiches to those who were waiting. I remember that Khamis' tea was delicious despite the filthiness of the cup it was poured in. I've always been amazed by the resilience of our people in the face of bureaucratic hurdles—they do not accept the label 'unemployed.' Even if the world collapses around one of them, he won't worry and sit at home all day—instead he will grab some tissues and sell them at stoplights and call himself a 'businessman.' It seemed that Khamis had found himself a job, something thousands of Egypt's young men had failed to do—one man's misfortune is another man's gain.

The young men began to talk about what they would do in Germany as if they had already received their visas, even though they all knew that the chance of actually getting a visa was very slim. Their laughter awakened the old man leaning on the embassy wall, and he gave them a bitterly fierce piercing stare. I wondered what the old man thought of us. Was he rebuking us for trying to leave our country at such a young age? Did he know that we cursed the West in our hearts, but could only find hope at the doors of its embassies? Or perhaps we reminded him of his son who had left and gone to Germany?

The old man leaned against the wall again and fell asleep sitting. One after the other we all fell into a deep sleep that wouldn't end until the first rays of sunlight. Khamis passed out cups of tea and some breakfast sandwiches before he disassembled his kiosk and disappeared just as he had come, before anyone from the embassy or the police saw him.

While the first man in line slept clinging to the iron door of the embassy to establish his precedence in line, the old man opened his eyes and stared into the nothingness. He then stood and came to take his place in line in front of me. Minutes before the embassy opened its gates, an elegant middle-aged man carrying a black bag came and stood in line in front of the old man. I became infuriated and went to him and said "Excuse me! We've been waiting here all night. What do you have against this hajj? Why do you want to take his place in line?" I expected some sign of gratitude or acknowledgement from the old man, but his face of stone-like despair turned to one of punishment and heartbreak.

"Sir, you don't understand . . . hold on a minute," said the elegant man. He then gave the old man five pounds and told him, "Now head on home, Amm Ahmed!"

The man took the petty cash and shuffled away, muttering incomprehensible words to himself. He hadn't wanted to go to Germany—perhaps he didn't even know where Germany was. He was merely reserving a spot for a 'better' man. I was incensed—no, ashamed—when I saw this. Had the elegant man exploited the old man, or had he merely presented him with an opportunity to earn five pounds?

I didn't have time to dwell on these issues of social injustice since my turn finally came to enter the 'embassy of deliverance.' I walked through the door of the stronghold and stopped in front of an Egyptian embassy employee who began to speak to me in German.

"Sorry . . . my German isn't . . . " I said, filled with disappointment that my future was still in Egyptian hands. I gave the arrogant employee all the necessary documents for my travel to and residence in Germany, including my letter of acceptance from the University of Munich, my credentials for a German language course at the university, and health insurance documents, among other things. The employee meticulously examined my papers as if he was looking for an excuse to refuse my request, but in the end he approved my file and informed me that the visa procedure would take six weeks. I left the embassy reciting from the Qur'an, "Oh Lord! Deliver us from this land whose people are oppressors!"

Six weeks later I went back to the embassy and received an entrance visa to the land of Karl Marx and Mercedes. I was one of the few who had this 'good' fortune bestowed upon them. I left the embassy and began to wander the streets of Cairo, and my feet involuntarily led me to the street where my grandfather lived and where I hadn't been for nineteen years. I don't know why I went there or what I was looking for in that place where I spent the happiest and saddest moments of my childhood. Perhaps I was looking for an old wound to take with me as a souvenir from Egypt, or maybe I was looking for an excuse for my escape. My grandfather's house had collapsed years before and the foundations of a new house stood in its place. These foundations heralded that more prestigious and higher quality construction would replace the buildings that had collapsed, but they also proclaimed that these would be buildings without any spirit. I stood in front of the place for a long time, watching over the bakery, the coffee house, and the mechanic's workshop. I marveled that the distance between my grandfather's house and these three places was so close when it had seemed so vast during my childhood. I didn't cry and I felt no pain. Memories both beautiful and dreadful began to flood my mind without corresponding to any negative or positive emotions.

I then went to my village to bid farewell to my family.

Translated by Andrew Heiss

Idris Ali

from *Poor*

Cairo
August 1994
Homeland. Torture. Departure.

THIS IS YOUR LAST DAY. Be strong. Don't hesitate. Cut and run. An exit with no return. The end of the game. You've tried many times before. Today your decision is final, coming after a desperate life journey. That steady misery. You're serious this time. Determined. A heavy pall blocks every opening before you. There's no escape but death. The only possible conclusion. A depression colonizing you ever since you were born. Your condition drops in bad weather. Murderous Africa, home of the sun and oppression and homicidal rulers: damned, desperate continent. You've never lived like other people. As the poet says, "Trouble: life's nothing but." A suffering woman answers, "There's no greater mess than life." Weariness. Sickness. Trouble. You've lived alone and you will go out alone, leaving this planet of the apes without regrets.

How stifling this heat is! The Gehenna of August. Cairo ablaze. Egypt's rich have left you to face the sun all by yourself. They've fled toward the happy coastline, as they always do, in their Mercedes, SUVs, express trains, and planes. Even government officials are managing the country wearing nothing but their bathing suits. The naked governing the unclothed. Montazah Beach used to be occupied by just a single king, then the men in tanks seized it. It's a catastrophe—they've converted all the beaches of the country into private Montazah picnic grounds! Their forces have amassed along the summer refuges of the poor—*So where are we supposed to go?!*—and overrun the Bedouin beaches. Now they hang signs over these places with names like 'Maraqya' and 'Maribella' and surround themselves with guards and gates.

Poor you, drowning in your sweat, with no access to even a breath of fresh air ever since they landed their private clubs across the banks of the Nile. This historic Nile that is yours. They've separated you from your Nile. So you've decided to die in its waters as a sort of lawful protest. A feast for the schools of tilapia.

Yes, the Nile. You won't set yourself on fire. You won't shoot yourself in the head. Nor will you jump from the Cairo Tower. You won't retreat. You're shameless, refusing all sleeping pills and tranquilizers. You curse the ancestors of Job, the king of patience, worms, and putrefaction. You laugh when they try to tell you that sturdy trees die standing. Empty slogans! Trees die standing, lying, or falling down. They die and goodbye! They're done—worthless. They turn into either lumber or kindling. But they don't then start to bear fruit. Ask Papa Hemingway who famously said, "You can crush a man, but you can't defeat him." Were those words ever true? So what's left of someone after he has been crushed? Should he dance while he's bleeding? Should he laugh underfoot? Is he supposed to flash the victory sign in the midst of defeat? Isn't this what our leaders do in the underdeveloped world, shouting, "We've won! Victory is ours!" If you're above all this, Papa Hemingway, then how should we explain your horrific end? In my opinion, suicide is the prerogative of the brave and noble.

Faced with a life of bother, it is dignified to leave by your own choosing. Assholes don't kill themselves. They flee sinking ships. It's the idiots who cling on and float and are later called heroes. Meanwhile, the assholes make off with the loot and then pick up their corruption and sabotage from other bases of operation. They're the ones who say, "When the flood comes, stand on your son," as the idiots rattle on their ancient slogans: Homeland! Resistance! Land! They tell us, "Stand up in defiance!" even though there's nothing left that deserves the honor of resistance. Not since they sold the homeland along with everything else they could sell, including "The Cause," "The Land!" and their depleted bases of operation. Our freewomen are forced to sustain themselves by nursing from their own breasts. Our freemen sit there trying and almost shitting, their dull hands reaching out toward mulberry leaves. You tell yourself: Better to go out stoned.

You hesitate when you reach the Qasr al-Nil bridge, the spot from which you've chosen to depart. You hesitate, but not because you fear death, for death's an inescapable fact. The struggle wells up inside you, almost splits you in two. A brutal, ugly struggle. An awful fury inside shakes you and you rebel. You continue walking, confused. You ask yourself: Why did you lose your nerve? It collapsed! You want to go back on your decision. You reevaluate despite the fact that you've decided and committed yourself.

As you walk, you pass by the sleek League of Idiot Tribes Building. This is where they deliver speeches and applaud and say all the right words. You sleepwalk to the edge of Intifada Square, which once upon a time witnessed the Revolt of the Poor, that uprising which the tank rider called "The Revolt of the Thieves," even though it was he who opened the country's gates to the worst kinds of thieves and who told the most famous thief, "Beware of Alexandria, Mr. . . . !" Isn't that funny? How did that hashash reason? That comedian exposed him when he referred to him, saying, "Someone taught us how to cheat and steal. . . ."

Why do you bother with all this crap? It's their country and they're free to do what they want with it. Or are these just pre-mortem hallucinations? You're beset by many cravings all at once. Hunger. Lust. Thirst. The urge to scream. You've got one chance to fulfill one desire. Let out a scream that'll rock the world. Then relax. Or burn yourself up with crying. But your tears have gone dry after mourning over so many events, over innumerable national disasters whose sole cause was that singular man in the tank. He took you up to heaven's heights, then smashed your necks on the bank of the Suez Canal.

In your depressive state, your sexual appetite is so dead that even Viagra is useless. The diagnosis is that your impotence is systemic. One of them blamed it on white chicken. But the Tagammu' Party guy tells you, with the conviction of one who really knows, that the Mossad is behind this debacle: they have agents working at the water reservoirs and distribution centers. Some have rumored that the government is trying to limit the population explosion, while one intellectual attributes the cause to a general state of futility. Regardless of the cause, what's certain is that it's a thousand times easier to manage a society of limp men than to deal with men whose complete sexual capacities are intact. Perhaps the cause of your condition is that you're womanless in a city that hums with beauties. And that's because those women are meant for export and the enjoyment of tourists.

And then there's hunger. That boorish guest who's clung to you since childhood. You're used to him by now. And you only ever knew love once in your life. Dina Tantawi, the girl from Bulaq who tortured you. Impossible love. Poor folk's love.

You've got no choice but oblivion. To quench your thirst. Your budget is almost enough to get you drunk. It's your day and you'll drink to the dregs. You'll swill beer in gulps until you've fallen over. If only you had enough for a bottle of whiskey!

One thing is certain: they serve nothing but alcohol in heaven! Rivers of booze—forbidden in this world, but permitted in the afterlife. On your way, you pass by the new restaurants, the ones with the plate glass windows blatantly designed to incite the masses. You stop to stare at the piles of meat on the tables. One of the city's poor stands next to you speaking to himself loudly, "Those bastards . . . . That's all food?" He's right. Why do they eat so conspicuously? You yourself are salivating just from how gorgeous it looks. You imagine: What if you got up the nerve and walked in? You'd be another one of those jerks. Once upon a time, any citizen could easily afford to walk into a kabab place and order a quarter kilo of meat with rice and salads. Now this has become difficult. Once you lost your mind by bringing an Arab friend into a famous kebab restaurant to "do him right." On that meal, you wasted your primary income, your allowance, your advance, and your royalties. And you sat there for the whole month singing, "They did him wrong."

If you wanted to purge your bowels of fuul and the like, don't think about these fancy tourist restaurants. Go to the liver sandwich carts scattered throughout the streets of the city, even though you know that they serve only the livers of diseased animals, smuggled out of the slaughterhouse before they're butchered and frozen. Don't forget about the livers of hippos, rhinos, and elephants that they serve. Fuckers! But there's nothing extraordinary about this at all. They've also fed you the thighs and breasts of injured birds, not to mention falcons, eagles, and crows. Even if you were condemned to death and they were to ask you, as they do, what you'd like to eat before they hanged you, you'd reply without hesitation, "Fifi Abdou, peacock steaks, and Courvoisier!"

Translated by Elliott Colla

Mohamed al-Fakharani

from *An Interval for Bewilderment*

"WHAT'S MORE HARAM . . . to steal or to be hungry?"

That's what Hilal blurted out at his mother. He hurled the drug money he made into her lap. She threw it on the floor. He ripped his shirt from the chest down to his belly. He grabbed the dagger from his jeans pocket and stabbed the back of his arm. He knocked the tin of the shack with his foot. He cussed the mother of the detective who imprisoned his father. He swore, "Screw it! I'm going to eat, get drunk, and make money. The 'government' and the whole world can suck it!"

Hilal and His Mother's Shack

"I have my period. Leave me alone tonight."

He pushed her to the bed. He grabbed her blood-stained underwear. He hardened between her thighs. He forced them wide open. She punched his side desperately.

"What do you mean 'I have my period,' you bitch?"

He held his hardened organ and pumped it inside her in quick repeated movements mumbling the name of one of the sex idols whose posters he had stuck facing him on the tin wall of the shack. He fantasized that he was making love to them instead of his wife. In pain, she pulled at the tattered sheet to cover her naked behind and her thighs from the gaze of two of her kids sitting in the corner of the shack watching the scene as if it were routine.

Badri's Shack

"Get the hell out of here!"

Farawla yelled at the flabby detective standing at the entrance to her shack. He pulled out his sweat-stained money from his pocket. His gaze drooled over her hard nipple like a ripe blackberry underneath a sensuously draped nightgown.

"I'll pay you whatever you want."

A whiff of warm scent escaped from under her waxed armpit. She inhaled her own satanic smell and exuded it in his face opening up a fountain of drunkenness in his head,

"Haven't you had your fill of the shack women? Or am I made of chocolate?"

She snatched the pocket knife out of the tin wall of the shack and pointed it at his jaw. He gritted his teeth. He smelled her fingers. She felt the coldness of the tip of his nose and the disgusting grease on the knife melted in her hand.

He was breathless with excitement. He swallowed. "Even the stray dogs have ripped you apart. Why not me?"

She looked at him with disgust, "Get me out of your head or it'll be the end of you tonight."

She pressed the tip of the pocket knife into his neck. He crumpled up the money. He growled. He withdrew his jaw so that the light of the dim lamp in the corner of the shack reflected a big fat cheek.

She said, spitting, "I'd rather sleep with a dog than have your drool over my body!"

Farawla's Shack

You, Hussein . . . .

Wander around the shacks with your hunger, your fear, your weakness . . . . You toughen up when you sit with your drinking gang in your place to the left of the gang leader, Hilal the Great. You take the bango joint from between his fingers after he lights it and draws a long drag that is just right for his hardhitting head . . . .

Now you are wrecked: You look around you and listen intently to the sounds in the dark in front of you, behind you, on top of you, so that you are not busted by the flabby detective, or startled by the light beams of the police truck in your eyes blinding you so that you are nailed to the ground. You regain consciousness at the sound of your own screams as the bare wire electrocutes your anus at the police station where you, they, and the nation are in the service of hell.

You will not go back to the shack now . . . your mother is probably in bed twisting her body from cruel hunger and her rotten liver as your father sits in the corner eating kabab and cussing at her . . . .

He will not give her or you anything.

You do not sleep or close your eyes, Hussein, until dawn. Only then do you know that 'the government' will not come to electrocute your anus.

An empty kettle, a water pipe, a piece of hashish, cigarette stubs, the smell of cooked meat, of menstruation blood, and perhaps a baby in his wife's belly. These are what remained of last night.

Badri kicks his woman so she falls off the small bed. Four drops of blood drip underneath her clothes. She is doubled over because of the cramps. (She had told him the night before, "I still have my period. Don't you dare touch me.") He pushes her on the bed and mounts her.

She wails. She sees him step over her with a rotten smell between his thighs right in her face. She climbs back into bed, she feels her bleeding, she spits on his back and shuts her eyes . . . .

To get to the door of the shack, Badri had to avoid five arms, seven feet, a belly and two of his children's heads. He turned over two on their backs and two on their stomachs until he found his shoes.

The tin door screeched as he opened it.

He spread out his arm across his forehead to block the sunlight in his eyes, squeezing them with his other hand to remove the sticky dirt. With the first step he took outside the shack, his shoe sunk into a pile of small warm shit, the fresh smell of which rose to his nostrils followed by a light smoke. He looked around and saw one of his children half-naked, jumping around in search for a stone to wipe his rear end. He pounced on him and wiped his shoe on his back. The boy fell over on his face and tried to get away from him. Badri cussed at him, "You piece of shit son of a bitch!"

He wiped his shoe and headed for the toilet. The boy took the rest of his clothes off, rolled on the ground rubbing his body in the dirt, and cussed back, "Fuck you!"

A narrow tin toilet. The gaps between the tin sheets allow any passerby or any person standing near the toilet to see what the person inside was doing. On the floor of the toilet there were scattered pieces of shit, wrinkled bits of newspaper, tattered pieces of cloth, dirty stones. In the corner, there was a small rusty tin container with slimy green water. There were two broken red bricks to sit on; between them was a hole overflowing with shit. On the walls there was graffiti of big breasts and women's violently open thighs ready for oversized male organs drooping with white liquid.

Only adults can use the toilet.

Badri stood in line immediately behind you, Hussein. He spat profusely. He wiped his nose with his hand then wiped his hand on his clothes. You felt his organ brushing against your rear end. It infuriated you. After the third time, you turned to face him. You smelled rotten corn beef between his teeth. You cussed him silently.

The toilet door opens. Someone comes out of the queue and yells, "Fuck having to stand in line! Fuck it man!"

Another one echoes, "Yeah, fuck it man!"

They run to the toilet. One of them draws out a small knife from underneath his clothes. "It's my turn you sons of bitches!"

Knives, razor blades, steel chains . . . .

You run away from the scene, Hussein. You hear screaming. You feel heat in the air, perhaps because of the blood spilt in front of the toilet.

Hussein . . .

You know that the best time to go to the toilet is during the day when they're watching a porn movie or at night during the TV serials. You will never forget the forty minutes you spent alone in the toilet when all the shacks were busy watching the last episode of Opera Aida. Seconds after you heard the music of the final scene, they were knocking violently at the door and cussing at you.

You stand in front, away from the fighting. You spot Badri's shoulder before his body disappears completely on his way to Afasha the kibdawi, or liver vendor. The thirty-year-old man with frizzy hair, a mustache that covers his upper lip, and two narrow hazel eyes, stands behind a counter, the lower part of which is marked in red paint: Human Liver; the upper part is glass covered with fly shit and dead mosquitoes. He has a pan in front of him covered with ink sitting on a glowing heater. On the ground, there is an old carton with bread inside it, crawling insects and strange smells.

No one knows . . . .

Why did Afasha the liver vendor choose 'Human Liver' as a sign? What was so attractive about that label? Why didn't he call it by its true name:

Donkey Liver or Dog or even Cat Liver. Perhaps he wanted to stress that it was good for human consumption. He went a long way in that direction and finally landed on 'Human Liver.' Maybe he meant to threaten any human being who might even think of messing around with his liver or bad mouth it in any way. It should be noted that Afasha was not ugly enough for him to be called 'afasha.' The word 'afasha' probably referred not to the man himself but to the liver he sold, which was disgusting, but he took it on as a personal signature. He was very strange, almost completely silent. No matter how much you hit or cursed him he would say nothing until you uttered something about the liver he sold. No one knew his real name.

Badri stops in front of Afasha. He spits twice. He wipes most of it with his finger on the glass counter. "Two loaves, Kibdawi."

He doesn't look at him. He stirs the liver with the green pepper and bits of mutton fat that splatters that familiar heavy scent so that no one can tell the real taste of liver even though everyone knows that it is the liver of cats or dogs or any other rotten source.

Afasha prepares the two loaves. He throws them on top of the tin counter to Badri who bites into one of them. "This dog has rabies, Afasha. I want a mixed one with cats and dogs."

Afasha grabs his knife. Badri snatches the second loaf and runs off. He'll pay at night.

While Badri stands at the edge of bewilderment, the shacks behind him and the tall buildings in the distance, you, Hussein, would be standing between the shacks, watching him perform his ritual of uncertainty.

Should he take the Ain Shams bus that is crowded with students and employees he can easily pickpocket? Should he take number 14 C where he can enjoy rubbing against women and university girls? Should he go back to the shacks and wake up Farawla the slut and drag her to a student flat in Madinat Nasr? Farawla is Badri's niece. He is fifteen years older than her. He slept with her for three years until she forbade him so he had to content himself with becoming her pimp.

And . . . .

Translated by Samia Mehrez

Hani Abdel Mourid

from *Kyrie Eleison*

IT WAS VERY OBVIOUS that the house was illegally built. True, it had been there for more than ten years, in one of the nicest spots in the area where several streets intersect and where there was ample space in front of it and to its right, but it was still illegal. It was built without authorization on a piece of land that was supposed to be part of the street.

Perhaps it was unfortunate that it was built two minutes away on foot from a spacious lot that was suddenly destined to become the seat of an organization under the auspices of the First Lady. That's why special attention and planning descended upon the street.

Before that building was erected, all illegal structures were demolished. It was difficult for Abu Amer's house to remain even if it were one of the landmarks of the area. His free-of-charge repair of police-station trucks as well as police-officers' and lieutenants' cars did not help him plead his situation.

The house was made up of two floors: the upstairs was for living and the ground floor had two rooms and another inner storage room. One of the rooms was a car-body workshop and the other was Abu Amer's coffee shop.

My father sat there all the time, for he and Abu Amer were great friends with mutual interests. Abu Amer was a weak man who had three daughters. The younger two, Sharbat and Adalat ran the coffee shop, which was why people called it the girls' coffee shop despite the big sign that he had placed on top of the coffee shop entrance and his name that was engraved on the backs of the seats and the aluminum tea trays.

The eldest daughter lived with her husband in Upper Egypt and seldom came to visit.

God only gave him one male child who came into the world with deformed legs and a brain development that froze at the age of four. You always saw him stretched out on a wooden bench and covered with flies, perhaps because he had no control over his bowel movements.

My father was a strong and violent man. He imposed his protection on Abu Amer and his daughters out of alleged decency. In public he benefited from the situation because he was contracted to re-do the body paint of the cars that Abu Amer fixed. In private, rumor had it that he slept with one of the daughters, with varying opinions on which one it was.

But everybody confirmed that the only one who escaped him was Damma, the sister-in-law of their sister who came from Upper Egypt for a change of air. She was innocent and fresh; she was afraid of speaking in front of anyone lest they should make fun of her accent. She was amazed at Abu Amer's daughters and their audacity and at all the stories that they told her before they went to bed. With her prolonged stay with them, she gradually started to work in the coffee shop. She learned how to prepare the drinks only, without having to interact with the customers except under the strictest circumstances. They did not rely on her completely except on very specific occasions, like when a complaint was made against Abu Amer and his daughters that they were selling drugs. They were summoned and promptly released but she stayed alone in the coffee shop for the whole morning. She was able to control the situation and Abu Amer was very happy with her. "That's the way to go! I want you to get good at this. You never know what lies in store for you."

There was a special taste to the days when important football matches are broadcast. Work at the coffee shop was tight all day. The number of customers increased and in the evening Abu Amer came back with grilled chicken. "Eat, everybody! Eat, Damma! We deserve a treat."

On the day of the match between Egypt and the Cameroon, Abu Amer's TV died just as the TV anchor woman was announcing the beginning of the match. If it were a bigger TV set or even a colored one he would have given it as a present to my father, but it was an old locally made pre-transistor era *Telimisr* that took ten minutes for the image—which initially looked like moving ghosts—to kick off.

All the customers transferred to another coffee shop on one of the side streets; even my father and Abu Amer went with them to watch the match.

Damma remained alone after Sharbat had gone up to the house to watch over her sister who was sick that day.

"Keep an eye on the coffee shop, Damma. I will go see Adalat and rest a little. When things get going, I'll come down to help you."

There were no customers in the coffee shop until he came asking for a cup of coffee. He sat sipping it in silence. One of the passersby greeted him.

"How are you, doctor?"

He was a drug and sex pills dealer. That's why they called him "doctor." Rumor had it that he was indeed a student in medical school but that he had been expelled after he was caught stoned in the auditorium.

He looked sad because he couldn't secure any merchandise on this special occasion of the match, until she approached him. "Are you really a doctor?"

When asked the question, he responded, as usual, "Yes, I am."

"What's your specialization?"

"Everything. I mean, I'm a doctor of all things."

"I have a problem that's bothering me. Where's your clinic?"

Perhaps he didn't believe that she was that naive. He must have thought that she was trying to seduce him. He may have started this as a joke but now he was aroused. So he cast his net.

In the storage room she complained of irregular menstruation and red pimples below her belly button.

He asked her as he held her breast if she felt pain. She said no. He continued fondling her breast. She felt uneasy and from time to time would say, "Doctor!"

And he would answer reassuringly, "Don't be afraid."

He took her. He didn't ever try to show his face there again. She never found out his name and she may still believe that the man who slept with her was a "doctor of all things."

Translated by Samia Mehrez

Cairo's Drug Culture

The material in this section only partially represents the very rich and quite startling literary renditions of the place of drugs in Cairenes' lives. Egyptians have always consumed drugs, and official estimates tell us that at least ten percent of Egypt's population today engages in various kinds of drug consumption (hashish, heroin, cocaine, cannabis, prescription drugs, glue, and so on). Unlike alcohol, drugs are not prohibited by Islam and have been traditionally available, affordable, and associated with various kinds of medicinal remedies, religious and social ceremonies, as well as creative and visionary energies and production. This is not to say that they are not outlawed and viewed as a social ill. Indeed, both the nineteenth and twentieth centuries have witnessed intermittent yet stringent anti-drug enforcement policies by the Egyptian state that have led to interesting shifts and transformations in the geopolitics of drug consumption (what gets consumed where) as well as its political economy (who consumes what).

Mapping drug culture in Cairo through literary representations over a whole century is therefore of considerable importance and significance, since it traces the changes that have taken place in drug consumption, state politics, class attitudes, as well as local and global practices and networks. Since drug consumption cuts across social class and is part of the life of both rich and poor, its diverse and contextually different literary representations illuminate a whole array of social phenomena and problems, from excessive wealth to excessive misery. What remains most stunning in this literary map of Cairo's drug culture is the extent to which drug consumption is simultaneously depicted as thoroughly part of both the public sphere and the literary field itself. Hence, the relationship between writers and drugs, literature and the representation of drug consumption is doubly complicated, since writers are at once chroniclers and actors: not just historians of drug culture but also part and parcel of that history of consumption and practice.

Perhaps the most remarkable example of the representation of drug culture in Egyptian literature is Naguib Mahfouz's 1966 classic, *Adrift on the Nile*, which shocked Egyptian readers with its daring representation of defeatism and escapism in Egyptian society just before the Arab defeat in the 1967 Six Day War, and subjected Mahfouz himself to a direct confrontation with no less than President Nasser himself. *Adrift on the Nile* is set in a houseboat on the Nile, where a group of men and women from various walks of life (a civil servant, a lawyer, a young woman student, a house-wife, an actor, and a journalist), intent on escaping a bleak outside reality, convene every night to indulge in hashish, promiscuous sex, and politically satiric hallucinations. Amm Abduh serves the gentlemen and the ladies, buys the hashish or kif for them but doesn't partake of it, and sees no contradiction between being a practicing Muslim and his role as "the guardian of pleasures" of the decadent crowd. Mahfouz's text uses hashish at both a realistic and symbolic level: we witness the realistic drug rituals of the more affluent, which the author then deploys to make a symbolic statement about the general malaise in the country on the eve of the defeat.

In contrast to Mahfouz's houseboat—the more privileged and private space for kif—Yusuf Idris takes his readers to the popular, lower class district of Batiniya, which was reputed to be one of the most important strongholds of hashish dealing and consumption during the 1950s and 1960s. Once again, drug consumption is used as a political metaphor in which the spiritual leader of the community becomes entangled. The young and newly appointed Imam of the mosque of Batiniya initially has trouble convincing the Batiniya drug addicts, who were "reared in banter and humor, for whom jokes and anecdotes were a staple diet" to perform their religious "duties" and come to the mosque to pray. When he begins to partake of their drug culture and develops an inner voice more seductive and true than his institutional one, the members of "that den of opium, Seconal and hashish," lured by the Imam's newfound passion, begin to answer his call for prayer. In both texts hashish is associated with a form of escapism but at the same time it is the medium through which a higher level of lucidity is achieved: the 'hallucinatory' dialogue between the characters in Mahfouz's text constitutes powerful political insights into the reality these characters are trying to escape. Likewise, Idris's Batiniya addicts respond to the Imam's voice only when they sense the inner call that transcends his authoritarian institutional role for which they have no need or respect.

Hashish is also frequently represented as a source of creative and poetic energy throughout the literary production of the twentieth century. In Albert Cossery's *Proud Beggars* the narrator tells us that Yeghen "loved the fantastic atmosphere of the smoking-rooms, the heavy smoke, opaque and stagnant like fog, and especially the sweet, lingering odor that stayed in one's clothes for a long time, more insidious than a woman's perfume. All this had a certain romanticism dear to his poet's soul." Khairy Shalaby's *The Hashish Waiter* provides a literary map of such 'smoking rooms' in downtown Cairo, ghuraz, or dens, of the literati's drug culture:

> People like us hardened hashish-smokers preferred to smoke in a real den, not in some café. . . . The more a den resembled a cave, cellar, hole in the ground, or chicken coop, the better the mood of the smokers and the more the imagination was aroused.

Likewise, in Yasser Abdel Hafez's novel *In Celebration of Life*, we witness how the patriarch of the Abou Id family, which had monopolized the cocaine business in the neighborhood, becomes the inspirational guru for the literati and celebrity figures, who, having had their drug hit, would get ideas from him for their film scripts, plays, and essays.

This rather laid-back representation of drugs and their positive impact on creative energy and the imagination will give way to more alarming literary scenes as hashish, which is considered a relatively mild drug, has gradually disappeared from the Egyptian market in the post-1980s to be replaced by more corrosive forms of addictive drugs, including heroin, cocaine, and other prescription and off-the-counter drugs. As we descend the social ladder, drug consumption becomes more dangerous, since the poor are driven to consume the cheapest and most hazardous forms of drugs. Essam Youssef's bestselling novel *A ¼ Gram* takes us into the underworld of increasingly prevalent drug abuse among young upper-middle class Cairenes, whose lives are shattered by their addiction to heroin. A thoroughly didactic novel that exposes the fatal consequences of addiction and has drawn unprecedented numbers of young readers, it also exposes and implicates the hypocritical state policies whose law enforcers are part of the horrors of this underworld. As we follow these multiple and diverse representations we are able to trace the changing map of drug culture as it is reconstituted across the city's topography and changing class configurations.

Naguib Mahfouz

from *Adrift on the Nile*

THE HOUSEBOAT LAY STILL on the leaden waters of the Nile, as familiar to him as a face. To the right there was an empty space, once occupied by another houseboat before the current swept it away, and to the left, on a wide bank of the shore, a simple mosque surrounded by a mud-brick wall and spread with shabby matting. Anis approached the houseboat, passing through a white wooden gate in a hedge of violet and jasmine.

Amm Abduh, the night watchman, rose to great him, his gigantic frame topping the slate and palm branches that composed the roof of his mud-brick hut. Anis made for the gangway of the houseboat, walking down a tiled path that was flanked on each side by a grassy space. To the right of the path, in the middle of the grass, there was a watercress bed, while far over to the left, a wilderness of hyacinth bean lay like a backdrop behind a towering guava tree. The sun's rays beat down, fierce and insistent, through an arbor of eucalyptus branches that spread from the roadside trees to shade the small garden.

He changed his clothes and went to sit, dressed in his long white tunic, in the doorway of the balcony overlooking the Nile. He welcomed the gentle breeze, letting it caress him tenderly, letting his eyes wander over the expanse of water, which could have been still and motionless, not a ripple, not a spar-kle could he see. But it carried the voices clearly from the houseboats moored in a long line on the opposite bank, beneath the evergreens and acacia trees. He sighed, loud enough for Amm Abduh—who was setting the small table next to the right-hand wall, a couple of meters from the refrigerator—to ask him: "All's well, I hope?"

"A disgusting, rotten atmosphere today," Anis muttered, turning toward him. "Drove away my good mood."

"But you always come back in the end to the good atmosphere here."

The old man never ceased to excite his admiration. He was like something great and ancient, rooted in time. Vitality leaped from his deeply lined eyes. Perhaps those deep furrows were what awed him; or perhaps it was the clump of thick white hair that sprang like date blossoms from the neck of his robe. And the robe itself, coarse calico, hanging like a drape over a statue, hanging straight down unhindered. No flesh, really, just skin and bone. But what bones! He was built like a giant, and his head grazed the ceiling of the houseboat.

There was an attraction about his whole being that was irresistible. He was a true symbol of resistance in the face of death. That was why Anis liked talking to him so much, in spite of their acquaintance of barely a month.

Anis rose and took his place at the table. He began to eat a chop, holding it in his fingers. He gazed at the wooden partition, painted with sky-blue distemper. He followed the progress of a small gecko as it scuttled across the partition to secrete itself behind a light switch. The gecko reminded him of the Head of Department. Why was that? A sudden question plagued him. Did the Fatimid Caliph Mu'izz li-Din Illah have any living descendants who might one day rise to claim the throne of Cairo as their own? "How old are you, Amm Abduh?" he asked.

Amm Abduh was standing behind the folding screen that concealed the outer door, and looking down at him from above like a cypress tree towering among the clouds. He smiled, as if he had not taken the question seriously. "How old am I?"

Anis nodded, licking his lips.

The old man spoke again. "Who knows?"

I am no expert when it comes to guessing ages, but more than likely he was walking the earth before a single tree was planted along this street. He is still so strong, given his age, that one can hardly believe it. He looks after the big floats under the houseboat, and pulls the boat on a rope to a new berth whenever it is necessary, and it follows him obediently; he waters the plants, he leads the prayer, and he is a good cook.

"Have you always lived alone in that hut?" Anis continued.

"There's only just enough room for me on my own!"

"Where did you come from, Amm Abduh?" he asked next, but the old man merely said, "Ah!"

"Don't you have relatives in Cairo?"

"No one."

"We have that in common at least . . . . You are an excellent cook, by the way."

"Thank you."

"And you eat more than is good for someone of your age."

"I eat what I can digest."

Anis contemplated the remains of the chop. One day, all that would be left of the Head of Department would be bones like those. How he would love to see him being called to account on Judgment Day! He began to peel a banana, and continued his inquiries. "When did you come to work on the houseboat?"

"When they brought it to this berth."

"When was that?"

"Oh . . ."

"And does it have the same owner now as it did then?"

"There has been one owner after another here."

"And do you like your job?"

"I *am* the houseboat!" Amm Abduh replied proudly. "Because I am the ropes and floats, and if I forgot my duties for a minute it would sink or be carried away by the current!"

His simple pride was appealing. Anis chuckled, and gazed at him for a moment before asking, "What is the most important thing in the world?"

"To be hale and hearty."

There was something mysterious and magical about his reply that made Anis laugh for a long time. Then he asked: "When was the last time you loved a woman?"

"Well!"

"Have you found nothing else to make you happy, after love?"

"Prayer is my comfort now."

"Your voice is beautiful when you call them to prayer," Anis remarked, and then he added merrily, "Even so, you're not too holy to go and fetch the kif, or bring back one of the street girls for us!"

Amm Abduh guffawed, throwing back his head with its white skullcap. He did not reply.

"Isn't that so?"

Amm Abduh passed one big hand over his face. "I serve the gentlemen," he said simply.

But no. No, it was not just that. He was the houseboat, as he had said. The ropes and floats, the plants, the food, the women, the prayers.

Taking a towel, Anis went through a side door to wash his hands at the basin, and came back, saying to himself that it was due to excess alone that most of the Caliphs had not lived long. He saw Amm Abduh busily wiping the table, his back bent like a bowed palm tree. Playfully, he asked him, "Have you ever seen a ghost?" ·

"I've seen everything," Amm Abduh replied.

Anis winked. "So there has never been a good family living on this houseboat?" he asked.

"Hmm?"

"O guardian of our pleasures! If you did not like this life, you would have left it on the first day!"

"How could I, when I built the mosque with my own hands?"

Anis looked now at the books on the shelves, which covered the whole of the long wall to the left of the door. It was a library of history, from the dawn of time to the atomic age, domain of his imagination and storehouse of his dreams. At random, he took down a book on monasticism in the Coptic period in order to read, as he did every day, for an hour or two before his siesta. Amm Abduh finished his work and came to ask if Anis wanted anything else before he left.

"What is going on outside, Amm Abduh?" Anis asked him.

"The same as usual, sir."

"Nothing new?"

"Why don't you go out, sir?"

"I go to the ministry every day."

"I mean, for relaxation."

Anis laughed. "My eyes look inward, not outward like the rest of God's servants!" And he dismissed Amm Abduh, telling him to wake him if he was still asleep at sunset.

Translated by Frances Liardet

Yusuf Idris

from *"Did You Have to Turn on the Light, Lili?"*
in *The Cheapest Nights*

IT WAS A JOKE at the start. Perhaps it was a joke in the end too. Actually it was not a joke in the real sense, but an incident, rather, which happened to involve those fabricators of jokes who were past masters of the art. It was not the fact that all those people who normally go to bed at dawn should rise at that hour in order to pray, which was the joke, or the fact that for the first time in the annals of the quarter of Al Batiniyya—that den of opium, Seconal, and hashish—the people answered the call to prayer which came from the minaret at the break of day.

Nor was there anything odd in their praying with their heads foggy with dope. Forgetting that they have already recited the Fatiha they recite it another time, but they forget the words and then they remember them in the middle of a prayer so they start all over again. The joke, actually, came just as they were about to end the prayer. The incident is still one of the cherished tales they are fond of recounting. People around there were drug addicts for the most part, reared in banter and humor, for whom jokes and anecdotes were a staple diet. No sooner would an incident occur than they would seize upon it, adding frills and embellishments until they made of it a fantastic epic to rival the best of their local lore.

Oddly enough, the first prostration had gone in perfect order, so had the second, and only the third prostration, the salutation, and the uttering of the words "There is no god but God and Mohamed is the Prophet of God" remained to terminate the prayer.

"God is the greatest!" called the Imam as he kneeled for the third prostration. They all kneeled after him, albeit a little awkwardly, their joints stiff from disuse as most of them had not performed their prayers for longer than they cared to admit. Ten long rows piously repeated "God be praised" three times, and waited for the final responses from the imam to conclude the prayer. When that failed to come on time some began to suspect their count was wrong. So again, slowly, they repeated it, but still the response failed to come. A few resigned themselves to waiting, only too glad to rest, their dizzy heads still laden with dope, but most began to wonder what had happened as it was becoming clear the situation was rather odd. Still, they were hopeful that the sheikh would presently pronounce the words "God is greatest" and all would be well. But the longer they waited the more their suspicion was confirmed that they were facing a crisis. All sorts of possibilities began to storm through their bowed heads which none of them dared to raise. Had the sheikh been suddenly taken ill? Or had he passed out, or simply died? Or could it be some devil had induced him to take a whiff of hash, and he was suffering the consequences now? Yet in spite of these conjectures they still expected the response to come and restore peace to their minds which by now had gone on a wild rampage in the realms of fantasy.

Exactly how long they waited no one was certain. According to some accounts it could have been two minutes or it could have been two hours, that is, if one were to disregard exaggerations which affirmed that the pause had lasted until echoes of the noon call to prayer began to reach them from Al Azhar. There are also those who insist they are still kneeling up to this moment.

But what was certain even to the most befuddled was that an unusual length of time had passed and that all was not well with the sheikh. He had certainly not pronounced the takbeer for which they were all waiting and which would have put an end to their kneeling posture, and the snoring wheezing out of all those drooling jaws.

At this point each one of them found himself faced with a problem he had never encountered before. What exactly should he do now, and what do the laws of religion say with regard to a situation like this? If one of them were to move and raise his head, would that annul his prayer, and possibly that of the entire congregation? And would he alone take the blame? Being freshly returned prodigals made them once again recall visions of a God who promised reward and punishment, wielding paradise and the bottomless pit of hell. To the newly repentant new transgression was more than they would want on their consciences.

But time was starting to weigh, and wicked thoughts began to assail them. Like scoffing for instance, not only at their predicament but at the thought of what might arise if the sheikh had got it into his head to take a snooze or, even worse, he had simply dropped dead. They would probably have to remain in that posture till the following day, or possibly till doomsday before someone discovered them, as the mosque was not a place people around there were fond of frequenting, for merely to walk past it stirred the conscience. But they were afraid to dwell too long on their devilish thoughts or on the ridiculous situation they were in, since they were irreverent by nature, and they dared not succumb to impiety for fear of adding to their sins. Even the most optimistic were forced to admit that they were in a real predicament when the light of dawn began to break, and the wan light of the electric lamp slowly faded. It was pitch black when they had started to pray and now with daylight appearing no doubt remained that the prostration was uncommonly long. The sporadic sounds of coughing, growing increasingly more frequent, were the only signs of impatience with a situation which did not promise to end soon. It was impossible to know what had happened without raising their heads, and if they raised their heads they annulled the prayer. None was willing to take the lead and bring upon himself the opprobrium of such a deed. All were waiting for someone else to start. The blame would then be on him. There was a vast difference between the guilt of one who leads and one who merely follows. The prolonged prostration was becoming an undisputable fact and it lasted until it defeated all doubts and misgivings and any inclination to laugh at the matter.

And since there is no joke so far, and since the real laughs haven't started yet, let us leave them as they are, prostrate, each of them fearing to be the first to trespass.

For that's exactly how I left them. I, Sheikh Abdel Al, Imam of the Mosque of El Shabokshi, in the quarter of Al Batiniyya.

Did you have to turn on the light, Lili?

Translated by Wadida Wassef

Ismail Wali al-Din

from *Saqqara Grief*

THE SIGNS OF FESTIVITIES began: banners, colored light fixtures, the decorated cloth tent. It was Fathi Abdel Sattar's wedding.

Family and relatives in brightly colored clothes busied themselves in Deir al-Malak in preparation for the long-awaited day, the day of the wedding, quite a rare occasion. The phone rang. The old widow who Fathi Abdel Sattar had married was calling to tell him that her son had returned from the Red Sea and that he meant him no good.

Fathi did not give much attention to that report. He finished getting dressed: the brown suit with the expensive and colorful necktie that he had bought on Suleiman Pasha Street. After he perfumed his face with the scent of jasmine he told the family that he was ready. The family went down to the cars that had been waiting since morning, followed by other relatives. The cars were decorated with flowers and laurel leaves.

After the call for evening prayer, Fathi Abdel Sattar was wedded to his poor relative who would move into his house and serve the whole family until the day she died.

After the ceremony, preparations began for the wedding party. The bridegroom would not spend the night with his bride in Saqqara but rather in the family home in Deir al-Malak. They gave him the children's room. They had refurnished it on the occasion of the wedding.

The men's party began inside the tent: a hired belly dancer from Fayoum and a good singer who performed popular folk songs.

The drinking started, beer bottles were popped open, and glasses and plates of mezza were circulated among the guests, who were mostly the young crowd from the village.

Masoud al-Garhi sat to the right of the groom; to his left sat the village teacher and at a distance sat the omda and the rest of the relatives, friends, and loved ones.

They brought in the drug tray: several jars, the reed, and pieces of expensive hashish—the real thing from the real place. Notables from neighboring villages arrived: Maraziq, Hawamdiya, Abu Seir. They brought their own excellent drug in celebration of the stunning groom in his Sufi gallabiya before the groom had changed the brown suit after the ceremony and wore a gallabiya made especially for the occasion. He fired several shots in the air. All the men competed in shooting as a sign of celebration. Dog barks could be heard in the distance.

At the right moment, when the singer's voice filled the village and the belly dancer dazzled eyes in her tight red glittering outfit, the bottles of whisky appeared. "A night like no other," said the omda to the groom. The intoxicated groom got up to dance in front of the guests with a thick wooden stick. Everybody cheered him on as he danced with the belly dancer.

The young crowd laughed and the singer applauded.

When the groom sat down again between his friends, the women disappeared behind the curtains and windows after they had enjoyed that great scene. The bride was happy deep down for having been chosen from among all the girls in Saqqara by this handsome, wealthy young man.

Night fell and the sky looked like a silver plate glittering with happy stars.

A young angry-looking man suddenly entered the tent. No one noticed him except Fathi, who was anxious about his presence at that particular moment. His heart raced as he got up to greet the newcomer, who had grown up with him in the alleys of Deir al-Malak. They were together in high school; time had not separated them.

The old friend was the son of the old widow whom he had married informally on an intoxicated night of drugs and drinking, just for the sake of the dear friend.

In a moment, the old friend who had just arrived from the capital fired three shots into the groom's chest before he had time to greet him.

He fell to the ground, unconscious. The wedding turned into a funeral, with wailing and weeping. The lights were turned off; the singer and the dancer disappeared. The groom was taken to Badrashin Hospital but he died before the emergency doctor could come near him.

Translated by Samia Mehrez

Albert Cossery

from Proud Beggars

THE SOUND OF VOICES and the brightness of the acetylene gas lamps welcomed him like a kindly place of refuge. At this hour of the night the Mirror Café was full of a rowdy crowd occupying all of the tables and strolling in slow procession across the dirt sidewalk. The eternal radio poured forth a flow of stormy music amplified by loudspeakers, drowning the magnificence of the words, the cries, and the laughter in the same confusion. In this grandiose tumult, ragged beggars, cigarette-butt scavengers, and wandering merchants gave themselves to a pleasant form of activity, like acrobats at a fair. It was like this every night: the ambience of a fun fair. The Mirror Café appeared to be a place created by man's wisdom and situated in the confines of a world doomed to sadness. Yeghen always felt amazed by this idleness and this delirious joy. It seemed that all of these men know nothing of the anguish, the painful uncertainty of a miserable destiny. True, poverty marked their clothes made of innumerable rags and inscribed its indelible imprint on their lean and haggard bodies; however, it hadn't managed to erase from their faces the shining joy at still being alive.

Curious population! Delighted with this fraternal and wonderfully comforting promiscuity, Yeghen made a path through the crowd. He found himself in his own territory; here his ugliness didn't offend anyone. On the contrary, by contact with these humble men, it acquired a kind of radiance. He was quickly recognized and greeted by friendly exclamations. Several times he was invited to have a glass of tea, but he refused on the pretext of undefined business. Actually, he wanted to find Gohar; he must certainly be waiting for him, deprived of drugs and prey to suffering. Gohar's suffering was the only iniquity that he couldn't tolerate in a world full of iniquities. He put all the generosity he was capable of into the gesture of offering Gohar his daily portion of hashish. To give this scrap of joy to a man—be it only a few hours' worth—seemed to him more effective than all the vain attempts of reformers and idealists wanting to lift sad humanity out of its suffering. Yeghen gloried in being the apostle of immediate, tangible efficiency in this domain. In his opinion, elaborate plans and wise theories destined to relieve a people's misery were only sinister jokes. He laughed derisively, taking care to maintain his public image.

. . .

He was advancing with difficulty through the throng when he felt someone take his arm.

"My dear Yeghen, do me the honor of sharing my table."

Yeghen turned around. The man was a notorious pederast of majestic corpulence wearing a green silk robe and an ample aubergine-colored coat. His hair and mustache were dyed and he wore heavy rings on his fingers. He was a very rich fabric merchant who prided himself on his literary taste.

The fat merchant's affability toward him always amused Yeghen because of the ambiguity that it cast over their relationship.

"Well then, how is the poetry?"

"Dying."

"Never mind! Come have a glass of tea with me. I'm eager to hear you talk."

"Excuse me, it's not possible. I'm looking for someone. I absolutely must find him."

"Ah, I understand," the man said, with a knowing wink.

"You understand nothing. I'm not at that game yet. Perhaps one day it will happen."

"Well, that would be a great day. I will be happy to count you among my friends."

"You don't mean it!" Yeghen protested. "With my face?"

"Don't forget that you have other charms for me. I'm sensitive to genius."

"In other words, you want to sleep with my genius."

They burst our laughing.

"But that also is impossible," Yeghen continued. "I don't have genius. Take care. I'll see you very soon."

"Your modesty becomes you. At least give me the pleasure of accepting a cigarette."

He held out a pack of expensive cigarettes to Yeghen, who took one which the man lit with a gold lighter.

"Thank you."

Yeghen left the fat merchant and resumed his search for Gohar. Where was he hiding? He didn't see him anywhere. He began to grow more uneasy, especially since he felt the presence of a little cigarette-butt scavenger behind him, glued to his heels, watching and waiting for the moment he would throw away his cigarette. The allure of this expensive butt seemed to exercise a kind of fascination on the little boy. He followed Yeghen's trail with the look of a starving dog. Finally, Yeghen had had enough of this pursuit and threw him the half-smoked cigarette.

"Here, you wretch! You won't be up my ass any more."

"May God forbid," cried the child, picking up the cigarette.

It was completely by chance that he spotted Gohar.

In this barber shop, a kind of hovel without a door lit only by the distant café lights, Gohar sat enthroned on the only chair, exhausted by fatigue, given up to the desolate wisdom of a universe crumbling in all its parts. Yeghen's voice made him jump.

"Greetings, Master!"

"You're finally here, my son!"

Yeghen bent to the ground, parodying a bow. The respect due his master did not exclude a joke.

"Always at your command. I hope I didn't disturb your meditations."

"Not at all. Sit down."

Yeghen ran and got a chair lying on the sidewalk, then sat down next to Gohar with a happy grin. Each time he was transported by the same happiness; one would have thought that Gohar's presence made the most unbelievable bliss possible. All of his sorrows, even those buried in his unconscious, disappeared at the sight of his master. He even forgot his ugliness.

In the intimacy of the barber shop, Gohar's silence acquired an ineffable power of eternity. Yeghen respected this silence; he knew that it hid secret, incommunicable joys. But suddenly he was alarmed by the feeling of a major oversight; even though never asking for anything, Gohar was surely waiting for one thing: the drug. He quickly took a folded paper from his pocket, opened it, and broke in two the piece of hashish it contained. He offered the bigger part to Gohar, who took it without a word, rolled it around in his fingers to make a ball, then raised it to his lips and began to suck on it. Already, he felt life slowly returning to him and blood flowing in his atrophied veins. He closed his eyes, savoring, in all its fullness, that delicious moment which follows extreme privation. A little flabbergasted by this too hasty manner of taking the drug, Yeghen didn't move. This oral drug-taking that Gohar appreciated because of its ease always startled him like sleight-of-hand. In his view, drug-taking demanded a more complicated ritual. Yeghen loved the fantastic atmosphere of the smoking-rooms, the heavy smoke, opaque and stagnant like fog, and especially the sweet, lingering odor that stayed in one's clothes for a long time, more insidious than a woman's perfume. All this had a certain romanticism dear to his poet's soul that Gohar swept away with one stroke by stuffing the hashish directly in his mouth. Each time, Yeghen experienced a kind of dread at this blunder. Even though he told himself that the desired effect was the same, he couldn't help regretting this lack of interest in the preparations and the decor.

In the shop's darkness, he indulged in his favorite grimaces, attentive to the slightest sign of the revival taking place in his companion's organism. He already enjoyed the idea of being able to talk with him soon. But Gohar still remained silent; only a faint panting indicated that he was slowly returning to life.

. . .

Bountiful magic of the drug! Gohar moved in his chair, opened his eyes, and smiled in the shadows.

Yeghen understood from this smile that he could finally speak.

"Well, master, what's new?"

"Quiet, my son, I had a memorable day."

Translated by Thomas W. Cushing

Gamil Atia Ibrahim

from *Down to the Sea*

A SCREAM RANG OUT from another ward.

The women were the first to burst into wailing, immediately thinking the worst. The funeral-tent pitchers and gravediggers stood gazing with a cheerfulness and calm rivaling that of the doctors and nurses. Shatara went out to investigate. One of the smaller dealers bellowed at him to "Get it sorted!" but Shatara refused to be sidetracked, telling them that he had come to visit Mr. Sayyid and he wasn't going to work today.

Ma'allim Sabah put a hand in his pocket and took out a ten-pound note. He offered it to Shatara, who took it without a word and put it in his pocket. "A quarter of hash, just to oil the wheels, sir," Shatara said.

Ma'allim Sabah put his hand in his other pocket and took out a small chunk of something wrapped in silver paper. The moment Shatara's eye lit upon it, he grabbed it and it was gone. Nobody could have told where he had hidden it.

"That's a whole half!" Ma'allim Sabah said crossly.

"Thank you, sir," Shatara replied.

He rushed away toward the stairs—and then turned and came back. "And a couple of pounds, for change, sir," he said. "Just to clear everything."

For the third time, the man put his hand in his pocket. Shatara knew that this would be the last time. Ma'allim Sabah was tight by nature, and taciturn, and when his fist came into contact with the skull of even the strongest of men, they fell down dead. Shatara received two from a roll of one-pound notes and dashed off, away from the balcony, toward the rear of the hospital and the mortuary and storehouses. He picked his way disgustedly across a gloomy square, inches deep in water from a leaking pipe, toward a building with a large entrance-hall. The room he wanted lay down a narrow dark passageway. He opened the door. There was no one inside, so he sat down to break up a cigarette and mix the tobacco with hashish.

Girgis the Copt pushed open the door with his foot. The smell of hashish drifted to his nostrils. He put his head round the door, spotted Shatara smoking, and opened his mouth in a guffaw. Words of greeting emerged with difficulty through his rotten teeth.

Shatara offered him his joint and Girgis the Copt took a deep drag, holding it down in his chest until his veins stood out and swelled up. Then he let the smoke out through his great nostrils. The hashish had been so well absorbed into his lungs that only the dregs of smoke came out of his nose.

Shatara inquired about work.

"Three deaths—difficult birth, train accident, heart failure," Girgis replied.

Shatara took out the two pounds from his pocket and asked him if they could get it over with. They went together to the mortuary and began to bargain with the families of the deceased, Girgis the Copt swearing by the prophets and apostles and the Blessed Virgin and the mercy of his forefathers that all he wanted to do was to serve them, and there was nothing in it for him. When everyone had agreed, Shatara took the death certificates and the down-payments.

He returned to the balcony. Ma'allim Sabah drew him to one side. Shatara gave him the death certificates. The man took them and examined them carefully, checking the dates, the seals, and the place of burial. Shatara stood silently by his side.

Ma'allim Sabah summoned one of the other dealers and gave him one of the certificates. Then he beckoned to a couple of assistants. He told them to go with Shatara in silence to finish the work, and to come back in the evening after setting up the funeral tents. Then Ma'allim Sabah put his hand in his pocket once more and took out fifty pounds. He gave them to Shatara, who led the others away to the mortuary.

The men and women on the balcony were tying up the loose ends of their talk unaware of the deals being struck around them. Everything had been finished up quietly—in fact Shatara had not opened his mouth. He had handed the certificates over to the man in silence, and had taken the money from him and put it in his pocket in silence, and led the dealers and the boys away without a word. It was as if death, the atmosphere of death, reigned over them; and when Ma'allim Sabah returned to his seat among the men he began a new topic of conversation.

Shatara went back to Girgis's room. He found the quiet gloom pleasant. He sat among the files and folders—dubbed 'the dossiers' by Girgis. He had nothing to do except sit among them in the gloom or roam the corridors of the hospital.

A small window looked out over the narrow central well of the building. A cold breeze blew in, making it refreshing to sit there, banishing the smell of dust and ancient things.

Nobody knew exactly what Girgis the Copt did for a living—or even whether he had been employed by the hospital to begin with. The faculty students saw him throughout their years of study and after they were appointed to their posts. The directors would come and chat with him and then leave him on his own, sitting there as if he were a part of the storehouses, like an antique fixture of the hospital.

Girgis said to his favorites among the new porters, nurses, and clerks that he had entered service in the time of Sultan Hussein, or a few years afterward. Producing a silver coin with the name of Sultan Hussein on it, he claimed that it was the first wage he had earned in his life. They asked him about this silver coin, how much it was worth in those days, and he told them that it was equivalent to a hundred pounds of today's money.

Girgis the Copt told Shatara that Dr. Sabir was making life difficult for him these days. Dr. Sabir had decided to get rid of him, cut off his livelihood. Girgis wanted to speak to Sabir's relatives. He and Shatara chatted away, joints in hands, the light breeze blowing in on them and bringing relief from the scorching heat, the heavy stench of the summer. The air was as sweet as the scented breaths which came wafting to their noses from the burning joints.

Every now and again Girgis's chest became congested with the smoke and he started to cough. He took out a soft khaki-colored handkerchief to blow his nose. "This handkerchief dates from the time of the British Army," he said each time. "It belonged to General Allenby." He tried to make Shatara hold it, but Shatara turned his face away, disgusted by the way the man's snot had stained the khaki black.

Girgis the Copt began to rummage in drawers and to open cupboards until he found a syringe and a rusty can. He took these things out into the hall and began to fumigate the whole place, drenching it inside and out. A penetrating smell spread everywhere, burning their noses and inflaming their eyes until Shatara almost choked. Girgis soaked the room, the dirty khaki handkerchief over the lower half of his face so that it covered his nose and mouth, turning round and round in the middle of the room until Shatara shouted at him to stop squirting, his nose was on fire.

"This stuff keeps the moths away from the dossiers," Girgis said, laughing.

Shatara snatched the syringe away from him and, sneezing, forced Girgis to sit down in his chair. He wanted to speak to him about a serious matter before they both died of this squirting. Girgis retorted that this squirting kept the moths and the rot away from the room, and Shatara had to comply with his wisdom.

Shatara rolled a joint. He asked Girgis whether he would go halves with him in buying a hearse. Girgis the Copt guffawed. He said that a hearse which carried Muslims could not carry Christians.

"Let's be secular about this—like the Wafd Party!" Shatara said, to surmount this problem.

As Girgis chatted, his guts began to distend. He started to rub his belly, lifting it up and squeezing the flesh. His wind clung to the wall of his bowel, refusing to leave him, so he began to lean to right and left, moaning and lowering his body beneath the desk, dipping his head down until it was practically on the floor. Then he came back up again, rubbing his belly and unbuckling his wide belt. Clad in shirt and drawers, thin and wretched and writhing in agony, he muttered prayers and blessings on all the saints. "Blessed Virgin! . . ." he cried.

Shatara watched him, laughing, but when Girgis's eyes reddened with pain he began to be afraid for him and pray for his release.

"Urine retention, my son, is more merciful than this!" Girgis said.

Girgis disappeared once more under the desk. There came a slight, faint smell. He relaxed and sat upright once more, sparing Shatara any more bobbing up and down. He had long since ceased to be shy about the caprices of his belly.

Shatara decided there and then to come down hard on the old trickster, and get it over with; after all, he had known exactly what he wanted from the moment he had come with the hashish. "The goods are ready tonight," he said. "Are there any customers?"

"The atmosphere's unsettled," Girgis replied gloomily. "The government is on the watch."

Shatara stared hard into the man's wrinkled face. He saw that Girgis was serious. He was not joking. He asked him why.

Girgis explained. After the arrival of the Zionists, he said, there were no Arab students around—and there were no anatomy classes.

Shatara laughed. "So it's a question of politics!"

'Politics is in everything,' Girgis replied. "If you ate beans for breakfast, it's politics, and if you had meat, it's politics."

By now, Shatara had lost all hope of making a fat deal. The woman who had died in childbirth was going to be buried out on the hill-road where it would be easy to get her. He kept his nerve and proceeded cautiously. "So everybody who eats beans and deep-fried patties is a statesman, then?" he said.

"Bravo," said Girgis.

Shatara thought. The woman's corpse would last for quite a few days before the rot set in and the worms started to nibble, because of the formalin in which it had been kept while in the mortuary. "Did the Pharaohs know about formalin?" he asked Girgis the Copt.

Girgis showed off his knowledge, the words coming out in fits and starts through his crumbling teeth. "The Pharaohs know about something more important than formalin," he replied. "Magic."

"So!" Shatara said to himself. "Magic is stronger than formalin!"

Girgis fetched a bowl full of meat and potatoes from the kitchen, together with some rounds of hot bread and three big tomatoes as red as apples.

Shatara began to gobble the meat and turn over many things in his head, which was spinning from the heat of the food in his throat and belly and his fist. He tossed a chunk of meat into his mouth, turning it around and lifting it on to the tip of his tongue so that it would not burn the roof of his mouth, and then gulped it down into his belly. His body was hot from the food, his eyes shone with the heat, his brain was blazing with fire. He needed, now he had come upon the locked treasure-house, to slaughter the ape at its door, to break the spell so that it would open to him and he could plunge his hands into the treasure. Then he could marry the girl. The one who undulated before him in her white garments. He knew her—but he could not divulge her name. He never even said it in his mind, he never linked her with her name; he only said to himself that she was "Her," because he was afraid of attracting the Eye to her beauty, her fineness . . . .

Shatara, overwhelmed by love for her, asked Girgis the Copt about the value of historical remains.

Girgis mumbled through the scraps of unchewed meat which hampered his speech. "History has more value than money," he lisped.

In Shatara's view there was nothing more valuable than money. He was wondering about the value of the birth certificate with which a person's history began. Was that worth anything?

Girgis spat out his reply. "A birth certificated as such, Shatara, has no market value. But Napoleon's birth certificate, or Hitler's, or Sultan Hussein's, or Gamal Abd al-Nasser's, or Sayyid Darwish's, or Muhammad Abd al-Wahhab's or Umm Kulthoum's—they are the same as treasure."

Shatara was drowning in the warmth, the heat which stirred up his lust for life, made him yearn for it. He dreamed of the soft life. "Ohh," he said at last in wonder. He saw things free of their stink, they had become as clear as the clearest air or the purest water. "Ohh. Just like treasure."

Girgis realized cannily that Shatara had found a buyer for the dossiers which were in his possession. They had talked about them last month. He decided to get Shatara stirred up again, one last time before he retired. "All these dossiers are money," he said now.

"So put me in the picture," said Shatara.

"Historical documents!" Girgis boasted. "The history of medicine. The history of hospitals in the Two Domains of Egypt and Sudan. The names, and the certificates of the very first years of medical students. The history of the first surgical operation. Documents, my son," he concluded. "Documents."

Shatara said, "A file—pardon me—how much does it sell for? These days, I mean," he added, so that Girgis would not submerge him in stories of trials and gold currencies, those things which did not concern him and which for the most part he did not listen to.

Girgis dipped his hand into the food. "These documents sell by the page, my son. One page will get you a gold guinea—a King George guinea"—and he went back to talking about guineas.

This is an obsession with him, Shatara thought as he munched, but he went along with his exaggerations. "You're sitting on a gold mine, Girgis," he said.

"A gold mine of history," replied the sharp old man. "Not of golden guineas."

"Let's exchange the history." Shatara said, serious now. "Let's change it into money!"

To open a treasure-house you needed an ape. The ape was Girgis the Copt. Her eyes were as wide as those of a charging bull. Her body alluring without the aid of clinging shawls. Her voice, as soft as an angel's, said "Good morning!" as she walked on past without stopping. Shatara knew people who bought old copper pots, antiques, the decorated doors of old houses, carved window-frames—but he knew no one who bought old files of paper.

They finished eating. Shatara lit a joint and puffed a few clouds at Girgis, who was at that moment champing on one of his own. They smoked together until the joints burned down between their fingers. They sat, each absorbed in his own silence, each speculating about what was in the other's mind, what gold-mine the other had under his feet.

"Shatara's a bastard," thought Girgis the Copt. "He'd sell his grandmother." They parted, to meet again soon.

Translated by Frances Liardet

Khairy Shalaby

from *The Hashish Waiter*

The Maarouf Quarter

Hakeem's hash den was particularly well situated relative to all the other dens in the Maarouf quarter, which is just behind Talaat Harb (formerly, Suliman Pasha) Street. The main drag in the neighborhood, Maarouf Street, runs parallel to Talaat Harb, beginning at Tahrir Square and cutting across Antikkhana Street—now Mahmoud Bassiouni—where the Library and Museum of Modern Art used to be. Back when we were the masters of our own time, we used to spend countless hours in the library and museum, listening to music, reading expensive books, and admiring the paintings. Maarouf Street ends where 26th of July and Tharwat streets meet in front of the High Court building, which looks out onto 26th of July and Ramses streets. There are a few similarly styled buildings attached to its solemn edifice: the Judges' Club and the Lawyers' Syndicate, which look out over Tharwat Street toward the Church of the Sacred Heart and the Railway Hospital on the other side. Maarouf Street and Talaat Harb Street are completely different though they're only a few steps apart. Taking a shortcut or two, we could get from Café Riche in Talaat Harb Square—where intellectuals, celebrities, and the cream of the tourist crop hung out—to the clump of hash dens in Maarouf in less than three minutes, but we'd arrive feeling as if we'd been magically transported to another life in another city inhabited by another people. The entire length of the street was packed full of countless people and objects: donkey- and horse-carts; handcarts; vegetables, fruit, and fish for sale; plastic and aluminum tableware in all shapes and sizes spread out over blankets on the ground, to say nothing of the knickknacks, the refrigerators stocked with soft drinks, and the stores all alongside: grocers', fuul and falafel stands, kushari stands, auto parts stores, bike shops, spray-painting, mechanics', and electricians' workshops, and coffeehouses. And on top of all that, little bits from all of the above being carried around in roving vendors' display cases. To say nothing of the tiny corner stores where they fixed locks and car doors and primus stoves, and where you could find cobblers who were pros at fixing worn-out shoes and getting them to shine again. These stores all had loads of customers who came by car and on foot and the most amazing thing was that they actually managed to squeeze their cars into whatever empty spots they could find, calmly parking amid a storm of noise and shouting, and the kind of relentless honking that could drive you mad. And yet, because Egyptians are so generous—and because of that alone—everything had to be allowed to reach its destination. Cars passed through the eye of a needle but no headlights were smashed, no fenders dented, no merchandise upset, no pedestrians injured. The traffic only ever stopped for a second or two before starting up again. If for some reason there were a backup, several passersby would take it upon themselves to start directing traffic and others would push a stalled car out of the way; even the mechanic might haul himself down to the car when called for. And then there were all the people who came to shop for vegetables, fruit, meat, fish, and bread: most of the customers were women of various social classes armed with baskets and palm-leaf bags. Some of them were housewives who looked like foreigners—or else even blonder, paler versions of foreigners—while some others were scrawny, dimwitted, fish-out-of-water maids who never stopped talking. Still others came barefoot and dressed in black on black from who knows where to sit out in the street and sell white cheese, butter, mish cheese, and pigeon chicks out of huge pans. Everyone who lived downtown came to do their shopping on that market street, which buzzed all day and all night and made anyone caught up in its throng feel like it was the earth itself that was moving. Yet all the same, the street was a fun place to hang out be it day or night. Life there was also as cheap as could be: rather than costing you the equivalent of a humble government clerk's monthly salary like a meal on Talaat Harb Street would, on Maarouf Street you could stuff your belly for two piasters. For one piaster, you could probably even get a sandwich stuffed with fuul, falafel, and fixins, or a chunk of delicious and filling roast sweet potato. You could sit at one of the street's many coffeehouses or snack bars and have a cup of tea with milk and smoke a water pipe for just two and a half piasters. As an added bonus, your eyes could delight in the sight of a stupendous crowd of women of all different ages, shapes, and colors; it was as if every house in the city had dumped its fair ladies out onto the street. They were dressed in simple house-clothes that showed off all their curves, especially those spots that were supposed to be covered up. The women walked along naturally, without any cares, without even the slightest feeling that they were being ogled, as freely as if they were walking around in their own houses. Their chests spilled over the cages, their breasts mingling with the pigeons and rabbits lying there with appallingly calm resignation; their cheeks mingling with pomegranates and apples and peaches; their armpits, white and flushed and depilated, with legs of lamb and veal hanging from large hooks. Nile perch, whitefish, and catfish shuddered in the air above fishmongers' baskets at the touch of lady-Nile perches. Nights on Maarouf Street had their own special magic about them. Traffic would die down after sunset and the muddy street would be washed down, foul water flowing between the disgusting pavement tiles. The air would fill with a heavy stench, like the smell of all the sweat that had fallen onto the ground during the day, and then be freshened by the smell of meat grilling over coals and of liver and brain being fried up in pans on clean, white pushcarts decorated with colorful glass and lights. The clamoring, fragrant fruits on display looked like a grandstand of flowers, like a festival of natural colors. The sound of bottles of beer and soft drinks being opened grew louder, as did the slamming down of pieces onto backgammon boards and of tongs clanging on marble countertops in coffeehouses. Umm Kulthum's voice rose up out of the radio and spread in every direction, only to be reflected back by echoes from every corner of the street. Life there seemed as easy, as calm, as pleasant, as perfectly gratifying as could be. The screeching neon lights created a canopy of joyful serenity that provided an infinite space for imaginations intoxicated by philanthropic emotions that felt moist and green and warm all at once; especially when you were just stepping out of one of the hash dens hidden in the depths of that big carnival.

Clear Path

There were several ways to get to Hakeem's den. You could get there from Ramses Street, in which case you'd have to pass by Galal's den. This was actually mildly embarrassing because Galal competed with our favorite den, which was no more than a coffeehouse built of wood and reeds in the middle of a large bank of ruins. All the houses around it—down Maarouf Street and Ramses Street—were, according to official government records, at risk of collapse. Their expected lifespan had run out more than half a century ago and many stern orders to evacuate the buildings had been handed down; yet despite their age, they had maintained the charm of their inventive design. Each house was a priceless architectural treasure, but they'd ended up looking like big-shots who'd seen better days and were reduced to trying—albeit in vain—to get some bastard somewhere to take pity on them. The residents hadn't been able to find somewhere else to live so they just stayed put, accepting responsibility for themselves, and, as far as the government records were concerned, the houses were simply condemned and abandoned. This, despite the fact that everyone could see that the houses occasionally collapsed, crushing the people inside. Even so, new residents would come and take over the ruins, salvaging the iron and wood, and building shacks, stores, hash dens, and workshops for spray-painting, locksmithing, and metal-working in the clearing. Boss Galal, who ran the most famous hash den downtown—if not in the entire city including the suburbs—was the man whose lead they followed. And follow they did because Egyptians have a peculiar fondness for thuggish crooks, and many derive great pleasure from doing what they say and submitting to them. Maybe even going so far as to try to outdo one another in vying for their affection; maybe they do it to get on their good side, or maybe so they can count on their backing when something comes up. Boss Galal was the most famous safe-breaker in Egypt. Paroled from a life sentence, he was ready to gut any police officer who tried to get in his way, or keep him from earning a living, or who simply irritated him. The police were all scared of him so they just let him have his hash den, figuring that was better than him gutting anyone or cracking any safes. His hash den was really nice: it was clean and orderly and it felt like a coffeehouse with its proliferation of chairs and colored tablecloth-covered tables lined up in rows inside and outside the large shack, which was as big as a soccer pitch. There was a counter made of marble and tile that was fitted out with all the nicest cups, kettles, copper trays, ashtrays, and water pipes used exclusively for smoking molasses-steeped tobacco, in addition to the coconut bongs used just for smoking hash. The boys who worked there were relatively clean and good-tempered looking, but having a powerful and influential boss had made them rude and arrogant. They'd raise the price of each bowl from half a piaster to a piaster, which was double the price of other dens, and the price of a tea to two piasters, in order—so they claimed—to preserve a certain level of clientele and keep the lowlifes out. The Boss, owing to his tact and the experience of a commuted life sentence, had succeeded in attracting a select group of customers. Only the most respectable types who were most prone to look stylish and show off were in attendance: journalists, artists, public-sector grandees, businessmen, and the sons of wealthy Revolutionary Officers, who'd taken the place of the pashas' sons, and who liked to tip excessively from a supply of unknown provenance. This got them the best service, and that set them apart from everybody else. The rest of us had to wait for the boys to serve the beys, who liked to take their time. If you had a problem with it well— pardon the expression—but don't let the door hit you on the way out. A lot of serious hash smokers, including our group of friends, avoided Galal's den even if they were friends of his. They were bound to get the best service if they went to smoke when Galal was there, but during the day when he was fast asleep, they were captive to the whims of the malicious little bastards whose attention could only be got with money. The way our group saw it was that getting high in a common coffeehouse—or somewhere like a common coffeehouse—took half the fun out of it. It took longer for you to get to the stage of being properly stoned because the crowd made the smoking a lot slower. The bowls would come ten at a time no matter how big the group was, so each person would only get one bowl to smoke each round and by the time the next ten came and the water in the bong had been changed, and the coals broken up into smaller pieces because last round's rips were so weak, your high would've already worn off. But then if someone dared to tell the boy to hurry up or order another bowl, he'd be told off: patience is a virtue, and God helps those who wait, and the world hasn't flown away yet and it isn't going to, and there's a silver lining in every delay, and on down the list of the ever-ready, infuriating platitudes. The staff was all a bunch of no-good, disrespectful thugs. Plus, they always had the radio turned up as loud as possible and there was no hope of getting it turned down because every-one had the right to listen. At the same time, everyone had the right to talk, but with the radio at full blast, everyone had to shout. The racket alone guar-anteed that you'd end up coughing away the deepest hits and get a headache no matter how good the hash. It was all in Boss Galal's interest, of course: you could never get stoned so you'd just go on smoking and smoking. Serious hash smokers like us preferred to smoke in a no-frills hash den that was noth-ing like a coffeehouse, where even if they did serve tea and coffee, it was a service on the side—it could be canceled at any moment for any reason. The closer the den was to being like a cave or a crypt or a burrow or a hideaway, the more it improved the high and stimulated the imagination. It doubled a hash smoker's enjoyment to be sitting there—wherever he was—doing nothing but smoking hash, hemmed in by a lot of stimulating limitations. No-frills hash dens, like bars, didn't try to do anything else. As soon as the customer sat down, he'd get one set of bowls after the other with a steady fre-quency that didn't waste a minute. The workers all had specific tasks: there was one to clean out the bowls, one to pack them with tobacco, one to stoke the coals and break them up, one to change the water in the coconut bongs, and one—or more—to serve the customers. These guys would kneel down on the floor in front of the customers, holding the bong in one hand and pushing coals down on top of the bowl with the other to make sure the hits were strong. Because they depended on tips, they were the lowest paid of all.

Down past Ali Mango's

Off of Antikkhana Street, there was another way to get to Hakeem's den, but there was embarrassment to be had in that direction as well. Boss Ali Mango had a small store on the corner where he sold cigarettes, packaged sweets, and soft drinks, but it was all a front for his real business: dealing hashish and opium. Boss Ali Mango was a clever guy, but opium had made him thin and a succession of jails had chewed him up. He was famous across every far-flung Cairo neighborhood for being hyper-thorough when it came to his superb product. His specialty was a top-grade hash called 'Blue Powder.' He always stuck to the same variety and only ever did business with the same grower in Lebanon. He was constantly inspecting each crumb he sold, too, even when the customer was in a hurry and didn't really care. The problem with Ali Mango was that he'd suck your blood and pretend he was doing you a favor. He was—of course—insistent, crusty, and transparent, but he was also as smooth and as poisonous as a desert snake. He had a face the color of wormwood, and he was so frail and his face so devoid of any lifeblood that you almost couldn't see him. He had thick lips, rotting teeth, and a chronically dry throat from the fat, unfiltered Wings cigarettes that never left his lips. He had hawk eyes, too, and was always alert. Buried behind a glass counter adorned with jars of toffees, caramels, fondant bonbons, mints, gum, lollipops, firecrackers, and balloons, he'd spot one of us walking past on the sidewalk across the street. He'd reel you in with a somber and peremptory wave of his veiny arm and a smile like a crushed tomato that still managed to brim with hospitality, decency, generosity, and shiny promises as if he were about to give you good news or an expensive present. His smile would win you over, hooking you by the neck so that if you ever did try to get away, it'd hurt and you'd give up. You'd have to go say hello to him, Brother!—which was what he'd undoubtedly say—for no reason other than just to be polite; that was the lie you'd tell yourself anyway. "So I guess we only know each other when there's business to do, huh?," he'd ask. "Aren't we supposed to be men, fella?" As soon as he'd see you heading toward him, he'd get up, leaning on his crutch, and dart through the gap in the counter toward the red refrigerator that stood beside the cigarette display case outside the shop. Ignoring your protests that a treat was wholly unnecessary, he'd open it and move a slab of ice out of the way. Feeling to see which of the bottles were cold, he'd pull out the coldest one. In the blink of an eye, *chikk* . . . "Here you go, Bey. Drink up"—and as you took the bottle, he'd always add, "Drink up to cool down! Ha! It's as hot as fire today! May God protect us from the flames of hell." As you began to sip from the icy bottle, he'd rub his long fingers against the back of his ear and, in less than a moment, stretch his hand out toward you. On his thumb, there'd be a lick of opium smelling pungently of a freshness that was alluring and harrowing all at once, like the freshness of sin.

"Give me your mouth and take this kiss," he'd say.

The rumor among novice opium addicts was that soft drinks ruined the effect of opium, and Boss Ali Mango was always joking about how gullible they were, "God Bless the Prophet! What are they on about? There's nothing that can spoil honest-to-goodness opium, not even lemons!" You'd continue standing there in spite of yourself and try to think of a way out. Veterans like us would advise you—heads up, indeed!—that the longer you stood there, the more screwed you were because he was going to offer you a joint next, "This hash is brand new. You can't even buy it yet. May God bless you and help you get your hands on some! I wouldn't put it past Him." Working on advice you'd been given, you'd ask him—grudgingly, no doubt—for a quarter qirsh, or maybe even an eighth. You'd apologize for the paltriness of the order, saying something about straitened circumstances at the moment, and you were bound to add that you didn't like buying on credit and didn't believe in borrowing, not a cent. You had to be careful not to look persuadable or hesitant when you said it, because he'd do his best to confuse you with encouragement, "Don't worry about the money. Since when is money the only goddamn thing that matters? We only know each other because of money? What's up, fella? How much do you want?" He was certain his loan would be repaid because you had no choice but to smoke the hash in one of the dens in Maarouf, right under his nose, right in the Mayor of Maarouf's backyard as it were. Boss Ali Mango had all the hash dens under his thumb and he could get at them any time he felt like it. There was nothing to stop him popping up when you least expected, like a heart attack. Being forced to pay up or else being humiliated was as insupportable as it was insulting. If you ever did get made a fool of in a hash den, even just once—and especially if it were over money—you'd never ever be able to get your honor back, no matter how much money you spent. The real problem was that Ali Mango would sell you a quarter qirsh for forty piasters—cheap as can be—but at the same time, his ex-wife Umm Yahya would sell it for only twenty-five. And it was the same hash, maybe even a lot better. Umm Yahya was very generous, too: her hash looked reassuringly plentiful and made you feel that what you were getting really was a quarter qirsh with a little extra thrown in to be nice; you could easily get ten bowls out of it. But he—God help us—had a toxic touch and was always taking a little off the top of the quarter qirsh till it ended up the size of a shriveled, old fava bean, which he'd wrap up in a quarter of a sheet of cellophane in such a way that it was impossible to open up, unless you did it slowly after you'd left when there was no point in complaining or throwing a fit. All you could do was get angry about what'd happened, so the best thing was to appreciate the wisdom of those who say, "Don't push your luck and leave it in God's hands." And so, walking past Boss Ali Mango's stand was risky, awkward, and totally frowned upon.

Translated by Adam Talib

Yasser Abdel Hafez

from *In Celebration of Life*

ASHRAF BEY, THE CHIEF investigator who was responsible for security in our area, was a model of masculinity in a poor and ignorant neighborhood. He used to swagger around, showing off his black uniform that was topped with his well-kept muscles. Personal information about him and his life was unusually scarce, even for an officer who had been transferred from National Security because of a mistake for which he may have not been responsible. On his part, he sought to beef up the enigma, perhaps in order to protect himself and his family for he had made many enemies, especially because he did his job like a sheriff in cowboy movies. His arrogant stride suggested that he believed that the evil in the world had to be confronted with firmness and that people like him were the ones who could protect human civilization.

He was a man constructed of endless stories that were generated at night and circulated by day in a surprising manner as if he were supported by a media industry that was responsible for his image. Every resident in the neighborhood could tell you a different story. People always mentioned him in any gathering and each one of those produced its own appropriate set of stories: families would talk about his valor and his respect for lost values but in the evening, during all-male gatherings, the silenced aspects would come out. Some would talk about his homosexuality that, from their point of view, explained his excessive cruelty in dealing with the riffraff and in extracting their confessions, a cruelty that focused on their sexual organs. Women—his mistresses from our neighborhood and others—reported otherwise: they spoke about his virility.

These tales kept a dwindling tradition of storytelling alive and reflected the desire for a master, a hero for people, before whom they could kneel every time he walked through the street, careful not to raise their eyes but wanting at the same time to see him.

What has God put in our souls for them to be so broken? Why should there always be someone who has the final word, whose raised hand would silence everyone?

Everyone remembered the details of the day when he arrested three miserable creatures who were burglars. He waited for them on the street when they were on their way out of one of the houses. He must have smiled at the alarmed and horrified look on their faces. They say he relies on the element of surprise. The added details to the story are beyond imagination but it is certain that one of them was wounded by bullets that totally handicapped him for life, just because he tried to resist. The others were rewarded for surrendering: a real hot beating and a select repertoire of insults that secret agents master well.

But these stories are nothing in comparison to the story of the most famous cocaine dealer in Cairo that he destroyed. The Abu Id family—led by Amm Nasr, then his son, Mursi—had monopolized the market for a long time. Amm Nasr had struggled to attain any kind of status in society after a train cut off his arm during one of his morning trips to work. Almost overnight he was transformed into Abu Id—'the one-armed man'—responsible for a woman and a number of kids who had never been taught not to scream when hungry. He found himself on the street surrounded by pity and condescension because he was not a civil servant in this country. As Amm Nasr became fully aware, your weakness is a curse that you carry on your head all the time.

How did he begin his career in the forbidden, the haram, as he likes to call it? No one has a concrete answer. But Mazhar, who likes to philosophize, says that he was one of those Egyptians who had been brought up on melodramatic films. So if people wronged him, he felt compelled to wrong them back. He also said that his career in the dope business started out of financial need.

His persistence in the business was only a coincidence brought about by the fame he gained from this newly acquired title, perfectly suited for an old-time criminal. This explanation was convincing to us and, as Mazhar's friends, we applauded his analytic abilities.

Indeed, Abu Id, the one-armed man, was a striking example of the ability of Egyptian cinema and art to deform its audience. Every year during the holy month of Ramadan he would stay in the mosque and weep and then confess the crimes he had committed over the years to the people of the neighborhood after the long tarawih prayers in the evening. He did not want to tell anyone his secrets but he would speak to the heavens in a very loud voice because one of the respected sheikhs had once told him: raise your voice in prayer so that God may forgive you. That's why everyone was keen on being in the mosque during Ramadan.

If the believers tried to organize an interesting and unusual campaign on television to urge people to pray in the mosque they would not find any better than Abu Id to be the star, for the man did not belong to that bland school that represented a true believer as a calm, smiling, modest, angelic man. Rather, he relied on his intuition: he behaved in the mosque as he did on the street and at home. Perhaps if he had had some education, he would have defended his style by saying that he was not schizophrenic.

Amm Nasr's performance during Ramadan rivaled the soap operas and riddle programs that are aired during the holy month. His oratory talent was a very attractive element. It was difficult for people to resist listening to him when he addressed his God: "What could I have done? You are my witness. I went to everyone in search of work but who would hire someone with one arm if those who have both cannot find food. For the sake of your Prophet Muhammad, forgive me."

The Imam of the mosque regretted that he had counseled him to pray aloud, because the size of the audience increased beyond the capacity of the mosque itself. People who had nothing to do with prayer seized the opportunity to win both earthly and heavenly gains: rival drug dealers who wanted to listen to the man's secrets and kids who tried not to giggle so as not to ruin the daily show. The decisive moment was when George the electrician and his son came to the mosque in order to learn about Islam. The sheikh tried to end the farce by suggesting to the man that God was not deaf and didn't need for him to raise his voice so high. But Abu Id got upset, especially when he saw the sarcastic smiles that surrounded him, so he yelled at the sheikh, "If I were in your father's house you could kick me out and if I were in your mother's you could hit me with your shoe."

Amm Nasr, which is the name no one calls him by, is a romantic figure produced by Abdel Nasser's regime. He did not surrender to the temptation of crime by giving up on all principles. He still debated the fate of the nation after Nasser's death during his sessions that expanded to include famous artists, thanks to his son. He complained constantly to his customers about his sons, who had practically taken over the business because they believed in nothing but money: Dealing in drugs, dear sirs, doesn't mean that we should become criminals.

The man was a real magnet for celebrity customers. They would begin arriving at his building after midnight, the entire first floor was for the powerful people who, after they'd had their drug hit, would spend some time talking to him. He was a real treasure: he inspired journalists with ideas and issues to write about; his stories to scriptwriters and filmmakers were never ending; and his jokes entertained a huge theater audience every night. The constant rows between him and Mursi al-Baghl, his eldest son, were an additional source of entertainment. He was a handicapped man with a small body and his son was huge, ugly, and dumb: a laughable couple. The father and son slowly realized, perhaps even unconsciously, that the customers enjoyed their relationship so they worked on it and made sure to add new episodes every night.

Mursi, the eldest son, announced after some preliminary steps that he would take over his father's business. He carried out his decision by isolating the father in one of the apartments in the building where his daughters-in-law both served him and barred him from leaving. He was no longer the prodigal son as his father had described him; he was now protecting himself and his family. "The old man has gone nuts. He wants to turn us in." That's how he responded to the questions of the customers. Many could not blame him especially in the light of the father's latest action that left no room for cooperation: he had consulted the sheikh of the mosque about his repentance when he felt that his end was near. The sheikh had counseled that he cleanse himself in two stages: first he had to get rid of his dirty money and corrupt business before he could proceed to sealing his repentance by going on pilgrimage and remaining there for a while to pray until he received the sign that his repentance had been accepted. The sheikh explained that he could not specify a particular sign since that was beyond the knowledge he possessed. No one knew how the repentance plan got to Mursi, who quickly terminated it not only by imprisoning his father but by threatening the sheikh inside his mosque, "If anybody comes near my father, I'm gonna screw him!" The sheikh knew full well that Mursi had terrifying strength and that he feared nothing: not God, nor the power of the state.

In no time at all, Amm Nasr disappeared from sight. Sometimes passersby would hear screams coming from the third floor in the cocaine building: "Mursi, you son of a bitch, let me out! Let me out, you fag!" But this was a call in the desert where only silent, stately cactus grew.

"The state cannot scare a man," was one of Mursi's important axioms. It accompanied his new reign as if he were laying the foundational philosophy of governance. And so it was, for in the world of crime you have to be straightforward. But when Mursi made this statement, aiming it sarcastically at Lieutenant Ashraf in particular, he knew full well that his strength was not enough to protect him. So, he started bribing all the civil servants with whom he did business, starting with the detectives who kept an open eye on the movements and times of occasional raids on the neighborhood. Quickly the parameter of his acquaintances that received gifts and sealed envelopes widened to the extent that people said he had reached key figures in the ministry. There was nothing intelligent about what he did; he was just responding to the changing times, for his father had been inspired in his own schemes and style by the local films of Farid Shawqi and Mahmoud al-Miligi. But he was brought up during the American era where the only rule was the rule of might. His constitution was based on Mafia movies: he adapted the scripts to his own environment without relinquishing the basic principles.

The conflict between al-Baghl and Ashraf Bey was inevitable. We impatiently awaited it. I, in particular, wished for it in order to get rid of Mursi's heavy gaze that was a subtle threat against my rebellion, which I demonstrated by ignoring him. The only reason he kept away from me was that one of his brothers had been my schoolmate. Even though he was something of a retard, I made a point of befriending him especially when Mursi was within view, parading his muscles in front of all.

We were almost certain of the rumor, "Mursi feeds Ashraf Bey. Otherwise why did he ignore him and spend his nights chasing insignificant creatures from that world, when Mursi not only mocked him verbally but made public his merchandise to the extent that we imagined he would open a shop to sell the stuff! 'Meditation Supermarket for all kinds of drugs and pills' and in a smaller font: 'Al-Hamdu li l-Allah we do not sell alcohol.'"

No one expected that the representative of state security was planning quietly, patiently, and cunningly to get Mursi. Maybe that's why people called him 'Sadat' until it became his title, and his name 'Ashraf' disappeared completely. One colorless afternoon my mother woke me up with a troubled voice: state security forces had surrounded the house. For years I will remember this sentence; it never went away. I think the first thing I will say to God when I meet him is, "Did you see the national security forces when they surrounded the house?"

Translated by Samia Mehrez

Hamdi Abu Golayyel

A Dog with No Tail

I Keep The Files Stored In My Head, My Friend

I smoked the joint. It was strong. I say that about every joint I smoke—that it's strong, that it's "good stuff"—but this one seemed particularly potent. One piece of hash makes five perfect cigarettes. If I'd been with friends I would've made eight, even ten, but instead I made just three. Convinced myself it would help me think about the novel. I rolled each one differently and told myself each time: I'll start with this one.

I always seem to start with the weakest, the worst. Some flaw in my make-up means I never do better than good endings. I lack the trick of picking the best things first. If I have two books, I'll start with the one I think inferior. When I sit down to eat I plan things out so that my last mouthful is the morsel I crave. I'm one of those people who saves the choicest cuts till last. This joint was the weakest. Number two in the rolling sequence. I'd rolled one before it and one after it.

As I made the first joint I'd been dying for the hash: craving the little crumbs as they trickled into the mouth of the cigarette. For the second (the middle) joint, I was overcome by sudden circumspection. I was, let's say, tight-fisted. It's not like falling off a log, after all. No mean feat for a man to get a bit of space to himself and start rolling.

The last joint was pure hash. The heaviest hash crumbs get lost in the mix and end up being poured into the last joint.

But this one would do the job. Reducing the amount of tobacco is a good idea. It was the sort of stuff that left you feeling at peace with yourself, that the world still lay before you. The fact that I'm currently wandering around my room is the most overt symptom of my enjoyment of quality product.

Thoughts shake me nearly to pieces.

At times like these I picture my life as files stored away in my head. Sometimes they unfold one by one, but sometimes they all spill open at once and childhood memories are jumbled up with the image of the last face I've seen. Right now, I'm seeing myself in Shubra. I was twenty, just returned from a stint working in Libya, and employed as a manual laborer while I looked for a job. I lived in a room in Ain Shams with four guys from the village. I was working for a demolition contractor. No, not demolition: demolition and construction.

Translated by Robin Moger

Raouf Musad

Ithaka

SHEEN USED TO LIKE going to church and listening to sermons, especially afternoon ones when shadows on the ancient icons blended with the murmurs of prayer and incense. He didn't like the dry and empty Protestant churches that had no icons or sermons or incense, nor did he like the Catholic churches, which he said intimidated him with their self-aggrandizing architecture and excessive gold. He sought refuge in Coptic Orthodox churches where he would sit in a remote corner. Once I asked him, "Do you feel guilty?" He answered, "Why, if God has created me this way?" He said that the only guilt he felt was toward his fiancée whom destiny had hurled into his arms. I said, "Don't worry, I'm married too and I get by both ways." He was afraid that the engagement would fall through or that he would be discovered on his wedding night. I tried to calm him down and said, "Just look at me. I'm married and I have kids and every thing's alright."

There was an old church in Maadi where he liked to be alone. For him going to church was like yoga for me. I do yoga on a regular basis and it helps me achieve some spiritual and intellectual clarity. But surprisingly, I don't like churches. I admire prayer out in the open like Muslims. During my bus trips to the desert, I would see them performing their ablutions with or without the little water available. They would flatten the ground with their bare feet if they did not have mats or prayer rugs. I consider their mode of prayer a salute to the universe and to nature. *Sheen* who was a non-Christian knew a lot about churches and preferred the older, simpler ones, those of the oppression in old Egypt: Sitt Dimyana Church (the Copts call her Saint Dumyana). I prefer the title 'Sitt' (Lady). You enter the church by going down a flight of steps that lead to narrow stone vaults. There was another faraway church that was almost empty, near the hashish joint where we used to go in Deir al-Malak by the old church of the monastery. I used to sit in the hashish joint run by a Copt from Sohag. When he found out that I was from Upper Egypt he asked where from. I said, "Asyut" and he said, "The best people!" "And yourself, mu'allim?" "From Sohag." I said, "The best people!" Sometimes he would offer to pay for a dozen rounds of hashish and sometimes I would settle my bill later, depending on circumstances. After presenting their supplications to the Archangel, visitors of the Upper Egyptian monastery would seek refuge from the Saints and God's unobserved commandments in the hashish joint. For a while they would forget the Day of Judgment. I would eavesdrop and I would envy them. They would lie and swear by the Virgin. Anything goes; they had no sense of guilt.

There wasn't much sex between *Sheen* and I. We were more friends than lovers. We would go to the office and chat or remain silent, listening to music and getting high. We would escape from our noisy homes, the busy streets, and subtle or open gossip and be together. The reason why I broke off the relationship, as I discovered later, was my great fear that I would open up a door I didn't know how or wouldn't want to shut. Now, when I think back, I try to understand what it was that I was afraid of. I cannot recall the reason. Sheer madness. It seems that social pressures, even when subtle, have an effect: just like drops of water that can tear down a mountain. Later, I got a divorce and I roamed the world like a vagabond then I came back to prove that the earth—bitch that it is—is round.

Translated by Samia Mehrez

Yahya Taher Abdullah

from "A Tale with a Moral"
in A Mountain of Green Tea

IT IS RELATED THAT an astute fellow of our time, who was poor, bald, and homeless, chose the company of the dead, and there he subsisted on the bread of charity, and there he took up his abode, for however long he might live.

When the poor, bald fellow had found all the roofed tombs occupied by the living, he chased away the mangy stray dog and took possession of its place: a hole with a narrow entrance which held the bones of a dead person.

"The dead person was without doubt someone of little consequence."

Saying which, he dug out the earth, soiled by the dog's running sores, also the bones of the unknown dead person, while the stray dog barked but didn't have the courage to take any action.

The poor fellow with his astute mind went off eastward and westward:

* People are in grades, animals are in grades, tombs are in grades, and those who live in tombs are in grades. Do grades continue on after death, O unknown one? Tell me, O you who have known your grade among the dead.

* Humans and animals, man and dog, a bald one and a mangy one, a dumb stray and a reasoning one. What's the value of reason, O mangy one? And you, O bald one, have you the answer?

* What is it that has so emaciated the two of them, has so tormented them, has so deprived them of sleep, has so violently dealt with them in the world?

* Has he who measures out the world two different measures by which he apportions? Why? May no good come to him, may his life be cut short.

The bald, astute man made a bundle of the knowledge he had acquired and tucked it away in a far corner of his consciousness lest he be accused, he who was knowledgeable of the military era he lived in, of profanity, or dissension. Then, making a pillow of his arms, he lay down inside the hole of the tomb, with the mangy stray dog having already beaten him to it and lain down on the mound of earth and bones outside the hole.

The bald man saw himself urinate and drinking his urine, and the bald man saw himself relieving himself and eating his excrement. The bald man jumped up from sleep in dismay, with a body that was cold though the days were those of the height of summer.

He said, "It's good to be in darkness and Allah is He who veils. Disobedience by Allah's servant means imprisonment or execution," and he immersed himself in the task of ridding himself of the knowledge he had acquired. When he had erased it from his consciousness, he had a sensation of peace and security, the comfort of peace, the gentle breeze of peace, the sweet taste of peace.

He stretched out his hands, gently and lovingly, and took the mangy dog in his arms and, bringing it down into the hole, he embraced it, and the two of them slept with an unsullied consciousness that knew no rancor, no distinctions, no demanding or prerogatives, and they opened their eyes only with the rising of the day's sun.

Today is one of compassion.

And the day for compassion is everyone's day, the day of the dead and the living, the dead being shown compassion through alms from a living person of means to a living person in need. The dead (*in the name of Allah the Merciful, the Compassionate*) (the phrases in parentheses are quotations from the Qur'an) are in the belly of the tombs: sons and husbands and mothers and fathers and grandmothers and grandfathers who complain not of hunger or of thirst, and children (*thanks be to Allah, Lord of the worlds*) who scream not for a toy or a breast.

And the living (Say: *I take refuge in the Lord of people*) are above the tombs, locked in a vocal combat: "A little charity prevents a big calamity" . . . "O precious one, would that it were I" . . . peep-peep . . . "O adornment of youth" . . peep . . . "Blind and crippled" . . . (*Did We not gladden your heart for you?*) "I am not asking for charity from Umm Agrama" . . . "For the sake of Allah, O beneficent" . . . peep-peep . . . "You passed on, O husband, and left me to degradation" . . . peep . . . (*Alif, Lam, Meem, this is the Book of which there is no doubt.*)

And the living (Say: *I take refuge with the Lord of Daybreak from the evil of what He has created*) are:

* Women: weeping, wailing, keening, cheek-slapping.

* And men: in sorrow more steadfast, in the matter of desire more frank.

* And a woman in all her situations is with waist and breasts and eyelashes and buttocks and vulva.

* And a vendor of mizmars, a stranger who has come from some distant place, with a hand and a pocket and a mizmar and a mouth and a heart. He piped to yearnings and mutual touchings and mutual bickerings and to dating and the meeting of eyes and to the turning away of faces and the

acceptance of the back of the neck—for the day of compassion is the day of males and females.

* And children, they are split up: a joyful group that blows on the *mizmars* and a joyful group that watches those who are blowing on the *mizmars*, and a happy group that hops about, and a happy group that claps, and a happy minority that brushes the dust off new shoes and shuns crowded places lest new clothes be sullied

* And Qur'an reciters and beggars with bodily defects and the guardians of tombs on a memorable day, for the days of the world are long and drawn out and the days of compassion are few and limited.

* And an astute poor man, who did not crouch in his hole, awaiting the family of an unknown dead person, in whom there is no benefit and from whom no benefit will come, but who roamed around the tombs, exhibiting his deformity until dusk had vanished and darkness had descended. Then he went back to his hole, having obtained by way of alms: dates enough to fill the palms of both hands twice over, six piasters, two pastries made with cooking butter, milk, sesame seeds and sugar, four pastries made with sugar and milk, and ten pastries colored with turmeric and containing neither cooking butter, sugar, nor milk.

He stayed in the hole for two days and part of a day until his provisions ran out, then he set off to see his neighbor, who was living in the next-door tomb to him. After greetings were exchanged, they made each other's acquaintance and conversation ensued. The astute poor man understood: that tombs, like houses, should be entered by their doors, and that the big boss was named the Pasha because he lived in the Pasha's tomb and that it was he who uttered the first word and he who had the right to the third word, his the hand that gave and his the hand that withheld. His mind was put at rest when he learned that everyone welcomed his presence among them, so he took courage and asked his neighbor for food. His neighbor, however, excused himself in terms that were not embarrassing, saying:

"I have an illness and do light work, my exertion being limited, and wages here are in like measure to one's work. Go to the Pasha and ask for work and you will find it. With us, O bald one, everything is worked out and taken into consideration; no one envies and no one is envied. The work is apportioned between us and law and order is demanded and, thanks be to Allah, there is law and order, so be not frightened and be not sad but, putting your trust in Allah, take yourself off to the Pasha. There you will find your salvation and there you will know exactly where you stand."

It was in a tomb that was like a palace, in fact it was a palace: it had air-conditioning, a refrigerator, television and radio, its floor was carpeted and its ceiling painted. The Pasha was sitting on a chair in the midst of his friends, respected of all and sundry, with smiling face and robust body clad in colored silk.

"Greetings, bald one," said the Pasha.

"Greetings to you, Pasha," replied the bald one.

Said the Pasha: "The one with eyes to see has read your record. We take precautions but we are not afraid. Look, bald one," and the Pasha turned a dial on a machine and the front of the machine lit up and pictures moved about on it, and the bald one saw the bald one urinating and plucking out the hair from under his armpits and screwing it up and throwing it to the mangy dog in play, and then there was the bald one striving to expel poisonous wind from his backside.

The Pasha stopped the procession of pictures and said, "The best of talk is that which is brief. You were not a spy for the Robber, and do not become one. Return to your hole and be as the beast that keeps guard over its prey. The summer is easy and you will overcome the winter by wearing animal fur; if the rain comes, then the roof of your neighbor—who guards you as you guard him—will protect you. Be the eye and the ear but be not the tongue, and do not ask questions. Strengthen yourself to keep awake by taking opium. Your food will come to you at the proper times, and all your desires will be answered. Work is work, O bald one. Take yourself off, O guardian."

Yes, he is the guardian of a hole whose exterior is dust and bones and whose interior is hashish and opium, cocaine and heroin, Max injections and LSD.

The bald guardian, who had chased away the mangy one and shut out its friendship from his heart, with robust body and robust, astute mind, as he stayed on his own in his watchfulness and silence, thanks to sucking opium, was a well of secret knowledge, being well-informed about what the rulers kept buried deep in their earthenware jars:

* The military Hashish Smoker grasps affairs with a hand of iron, strikes with iron, brands with iron, hangs on suspicion, and the men of the tombs, who are under the Pasha's orders, are his men.

* And the Robber who lives in security under the shadow of the Hashish Smoker has gathered wealth for himself, and his supporters have increased in number and have spread like the reaping locust, openly proclaiming insurrection, and he may gain possession of the dust of the ground and shortly sit upon its hill.

* And the Pimp lives under the shadow of the Hashish Smoker and declares his loyalty to him all the time, but he is of an evil nature and is playing a double game.

The astute bald one weighed up with a jeweler's balance the strength of the opponents, and it was clear to him that the Robber's scale was the heavier. This would mean the waning of the big boss's power, or his being lopped off, and the imprisonment of his followers, except for those who had declared their loyalty right away. The storms of the following considerations played about in the mind of the astute bald one:

If I declare my loyalty to the Robber—after his success—I shall have saved both body and soul; and if the Robber's action fails, my soul will be of little importance and my body will be tortured. In dawdling lies indecision, which is to be despised from all angles. Fate has envied you, O bald one—or shall cowardice be the food of the indolent, the easily satisfied and the degraded till the day of Judgment? In gambling, there may be the loss of one's assured daily bread and of a body with a bald head or the winning of the wealth that lies under the bald one's body. You could, O bald one, achieve the Pasha's title, who is betting on the military Hashish Smoker, when you risk yourself for your people, the inhabitants of the tombs, and thus would I gain his palace and the expensive things it contains, and I would seat his women on my lap. The days go round and wealth goes round among people, and he who is strong triumphs. Gamble, O bald one, gamble.

The Pasha, who has for some time been burying his bald head under a large turban of Indian silk, after anointing it with French unguents of delightful fragrance that are beneficial to his sores, took off his turban and, folding it up, thrust it into a box inlaid with mother-of-pearl and ivory and kept it as a memento of his arduous battle. Bare-headed, he advanced upon the man who was wearing a suit so that he might put on him the crown of government, after which he returned and seated himself on the throne of government, guarded by soldiers, and listened to the suit-wearer reading out from a book the ceremonials of coronation and teachings of the crown:

"O bald one, O Ibn Habis, O bald one,

You, if your brother falls, will fall."

"Who are the Yankees?"

"Some fools overtaken by the corrupt belief that the Yankee is comparable to death in that both rob you of your shadow. This, by Allah, is not giving him his due, for the Yankee has a great shadow—which death has not—and the Yankee obscures with his shadow all other shadows, though the shadows remain shadows in one great shadow—which death does not do. The Yankee is of us, is in us, is through us."

"Why were the Yankee men strong?"

"The élite are a minority, possessors of wealth, and wealth is a strength. The elected are people of insight and they are in greater numbers than the élite, though it is the élite who find out the blood group of the elected and mix it with some blood of their own type until the body of the elected becomes sound: a sound mind in a sound body."

"Are there any other differences between the élite and the elected?"

"The élite are élite and the elected elected—the differences are evident to everyone with eyes to see. To expatiate further would be helpful: a truncheon isn't a neutron bomb, nor a fridge a pitcher."

"And what is the difference between the Yankee and his supporters?"

"All is one and one is all. There is reason in being far from reason, and there is reason in being near to reason, and daring is better than fear, and he who has seized the opportunity has reaped numerous benefits—and now listen to this tale with a moral: It is related that an astute fellow of our time, who was poor, bald, and homeless, chose the company of the dead. Over there was his home and over there he was nourished by bread given in charity, and over there he became enlightened as to what had made him emaciated and what had tortured him and deprived him of Sleep and what had so roughly dealt with him in that world that has two ways of measuring out . . . ."

Translated by Denys Johnson-Davies

Bahaa Abdelmegid

from *Sleeping with Strangers*

THESE DAYS YOU WILL see Basim downtown, sitting at the al-Bustan Coffeeshop, or holding hands with a girl, maybe Japanese or American, or a tourist from somewhere. You can also see him in a perfume store, or in a tourist shop that sells papyrus. He looks the seller in the eye to make him understand that he has a female client with him who is looking to buy, and so he should jack up the price of his wares so that Basim can get his cut of it. You'll see him wearing clothes that look like what foreigners are wearing, their formal outfits and casual styles. You'll see his face, radiant like the faces of foreigners. He walks like they do, too—with energy, overconfidence, and wonder. He smiles with confidence and experience.

At the end of the night, he will go to one of the dark, narrow side streets in the Kom al-Samn district to buy heroin. It's to help him relax, and to sleep deeply. He will dim the light in his room as much as possible. That way it won't remind him of the neon light the Americans used to inflict on him as a kind of torture, until he confessed to beating his wife. He will open all the windows in the biting cold of winter, in order to see the stars. In the daytime, he will intentionally look at the sun he was deprived of seeing in prison. He recalls Mado and how he preached to him of salvation. A year after he comes back from America, he will come to rely on a Jewish Canadian girl named Judy, whom he came to know in Sharm al-Sheikh after she had visited Israel. After they had met several times, she claimed that she was his blood relation, since Arabs and Jews come from one race and are cousins. She declared that the reason she clung to him was that she saw in a vision that the Adam>s rib from which she was created was the same as the one that belonged to an Egyptian; that he had come to America to look for her, but failed to find her there because she wasn't American. And so she came to him to complete his missing part, and to search for the meaning of the east between the legs of an Egyptian man whose semen might grant her the essence of eternal life.

She is the daughter of a wealthy Canadian who owned a number of businesses. Basim invites her to live with him and she welcomes the idea; although the apartment is hardly suitable for living in, she will say it's not important. She will buy some indoor plants to give him a feeling of living in a natural forest, and she will hang on the walls a picture of a beautiful girl carrying a child in her arms, or a piece of carpet she bought from an old man in the Tentmaker's district, which will breathe life into the apartment. In one corner, you will see some English-language novels by Stephen King or John Grisham, or a novel with an old jacket by Charles Dickens, *David Copperfield,* or Jane Austen's *Pride and Prejudice.* And from the current era, you will find a single Arabic novel, Alaa Al Aswany's *The Yacoubian Building.*

You will find a small cat which will grow to full size over the course of the few times you visit him. He will tell you that he bought it at the Friday Souk in the Sayyida Aisha neighborhood, and that Judy took pity on it, being so thin and emaciated, and that she treated it, especially in its sensitive spots, and fed it until it grew bigger. She is afraid for its safety from the male cats that lie in wait for it on the staircase. Basim will tell you that he knows for certain it isn't a purebred Siamese cat, but is a mixed breed. He doesn't keep the cat from coming in and out, although he had made a square-shaped iron door for her. The door had another benefit for him, as protection for his empty apartment against thieves. When Judy commented that it looked like a prison door, he said, "Life is one big prison."

She will pay the rent for the apartment, which has no furniture other than an old sofa that his mother had let him borrow, and a filthy mattress covered with semen, bloodstains, and sweat from long nights when foreign girls who came for different reasons slept on it. The apartment is lit by fifty-watt bulbs. She will buy him a Volkswagen, and she will pay his electricity and water bills, and pay the rent for him for the previous year and the next. She will go with him to meet tourists and share in his profits, but woe unto him if he should have sex with another woman. She will think about having a baby one day, but she is afraid of giving birth to twins because her mother gave birth to fraternal twins, of which she is one. She will be very happy about being friends with Nadir. She will say that he is romantic, and that girls will cheat on him a lot because he is so nice and easygoing. She will say he is a genius and he will make a great writer because of his sensitivity. She will go with Basim after Nadir pulls some strings for them so they can work in the Auberge Hotel in Fayoum: Basim in reception, and Judy as head of cleaning services. Nadir will also serve as a witness to their urfi marriage, after the hotel's manager said it would be necessary to smooth the way for them to reside and work in the hotel, and so that the Jews and Arabs could reconcile with each other with this marriage.

Translated by Chip Rossetti

Mohamed al-Fakharani

from *An Interval for Bewilderment*

Hussein
You went into Orphanidis only once to buy a bottle of 'Amprator Brandy' as a present for Hilal for no particular reason. The forty-year-old salesman treated you with respect so you felt safe. You walked quietly out of the shop

and strolled along the street. You did not hide the 'Amprator Brandy' in the folds of your clothes; you did not run or feel anxious. A couple of meters away from Orphanidis you ran into Sharnoubi standing near Cinema Rivoli. The size of his wooden rectangle had increased. It was now filled with videotapes and CDs, secret ointments in small tin boxes in the corner of the rectangle, a mobile phone in his hand.

You walk on for another couple of meters and you hit the Cave de Korintous liquor store: a small, faded glass window behind which a few brands with hardly legible price tags were lined up. The store is known for carrying the brand of "The Red Greek Soldier," which is hard to find elsewhere. Inside, the bottles are lined up without any order on worn-down wooden tables.

You continue on 26th of July Street until the intersection with Talaat Harb Street. The À l'Américaine coffee shop is to your right across the street from another liquor store:

Vignobles Giancus

You notice that the store has been renovated; the sign outside is clearer and well-lit. You move on, leaving the garment stores behind in the dimmer light . . . .

You continue on Talaat Harb Street until you reach the statue of Muhammad Talaat Harb when you find yourself confronted with several choices: Mahmoud Basyouni Street to your right, to your left Sabri Abu Alam Street or Qasr al-Nil Street that runs parallel to Talaat Harb that stretched ahead in front of you. You notice Groppi's in front of you; it opens onto both Mahmoud Basyouni and Qasr al-Nil.

Hussein
You love those streets. After you drink Codiphan with the gang, you take a break, wash up, and hit on girls. You put on your clean outfit and you go downtown. You go to a movie, you follow girls around, you walk gingerly behind them; you prefer science fiction movies that are hard to come by.

You choose to continue on Talaat Harb because it takes you directly to Tahrir Square. You get to Cinema Metro to your left on Talaat Harb; a couple of meters away you find Cinema Miami, the Talaat Harb Mall, fast food stores. As you walk, you see young girls selling tissue paper. You suspect that two of them are sisters because they look alike. One of them has the tissue paper in front of her, a copybook in her lap, a school book and a pencil; her old cheap school bag is beside her.

You verify that the girls are sisters when you see their thirty-year-old mother waving at them from across the street with her newborn in her arms and a bag full of tissue paper packets.

When Talaat Harb leads you into Tahrir Square you find yourself in front of Kentucky Fried Chicken . . . .

This is the work zone of "the fag with a license". . . .

Fawzi

He is around forty, somewhat big, with masculine features. When he comes into the coffee shop with his cardboard box one of your friends points at him and says, "This guy is a fag." You will not believe it but you will reconsider when he comes up to greet you with a soft, high-pitched voice that will encourage you to look straight into his eyes. You will see that deep watery purple and the line of kohl on his lower lid. He smiles and looks at you for a moment to find out if you're interested.

Fawzi might surprise you with a direct question. Quickly he tries to logically convince you that he didn't mean what you thought and got upset about.

Once he asked you, Hussein.

He asked you directly as he had done with Hilal.

You still fear that purple in his wide eyes and his soft voice.

Fawzi made you uncomfortable initially because your ideas about homosexuals can be summed up in their being more like evil spirits, closer to vampires or madmen or a mix of both. It had never occurred to you that they can be unthreatening and peaceful to a great extent, until the armies of ants start moving under their skin, pinching their bodies, collecting at one spot and pinching it incessantly so that they are possessed with a desire to destroy themselves and the whole world.

Fawzi grabs a chair and sits down next to you the first time you see him. It's not a problem since your friends know him. He begins with a dirty but smart joke and a funny story about a slut. He tells it in a low voice. You laugh because he is really funny and witty. He moves to give you five but you do not open your hand to him. He puts sugar in your tea and stirs quietly. He rubs his knee against yours. You move yours away. He tries again, and again, and again. You like his insistence but you also find it disgusting. Maybe you can play on his desire: you cunningly leave him your knee, wanting him to think that you are seriously considering it. He moves his knee away. He giggles because he was sure from the very beginning that you were not into this.

He asks you one more time in your ear, "Do you want meat?"

When you remain silent for a couple of seconds he produces his license from the bottom of his cardboard box and says, "I'm an old time peddler."

That's why they call him "the fag with a license."

Translated by Samia Mehrez

Essam Youssef

A ¼ Gram

THE ACADEMIC YEAR BEGAN, and, as usual, I did not go to university. Every now and then, I met my neighbors who lived in the nearby buildings. When they saw me, they insisted that we share some hashish gathering. They knew that I traveled to America often, and that I spent time with friends between Dokki (another suburb of Cairo) and Mohandiseen. One of these neighbors was a police officer called Hossam. I did not meet him often, but whenever I did, we shared some hashish. On one of those days, I met my friend Sherif, the king of dens, who had started using brown sugar regularly. He surprised me by asking,

"Do you know what happened to Hossam?"

"What happened?"

"He's been fired."

"Man, no. Why?"

"He was on a mission to Suez, and he bought brown sugar."

"You're kiddin'? Hossam uses brown sugar?"

"Of course, he's been using for a long time. The dealer out there ripped them off and gave them fake brown sugar."

"And?"

"Hossam took out his pistol and fired, and Suez turned upside down. The chief security officer found out, and of course Hossam was fired."

"What did his father do?"

"Nothing. What could he possibly do?"

From this conversation, I found out that Hossam used brown sugar. Days passed until one day I saw Hossam sitting in his car with his girlfriend Doua'. During a long conversation, I blurted out,

"Shouldn't you have told me that you use brown sugar?"

"Who told you?"

"I found out. This can't be a secret forever? Tell you what: let's shoot up together."

"Do you have money?"

"I do. How much do you want?"

"Let me take care of it this time. Get in."

I got into the car, was introduced to Doua', and we talked,

"Hi. How are you?"

"Hi. This is the first time we've met."

Hossam said, "This is Salah. He is either in America or with his friends in Mohandiseen and Dokki. I knew you must be a shooter. It shows. But because you always disappear, I didn't notice you doing it. How could you go to America and not be a junkie? That's not even an option."

"For your information, there is no brown sugar in America. It's all coke and marijuana."

"And what's coke like?"

"Nice, but not like brown sugar. Brown sugar is nasty and a son of a . . . . And where are we going?"

"We're almost there. A nearby deli. Poisonous brown sugar. This is Doua's route. Tell him about it, Doua'."

"She is called Om Sayed, in Gayara. There is a black door over there, if it is closed, they're open; if the door is open they're closed."

"Wow! Awesome system!"

Hossam asked me, "Where do you get the stuff, Salah?"

"Frankly, I don't buy, but my friends do from places like Boulac or Kit Kat. Tell me, exhaust pipes or needles?"

"Oh, no! You're ancient. Needles, ma'lem."

"What are all those parked cars? Clearly, Om Sayed is obviously a hit."

It was the first time for me to shoot up with Hossam and his friend Doua'. Hossam parked the car on a quiet street, and in less than five minutes, he prepared all our needs: lemon, needles, a coffee cup from the glove compartment, and a bottle of mineral water which was next to me on the backseat of the car. It was the first time I had used brown sugar with a female. Obviously, there was affection between her and Hossam. They were overwhelmed with feelings of love and tenderness after shooting up. Hossam started talking: so and so shoots up, and so does what's his name, and so on. Dozens. Sherif has just come out of Switzerland.

These facts blew me away and so I said, "How tragic! We are talking about more than ten guys on the same block."

"This is not all. Even what's his name, doesn't he also sell the stuff? In small quantities, though. But this brown sugar is good. He buys it from the Bedouins living in Suez."

This was how I found out about a new place that sold brown sugar.

I went back to the group at the university. Every now and then, I met Rico, Hussein, and Mido. Baha' appeared after he had spent about two months in Switzerland, I mean, the hospital. Of course his health was much better, and he declared his new point of view, "I understand the system: not to shoot up every day. Once a week is enough or once every ten days. This will pass. Otherwise, it'll be down hill." . . .

On Thursday night, at the beginning of the month in the winter, I was twenty-one years old. After a couple of joints and beers, I went out. At the elevator, I found Mido and Zoni together and hurriedly said,

"Hey Mido? I was just on my way to see you."

"We beat you to it. How've you been?"

"You know how Thursday is Satan's birthday. A couple of joints, and a couple of beers, and so on. Tell me, what will we do? The Jackies? Or al-Baron? What's the plan?"

"Neither. We're going to worship."

"Come again, Mido? Are you going to beg or what?"

"Beg? We decided we would spend some time in a mosque."

"I didn't get it, Hussein?"

"Seriously. Come with us."

"Come with you? Where, Zoni? I don't understand."

"Come with us. You'll enjoy it. Believe me, it will be a lovely experience."

"We always go everywhere together, and I can't let you down today. No way. But I'm drunk, boys. What should I do, Mido?"

"Go and take a shower and you'll sober up. Get two or three gallabiyas with you and a blanket and a pillow. We'll wait for you."

"It just isn't possible, Zoni. Can't believe it! I'm drunk and was on my way to the Jackies to find myself going to worship instead"

"Let's go. Try. If you don't enjoy it, leave. No problem."

"Fine. Give me half an hour. I'll take a shower and get ready."

"We'll be in the car."

I quickly took a shower, got dressed and went to my parent's room. I told my mother, "Mama, I need a blanket and pillow because I'm going to worship."

"Going to worship? With who?"

"With Zoni and Mido, Mama."

"I don't understand, but good, khair."

"Is there anything you need, Baba. I'll be back in a few days."

"What on earth would I want from you? Leave me alone. You've completely lost your mind."

"I'm sure you don't believe me, do you? I swear I'm going to worship."

"May God bless you, son. *Surely, you do not guide whoever you love, but Allah guides whom He wills*" (Qur'an 28:56).

"Bye, bye."

I left them in a state of shock. They could not understand, but they were used to surprises. There was always something happening in my life.

I asked Mido when I got into his car,

"What is going on, Mido? Explain to me. I don't understand."

"A couple of weeks ago, after the Friday prayer, I met the kind Sheikh Omar el-Mahdy, a blessed man. He came by today and told me he is going out to worship and wants me with him. He is respectable and has a radiant face. I felt I wanted to obey him, and frankly one needs to be closer to God. We've gone overboard. Between you and me, it is an experience. We have nothing to lose."

Translated by Loubna A. Youssef

Epilogue

Sherine Aboul Naga

from Cairo Treason

CAIRO, THE CITY OF seduction that hides its forgiving face in the corners of alleyways, under the bridges, and on top of a pile of sand and cement hurled in front of a building.

Cairo does not like those who take its power and might lightly; Cairo frankly does not like the headstrong. Cairo likes those who are complicit with her. Only then will she conspire with them. And to be complicit with Cairo requires an entire lifetime.

Translated by Samia Mehrez

Sonallah Ibrahim

Cairo from Edge to Edge

MORE THAN ONCE I deserted my home city where I experienced the long and short ends of freedom. More than once I left it, embittered, enraged, determined never to see it again. More than once I abandoned it, haunted by its Citadel with its minarets, only to return again, meek and humble. To this very day I cannot explain my inability to live in any other city on the face of the earth.

Translated by Samia Mehrez

About the Authors

AHDAF SOUEIF was born in Egypt in 1950. She earned her PhD in linguistics in 1973 from the University of Lancaster. She divides her time between England, where she writes for English-language newspapers, including *The Guardian*, and Egypt. Her first collection of short stories, *Aisha*, was nominated for the Guardian First Book Award. This was followed by the publication in 1992 of Souief's first novel, *In the Eye of the Sun*. In 1999, her second novel, *The Map of Love*, was shortlisted for the Booker Prize. Soueif is founder and chair of PalFest, the Palestinian festival for literature, and is also the recipient of the Lannan Foundation Award in 2002 and the first Mahmoud Darwish Award in 2010.

AHMAD HUSSEIN (1911–82) was a controversial political figure and a student activist who pioneered the 'piaster project' in 1931, which called for all Egyptians to donate one piaster each to support the Egyptian economy. He also encouraged an Islamic political movement and established the National Islamic Political Party. He authored several works including a 1,500-page *Mawsuʿat tarikh Misr* (Encyclopedia of Egyptian History).

ALAA AL ASWANY was born in Cairo in 1957. Educated in Cairo and Chicago, he is a dentist by profession and a columnist for several Egyptian newspapers, where he writes on literature, politics, and social issues. He became an internationally bestselling author after the publication of his much-acclaimed novel, *The Yacoubian Building*, which has been translated into twenty languages and adapted into a major film production. His other works include *Chicago* and a story collection entitled *Friendly Fire*.

ALBERT COSSERY (1913–2008) is a French-speaking writer of Egyptian origin who was born in Cairo but settled in France from 1945. He published eight novels set in Egypt and other Arab countries, which portray the contrast between poverty and wealth, the powerful and the powerless, in a witty although dramatic style. In 1990 Cossery was awarded the Grand Prix de La Francophonie de l'Academie Française and in 2005 the Grand Prix Poncetton de la SGDL.

AMIRA ABOU-TALEB was born in 1967 in Alexandria. She moved to the USA where she received a BA in mass communications. After a fifteen-year advertising career between California and Cairo she left to become a full-time mother. She is currently studying for an MA in Islamic studies at the American University in Cairo (AUC). She was awarded the AUC Layla Fawwaz prize for best graduate essay in 2005. "Harir wa shawk" (Barbed Silk) is her first work of fiction.

BAHAA ABDELMEGID was born in 1967 and is professor of English Literature at Ain Shams University. He is the author of four novels and one collection of short stories. *Saint Theresa* is his first novel and has been translated into English by the American University in Cairo Press along with his novella, *Sleeping with Strangers*.

CHAFIKA HAMAMSY grew up in Zamalek. She received an MA in English literature from the American University in Cairo and for many years headed the catalog department of the American University in Cairo Library, where she later became a consultant. Hamamsy began writing after her retirement. She is the widow of the leading Egyptian journalist Galal al-Din al-Hamamsy.

COLETTE ROSSANT was born in Paris but spent most of her childhood in the Garden City district of Cairo. She has had a major career as a cookbook author and cooking show presenter and is the winner of several awards. She lives in New York and has been a culinary partner in two New York restaurants.

EDWARD SAID (1935–2003) was born in Jerusalem but his family fled Palestine for Cairo in 1948. He eventually attended Princeton and Harvard universities and settled in the U.S. where he became a professor of comparative literature at Columbia University, a celebrated intellectual, and a leading advocate of Palestinian self-determination. Said was a literary critic, writer, and musician and has been ranked among the most influential thinkers of the twentieth century.

ESSAM YOUSSEF was born in 1965 in Cairo to literary parents and earned a BA in English literature from Cairo University. He was the director of the Egyptian International Company for Environmental Protection (EICEP) and in 2007 started Montana Studios for Cinema Production. *A 1/4 Gram* is his first novel.

FATHY GHANEM (1924–99) studied law and worked for the Egyptian Ministry of Education until he began to devote his time to political and fictional writing. He was editor of the weekly *Sabah al-khayr* magazine and editor-in-chief of *al-Gumhuriya* newspaper. He also wrote for *Rose al-Yusuf* magazine.

GAMIL ATIA IBRAHIM was born in Giza in 1937 and has worked as an accountant, a music and math teacher, and most importantly a journalist. He lived in Morocco and Switzerland and is a founding member of *Gallery '68*, a literary magazine that became the mouthpiece of the writers of his generation. He published several works, among them a trilogy entitled *Thawra* (Revolution) published in 1952, 1954, and 1981 respectively.

GHADA ABDEL AL was born in al-Mahalla al-Kubra in 1978. She is a pharmacist by training who started a popular blog that later became her first book, *I Want to Get Married*, which was a bestseller at the Cairo International Book Fair in 2008. The book has been turned into an equally successful television serial that was aired during the month of Ramadan in 2010.

GHALEB HALASA (1932–89) was born in Ma'en in Jordan and later toured the world. He moved to study at the American University in Cairo in 1953 but was deported in 1976. The existentialist project he championed explored the depths of what Sartre called "the sin of existing," while maintaining the collective Arab dream of a firm sense of identity and social justice.

GHAZI ABDEL RAHMAN AL-QUSAYBI was born in 1940 in Saudi Arabia. He is a law professor and has held many ministerial positions in Saudi Arabia. Al-Qusaybi has also served as Saudi ambassador to the United Kingdom and Bahrain. He is a poet, an author of several novels, and has also published various books on a variety of topics such as development, globalization, and religion.

HALA EL BADRY was born in Cairo in 1954. She worked as a correspondent for *Rose al-Yusuf* and *Sabah al-khayr* in Baghdad. She is deputy-editor-in-chief of Egypt's *Majallat al-idha'a wa-l-tilivizyon* (Radio and TV Magazine) and the author of several novels, including *A Certain Woman*, which was awarded Best Novel of the Year at the Cairo International Book Fair in 2001.

HAMDI ABU GOLAYYEL was born in 1967 in Fayoum. Of Bedouin origin, he later moved to Cairo. He is the author of three short-story collections and two novels, the first of which is *Thieves in Retirement*. He is editor-in-chief of the Popular Studies series, which specializes in folklore research, and writes for the Emirates newspaper, *al-Ittihad*. He was awarded the Naguib Mahfouz Medal for Literature in 2008 for his *al-Fa'il*, which was published in English translation in 2009 by the American University in Cairo Press as *A Dog with No Tail*.

HAMDI EL-GAZZAR was born in 1970 in Cairo. He has a degree in philosophy from Cairo University. Since 1990 he has published several short stories and articles in the Arabic press, as well as writing and directing three plays. *Black Magic*, his debut novel, was awarded the Sawiris Foundation Prize in Egyptian Literature in 2006.

HAMID ABDEL SAMAD was born in 1972, in Giza. He holds a BA degree in literature and linguistics (English and French) from Ain Sham University and later studied in Germany and Japan. He was nominated for the Arabic Booker prize in 2008 for his novel, *Wada'an ayyatuha al-sama'* (Farewell, Heaven), which later led to terrorist threats by Muslim extremists in Germany, where he was placed under mandatory house arrest by the German police authorities for his own protection.

HANI ABDEL MOURID was born in 1972 and is an information systems specialist at one of Cairo's public libraries. He was awarded reader's choice awards in 2002 and 2008 for his novels, *Ighma'a dakhil tabut* (Passing out in a Coffin) and *Kyrie Eleison* respectively.

HASSAN HASSAN (1924–2000) was born in San Remo, Italy, the son of Prince Aziz, the nephew of King Fouad I, and thereby a great-grandson of Khedive Ismail. He was a painter and a pianist and died shortly before his book, *In the House of Muhammad Ali*, was published.

HUDA SHAARAWI (1879–1947) Pioneer Egyptian feminist leader and renown nationalist. She was married to Ali Shaarawi, a leading Egyptian nationalist and helped lead the first women's street demonstration during the Egyptian Revolution of 1919. She was elected president of the Wafdist Women's

Central Committee. In 1923 Shaarawi founded and became the first president of the Egyptian Feminist Union, which sent her to an international feminist conference in Rome. Upon her return, she removed her face veil in public for the first time, a signal event in the history of Egyptian feminism. She wrote poetry in both Arabic and French.

IBRAHIM ASLAN was born in Tanta in 1937. He published his first collection of short stories in 1971. *The Heron* is his first novel and was listed among the best one hundred novels in Arabic literature and also made into a popular feature film, *Kit Kat*. He was culture editor in the Cairo bureau of the London-based daily newspaper, *al-Hayat*. He has a weekly column in *al-Ahram* daily newspaper.

IBRAHIM ISSA was born in 1965 and is one of the most outspoken journalists against the current political regime in Egypt. He was editor-in-chief of the daily newspaper, *al-Dustur*, until 2010. He has been prosecuted for slander and had his works banned several times. He was awarded the Goubran Tweeny (WAN) journalistic award in 2008. Issa also hosts a regular television show.

IDRIS ALI (1940–2010) One of Egypt's leading Nubian writers, Ali authored three short-story collections and six novels, including *Dongola* (American University in Cairo Press, 2006). Self-taught in literature, he attended the Religious Institute of al-Azhar and was living in Cairo at the time of his death.

IHAB HASSAN was born in Cairo in 1925. Originally an engineer, he switched to studying literature at the University of Pennsylvania, and earned two degrees in English (an MA in 1950 and a PhD in 1953). He is the winner of numerous awards and fellowships, including the Guggenheim Foundation Fellowship. He has authored fifteen complete works and over two hundred articles.

IHSAN ABDEL QUDDUS (1919–90) graduated from the Faculty of Law in 1942 and while still a legal trainee joined *Rose al-Yusuf* magazine as a journalist. In 1944 he began writing film scripts, followed by two collections of short stories featuring memories of a young man on a visit to Europe. He was inclined toward the sentimental novel. He received many state awards for his prolific writings, and many of his works have been adapted into movies and television series.

ISMAIL WALI AL-DIN was born in 1939 and studied architecture at Cairo University and worked for the Armed Forces until his retirement. A prolific writer, he has published more than twenty novels. Between 1975 and 1995, many of Wali al-Din's novels were made into movies, such as *Hammam al-Malatili* (The Malatili Baths), *al-Batniya*, and *Bayt al-Qadi*.

KHAIRY SHALABY was born in 1938 in Kafr al-Sheikh in Egypt's Nile Delta, and has written seventy books, including novels, short stories, historical tales, and critical studies. His works are heavily influenced by his love for *sira* (traditional oral epic poetry) and his pride in local heritage. He was awarded the Naguib Mahfouz Medal for Literature in 2003 for his novel, *The Lodging House*, and has received several other distinguished national and regional awards. His novel, *The Time-Travels of the Man who Sold Pickles and Sweets*, is published by the AUC Press (2010).

KHALED AL KHAMISSI was born in 1962 and is a writer, film director, and producer. He received an MA in political science from Sorbonne University. He is a journalist who contributes weekly articles to numerous Egyptian newspapers. *Taxi* is his first book and has been a bestseller since its release in January 2007. *Safinat Nuh* (Noah's Ark) is his second and most recent work.

LAILA OSAYRAN is a Lebanese writer and activist. Osayran started writing in the mid-1950s and spent time in Palestinian camps in Jordan following the 1967 Arab defeat against Israel. She published a novel based on her camps experience in 1972. She is also known for her advocacy of women's rights. She has published over twelve novels. She died in 2007.

LATIFA AL-ZAYYAT (1923–96) was born in Damietta, Egypt. She was a student activist at the Faculty of Arts, Cairo University in the 1940s when she was part of the leftwing and feminist movements on campus. She was later imprisoned by President Anwar Sadat for campaigning against normalization with Israel. Al-Zayyat was Professor of English at Ain Shams and head of its Department of English Literature from 1976 to 1983, publishing several critical studies and short stories. Her novel, *The Open Door,* was made into a popular movie in 1964.

LEILA AHMED was born in 1940. She is an Egyptian-American professor of Women's Studies and Religion at the Harvard Divinity School. She earned her graduate and undergraduate degrees from the University of Cambridge, before moving to the United States. She is known for her groundbreaking work on the Islamic view of women as well as women's historical and social status in the Muslim world.

MAGUID TOBIA was born in 1938 in Minya, Egypt. He is an author and script-writer who has won several awards including the National Medal of Science and Arts. He contributes regularly to *al-Ahram* daily newspaper as well as to several magazines.

MAHMOUD AL-WARDANI was born in 1950 in Cairo. He began writing shortly after leaving university and is the author of three volumes of short stories, six novels, and three works of nonfiction. His stories have appeared in translation in English, German, Italian, and French. Al-Wardani has served as deputy editor-in-chief of the weekly Cairo newspaper *Akhbar al-yawm* and as editor of the opinion page of the daily *al-Badil*.

MEKKAWI SAID was born in 1955 and began his career by writing scripts for documentaries. He published his first selection of short stories in 1981, and in 1991 was awarded the Suad al-Sabbah Award for his novel *Firan al-safina* (Ship Rats). His novel, *Cairo Swan Song*, was short-listed for the Arabic Booker Prize in 2007.

MIDHAT GAZALÉ was born in Alexandria, Egypt in 1930(?). Formerly the president of AT&T France, he is currently a special science and technology adviser to the Egyptian prime minister. He is the author of works on mathematics in both French and English. He was made Chevalier dans l'Ordre national du Mérite in 1981.

MIRAL AL-TAHAWY was born in 1968 into the Bedouin al-Hanadi tribe in Egypt. As an adult, she left to study at Cairo University. She studied Hebrew, Persian, Urdu, and English at Cairo University. She writes short stories and novels in Classical Arabic, and credits her liberal-minded father with the fact that she obtained an education despite living in traditional seclusion. She is the author of *al-Khiba'* (The Tent), *al-Badhingana al-zarqa'* (*Blue Aubergine*) and *Naqarat al-ziba'* (*Gazelle Tracks*), all of which have been translated into English by the American University in Cairo Press. Her work has also appeared in the UK's *Banipal* magazine. She was awarded the AUC Naguib Mahfouz Medal for Literature in 2010 for her novel, *Brooklyn Heights*.

MOHAMED BERRADA was born in 1938 in Rabat, Morocco. He was educated in Morocco and Cairo, where he studied Arabic literature and criticism at Cairo University. He holds a PhD in literary criticism from the Sorbonne. He is one of Morocco's leading writers and literary critics and the author of several short stories, novels, and works of literary criticism.

MOHAMED AL-FAKHARANI was born in 1975. His work as a geologist enabled him to visit many remote areas in Egypt. He authored three short-story collections prior to the publication of his first novel, *Fasil li-l-dahsha* (An Interval for Bewilderment), which addresses the marginalized in society and created a stir in the literary community due to its daring language and subject matter. His short-story collection entitled *Hayat* was awarded the Dubai Literary Award.

MOHAMED MANSI QANDIL was born in 1949 in the Egyptian Delta city of al-Mahalla al-Kubra. He graduated from the faculty of medicine at Mansura University. He has published several novels and short-story collections as well as children books. In addition to receiving the Sawiris Foundation Award in 2006, one of his short-story collections was awarded the State Incentive Award in 1988.

MOHAMED SALAH AL-AZAB was born in 1981 in Cairo. He has published several short-story collections and four novels. He won the Supreme Council for Culture Award for the short story twice, in 1999 and 2003, as well as the award for best novel in 2003 along with several other awards from Kuwait, the Emirates, and Libya.

MONA PRINCE was born in 1970. She received a PhD in English literature from Ain Shams University and is currently assistant professor of English literature at Suez Canal University. She is an essayist, translator, short-story writer, and novelist. She has published one collection of short stories and two novels, in addition to uncollected short stories and essays in different local and regional magazines and newspapers. Her short story collection and her first novel, *Thalath haqa'ib li-l-safar* (Three Suitcases for Departure), have earned her distinguished national and regional literary awards.

MOURID BARGHOUTI was born in 1944 near Ramallah, Palestine. In 1966 he left to study at Cairo University and was not allowed to return home until thirty years later. One of the Arab world's most prolific and renowned poets, he received the Palestine Award for Poetry in 2000 and his novel, *I Saw Ramallah*, was awarded the AUC Naguib Mahfouz Medal for Literature in 1997.

NAGUIB MAHFOUZ (1911–2006) is probably the best-known Arabic writer of the twentieth century. He studied philosophy at Cairo University, graduating in 1934. Throughout his career he held many positions in the civil service within the ministries of Awqaf and Culture until his retirement in 1973. Mahfouz has written over forty novels and short stories, many of them about the Cairo neighborhood of Gamaliya, which he knew intimately. He was awarded the 1988 Nobel Prize for literature. His most noted works include *Children of the Alley* and *The Cairo Trilogy*.

NAWAL EL SAADAWI was born in 1931, in a small village outside Cairo. Having studied medicine at Cairo University, she practiced as a doctor and psychiatrist beginning in 1955. She wrote her first book, *Memoirs of a Woman Doctor*, in 1958 and continued after that to write about women's issues and gender inequalities. An outspoken critic of the government of Anwar Sadat, she was imprisoned in 1981, and in 1988 her name appeared on a fundamentalist death list. She left for the U.S. with her husband, novelist, Sherif Hetata. She has recently returned to Cairo where she writes for several papers.

RADWA ASHOUR was born in 1946 in Cairo. She graduated from the Faculty of Arts, Cairo University, and has a PhD in African-American literature from the University of Massachusetts at Amherst. She is currently professor of English and comparative literature at Ain Shams University and is co-editor of *Dhakira li-l-mustaqbal: mawsu'at al-katiba al-'arabiya* (2004), a version of which was published in English translation by the American University in Cairo Press as *Arab Women Writers: A Critical Reference Guide, 1873–1999* (2008). Her works include five volumes of literary criticism, several collections of short stories, and novels. As a translator Ashour co-translated, supervised, and edited the Arabic translation of volume 9 of *The Cambridge History of Literary Criticism* (2005). She has also translated Mourid Barghouti's *Midnight and Other Poems* (2008). Her novel, *Granada*, won the Cairo International Book Fair Book of the Year award in 1994. She was awarded the Constantine Cavafy Prize for Literature in 2007.

RAOUF MUSAD was born in 1937(?). He was raised in Egypt as a Protestant but later renounced his faith. He was imprisoned during the 1950s along with many of Egypt's leftist intellectuals. After his release, he left Egypt, finally settling in the Netherlands. His writings reflect a concern for minority rights and discrimination and are noted for their audacious representation of many taboo subjects. He is the author of several noted novels including *Ostrich Egg*, *The Temper of Crocodiles*, and *Ithaca*.

ROBERT SOLÉ was born in 1946 in Cairo. He moved to France at the age of eighteen and studied journalism at Lille University. He writes in French and works for *Le Monde*, for which he has reported from several locations, including Washington and Rome. He is the author of more than ten novels, all of which revolve around Egypt and Egyptian history. Several have been translated into English.

SALWA BAKR was born in 1949 and has become one of Egypt's most respected novelists and short-story writers. She graduated with a degree in business management and another in literary criticism. A leftist and activist from her university years, she was imprisoned in 1989 for her support of the Egyptian labor movement. She is the author of several short-story collections and novels that have been translated into English as well as many other languages. She won the German national radio award for literature in 1993.

SAMIA SERAGELDIN was born and raised in Egypt, educated in Europe, and emigrated to the United States with her family in 1980. She holds an MS in politics from the University of London, and is a writer, political essayist, editor, and literary critic. She is also a part-time instructor at Duke University.

SHARIF HATATAH graduated from medical school in Egypt in 1946. He participated in the founding of the Association for Health Education in 1969 and the Arab Women's Solidarity Association in 1982 and has worked with the International Labor Organization. He has written on many subjects, including travel, politics, and health, but since 1968 has devoted himself to novels. He has translated some of his own works as well as some of the works of his wife, Nawal El Saadawi, into English.

SHERINE ABOUL NAGA is a literary critic and professor of English at the Faculty of Arts, Cairo University. She taught at the American University in Cairo and in Berlin and has authored several papers on issues of gender and cultural politics and discrimination. She is also a regular contributor to several Egyptian newspapers and journals. *Khiyanat al-Qahira* (Cairo Treason) is her first novel.

SONALLAH IBRAHIM was born in 1937. After studying law and drama at Cairo University, he became a journalist until his imprisonment in 1959 as an advocate for the Left. Upon his release in 1964, he returned briefly to journalism in Egypt before moving to Berlin to work for a news agency and to Moscow where he studied cinematography. He returned to Egypt in 1974 and since then has dedicated his time to writing. Ibrahim is well known for his documentary novels, which employ a literary style unique in Arabic writing. He is the author of several novels and short stories, as well as a dozen children's books. In 1998 his novel *Sharaf* received the award for best Egyptian novel at the Cairo International Book Fair. He declined the Egyptian national novel award in 2003 in protest against state policies and practices in general.

TAHA HUSSEIN (1889–1973) was one of the most influential Egyptian writers and intellectuals of the twentieth century. He was the first graduate to receive a PhD from and become a professor of Arabic literature in the newly established Fuad al-Awwal Univerity (now Cairo University). Perceived as the figurehead of the modernist movement in Egypt, he earned the title of Dean of Arabic Letters. He was an encyclopedic figure: a translator, poet, and essayist. He also wrote many novels, though in the West he is best-known for his autobiography, *al-Ayyam*, which has been published in English as *The Days* (1997).

TAWFIQ AL-HAKIM (1898–1987) was a leading Egyptian playwright of the twentieth century. He was born in Alexandria and studied law in Cairo and furthered his studies in Paris. He introduced a new style of theatrical writing and authored over one hundred plays and many other literary works.

YAHYA TAHER ABDULLAH (1938–81) was born in Luxor, Upper Egypt, his village remaining a main source of inspiration for many of his works. He studied agriculture and worked briefly at the Ministry of Agriculture. His first collection of stories was issued in 1961. He is known for his oral recitation of his stories to accommodate a population that is not fully literate. He died in a car accident in 1981.

YASSER ABDEL HAFEZ was born in Cairo in 1969. He has a law degree from Ain Shams University in Cairo and started working as a journalist at the age of eighteen. He has been worked for the literary magazine, *Akhbar al-adab*, since its establishment. *Bi-munasabat al-hayah* (In Celebration of Life) is his first novel.

YASSER ABDEL LATIF was born in 1969. He graduated from Cairo University with a degree in philosophy in 1994. He has published two collections of poetry and is also a screenwriter for several documentaries. He volunteers his time conducting writing workshops to assist aspiring writers. In 2005 he received the Sawiris Literary Award for his first novel, *Qanun al-wiratha* (The Law of Inheritance).

YUSUF IDRIS (1927–92) graduated from medical school in 1951 and practiced medicine for several years. His first collection of short stories was published in 1954. In 1960 he gave up medicine to become editor of the Cairo daily newspaper, *al-Gumhuriya*, and continued to write and publish prolifically until his death in 1992. He is deemed one of the great figures of twentieth-century Arabic literature. Many of his works are written in the Egyptian vernacular, and he was considered a master of the short story. He sought to lay the foundations of a modern Egyptian theater based on popular traditions and folklore. He was nominated several times for the Nobel Prize in literature.

Bibliography

Ahdaf Soueif, *In the Eye of the Sun*. London: Bloomsbury 1992.

_____, *The Map of Love*. London: Bloomsbury, 1999.

Ahmed Hussein, *Wa-ihtaraqat al-Qahira*. Cairo: al-Matbaʻa al-ʻAlamiya, 1968.

Alaa Al Aswany, *The Yacoubian Building*, trans. Humphrey Davies. Cairo: American University in Cairo Press, 2004.

Albert Cossery, *Proud Beggars*, trans. Thomas W. Cushing. Boston: Black Sparrow Books, 1981.

Amira Abou-Taleb, "Harir wa shawk," in *al-Sabiʻa wa-l-nisf misaʻ al-arbiʻa'*, trans. Amira Abou-Taleb. Cairo: Kutub Khan, 2009.

Bahaa Abdelmegid, *Saint Theresa* and *Sleeping with Strangers*, trans. Chip Rossetti. Cairo: American University in Cairo Press, 2010.

Chafika Hamamsy, *Zamalek: The Changing Life of a Cairo Elite 1850–1945*. Cairo: American University in Cairo Press, 2005.

Colette Rossant, *Apricots on the Nile: A Memoir with Recipes*. New York: Washington Square Press, 2004.

Edward Said, "Homage to a Belly Dancer," in *Reflections on Exile*. Cambridge: Harvard University Press, 2001.

_____, *Out of Place*. New York: Alfred Knopf, 1999.

Essam Youssef, *A ¼ Gram*, trans. Loubna Youssef. Cairo: Montana Production, 2010.

Fathy Ghanem, *Bint min Shubra*. Cairo: Dar al-Hilal, 1986.

_____, *The Man Who Lost His Shadow*, trans. Desmond Stewart. London: Heinemann, 1980.

Gamil Atia Ibrahim, *Down to the Sea*, trans. Frances Liardet. London: Quartet Books, 1991.

Ghada Abdel Al, *Awza atgawwiz*. Cairo: Dar El Shorouk, 2008.

Ghaleb Halasa, *al-Riwaʼiyun*. Damascus: Dar al-Zawiya, 1988.

Ghazi Abdel Rahman al-Qusaybi, *Shaqqat al-hurriya*. London: Riad El-Rayyes Books, 1994.

Hala El Badry, *A Certain Woman*, trans. Farouk Abdel Wahab. Cairo: American University in Cairo Press, 2003.

Hamdi Abu Golayyel, *A Dog with No Tail*, trans. Robin Moger. Cairo: American University in Cairo Press, 2009.

———, *Thieves in Retirement*, trans. Marilyn Booth. Cairo: American University in Cairo Press, 2007.

Hamdy el-Gazzar, *Ladhdhat sirriya*. Cairo: al-Dar Publishing, 2008.

Hamid Abdel Samad, *Wada'an ayyatuha al-sama'*. Cairo: Merit Publishing, 2008.

Hani Abdel Mourid, *Kyrie Eleison*. Cairo: al-Dar Publishing, 2008.

Hassan Hassan, *In the House of Muhammad Ali*. Cairo: American University in Cairo Press, 2000.

Huda Shaarawi, *Harem Years*, trans. Margo Badran. Cairo: American University in Cairo Press, 1986.

Ibrahim Aslan, *The Heron*, trans. Elliott Colla. Cairo: American University in Cairo Press, 2005.

Ibrahim Issa, *Maqtal al-rajul al-kabir*. Cairo, 1999.

Idris Ali, *Poor*, trans. Elliott Colla. Cairo: American University in Cairo Press, 2007.

Ihab Hassan, *Out of Egypt: Scenes and Arguments of an Autobiography*. Carbondale: Southern Illinois University Press, 1986.

Ihsan Abdel Quddus, *Ana hurra*. Beirut: Dar al-Ma'arif, 1958.

Ismail Wali al-Din, *Ahzan Saqqara*. Cairo: Maktabat Gharib, 1980.

Khairy Shalaby, *The Hashish Waiter*, trans. Adam Talib. Cairo: American University in Cairo Press, forthcoming.

Khaled Al Khamissi, *Taxi*, trans. Jonathan Wright. London: Aflame Books, 2008.

Laila Osayran, *Shara'it mulawana min hayati*. London: Riad El-Rayyes Books, 1994.

Latifa al-Zayyat, *The Open Door*, trans. Marilyn Booth. Cairo: American University in Cairo Press, 2004.

Leila Ahmed, *A Border Passage: From Cairo to America—A Woman's Journey*. New York: Penguin Books, 2000.

Maguid Tobia, "Five Unread Papers," in *Flights of Fantasy*, trans. Nadia Gohar, edited by Malak Hashem and Ceza Kassem. Cairo: Elias Publishing, 1985.

Mahmoud Al-Wardani, *Heads Ripe for Plucking*, trans. Hala Halim. Cairo: American University in Cairo Press, 2008.

Mekkawi Said. *Cairo Swan Song*, trans. Adam Talib. Cairo: American University in Cairo Press, 2009.

Midhat Gazalé, *Pyramids Road*. Cairo: American University in Cairo Press, 2004.

Miral al-Tahawy, *The Blue Aubergine*, trans. Anthony Calderbank. Cairo: American University in Cairo Press, 2002.

Mohamed Berrada, *Like a Summer Never to be Repeated*, trans. Christina Phillips. Cairo: American University in Cairo Press, 2009.

Mohamed al-Fakharani, *Fasil li-l-dahsha*. Cairo: al-Dar Publishing, 2007.

Mohamed Mansi Qandil, *Inkisar al-ruh*. Cairo: Dar al-Hilal, 1992.

Mohamed Salah al-Azab, *Wuquf mutakarrir*. Cairo: Merit, 2006.

Mona Prince, *Thalath haqa'ib li-l-safar*. Cairo: Markaz al-Hadara al-'Arabiya, 1998.

Mourid Barghouti, *Checkpoints*, trans. Humphrey Davies. Cairo: American University in Cairo Press, forthcoming.

Naguib Mahfouz, *Adrift on the Nile*, trans. Frances Liardet. Cairo: American University in Cairo Press, 1999.

_____, *The Day the Leader was Killed*, trans. Malak Hashem. Cairo: American University in Cairo Press, 1997.

_____, *Midaq Alley*, trans. Trevor Le Gassick. Cairo: American University in Cairo Press, 1975.

_____, *Palace Walk*, trans. William M. Hutchins and Olive E. Kenny. Cairo: American University in Cairo Press, 1989.

Nawal el Sa'adawi, *Memoirs from the Women's Prison*, trans. Marilny Booth. London: The Women's Press, 1986.

Nawal El Saadawi, *Walking Through Fire*, trans. Sherif Hetata. London: Zed Books, 2002.

Radwa Ashour, *Hajar dafi'*. Cairo: Dar al-Mustaqbal al-'Arabi, 1985.

_____, *Qit'a min urubba*. Cairo: Dar El Shorouk, 2003.

Raouf Musad, *Baydat al-na'ama*. London: Riad El-Rayyes Books, 1993.

Robert Solé, *Birds of Passage*, trans. John Brownjohn. London: The Harvill Press, 2000.

Salwa Bakr, *The Golden Chariot*, trans. Dinah Manisty. London: Garnet Publishing, 1997.

_____, "Zeenat Marches in the President's Funeral," in *My Grandmother's Cactus*, trans. Marilyn Booth. London: Quartet Books, 1991.

Samia Serageldin, *The Cairo House*. Syracuse: Syracuse University Press, 2000.

Sharif Hatatah, *The Eye with an Iron Lid*. London: Onyx Press, 1982.

Sherine Aboul Naga, *Khiyanat al-Qahira*. Cairo: Madbouli Publishing, 2008.

Sonallah Ibrahim, *The Smell of It*, trans. Denys Johnson-Davies. London: Heinemann, 1971.

————, *Zaat*, trans. Anthony Calderbank. Cairo: American University in Cairo Press, 2001.

Taha Hussein, *The Days*, trans. E.H. Paxton. Cairo: American University in Cairo Press, 1997.

Tawfiq al-Hakim, *The Return of the Spirit*, trans. William M. Hutchins. London: Three Continents Press, 1991.

Yahya Taher Abdullah, "The Story of the Upper Egyptian," in *The Mountain of Green Tea*, trans. Denys Johnson-Davies. Cairo: American University in Cairo Press, 1992.

Yasser Abdel Hafez, *Bi-munasabat al-hayah*. Cairo: Merit, 2005.

Yasser Abdel Latif, *Qanun al-wiratha*. Cairo: Merit, 2002.

Yusuf Idris, "Did You Have to Turn on the Light, Lili?" in *The Cheapest Nights*, trans. Wadida Wassef. London: Three Continents Press, 1989.

————, "The Siren," in *Rings of Burnished Brass*, trans. Catherine Cobham. Cairo: American University in Cairo Press, 1990.

Glossary

arghoul wind instrument.

'awra parts of the body that should not be exposed, according to Islam.

Badr al-Budur name of a princess from popular stories.

bikbash a title for a clerk or civil servant.

al-Bukhari The scholar who compiled the most famous collection of the sayings of the Prophet Muhammad.

Eid al-Adha the Islamic Feast of the Sacrifice.

fallaha peasant woman.

Fatiha the opening verse of the Qur'an.

fawazeer riddles.

futuwwa thug.

fuul cooked fava beans.

gallabiya a loose-fitting, long garment for comfort and ease of wear.

Hadith saying of the Prophet Muhammad.

halawa sweet sesame paste.

haram literally, prohibited by religion; not permissible; unacceptable.

hashash a person who consumes hashish.

hijab Islamic head cover for women.

al-'izba farm, estate.

kassaba linear measure equal to 3.55 meters.

Kefaya opposition group formed in the early 2000s in Egypt to promote democracy and constitutional change.

khamaseen hot and sandy spring winds.

khawaga title or form of address used for Westerners, with or without the person's name

koshari a popular dish made of rice, macaroni, and lentils and served with fried onion, garlic, and vinegar topped with a hot sauce.

kubbaya drinking glass.

Laubali a type of nostalgic song particular to the Egyptian countryside.

ma'allim a term of respect used to address a small-business owner.

Mahallawi 'from Mahalla'; Mahalla is a city in the Delta known for its textile industry.

mawwals popular vernacular poems set to music.

mulukhiya Jew's mallow; green leafy soup with fried coriander and garlic.

mizmar reed wind instrument.

musaqqa'a a Middle Eastern dish similar to the Greek moussaka.

niqab face veil.

omda mayor of hamlet, town, or village.

oud stringed musical instrument; lute.

qirsh a measure of hashish.

Rumi (*not* the poet) literally 'Roman'; meaning of Greek (Byzantine) origin; foreign.

shibshib slipper.

Sitt literally, 'woman'; used as a title of respect to indicate age or class.

suffragi butler; waiter.

takbeer single word used to describe the phrase 'Allahu Akhbar' (God is the Greatest).

tarawih supplementary prayers performed by Muslims during the holy month of Ramadan.

tarha traditional head-cover for women, loosely wrapped around the head and shoulders.

Tawjihiya Egyptian national high school certificate; now called Thanawiya 'Amma.

thob traditional wrap worn by women.

tisht large brass basin.

Ummina al-Ghula mythical figure of an ogress in children's stories.

urfi traditional or common law; an *urfi* marriage is one without an official contract.

waqfs perpetual, nontransferable, and non-salable estates administered by a Ministry of Waqfs.

zagharid ululations; shrill, trilling cries of joy.

zalabya a kind of donut cooked in oil and sprinkled with sugar.

zar spirit appeasement ceremony; popular dance trance meant to quieten possessive spirits.

Index of Authors